D1531350

White Ice

CELIA BRAYFIELD

VIKING

VIKING

Published by the Penguin Group
Penguin Books Ltd, 27 Wrights Lane, London w8 5tz, England
Penguin Books USA Inc., 375 Hudson Street, New York, New York 10014, USA
Penguin Books Australia Ltd, Ringwood, Victoria, Australia
Penguin Books Canada Ltd, 10 Alcorn Avenue, Toronto, Ontario, Canada m4v 3b2
Penguin Books (NZ) Ltd, 182–190 Wairau Road, Auckland 10, New Zealand

Penguin Books Ltd, Registered Offices: Harmondsworth, Middlesex, England

First published 1993
1 3 5 7 9 10 8 6 4 2
First edition

Typeset by Datix International Limited, Bungay, Suffolk
Set in 12/15½ pt Monophoto Times
Printed in England by Clays Ltd, St Ives plc

A CIP catalogue record for this book is available from the British Library

ISBN 0–670–84100–5

ACKNOWLEDGEMENTS

I owe an immense debt to Veronyka Bodnarec, not only for her advice and encouragement during the writing of this book but also for the many hours of casual conversation about Russia and its citizens, from which I have freely borrowed themes and anecdotes. For my original reading list on Russian life and history I am most grateful to my cousin, Yvette Jansco. Additional books recommended by Tony Cash, Tim Hodlin and William Gill were of great help. My thanks are due to Joan Benham for her inspiration and patience in teaching me enough Russian to catch a trolley-bus in a very short but pleasant time.

Those whose advice and experience I have drawn on for the contemporary section of the book include Glynn and Carrie Boyd Harte, Janet and Rodney Fitch, Clare Francis, Thomas Gibson, Elaine Mayson, Biddie Saliba, Camilla Shivarg and Dr Fabien Stein. In addition, several friends were kind enough to agree to read the original manuscript and give me comments from their particular perspectives – for this considerable kindness, and for their flattering reactions, I am grateful to Alfreda Thorogood and David Wall, Marina Vaizey and Paul Haley.

White Ice is dedicated to Andrew and Margaret Hewson, who sustained me through this book and many others by their friendship, care, patience and judgement. Finally, none of this would have been possible without the kindness of the late Charles Cahn, who first invited me to the ballet.

It is amazing how complete is the delusion
that beauty is goodness.

Leo Tolstoy, *The Kreutzer Sonata*

PROLOGUE
London, 1991

She despised all superstitions except one, her own personal
item of folklore. If she could steal the early morning for
herself, then she could win the rest of the day. Because she
had come to believe this, and because her lover used to
grumble if she left him before sunrise, she preferred to sleep
alone. Her energy frightened people; lately, it had frightened
herself.

Needing to win this day more than most, Bianca Berrisford
arrived at her offices in time to meet the overnight courier
from the printers. He handed her the proofs of the catalogue
for her firm's sale of Russian art and jewellery, a rush
job, begun too late; only she knew the true reason. She
approved the proofs with confidently scribbled initials, then
settled down to read them and marked them for immediate
return. Lastly, she recalled that the signature of at least
one other director was needed. Waiting was torture to her,
but she would have to wait.

She walked around her desk, looking at the catalogue
cover from different angles, approving its design. The Berrisford family had been in the art business for three generations; people said that Sotheby's were all hype, Christie's
were all starch but Berrisford's were all style.

Bianca Berrisford was a success, a typical member of the
family in that at least. She had changed the firm from a
dusty second-division house to the leader in London's art
market, and one of the most respected businesses in the

international field. When Berrisford's were on a roll, they could lead world markets by the nose.

Lately, the markets had been going nowhere. London needed more than a few Japanese buyers hoping to find a few little Renoirs cheap. Odd how failure had a scent, an aroma so subtle it was like the smell of approaching rain, indefinable but indisputable. She could smell it now. She was not frightened. Failure promised peace of a kind, the calm which would follow the final destruction. Peace and freedom. There had been moments recently when she had truly longed to fail, when it seemed misguided to struggle when the end was inevitable.

When she weighed her options, one consideration was heavier than the others. If she failed, her husband would be right. Her ex-husband. Every day she heard the echo of his voice like a church bell, promising to ruin her if she did not do the job herself. Lovat kept promises; in other circumstances it would have been a virtue. Now she was tired and her will to win was failing, but Lovat was the goad which kept her going. She had to struggle. If she failed, he would claim it as his victory.

Bianca had the double-edged gift of seeming calm when she was distressed. Anguish drained the expression from her pale face and tautened its softness. Her thick, level brows contracted, her nostrils flared, her lips compressed. Behind her birchwood Biedermeier desk – her office was always furnished with a lone, magnificent example of the style currently most coveted – she sat very straight, her shoulders braced in defence, as still as marble, listening to the sounds of people arriving for work.

There was a knock at the double doors and she got up to open them. Two porters in the Berrisford uniform of grey-striped shirts and green felt aprons brought in a painting and installed it with the care due to any putative masterpiece on the picture rail which extended around all four walls. Behind them her father arrived, bestowing camel coat, felt hat and black umbrella on her secretary before taking up a proprietary pose in front of the picture.

'You look tired.' This was his usual greeting to his daughter.

'Oh well ... the boys, you know.' She played her fuzzy maternal smile and glanced at the plain silver frame on her desk which displayed the photograph of her children. He said nothing. First blood to her.

Bianca had three sons and a daughter. She had discovered very early in parenthood that three sons amounted to an ace in the hole. From the obstetrician onwards, almost every man who found out that she had three boys looked at her with dizzy worship.

Career mothers who discovered that she had three sons stopped asking her how much time she spent with her children. When the Italian waiter at the Caprice discovered that she had three sons he ceased to feel awkward about giving the bill to her rather than her male guest. Middle Eastern customers could look her in the eye when they discovered that she had three sons. Nobody argued with the possession of three sons, especially not her father, who had two daughters. Bianca despised anyone who conceded when she played her three sons as trumps, and took special pleasure in turning her father's own prejudice against him.

'What do you think of it, now it's been cleaned?' She stood up and went to examine the picture, peering closely at its surface where she knew that there had been damage to repair.

'Without doubt one of the finest portraits we have ever sold,' her father announced.

'I can agree with that.' The restorer had left just enough in the way of dirt and scratches to make it appear that the painting had not been touched.

'A landmark in the history of portrait painting. Realism, narrative, almost allegorical use of detail, that Russian richness and a truly European refinement . . .' Tall, slender and grey, Hugh Berrisford began to sway like a violinist, moved by his own eloquence. His hair had receded at his temples, leaving a high forehead, smooth and polished with the faint outline of his knotted old-man's veins just discernible when the light struck in a certain way.

'It's an extraordinary picture,' she said.

'Extraordinary to think of such very great talents undiscovered and unappreciated, behind the Iron Curtain, for *decades* now . . .'

'Yes, isn't it?' The day had begun. Events would now invade the anxious limbo of her early morning, people would crowd into her loneliness. The catalogue cover was a reproduction of the portrait, and Bianca picked it up at arm's length to compare with the original.

A masterpiece. The painter had chosen a young woman with abundant dark red hair and caught her alone before her dressing-room mirror, throwing herself sidelong glances from beneath her short lashes. She had sharply angled black eyebrows, like circumflex accents, which gave her face an indelible air of cheap pertness, for all she had tried to soften their line with greasepaint.

This was the face only her mirror knew; after a few minutes of looking at the painting there was an uncomfortable impression of having violated the privacy of the girl's toilette, but at the same time fascination with her character. She was alone, rehearsing a repertoire of flirtatious gestures, certainly for the benefit in due time of the lover who waited

4

offstage but also it seemed because she was compelled to coquet even with her own reflection.

The title appeared below the picture. *Prima Ballerina Lydia Kusminskaya*, painted in 1912 by Zinaida Serebryakova. The portrait had a disconcerting graphic quality; its clarity and detail were so emphatic and the subject so enduring that the picture could have been finished yesterday by a modern photorealist.

Despite her grand title, Lydia Kusminskaya seemed to have been about twenty years old. She was pretty, her costume was decorative and her surroundings attractively arranged, but the whole effect of the picture was disconcerting. The subject was charming but the painter was not beguiled. The composition had a knowing quality, an atmosphere of pitiless feminine intimacy, a wealth of disingenuous observation. The foreground clutter of paints and grimy puffs was minutely observed and every object in the composition implied a reference to the politics of seduction.

The young dancer was still in full costume, a black tutu encrusted with sequins and feathers, suggesting Odile, the false princess in *Swan Lake*. The heavy make-up was distinct, but it was clear from her unbound hair and her heightened physical condition that she was pausing in the act of undressing after a performance.

In the shadowy background of the room pale garments and ribbons lay in disarray around a rose plush *chaise-longue* with a deep gold fringe. The outline of a door could be seen, half opened as if a visitor was expected. A bouquet of some fat, creamy blooms spilled from a bamboo stand in a far corner but a fragment of wilting lilac blossom which lay discarded between pincushion and hairbrush seemed to be of more significance.

5

'Excellent. I was afraid the necklace would lose its importance but if anything it stands out more – what do you think?'

'What?'

Hugh Berrisford acted as if he had hardly heard his daughter speak to him from the less exalted plane of existence which she occupied.

'This is the proof of the catalogue cover. Come and look.'

Her father unwillingly turned his attention to the practicalities of marketing.

The necklace, not the woman, was the focus of the whole painting. Both the girl's small hands rested avidly on her chest, drawing all the viewer's attention to the object which she had paused to admire. Her necklace seemed to be creeping close around the base of her neck like frost fronds advancing across a windowpane, a chill rime of diamonds. So many diamonds, massive stones and primitively cut, so skilfully painted that every tiny lance of light from thousands of facets seemed to have been recorded and the texture, and the effect of brilliance, was perfectly conveyed. If the viewer stood close to the painting the necklace became nothing but a mass of tiny brush strokes; two paces backwards and it appeared as a dazzling jewel.

The piece had a pagan look. It was not delicate; the jeweller's aim seemed to have been to attach together as many of the largest stones as he could find. The mass of huge, crude gems had been cunningly painted, but the artist had been unable to admire it. Instead she had issued a satirical invitation to the viewer, to consider whether the necklace was truly more valuable than the young woman who displayed it to herself with such possessive pride. The tiny dashes of paint, the delicacy with which the minute points of light refracted into the shadow under the sharp chin were rendered, the suggestion that the jewels weighed down the soft neck, were all remarkable. On the neck itself, the artist had worked with passion.

The parchment pallor of the young dancer's flesh, palpitating invisibly with vitality, the rises and hollows of the collarbones, the light sheen of perspiration, the fine skin, the blue veins and the flush of colour at the earlobes suggesting a hectic excitement, all these had been captured with a mastery which forced them on the eye and demanded that the content of the picture should be acknowledged.

The printer's proof on which the painting was reproduced had a wide green border. The green was dark, the colour considered evocative of the English at their most aesthetically refined – gardener's green, forest green, British racing green. The name Berrisford's appeared in fine gold lettering above the picture, and below it the words 'The Eagle and The Firebird: Sale of Russian art and jewellery at our London saleroom, 11 June 1991 at 11 a.m. By Invitation Only.'

Bianca Berrisford walked away from her father and spent a few moments looking down from the tall window of her office to the short, straight Mayfair street. It was empty except for a traffic warden patiently patrolling the line of legally parked cars, waiting to catch a few minutes of offence in her ticket book.

A year ago the narrow pavements would have been peopled by men and women in beautifully tailored dark suits, getting in and out of chauffeured cars, making for one or other of the plate-glass doors of the great art traders of London. No one was buying art this year, and people were only selling if they had no option.

A year ago, if she had leaned backwards a trifle, she would have been able to see the rear entrance to Fortnum & Mason, and those doors also would have swung constantly open to admit mostly the curious who wanted to see the most expensive store in London but among them a reasonable number of people who treated it simply as a convenient place to buy clothes. Now the doors were still. No one was shopping.

A year ago it would have been impossible to get a taxi in that street. Now the only vehicles which moved were cruising cabs, the drivers anxiously scanning the pavements for passengers. Theatre tickets and restaurant tables were easy to get now; people laughed at the touts outside *The Phantom of the Opera*.

Every now and then Bianca drew a deep breath, as if the spring air, heavy, cold and humid even for London, was painful to breathe. It was an uneven respiration not unlike the prelude to weeping; her thin, square shoulders rose and fell in silence, only the changing light on the folds of her shirt indicating movement.

She was wearing what she called her Fuck You I'm Rich shirt; the waiting list for it at Gucci was six months long. Some things were still in demand. Red, gold and black, acanthus leaves, leopard spots – she thought the design was a dog's breakfast but if she could impress a few more fools by wearing it, she would.

Her father saw that she was in distress and was disturbed. He considered his daughter's energy neurotic. She would have been beautiful if she had ever achieved serenity. Hugh Berrisford had well-developed opinions about beauty, as he had about many things. He considered that women with his daughter's looks – cool, pale, rounded, aqueous, with soft, indefinite hair and eyes the colour of river mist – could only achieve beauty if they were tranquil.

Her trouble, he considered, was that she had lived too many lives, tried too many roles. Her energy was a torrent which had torn up and borne along art, children, husband and family; too many directions, too many people in the one being. She did not understand the virtue of restraint.

Of course, he had tried to teach her, but Bianca had always smouldered with a quarrelsome inner fire which had heated her resistance and fuelled her ambitions. Her tenderness, love, care – he assumed that being female she had once had these qualities – had scorched to death in the heat and now her heart was burned out. Now she was clinging to her territory like a stubborn tree stump, already hollow in the centre but too deeply rooted to be destroyed. It had been more and more difficult to pity his daughter as she moved into the fullness of her womanhood, but Hugh always did his best.

Now he perceived strong emotion. Her feelings were destructive; anarchy, chaos and havoc attended them. He soothed himself, reasoning that she was looking at a picture of her lover's grandmother, her lost lover's grandmother, and was therefore moved by grief. That he himself was at the root of her distress did not occur to him.

Bianca left the window and distracted herself in appreciating the technical accomplishment of the picture, turning it towards the diffuse morning light from the windows, holding at arm's length the knowledge that the portrait of Lydia Kusminskaya and the necklace around her plump young neck represented to her the difference between survival and ruin.

Below that knowledge was something darker and even more threatening: a suspicion; when she was at ease with failure she addressed it directly. Being also at pains always to be honest with herself she periodically hauled this terrible doubt into the full light of her consciousness and examined it, found it reasonable, reiterated the worst consequences to herself, and then let it slip back into the shadows. When she did that the cupidity of Lydia Kusminskaya's expression seemed more obvious.

She felt breathless and there was a burning pain in the centre of her chest. In her mind's eye she could see Lovat again on the day she asked for the divorce, suddenly seeming taller and so dark he was almost a silhouette. 'You have no conception of what you're getting into and it will be an utter, absolute and miserable catastrophe. And never think you can ask me for help, Bianca. After what you've done to me, there's nothing I won't do to finish you – *and* your bloody family.'

Her hand did not shake and her gaze, the intense, drilling stare of an artist, did not waver. She took the catalogue proof from her father and when she spoke her voice was well modulated, something else he had always disliked. Her speech seemed to him to be overcareful, as if acquired through elocution lessons to replace a vulgar accent when effortlessly superior diction was part of her birthright from him.

'It has come out better this time, don't you think? You can get a much better idea of the quality of the work now, can't you?' She did not call him by his Christian name, as he would have preferred, or by an affectionate paternal diminutive, as she would have wished. This also was a detail on which they could not agree.

There was a silent pause while he unfolded his spectacles to scrutinize the proof.

'I suppose it is an improvement,' he said at length. 'If you are set on using the portrait.'

'You know I am.' Immediately, her voice was hard with irritation. 'We've been through this already.'

'I just . . .' If asked, Hugh Berrisford would have agreed

that his daughter was becoming angry at this point, but would never have considered her feelings to be any reason for hesitation in the expression of his own. 'I just think we'll only sell the Orlov necklace once in our lives and it's worth doing in the best possible way.'

'This is the best possible way.'

'You can't expect people to pay five million dollars . . .'

'Pounds.'

'You can't expect them to pay that kind of money for a necklace and not show them a photograph of the real thing.'

'You agree that this is a superb portrait . . .'

'Yes, but it doesn't do the thing justice and it's confusing to people. They'll think the picture's on sale itself, not the necklace.'

'The picture *is* in the sale.'

'I am aware of that, but the necklace is the major piece. How many other portraits are there on the list. Three? Four? Yes, it's an important work but you must take into account that the market for Russian art is still developing . . .'

His daughter ceased to hear him. Since she had realized that her father was less than a god, which had happened almost thirty years ago, his lecturing tone of voice had triggered an automatic failure in that part of her brain which received advice.

'You need to show people the necklace and only the necklace,' he continued, unaware of her response. 'The portrait will get thirty thousand, perhaps. It's good and now there's all this interest in Russian art this is something we can hope to sell well. I grant that the ecology of the art market is changing but still in this sale the Orlov necklace is the thing, it's what people will talk about, it's historic, it's sensational, people will come just to see it sold, and that's what the catalogue cover needs to say, and say loudly and clearly.'

'What makes the necklace unique is its story. What makes it sensational is its associations, and the picture tells you everything. Here's Kusminskaya, a few moments after she left the stage wearing the necklace given to her by her lover, Prince Orlov, the last descendant of a noble house which had served at the courts of the Tsars for centuries. Their love affair was the talk of Europe; whoever buys the necklace buys the glory of imperial St Petersburg, the romance of the Ballets Russes, the tragedy of . . .'

'My dear, you don't need to sell it to me . . .'

It was an unfortunate allusion, raising immediately in both their minds the fact that at that moment Hugh Berrisford could not have bought a strand of rhinestones at Woolworths, and that it was his bad judgement, in financing other covetous but equally ill-provided buyers in Berrisford's saleroom, which had brought them both to the brink of bankruptcy.

Hugh sensed unpleasantness ahead and avoided it. At the same time, he avoided acknowledging that he had no authority now to choose Berrisford's catalogue covers, that he had, in theory, retired, and that his daughter was now the head of the firm.

'But I suppose . . . if your mind's made up, Bianca,' he said after a pause, employing an ingratiating smile which contorted his small, lined face. His eyes were so deep-set that their colour and expression could not be distinguished.

'Yes.' She was biting her lower lip, an unconscious movement she had used since childhood to bite back everything she wanted to say to her father.

'We're agreed then.' It was intended to sound like a magnanimous concession.

'Yes, I suppose we are.' She stood up and walked out to her secretary's office with the proof, needing to put distance between herself and her father. 'Now you'll have to excuse me,' she told him through the half-open door. 'I want to look in on the chap doing the authentication before all the Foundation people get here.'

He looked pained. The Foundation for Art in Britain, commonly reduced to the acronym FAB, was in truth another extension of Bianca's war with her husband, a body convened to raise money to keep works of art in the country while Lovat's dealership specialized in finding neglected masterpieces for Japanese banks. Hugh was also on the board, and was afraid that here, too, his daughter would overshadow him.

Descending the narrow, curved staircase at Berrisford's, no one would imagine that the business was falling to pieces. The decor was fresh and flawless, the walls dragged in muted shades of green, the heavy rush carpeting exuded a faint scent of spice. Young men with slick haircuts, young women with interesting large earrings, moved in and out of quiet rooms where screens flickered in silence. A large Aubusson in shades of gold and grey softened the light in the stairwell. Periodically a Chinese Chippendale *fauteuil* issued the passer-by an invitation to sit and be uncomfortable.

Under Bianca's direction the firm emphasized its modernity. Not for Berrisford's the dusty clutter of picture frames, stopped clocks, folded tapestries and rolled carpets which characterize the premises of other auction houses. The offices were spacious and bare.

Berrisford's had been the first to realize that the trade in beautiful things would appeal to the leaders of the new consumer culture. Their salerooms had been crammed with the new rich, brokers and dealers, property developers, bankers and arbitrageurs, people with no respect for tradition and much attraction to a public, socially admired and ethically irreproachable means of displaying their wealth. The quiet coteries of art dealers had been almost literally elbowed aside as the new rich fought for their trophies with the frenzy of feeding fish.

In the first-floor saleroom the walls were painted red to generate warmth and excitement. To Bianca this room always recalled their famous 14 May sale – at the outset a mob scene like the rest but then the madness had died down, the buyers themselves awed by the prices to which they had pushed each other. When the chief auctioneer had brought down his gavel almost timidly on the first record sum, applause had broken out. The next picture broke that record. In all they had sold seven Matisses, each for more than the one before.

There were perhaps five hundred people in the world capable of paying more than ten million pounds for a picture, and Bianca talked to most of them in the course of a year. Even the newest and least sophisticated collectors were muttering about price stability. The total business done at Berrisford's on 14 May 1989 was more than the turnover they projected for the first half of this year.

A small sale of furniture was in progress that morning.

'Five thousand pounds, ladies and gentlemen. Five thousand pounds. Five thousand pounds.' She had taken Patrick on six months ago, from the Scottish National Gallery. He was young and overconfident, a born auctioneer and he knew it. They found his accent easy to understand in the New York office. It pained him to be knocking down a signed Louis XVI writing table at such a low price.

'Five thousand pounds, five thousand *five hundred*, thank you, Sir, five thousand five hundred . . . can I hear six?' He almost skipped with pleasure behind his desk. With his blond hair springing straight up like a brush and his hand-painted bow tie, he was optimism personified, but the room was cold and within a few minutes the porters reluctantly stepped forward to move the piece and the dealers wrote £5,500 in the margins of their programmes without much comment.

Patrick took off his wire-rimmed spectacles and polished them. He had just married a very promising young woman in the Oriental department. She was pregnant although she might not yet be aware of it – Bianca could tell, by instinct, sometimes almost from the moment of conception. If Berrisford's went down, what would happen to them?

She hurried away, unwilling to allow her mind to dwell on all the consequences of failure. The Russian sale would be a success. She would make it a success. It was simple. Whatever had to be done, she would do it.

Nobody else now knew exactly how dangerous the situation was. The accountant knew that the handsome large company cheque books with the copperplate insignia of an old-established private bank could not be used at present. The directors knew the size of the last year's loss, and that a similar loss could not be sustained again. Bianca and her new financial director knew that loans outstanding to buyers at the year's end would exceed thirty million pounds. The sales director knew that his department had done half as much business this year as last. Bianca, Hugh and Hugh's former assistant knew that the collection of uninspired Impressionists which the firm itself had bought for almost a million was unlikely to be sold at current prices. The only hopeful secret was kept by their lawyers, who had found a loophole in the contract for the new offices which they could not afford.

Other senior staff knew that mortgages had been raised or extended on several Berrisford's properties in Europe, but not the exact figures involved. There were two bank managers in London who had lunch with Bianca occasionally and did not know that they were rivals.

The shareholders knew that the firm had reported losses, and that Lovat Whitburn would buy their shares if they cared to sell them. He already owned 38 per cent. Ten years ago Whitburn had been a director of Berrisford's, and the architect of their success. He had also been Bianca's husband. There was a body of opinion which put all the company's troubles down to Bianca's relentless impulse to fight Lovat for every dollar and yen in the art market. She considered that she was only defending herself.

At the ground floor there was at last an impression of busyness. The uniformed doorman bustled in and out as he admitted the visitors who struggled with their bags, packages and cardboard boxes. At the long counter she saw people waiting patiently.

'The market *is* a little slow just at the moment but . . .'

'I can't seem to find a signature . . .'

'Of course, since the Americans stopped coming . . .'

'A very *good* copy of an eighteenth-century pattern . . .'

'We can't advise our sellers to look for that kind of price in the present climate, but we are planning a sale early next year and if you still wanted to sell then . . .'

To herself, Bianca called the front office the *salon des refusés*. They had opened a separate suite for liquidators. She used to train the staff herself. Buyers and sellers are all this business is about. Never forget that everyone who you see is selling something they love because they need money. And they all fantasize about what it might be worth. Of course, they'll always say it was a piece of junk they inherited, but the chances are that in the piece of junk are their childhood memories, their family pride, their love for their favourite aunt. They've lost their jobs. Their businesses have gone bankrupt. They can't pay their mortgages. They need holidays and can't afford them. Their wives are leaving them. They're in pain. Be kind. Be gentle. Ask them what else was in the bequest, if they're interested in collecting. And don't use the word 'recession', or even think the word 'slump', or tell them the market is collapsing and there's nothing scheduled after the big Russian sale. Be positive.

Crumpled newspapers and cardboard boxes littered the room. All the hard horsehair Victorian couches against the wall were full and people were standing patiently in small groups, silent except for periodic coughs. There had never in Bianca's memory been so many people so anxious to sell, or, alas, so few people able to buy.

She continued downwards to the strongroom in the basement, pausing to slide her security card through the automatic lock which released the bomb-proof doors. Ever since a gang of thieves had rammed a truck through the window of Asprey's in Bond Street a siege mentality had prevailed in the commercial heart of Mayfair. Bianca, complacently aware that Berrisford's security was already the best, had admired the villains' nerve; she always admired nerve. Her own capacity for bone-marrow recklessness was criticized constantly, but without it she knew she would have remained a shapeless, spineless creature hiding under her family like a slug beneath a stone.

The elderly man sitting beside a pool of bright light in the far corner of the room had no recklessness about him. He was small, bony and yellow-skinned, but gave the impression of having once been a plump man. His smile was thick-lipped and wide, like a fat man's smile, though his teeth were stained.

'Mrs Berrisford! So beautiful!'

17

She was not and never had been Mrs Berrisford, but people always called her that and she never corrected them. She did not correct people who called her beautiful either, but in this instance the man was referring to the array of jewels blazing from their cases at his side. They glittered as if they were alive; they seemed to move, a luminous slick of lava cooling from white to red hot as it spilled over the table.

'Yes, Mr Wyngarde, they are beautiful, aren't they?'

'Magnificent. Mag – nificent.' The heavy, elided vowel sounds indicated his origin. Wyngarde had been born in Russia as Vinogradov and her father had made one of his weighty jokes of the name for them as children, calling him Mr Vineyard.

'I feel really, truly . . .' With both hands clasped to his heart, he almost bowed over the gems. 'Well, truly, it's an honour to have . . . to be . . . for once in one's life . . . even for one half hour . . . just even to see them.'

His obvious emotion reassured her. 'I'm glad you like them.'

'Like them . . .' When she was younger he would have pinched her cheek. Even now he was tempted; adorable, the way she pulled down the centre of her mouth so the upper lip was almost straight, twitching her nose, her eyes mysterious, blue or grey, one could not quite decide, and the eyebrows also rather flat, something which could have been ugly but was with her quite distinguished. 'One does not like pieces of this quality; one loves, reveres, worships perhaps . . .'

'All I need is authentication, Mr Wyngarde. Do we have any problems?'

'I don't think so, I don't think so. Certainly not, no, nothing, nothing I can see.' He folded his arms, resting his curved, bony spine against the edge of the table, as if to show he could turn his back on the jewels and trust them. Gold and silver, diamonds, emeralds, sapphires, rubies, pearls, amethysts, brilliant lacquer and semi-precious stones glowed under the strong light. Always methodical, Mr Wyngarde had arranged their cases in straight lines.

'The Empire-style Cartier was all catalogued, all this Fabergé is exactly, *exactly* as the workshop drawings, this . . .' He turned to pick up a diamond hair ornament like a miniature ostrich feather. 'Countess Ouvarov was photographed with it and you see it is the same, these curled pieces, unmistakable . . .' He replaced the slender ornament with a precise gesture. His hand hovered for an instant over the dazzling array and descended slowly to pick up a plain gold watch, its case decorated with a double-headed eagle and a crest in small diamonds. 'And this, Stolypin's watch, again, beyond question, documented . . . what a treasure, what a story it could tell, how close to the assassin's bullet, how close to history itself . . . no, my dear, I can't find any problems for you.'

'That's good.' Why did she still disbelieve him?

'Now we have known each other many years so you won't mind me asking you something.'

'Of course not . . .'

'I understand of course that you have given the Orlov necklace to someone else.' He paused, pained but wishing to appear disinterested. Her doubts immediately sprang forward like demons. 'But I would be so very pleased just to see it, just to look at it . . .'

Without a word Bianca stepped forward and picked up a case of pale birch wood. It was lined in white satin, with a coat of arms embossed in gold, the field quartered and divided between two rampant lions and two eagles. The case contained a mass of diamonds. 'This is the one, Mr Wyngarde, or so we have been told.'

'So you have been told, yes.' Now he was in an agony of embarrassment, perspiration breaking out along his temples, his blubbery mouth stretched into a mask of tragedy.

'But in your opinion,' she prompted in a soft voice.

'Well, my opinion . . . we have known each other many years, Mrs Berrisford.' He was speaking so fast the words were barely distinguishable. 'I tell you the truth. I don't think so. In fact, I am sure. Yes, this is the Orlov crest, but the box is obviously new. The necklace was a family treasure, made in the eighteenth century, there is a description, the workshop records, its style was considerably less delicate. And the stones themselves, I would expect a cut typical of gems cut in Russia at that time, a little bit crude, shall we say, gives jewellery a pagan sort of look. Not the European cut of the next century. Also these are not well matched, some are grey, some a little yellow, the drop stones have been added much later, and there's no record that coloured diamonds were used in the Orlov necklace, in fact they are described everywhere as very fine blue-white. The style of the setting is a little bit like, it's true, these little scrolls – but not identical. The Fabergé records describe some yellow stones set for Kusminskaya in 1913, so that clinches it for me as you might say. I don't . . . I'm sorry . . . not to disappoint you, but it is not the Orlov necklace.'

She was silent, wishing she had not heard him, ridiculously wishing the silence could roll backwards over their conversation.

'Of course, you will ask another opinion . . .'

She shook her head at once, knowing what she would do. The fewer people to see the necklace now the better. 'Thank you, Mr Wyngarde. Someone had to tell me.'

'Yes, someone, but I wish it had not been me.'

'Don't say anything.'

'Of course. You can always trust me.'

'I know. I am grateful to you, really.'

After he had gone and all the jewels, except the necklace, had been put away, Bianca sat on the tabletop like a schoolgirl and waited to feel something. Mentally, she rehearsed her decision, trying to scratch the numbness that filled her mind. I am going to commit a major fraud, she hectored herself. The sale will proceed as planned. The chances of discovery are at least fifty per cent. The scandal would be catastrophic. Far worse than any of my father's mistakes. And it will be the end. Berrisford's will be finished. Bankrupt. Seventy years, three generations brought to nothing. Shame on the family, shame on the business, shame on the whole country. The trust of the world in the London art market will be destroyed. And Lovat will be right.

No emotion arose. The peace which would follow failure was so palpable she felt as if she could stretch out her arm and pick up a handful of it.

CHAPTER 1

St Petersburg, Russia, 1902

The heart of St Petersburg was artificial in everything; in scale, situation and magnificence. For the sophisticated few who had travelled and lived in untidy, organic towns where every landmark masked a squalid alley, there was an unnatural excess of splendour.

The city's beauty had been calculated in the subtlest detail. It had the atmosphere of a pantomime stage set. To stand out against the snow in winter, the buildings were painted the colours of sugared almonds – apricot, aquamarine, turquoise and pink. In them was conducted the hopeless business of the Imperial Russian government, affairs of chaos, corruption, misery, bankruptcy and brutality carried on behind walls fit for fairy castles.

The city was built as much on water as on land. At the command of emperors of all the Russias, St Petersburg had risen from marshlands intersected by countless rivers. Between its buildings and at the end of its streets flat expanses of water, grey and shallowly indented like vast sheets of hammered pewter, reflected the pale northern sunlight upwards, shortening perspectives and casting melodramatic shadows above pediments and lintels. Immense baroque façades were illuminated from behind like scenery flats. Noble vistas which led from palace to statue to cathedral in the ideal style were cut short at the water's edge.

Wealthy citizens promenaded in their carriages around the embankments and parks contrived to idealize the grey sprawl of the river Neva. Its little sister, the Fontanka, lined with the family palaces of the aristocracy, was decorated with pretty bridges each guarded by a small corps of statues. At the point where the eye might be weary after a long stretch without a diverting feature, two cathedrals, their huge domes thoughtfully counterpoised, were deployed to break the monotony.

The finest architects and craftsmen in the world had been imported to realize this vision. Italians, French, German, Dutch and English, they adorned the face which Russia wished to show the world with features which, for all their harmony, still recalled their home countries, and so one panorama whispered Canaletto, another Turner, a third Rembrandt, and the vital, throat-rending roar of Russia herself was suppressed.

While the city was created to lure travellers, only the most adventurous or discontented of its own people voyaged abroad. As a race they were bold on their own territory but hesitant outside it, knowing that their dream homeland was a sham and feeling themselves inferior. St Petersburg was the mask which Russia had painted to show her superiority to the world, a gracious, cultured and European decoy behind which her Asian lineage, barbaric and hot-blooded, was disguised.

This, like many great deceptions, had been undertaken for the highest motive: for love and duty. The man whom his people believed had been appointed by God to lead them, the Tsar Peter the Great, had decreed that the glorious city should be created at a strategically useful position on the mud of the Neva estuary, and so it was done, and his descendants and adherents for more than two hundred years had continued the work, pouring out their incalculable wealth to raise gold spires on the ooze. If their infallible and beloved Tsar had commanded that the greatest city in Europe was to be raised on a swamp, then it was God's will and would be done, no matter what the cost in gold and human lives. As Russians they were already passionately in love with the idea of sacrifice. Furthermore impossibility was a concept which they could not precisely define; so many impossible things happened in Russia.

In this vast theatrical illusion, theatres themselves acquired unusual dignity. A public theatre was a building fit to command a square of its own. The palace of every noble family included a gilded miniature auditorium. The Russians of St Petersburg built their theatres in the same propitiatory spirit that a Roman would have built a temple or an Englishman a garden. In place of Mithras or Nature, the god whose favour was needed was Civilization, in whose train all the Muses were presumed to dance.

At the sanctum of the entire land a palace was built adjacent to the Imperial seat for the sole purpose of enshrining the arts, and a theatre built in it for the Court. The theatre in the Hermitage was designed to resemble a miniature temple, with statues of Apollo and the Muses posed between columns of rose-red marble. On the performers' side it was generously constructed, imposing minimal restraints on the productions which could be mounted. The audience's portion was small, no larger than many of the city's ballrooms, and decorated with restraint, which, to little Lydia Kusminskaya's childish eye, was not at all satisfying.

'Heavens, it's tiny. And it's all Greek.' She stood on her toes at the edge of the stage, peeking through the spyhole in the drop curtain. Five companions from the Imperial Theatre School pressed impatiently around her, but she ignored them. The backstage area was a cavern; the scenery was dwarfed by its size, its boundaries were lost in darkness, and bitter cold persisted in the corners which were too distant to draw warmth from the massive stoves which heated all the surrounding structure of the palace.

Through the spyhole Lydia could make out a rectangular room, shallowly tiered and set with orderly rows of gilt-framed armchairs which gleamed dully by the reduced light of the great crystal chandelier. Two carved thrones with embroidered brocade slipcovers awaited the Tsar and Tsarina, but the auditorium seemed a mere box by comparison with the vast space behind the stage, and it was far too classical for her taste. To Lydia, elegance meant gilding and elaboration. The white capitals of the columns, which gleamed in the half darkness, were superbly carved but did not impress her. Her little round mouth drooped in disappointment. 'There aren't even any boxes or any paintings. I thought it would be bigger. And more decorated.'

She had expected the court auditorium to be more gorgeous than any other in St Petersburg and felt her disappointment as a personal slight.

'Let me see! Let me see!'

'Be quiet, Marie, it's my turn next.'

'Come *on* Lydia, move over.' The other girls urged her but did not push. Although she was the smallest of them, Lydia was acknowledged the strongest; to reach the peephole she had been standing on full point for some minutes without wavering in the slightest, a feat none of the others could match. She was also the quickest to resort to using her hairpins as weapons.

'There you are, Olga, but it's not much to see.' Lydia at last lowered her heels to the floor and moved aside in favour of a tall, pale girl who at once exclaimed:

'Oh! It's so beautiful! It's all marble! I can't believe we're going to dance in such a beautiful place. But it's so small –

how can we possibly think about our dancing when we're only six feet away from all Their Majesties?'

Scuffling and whispering, their blocked shoes tapping on the bare boards and tarlatan skirts scraping their knees, the girls discussed this question. With their fluttering hands and sharp shoulder blades they jostled like a brood of half-fledged birds, awkward and graceful in the same moment.

They were alike in so many features that they could have been sisters. Their high-cheekboned faces were refined, flattened and poised on elongated necks. Their shoulders were level, their calves round, their thighs straight, their hips flat and their waists slim but round and firm. The sway of each spine, the articulation of every joint, was identical. However diverse the forms decreed by their genes and hormones, they had been shaped alike by their daily regime of exercise. As their soft bones lengthened, the pull of muscles meticulously trained to move in unison had made their form the same.

Their ears were attuned to music, their eyes were taught to watch their mirrored reflections and their minds were drilled to judge themselves and never be satisfied. So the dance had claimed them entirely, sacrifices to their nation's glory no less than the three hundred men who had died in the hazardous process of gilding the domes of the new cathedral of St Basil, and they were proud to be members of the Imperial household and to have the privilege of entertaining the Tsar, his family, his nobles, his foreign guests and the elite of his country.

'Well, if I were the Tsar I'd have a really splendid theatre,' Lydia continued in a wounded tone.

'Holy Mary!' Olga's narrow fingers flew to her lips. 'They'll all be right under our toes. I think I'm going to faint.'

'Oh don't be silly. You've danced for Their Majesties lots

of times.' At the Maryinsky Theatre, where ballets were performed twice a week and Sunday's performance was always attended by the Court, small divertissements and tiny roles in crowd ensembles were always included for the school students so that they should become accustomed to the stage as early as possible.

'But not so close, not so close.' Olga sounded as if she were going to weep. She was acknowledged to be excessively sensitive.

'Just think – how frightful if they saw our knickers!'

'Lydia! How can you be so vulgar!'

'Olga! How can you be so stupid!' She pulled faces and flounced her skirts, but no one defended her. The disapproval of the others pricked like needles. Lydia hated to feel excluded from the group. She had only intended to lighten Olga's gloomy mood. Normally she could trust her wit to mask her sharpness, but when it came to questions of taste it was so easy to go wrong.

'Trust you to spoil everything. You've no sense of propriety at all.' Olga seemed ready to shed tears at any moment.

'Ssh! Sssh! everyone – the boys!'

'Not in front of the *boys*, Lydia.' Performances were the only opportunity which the school pupils had to escape for a few instants from the institution's strict chaperonage. From the wings stepped forward two slim adolescents, subdued by the grandeur of their surroundings and by the sudden transformation of their schoolmates into miniature women. All the young dancers, who were to portray Parisian ballet students, were costumed in severe smocks and pinafores, exaggerations of the uniforms they wore every day at school, whose design had not changed for seventy years; mysteriously this dress made the boys appear younger but conferred a precocious maturity on the girls.

'Leo! Nico! Do come and look.' Little blonde Marie Kozhukova bubbled with vivacity that was natural, like a spring; she was being friendly rather than flirtatious and one after the other, the two boys stepped up awkwardly to the curtain to see where their audience would shortly be seated.

'What wonderful shadows.' Leo, the taller and darker of the two, moved aside to stand by Lydia. 'The statues of Apollo and the Muses look as if they're almost ready to step down from their alcoves, don't you think?'

'No.' She responded promptly, and was rewarded by stifled sniggers from her companions. Leo was always trying to get her attention with such pretentious observations but what was the use when his ears stuck out like bat's wings?

'Lydia never thinks, Leo, you ought to know that.' And Olga was always trying to get Leo's attention by being sweet to him. He ought to pay her more notice, she was nearly as pompous as he was. Contented to have spurned a suitor, Lydia twitched her neck to toss her curls, hoping that the stage lighting would show up the full depth of their colour. Her hair was a rich dark auburn and when it was plaited for the school day she boasted the longest and thickest pigtail in her class.

On hearing a silly slight against his beloved, Leo froze with disapproval and stepped back with Nico in disdainful silence. He seemed unaware of his humiliation, which Lydia ascribed to his hopeless arrogance and her companions to the fact that he adored her so passionately that in his eyes she could do no wrong.

'There aren't any boxes – where will Chinchilla be sitting?' Olga wisely decided to change the subject. Chinchilla was their nickname for the ballet's administrator of special services, a tall, heavy man with a thick head of black hair striped by a forelock of premature grey. Although danger-

28

ously attracted by modern ideas, his artistic judgement was superb, particularly when he organized these entertainments for the Imperial Family, and the whole company lived in hope of his approbation.

'He always sits in the Administration's seats.' Nico spoke with authority.

'But he won't be here tonight, will he?' Olga's huge eyes expanded with anxiety. 'Since he fell out with the new director?'

'He's still in with the Court, though.' Gossip was an important weapon in the battles for distinction which the dancers would wage violently for the brief duration of their stage lives. Lydia, in addition, enjoyed gossip for its own sake.

'And Kchessinskaya,' Lydia added, pausing involuntarily as she uttered the name of the prima ballerina, 'he was smart enough to get her on his side years ago.'

'They say he supported Mikhail Mikhailovich and that idiotic questionnaire he sent everyone.' In a transparent attempt to gain support for his ambitions towards modern choreography, a soloist called Mikhail Fokine had written to all the senior dancers in the company demanding to know if they felt ballet needed fundamental reforms.

'That was two years ago and anyway I don't believe it, Chinchilla would never have approved of anything so ridiculous.'

'Mikhail Mikhailovich is one of his little favourites.'

'Chinchilla kept himself well out of the whole affair.'

'And Tamara Platonova told me that Chinchilla told the director that only in Russia would ballet dancers have the intelligence and the sense of artistic responsibility to do such a thing, because it is only in Russia that the ballet is truly an art whereas in the rest of the world it has become nothing more than a decadent entertainment . . .'

'In a pig's eye!' Lydia's piercing laugh echoed in the void of the stage. 'He knows how to lay it on all right!'

'And decadent entertainment – now in that he's a real connoisseur!' Marie was almost bouncing with amusement.

'Chinchilla can't go wrong with the Court now,' announced Leo, whose deep-set eyes caught fire at the mention of anyone connected with the avant-garde set which he idolized. 'The Academy of Arts are backing him. All the people who went to Paris said his exhibition of paintings was a *succes fou*. I've heard people say he'll have all Europe at Russia's feet.'

'Grand Duke Vladimir is still on his side, I suppose. He's definitely in with him. Hasn't he agreed to finance Chinchilla's next show in Paris? Oh dear, I shall be so nervous if he's here tonight.' If Chinchilla had a failing, it was his leaning towards skinny neurotics like Olga. He had already acclaimed Anna Pavlova, who was as weak and thin as a bundle of sticks, and always seemed to have a special word to encourage Olga although she was, if anything, even less suited to the dance. No matter. It was easy to deal with such feeble competition.

'Oh, then Chinchilla's bound to be here,' Lydia assured her companion cheerfully. 'And I expect he'll sit on one of the aisles, because he always comes in late from backstage. Maybe he'll sit with the Grand Duke.' Olga wavered visibly with apprehension. 'But it will be dreadful, he'll have to disturb everyone,' Lydia continued, as if oblivious. 'It's such a badly designed theatre – why didn't the architects think of things like that?'

Nico sniffed humorously. 'Italians – what do they know?'

'It *is* beautiful,' Olga protested.

'But not practical, you must admit. Why are we Russians always running after foreigners thinking they know

30

something we don't – we ought to have more confidence in our native artists, they're just as fine and who else could express our national spirit?'

The two junior lovers of art, whose eyes never fell on an ugly object from waking to sleeping, fell into the fashionable argument with enthusiasm.

A moment later Olga let out a hysterical shriek. 'The toad! The toad is coming!'

The school's governesses were known by this charming nickname. Olga sprang aside, her ribs heaving with fright. 'Its Varvara Ivanova – help!'

Nico and Leo fled to the wings as one boy. The school rules on chaperonage were inflexible. Boys and girls had separate lessons and their dormitories were situated far apart. They met rarely and were absolutely forbidden to talk to each other. One of the great bonuses of a performance was the opportunity of a stolen exchange.

'Queen of all the toads. Now we'll catch it. No puddings for a week!' The thought of seven days without a jam pie at last subdued Lydia's spirits.

The stern-faced directress bustled swiftly towards the group, her black skirt swirling in agitation from her cinched belt. With her tiny waist and full bosom Lydia thought she looked more like a large angry ant than a toad, especially when she waved her arms in fury.

'You wicked girls. Do you think you can wander around in the Tsar's own theatre as if it was just anywhere? And why aren't you wearing your wraps? You were warned particularly about getting cold. Especially you, Spessitseva, no wonder you're always sick.'

'Please, Madame, we only wanted to see . . .'

'We've been looking everywhere for you. Why aren't you warming up? Take that smile off your face, Kusminskaya,

31

there's no cause for amusement, I promise you. Now behave yourselves, go back to the dressing room and practise. You'll disgrace us all anyway, no doubt.'

The girls filed off the stage, shamefaced until they were halfway down the corridor backstage and out of the governess's sight, when they began to recover their spirits.

'The stage here goes right out to the stalls, doesn't it? I can't believe I'll be dancing so close to the dear darling Tsar he'll almost be breathing on me.' Marie led the way to their dressing room.

'Dear darling . . . since when, Marie?'

'Oh don't be silly! I don't mean anything romantic and you know it, although he is wonderfully handsome, you must admit.'

'You're not taking over La Kchessinskaya's role yet, then?' Lydia's teasing was not completely idle. She had a fine piece of gossip about La Kchessinskaya, their prima ballerina.

'That would be the day! I'm not ready to end my career before it's even begun, thank you!'

Mathilde Kchessinskaya, a petite woman of intense glamour, arrived for class every morning in her own carriage drawn by three thoroughbred ponies. In summer she was swathed in lace; now, in the winter, muffled in sables, she herself seemed like a forest beast, quick, supple, ferocious, with glowing eyes and a decisive long nose poking from the depth of the pelts. She was a goddess to them all not only for her dancing but even more for the skill with which she managed her many intrigues. Kchessinskaya was a woman who made the whole world dance to her tune, and was moreover feted and adored in consequence.

In the empire of the ballet, Kchessinskaya ruled absolutely. She owed her untouchable position to the fact that, as a young prince, the Tsar Nicholas II had fallen madly in love with her. She had been a promising student of seventeen, but his favour swiftly raised her above her equally gifted rivals.

Their affair had continued at epic emotional pitch for four years, until his father's death brought Nicholas to the throne and compelled the lovers to part. Tsar Nicholas married the German Princess Alice and Kchessinskaya was commended to the care of his uncle the amiable Grand Duke Sergei. She was a magnificently strong dancer, and her vibrant personality positively burned on the stage, but her present eminence as prima ballerina *assoluta* was owed to the Tsar's patronage. She exploited it to the full; whenever she was crossed by the management, she appealed directly to the Emperor.

By this means she had annexed all the plum roles to herself, made sure she starred in all the most prestigious performances, demanded the richest gifts and even procured the resignation of the Director of the Imperial Theatres only eighteen months ago. He had displeased her by insisting that she wear the traditional hooped skirts for the role of La Camargo in a ballet designed in the style of Louis XV. Kchessinskaya preferred a lighter, more flattering costume, and so, after a public squabble, the Director lost his position over a petticoat. Shortly afterwards Chinchilla, the disgraced Director's young protégé, had almost been expelled by the new management, but he had prudently admired Kchessinskaya in his years of ascendancy and she rallied support for him.

Her appetite for scandal was insatiable. Now she had taken up with another of her former lover's cousins, the shy, good-looking Grand Duke André, who was younger than her by almost seven years. And furthermore she was carrying his child, and had retired formally from the stage a few days earlier, with her pregnancy quite visible to the informed eye.

'You're very wise, Marie.' Lydia crossed the empty

dressing room dramatically and perched on a battered gilt chair in a far corner. 'Especially since Kchessinskaya is dancing tonight.'

There was an immediate sensation and the girls crowded around in excitement.

'She can't be!'

'The scandal!'

'With the Tsar *and* the Grand Duke Sergei watching!'

'I don't believe it!'

'It's true, I promise you. Her name went on the notice board at the very last moment this afternoon. Tamara Platonova overheard the whole thing when she was sent to see the Principal and she told me herself.'

'It must be true then.' Tamara Platonova was a senior student whose honourable character was very much respected; if she had passed on the news then there could be no doubt.

'But won't she . . . I mean, won't it . . .' A deep blush rose up Olga's fine white neck as she tried to put the scandalous thought into words. 'I mean, you could see already . . .'

'Yes, they've been letting out her costumes for weeks. It's absolutely obvious.'

'And there's nowhere to hide on that tiny stage.'

'Her parents must be dying of shame,' Olga announced in a pious tone.

'Well, they're taking long enough about it. How many years is it since she left her father's house for that little villa the Tsar bought her?' Lydia suddenly checked herself, realizing that she was again about to cross the borders of good taste.

'And she's dancing Camargo again – one in the eye for the old Director, eh?' Marie chuckled and turned to the mirror to rearrange her curls. 'Well, I bet she's sorry she turned down that hooped skirt now.'

Before they could settle down for a long exchange of gossip the brisk footsteps of Varvara Ivanova were heard in the corridor and the girls fled to the barre to begin their pliés.

An hour later, arranged in a charming tableau on the stage, they strained their eyes against the glare of the lights to make out the noble figures beyond. The drop curtain, painted to show the audience a mezzotint scene of the river and bridge outside, rose slowly to reveal the small auditorium shimmering like rough seas by moonlight. Lydia realized that after all she was not to be cheated of a glorious vision. Jewels and gold, rich brocades, braids and embroidery sparkled even in the halfdarkness as their wearers applauded the opening scene.

From Christmas onwards, while the city lay under fathoms of snow and the river Neva froze to such a depth that the people used it as a highway, the Winter Palace indulged in a frenzy of merrymaking that lasted throughout Epiphany and reached a crescendo at this time, the week before the beginning of Lent. Then quietness and relative austerity would reign for forty days and forty nights: no balls, no state dinners, and no ballet.

Now however was still the time of lavish celebration. At the start of a new century, with the vigorous new Tsar and his lovely bride cherished in the splendour of St Petersburg, there was the sense that a great and beautiful new era had dawned for Russia. The harvests had been good, so the peasants were content. After centuries of darkness and struggle, enlightened government was leading the country into the future. Only the superstitious, the disloyal and the wicked could still believe that catastrophe was somehow a part of the nation's destiny. The Court agreed that informed folk felt otherwise.

No information ever reached this jewelled enclave without first being groomed for the occasion. The Court heard only official facts and rumours and, like the rest of the country, placed little reliance on information which had been managed from its origin. Nothing that had happened in recent years seemed beyond reasonable explanation. Peasants and factory workers had rioted, but this was the natural consequence of their terrible conditions, which were being improved. Students protested, but the young were always extremists. It was true that an incontrovertible assassination occasionally took place, but the murders had been incited by foreign agitators and the police had caught them. Russia was blessed with many able statesmen to take the place of the victims. In the Court theatre, on another glittering evening among many, the noblemen stretched their legs in the braided uniforms designed for them by Peter the Great himself and contemplated the coming years with confidence.

The audience was quiet but animated. Their excitement warmed the entire auditorium, making the girls' blood tingle in their veins and their feet itch to be moving. Lydia could make out the shapes of jewelled aigrettes and tiaras, nodding like sparkling flowers in a breeze. She sensed the silk dresses heavy with the weight of their gold-thread embroidery crushed carelessly together. As the applause died down it was even possible to hear the rattle of the long ropes of pearls, of which most of the women would be wearing as many as their necks could carry.

> *Now I know*
> *That Chinchilla is out there*
> *I am so*
> *Afraid I'll die of fear.*

Without disturbing her cherubic smile, Marie hummed the

little song which the girls had made up to warn each other that their exacting overseer was among the audience.

'Where?' hissed Lydia, her piquant simper deepening with the effort of whispering from the side of her mouth.

With a blink of her round doll's eyes Marie indicated the left side of the auditorium, and Lydia saw the dark bulk descend heavily into the gold armchair at the end of the third row. Another large figure stirred beside him and the Grand Duke Sergei's bull-like grunt resonated in the hush. All the Tsar's uncles were huge men. A few rows further back were the most favoured seats, where she could distinguish the Tsar Nicholas and his family, so smothered in precious stones and cloth of gold that they resembled those old icons which seemed to move by the flickering light of their lamps. The Tsarina sat stiffly, wearing a gauze veil under her tiara.

As the music gave them their cue, Lydia dragged her attention away from the half-hidden splendour of the Court and the girls regrouped around the handsome figure of Nikolai Legat, who created the role of the dancing master as a caricature of one of the legendary teachers at the Imperial School, an elderly and choleric Swede who sat wearily in a chair directing the pupils with febrile gestures of his violin bow. For the devoted balletomanes this piece was a delicious tapestry of allusions and private jokes. Legat's own talent for drawing caricatures was hinted at in his performance; wicked details such as this were Chinchilla's hallmarks.

The girls performed an opening divertissement based on their daily class, each having a few bars of solo dancing to display her talents. As Lydia stepped forward to prepare her opening steps a radiant calm posessed her. It was very quiet; she heard little, but felt the music running in her body like blood and when her cue came she flew into motion without

37

knowing what she did. The Court, the audience, her teachers and the other dancers were distant presences. Inside her being she was all-powerful. Her limbs took possession of the air as if their proper space was already marked out. There was no doubt, fear or hesitation and as she came to rest and her normal consciousness returned she knew before the applause that she had briefly created perfection.

In one corner of the auditorium the applause redoubled and she paused for an instant, glancing into the wings to see if she might be granted a second curtsey, but a gesture from the startled *régisseur* sent her to rejoin the others at the back of the stage. Tingling with pleasure she fell into line beside Marie and the girls turned and froze into a tableau to complement the first of the soloists.

Tinkling and rattling in her costume sewn with coins, an older dancer made her entrance and paused for applause in the stylized attitude typical of the gypsy dances which were currently a fashionable addition to every work.

'I can't bear to watch, she'll end up flat on her face, I know it.' Marie lowered her eyelids as the older girl passed them, already white with the effort of forcing her feet through the rapid sequence of steps.

'Why in the world did they give her this one? The poor thing – she just isn't fast enough.' Lydia herself excelled as a *gitane*. When it was her turn she would show them all; her legs were simply made for those wild turns.

The two girls solemnly rearranged their arms for the next dance and exchanged glances of disgust as Anna Pavlova wafted through the romantic variation, gossamer wings quivering at her nothing of a waist.

'God, she's pathetic,' Marie hissed under cover of the applause. 'Why doesn't she eat more, she looks like a ghost. However did she get chosen for this?'

'Kchessinskaya insisted. You know she's making a pet of Anna Matveyana.'

Close, chassé, demi-plié in fourth, port de bras, don't forget your head . . . they heard their teacher's voice in their minds as they regrouped for the final variation. Deliberately the conductor extended the pause in the music. A faint spray of reflected light signified the audience fidgeting in anticipation. The baton rose in a grand sweep, plunged the orchestra into a brilliant crescendo, and all at once Kchessinskaya had leapt into the centre of the tableau and was acknowledging rapturous applause.

The music resumed and the great ballerina darted across the stage, her shoulders never losing their imperiously coquettish tilt while the extraordinary power of her pretty limbs propelled her across the boards like a lightning bolt. At the age of thirty many dancers were past their best, but Kchessinskaya's strength was still a marvel, enough to carry her through the most dazzling athletic moves with her smile bright and every appearance of ease. Her diamond earrings, famous as the Tsar's gift and the cause of another victory over the directorate, flashed with every snap of her head as she finished the final series of pirouettes.

Criticism was all that the girls heard, and naturally it made up most of their own conversation. With Kchessinskaya tonight there was nothing to criticize as they scurried away for their wraps at the interval.

'Wasn't she ill yesterday?' Marie made a feeble effort to start the conversation.

'Not much wrong tonight,' responded Olga with frank envy in her voice.

'My mother says a woman can never be the same in that condition,' volunteered an olive-skinned girl. 'Did you notice how she moved all those attitudes round so His Majesty couldn't catch her in profile? So, so clever.'

'And I swear she's had the roses sewn lower at the front of her dress.' The Camargo costume was always swagged with garlands of silk roses to recall the dancer's famous portrait by Boucher.

'I don't see the point – we know, everybody knows and surely His Majesty must know as well. She ought to go away quietly until it's all over.'

'No, why should she? Nobody's offended. It's one thing to be pregnant, but looking pregnant – that's quite different, isn't it?' Lydia pulled a chair over to the blue and white tiled stove whose warm mass occupied the entire end of the room.

'I don't see why, surely being pregnant is all that matters.'

'No, it's how you look as well.' Marie joined Lydia in the warmth.

'How you look is most important really,' Lydia continued abstractedly. 'You can be what you like, after all, but if you don't look it then nobody can be sure and it doesn't really matter. After all, nobody will be scandalized by La Kchessinskaya tonight, will they? I think she's doing everything absolutely properly. After all, if she didn't dance, His Majesty would have to know why.'

'Kusminskaya! Why were you born a guttersnipe!' The door flung open to reveal Varvara Ivanova, fortunately too full of the urgency of her message to have heard the improper conversation which she had interrupted. 'They can see at the back of the house that you're wearing old shoes! Surely you could have worn new shoes for your Emperor? Change immediately! And the rest of you' – her gaze raked the room with disapproval – 'stop dozing like a litter of stray cats and make sure you look perfect. You're all to be presented to Their Majesties after the performance. I don't want to see a hair out of place. Spessitseva! You've tied your ribbons the wrong way. Somebody help her! And all of you – five minutes!'

The virago swept away, and while the other girls leaped to the mirror with squeaks of excitement Lydia changed her shoes in silence while she calculated her response. Now more than ever she was anxious to behave correctly, and aware that whatever instinct dictated the behaviour of her companions, she had been born without it.

Her dancing often set her apart and after tonight's strange interlude of possession she was inclined to believe that she was exceptionally gifted. There could be no doubt that their sudden summons before the Imperial Court was as a result of her performance. The curious, alarmed little looks which she caught obliquely from the mirrors confirmed it, as well as the fury with which the directress had picked on her. Her strength was undeniably special. In the school everyone knew everyone else's weakness, and physically little Kusminskaya had none of gravity; thus what was simple for her was an ordeal for her companions, and their fears were not her fears.

Her faults seemed harder to correct. She was accused of lacking feeling, of being unmusical, even of having no soul, and these qualities seemed hopelessly nebulous. Practice, she assured the others sincerely, would easily make them strong, but how could one practise feeling? They said she was insensitive. Olga frankly called her vulgar and asked what else one could expect of a merchant's daughter. She had become wary.

Ambitions are born at the beginning of adulthood. There was a consensus among the students that to dance the great roles, the princesses in the huge five-act ballets, was the only proper ideal. Lesser spirits might aspire simply to please their parents or to marry well. The pretentious group, among whom Leo was prominent, dreamed of creating a great art which would transcend the classics. None of this moved Lydia. Dancing was too easy for her. She had an unformed sense that the real world was on the other side, beyond the orchestra pit, across the footlights, among the men with decorations and the women with jewels. Despite the tears and blood shed for it, the ballet was nothing of any significance to her, although she dared not voice this sentiment, even to herself.

Lydia uttered a few exclamations to show that she shared the general elation and returned to the stage with the others. She felt that her progress was to begin. In less than an hour she would make the mystical journey across the footlights and stand among the courtiers, and the Tsar himself would speak to her. She was so nearly in a trance with the knowledge that if Marie had not seized her hand and pulled her forward she would have stood still in the wings throughout the entire second act.

Shepherded by Varvara Ivanova they were conducted through the empty theatre to the salon beyond, where the audience gathered to drink champagne before moving on to supper. Striving not to gawk like yokels, Lydia and Olga led the demure enfilade. The crowd parted to admit them, and halfway down the room they heard the soft clapping of many gloved hands.

The room was still intimate in scale, but elaborately decorated. Rococo mouldings, white palm fronds, treillage and gilt rosebuds overlaid walls of bird's-egg blue. The light from six gilt chandeliers gleamed on Court dresses by Worth and Nicaud, jewellery by Fabergé and Cartier. The air was rich with perfumes, tobacco smoke and the faint aroma of consommé from the distant dining room. It was necessary to take care and watch each footfall, for when the women turned to look at them their long stiff trains swept unexpectedly across the polished wood floor.

The Imperial Family themselves wore so much gold and silver that they seemed to stand in a haze of light. The Tsarina wore silver silk brocade embroidered with gold thread, and as she greeted each girl in turn the white ermine which edged her sleeves brushed their hands. Behind her Lydia briefly saw the short round figure of the Court nurse, formally clothed in a peasant sarafan sewn with gold which billowed around her as she bent to pick up a three-year-old girl.

'So, at last – the young lady who is to be the new glory and adornment of our ballet.' Lydia curtsied immediately, feeling faint as the Tsar himself turned his sad brown eyes upon her. She sensed beside her the agitation of Varvara Ivanova, who had been prepared to present Olga first. The Tsar was extending his hand towards her. Automatically she curtsied again, then almost leaped upright, struck by the idea that she ought to have taken his hand instead. Beside the Court ladies in their stiff dresses she felt grubby and half-naked in her costume. She was so confused that she felt tears start in her eyes.

'Charming child,' murmured a resonating deep voice, quickly echoed by others. 'Charming, charming.' Lydia froze with uncertainty.

'Take care not to grow up too fast,' His Majesty continued. 'Tell me your name.'

'This is Lydia Alexandrovna Kusminskaya,' Varvara Ivanova announced immediately, struggling for control of the situation. 'Olga Sergeyevna Spessitseva, Marie Stepanova Kozhukova . . .' Almost in panic the girls placed their right feet forward, swept their left back and sank to the floor in a ragged succession. At the end of the line Leo and Nico bowed so low that they swayed off balance. Nausea gripped Lydia's throat. Surely their horrible gauche display would be a joke in the Court for weeks.

The soft applause broke out again. Surrounded by tall people, Lydia could see nothing but she heard Kchessinskaya's name murmured around the room, and the ballerina's unmistakable high laugh as she acknowledged compliments. The focus of attention mercifully moved away from them. She saw the Tsar lean over the shorter figure of a Court page, muttering an order while his eyes were clearly looking for the ballerina's arrival. The boy hurried away while the stiff figures around them stirred and regrouped themselves. Expressionless, the Tsarina proceeded to a far corner of the room.

The awkward atmosphere vanished as Kchessinskaya approached on the arm of the Director, the bouquet of orchids and tuberoses which she had received on stage held lightly in the curve of her arm. She had changed into a silk dress of the pale lilac blue which was the absolute rage of the moment. It was oversewn with tiny pearls, and so lavishly embroidered with corded silk that the tactful ruching of the waist seemed a natural decorative touch. Behind her, appearing small and with no special presence in their evening clothes and normal make-up, the remaining dancers followed in a procession.

The crowd fell silent, momentarily transfixed as the presentations began, and then recalled the need to pretend that there was no cause for prurience and began gossiping at once.

'We are sad to hear of your retirement.' The Tsar was speaking to Kchessinskaya.

'I shall be sad to leave the stage, Your Majesty.'

'You will be a great loss to our ballet.' The words were

formal banalities but the tall man whose uniform blazed with decorations and the tiny woman in flowing silk had the appearance of old friends in relaxed conversation.

'Your Majesty is too kind.'

'Are any of Madame Kchessinskaya's ballets to be given next season?' This inquiry was to the Director. It was a pointed question and a shiver of interest passed through the onlookers.

'Only *La Bayadère*, Your Majesty. At Madame's request. She has given the role to Mademoiselle Pavlova.' The younger dancer immediately dropped to the floor in a curtsey, acknowledging her mentor with a graceful inclination of her long neck.

'The generosity of a great heart.' The complicity of the former lovers was beyond doubt. The official information was that the marriage of the Tsar Nicholas and the Tsarina Alexandra was a great love match, but all St Petersburg knew that Nicholas had evaded marriage for years and had been forced to give up Kchessinskaya only when it was clear that his father was dying. The real generosity to which he was alluding was hers in accepting that loss with extraordinary grace, and now his in blessing her new alliance. All around the couple there was a warm outpouring of breath as the Court savoured the true meaning of the exchange.

'It seems that every year a new generation of great dancers is born in our country,' the Emperor continued, gesturing towards the children. He leaned forward and said something inaudible, then gestured to the page.

The Director nodded to Varvara Ivanova who surreptitiously took hold of Lydia's arm to pull her forward. 'You are all to receive a gift from His Majesty's own casket,' he informed them in a ringing voice, and while her companions exchanged nervous glances Lydia immediately grasped his meaning.

45

The page stepped forward with a tray draped in red velvet, on which were arranged eight black leather boxes stamped in gold with the Imperial eagle. The Director selected one and presented it to Lydia, who curtsied to him, then to His Majesty, and then, amidst the cloying aura of tuberose, received a kiss on both cheeks from Kchessinskaya.

'The little pets!' she exclaimed, tipping up Lydia's chin as she rose. 'Such a sweet, surprised little face! Just like a violet, isn't she? Show us His Majesty's gift, little one.'

With the bright sable eyes encouraging her, Lydia opened the box with graceful gestures and then gasped with surprise at the sight of an oval hoop of gold, a bracelet chased with scrolls, lying inside it. At Kchessinskaya's prompting she turned the box around and displayed the gift to the approving crowd.

'You will treasure this gift for ever ...' She nodded, unable to find her voice, patting the bracelet in its place with timid fingers. 'Although I am sure it will be the first of many tributes to such a gifted young artist.' There was another burst of animated comment. Clearly La Kchessinskaya did not pay such compliments lightly. 'And now this little angel ...' Olga was at her side and Lydia stepped back swiftly to make room.

In a few more instants it was over, and as they were led away to more salon applause Lydia saw the footmen opening the doors to the dining room and caught a whiff of rich soup which almost made her stomach rumble. She was extremely hungry. Their maids, who were waiting to help them change into their thick outdoor clothes, also had baskets of pastries and hot milk which had thoughtfully been sent up from the kitchen.

A heavy square coach of ancient design, known to the

students as an antediluvian, waited for them by the artists'
entrance to the theatre. In the winter it lurched through the
snowy streets on iron runners in place of wheels. The wicker
baskets containing their costumes were loaded behind, the
coachman pulled the rugs off the three heavy horses and
they set off along the icy river embankment. It was snowing,
tiny flakes blown in thick gusts by the wind. Lydia realized
that her hands were still pressing the black leather box to
her heart.

'I wonder why she chose Anna Matveyana to take over
La Bayadère?' Marie spoke drowsily, pulling the rug around
her face. 'She works so hard and she is very lyrical, of
course, but it's supposed to be terribly demanding. I'm sure
she isn't nearly strong enough.'

'Then everyone will always remember La Kchessinskaya
and how marvellous she was.' Lydia yawned. The reasoning
seemed simple to her. 'Don't take all the rug, Marie. My
knees will get cold.'

'Why of course! How clever you are, Lydia. I'm sorry,
here's the rug back. If Anna Matveyana is a disaster then
Kchessinskaya will seem all the better. That must be why
she's making a favourite of Tamara Platonova too. I heard
her promise to give her some of her costumes.' It was
natural to them all that a student should qualify unofficially
in dance company politics at the same time as her formal
graduation.

'I heard she isn't really retiring.' Leo, whose father was a
dancer in the company, spoke with his usual authority. 'It's
all a sham. Once the baby's born they'll ask her to come
back. So she doesn't want to give herself any competition.'

'I'd never be able to do that,' Olga suddenly whispered in
the darkness.

'Do what?' Lydia mistrusted her companion's morbid tone.

'See the man I loved married to another woman,' responded Olga.

'When you're officially protected by his uncle *and* pregnant by his cousin too – yes, that must be quite a challenge,' responded Lydia with gaiety, forgetting the need to eschew vulgarity. But sleepy laughter warmed the carriage and she realized that her status had altered.

The boys were made to descend first and give the girls their arms as they left the carriage, a chivalrous drill which enabled Leo to slip a note into Lydia's pocket. She frowned with irritation but in the meagre light of the school entry he saw nothing and was soon hurried away.

'Hurry to bed now, girls, but don't wake the others,' was Varvara Ivanova's parting instruction. Twenty girls slept in their dormitory, and a maid dozed in a chair at one end of the long room. Marie and Lydia were close together in a far corner and were permitted to share a night light while they undressed. Under cover of brushing out her long hair and braiding it loosely for the night, Lydia pulled a small box edged with paper lace from her night stand. Here she kept everything precious to her, and she intended to put the Tsar's gift with the collection of two sweets wrapped in silver paper which were too pretty to eat, a spray of velvet forget-me-nots which she had picked up in the street, a tiny silver charm like a violin and a tortoiseshell comb edged with brilliants. The last of these two items had been the property of other girls, and so Lydia kept her treasure box to herself.

'What's in there?' Marie sat on the edge of her bed and rubbed her sore toes.

'Oh, just hairpins.' To confirm the truth Lydia pulled the last few pins from her braid, dropped them into the box and put it quickly out of sight. Marie seemed uninterested, although something was on her mind.

'Lydia,' she whispered again, 'do you have a friend?'

Friendship was a formal affair among the girls. If two agreed to be friends they pledged themselves to reserve all their confidences for each other and to walk into dinner together every evening. Knowing that she was, if not exactly unpopular, then at least a girl regarded as different by the others, Lydia was resigned to remaining without such a special companion.

'No, I haven't got a friend.' Maybe Marie would say something sympathetic.

'Well then . . . Lydia Alexandrovna, will you agree to be my friend and tell me all your secrets?'

A proposal from sweet-natured Marie, whom everyone loved and whose father was said to have been a count from a really old noble Polish family – Lydia almost forgot to whisper.

'Oh, heavens – Marie! Do you really mean it?'

'Yes, yes, of course I do. I've always liked you, Lydia. You're going to be a wonderful dancer, everyone says so. And you're terribly clever. And you've got beautiful hair, not like mine.'

'Well, of course I will.'

'No, you have to say it properly.'

'Oh yes, of course. I Lydia Alexandrovna agree to be your friend and to tell you all my secrets.' Furtively, in case the maid should order them to bed immediately, they exchanged kisses on the cheek.

'Well, go on then.'

'What?' Lydia was alarmed. Was there another point of school etiquette of which she was ignorant?

'I saw Leo give you a note, Lydia.'

'Oh, that . . .' It had fallen to the floor and she swept it up with disdainful fingertips. 'Do you want me to read it to you?'

'Yes, *yes!*'

'It's a poem. "She dances as one of the immortals among the stars of heaven. The goddesses marvel at her celestial beauty. Among the muses, Apollo favours her alone." Oh how awful! Isn't that silly?'

'Oh, no. It's really romantic, Lydia. Imagine, you are the first of us to have an admirer.'

'You can't count Leo as an admirer, he's only a boy.'

'Well, I think you're very lucky.' Disconcerted to find her friend so unmoved by love, Marie gathered up the folds of her nightdress and climbed into bed.

'I tell you what,' Lydia whispered, realizing that the pact needed to be sealed immediately if Marie were not to regret her proposal. 'Let's do something. After we blow the night light out, let's wait until the maid's asleep and then look at our bracelets in the moonlight. The sky's clearing, there ought to be plenty of light soon.'

Marie found this a suitably exciting adventure and half an hour later the blind was quietly raised and the new friends lay in bed turning their little hoops of gold in the colourless light of the moon. Their enclosed world was full of magical talismans – Cinderella's slipper, the Swan Queen's feather, Giselle's fatal necklace and countless roses and lilies symbolizing eternal love. Lydia knew with complete certainty that the Tsar's gift was her own token of fortune. An hour later when Varvara Ivanova passed on her final patrol she found the new ornament of the ballet sleeping with her arms crossed like a corpse and the bracelet pressed firmly against her heart.

CHAPTER 2
Chelsea, London, 1968

'Why do you want to be an artist, Bianca?' He smelt of sweat, Kents and beer, in quantities; at least twenty cigarettes, at least six pints and as much sweat as a healthy mesomorph could work up through emotional exertion alone in the first half of a close summer night in Chelsea.

'I don't want to be an artist. I want to die.' He taught her screenprinting. Bianca did not see her future in screenprinting, and in any case he had already written his report on her. She normally preferred to be polite, but in his case it seemed appropriate to make an exception.

'You don't really mean that.'

'Of course I bloody mean it, why do you think I bloody said it?' She thumped the windowsill with her fist and felt the hurt with surprise. It was reassuring to feel something, even pain. As the necessity to choose her future course of study had grown more acute, anxiety had numbed all her senses. Now the echoing canyon of the summer vacation was opening ahead and she was unable to choose a direction.

By chance at that moment the Rolling Stones completed their farewell to Ruby Tuesday and the nearby group of men whose recurring guffaws had almost drowned their conversation had nothing to amuse them. Bianca's voice resounded across the room above the general buzz. A few heads turned, but Bianca, adept at averting attention, assumed a bored expression and an inactive slouch so that the curious found nothing to interest them and the party soon resumed its volume.

'You don't want to die, Bianca.' His hand, holding hers, was clammy. Perhaps the beer was starting to ooze out of his pores.

'I do want to die. I can't draw, I'll never be able to draw . . .'

'You've got a lovely sense of colour . . .'

'I can't draw, everybody hates everything I do . . .'

'No they don't, you've got it all wrong . . .'

'I have *not*. Will you listen to me, for God's sake? I can't draw, nobody likes my work, I've no ideas, I bore everyone, I even bore myself. I've nothing to live for, I've never fallen in love and I'm nearly twenty, and I want to die.' At last he relaxed his damp grip and she pulled her hand away with relief.

'But I love you, Bianca.'

'Oh, God.' She rolled her eyes and for an instant felt as if this minor motion would overbalance her. Drink was not a factor; she hated the taste of beer and had struggled through the minimum quantity necessary to participate in the evening. Unhappiness had sapped all her energy. She felt exhausted. For support she leaned against the wall and regarded the man who taught screenprinting. With his wild brown hair hanging over his low eyebrows, he was preparing to move towards her.

'I do, I love you, Bianca.'

'I want to go home.'

He paused, shaking his head slowly like an ox choosing between two gates. 'This is your home, isn't it?'

'Oh God, yes, it is.' That was her weeping fig tree behind him, and she was the person who had started to paint the opposite wall pink last weekend and stopped because it had not come out the right colour. She could smell her sister's joss sticks from the next room. Above her head she could hear her mother, or her father, or maybe her mother's lover, or any combination of these – who cared? – clattering around on the varnished floorboards.

She had a memory of a voice in another party an hour or so ago, gaily inviting everyone home for coffee. Hermione, her sister, had already collected five friends who had been sitting at the square pine table with a large lump of dope and its attendant paraphernalia scattered around them when the rest arrived. Now the room was full of people and hazy with marijuana smoke; Hermione and her friends were grating some of their stash into a large bowl of chocolate cake mix, arguing over the quantities with benevolent intensity.

There was a ludic, end-of-term craziness in the gathering which made Bianca sad because she was excluded. The full length of her back was now against the wall and there were so many people around them that she could not move away. Breathing beer fumes, the printing tutor put his hand on her shoulder. He could hardly rape her with thirty people in the room. Since she was Bianca Berrisford, it was unlikely that anyone in the world of art would consider raping her anyway. It might be fatal to their career.

To be a Berrisford was to belong to a great dynasty. From the beginning of the century the family's tentacles had reached out to embrace the entire world of art, and from the outset had recognized that they were also artists who only bought or sold. Now, when the creative eruptions of the Sixties were at full violence, the family stood for the moneyed, sophisticated elite who would guide the new Britain, loaded with talent and bright with money, to a position of worldwide eminence.

Bianca's grandfather had been a great painter, a Royal Academician whose pretty reveries were now unfashionable but might be technically admired; his proud younger brother founded a gallery to sell his work. Bianca's grandmother, arthritic as she had become, was still an accomplished amateur watercolourist; her father in his turn had turned his uncle's gallery into the famous auction house that bore their name.

Her mother made silver jewellery which just at that time was acutely fashionable. There was an aunt by marriage who sculpted, a runaway cousin who photographed, a huge diaspora of relatives who administered, or curated, or restored, or lectured about or financed art. The ex-wife of the son of one of her grandfather's uncounted illegitimate children ran a venue for happenings in a derelict fruit warehouse in Covent Garden, and was warmly acknowledged by the clan who held creativity to be their blood bond.

Their handsome white villa stood proudly in its garden in the heart of Chelsea, with a blue plaque over the door commemorating her grandfather's residence. The house was permanently awash with artists, gallery owners, collectors, publishers, academics and thin, hollow-eyed art groupies, all jostling in their orbits around the Berrisford star, eager to believe that culture was breaking free of upper-class control, that they would be on the barricades in this social revolution and that a new class of art patrons would finance a new Renaissance.

To be born a Berrisford was to accept art as an inevitable destiny. Bianca had never questioned her path in life, only her own fitness to follow it. She was, however, well accustomed to admirers who were merely dazzled by her heritage.

'What I hate about people like you' – she folded her arms and leaned heavily into the wall – 'is that although you say you don't care about things, actually you do.'

'I care about you, Bianca. You're beautiful and talented and . . .'

'My mother is beautiful. My father is rich. My grandparents were talented. Could your judgement have been influenced at all, do you suppose? I seem pretty ordinary to me.'

'But you are good, Bianca, honestly you are. Look, come and do printing next year with me and I'll prove it to you.'

'Oh, don't listen to him, love.' The noisy neighbouring group suddenly surrounded them. 'Don't let him talk you into mucking around wi' printing. Come and do sculpture wi' us.' She eyed them with gratitude, six large men in frayed Shetland sweaters standing with glasses clamped firmly in their fists and smiles on their ruddy faces. Undoubtedly they were affecting their broad Northern accents to emphasize the integrity which a man or an artist could claim with birth into the industrial working class.

'Half an hour!' Hermione, her face flushed with the effort, manoeuvred a large baking tin of cake mixture into the oven and slammed the door. 'Half an hour, everybody. Who wants to lick out the bowl?' Eager hands reached forward and she passed them their prize, taking care to keep her hair under control. It flowed around her shoulders like a glistening brown-grey river, caught in swirls and eddies by the numerous beads decorating her velvet smock. Hermione was three years younger than Bianca, but people often assumed that she was the older sister since she was already an accomplished earth mother, deep-bosomed, mystical and fond of cooking.

Unconsciously, Bianca ran her fingers over her own cropped head. Intent on baiting the printing tutor, the sculpture students closed ranks around them both.

'Sculpture's where it's at, really. It's cool, is sculpture.'

The slim, freckle-faced man winked at his comrades over the rim of his glass and the tutor shifted uncomfortably from one foot to the other.

'Aye,' the black-haired one added, 'come wi' us and do some welding, love. It's a groove, you'll like it.'

'Forget all that poncey drawing lark. We don't do none of that in sculpture.'

'That's for poofs, drawing is.'

'Aye.'

'You can get good and mucky doing sculpture.'

'Aye, we like to get our 'ands dirty in sculpture.'

Intimidated, outnumbered and with his masculinity tarnished, the printing tutor backed away, accepting defeat. 'I really think you ought to consider screenprinting,' was his final feeble offer.

'Aye, come up an' see my etchings, 'n all,' muttered the freckled one with derision, and his companions laughed.

They were the kind of men who ran in a pack to give themselves courage. Individually they were nothing but provincial boys overawed by the metropolis; honest, uncomplicated, kindhearted and vulnerable on account of those qualities. Together they could impose their own perspectives, they were a company who could stand with their shields edge to edge and repel their enemies.

The dark-haired one shouldered through the crowd to the kitchen and returned with beer in glass bottles.

'Can you drink Newcastle Brown?' he asked with concern, suddenly aware that the band had captured one of the glossy Chelsea girls whose excessive self-esteem and disinclination to date Northern lads had been the cause of much bitter humour since their arrival in London.

'I don't know. Let's find out.' She gave him a fleeting smile and put the bottle to her lips before they distanced her any further by producing a glass. 'What do you work in?' He had a strong face, with thick eyebrows, a slightly Roman nose and downturned, heavy-lidded eyes. There was something classical about him, and she had a flash vision of him chipping granite.

'Tungsten tubes. Lights.'

'Oh.' From the kitchen area rose a rich aroma of chocolate cake with the sharp tang of hashish. Hermione was clattering plates.

'But they're very open, any medium you're drawn to you can have.'

'Uh-huh.'

'Plastic, steel, concrete – there's even a bloke working in video. I was surprised, I must say. They don't seem to consider the expense very much down here.'

Bianca felt the leaden cloud of tiredness stealing around her once more. She had no desire to work in plastic, steel, concrete, video or tungsten tubes. Her foundation year at art school had taught her one ugly fact about herself – she was dull. No medium excited her, no course truly attracted her, no subject drew her except the human body. The realms of space, planes and light, the adventurous textures and the gigantic statements lured the other students like new worlds while she was content with faces and bodies. She admired people who created heaps of tin cans to criticize the throwaway society, or multiple nipples on video for the sake of liberating human sexuality from centuries of repression, but for herself she wanted only to catch the curve of a shoulder or the motion of an arm.

Her tutors muted their disapproval but it was constant. If she painted a woman in a room, they gently suggested that she remove the woman. Her melancholy study of an old man's face had prompted the comment that the light on his nose was the real focus of the picture. There was no advance between her work and the genteel studies of his lovers in his garden for which her grandfather remained famous. She was hardly fit to create a picture postcard.

The lights were dimmed to their lowest, temporarily causing a lull in the conversation. At the stove, Hermione ignited a bunch of sparklers and began to stick them in her Indian joss-stick holder, squeaking as she dodged the sparks. A thoughtful soul turned up the lights sufficiently for her to complete the task. There was a cheer as the cake with its blazing crown was raised to shoulder height and carried into the throng.

'What about collage?' Bianca asked, without enthusiasm.

'There's several blokes doing that. *Objets trouvés*, old cans, bits of cars.'

'Hmmn.'

'What do you think you'd be interested in?'

'Cake, anyone?'

'Hey, thanks love!'

'Oh wow!'

'Really great.'

As they extracted hot, crumbling helpings from the baking tin, the other men regrouped and left them to develop their own awkward conversation. She sensed that he was superior among them, that it was natural for him to carry off a prize female such as herself, and that the rest would support him proudly in the adventure. Bianca was well accustomed to the role of a sexual trophy, but was certain that this man had no desire to capture her.

'Thanks, Herm. It looks good.'

'Have this end, it's burnt at the other.' She beamed at them both, looking from one to the other with curiosity, her Tibetan earrings tinkling as she turned her head.

Bianca swallowed a handful of warm crumbs, pulling a face at the bitter aftertaste, and returned to the conversation.

'I don't really know. Bodies, I like working with bodies.'

'Performance art, you mean?' He was holding his own slab of cake uncertainly, as if hoping someone would take it away from him.

'You don't have to eat that. She won't be offended, she's cool about everything, my sister. There's not enough sugar in it anyway, it tastes awful.' He nodded thankfully and returned his portion to the tray as it passed. 'God no, not performance art. I just like people, the peopleness of people. The human essence. You know.' She had at least developed a convincing rationale for her deficiency.

'That's original.'

'No it isn't.' For the first time he looked at her directly and against all probability she read his expression as sympathetic. She felt uncertain. 'People have been painting each other for millions of years.'

'There must be something in it, then.' Another unlikely occurrence, her mouth was smiling.

'I'm sorry, you were being sarcastic.'

'I wasn't, not entirely. What's art for if it doesn't tell people something about each other?'

'Is that what you're doing with your lights?' At the back of her mind was a rumour she had recently heard which seemed to have some relevance.

Defensively, his eyes flickered. 'Well, folk can certainly see each other better when I switch them on. Tell me something . . .'

'What?'

'If you have so much trouble with who you are and your family and all, why don't you move out of here? Don't get me wrong, I'm not giving you advice, but I can see it must be tough for you and, well, they're literally on top of you, aren't they?'

The notion had occurred to her many times, but life outside the Berrisford galaxy had seemed shadowy and unreal. Now that this big man, with his vivid features and deep voice, and the extra dimension of being an absolute outsider to the Chelsea scene, was positing the idea, it seemed more tangible.

'I should, shouldn't I?' He nodded and there was an energy connecting them which she could not interpret. 'You know, I have been thinking about sculpture. I was quite interested in maybe doing body moulds or something.' Tentatively, she picked at her fingernails, her eyes averted to hide her full intentions. In an American avant-garde art magazine she had seen pictures of work moulded directly on models and realized that the technique would enable her to appear interesting while concealing all her faults.

'We'll be seeing you next year, then?' He spoke too eagerly – a sign, at last.

The room was changing. A few people were settling down on the floor, ready for a long stoned night. Van Morrison was remembering Cypress Avenue. The rest, with other tastes or invitations, realizing that there was no longer enough dope to share, were moving languidly out into the garden and then on to the street. The dark man's friends were arguing about their next party and how they would reach it.

'I'm the one with a car,' he told her, shrugging helplessly as he was pulled by the sleeve towards the door.

'So is the lass on for it, or what?' demanded the freckled man, half from Bianca herself.

'On for what?' She had not felt flirtatious for months, but

now she followed them to the door and leaned teasingly against its edge, still smiling.

'This is Joe – don't mind him, he's one of them unmannerly Northern lads.'

'Pleased to meet you,' Joe responded, shaking her hand with enthusiasm. 'So are you coming to do sculpture wi' us, or are you going to do printing wi' that daft git?'

'She'll be wi' us, Lovat, in't she?'

'Gotta be.'

'Bound to be.'

'Cut it out, fellas.' They tumbled drunkenly up the stone-flagged stairs to ground level and disappeared in the darkness one by one. The sticky yellow glare of the street lights coated the leaves of the magnolia tree beside the house and Bianca noticed that the sky was lightening beyond the high brick walls of the garden. The dark one paused at the head of the stairs but she closed the door rapidly before she could say something stupid.

'Do you think I should do sculpture, Herm?' Her sister was lying sprawled on the window seat like the death of Chatterton.

'I think you should listen to the voice inside you and do what it says.'

'Bianca, do you know who that *was* who was trying to pull you?' The second voice belonged to Shona Crawford-Pitt, who wore velvet bows in her thick blonde hair, and smart loafers with her jeans, and was the most obvious of all the people who tried to attach themselves to the Berrisfords because of their name.

'Don't be daft, he wasn't trying to pull me. Lovat, his name was, I heard the others say it. He's a second year, isn't he? Oh no!' Finally the faint memory of a new rumour sharpened in her mind. 'That's not the one who's doing the bank job, is it?' The sensation of the last weeks of term had been the second-year student who had been commissioned to produce a work for the atrium of a large American bank. A corporate contract of that size would have been a coup for a major mature artist; for a student, let alone a mere second-year student, it was either tantamount to a certificate of genius or proof of absolute moral bankruptcy: the body of the college was passionately divided on the issue.

'Of course it is! You goof, that was the great Lovat Whitburn.' Even when she was stoned Shona's patrician squeal was enough to crack glass.

'Oh, God, *that* ghastly breadhead. What a pity. He didn't look like a class enemy.' Hermione rolled over to pass the joint.

'Herm, you're so uptight! What's wrong with someone doing a gig for a bank? Money doesn't make you a bad person – why am I telling you this, of all people? Daughter of the Affluent Arts, you should know.' Shona swallowed a mouthful of smoke the wrong way and coughed violently. 'Shit! Now look what you made me do. Anyway, whatever you think about him he's a real turn-on, you must give him that. I mean, all that rough trade in sculpture's pretty juicy but he's just pure sex on legs – eh, Bibi?'

'Whatever turns you on.' Bianca replied, preoccupied. She did not care for pet names and the fuss everyone made about sex mystified her. She had tried it, conscientiously, with several pleasant men, hoping to feel some transcendent emotion that would give meaning to her life, but finding instead that it was a messy and disappointing pastime. Picking up the last few crumbs from the cake tin she strolled away to her bedroom, preoccupied with her future.

The Sunday morning was bright and warm by the time she

was fully awake and for the first time for many years she saw the day's tasks lying before her in a clear and inviting succession. Persuading the Berrisfords to accept her decisions required a strategy which by now was well practised. The family cowered under the prevailing disapproval of her father; as a small child Bianca had discovered that he would always refuse any straightforward request and spend much time explaining why she was stupid to have made it. Her mother, who spoiled the girls to disguise her profound boredom with them, would agree to anything. The person most attuned to her interests was her grandmother, but the older woman was a natural peacemaker, reluctant to intervene in conflicts between her son and his wife. The best procedure, therefore, was to gain the approval of both mother and grandmother and persuade her father that the matter was a female, domestic affair that was beneath his interest.

Having resumed her worn black velvet jeans and tie-dyed T-shirt, Bianca made her way up to her parents' domain, her bare toes curling uncomfortably around the treads of the wrought-iron staircase which led upstairs. There was no time to lose. Hugh and Olivia Berrisford normally entertained on Sunday and soon her mother would be ricocheting around her kitchen in a bad temper.

She walked slowly, composing her argument, anticipating possible objections: the expense, how it would look, what people would say, whether such a move were suitable for a family in their position. The house was so quiet that the footfalls of her mother's Abyssinian cats were clearly audible. Hushed and deserted, with many pictures facing each other across the rooms, it felt like a museum. Bianca checked the terrace, to see if perhaps her mother was outside, but found only the Portuguese maid laying the long teak table for an alfresco buffet. Her father, she discovered, had been driven to the airport to meet an important guest. Her mother was presumably in the process of dressing.

The back stairs led directly from the library to her mother's dressing room, through a door concealed in the white-painted panelling which had charmed her from infancy. As she mounted the narrow treads she became aware of a rhythmic tap, perhaps a blind slapping against the frame of an open window in the slight breeze.

The dressing room was humid and scented from a recent bath. Indeed, the foamy water was still in the free-standing marble tub and she saw wet footprints on the carpet leading towards the bedroom. Bianca knew she should follow them at once; Olivia liked her children to be unembarrassed about nakedness, it demonstrated the family's modernity.

At first she thought there was a new piece of sculpture in the corner of the room; the attitudes of the bodies were strikingly artificial. She walked into the centre of the room, idly wondering why an erotic piece had been put in the bedroom when such works were usually given prominence downstairs. Then she noticed the tangle of damp towels beside the figures, and registered the regular heave of the man's buttocks, and his back knotted with the strain of supporting the woman's long body against his own. She saw that the higher pair of feet were her mother's, projecting above her lover's shoulders, and realized that the noise which she had heard was the slap of their flesh together. Otherwise they were fucking in silence with their eyes shut, distant and self-involved, each intent on their own gratification.

Shocked, Bianca ran backwards to the doorway so fast that she collided with the wall. Her mother's lovers were another celebrated feature of the ménage, another flaunted proof of the family's bohemian heritage. All her life she had been accustomed to being introduced to the succession of uneasy, flattered men who lit her mother's cigarettes, fetched her drinks, drove her car, loitered in her workshop and contributed a background of eroticism to the drama of her life. Often the men were of her own generation; this one, from his heavy contours and the shake of his over-mature flesh, was older. Their exact significance was something she had always avoided thinking about; to come across it by chance was ugly.

She turned and ran away immediately, then sat in the garden for almost an hour trying to still her thoughts. Anger was predominant. It seemed as if there was no corner of life that her family had not colonized; even sex, the proper playground of the young, belonged to them. She was at a loss for a place to go where she could be herself.

The beauty of the garden was soothing. Many of the trees and shrubs appeared in her grandfather's paintings, smaller or even newly planted. Now they were sprawling old growths with thick trunks bearing the scars of many prunings, green with algae because moss would not grow in London. The rose bushes were leggy, their long stems bowed with heavy, richly scented flowers. The apple tree carried green infant fruits and its last exhausted blossoms together. An early shower, whose dampness lingered in the shady corners, had brought down a sprinkle of petals and stuck them to the flagstones.

Convivial voices drifted over the walls from the Queen's Elm pub to the north and the Arts Club to the south, a sound which told Bianca the time. There was a brief interval on a Sunday in Chelsea when a quorum of inhabitants sleepily dragged themselves out for a slalom between the licensing restrictions of the Lord's Day. In the course of

65

quitting the pub in time to claim a restaurant table before the bars closed at 2 p.m., too much beer was sunk too fast and in summer, when outdoor drinking was preferred, the race was a noisy one. Bianca had grown up listening to the muted chatter with the accents of surly barmen urging their clients to drink up.

In the house the lunch guests would be arriving. Bianca recalled her intention and decided to talk to her grandmother before she was swept up in the event.

Some years earlier, Hugh Berrisford had decided to buy a dainty white house sharing a common garden wall with his home and extend the villa bearing the plaque of Walter Berrisford R.A. into an urban approximation of the dynastic country estate. The shared wall was pulled down, and a celebrated architect retained to gut the new dower house and incorporate a studio for her grandmother. When Bianca and Hermione were children the studio had been an enchanted cave where new marvels could be discovered every day. Until her eyesight deteriorated, Charlotte Berrisford had painted tiny pictures on wood, inspired by traditional Russian enamel painting. She told her granddaughters stories about the creatures she created with tiny brushes and glowing colours, dragons, mermaids or talking birds, with flowing manes and tails. Charlotte had spent seven years in St Petersburg before the Revolution, living with an aristocratic family as their governess and everything Russian held an irresistible nostalgic glamour for her.

Her son despised this attachment, but it was Charlotte's defence against him. He deplored her collection of icons, and was rude to the shabby, gentle friends, émigrés and exiles, who were forever dropping round to drink tea in glasses, smoke stinking cigarettes and hold long passionate philosophical arguments with his mother.

'She's not entertaining another bloody Boris, is she?' he would demand of his daughters, 'because I can't stand to breathe the same air. Tell me when he's gone, for God's sake.'

Bianca found her grandmother fussing over the cactus garden which enjoyed the roof light, a small, quiet figure in slacks with a red cotton scarf around her short white hair.

'I hate these things not needing water.' She picked a dead flower from a succulent which trailed over the raised edge of the bed. 'They're not like plants at all. There's nothing you can do for them. Hello, darling, you look cross.'

'I wanted to talk to Olivia.' It was also mandatory in the family to call parents by their Christian names.

'That makes a change. Anything important?' She dropped a handful of dead flowers into the wastebin and lowered herself into a seat to listen. All the old woman's movements were slow, and her eyes characteristically focused in the middle distance, as if she were following the flight of a bird. She appeared untroubled, which Bianca found comforting.

'Well – it isn't that I'm not happy at home and of course I'm very lucky that the house is so big that we can have our own part of it, but – I want to have a place of my own.'

'Does this mean that you want to stay at Chelsea after your foundation year?' It was always a relief to talk to Grandmother who, if not truly wise, was always interested and never angry. Bianca pulled up an old bentwood chair and sat across it, leaning over the back.

'I've decided I want to do sculpture. I'm really interested in moulds, Gran. And I think – something pretty big. And they have got the facilities here and they encourage that kind of work so – why not? And really, I am a bit frightened of leaving all this and going off somewhere in the provinces where I'll get flak for the way I speak and everything. It's bad enough as it is.'

'Is it?'

'Yes, of course it is. At least here I'm not the only rich kid on the block.'

'Well, that is true, I suppose. So where do you want to move to?'

'Oh, not far. Just to be independent, you know.'

'Have you thought about what it will cost?'

'I can rent something, I'm sure.'

'And what about your sister?'

'Hermione's going to India when she finishes school, isn't she?'

'Well, that's everything considered, isn't it?'

'Yes.'

They fell silent, two women with more than half a century between them and the same fear in their hearts: of Hugh Berrisford's temper. The central problem of the family was always the same, to manoeuvre the critical patriarch over the ditch of his own arrogance to a place of reason.

'Help me, Gran,' appealed Bianca suddenly.

The older woman looked at her granddaughter. Her short hair was straight and fine, standing up on top of her head like coconut fibre and flopping over her big blue-grey eyes. She was full of the fresh, clear, new-grown beauty of youth, and full also of pain, crippled by the softness of a new soul facing the hard world. However, the older woman had seen worse hardship than being young, beautiful, rich and well connected, and did not understand the malaise of the juvenile overprivileged.

'There's nothing I can do, you know that.' Feeling uncomfortable, she went to the sink where she washed brushes to rinse her fingers under the cold tap.

'Yes there is, you can talk to him, he does listen to you.'

'He listens and then he dismisses whatever I've said. I'm

68

not going to be some music-hall mother forever nagging my son, however much he deserves it. I should think he would be pleased that you want to be independent. Most parents expect it of their children nowadays, don't they?'

'Hugh isn't most parents.' The light of hope dimmed in Bianca's eyes. She sighed and dismounted from the chair. 'I could just leave, I suppose. There's nothing to stop me. I'd have to live off my grant, but . . .'

Sensing the potential for a greater conflict, her grandmother became alarmed. 'Don't do anything extreme, Bianca. Remember we will all have to live here after you've gone.' The girl was drifting towards the door as if she had not heard. 'Look, dear, I am on your side, you know I am. Let me just think of the best way to go about it . . . Bianca? Please, dear, don't do anything you'll regret . . .'

'Anything *you'll* regret, you mean.' It was unkind, but Bianca felt doubly hurt, and thus goaded into taking action. 'Got to go now, I promised I'd be over there when the people came. Bye, Gran.' She blew an insincere kiss and ran away down the path to the big house without looking back. Yesterday she would have wept at her grandmother's feebleness. Today she fixed more resolutely on her intention.

On the terrace she saw a full complement of guests already assembled. The Sunday lunch party was a defiant social statement for Hugh and Olivia Berrisford. By choosing to entertain in London at the weekend, they challenged the convention of the establishment upper class, who had country houses for weekend parties. The Berrisfords belonged to the new elite who fancied themselves as classless. They despised people with titles and nothing else to recommend them; their most prized guests were the well-born Labour politicians who had refused their hereditary peerages;

if neither of these was free, they made do with new money, new power and the artistic meritocracy. Youth was also much esteemed, and the girls were always under pressure to bring friends, the more outrageously dressed the better.

The striking figure of Olivia was already inviting the throng of guests to eat. She was dressed in a long suede waistcoat over a flowing white jersey catsuit, with her blonde hair pulled severely up and back into one of her own heavy silver clasps. Her eyes were unequivocally blue, heavily and perfectly made up below thin, arched brows, and in the sharp sunlight her false eyelashes cast shadows over her cheekbones. Hugh was at her side, of equal height and similar colouring. They made a handsome couple. Her mother had a bright-eyed, hopped-up air; Bianca wondered if her lover was still in the house.

'Bianca, my dear. Come and meet Pierre Dumesnil.' Her father presented a slender, colourless man with a mobile face and a fresh black cotton shirt. 'Even you will have heard of Pierre, the hero of the Sorbonne riots. He's our guest for a week and he's been asking me what sort of support the Paris students are getting over here – you can answer that, can't you?' He leaned over her intimidatingly, making it sound as if the question was completely beyond her comprehension.

'All the politicos are in Paris already.' Bianca shook the Frenchman's hand, conscious that she was on display before the company. There was a ripple of interest. 'A whole group have been out there since the beginning of term – the International Socialists anyway. You understand that in London the university doesn't really have a campus or anything, everyone's spread out all over the city. I think it's easier to organize people when they're together.'

'But the students don't make demonstrations here in London?'

'Oh yes, everywhere – riots for democracy, people tearing up their exam papers, barricading the classrooms – maybe the problem with art students is that they love their work too much to rip it up.'

'And your work? Would you destroy it for a cause?'

'I destroy it all the time in the cause of making it better.' It was a pat answer; she was adept at playing the genius in bud. The company was well satisfied. Her father relaxed his inquisitorial stance, accepting their approval, and Bianca decided to seize her moment. If anything counted with her father it was the opinion of his peers. She felt her stomach heave as she drew breath to speak again.

'I do intend a little personal protest of my own.'

'Oh yes? And what's that, may I ask?' He was unable to hit the hectoring tone in which he normally uttered those words. She saw that she would succeed.

'I've decided I want to move out, Hugh. I want a place of my own. I need . . . I feel that I'm my own person and I need to be more on a level with the other students. All this is wonderful . . .' With a bold gesture she indicated the laden buffet, the smart guests settling down on the matching hide sofas in the library and the maid, her wide backside undulating in her egalitarian non-uniform blue jeans, smiling as she poured champagne. 'Wonderful, I'm terribly happy at home, but it's a barrier, do you see? I need to be part of a wider life now. My head needs to be blank, free, empty even – you do understand?'

The hero of the Sorbonne felt included in her appeal. 'But of course, it's normal, no? The little bird leaves the nest?' She could have kissed him.

There was a pause so small that only the family registered it. 'My dear, your mother and I thought you'd never ask, didn't we, Olivia? We've been wondering where we went

71

wrong, having these unnatural children who never rebelled. We're so pleased to know you're *normal*, Bianca. Just don't forget to put on a clean T-shirt when you meet the landlord.' There was general laughter, and while the guests were telling each other what magnificently liberal parents the Berrisfords were, and how lucky therefore were their children, he added in a low voice, 'We'd better talk about this later, don't you think?'

Later, when the guests were gone, her mother elsewhere with her lover, and Pierre taking a shower, the interrogation took place. She sat squirming on the terrace wall while he berated her. Where would she live? How much would it cost? How would she travel to college? What about the mess of her work, the damage caused by her ghastly friends, the criminal responsibility if drugs were consumed on the premises? Had she thought this through, really thought it through? Who on earth would rent a flat to an unprepossessing slut with paint in her hair? How would her sister manage on her own? And when she was thrown out, did she suppose she could come back home as if nothing had happened? He was appalled by her stupidity, amazed at her selfishness but, as she sat in pretended meekness and silence, they both knew that he could not withdraw his consent and that with the French lecturer still in the house he would not cross the border into full-blown rage.

King's Road and Fulham Road flowed through Chelsea like the Tigris and the Euphrates cradling the new civilization. Bianca found a room the next day, in a flat on the top floor of a mansion block that was a crucial half mile further towards the shabby West and a radical couple of blocks closer to less fashionable Fulham Road. It was reasonably large, with a sloping ceiling and a wide three-part window giving on to a decorative balcony just big enough for the flower pots donated by her grandmother. Her flatmates were a sweetly devoted couple studying fine art and another man who played French music-hall songs on the piano all morning.

She painted her largest wall in undulating bands of pink, green and yellow, this time getting closer to the intense hot-country hues she had been striving for in her parents' basement. Hermione, now in full possession of that apartment, painted a mandala all over her old wall. She liberated two red geraniums from the municipal concrete cones in Sloane Square. From home she took a mattress and red sheets, and before Pierre returned to Paris she cast his hands in plaster in half a dozen poses and set them on the window ledge to point her way forward.

Sculpture, as she anticipated, proved a highly acceptable choice of direction for the new year, and moulds also a speciality which extracted further approval. She heard the word of accolade, 'interesting', from all sides, except from her parents. Olivia gave her a dense look of complete non-comprehension and never referred to her work again, while Hugh uttered a disappointed 'Ah!' followed by 'I suppose you didn't consider something rather less derivative?'

As time progressed Bianca found as she had hoped that the techniques were easy to master and disguised all her shortcomings. She walked more and more rapidly to the studios each day, kicking up the fallen plane leaves in the streets with something close to vivacity. The terrible lethargy of the past months lifted. I've got away with it, she affirmed, smiling to herself, I've conned them. Now they'll never find out that I have no talent.

Although he had been a catalyst in the whole process, Bianca gave no further thought to the dark-haired Lovat Whitburn until he boldly sat down beside her in the canteen

on the pretext of sharing the sugar bowl. He immediately
lost his nerve and could think of nothing to say. In the
hideous silence which ensued, she noticed that his hands,
with their long thick fingers and square palms, were in their
way as expressive as the Frenchman's but somehow very
British in their solidity and clumsiness. She watched in
fascination as he stirred his cup.

'I am doing moulds after all,' she told him with satisfaction. 'I'm really enjoying it, too. I'm glad I took your
advice.'

'What advice?' he returned, defensive.

'To do sculpture this year. You remember trying to
persuade me.'

'That was the others. But you – uh – you look happy,'
he ventured, almost swallowing the words because he was
nervous. He meant that she looked beautiful, but whereas in
her home she had seemed limp and uncaring, and so not
difficult to approach, here in public she was fully alert.
All around them students sprawled or slouched, but she
sat with a straight spine, graceful but intimidating. Her
gaze darted past him to the door, to the counter, to the far
end of the room, registering everything that happened,
making him feel that he must be the least interesting person
in view.

'How are your tubes?' she inquired, in a tone which might
have been facetious.

'I bust one this morning.'

'Oh.'

'Could've kicked myself. It had just come from the
workshop and I was unpacking it. Dropped a screwdriver.'
His hand was resting on the table's edge and to his amazement, she reached out without warning and turned it
palm-upwards.

'I do like your hands.'

'I'm quite fond of them myself. Wouldn't be without them, actually.'

'I've moulded some hands. It was quite an interesting thing to do. Can I do yours some time?' The question was asked without any implication that her interest was more than visual, which piqued him. Lovat was accustomed to the admiration of women.

'I'm pretty busy at the moment.'

'Oh well, then.' She released her clasp with a good-humoured pat and reached for her coat, preparing to leave, and he turned towards her in alarm.

'But I could – well, how long will you take? I mean, what are you casting in?'

'Just plaster.' She made it sound very obvious, as if he was a fool for asking.

'Maybe Saturday?'

The day began awkwardly at 3 p.m., with both of them tongue-tied, curious about each other, disturbed by the quality of attraction they felt. The thrills and lurches of a young desire were familiar to Lovat, but he associated the feeling with women who were simple to bed and even simpler to forget. He had learned early in his adult life that for him it was hardly necessary to make the effort of seduction; at home in the North he had been acknowledged as a heart-breaker at every school dance or junior social. In London he had only to appear in a pub or at a party for several girls to seek him out, manoeuvre introductions or even approach him directly, and then remain by his side until he chose to suggest sex. He sometimes accused himself of sleeping with women only to amuse his friends. It occasionally embarrassed him that he could not remember names or bodies a few days later, but for the most part he did not consider these liaisons of any significance.

People said that Lovat lived for his work. It was a part truth; he was eaten by a need to do something great, but unsure what it might be. For the moment, tungsten tubes served to orient his life. His father had given him a vision of life as a quest for greatness, but the journey required a helpmeet. 'A man doesn't get far if he hasn't got the right woman behind him' was an observation he had heard a thousand times, his father's formula for complimenting his mother.

Lovat carried an ideal of this 'right' woman in his heart, a woman who would require pursuit, a nymph-like figure who was forever on the point of vanishing in a dark forest but who, if captured, would somehow guide his path and assure his fortune. He had not expected the nymph to carry a famous name. He had not foreseen that he would desire her.

Bianca did not know that she desired him. She was aware of a leaping anxiety in his presence, but did not distinguish it from the nervousness she normally felt with anyone of proven artistic worth. She allowed the practical business of making the moulds to distract her, unaware that her lowered eyes and over-controlled movements appeared subtly flirtatious.

'This place is a mess – how can you stand it?' he inquired, intending the kind of weighty joke which made up most of his conversation with his men friends.

'I'm sorry, I know I'm terribly untidy.' She raised her head, alarmed, and slopped liquid plaster on to his jeans. 'Oh my God, help! I'm so sorry, really, I just wasn't looking . . .' She sprang aside like a panic-stricken animal, looking for a cloth. 'Here, let me – no, you do it, I'll make it worse, oh God, I'm *so* sorry, how could I have done something so stupid, I've ruined your jeans . . .' They were, now she noticed, newly washed and even ironed.

'No matter,' he told her, taking the rag and wetting it to wipe the white splash away. 'You said you were untidy.'

'Yes.' Her smile was curious, curling her upper lip. He felt obscurely reassured by her readiness to be criticized.

'The plaster will set if you don't pour it.'

'Oh God, yes. Oh no, it's set already. Damn!'

'Have to make some more, then.'

'You must think I'm an idiot.'

'Not necessarily.' This time she laughed and they both relaxed.

It was early evening by the time Bianca had finished. He invited her to see his celebrated light sculpture, which she knew even his closest friends had not been shown. It undulated across the floor like a great white snake. Lovat was gratified that she stood watching in awe as he fiddled with switches to demonstrate how he intended it to be illuminated in an endless, seemingly random pattern. She knew exactly how to respond, with judicious praise framed to sustain the artist in the lonely business of creation, but as he accepted her compliments she felt for the first time that she understood the excitement of such work.

After that it seemed natural that they would meet frequently to see what progress each was making, and then to share meals afterwards, and then to stay together for hours because they enjoyed each other's company. She discovered that the group among whom they had met were not his regular associates. Apart from the red-haired Joe, a friend from the Northern college where they had done their foundation year, Lovat was solitary. He worked long hours, constantly refining and changing, and for amusement drew notebooks full of imaginary projects.

Conveniently, the night bus to Hammersmith ran along Fulham Road, and Lovat spent many hectic journeys being thrown across the seats of the speeding double-decker, burning with excitement while he argued with himself that he should make a move, grab hold of her, kiss her, do something to secure her once and for all. Free fucking was the watchword of half the student community and he called himself a fool and a coward for holding back. It was just that she was Bianca Berrisford, and forgetting her would not be an option. He knew that once he touched her his destiny would be fixed.

Bianca gave him none of the conventional signals because she did not know them. Almost alone among the female students, she had never considered Lovat as a prize, either for his gifts or his looks. The business of evaluating men according to their sexual attractiveness was distasteful to her, and she had never imagined that she would attract the attention of such an eminent talent. Fear immobilized her. Since she admired him, she supposed she must love him. For all that he praised her ideas, she was afraid that if he knew her intimately he would find out how dull she was. If they made love, he would discover that she had no capacity for passion. She stood still in detachment, watching herself wait for the move which now seemed inevitable.

On a rainy night towards the term's end, her three co-tenants conspired to mate them, announcing with firm, encouraging looks that they were all attending an all-night Warhol screening at the Institute of Contemporary Art and would not be back until the morning. As soon as the door slammed behind them Lovat catapulted himself across the kitchen to kiss her, holding his breath with apprehension so that they were forced to break apart gasping ninety seconds later.

Bianca's pale skin had reddened with the force of his kiss and her face was expressionless.

'You do want to do this?' he asked with anxiety.

'Yes,' she said, her voice faint with shock. 'Yes, I do. Really. I'm sorry, it was just I wasn't expecting . . .' Terror of losing him finally moved her into action. If she could pretend talent, well, she could pretend passion too. She reached up to kiss him again and he felt her hands, still chilled from the street, steal under his sweater to touch his back.

After a while he pulled off her shirt and the black satin waistcoat she wore over it. He was eager to see her breasts, to be surprised by the hidden physical woman inside her clothes. They were pale, even paler than her face, but heavier and rounder than her outward persona hinted, suggesting a voluptuous nature reserved. For a long while she sat on the edge of the table while he held them, her lips brushing his forehead, listening to his halting breath, becoming aware of a sweet, hot tension in her body.

In time they moved to the bedroom. Lovat seemed unable to speak. In the dim light his eyes appeared huge and black; she sensed from his ragged movements that he was making an immense effort to control himself. She wanted him to fail, she wanted him inside her, out of control. She strained his body to hers, winding her legs around him, holding him in her arms, wanting to heal him, please him, to release the frenzy which he was fighting. His body was so hot that the sweat dried as it appeared and her lips stuck to his throat.

It was easily done and within a few moments he was screaming in climax as if in pain. The full weight of his body fell on her. It was then that her own flesh asserted itself, convulsing in a series of contractions which would have been pleasurable if she had been expecting them.

Lovat opened his eyes and pulled himself up on his elbows again, scanning her face uncertainly. 'I'm sorry,' he whispered, 'I didn't mean to do it like that. I couldn't help it, you're too beautiful.' She said nothing but he could see the strange, curled smile on her lips. The hand which caressed his face was warm. He felt helpless with tenderness.

Later in the night he tried again, anxious to give her a sexual experience that would prove his mastery. He was afraid that other lovers had been better. With other women he could last an hour or more and stay in control until the end. Bianca was conscious of her own enjoyment at first, but the more heated her responses became the more power she had to arouse him. The challenge was irresistible. The touches which pleased him were so easy to find, so thrilling to try. Was it so bad to want to give a man pleasure?

At the end it seemed as if he lost consciousness for a few instants. When he came to, his limbs tensed and his eyes focused, he looked at her with a pleading expression she had never imagined that his imperious face could wear.

'We will always be together like this? Bianca? You won't ever leave me?'

She kissed his forehead and promised what he asked.

In the months which followed she discovered that she had promised to marry him. At first she was delighted to be with him among the other students as an acknowledged pair, and then astounded to find that they were regarded in that community as a golden couple, blessed with all the good gifts: ability, beauty, style, connections and wealth.

Lovat seemed to be planning the progress of their love according to a preordained scheme. He asked to meet her sister, who endorsed him at once as a suitable prospective relative and elected to cast his horoscope.

'There's definitely a karmic link,' she told them, shuffling her smudged and much-corrected charts. 'This is how I can tell – see, Pluto here and here, seventh and twelfth houses, and the trine there, Bianca, through your fifth. Ideal aspects between Mars and Venus, absolutely ideal. You're fated for each other.'

'Well that's a relief.' Lovat was only partly joking. 'I was worried you might say she could do better.'

'You're very good with Hermione,' Bianca told him afterwards. 'She drives most people crazy with all that hippy stuff.'

'She's only a kid and I suppose with your parents you've both got to do something to find your own way.'

His parents were the next item, and they travelled to Northumberland by overnight coach for a weekend visit. Bianca was astonished to be met at the station by a uniformed driver with a Bentley limousine, who took them to a grey stone manor house standing in a newly planted and very vulgar garden.

Inside she found that the Whitburns were an imposing couple with faces reddened by the winter's hunting. His father in particular had an accent as broad as the one Lovat had affected at their first meeting. He had made his way up in the remnants of the Yorkshire wool business; Lovat's mother had once been his house model. A younger brother and sister home from their boarding schools helped to break the ice. Their household was a pleasant mixture of nouveau riche formality and warmhearted common sense. When his mother asked when the wedding was planned to take place Bianca discovered that Lovat was serious.

'Hasn't he told you, love?' There seemed to be acceptance in the family that Lovat would always surprise them. 'Isn't that a typical man? He wrote us he was bringing his fiancée.'

In the night when he left his room to join her, she asked, 'Did you call me your fiancée so that they would give us bedrooms next door to each other?'

'What else should I have called you?' He could switch

from affection to mild contempt with unsettling speed. 'We are engaged, aren't we?'

There was no real question in his voice. Bianca was confused and excited. 'I suppose we are,' she agreed, unwilling to admit that she had misinterpreted him.

'I didn't think you'd want a ring or anything. That kind of jewellery isn't your style, is it?'

Again, she agreed to avoid argument. A thundering great conventional engagement ring, something like a star sapphire in diamonds, would have annoyed her father intensely.

Her new confidence in their future faltered at once. She proposed the next step, for Lovat to meet her parents, and he dismissed the idea.

'God, that's so bourgeois,' he yawned.

'I don't see why,' she argued. 'You wanted me to meet yours. I'm not expecting you to like them or anything but – I mean, I thought you'd want to.'

'Well, I don't. So you needn't suggest it again.' She was bruised, but after a while realized that there had been fear in his vehemence, and for the first time saw that he was not free of provincial insecurity. Instinctively she used opportunities to build his confidence and familiarize him with the matrix of smart people in which she had been raised. Within a few months it was becoming awkward to explain that Lovat and her parents had never met.

When he at last agreed to visit their house, Hugh was sufficiently annoyed by Lovat to satisfy his eldest daughter completely. Counting on the influence of their lunch guests once more, she chose to present Lovat casually in their midst and was gratified by a dead silence in the crowd. Her nerve failed her on the word 'fiancé' and she stumbled on to introduce him by name. She was surprised to notice that he was almost rigid with tension.

Her father reached out to shake Lovat's hand too heartily and too fast, then drew him to his side with a compelling hand on his shoulder. 'Charlotte, my mother,' he announced, introducing Bianca's grandmother. This was one of his common tests, designed to make the conventional startle at its informality. Lovat took it on the chin and talked to the older woman with an attentive chivalry which obviously charmed her.

The lunch progressed normally, but at the end Lovat insisted they should linger until the family were alone, and then disappeared into the library with her father. Afterwards they gave the same account of the meeting.

'He's a difficult bastard, isn't he?' Lovat spoke with ferocity. 'I can see why you and Hermione have got problems.'

'A very difficult young man you've picked there,' Hugh announced at the first opportunity, but would not be drawn any further.

'I am surprised at your choice, Bianca,' her mother added, also looking uncomfortable. 'Why on earth, when there were so many others . . .' She looked away and lapsed into silence, her face drawn.

In the face of such hostility, Bianca felt justified in omitting to mention that they were planning to marry. It was still hardly real to her. As the spring mellowed into summer she felt she wanted to be more certain.

'If we're getting married . . .' she began as they waited at the bus stop one raw windy morning.

'Which we are,' he assured her at once, pulling her aside so that the rest of the queue need not overhear their conversation.

'Can we just – do it? Run away or something? I just don't want to get into one of those awful huge weddings with all the relations fighting and everybody being hypocritical and snobby and vicious . . .'

'Whatever you want,' he agreed, his face clear and smiling. 'Wherever you want. However you want. Waterskiing in Hawaii. In the gorilla cage at the zoo. Down an emerald mine in Brazil. On top of a number nineteen bus . . .' The named vehicle, already crammed with travellers, sailed past the stop leaving the queue to huddle deeper into their coats.

'I just want to wake up one morning and have you say we're doing it today,' she told him, still not fully believing that it would happen.

'It won't be before graduation. But after that – you'd better watch out, girl.' She loved being called *girl*. She also loved the implication that this marriage was something into which he was going to trap her, not the other way around.

Her parents were in Tuscany when he rolled over as she brought him his morning coffee at midday, reached for his watch and shouted, 'Shit! We've got to be there in half an hour. Blast! Where the hell has Joe got to?'

Hurling the sheet aside he scrambled to his feet and waved at her with one hand while trying to turn his jeans right side out with the other. 'This is it, love. This is the big day! We're getting married! Come on, you said you wanted to be surprised – get dressed! Hurry!' He saw her expression and added, 'Don't worry, love, I've taken care of everything.'

She was about to accuse him of joking when the doorbell rang and Joe appeared, pink eyed and smelling strongly of vodka and cigarettes. He extended towards her a fist carrying six creamy roses tied with a white ribbon. They were a variety she recognized, Pascale, specially grown for her grand-mother's favourite florist in Sloane Street.

'I'm not late, am I?' Joe had never previously arrived for an appointment less than a day in arrears. He was groping for something small in the upper pocket of his jeans jacket. Lovat hustled him into the kitchen and Bianca wonderingly deduced that it was the ring, her ring, and that this was not a joke.

The nineteen bus deposited them close to Chelsea Registry Office, where Hermione was skipping up and down the pavement in a dress composed almost entirely of fluttering multicoloured ribbons. In the waiting room they found a random sample of Chelsea life: an overpainted blonde divorcee, a property developer in a white suit, a group of uneasy Irish with white carnations pinned to their lapels and two West Indian families in bright printed robes.

Until she stood before the registrar and heard him read the words, the question of whether Bianca would have Lovat as her husband had never been formally posed. She had allowed herself to be washed along by his conviction and it had been a soothing, flattering and delicious experience. The wedding itself seemed to pass in the blink of an eye and immediately afterwards they were wafted to the overgrown sanctuary of Brompton Cemetery where they reclined in the long grass between the carved Victorian gravestones drinking champagne straight from the bottle while Hermione read poetry. The rings – for Lovat had one also – were plain wide bands of gold, standard issue for the visually aware modern wedding. He always got everything right.

The Whitburns, who arrived in London a few days later, had obviously expected no less than a surprise announcement from their eldest son. Over dinner at the Savoy they presented him with a cheque in a large white envelope with a silver deckle edge. Lovat was embarrassed by the vulgarity of the gift, but Bianca enjoyed the bourgeois simplicity of her new parents-in-law; there was also a strong hint that the Whitburns were concerned that the Berrisfords should not see them as provincial fortune hunters, which the young couple both saw as an assertion necessarily and correctly made.

Olivia and Hugh, when they returned from Tuscany with walnut-brown tans to pick up the reins of their London life, were harder to read. Both were predictably at pains to express their approval of the marriage, although it had clearly startled them. Hugh issued statements of endorsement which lacked his usual supple loquacity. Olivia, having almost warmly invited the newlyweds to dinner, turned grey and faint over cocktails and withdrew to bed. Hugh diagnosed a migraine, although she had never suffered from one before.

This left Charlotte in the role of hostess at the table, and apparently on a whim she rose after the dessert, walked round to take Bianca's hand and said, 'I think it's time for us to leave the gentlemen to their cigars, dear. We can get on with the coffee upstairs.' Lovat nodded and so Bianca followed her grandmother out of the room, presuming that this too was part of his orchestration of their marriage.

The older woman's papery cheeks had blotches of high colour and her eyes were watery with emotion. To Bianca's surprise, Charlotte embarked on a tirade of criticism masked as concerned questioning.

'How well do you know Lovat – I mean, really know him?' She began, passing Bianca her tiny cup of coffee.

'We've been together almost a year now, I know his friends, his family – what else is there to know about a person?'

'I mean, are you sure you can trust him?'

'Of course I'm sure, I wouldn't have married him otherwise. Do you think he's after money or something? Because he isn't, his parents are loaded, they want to buy us a house. They're not sophisticated people, but money's no problem. And Lovat is brilliant, Charlotte, everyone says so. I can't believe I'm lucky enough to have him.'

'I don't think he's interested in money, that isn't what I meant at all. I'm just wondering if perhaps there isn't something he might be concealing from you.'

'Like what?' Bianca was beginning to feel angry. How typical of her family to plan this devious way of attacking her, instead of coming straight out and saying they were angry that she had got married without letting them take charge of the whole process.

'Well, like his history before he met you. With women, I mean.'

'He isn't concealing anything. The whole college knows. He screwed every cheap cunt between the Chelsea Potter and the Queen's Elm.'

Bianca was satisfied to see the older woman flinch at her language. She felt she had at last found the strength to defend herself. It was the first noticeable benefit of her new status as a wife.

'If you don't want to discuss this . . .' her grandmother persisted in a stiff tone.

'I'll discuss whatever you like,' Bianca replied quietly. 'But if you all don't like my marriage, why not simply say so? It won't alter the way I feel. I love Lovat and I trust him completely. But you're entitled to your opinions.'

The old woman sighed with exasperation and was about to say more when the men's heavy footsteps and loud conversation were heard from the stairs. A few seconds later they entered the room in a pall of cigar smoke, surprisingly convivial together. As her husband sat down beside her Bianca took his arm, enjoying the comfort of his protection.

CHAPTER 3

Atlanta, Georgia, 1964

The prisoner was a white male, fifteen years old. He was in fact very white, without the sun-reddened complexion of a local boy. Fear might have drained the colour from his face, and maybe he studied hard and did not get out in the sun much. It was not the pallor of poor nutrition or illness; although he was slender, he gave the impression of milk-fed good health. He stood well, without fidgeting. His thick cornsilk hair needed cutting, it was falling in his eyes and touching his protruding ears. Apart from that there was no sign that he was the rebellious type. His attitude to the court had been respectful, his expression was grave and the judge considered that he understood the seriousness of the charge. In fact, he had seemed close to tears at the beginning of the hearing.

His mother had travelled from their home in Ohio. She was apparently a decent woman; her entire manner in the courtroom advertised that. Small and neat, wearing a good suit and a hat in a hard shade of turquoise, she sat with her hands clasped on her purse and her knees pressed together as if to draw herself apart from the doubtful characters on either side. When the judge looked at her a second time he concluded that she was older than he would have expected.

The father was a supervisor in an insurance company. This was their only child and indeed he had a certain air of having been over-protected, not allowed the freedom to run about with his pals. Too docile, too dutiful, his boyish energy suppressed. The probation report showed that his school had no complaints about him other than poor grades in the past few months and he sang in the choir at the Christian Science church in Cleveland. Six or seven years ago he would have been a perfect living Norman Rockwell kid; in another six or seven years, the judge considered, he would be a fine young American. Right now it seemed obvious that he was just kicking over the traces; it would be plain irresponsible to send him down to juvenile hall to learn criminal behaviour from no-hope negro kids.

'Alexander Thomas Elliott Wolfe' – the judge gave him a smile which was intended to be reassuring but looked to the prisoner as if the old boy was trying to stop his false teeth from falling out – 'I find you guilty of the charge which has been brought against you, namely of stealing two packets of cigarettes from the Peachtree gas station on International Boulevard here in Atlanta. You pleaded guilty, I consider you have shown remorse and as this is your first offence I am going to give you a year's probation and send you back to school to work hard and stay out of trouble.'

'Thank you, Sir.' The prisoner used a very quiet voice. The mother nodded as if she had been asked to agree with the verdict, half rising in her seat as if she intended to repossess her child immediately.

'And remember, son, whatever your problems are, or whatever you think they are, you'll do better to stand your ground and face them than to run away.'

'Yes, Sir, I will remember that.' Damn, that Southern drawl had crept into his speech; they would think he was ridiculing them and the act would be spoiled.

In the daydreams which passed more than half of Alex Wolfe's waking time he sometimes chose to be an international confidence trickster, a Cary Grant figure on the

French Riviera who suavely persuaded beautiful women to give him their money and jewels. He had discovered that he had a very useful ability to appear as whoever people wanted to see. The good student or the ideal date were roles he could play to perfection; the prodigal son obviously still needed practice. He enjoyed these performances for the secret sense of power over his duped audiences which they gave him. Perhaps he ought to be an actor. The drama teacher was more and more inclined to make a pet of him, but his father never lost an opportunity to point out that showbusiness folk were immoral, lazy, spendthrift, antisocial trash.

'Alex, I can't understand you,' his mother began as soon as they left the court. She had a taxi waiting to take them directly to the airport. 'What in the world possessed you to run away like that? I could hardly believe it when the call came to say you were in Atlanta. Atlanta! Do you know what it's costing me to come and bring you home? Why did you do it?'

'I don't know.' He stared out of the car window. She pulled at his shirt sleeve, the most violent movement he had ever known her make.

'You will answer me, Alex, you will. I'm your mother, I have to know what has come over you. You are a beautiful child, a true offspring of the spirit, and you have had a good spiritual education but to do something like this you must have fallen into an error of thought. If I know what it is I can explain it to you.'

He sighed, but not so that she could see. His mother was forever trying to invade his mind to clean it out. The only defence was to keep his thoughts so indefinite that they could not be grasped. 'Nothing's come over me, Mother. I just didn't want to spend the weekend in Bedford Heights. I just wanted to go someplace.'

It had been a beautiful moment, when the idea had come to him. He had gone out at her request on Saturday morning to shovel snow off the driveway, and some blessed random impulse had prompted him to put down the shovel and walk on, out into the street.

Bedford Heights was a very quiet neighbourhood. As its street life went, a defective fire hydrant was a major event. A pedestrian was unusual, but on a winter Saturday morning all the inhabitants were snug inside their spacious, low-roofed homes. There were a few tyre tracks which indicated that some fathers had taken their sons to sports coaching.

The silence had been stifling. He had heard only his own footfalls and the thin whine of the wind in the trees. It was a noise which he imagined came echoing from the distant wastes of Canada, of the far-off howl of the tundra, the lament of the great forests for the dead lakes and from further still the sound of nothing, the base note of the emptiness of the world. It would whistle away across the great plains, picking up the hiss of dry corn stalks and the rumble of running cattle until the heat of the South warmed it and the crash of the sea swallowed it and it returned to its source. Maybe it went to God. In the Bible it said that the Spirit held the wind in his fists.

He saw himself as an atom in the air, a particle of some mysterious inert gas whirling alone among the common myriads of nitrogen, skimming the ice on the lake, tumbling around the great ugly buildings of the city centre, soaring in the updraft from a heating duct, skimming through the wing feathers of a flock of geese.

In time his thoughts became blurred. All his being had been impelled to move and he had begun to run, his swift economical stride carrying him around the corner and away towards the estate's gatehouse. Running was dangerous,

nobody ran in Bedford Heights, it would draw attention to
him. He pulled himself up and tried to recapture his reverie
but nothing came into focus except the bitter cold hurting
his bare hands.

He had stuffed his hands in the pockets of his red plaid
work jacket. Stretching his fingers in the warmth, he touched
some bills, money awarded by his father for doing chores
around the house. The tariff for yard sweeping, car washing,
table setting and the like, written in Elliott Wolfe's very
small even hand, was taped to the kitchen wall. His father
prided himself on having taught his son the value of money
from his earliest years. Once a month the boy was treated to
a ride to the bank to deposit his earnings. The ride was due
in two days' time. He had almost forty dollars. The impulsion
of his imagination had made his feet so restless that it was
almost painful to set them down on the sidewalk. He had to
move. Accordingly, he made for the highway, hitched a ride
downtown and went to the bus station.

Atlanta had been the first destination on the timetable
within his budget. It had seemed to promise the oblivion of
the Southern heat, but getting there had been less exciting
than leaving Bedford Heights, and staying there with only
two dollars and a quarter was obviously unfeasible, so he
had stolen the cigarettes in the hope that he would be picked
up and somehow sent home. The juvenile court had been
outside the scope of his imagination, but Alex had the blithe
certainty of a coddled suburban child that no real harm
could ever come to him and the experience had not shaken
this belief.

'Cigarettes.' His mother's mouth was compressed to a small
cerise slit. 'You know tobacco is one of the depraved appetites
that proceed from an unconscious error. This is how sin begins,
a little thought with no reason behind it that leads us to evil.'

'I didn't smoke them, I just took them so that the police would come.' He did not bother to elaborate.

'You are such a mystery to me.' She looked at him without affection, reminding herself that suffering was a gift with which she could refine the spirit within. 'You realize you will have to see a' – she baulked at the term probation officer – 'a *person* when you get home? Every week? For a year?'

'Yes.'

'Well, what are we going to do about it, Alexander?'

'I don't know, I guess I'll go after school or something.' She had evidently set off on another of her incomprehensible flights of anxiety.

'You little fool, that's not what I mean. I mean, what are we going to do? To tell people?'

'Why do we have to tell people?'

'It will be remarked. Be sure of that. Oh yes.' She clutched her purse more firmly to her side as if holding tight to it could preserve the family's privacy. 'People will be curious, they always are.'

'So?' The car stopped at doors to the departure hall and he helped her to get out as she had trained him to do. People noted the chivalrous effect he created. He did not feel at all gracious towards his mother, but Alex was a youth distinguished by an innate delicacy of movement and could not be clumsy if he tried. She gave him money and he paid the driver.

'I cannot believe your stupidity, Alexander. How long are you going to remain a child in knowledge? Do you want the entire neighbourhood to know that I have a criminal for a son?'

'But I'm not a criminal.'

'Why do you think you were arrested and taken to that

court? You're a thief, that's all. My son is a thief.' She was pulling down on his arm so that she could hiss in his ear and avoid raising her voice and being overheard. He caught her sickly floral scent, a smell which he associated with all those angry, furtive conversations in which she had told him what to say or how to act for the benefit of other people. These were the only occasions on which she ever came physically close to him.

'We'll tell them you're going to a tutor,' she decided suddenly, 'anyone who had seen your grades would certainly have no trouble in believing that.'

He picked up her bag and pulled open the door. 'And you can thank me that I have not told your father you were arrested.' She reached into her purse and gave him their tickets to present at the desk. 'Not to save you any embarrass-ment, oh no. But to save him. Your father lives in error in spite of the best we can do. He has no spiritual defences, he believes that a shock could give a man a heart attack. Your father is to be sixty years old next year and we can thank God that he is still with us because many women lose their husbands long before sixty. So you be sure never to breathe one word of this, Alexander, because that word might make me a widow.'

'Yes, Mother.'

'I had to tell him where you were, or course, but we can say you were just picked up as a runaway.' It was an order, not a suggestion. She sat down on the worn upholstered bench to wait for their flight call and looked around her with an air which was both inquiring and accusatory. Alex knew the mannerism well; it meant that he should fetch her something to drink.

Elliott Wolfe was a man so devoid of imagination that he could not be interested in anything. He sailed slowly through life on an even keel of mental limitation, feeling neither enthusiasm nor anxiety. When the newspapers or the TV presented him with evidence that the world could be magical or bizarre, he dismissed it as exaggeration. When his colleague in Sales explained that syphilis was being spread by Moscow-trained female carriers as part of a Communist plot to undermine the health of the young men of America, he was disappointingly unimpressed with the hypothesis. He was probably the only man over the age of thirty in his city who had never contemplated the peaceniks demonstrating in Washington and seen in his mind's eye the Russian army on May Day parade down the Memorial Shoreway, with Khrushchev in the first tank grinning, gorilla-like, leaning on his arms.

Elliott's intellect lacked any but the most basic dimension, and he was able to resist his wife's faith with complete non-comprehension. Although this pained her, she found security in the narrowness of his mind and was happy to dwell within its boundaries. The word 'why' seldom crossed their lips. When she offered him her version of their son's escapade he accepted it as she expected he would, without asking the questions which would have occurred to a person of normal curiosity.

His anger, a feeble force, was reserved for the foolish waste of a month's earnings. He decreed that the shortfall should be recouped by greater industry in the coming month, and wrote out an appendix to the schedule on the kitchen wall: 'Straighten out garage: $2. Wash windows: 10c each. Paint window frames: 25c each. Paint back fence: $1.'

'I want you to notice, son, that I have set down a rate for the entire job here, not a rate by the hour.' His liver-spotted hand moved slowly over the figures. 'These sums are estimates, what I think each task should be worth to the

95

household. I am not proposing to pay you by the hour or by the day, because when you pay a man on time it pays him to be idle. Pay a man for the task and you'll get it done and finished in the best time he can manage because that way he'll make the most money. Now that's a good lesson I'm giving you – you remember that.'

Since outside painting would not be practical until the snow melted, Alex began with the garage the next day after school. It was already neat and ordered, but his father wanted a space cleared for their old refrigerator, which would need to be stored now that a new one had been purchased. At the back of the oil-stained area occupied by the family Ford towered a wall of old packing cases which needed to be disassembled and rebuilt higher with a place for the discarded appliance. The Wolfes did not throw away their old household equipment, but preserved it with care in case it should be needed one day. Elliott and his wife shared the belief that catastrophes were always poised to strike their home. After death and accident, scarcity was their keenest fear. Alex put these worries down to working in the insurance business and being too familiar with other people's disasters.

He set up the stepladder and began methodically to bring down the highest cases. Old heaters, a toaster, outgrown shoes and worn clothing were stacked on top of each other, a dusty record of the family's life. There were boxes of PTA records, bundles of the church magazine, issues of the recipe circle's bi-annual booklet. Near the bottom he knew he would find his old toys and the glass bottles from which he had taken milk as a baby, their perished rubber teats wrapped separately in blue surgical paper. Several boxes contained paper dress patterns and precisely folded remnants of fabric; his mother held that the clothes she made herself were far more stylish, and of course more economical, than anything store-bought. At the front of the pile where she could reach them easily she stored her jam jars; by this season one third of them would be empty.

By the end of the morning he had the pile down, and the space for the refrigerator measured and marked out. Elliott Wolfe undertook no physical work of any kind himself. When the new fridge was delivered he would give his wife a quarter to give to the men to carry the old one out to its new home.

Putting back the boxes was quicker work than taking them down, although it had to be done carefully so that nothing was in danger of falling. The stack grew fast and the anticipation of finishing made him careless. He picked up one of the older boxes, containing mostly his infant clothes and yellowed leaflets on child development, and hoisted it roughly to shoulder height. The side of the case broke away in his grasp and the contents spilled on the ground.

With three new carpentry pins the box was easily reassembled, and he began to pick up what had spilled out of it. Here his mother's obsession with order at last betrayed her. Without question, everything needed to be refolded and packed neatly. Alex was straightening a small bundle of papers when he saw, among the recipes for baby dinners and patterns for romper suits, the corner of a letter with a strange stamp, bearing the head of a woman in a helmet.

He pulled the letter from the bundle and looked at it. It was addressed to his mother in erratic brown ink writing, and readdressed in a more disciplined hand in blue. The letter inside was completely incomprehensible apart from his mother's name: Marie.

For some time Alex had known that his mother's silences were more eloquent than her words. She was most strikingly dumb on her life before her marriage. He had no idea where she had been born or who her folks were. The Wolfes, his father's family, he was told had lived in Ohio for three generations, and before that had emigrated from 'the middle of Europe'. This was a euphemism for Germany which most families in their circle used. There was a black morocco photograph album with black silk tassels which contained some yellowed old photographs of Wolfes at harvest suppers or works outings, a few formal family portraits, his parents' wedding photograph and his own christening picture. Visits to his father's brother in Akron were made at Christmas or Thanksgiving.

If he asked, Marie would say, 'My life began when I met your father, Alex. Surely that is all you need to know.' When he pressed her further, she changed the subject. To a youth with a burgeoning sense that he could not follow his parents' way of life, the denial was a goad.

The letter might lead to the answers he wanted. He put it in the pocket of his work jacket and completed his task. Later he transferred it to the inner pocket of the jacket which he wore to school, where it lay forgotten for three months until he walked Jennifer McIlwaine to the bus stop after a movie and decided to pass the time until the bus came in kissing her. She put her hands against his chest to make him keep a decent distance apart, and felt something crackle under her fingers.

'What is that?' she asked him, playing for time. She had picked Alex Wolfe to date in the hope that he might let her off without an hour of heavy petting at the end of the evening; other girls he had dated said he was really quite a gentleman.

'This old letter.' He pulled it out to show her. 'I found it in our garage. It's addressed to my mother but I can't read it. Maybe you can?'

98

'I believe it's in French.' Intrigued, she scanned the uneven lines. 'This word here, *Chère*, that's kind of like *chérie*, isn't it?'

'Why, so it is. I never thought of that.' Words in any language were difficult for Alex. He was in awe of girls like Jennifer who could read a book in a day and seemed able to chatter for hours, never lost for expression. His head was full of things he wanted to say, but nothing ever came out right, especially if he had to write it down.

'Hey listen, maybe my sister can tell us what this means, she's a senior and she's doing some French, I think. If you give it to me I could show it to her tonight when I get home.'

Her eyes were bright with interest and sympathy, but he hesitated, suddenly afraid of losing the only reason he had to suspect that there might be a romantic secret in his origins. 'Gee, I don't know, it is kind of special to me. It isn't that I don't think you'd take care of it or anything . . .'

'Oh, sure. Listen, I understand, really I do. Of course you must keep hold of it. But if you like you could show it to my sister yourself.' She recalled that she had found the letter in a place which might be described as lying close to his heart, and was attuned to his unspoken yearning for mystery. 'Why don't you come over to our house on Saturday?'

The older McIlwaine girl could only pick out a few words in the letter, but confirmed that they were in French, although the writing was so elaborate it was barely legible. She offered to ask her teacher for a translation and he agreed to entrust it to her. The three of them passed a delicious afternoon speculating on the significance of the find. The girls, who were very alike in their cleanly rounded limbs and fleecy fair hair, both favoured the idea that it was a love letter, perhaps the tragic last farewell of a wartime sweetheart, but Alex could not imagine his mother being

loved. Lately she had taken to emphasizing that chastity was
the cement of civilization and progress.

Word came back that the French teacher would like to
talk to Alex privately, and so he and Jennifer went over to
the high school and the two girls accompanied him to her
classroom door. She was young for a teacher, with very
glossy long brown hair which she wore pulled back in an
artistic-looking wooden slide. She sat beside him and he
glimpsed black lace inside her orange sweater.

'Well, Alex, I thought I ought to talk to you face to face
about this letter because I really don't know if I would be
doing the right thing in telling you what it contains. Now
tell me, what about your grandmother, your mother's
mother?' By her soft accent she was a Canadian. He felt as if
her voice was stroking him.

'I wish I could tell you about her, honestly I do, but I
don't know anything. Mom just clams up if I ask her
anything about where she came from.'

There was something about him that was so eager and
fresh, his eyes were so clear and he stammered slightly, his
full lips rosy and wet, that the teacher's misgivings evaporated.

'And you really want to know all that, don't you?'

'Why yes. I want to know about all of my family, not just
half.'

'I think that's very natural, Alex. But your mother is
keeping a secret here, and perhaps for good reasons, so she
could get mad if you find out.'

'I do understand that being a teacher you might be on my
parents' side.' He sounded so reasonable but he looked
crushed. His shoulders drooped inside his jacket.

'There aren't any sides in this,' she told him with a
sympathetic touch on his arm. 'I would like to tell you

what's in the letter and actually I think it's important that you know.' She paused, asking herself if she had gone crazy, then opened her folder and took out the envelope. 'Now there are a few words in this which I didn't recognize, they seem like little pet expressions which people might use with a child. But the gist of this letter is that your grandmother is writing to your mother to say she has heard that she is married now and that she has a child of her own. And she says – and it's really quite emotional, Alex, I think she must have had very strong feelings here – that now she is a mother herself perhaps she understands what mother love is, and how much she is missed back home.'

'So it sounds as if she ran away or something?' Alex felt almost betrayed. If his mother too had run away from home, why had she been so stony towards him when he did the same?

'And then your grandmother writes that she is alone now, which I don't fully understand because then she goes on to ask your mother to write saying that the letter would be received with great joy by herself and her brother and everyone at home. And there you see she has set down the address, which is in the town of Nice in France.'

As she spoke she saw the young man begin almost to glow with excitement. His great grey eyes grew wet with tears and he quickly turned away his head and felt for his handkerchief, wiping his eyes under cover of blowing his nose. The French teacher was herself quite breathless with feeling when she finished. She took his hand in both of hers and squeezed it. The heave of her chest, the slight quiver of her breasts, was the most erotic thing he had ever seen. Alex was dizzy with emotion.

'If there's anything you'd like to talk to me about, I'm always here,' she told him when they parted after a little more discussion. She leaned against the door after she closed it, wondering what the boy possessed which had caused her to lose her head that way.

That spring became a season of wonders. The poignant secrets of his past were nectar to Alex's starved spirit, filling him with energy and hope. Until then he had been a reserved and rather perverse boy. He could have been an athlete, but he lacked aggression and hated to get hurt, so that even on the running track boys with less ability but more drive could beat him. His father, a pigeon-chested weakling all his life, saw no merit in sports.

In the classroom Alex was equally hamstrung by his parents' prejudices. His mother abominated science, his father the arts, and so his interests were doomed to frustration. In addition, even the teachers most taken with his pleasing manner had to acknowledge that his intelligence was weak. He was always attentive in class but much too quiet, and he had an absolute inability to extract facts from print. Socially too, Alex Wolfe was an outsider, rejected by every clique, not in need of close friends or ambitious for a sweetheart. He could have scored with the girls, but liked them too much to want to quarrel over doing dirty things with them.

In a matter of weeks all these obstacles disappeared. Alex found himself in a gentle, female world in which he was a source of fascination. Interest and sympathy bathed him like the water of life and the emotions which had previously been obscured in the mist of his mind became recognizable forces. His grades improved and he qualified for the track team. His probation officer concluded that running away had just been a typical episode of sophomore nerves, and Alex Wolfe was no longer a cause for concern. Jennifer McIlwaine, bewitched by the romance of his ancestry, became absolutely gooey over him and when he next kissed her she unhooked her brassiere herself, although she was grateful when he explained that he really respected her too much to go that far.

Alex Wolfe was in love. The object of his passion seemed to him the wisest, kindest, most accomplished and most beautiful woman in creation. In the smothering quiet of his home he lay awake half the night either wondering what he could do to follow the revelation of his French grandmother or masturbating over the memory of the French teacher's quivering breasts. In the end he helplessly brought both problems back to their source and returned to her classroom.

She startled like a guilty cat when she saw him, then recovered and sat him down at the same desk.

'I wondered if you could maybe give me some more help – if you aren't too busy? Do you think – I mean – I thought' – he took a deep breath, kept his eyes on the desk and ignored what he could feel – 'I was thinking maybe I could write to this address.'

'You could write? But, this was fifteen years ago, Alex. Have you thought that she might have moved in all that time?'

'Well, yes, but I won't lose anything if she has, will I? She sounded so unhappy and I hate to think of some old lady all alone, who is my grandmother, never knowing anything about me and maybe dying or something.' He noticed that the skin of her neck creased in several places, wonderful marks of maturity. She smelt of face powder and there were smudges of make-up under her chin.

'What a very good sentiment, Alex. You really have what French people call *tendresse*, tenderness.' Again, she was moved to help him. With all the uncaring, destructive young men there were in the world, surely this one deserved appreciation for his fine heart.

She had that awesome facility of expression that he admired in most girls. The letter she composed said what he intended far better than he could have put it, and she thoughtfully suggested that she should add a postscript explaining that someone had helped with the translation.

'Where is this place Nice, exactly?' He pronounced it awkwardly.

'You say it like niece, niece like nephew,' she corrected him. 'It's in the South of France, the major city of the French Riviera. I haven't been there myself but I think it has palm trees and some beautiful old buildings.'

A piece of fantasy made real; somehow he had suspected as much. 'Could I possibly ask one more thing? May we put your address here? Because if she should write back and my mother saw the letter . . .'

'Oh my goodness, I never thought of that. We would be in trouble, wouldn't we?' She turned to look him full in the face and she seemed so beautiful he thought he would pass out right there. The conspiratorial 'we' was sweeter than birdsong. 'You do realize that this is something I should not be doing, Alex. If people found out I would lose my job.'

To his heated sensibilities this sounded like encouragement. Alex shut his eyes and planted his lips on hers, reaching out to hold her and finding her upper arms. After a moment of shock, he felt her respond. Her mouth was confident, almost greedy, but all at once she pulled away.

'Is that what you really came for?'

'No. Yes. Both. I mean, I do want to send the letter.'

'Just let me think, Alex. Give me a moment.' She sat with her hands in her lap, considering. The help she had already given him was quite enough to cause a scandal. He was such a nice boy, so obviously unhappy and looking for a path in life. He seemed level-headed, trustworthy. It must be right to help him. In the fall she was moving back to Quebec to get married. Her evenings were lonely but she was still swallowing her pill every day. In all probability, no one would ever find out.

The letter was sent. He came to her apartment on Friday, telling his parents there was extra training after school, and with the gentle patience of a born teacher she showed him how to make love. It proved the most successful study he had ever attempted. In the realm of the physical he had complete confidence; his body always did whatever he asked of it and when he asked it to give him pleasure, and to give the woman pleasure, new instincts were born to direct him. Her secret hair, as he called it, mesmerized him; he felt he could pass a whole day nuzzling at the glistening mysteries beneath, while his cock swelled with impatience and her fingers stroked his neck.

He visited every week, still respectfully dating Jennifer on Saturday nights. The fact that this first love was doomed, that she was promised to another man and must leave him in the summer, seemed ideally poignant and freed them both to ecstasies of melancholy.

In the interludes between lovemaking he began to ask her about France. The glamour of being, as he supposed, partly French himself now illuminated all the gloomy corners of his mind. She related every detail of her student year in Aix-en-Provence, and he envisioned the lavender fields and the bakeries so passionately that the smells seemed to fill his nostrils. He began to repeat words after her, savouring their strangeness, and so she set him simple exercises and loaned him books which he read through the empty nights at home, burning out his torch batteries under the blankets.

In time the next phase of the miracle came to fruition, and a cheap blue envelope arrived from France. The handwriting was small and tremulous but the sense was as dramatic as he had hoped. His grandmother was moved to the very depths of her heart by his letter. Inexpressible joy filled her life and made her forget all the terrible things which had happened in the past. There were three pages in the same operatic vein, then a cascade of demands for photographs and details of his life, and finally more professions of love and joy before the signature.

'I think we did the right thing,' the teacher concluded as she put the letter in his hand. 'Imagine that poor woman pining for you all these years.' They reflected that when the term ended they too would pine and held each other more closely.

She composed a reply and he dispatched it, but Alex began to entertain the idea of meeting his grandmother face to face. He imagined her in a dozen different ways, white haired or pepper-and-salt, dressed in black lace, or in lavender chiffon, with a stick, a parasol, maybe some species of French lapdog, always smiling, always holding out her arms to him. Soon the craving to know was always with him, and he started to form plans. Finding that his life seemed more his own if he had a secret to keep, he told no one, but extracted from his lover the procedure for applying for a passport and buying an air ticket.

When his father drove him to the bank he went in, sat down for a few minutes, then came out again with the cash from his redoubled chores still in his pocket, and when he returned home he hid it in the toe of one of his snow boots. He learned to forge his father's signature. The birth certificate and the passport application were easy to get. His final inspiration was to volunteer to help at the church summer camp on the lake at Port Clinton. It was not a paid job but the tips were generous, and it set the seal on his parents' reassurance that his previous escape was just an isolated adolescent aberration.

If the work was hard it helped him to forget the tearful parting with his lover at the term's end.

By October he had more than enough money. His father fell ill, which meant that the house was invaded by a succession of women from the church who sat with the sufferer reading him the arguments of Mary Baker Eddy to help the old man understand that his gallstone was an illusion of the material world. Seeing the opportunity for an escape which would not be noticed for days, Alex offered to stay with the McIlwaines until his father was better, so that one of the church women could sleep in the house overnight.

It was a Friday. He left school with his hiking pack and took a bus to the airport, mentally saying farewell to the towering, featureless buildings, the gangling men in dungarees on the street corners, the sign forbidding agricultural vehicles to be driven in the city and everything else which he despised about Cleveland.

He bought tickets and was in Paris within twenty-four hours. Delighted at his ability to buy a sandwich and decipher destination boards, he transferred to the Gare de Lyon and sat up all night on the train to Marseilles, listening to the strange metallic sounds of the railway.

At Marseilles he caught a few hours of sleep on a bench, then boarded a smaller train for Nice. As the morning sun rose his compartment grew hotter and hotter. People, French people, looked at him incuriously and grumbled at the heat, animated brown faces with black eyes and bad teeth. He strained his eyes against the light to see the landscape, the houses with their red-tiled roofs, the pine trees and at last the glittering blue sea in the distance. The Mediterranean! Yesterday it had been only an exotic shape in an atlas, and today it was gleaming behind the rocky hills, a thousand times more real than the steely expanses of Lake Erie.

Restless with excitement, he got up and spent the rest of the journey hanging out of the window at the carriage door, breathing the warm resinous air. Names brilliant with romance passed on station signs: Juan les Pins, Cap d'Antibes, Cannes.

At Nice, light-headed with tiredness and agitation, he almost ran out of the station, brushing aside unheard the well-dressed man with a pink carnation in his lapel who advanced to offer the good-looking boy accommodation. A kiosk was conveniently placed in his path and he bought nougat and a map which promised wonders. The casino, the opera, the flower market and the Promenade des Anglais danced invitingly under his eyes, but he collected himself and referred to the index to find his grandmother's address. It was in the extreme south-west quarter of the city.

The walk was long and full of marvels. He passed shops crammed with shiny sugared fruit, stalls loaded with carnations, news stands buried under piles of foreign periodicals. There were gardens overflowing with palms and bright subtropical flowers. The main boulevard was crowded with people in light summer clothes and the smells of burnt sugar, garlic and bad drains delighted his nose.

Eventually he made his way to a residential district, where villas painted pink and orange were shuttered against the sun and fragrant rosemary and lavender bushes spilled over their walls. He was close to his destination when he unexpectedly came upon a crazy fairy-tale church, with multiple fat domes in Walt Disney pastels and palm trees in its garden.

He walked uphill, with the sparkle of the sea far behind

him, and at last came to a house which bore the number he sought. It was in a street of similar two-storey buildings in Thirties style, with Villa les Gazelles worked in the wrought-iron screen across its frosted-glass door. The geraniums in the garden were old, stunted plants with small flowers and the rosemary had sprawled so far that the bush had torn itself in two and was half dead.

Alex paused and drew a slow breath. His search was over. After travelling for two days, four thousand miles across an entire ocean, he was outside his grandmother's house. It had a somnolent air, but in the breathless heat of late afternoon the whole town seemed to be dozing.

The bell did not ring the first time he tried it, so after an interval he tried again with more pressure and heard not one but several buzzes inside the house. Silence followed. He thought after a while that he heard a sound, but could not be sure. Perhaps she was out, perhaps away. He had money, he could find a hotel or a students' hostel.

Very slowly the door opened four inches and he saw a brown face with straggling black hair above it.

'*Vous cherchez quelqu'un, Monsieur?*'

He pulled the blue envelope from his shirt pocket, pointed to the address and made the announcement which he had prepared:

'*C'est moi, Alex. Je suis Alex.*'

A hand, all veins and sinews, reached for the envelope and he passed it over. The door closed three inches, and he heard a whispered conversation, then it opened wide and he saw two small women, wrinkled and stooped but not like any old ladies he had ever seen in his life. The one who had opened the door wore a black dress with her hair pinned firmly in a chignon.

The other one was pale-skinned and dishevelled, clutching

around her a stained peach satin wrapper edged with feathers. Her hair was short and the colour of rust, her eyes painted thickly with black liner. Her lips were colourless, but the red lipstick had run into the deep lines around her mouth. She was holding the wrapper together at the neck so tightly that she seemed to be throttling herself.

'*Mais c'est lui! C'est vraiment lui! Personne d'autre! Son image vivant!*'

Her voice was a crow's screech. She clutched her heart. The two conferred rapidly in another language full of harsh sounds, and then she stepped towards him, smiling and opening her arms, revealing a nightdress from the neck of which hung a length of torn lace. Her clothing released a wave of thick, musky perfume. The gesture was exactly as he had visualized it, but the rest of the picture was strange beyond his imaginings and all the more thrilling.

'Alex!' Her bare foot stamped on the dark parquet, and she tossed back her red head, commanding him to respond.

He stepped forward and leaned down to embrace her. 'Grandmother!'

CHAPTER 4

St Petersburg, 1905

'My sister says she has half my clothes finished already.' Marie turned over the next page of her letter. After Easter, in a few months' time, the class was to graduate, find places in the Imperial ballet company and emerge in the wide world. The girls who had lived in the school building at Theatre Street and worn the plain uniform garments for ten years past would go home, some to a veritable trousseau of new clothes. 'Two visiting dresses,' Marie continued, 'and two evening dresses, with gloves, stockings . . . but she says she will wait until I come home to look for my new boots – oh, she's such a bitch, look what she says here – "because I'm sure you will have acquired some new corns or bunions or other unimaginable disfigurements by now and we will have the devil's own job to find anything to fit you".'

'You're so lucky. God knows what my mother will have got ready for me. I expect she'll complain, she always does. Maybe if I write to her and drop a few hints she'll get the message.'

To train themselves for society, Lydia and Marie had pledged to speak only in French to each other for the rest of the term, so they would be as fluent in the language of the elite as any coddled debutante from the Smolny Convent. French made them both more animated and they chattered like a pair of finches as they crossed the inner courtyards in the school complex on their way to the bath house.

They paused for an instant, oblivious of the lacerating

cold, to look up to the windows of the rehearsal room on the first floor, where dancers appeared in silhouette against the drawn blinds. All the windows in the school had been provided with opaque blinds since the Director had discovered that a rehearsal room elsewhere in the city was vulnerable to balletomanes who rode upstairs on the omnibuses to catch sight of the dancers at work. The double windows cut out all sound, but it was still possible to see poor Tamara Platonova fumble her turns and some of the onlookers turn aside to hide their sneers.

'Poor thing, and she works so hard too.' Marie put away her letter and blew on her fingers. 'Whatever problems we've got they can't be as bad as hers. Especially not you, with your steel feet. Lucky for Tata she's so sweet, she can get by on personality. Or do you think her father pulls strings for her?'

Lydia shook her head as they proceeded onwards along the icy path. 'He can't any more, he's lost his job – haven't you heard?'

'No! Poor Tata. And she's got no one to look after her, has she? That's the kind of news that really makes me count my blessings. I don't know what I'd do if it wasn't for my sister – she's the lucky one really to have married so well and be able to look after me.' It was the simple truth. Every ballet school pupil was the child of parents who were either dead or impoverished. Even the children of older dancers, or of singers or musicians in the Imperial train, were well used to tight circumstances at home. Others, like the fragile Olga, had come straight from the orphanage. They were always conscious of poverty snapping at their heels.

They lived in a no-man's-land between starvation and opulence. The luxury of the ballet's *mise en scène* was held to be one of its cardinal qualities. Productions called for scores of people to be on stage, for lavish scenery and elaborate effects, horses and chariots, even gilded barges with silk sails gliding over the lakes at the Tsar's summer palaces in the country. The costumes were made of the finest fabrics, trimmed with rich furs, braids and ribbons, and worn with the dancers' own jewels. Beyond these sumptuous illusions lay the genuine splendour of St Petersburg society, and the Imperial Court. Behind, however, was the monastic simplicity and discipline of the school. This they would never leave, even after graduation. Daily classes and rehearsals, plain clothes and bare board floors would remind them of the instability of their lives, in which an accident, an illness or an injury could throw them back into deprivation.

The young dancers had the *épaulement* of goddesses, imposed by fine training but finally enhanced by knowing their own good fortune. However harsh their teachers might be, however strict their regime, at school they could eat meat three times a day, be educated, have their morals guarded and their manners guided and if they worked hard and behaved properly would at last be released into a glittering world with a livelihood and excellent opportunities to improve on it; those with real gifts would be rewarded, although political agility was at least as important as artistic talent; the average performers could still find lovers, and for the girls, like Marie's sister, perhaps even husbands, who would provide for them. For Lydia and Marie the day of release was intoxicatingly close; they lapsed regularly into fevers of anticipation.

They passed under a broad archway into the smallest courtyard, picked their way around the stacks of firewood, and entered the wooden bath house, which seemed to Lydia like Hansel and Gretel's cottage in the forest in comparison with the school's classical buildings. Faint light radiated from the tiny windows into the gloom of the winter evening.

It was deliciously warm after the bitter cold outside, and the smells of smoke and the wet, resinous wood were unique to the place. In the dressing room they shed their heavy coats and unlaced their boots. The maids helped them remove their long white pinafores and their serge dresses of plain blue. They pulled off their petticoats and their white cotton undergarments with modest lace edging. Wrapped in towels which were harsh from much laundering, they decided to sit in the steam bath and climbed up the wooden benches against the panelled walls. The maids threw water on the stove filled with stones in the middle of the floor.

'Here.' Lapsing into Russian, Marie handed the nearest woman a small brown bottle. 'Put some of this in the water – it's juniper balm, my sister says it's good for making your muscles relax.'

Billows of steam shot to the ceiling and spread out in a cloud. Lydia pinched her nostrils to keep them from being scalded until the temperature moderated. 'Go on, Marie, tell me about your clothes again.'

Marie obligingly recited descriptions of her dresses. Lydia had an extraordinary passion for everything pretty, for clothes, costumes, knick-knacks, flowers; if she could not own these things, it was almost as good to hear about them. 'Do you think your mother will get you anything?' her friend finished hesitantly.

'I don't know. I hope so. I know what I'd like, I've been dreaming about it. I want a black and white hat, with feathers . . .'

'Ooh, yes. Everyone's wearing them this year, my sister says.'

'And a polka-dot dress to go with it, with a low waist.' The languor induced by the steam was blown away by her enthusiasm and she got up to demonstrate, drawing imaginary seams around her naked body. She had already passed hours sketching the dresses of her dreams in her school notebooks. 'And something with those contrast-colour revers, cream and delft blue, or cream and red, maybe a coat, you know, with the buttons in cream.'

'Gorgeous! I wish I could have something like that too.'

'We'd look like sisters.' The heat and the excitement had made her breathless and Lydia lay down again. 'I do wish I had a sister like you.'

Marie's little hand, its fingertips scarlet with the heat, reached blindly across to pat one of hers. 'I'll always be your friend, Lydia. We all love you, you know that. And you know there's always Leo . . .' She giggled and turned over to watch her friend's reaction.

'He hasn't given you another note?'

'I almost forgot it – it's in my pocket.'

'You ought to be kinder to him, he's absolutely devoted.'

'Yes, and absolutely dull.' Leo had graduated the previous year, but the senior pupils and the dancers often worked together. Marie was now Leo's partner in the pas de deux class and a week seldom passed without another poem, or a little present, being smuggled to Lydia by her friend. Her adolescent contempt had matured into mere irritation, but now that the world was about to open before her the idea of an admirer, albeit a poor one, had its attractions. Not that she had any intention of throwing herself away on a dancer. There had been a number of notes from a number of men, even one or two fan letters which she had not been allowed to see, and she had a sturdy sense of what her worth would be once the market opened.

'I think Leo's going to ask if he can partner you next season.'

'Oh. Is he?' Clearly, he had asked the kind-hearted Marie

to sound her out. The deference was flattering. It was now beyond question that she was one of the outstanding dancers of her year. Leo himself was perhaps not so gifted; fervent in private, forever planning and arguing in pursuit of his ideals, he was still reserved on stage. He was attending classes with Mikhail Fokine, and made no secret of his ambition to follow him as a choreographer and try all kinds of modern experiments. He could have set his sights on partnering one of the senior ballerinas, and equally Lydia was hoping to be chosen by one of the first dancers. 'I think it depends what they give me, doesn't it? I don't know what parts the Director is going to choose for me, do I?'

'He wants me to tell you something – something really big – but you mustn't breathe a word, all right?'

'Oh yes!' Nothing was more delicious than a secret.

'Leo's father told him they were going to give you a debut.'

'No! Marie! How wonderful!' She sat up again, gasping in the heat. 'Is he sure! Who told his father? Oh, I can't believe it! I can't breathe! I can't talk in this heat – let's get out of here, quickly.'

They emerged from the steam, gasping, and blundered towards the washroom where they let their damp towels fall to the floor and ran to stand on the duckboards while the maids ladled cold water from buckets over their bodies.

'Does he know what they've chosen?' Lydia took a meagre splash of water on her back before gesturing to the maid that she had had enough and turning around. She hated all cold in general but everyone said cold splashes improved the beauty of the bosom, so she endured longer rinsing for her front.

'No! Aieeh! That's freezing! No, all I know is that they've decided you shall have a debut performance before the summer, some time in May. I'm so proud of you, Lydia. It's wonderful – there hasn't been a debut for years. Doesn't this prove what I've always said? You're a real star.'

They moved to the wooden benches and lay down to be scrubbed. 'Not too hard,' Lydia ordered abruptly. 'I hate having my skin scoured off. If I can't have pretty dresses at least I've got a good complexion – until you stupid women spoil it.'

The next day she was called to the Director's office to receive the great news. The role chosen to introduce her to the public of St Petersburg was a special pas de deux tucked away in the famous excitements of *Paquita*; it would be a little gem choreographed by Marius Petipa, the supreme genius of the company who had recently retired at almost ninety years of age. The title role was to be danced by La Kchessinskaya herself, whose return to the stage after the birth of her child had been as prompt as predicted.

Paquita was a long, elaborate classic with a vague Spanish scenario, calling for a huge corps drilled like guardsmen, successions of brilliant soloists, and costumes based on a wide traditional tutu decorated with black chenille net and pompoms. She would be able to show off her speed, strength and suppleness, to part her hair severely on one side in the prescribed style for all pseudo-Spanish pieces and pin a silk rose under her right ear. The music was easy stuff, circus tunes which she was well able to follow. Better still, her partner was to be Sergei Legat, Nikolai's brother, one of the most popular men in the company with the public and his colleagues. Lydia was struck dumb with such favour.

'Well, child?' the Director inquired, peering at her with narrowed eyes. 'Are you pleased?'

'Oh! Monsieur le Directeur, do please forgive me,' she almost whispered, 'of course I'm pleased. Thank you all, so much.' Still lost for words, she darted forwards, seized his hand from the desk and kissed it.

The elderly man recoiled with amusement and a distinct blush on his cheeks above his sparse brown whiskers. 'Well, I believe you now, at any rate. I have sent a note to your parents to let them know the date, and to tell them that you will have one full day of leave after the exams to visit your family, and two half days after that so that you can go shopping with your mother. And don't get so carried away that you let your mathematics disgrace you – your reports haven't given us as much confidence as your dancing.'

There was no real reproof in his words. The ballet masters unanimously nominated Lydia Alexandrovna for rapid success; the school tutors reported that she had intelligence but no ambition beyond the stage and no weakness for ideas. All round, she was an ideal product of their labours – beautiful, gifted and delightfully traditional in her outlook.

Lydia assured him that she would work hard, rapidly muttering the insincere promises she had made her teachers every year, and dashed away to spread the great news. Not until the evening, when she sat with Olga stitching shoes after dinner, did the shadow of her home fall over her cheerfulness.

'Where are you going to live next season?' she asked, suddenly envious of the girl without parents who could make her own choice of home.

'With my brothers and sister – Anatole and I have found a couple of rooms and with three of us in the corps de ballet we'll have enough to live on and be able to have our dear Pierre with us.' Olga's gestures, always affected, were even more artificial when she skirted the subject of the orphanage where her youngest brother still lived. Pierre had weak lungs and the school had refused to accept him. 'You'll be going home, I suppose?'

'Yes, I suppose so too. I don't want to, Olya. I'm dreading it, to tell the truth.'

'Because your father's ill? But at least you have a father and you know him. Think of us – our bitch of a mother screwed around, lied to us all her life and now she's dead we'll never know who he was.'

'It's not that. Where they live isn't my home. It's just the dustbin we were thrown in when we lost all our money. I've hardly ever lived there. I can't remember much about it, except it was a horrible place. Where we lived before was beautiful, I remember that . . .' She paused with her needle in mid-air, trying to recall her life in the handsome red house where she had been born and which she counted as her real home. All that came back were impressions of deep, soft pillows with lace and ribbon borders, of sticky little cakes made with cream cheese, a sweet young nursemaid who tickled her, and her mother, a beautiful young woman with long auburn hair, opening a drawer in her dressing table filled with suede gloves the colour of doves' wings and asking her help to choose a pair.

'Oh, how sad. Poor Lydia. I always envied you for having a family, I never thought you might have troubles of your own on their account. Of course, your mother doesn't visit you ever, does she? And you always have to board in the holidays. Forgive me, I'm so selfish . . .' For all her sympathy, Olga was watching intently as Lydia stitched her shoes, hoping to discover a better way of doing it.

'Oh, it's not so bad. My mother has enough to do looking after my father, I expect.' Lydia had indeed worked out a way to reinforce the instep, but she had no intention of giving away her secrets, especially not to Olga, whose major gifts seemed to be an exquisite line and a flirtatious way with critics. Casually, Lydia leaned towards the lamp, moving her hands out of Olga's sight. 'So tell me, what will you do about your clothes?'

'Dream! Pray! Walk about naked, maybe? I can't begin to think about it . . . wait a minute!' She held up her hand as if for silence and stared ahead into the dark corner of the sewing room. 'Oh! How horrible! Lydia, you mustn't go, you mustn't go home. I can see things, people being cut up. I can see a man with his head split like a muzzle in the butcher's. It's revolting, everything's hanging out of it.' Her delicate hands flew to her eyes to rub them, and her needle fell to the bare floor with a tiny noise. Lydia frowned, annoyed. Of all Olga's pretensions, she found her clairvoyance the most irritating. 'But there's a man there, too. Yes, I can see him quite clearly. Fair hair and a high forehead. He's not kind, but he does kind things. And this is *the* man, the one for you . . .'

'Can you see the maths exam paper as well?' Wrapping her shoes in their ribbons, Lydia put them away in her bag and pulled out a textbook.

'You shouldn't joke, I have the gift, you know I do. Oh God, where's my needle?'

'Don't you have a vision of it lying in the crack between the floorboards?'

'Oh, shut up. I can't find it, lend me yours.' Smiling, Lydia passed her felt needle book. 'Seriously, Lyduchka, don't go home on Sunday. Something terrible will happen if you go, I know it.'

'Yes, and something terrible will happen if I don't go. I'll have no roof over my head.'

When Sunday came, her entire body was heavy with reluctance. She found she could barely remember what her mother looked like, nor when she had last visited. As Olga had remarked, she came to the school very seldom, although their old maidservant, Douniasha, had called often in her younger days. And Lydia had not been home for years. The older girls were not allowed holiday visits at all – a rule introduced, so school legend held, because a girl called Mad Ann had contracted a scandalous liaison with a Horse Guards officer during a trip to see her family.

This neglect was no mystery to Lydia. She knew that her poor mother was not worn to a shadow by her father's illness, but because she was so devoted to her younger child, a son, she hardly remembered that she had ever borne a daughter. While some families reluctantly dispatched their girls to Theatre Street, compelled by poverty to overcome their misgivings about the immorality of the theatre world, the Kusminskis had packed off Lydia Alexandrovna at the age of eight without a backward glance and turned towards their miraculous boy. She had rarely seen her brother in the intervening years, and remembered him as an infant in a sailor suit with a sulky expression and a piercing scream which he let loose when anything displeased him.

Everything had gone wrong for Lydia after the boy had been born. Her mother had given up hoping for another child, and his birth had been greeted as a miracle from heaven. Then her father's business partner had cheated him, and he had fallen ill and seemingly lost his health for ever. They had passed from prosperity to poverty in no time, losing their home, friends and possessions one after the other, and then all the family turned to little Dima as their only hope, and Lydia became nothing more than a great insolent girl with an insatiable appetite, nothing but a burden on the household.

Their apartment was not far away from the school. On Sunday she set out early after Varvara Ivanova had warned her that there was to be a demonstration that day by some striking factory workers who planned to march through the city to petition the Tsar. The sacred right of every Russian to appeal directly to the Emperor for justice had been much invoked in recent years and columns of marchers with banners, placards and shouted slogans were a familiar sight. Lydia wondered if the queen toad's concern was for her safety or her allegiance, since support for the workers was growing among the dancers and Mikhail Mikhailovich and his set were forever calling meetings to vote motions of sympathy.

She heard the crowd as soon as she bade the uniformed doorman good morning and stepped out into the street. They were singing hymns, the rich deep voices of the men resonating in the clear air above the rumble of thousands of feet in heavy boots shuffling slowly forward. As she began to skirt the impressive bulk of the Alexandrinsky Theatre her nostrils caught the sickly tang of incense.

Beside the theatre's massive colonnade a group of twenty guardsmen were drawn up in four lines and waited at ease, their horses shaking their manes and watching the passing multitude with curiosity. Their officer, a fair-haired young man whose nose shone red with the cold, drew them to attention as Lydia passed and saluted her, calling out, 'Good morning, Mademoiselle,' in a ringing voice.

Alarmed, she looked behind her to be sure they were out of sight of the school before dropping him a curtsey and continuing onwards, her cheeks a little pink with the flush of flattery. Her way lay across the small park which separated the theatre from the road. Crisp new snow lay almost undisturbed over the shrubs, with only the little crosses of birds' feet tracking across the ornamental lawns.

Ahead the breadth of the Nevsky Prospekt was choked

with a grey mass of people. The snow beneath their feet had been churned almost to slush. She paused, amazed at the uncountable number of men flowing slowly down the city's main avenue, and even climbed on a bench to see how far in each direction the river of people extended. There was no visible end to the crowd, it seemed to go on for ever.

The men were bundled in their thick padded coats. Beneath their caps, padded or worn over scarves to keep out the cold, their grimy faces were calm. Many were stooped over, whether from toil, tiredness or in prayer she could not tell but such a number of bent backs gave the impression of pathetic supplication. Some had the beatific expression of men moved to ecstasy in church. When their eyes fell upon her a few of them made gestures of respect but most passed on with glazed looks as if they saw nothing. They moved as if in a trance, very slowly, almost shuffling, carrying placards demanding bread and justice in their hands, icons on their shoulders, or cheap print portraits of the Tsar decorated with paper flowers and fluttering ribbons. Here and there were small groups of priests, swinging censers and leading the singing.

Perplexed, Lydia walked along beside the crowd for a short distance and then returned. Her home lay on the far side of the road, and, peaceful as they were, she was afraid to plunge into the tightly packed mass and struggle across it; they would surely sweep her along with them. Every Russian had heard stories of crowds suddenly maddened by panic, trampling hundreds to death before they came to their senses.

'Captain Orlov's compliments, Mademoiselle.' She heard horses behind her and turned to see an ensign and three guardsmen draw to a halt. 'He is concerned for your safety. May we escort you across the Prospekt?'

'Can you make them let us through?' Lydia looked doubt-fully at the river of petitioners.

'Of course. They mean no trouble to anyone, Mademoiselle. You can see they're harmless beasts. And they're not drunk, not yet anyway. Which way are you going?'

'Up to the Gribojedeva Canal. I only need to get across and then I'll be fine.'

Still in doubt, she looked back towards the theatre where the rest of the guardsmen remained. The officer saluted her again and she inclined her head in acknowledgement, reflect-ing that if any of the school staff passed by and saw what was happening she would be punished for flirting, probably by the revocation of her famous debut. Best to move on at once. 'Why – thank you, thank Captain Orlov, very much. You're so kind. Shall we go?'

The ensign, who under his gleaming braid and buttons was hardly older than she was, ordered the men forward and they approached the edge of the crowd. Calling out, 'Make way now, let the lady pass!' they stemmed the flow of the crowd and Lydia walked through them like Moses through the Red Sea, suffering nothing worse than the stink of thousands of unwashed bodies. The distant pavement seemed very far away, but she kept her eyes on the icy road and stepped out at a steady pace beside the horses. Quite a few of the men bowed as she passed or touched their forelocks, although they made no sound except the continuous singing. From the centre of the mass the hymns merged into a cacophony, one refrain running up against another because one group could barely hear the next along the column.

To her embarrassment the ensign insisted on accompany-ing her with his party as far as the canal side, where her route left the main street. 'What will happen to them all?'

she asked, still overcome by the vastness of the crowd. 'There are more people here than I could ever imagine in the world.'

'Or me.' The ensign regarded the ragged mass with a cheerful shrug. 'They won't be able to get to the Winter Palace – their leaders will be received, which is more than they deserve since this is an illegal demonstration, but there are barricades all around to turn them back. Then the officers up there will order them to disperse peacefully and they'll go home having got cold and hungry for nothing.' Young as she was, Lydia could tell that he was speaking from self-importance rather than experience.

'Don't they realize that?'

'They haven't the intelligence – and the strike leaders whip them up into hysteria so the few who can think don't. But if they carry on in this church procession style there won't be any trouble. Our company is part of the reserve, we've been posted all over the city just in case.'

'Well, you can tell your captain I'm terribly grateful to him, I'd never have got through without you.'

'I'm sure he'd want me to say that it was a great pleasure to be able to assist a lady, Mademoiselle.'

He saluted with a carefree flourish and prepared to part the crowd once more to return to his post, while Lydia, happy that she had behaved with the ideal modicum of coquetry, set off along the canal bank. The Gribojedeva, named after the playwright, was narrow and ran between high red granite embankments through the heart of the city. Even in summer its water was so still that it seemed dead. Now great baulks of timber were frozen in the ice, although here and there an intrepid party foraging for firewood had prised a log loose with crowbars, leaving jagged lumps to freeze over once more.

The motionless waterway ran in a straight line to join a small river, interrupted by the gaudy pile of the Church of the Bleeding Saviour, an edifice in the traditional style built on the spot where the Tsar Alexander II had been assassinated. This tragedy had taken place in the year of her parents' marriage, and the church, a harshly coloured aberration in the street of gentle browns and russets, always struck Lydia as an ill omen. Halfway to it, on the same bank, was a flat-fronted dun building that was bare of ornamentation and obviously older than the larger constructions with art nouveau bas-reliefs which had sprung up around it. Lydia's family were squeezed into the low-ceilinged rooms on the top floor.

She remembered that once they had lived on the opposite bank, in the fine red house which had been all theirs. When her father had fallen ill they had sold it, and moved over the still water to the rooms rented by the widow of one of his former business friends. The apartment was so badly arranged that the main room had only one window, and she was glad to have called it home for less than two years.

On the staircase her steps grew less and less brisk as she climbed. Wretched memories sprang out of every doorway, telling her that this was her true home, that the ordered and privileged world of the dance was a silly dream. The real Lydia was an ordinary chit of a girl who laid her head to sleep in a maid's room under the roof, not the dazzling dancing nymph loaded with bouquets and votive poetry.

She remembered the family's arrival, a sad caravanserai, grumbling men manoeuvring their furniture through the mean doorway. Her father, wrapped in a quilt, had been carried upstairs like a child. He had glanced into the dizzying depth of the stairwell and her mother had called out, 'Shura, for heaven's sake, take care – are you mad? Do you want to make this good man drop you?' And he had whispered to Lydia as he was set gently down, 'Next time I'll be going down in a box, my dear. Maybe I'll be still enough for her then.'

With dragging feet she crossed the bare boards of the landing and knocked at the door. Their name, Kusminski, was written on a curled card fixed to the jamb with a rusty pin. There was a long interval before she heard footsteps, then the door opened and her mother welcomed her inside with a nod and a few grunted words of greeting.

The news of the great crowd marching down the Nevsky Prospekt was received with no interest by her mother, whose whole manner suggested that this visit was merely a necessary ordeal. Stale smells mingled in the atmosphere: cooking fat, medicines and the disgusting emanations of a diseased digestion.

'Here's our little Dima.' Her mother led her to the gloomy salon where the boy was reclining by the stove. 'Always with a book in his hand – Dima, show your sister what you are reading now.' He looked up in silence and showed her the book, a lanky nine-year-old whose overlong blond hair hung straight over his eyebrows. 'You see, German, he reads German already. Nine years old! Can you imagine, to be blessed with such a clever son? Dima will be the salvation of this family, I know it.' The child did not stand up to greet her and neither their mother nor her own mother, a dark figure bustling in her wake, prompted him to remember his manners. Although the room was warm, he wore a knitted scarf tucked into the neck of his smart blue jacket.

'I was clever, at that age. Latin and Greek. Poetry ... Ovid, Catullus ... the wars, the wars, always about their wars ...' The hoarse old voice on the far side of the stove faded to silence. Until he spoke she had not noticed her father; he had shrunk to something yellow-skinned and bowed like a crescent moon, his face below his coarse knitted cap half a skull already.

'I wish he'd keep quiet, he'll disturb the boy.' Her mother in contrast had swelled to an unhealthy bulk, her once-fine bosom subsumed by fat, her rosy cheeks now pallid cushions. Her hair was worn in the same style, held up by combs, but they had been inserted unskilfully, at crazy angles, and locks were bidding to escape. Lydia had always recalled her mother wearing filmy blouses, soft and delicate against her cheek when they embraced, but now she wore a grey shirt that was almost mannish, with a button hanging loose and darned patches under the arms where the rubbing flesh had worn the fabric.

'I'm going to write to my cousin and see what he can do about getting our Dima a place in the Gymnasium,' she continued. 'He was a lawyer, he should know somebody. The boy needs to have his mind stretched, his teachers don't see that he's bored, they don't challenge him enough. And he needs to get out of this dreadful city, out in the country so he can run about and get some colour in his poor cheeks.'

Her father looked from one person to another, obviously struggling with the fact that there was a stranger in the room. 'A girl, is it a girl? What's she come here for?' Getting no response, he retreated for a moment into his muddled thoughts, his fingers picking at his frayed cuffs. 'I remember something. *Passer mortuus est meae puellae, Passer deliciae meae puellae.* That's Latin, I remember it. The sparrow's dead. Couldn't see any sense in it, but I learned it all the same, when you're a boy you have to learn.' He coughed, a weak, wheezing noise like a worn-out harmonium.

'We thought he might not last the winter this time.' Lydia's mother spoke as if her husband were not in the room. 'Night after night he was coughing like that and keeping us all awake. Poor Dima was exhausted going to school in the mornings. Here around his eyes he was quite grey. Of course he has such fine skin it shows immediately the state of his health . . .'

'And he is delicate, your brother. We have to take very good care of him. Country air is what he needs. If we had our dacha still it would be different.' Grandmother drew Lydia away to the table, which was covered with a fringed red jacquard cloth much spotted with grease. She alone seemed to be unchanged, a white-haired old woman in black with small, round brown eyes. The whites were tinged with yellow, but there was still vitality in her look. At the neck of her dress she wore a pink cameo brooch which seemed to dig uncomfortably into the wrinkled flesh above it. The brooch was finely carved with the head of Diana, her long locks caught in a fillet with a crescent on the brow, her small mouth curled in a smile. It was the only beautiful sight in the room. 'It's only by the grace of God and because we are so careful that Dima is still with us. One cold after another . . . ah, at last, there you are, girl – now we shall have some tea.'

A young girl entered the room carrying their samovar with arms so thin that it seemed doubtful that she was capable of bearing the weight. She proceeded towards the table with such exaggerated care that Lydia was put in mind of a wirewalker she had once seen at a circus. When the steaming silver pot was set on the table she looked around at her mistress with an inquiring expression in her dull eyes.

Lydia's mother nodded and the maid withdrew almost as slowly, returning a few moments later with cups. 'What happened to Douniasha?' Seeing the servant who had cared for her as a child and loyally served them all through fat and lean years without complaint was the one aspect of the visit which had offered Lydia pleasure.

WHITE ICE

'We had to get rid of her.' Her mother passed a cup brimming with watery tea. 'What a disaster that woman turned out to be in the end.' She shook her head.

'What happened? You never told me anything about it. I can't imagine old Douniasha doing anything really bad.'

'Neither could we, but we should never have trusted her, never.' Grandmother joined the lamentation, her eyes bright with indignation. 'A woman like that, who had lost her own children – we ought to have foreseen it.'

Lydia had a dim memory of Douniasha's arrival from the railway station, a big woman with stooped shoulders and bony hands whose touch was nevertheless soft and gentle. Her mother's family had once been country gentry, comfortable in a small way but without enough wealth to survive the reforms of the past decades. There had been bad harvests, and an epidemic of a terrible fever which had carried off half the peasants on their diminished estate. Douniasha had lost her husband, three children and her own parents and had arrived with a note from Grandfather commending her with the words, 'She is a good woman and I cannot bear to see her starve with the rest.'

'She was kind – she used to fry potatoes for me.' Lydia searched her memory for more evidence for the defence and was surprised at her mother's angry retort.

'Did she? Well, I'm not surprised at that either. She was always half mad, if you ask me.' She dropped her voice to a whisper so that Dima, still reading by the stove, could not hear. 'Don't you realize? She almost killed your brother. She let the stove smoke. We had gone to church. The whole place was a cloud of charcoal fumes. He could have suffocated. Babushka and I only just got back in time – he was hardly breathing, I thought he'd die right there, right then ...' The two women crossed themselves quickly,

130

exchanging glances and nodding, agreeing with each other on the gravity of their old servant's crime.

There was a rasp of breath as her father rose to his feet, pausing unsteadily before shuffling towards the table. They ignored him as he fumbled with the chair, dragging it out with difficulty so that he could lower his frame to sit. Since no move was made to pour him tea, he began to draw long, unsteady breaths and try to speak, but the effort was too great and he sat helplessly, his clawed hand twitching on the table top as he tried to summon the strength to make a gesture.

'I think Father would like some tea.' Lydia tried to speak without making it sound like an accusation. One cup remained on the tray. Her mother gathered her skirts and walked heavily across to her son.

'Dima, my dear' – she put her hand on his arm – 'come and have some tea.'

'I want to read,' he replied without looking up from the page.

'Won't you come and have just one cup with us?'

'I wish you'd leave me alone.' His full pink lips drooped with distaste.

'Very well, dear. You keep on with your reading if that's what you want.'

She returned to the table and filled the last cup for her husband with very little grace.

Lydia sat in silence, contemplating the home to which she was to return in a few months' time. Her mother and grandmother seemed to have become more than half crazed in their obsession with her spoiled pet of a brother. The boy was already looking at her with undisguised resentment. Her father had truly lost his mind, and would die perhaps as much from neglect than as a consequence of his broken health.

Her family, she appreciated now for the first time, had never given her natural affection, only loaned it until her brother, the more worthy recipient, had appeared. Even he was not loved for his own sake; mercantile to the marrow, they invested care in him looking for a good return when he was old enough to follow a profession.

Among other children who had no parents at all, Lydia had never pitied herself. Her fallen family were part of her lot in life and she had better gifts in her good health and strong legs. Sitting among them now, seeing how misfortune had poisoned their spirits, she felt nothing for them, only a gnawing anxiety for her own future.

The room itself had a madhouse air, the few remaining items of simple furniture standing on the thin rug like strangers on a railway platform, in no relation to each other. There were light patches on the dirty walls where there had once been pictures and dust lying thick in corners where the simple-minded servant had not noticed it and no one had corrected her. In one corner the roof had leaked, the wallpaper was peeling and marked with streaks. The samovar, she noticed, had formerly been used in the butler's room of the old house; she remembered their old silver one, in whose shiny fat belly she had watched the reflection of her face distorting as she moved her head from side to side. This cheap nickel-plated vessel, chased to the depth of mere scratches with scrolls, showed brassy patches around the handles from use and stood crookedly on the table, having obviously been dropped and never mended.

'So you'll be graduating at Easter,' her mother began with a weary air of responsibility. 'And what then?'

'I'll become part of the Maryinsky Theatre company and dance in the ballets and operas there.'

'What are they going to pay you?' The question was put so rapidly that her mother almost spat.

'Sixty-five roubles a month to start.'

'Sixty-five! Can't you get more?' Both women were leaning intently towards her.

'Everybody gets the same in the beginning. As you rise in rank so your salary goes up. That's the system.'

'Hum. Herr-um. Well, I thought it would be more. You're supposed to be good, aren't you? That's what the letter said.' Her mother grunted and Lydia felt that she could almost hear her thoughts as she planned how to spend the meagre sum. 'Well, and I suppose we shall have to turn the girl out of her room for you.'

'She can sleep in the corridor.' Her grandmother was clearly eager to make Lydia feel at least minimally welcome.

'And I am to have a debut performance in *Paquita* in May. The Directorate can arrange tickets for you if you want.' Lydia tried to make the invitation sound unattractive, but the effort was unnecessary.

'We don't go to the ballet,' her mother exclaimed with vehemence. 'What an idea! Do they think we're millionaires with nothing better to do than get dressed up to amuse ourselves? Even when we had money we didn't fritter it away on entertainment. Your father always said a business-man should attend to business and not waste his time buying pictures and keeping musicians who only drink and laugh at you behind your back. And what would we do with Dima? He would be tired out, poor lamb.'

Her mother's contempt withered Lydia's heart. She wanted to cry, but being well used to injuries she sat silent, trying to calm herself by listening to her breath. The voice of one of the teachers echoed in her thoughts, recalling the soothing discipline of school: 'Don't breathe into your stomach so you stand there heaving like a horse, breathe invisibly, down your back, here'; and she felt the pressure of a teacher's warm hand over her ribs. In a little while the inner emptiness closed over like a hole in the ice freezing anew.

The maid, who had been waiting uncertainly by the doorway, asked if she should serve lunch. The meal consisted of a thin soup followed by buckwheat cooked with chicken fat which had a whiff of putridity that too much pepper could not disguise. Dima stirred his portion reluctantly but the adults ate every scrap and wiped their plates with bread like peasants.

There had been no mention of clothing and now that Lydia had seen the pitifully reduced style in which they were living she feared that there would be nothing to give her. The best she could hope for would be an old dress of her mother's. With a heavy heart Lydia chose her moment to open the subject.

'I won't be able to wear the school uniform once I'm in the corps,' she began. Her mother gave her a sharp look which suggested that whatever she was about to say would be unpleasant to hear. 'So ...' Her nerve failed and her mouth could find no more words.

'She's surely not expecting us to clothe her when she can see that we can hardly even feed ourselves.' Her mother spoke to her grandmother in the same tight voice full of anger that she had used to talk about her invalid husband.

'I'll get a grant from the school – a hundred roubles,' Lydia added rapidly. 'But I have to buy shoes and tarlatan for my practice dresses.'

'A hundred roubles – well, you'll just have to make do with that.'

'But it won't be nearly enough – don't you understand? I haven't any other clothes, we've got to buy everything.' By a supreme effort of will Lydia kept her voice from rising to a scream.

134

'It's no use her telling us what we've got to buy, is it? We've nothing to give her, no money and nothing to pawn.'

'You can't get blood out of a stone, you know.' For the first time since her arrival, Dima looked as if there was some possibility of pleasing him.

'But what am I to do? I can't walk the streets in my practice clothes.'

'How dare you come home to us with your worries! Can't you see we've got enough troubles of our own? We're sitting here in rags and you want new clothes – you must be mad.' Her mother rose to her feet and Lydia flinched, an old reflex remembered from the days when her mother was always angry and she was slapped almost every time she spoke. 'I do the best I can, you know. I have some pupils, stupid girls but if their parents want to pay good money to give them some ladylike accomplishments I won't complain. It's better than taking in washing – oh, yes, we've been reduced to that before now. But you'll be better off than us, you'll be earning money, or so you tell us. If you want clothes you can surely provide them for yourself.'

Her grandmother looked on Lydia's downcast face and tried to soften the truth. 'Lydia, if they're going to pay you this salary, perhaps you could ask for a loan, an advance – to be deducted from your future earnings.'

'Of course, that's the answer,' her mother broke in at once. 'There, that's settled. They'll give you a loan. Don't ask for a kopeck more than you need and be sure to buy sensible things which will last. I know a woman who can fix you up with some good quality stuff at the right sort of price. I got this blouse from her, you wouldn't believe what I paid for it. We'll go shopping together. And maybe there'll be enough to get some flannel for a shirt for Dima, he grows so fast I can't keep up with him.'

The samovar reappeared and they drank more tea. With all the business of the visit concluded the atmosphere loosened. Lydia offered them titbits of gossip about the Court and society, how the Tsarina had looked during her pregnancy, how her long-awaited baby son behaved at his christening, how the Grand Duke Nikolai was so crazy about his actress mistress that he refused to marry even though he was past forty, how a young officer had tried to take home treats for his children from a Court banquet in his helmet then forgotten and put it on, raining grapes and sweetmeats on his own head. Mother and Babushka swallowed every tale with relish, their dull eyes gleaming with such a greed for high living that Lydia grew disgusted and decided to leave, although the afternoon was still bright.

They sent her away with far more enthusiasm than they had received her, calling advice about the loan down the stairs after her.

By the Church of the Bleeding Saviour was a park, one of several lovely green spaces which led one after the other to the Field of Mars where Douniasha had taken her to watch the guards parade, and then to the Neva's edge. As a child she had bowled her hoop in these gardens, and the fantastic shapes of the iron railings had appeared in her nightmares as serpents. Now in the dead of winter the tall lime trees were leafless and the paths empty. A couple of hardy sparrows hopping from twig to twig sent tiny showers of snow falling through the chill air.

As she walked to calm herself, she heard a distant, muffled crackle as if a hundred corks had been popped at one command. It was a sound that was familiar, although she could not place it. Across the open spaces she heard faint cries from several directions and she halted, recalling with foreboding thousands of men marching to the Winter Palace. She imagined the docile crowd running mad with fear if soldiers attacked them.

At the far end of the gardens a riderless horse, reins and stirrups flying, galloped into view, gathering speed across the snow-covered grass. Immediately the animal's terror infected her; she felt her blood leap and her heart stick in her throat as if it would choke her. The crowd was coming, she would be killed if she was in their way. She turned and ran back towards the gate, quitting the path to bolt directly between the trees, her long, swift strides kicking snow high in the air behind her.

Within a few yards her heavy skirts had wound themselves around her legs and forced her to stop. The shouting was suddenly distinct, and with it a distant roar of a huge crowd in motion, the constant tattoo of shots and bugle calls sounding clear above the din. As she tore at the obstinate swathe of fabric around her knees, she saw a dozen men now running across the open space in panic. A slight rise in the ground gave her a longer view. The further gardens were covered by an agitated grey mass, men and horses barely distinguishable as they struggled together.

The desperate group in the park were a mere hundred yards away and dashing in all directions in their confusion. A group of cavalry wheeled into view and bore down upon them, their swords raised. She saw one man throw up his arms and pitch forward, shot by the officer who was urging his men forward. Then the horsemen overtook the rest, and she saw blood spout across the snow as they were cut down.

Her skirts untangled at last, Lydia grabbed their weight in her arms and ran towards the gate with all the strength in her legs. The sounds of fighting were all around her. Another group of strikers were running down the street outside her family's home. She tore towards the church; the nearest door was locked but in the porches surely she would be safe.

She made her way around the wall to the next door, fighting for breath. Many more figures were running down the far bank of the canal, away from the Nevsky Prospekt. She could see them clearly, young men in students' caps, granddads who struggled to keep the pace, a hatless priest with his long hair flying dragging a boy by his collar. As they came closer she saw that among the marchers were ordinary citizens swept along by the mob. Two young women in stylish fur-edged coats were floundering at the rear, hobbled as Lydia herself had been by their skirts and desperately manhandling a screaming child who was too big to carry and too small to run.

A group of workers bolted up a side street only to reappear in a few seconds with terror on their faces; after them rode more troops, fifty at least, and they ploughed into the panic-stricken crowd from the side. The rear of the group turned and ran back, and she saw a massive young man with a farrier's apron over his coat seize the child from the arms of the stylish young women and charge onwards. From the mêlée the body of a man was pushed over the railings and fell on to the ice of the canal; his tongue tumbled hideously through his severed throat, trailing with it a skein of guts.

The next door was also locked. The priests had prudently barricaded themselves inside. Lydia squeezed herself into the porch and hammered on the wood, hurting her fist. The Prospekt was too far away to see, but she guessed from the volume of people pouring down the embankments that there was worse fighting there. More soldiers had crossed the park; they passed her without noticing and sped down the street to attack another group of rioters.

The park itself, so peaceful a few minutes ago, was an

apocalyptic scene. Everywhere the snow was stained with blood. Hundreds of men fled crazily in every direction, stumbling over the bodies of their comrades. The soldiers, uniforms bright even in the failing light, pursued in tight groups. As she watched one hussar rode into the basin of an ornamental pool, his horse struggling on the ice while he hacked at the legs of two boys who had climbed the fountain.

Some men, old and exhausted, got down on their knees by the corpses, shouting, 'Death to the Tsar, Death to the Murderers!' and waiting with rolling martyrs' eyes for the cavalry to dispatch them. A man had fallen back on a park bench as he died and lay sprawled there like a sunbather in summer. One arm hung low, the shoulder almost sliced away. There seemed to be more soldiers at every moment, galloping from the direction of the Field of Mars.

'Let me in, for God's sake, let me in! Aren't you men of God? People are being killed here, help me!' Lydia hardly knew she was shouting, but her whole arm was bruised from battering uselessly at the closed church door. At least if she turned her face away from the bloodshed she would be spared the sight of men cut up like carcasses in an abattoir.

There were horses behind her, very close. She shut her eyes and prayed to die quickly, not be trampled under boots and smothered in the snow. Hands pulled her bodily away from the doorway. She screamed as she was lifted in the air. Something bruised her legs, something grazed her face.

'Don't worry, Mademoiselle, don't worry, you're all right now, you are safe, I've got you.' Her whole body was shaken with a horrible jostling motion. Her waist was being crushed. The voice was a man's and he was speaking in French. 'Don't scream, please, I beg you, this horse can't bear to hear a woman scream. Here, catch hold around my neck . . .'

Her left arm was pulled upwards. She felt the speaker's chest, his shoulder and collar, buckles and straps, and by her right hand the coarse hair of the horse's mane. Her frenzied fingers seized whatever was beneath them.

'That's good, hold tight now. For God's sake don't scream. We're setting off now, you'll soon be home.' The horse jolted into motion, tossing her around so violently that she needed all her strength to keep hold of her rescuer. Around them she heard other riders. The smell of the sweating animal was reassuring, and the man gave off an aroma of a fine cologne, an absurd drawing-room perfume in such a moment of horror.

In a few moments she grew accustomed to the animal's stride and dared to squeeze open her eyes. The horse was black, and they were crossing a small square. She recognized the statue of Pushkin. There were guardsmen riding on each side. They were turning towards the palace in the corner. The noises of fighting had diminished.

'We're making for the Fontanka river.' The man was speaking close to her ear and she felt his moustache scratch her cheek. 'We came that way, it was quiet, we can get you to Theatre Street the back way if we're lucky.'

The horse swerved to avoid the body of a man which lay alone in the centre of the street. Lydia almost lost her grip and gasped in fear. 'Don't worry, I'm always lucky,' he went on in a pleasant voice, for all the world as if making conversation to a dancing partner. 'At poker, at life – maybe even in love, huh? What do you think, Mademoiselle?'

'For God's sake don't joke – they're killing people everywhere. How can you talk like that?'

'Forgive me, Mademoiselle, I didn't mean to distress you. This is a mess, it's a tragedy, but still it's not the Manchurian front, you know.' He spoke so lightly that she could not judge whether he was an experienced soldier or a posturing cynic. 'Anyway – don't you want to know how I know where you live?'

'I thought . . .' She was so shaken that reasoning was impossible. 'Well, our uniform, everyone knows the Theatre School coat.'

'Indeed, although, if you'll pardon a compliment in these circumstances, it is rarely so elegantly worn. But the uniform isn't everything – and come to that, you don't recognize ours either, do you?'

Since he was clutching her firmly to his chest and she was holding on for dear life it was hard to see the details of his dress. The coarse khaki battledress scraped her cheek, and from the corner of her eye she could see the collar, with a crown and a dusty blue flash edged with gold, regimental badges which meant nothing to her. 'Well, surely at least you recognize my ensign? Who escorted you across the road this morning?'

The youth was riding almost at their horse's shoulder and saluted as he was named. 'Oh my goodness, you were outside the theatre when I left.'

As they reached the edge of the Fontanka two men were ordered ahead to survey the embankment, and called 'All clear!' at once. The officer's horse halted at the junction and began sidestepping in agitation.

'Excuse me just a moment.' He reached around Lydia's waist to change the reins from one hand to the other, turned the animal's head and sent it on with a jab from his spurs. 'Yes, absolutely correct. I'm the man whose heart you broke when you stuck your nose in the air and refused to give me a civil good morning.'

'Oh, don't be silly.'

'I was inconsolable.'

'You were bored.' She was beginning to feel annoyance, not only at her rescuer and his world-weary pose but also at herself, and beyond that at fate itself. This was not the style of scintillating badinage she had imagined herself adopting with a guards officer, nor the circumstances ideal for such a meeting. She was in pain, too, from being battered by the pommel of the saddle and the rest of its hard protuberances as the restive horse carried on in broken strides.

'Well, perhaps you're right. But when I saw that rabble running back down the Prospekt I knew for the sake of that lady who wore her coat so elegantly I had to get to the Gribojedeva bridge before them. I'm only sorry we frightened you so much.'

'Oh – but – you did save my life. I am grateful, really I am ...' Lydia had never been so profoundly thankful for anything; the Alexandrinsky Theatre was almost in sight and she was almost fainting with relief but her words sounded perfunctory. 'Oh, no! I mean that! I do! Why can't I say it properly?'

'Quiet, now, remember my poor horse. Let's see if we're clear to cross.'

Three or four young men were running across the bridge ahead as fast as their powerful legs could carry them. Again two guardsmen rode ahead to reconnoitre, and one turned and rode back immediately.

'There're quite a few coming down the Prospekt, Sir, but we'll have no trouble if we keep together.'

'Last time, Mademoiselle, hold tight.' The officer gave the order to go forward and all eight horses sprang away together, reaching a gallop in a few strides. Lydia caught a brief impression of ragged crowds behind her. Then the horse bounded away at a diagonal, again to avoid a fallen man, and she lost her grip, but the officer's arm was like rock around her waist and she found herself safe. On the ground lay the obstacle, a powerful body in a patched grey coat, still alive, legs moving weakly in the ploughed snow.

It seemed that the horses had hardly slowed to a trot before they turned into the haven of Theatre Street and halted at the school gateway. Half the troop was already waiting there, guarding the entrance. Lydia gave a last scream as she was lowered to the ground and discovered that her hair had fallen down and become tangled in her rescuer's buttons. He swiftly caught the ends and pulled them free, his lips twitching with a suppressed smile, then dismounted and walked with her to the door. It opened as they approached to reveal the Director with Varvara Ivanova at his side.

'Kusminskaya! Thank God you're safe!' The directress's long, cold hands reached out in an awkward gesture.

'You are the one we should thank, Captain ...' An awesome figure in the school, the Director suddenly seemed ineffectual, almost ridiculous, beside this fine tall man in uniform.

'Captain Orlov, at your service. Frankly we are fortunate to be protecting His Imperial Majesty's artists rather than hounding those miserable misguided cattle. Are any more of your students missing?'

'Three now. Nijinsky's back with his head split open, but not Bourman and Babitch, or his sister who was with them.' The directress hugged Lydia to her side, making her feel like a helpless child. 'What's going on, Captain? What happened up there?'

'I know they tried to advance beyond the barricades at the Palace Square; there was some firing then, and a charge, but they dispersed and we thought it was all over. I was waiting for orders to go home when the mob came pouring down the Prospekt. We'll know tomorrow. But there's fighting all over the city and hundreds dead, if not thousands. Mademoiselle Kusminskaya has endured some dreadful scenes today, with great courage, I may say. But those people who are still unaccounted for – well, we'll do our best, but I fear for them. Which direction did they take?'

Before he left, Lydia was bidden to thank Orlov again, an order so humiliating that she could hardly speak for annoyance. A deadly tiredness was taking hold of her, and a few minutes later when the senior tutor came to fetch her she found she could barely move.

The next day she was as stiff as a plank and covered with black bruises. For weeks afterwards the scenes of the day recurred in her dreams. Night after night she woke, chilled with sweat, seeing the dead man fall into the canal, or the young blacksmith with the child in his arms decapitated by a sabre stroke and the screaming infant bathed in blood.

The two missing students returned safely, but Babitch's sister had been torn out of his arms in the crowd and lost for ever; the commander of the guards ordered that all the dead should be buried before daybreak, lest more riots should break out when the bodies were counted, and no trace of the pretty young woman was ever found.

Despite Orlov's guard, the rioters broke into the Alexandrinsky Theatre at the end of the street, but at the Maryinsky, across town, the ballet performance continued without interruption.

Vaslav Fomitch, a Polish boy a couple of years below Lydia, had also been trapped in the riot, hit by a cossack and his forehead split open. They were both allowed two days of rest to recover from their injuries, and given extra tuition while their colleagues were at class. It was not a success. Vaslav was notoriously stupid, and Lydia was possessed by raging terrors which tore her mind to shreds.

In the dark corners of the school's many corridors she imagined indefinite bloody horrors lurking. Everyday noises, a rattling music stand or plates clattering in the kitchen, startled her out of her skin. One day she left a classroom on the top floor and froze at the head of the stairs, imagining herself falling to the bottom.

In a few days all her fearful imaginings devolved upon her home and family. 'They're cursed,' she told herself, 'they must be. Nothing but tragedy around them, always. Someone sinned, someone put a jinx on them. It's abnormal, so much bad luck.'

By day she fretted and at night she lay awake, fearful of sleep and dreaming. 'I can't go back home, I can't,' she confessed one night in a whisper to Marie. 'I'll never be able to walk down that street again without seeing those horrible things. And my wretched family – if you'd seen how they were living. I can't bear it, I can't even think of them. What can I do? Where can I go?'

'You can stop whispering and let the rest of us get some sleep,' hissed a voice from the far side of the dormitory.

'Oh shut up, Olga! We put up with you tossing and turning like a dervish all night – have some pity for poor Lydia.' Marie got out of bed and fussed over her friend like a nurse, smoothing out her pillow. 'Oh, you've been crying, you poor thing. But you must sleep, you'll be worn to a shadow. Here.' She raised the blind a few inches to give herself some light and searched her night table for a book. 'Look, here are my maths notes, put them under your pillow and then your head will be filled with algebra and there'll be no room for bad dreams.'

'You want me to swap one nightmare for another?' Lydia tried to raise a smile.

'Come on, everyone knows that putting the book under the pillow helps you revise. Don't worry, dear friend ... listen, I've been thinking, would you like to come and live with us? I'm sure my sister would agree. Shall I talk to her?'

'Oh! Marie – would you? You're so kind to me, I don't deserve it.'

'Of course you do, you're going to be a star. Out of all this bad some good must come. Now shut your eyes and try to sleep.' And Lydia laid her head on the damp pillow, her turbulent mind becoming quiet at last.

Her remaining worries miraculously resolved themselves in a few weeks. Marie's sister readily agreed to lodge her in exchange for a reasonable rent. She was again summoned to the Director's office, informed that her grandmother had called and given a small package wrapped in newspaper. Inside was an old red morocco box containing the cameo brooch, and a note: 'Dear child, if I could protect you from our misfortunes I would. You have seen how things are – this is the best I can do, the last treasure I have. The beauty of my youth is long gone, take this to enhance yours.' The address of a pawn shop followed, and a postscript warning her to say nothing to her mother.

With a heart now lightened almost to euphoria, Lydia sailed into her examinations, passing with better marks than her most generous tutors had predicted. Shortly afterwards her first morning of shopping came around, a marvellous foretaste of the freedom to come. With Marie, she enlisted the help of Tamara Platonova, who was clever at making every kopeck count. In the pawn shop they haggled half-heartedly over the price for the brooch, well aware that nothing would soften the broker's heart; he admitted that it was a good piece and gave more than Lydia had expected. Elated, the three of them plunged into the clamour of the Jewish market.

Their sleeves and skirts were pulled in every direction as the eager traders tried to entice them to view their wares. The market was housed under a glass dome, which magnified its noise to a deafening volume. Ignoring the dull booths stocked with good plain clothes, Tamara Platonova led them to a little shop in the heart of the bustle, a narrow cave crammed to the ceiling with neatly folded garments. Everything was second hand. The elderly couple who owned the business greeted them like long-lost friends and the wife scrambled again and again up her shaky step-ladder, muttering, 'I know I've just the thing here, just right for your colouring, now where was it? What size did you say? Ah, here it is. Or maybe you'd like something else, a little brighter, now let me see . . .'

Lydia chose a dark green tailored suit. The label inside was French, and in no time the old man pinched the shoulders to fit her with his crooked fingers and slipped a line of pins along the seams. Then she asked to see evening dresses, ignoring the disapproval of the older girl, and Marie's urging to buy a good warm coat. When she tried on a pale pink mousseline with jet beading at the hem there was a sudden silence before her companions reluctantly admitted that she looked gorgeous. The old man shuffled away and came back with an opera cloak of raspberry velvet which he lowered around her shoulders.

'It's lovely but it's far too much,' Lydia said at once when she saw the price on the label tied to a buttonhole.

The old couple exchanged a few words in Yiddish. 'Take it,' the old man ordered, 'pay when you can. You've got a lucky face, one day you'll have all the beautiful things you want and then you won't buy from us any more. And anyway, we know where you work, don't we?'

Lydia regarded herself in the mirror, turning this way and

that to admire the rich fabrics. 'Thank you, you're too kind.' She inclined her head graciously as she had seen Kchessinskaya do when complimented on her dancing.

'Do you think he's right?' she asked as they emerged from the crush of the market half an hour later, carrying her parcels between them. 'Have I really got a lucky face?'

'How ridiculous! You'll be believing in gypsy curses next.' Marie tucked the package containing the suit under her arm and they set off for Theatre Street at a brisk pace. 'My sister always said that for a dancer, working hard was all the luck you needed.'

'Oh. Well, Tamara Platonova, what do you think?'

The older girl hated to be unkind. 'You must have something – Minna and Samuel never trusted anyone else like that.'

For hours the sun had been making heroic efforts to pierce the cloud and at last succeeded in sending a few weak rays down to the Nevsky Prospekt. The wide pavements were crowded with people going about their affairs, and the roadway rumbled with vehicles. Here and there the snow was already melted through to the cobbles. There was a smell of spring in the air. Lydia tried to envisage the avenue as she had seen it on the day of the massacre, but already her memory was weak and the gory details which had obsessed her a few weeks earlier were gone.

'I'm so happy,' she said suddenly. 'I must be lucky, I feel it – I was in despair and then everything just changed! Oh, I wish I could run but there are too many people!' She flung her arms round Tata's shoulders and kissed her, then turned to Marie. 'Thank you for being my friends! Thank you for coming shopping with me! No more school! No more toads! Everything's going to be wonderful for all of us, I just know it!'

CHAPTER 5
London, 1969

'I had a letter from the James A. Templeman collection the other day.' Hugh Berrisford paused, his hand hovering over the slices of beef, graduated from raw to burnt, on the serving dish which the maid held at his elbow. 'They had the gall to send a list of works which they said they would be interested in purchasing. A *list*. Would you believe it?'

Six faces around the dining table were turned towards him, ready to believe anything. On his right sat Cheri Tuttlingen, her flawless teeth bared in amusement. She had round, soft, shiny cheeks like newly risen dough. Through a thin and much extended web of blood ties she had claimed the maiden name of Guggenheim, which had seemed an excellent reason to open a gallery within a nightingale's song of Berkeley Square, which had then licensed her to go shopping for art's sake. People in New York had told her that Hugh Berrisford was the best man to see – amusing, deliciously British but not *dusty* like some of them.

'It was like a *shopping* list.' Hugh poured a precise puddle of gravy beside his meat to demonstrate his distaste. So much for those who could even mention art and commerce in the same breath. Cheri's smile faded. 'Terracotta figures from the frieze of Civitalba depicting the intervention of Apollo in the attack on Delphi, circa AD 190. Marble figures from the acropolis of Pergamum, circa 200 BC, or Roman copies thereof. Etruscan *figure rose* vases, fourth century, depicting Romans and barbarians in combat . . .'

149

Hugh paused to allow his guests to digest the story so far. Cheri's husband, described by *Fortune* magazine as one of the ten most dynamic men in the world, sat beside Olivia. She had wiped her fingertips elegantly across his crutch as he stood aside to let her pass through the dining room doorway and now, being satisfied as to the potential dimensions of his cock, she was curious to see if *Fortune*'s assessment would prove correct. Donald Tuttlingen had made his money in haulage, doubled it in hotels and lost part of it in Hollywood. He sat with his body tipped eagerly forward, checking the details of the Berrisfords' covetable lifestyle and enjoying the anticipatory swell in his underpants. If paintings kept his wife happy she could have as many as she wanted.

'Do you get letters like that very often?' Lovat had eaten rapidly, his brows pinched in concentration as he listened to his father-in-law.

'No, I'm happy to say. People often ask us if we can track down something they're particularly interested in, but this was something different. Specific works, most of them well known and already in private hands. . . the aroma of rodent was overpowering.'

A murmur of amusement confirmed his audience's appreciation. Lovat prompted him to finish the story. 'So, how did you handle it?'

'Well, I know old Templeman, oil and shipping, mostly oil, known him for years, sold him a few paintings for his Manhattan place, Rubens and not-quite-but-near-enough Rembrandts. I just rang him up and said if I ever heard that the present owner was fed up with the Civitalba frieze or was ditching the Pergamum marbles, he'd be the first to know. But in the meantime I wouldn't send his little note on to my friend Inspector Sutton of the Fine Art and

Antiques Squad in case he was moved to talk to his chums in the FBI and they came riding down on him with all guns blazing.'

There was a hearty roar of laughter around the room. Olivia had recently decided to line the walls in polished copper sheeting, which reflected the eight diners in exactly the colour of an Etruscan *figure rose* vase, and distorted their shapes like a fairground hall of mirrors. Bianca found the whole effect revolting. It seemed that evening she had wasted half her life at her parents' long mahogany table listening to her father manoeuvre people into becoming buyers.

'I'm not sure I understand. You mean he was asking for specific statues which weren't on the market?' Lovat had recently discovered that naivety, straightforwardly expressed with the merest hint of his Northern accent, could be a great asset. You learned a great deal fast and disarmed your informants. In Hugh's case, he was flattered by his son-in-law's interest in his work, balm to his ego after the lifelong disdain of his daughters.

'And were never likely to be on the market, dear boy. Oh yes, it isn't all sweet golden aestheticism in the world of art, believe me. I don't think old moneybags had anything to do with it, just some pushy young assistant curator in California. It's quite common for unscrupulous collectors to express an interest in a major piece which they know full well is already in a museum. What they're really doing, of course, is asking for a volunteer to nick it.'

'My Ga-a-ad! The shit morals some people have.' By 'some people' the speaker intended the group to understand 'all Americans'. Lee McGrath, a native New Yorker, was a whizz at the British technique of encrypting sneers in polite company so that the victims never heard the bullet that killed them. The *Guardian* newspaper paid her handsomely to badmouth her native country in her weekly column, View Across the Pond. The eighth guest at the table was her lover, Remi Ogunsoye, twenty years her junior, whose declared profession was hustling Arts Council sponsorship for the first annual London festival of West African cinema.

'Do you think the art business is more corrupt than any other?' interjected Lovat, nimbly offering Hugh the opportunity to emphasize his own honesty while impressing upon his prospective customer the rapaciousness of all his competitors. In a year as a Berrisford-by-marriage he had become a skilled player at these events, contrived to be elegant, modern and at the same time cosy; he called them simply family dinners. Bianca referred to them as Mafia weddings.

'Ah well! Every man likes to think there are more sharks in his swimming pool than in the one next door, doesn't he? My father always told me that there was no such thing as an honest art dealer, but then he was a painter, so you'd expect him to be prejudiced. It's not all rich men's conspiracies, but you have to be awake. The thing is, I think, it's a *very* small world, we all know each other, and between our specialists we know most of the major works in all our fields. So what you have, I suppose, is honesty among thieves. We have to be able to trust each other somewhere along the line.' Hugh smiled around the table, pleased with himself for having hit integrity and heritage in a left-and-right. 'Now, Lovat, how's life treating you these days?'

'Rough,' his son-in-law replied. No apology, no self-deprecating shrug, no smile, no bitterness.

'No commissions, is that what you mean?'

'Not since that first one. And to be honest, I'm wondering what to do to get my work seen. It's so big.' He turned courteously to Cheri. 'I'm a sculptor, I work in light, glass tubes glowing different colours; the last piece I did was sixteen feet long, and the one I'm working on now is nearly the same size. There've been a couple of galleries interested, but they haven't got the space.'

'Why don't you make something smaller?' Cheri gave him a glowing smile and tucked a stray swag of backcombed blonde hair behind her ear with her fingertips.

'Actually I'd like to make them bigger. My idea is to do sculptures that can have some meaning in a city. Ideally I want my work to be something beautiful that everyone can enjoy as they go about their daily lives. They really need to stand outside, and not be dwarfed by buildings.'

'Oh, yeah, I see, so they have to be big, I got it.' She swayed to one side as the maid cleared the plates. There was only one picture in the dining room, a portrait of a lady in an Empire dress. She might have been the Empress Josephine, the painter might have been Pierre Paul Prud'hon. Hugh had selected it partly as a test of his guests' knowledge of painting, partly because it was discreetly sensual and contributed to the feeling of wellbeing in the room, and partly because he had been able to buy it cheap. It was a work of museum quality, a painting which boldly proclaimed the accomplishment of its creator in every fold of muslin and wisp of auburn hair. People were often moved to touch the dimple in her cheek. She reclined on a lion skin, pretending not to be aware that her honey-coloured breasts were about to spill right out of her inadequate bodice.

The room was not large. Below the Empress the carved limewood fireplace glowed from reverent applications of oil. The light from the George III candelabras caressed the apples, grapes and pomegranates without revealing any trace of tool marks. Curtains of heavy forest-green silk had been lovingly dressed into even pleats. The mingled scent of cloves and lavender rose from a Chinese porcelain bowl and for a moment, Cheri Tuttlingen thought she heard horses' hooves clip-clopping in the street outside. Eating at ground level was mystically calming to her – in New York she performed no vital function below twenty-seven storeys, unless getting into a car counted as vital. She decided that she never wanted to look at another wall of Mark Rothko sludge in her life. The mere thought of Kandinsky gave her a headache.

'Bianca is also a sculptor,' Lovat continued, smiling at his wife across the table-centre, a little glass tank containing ten identical red tulips with four-inch stems. Olivia had a penchant for doing aggressively modern flowers to round off the eclectic range of her interiors. 'She works very, very hard. Her first exhibition is coming up in a few weeks.'

Bianca automatically dropped her eyes, wishing that Lovat would not always push her and her work forward when they were in company.

'How interesting. What kind of work do you do?'

Bianca explained as briefly as possible, hating to be put on display. 'But really, what Lovat's doing is much more interesting,' she finished.

Cheri noted the look of pure adoration which accompanied this conclusion, but Lovat said, 'Don't be silly, darling. She's always putting herself down.'

'Could I perhaps come and see what you're doing, come around to your studio maybe?' Cheri briskly demolished her portion of soufflé Grand Marnier without tasting a morsel.

'We'd love you to do that.' Lovat tasted his thimbleful of Sauternes, noting its qualities for future reference, remembering that it was permissible to call such a drink a pudding wine. 'Bianca's studio is in our home, you could see her first and then she could walk you around to my workshop. It's just around the corner, I've found a place in the railway arches. Very Gustave Doré, especially in the winter. We're in Notting Hill Gate, just across the park.'

He looked at his wife again. Her left hand was lying on the table beside her plate, fingers folded under the thumb, and he wanted very much to reach across and touch it. She was wearing a dark brown dress with a high tight collar and long cuffed sleeves. Candlelight refined the pure planes of her face. With her limpid eyes and short hair she looked like one of Botticelli's portraits of young men. He felt as if he would dissolve with the softness of love, but at the same time he knew that if she were not close enough to touch he would be burning up with fear in the company of people who seemed unattainably richer, smarter and more powerful than him.

For Lovat, the first year of their marriage had been a series of sickening oscillations between private bliss and terror in public.

The couple had found themselves alarmingly alone. The cheerful, casual crowd of college friends had scattered. Of Lovat's friends, Joe was the only one left in London, working for a large design group near King's Cross, and he visited their flat every week, but a friendly and well-behaved supper for the three of them was not the same as the old, long evenings in the pub. Their other regular visitor was Shona Crawford-Pitt, who marched round dutifully as if she were visiting a hospital. She was entertaining and warmly interested in everything they did, but Bianca still considered her to be a social climber and did not really like her.

They were both struggling to find buyers for their work, both working in their studios alone all day. Neither would admit their loneliness, or the long periods spent in mental limbo when all their ideas seemed too weak to carry out. Bianca longed for her sister Hermione who had been in India for a year. Lovat gave her pep talks, which made her feel even more inadequate than before.

'Do you think Cheri will come and see us?' he asked as he drove them home in their new dark blue MGB GT. It was November, and a light, icy drizzle was falling invisibly in the night.

'Of course she will.' Bianca yawned and ran her fingers through her hair.

'How can you be sure?'

'She's that type. She buys things to own what they mean to her. She'll buy old paintings from Daddy so she can own stability and continuity and all that, and she'll buy something from us because we're young and in love and she wants to own that too.'

There was a pause. He found her casual insights proof that she was a creature from the smart metropolitan world which he would never be able to inhabit. He suddenly demanded, 'Do you love me?'

'You're always asking that.' She curled round in the seat and leaned on his shoulder. He stroked her knee fondly as he changed gear.

'I'm always wondering. What do you see in me?'

'Everything. You're real, that's what I love most about you. You're not full of shit like all those people. You're plain and honest about things, you don't make an entertainment of your life, turning everything that happens into a witty little dinner-party story.'

'You haven't said that you love me.'

'I love you,' she breathed the words in his ear and slipped her hand down the open neck of his shirt, causing him to take the corner into Fulham Road wide and skid on the greasy street.

'You just love my body, that's different.' His laugh was mildly nervous. Bianca was more passionate than he had ever imagined a woman could be. He had unconsciously expected that in marriage some of the hecticness would vanish from their sex life, but after almost two years together, feelings wilder and deeper than they had believed existed were let loose in their bedroom. Wanting to make him feel secure, she never refused him, or reduced making love to a mere routine of life, but the hungrier she was for his flesh, and the more his desires became needs, the more unsafe he felt.

'Are you complaining?' She kissed his neck.

'Aha! I knew I was right! I'm just your plaything, your sex toy – and when the batteries run down you'll toss me aside . . .'

She caught the hard edge of grievance in his voice and withdrew, feeling hurt. 'You're serious. I can't believe it.'

'No, of course I'm not.'

'Maybe you ought to have married some frigid cow who has a headache every night.'

'Darling, I was just teasing you, can't you take a joke?'

'Why do you always do that, Lovat?' Wanting him to confess, she put her hand on his on the wheel. He shook it off on the pretext of turning down the stereo.

'Do what?'

'Say it's a joke when it isn't?'

'Oh come on, Bianca, don't be paranoid. I was just kidding.'

The car reached a red light in Holland Park, which was inconvenient since their feelings were running high and the distraction of driving was helping them keep control. Behind them a line of vehicles was forming. After thirty seconds of silence, Bianca suddenly opened the car door.

'I'm going to tell everyone in this traffic jam that I love you – then will you believe me?'

She was out on the street before he could grab her, and running backwards towards the first vehicle, a taxi whose driver had lowered his window. 'I love my husband,' she told him, leaning into the cab.

'*Mazeltov*,' he answered with resignation.

She pulled open the taxi door and told the middle-aged couple inside, 'I love my husband.'

'So do I,' the woman rejoined, hugging the man's arm. 'Mine not yours, I mean.'

The next car was occupied by four youths drinking beer. 'I love my husband,' she shouted at them. They raised their bottles and cheered.

'I love my husband,' she screamed up at the bus driver, who looked at her warily, wondering if she was one of those love children always on drugs. She jumped on to the platform of the bus and told the conductress and the three passengers.

'I love my husband,' she said to the young man of Middle Eastern appearance driving a white Mercedes.

'Lights are changing,' he warned her, smiling all the same. She darted on to the next car, then jumped on the pavement and ran back towards the head of the jam, skipping and whirling with her arms outstretched, shouting, 'I love my husband, everybody!' to the canopy of plane trees above.

At the head of the queue Lovat pulled over to the kerb and the taxi pulled out and drove on, followed by the other vehicles. The four drunks gave him a blast on their horn as they passed him, and the other drivers, waving and cheering, did the same, while he sat behind the wheel staring ahead, angry and embarrassed.

Bianca joyously pulled the car door open and threw herself back into her seat. Her hair was wet and her dress beaded with moisture.

'There! I've risked my life to tell the whole world that I love you. Now will you believe me?' She leaned across to kiss him and he flinched away.

'I think you're mad,' he said. His voice was thick with suppressed violence. The traffic lights turned red again, but Lovat shoved the car into gear and shot into the street regardless.

The money which had been his parents' wedding present, with the matching sum which her parents had then been obliged to add to it, had been used to buy a first-floor flat in a tight, steep crescent in Notting Hill. The area was half occupied by lightly gilded young artists like themselves and half public housing owned by Kensington and Chelsea council. For fifteen years it had been London's unofficial ghetto, the only area of the city where the cards that landlords pinned up in corner newsagents to advertise accommodation did not include the words 'no blacks'. Cheap in consequence, it had lately attracted rock musicians, underground magazines and hippies of all persuasions. For Lovat and Bianca its chief virtue was its distance, geographical and psychological, from Chelsea.

The apartment had two rooms. Overlooking the street was Bianca's studio, the fashionable stripped floorboards already ankle deep in debris. Behind it was their bedroom, painted plain white, with a low bed in the corner.

They lay side by side for hours without touching, each wrestling the serpents of their emotions in silence.

When the night was at its deepest she felt Lovat roll over and stand up, then leave the room. For a fearful instant she imagined that he was going to put on his clothes, walk out

into the street and leave her. The bathroom light suddenly
glowed from the corridor and she was reassured. She heard
the lavatory flush and the shower running.

He came back and she felt a wash of relief. Then his
weight depressed the edge of the bed and his hand, still
damp, reached for her face on the pillow, fumbling in the
darkness. She lay perfectly still, reminding herself that he
was the one who had picked the quarrel and making up was
now his obligation.

The bed creaked and she felt him lean over her. In her
stomach she felt a flash of fear, sensing his weight and
strength above her. Then she smelt his breath, and his
mouth pressed lightly above the bridge of her nose, in the
place which Hermione her sister called the Third Eye. The
fullness of his lips was trembling. There was a catch in his
breathing. Something touched her cheek; it was wet, a tear,
and it ran down towards her hairline as if it had been one of
her own.

Bianca reached up with her arms and pulled him to her,
and soon afterwards drew up her legs and wound them
around him, and let him make simple, selfish love to her.
Her overpowering desire was to tell him that she loved him,
but then the words were impossible between them. She had
an obscure sense that she had been tricked, but could not
explain to herself how or by whom.

In the morning they lingered over their coffee in the
narrow kitchen, unwilling to part with so many raw places
unhealed. Eventually Lovat said, 'Time to go to work, I
suppose,' pulled on his denim jacket and slipped down the
stairs and out into the street, looking up to wave to her
before he turned the corner with, she realized in slight pique,
complete confidence that she would be at the window to
return the gesture.

Within an hour he came back. She was sitting by the window drawing at a flat table, which she had discovered she preferred to an easel. Nothing at all of any interest had come into her mind for weeks; she had made a drawing of one of her old hand moulds and was playing around with it, trying to think of new ways to catch the articulation of the joints. He came into the apartment without her hearing, walked silently up behind her and laid a long-stemmed yellow rose beside her paper.

'Can you leave that?' He spoke roughly, his body twisting as if his feelings were buffeting him like a wind. 'I can't concentrate. We could go for a walk or something.'

'Where shall we go?'

'I don't know, you choose. I just want to be with you . . .'

'I know.' She stood up and held him, marvelling tenderly that a man could be so helpless. 'Let's go West, young man.'

They walked out into the morning with his arm around her shoulders and by noon had ventured far beyond Shepherd's Bush into a region of decaying Victorian cottages and flyblown suburban shops. At length they reached a park, with a banal Chinese-style bridge over a pond of Canada geese and an expanse of muddy football pitches beyond. The wind scraped their faces as they walked arm in arm down a straight path lined with leafless trees.

A children's playground completed the civic amenities. A few women, already stout and bundled up in winter coats and scarves, stood talking in a group while their children climbed on and off the merry-go-round. Another mother stood apart, pulling and pushing a shiny new pram with one hand and holding a black mongrel dog on a leash with the other.

'It's a different world down here, isn't it?' Lovat had not spoken for half an hour. His hands were thrust deep into his jacket pockets against the cold.

'I suppose this is the real world. We just live in a fantasy bubble.' Bianca curled her freezing toes inside her boots.

'Do your feet hurt?'

'No.'

'You're sure?'

'Honestly.'

'We can take the bus back, I've got money with me.'

With one accord they turned slowly and began to retrace their steps. The woman with the pram, cheaply smart in a red coat, was walking twenty yards ahead of them, with her dog trotting obediently at one side and a small boy jumping and running on the other. She stopped, braking the pram with care, and reached into it to pick up the baby and rearrange its covers. As they passed her the infant stared moonily at them, sucking its tiny fingers. The mother's face, which had only recently lost the bloom of youth, was illuminated with tenderness.

'Enormous eyes babies have.' Bianca smiled and coincidentally the child smiled also.

She felt Lovat consider what he was about to say, then draw a deep breath. 'You wouldn't ever want one of them – would you?'

'Yes. Yes, of course I would.' A ridiculous delight began to bubble under her heart.

'You never said ...' They stopped walking and turned towards each other.

'We never talked about it.'

'You really would, I mean, really? A baby and all of that?'

'Of course I would. Maybe even two.' His hands were gripping her arms tightly.

'But I mean, like now? Or ...'

'I think it takes a while to happen, doesn't it? Nine months or something?'

'Does it, then? Well, we can't waste time hanging about

here talking, can we? Best get home and get on with it.' And they forgot their blisters and ran out of the park hand in hand, then stood at the bus stop giggling like children because the other people waiting could not possibly understand what a huge decision they had just made.

Bianca stopped taking her contraceptive pills, but the next day it seemed that something settled upon so lightly, by a couple who were doing nothing more than healing a quarrel and smoothing down their doubts, could not ever become real. But to her surprise, events rushed from every direction to confirm their hasty promises. Within a few weeks she knew she was pregnant, and their life turned a corner and careered away from them on a new course.

'I'm going back to school,' Lovat announced one evening, with the obvious expectation that she would be pleased. 'We can't start a family like this. We'll have to get a bigger place and I'll have to get a job, at least for a while.'

She knew at once that he was withholding the most important piece of information there was. 'What are you going back to do then?'

'I'm going to Sotheby's to do the Art History course.'

'Where's that going to get you?'

'Closer to a wage packet, I hope.' He had grasped that people in London had salary cheques, not wage packets, but at that moment it suited him to emphasize his disadvantages. 'Face it, Bianca, you're having a baby and I haven't sold a single thing since I left college. It's time to think seriously.'

'You can't give up because of me . . .'

'I'm not giving up, just adding another string to my bow, as it were. I won't live off my parents, Bianca, and I know you wouldn't want anything from yours. I'll still be a sculptor, don't you worry. But we can't afford a bigger flat and two studios, not right now.'

She was deeply disturbed, but he refused to discuss anything more with her, and soon a new energy took over her mind and washed away all her old anxieties. From the first day that she found the waistband of her jeans uncomfortable the sweet, rich pleasure of pregnancy filled all her life, and then anything which was to be done for the baby's sake was just another part of the blessing.

Miraculously, the baby-to-be brought about everything which she had wished for in her family. Her father retreated from her, as if at last acknowledging that she was a woman, with a right to womanly concerns which were beyond his comprehension. Her mother seemed simply defeated. She shot Bianca a poisonous glance which conveyed powerfully that she was not ready to be a grandmother. They received the news with hardly a word, gave Lovat more money to match the second gift of his own parents, retreated for a few weeks and then, having formulated appropriate behaviour for this new situation, began asking them to lunch instead of to dinner.

A few days after Bianca felt the mysterious flutter of the foetus within her, Hermione suddenly returned from India, not an inch thinner than when she had left but with the forelock of her hair bleached almost white. She enrolled herself in a cooking school nearby and visited Bianca every afternoon with a bag of buttery, misshapen 'experiments', to inquire if her sister felt connected to the Great Mother, the primary goddess, the wellspring of all life, and to hold a variety of pendulums over the swelling in an attempt to divine the baby's sex.

Their grandmother, Charlotte, felt compelled to bury the hostility to Lovat which she had maintained sturdily for months, and the two rapidly became excellent companions. 'I can mother him, and I could never mother your father,' she told Bianca. 'Your father would never say that he was worried about anything, but Lovat really talks to me. He's so young, poor lamb.'

'I'm younger than he is.' Bianca was a little jealous, seeing her husband elicit from Charlotte a quality of affection which was different from the indulgence she gave her granddaughters. 'And I'm the one who has to have this baby.'

'You're a woman, and women endure better than men,' was the response.

Charlotte left her usual position of neutrality on the sidelines of the family, and fussed around Bianca, looking for useful actions to perform. Her presence was soothing, and when Lovat found them a new home she took over the entire task of organizing the move.

'This is what I call a real little home,' she exclaimed, standing among the packing cases with a clipboard. 'You're very quiet, darling, don't you like it?'

Bianca, by now thoroughly tranquillized by her hormones, looked around the building with a vague expression. 'It's a house, not a flat, that's all. Lovat says he thinks a family ought to have a house, and there are no small houses in Notting Hill and it's not a family area, so here we are in Chelsea, more or less.'

'He's quite right, children need a garden, they can't run around in a flat. You'll be just down the road, darling, so convenient. And we'll have a wonderful time decorating it, you wait and see.'

'Where do you want this, love?' The contractor stood in the doorway with the case containing her tools and clay on a trolley.

'Oh, out the back in the garden shed.' Bianca waved him to the rear of the house. Albion Street SW3 was a charming strip of Victorian artisan housing on a much smaller scale than the buildings in their old crescent.

'Don't you want it in your studio?' Charlotte stepped forward and peered up the stairs as if looking for a signpost.

'I'm not having a studio, there won't be room with the baby. I'll just work on the kitchen table. The materials can live in the coal hole. After all, I'll be a mother first, plenty of time to catch up on my work later. And I'm sure the experience will change me, make me want to do different things . . .' Bianca felt completely disinclined towards doing anything but reading baby-care manuals and shopping for nursery equipment. She was looking forward to the baby as a cast-iron excuse to escape from her destiny as a Berrisford.

She sat on the stairs, suddenly feeling her back ache for the first time. 'What was it like when you had Hugh, Charlotte?'

'Oh goodness, you can't expect me to remember that, it was more than fifty years ago and the war was on.' The older woman was looking intently at the plain white marble mantelpiece, a sure sign of evasion. Bianca knew better than to press her.

A few weeks later she asked Olivia about her own birth. 'Oh darling, I really can't remember,' was the careless reply. 'I had so much gas-and-air I was completely stoned most of the time.'

Bianca felt a wrench of deep loneliness, from which only her sister could rescue her. 'I just wish they'd both behave the way families are supposed to, for once,' she complained. 'It's not that I want them to knit or anything, but some corny advice and a few old wives' tales would stop me feeling as if I was the only woman in the world ever to do this.'

'In India,' Hermione told her, 'birth takes place in the home, with all the women of the village singing and the mother and grandmother and the midwife supporting the woman in a squatting position.'

'If we asked our mother or grandmother to do that they would probably say they couldn't remember which end the baby comes out of.' Bianca folded her new cot sheets crisply and put them into a drawer in the room designated the nursery.

She floated through the last months of her pregnancy in a haze of fecund happiness. Every bodily development seemed to promise her a new life as a new person. She had let her hair grow, which it did at a remarkable rate, reaching a short, sleek bob in a few months. Gliding along, belly first, in dungarees and clogs, she hugged her tight-skinned stomach as if it was her best friend. 'I don't want to have this baby,' she admitted to her sister with a silly smile. 'It's so beautiful where it is.'

'You may find you're bucking the laws of the universe there. And it doesn't care for it, let me tell you. Do you want me to make you some raspberry-leaf tea?'

'What does that do?'

'It's an ancient herbal remedy against the pains of childbirth. Doesn't taste too bad.'

'All right, but I want to hug you first.' Hermione found her sister's thin arms around her shoulders and they embraced awkwardly around the bulge. 'You fill up such a big hole in my life, Herm. Don't go off travelling again, will you?'

The birth took place on the exact day predicted, took five hours and seemed to cause the mother so little distress that the midwife complained of feeling redundant. Lovat seemed to be suffering from the same sensation. Having delivered his wife to the maternity hospital, and waited to view the baby, he seemed confused and stood awkwardly by the crib at the foot of her bed not knowing what to say.

'This isn't the right time, but I must tell you,' he

announced at last. 'I've been offered a job so – well – I'm taking it.'

'But that's wonderful,' she told him, still tired and feeling as if everything were taking place behind an invisible curtain that muffled sound and feeling. 'What job is it?'

'You remember that American woman, Cheri Tuttlingen? I'm going to manage her gallery. Twentieth-century sculpture is going to be the main thing; Cheri's going back to New York for half the year and I'm to buy for her in Europe.'

'That's wonderful,' she said again with a dreamy smile.

'Well, not that wonderful. I've got to go to New York next week, just for a few days.'

'Oh, don't worry about me, I'll be fine. Hermione will look after me.'

'That's all right then.'

'Of course it is, darling. You're acting like it's the end of the world.'

If Bianca had been happy before, she was now permanently ecstatic. Her energy switched from the inner marvels of her womb to the wonderful child in her arms, and all her thoughts, dreams and reactions became attuned to him. Her sleeping and waking followed his. Her ears heard his smallest murmur before any other sound. Finding herself possessed of the most perfect natural instinct for everything the baby needed, Bianca was grateful, but guilty, that Lovat was often absent or preoccupied and so unable to break the glorious spell that bound her and the child together. He seemed anxious to make love to her as soon as he could, and since her healthy young tissues recovered rapidly they went to bed the moment she was home while the baby slept in his carrycot, but a new dimension of her soul had opened and what had filled her being before was now just one sensation among many others.

The child was named Tom, and far from being the perplex-
ing, distressing, howling creature which she had anticipated
he fed and slept with enthusiasm and seemed determined to
pass all the milestones on his developmental chart ahead of
time. She breast-fed him. He was deliciously greedy; feeding
binges sometimes lasted half the day. He lay heavy and
robust in her arms and was soon able to smile with satisfaction.

Hugh and Olivia approved of none of the decisions she
made about the baby, from the colour of his clothes –
traditional baby blue – to her decision to bring him up by
herself, without the help of the nanny for whom a room lay
waiting at the top of the new house. They protested that she
would change her mind, but instead of falling into resentful
silence she cheerfully said, 'Oh, no, I don't think so. Not
until the next one, anyway,' and was amazed to see her
mother twitch her lips with annoyance and her father step
back and swallow his criticism.

She had found a means to ally herself with convention,
and together they prevailed. As weeks went by, her
confidence flowered; Tom thrived visibly. Their friends and
the wider circle of the family's acquaintance nodded approval
and her parents felt unnatural and were forced to keep
silent. Bianca gave herself over entirely to righteous motherhood.

The next consequence of the baby was that Shona, now
again a close neighbour, dropped in one afternoon. Her face
was completely creased with happiness. 'I want to ask you
and Lovat to do us an *enormous* favour.'

'Us?' Bianca leaned against her new washing machine,
folding nappies with a practised hand.

'Oh of course, I haven't told you. I've been seeing Joe,
you know.'

'Joe?'

'Your friend? Lovat's friend? Joe with the red hair? Your best man, remember?'

'Oh my goodness, of course. I just didn't connect . . .' She had never imagined that Shona, whose father was a baronet and a Lord Lieutenant of some East Anglian shire, would look twice at Joe, whose pose in life was aggressively that of the Yorkshire tyke, the North Country working-class lad. Nor had it seemed obvious that Joe would find Shona attractive.

'Never mind, darling, you've been so wrapped up in your adorable baby. The thing is, we do so want to get married like you two, but my father doesn't know yet, and Joe's scared shitless he'll make a scene, and so he thought that if we could ask you and Lovat to come down for the weekend it might take the curse off the whole affair a little. What do you think?'

'I can't leave Tom, Shona.'

'No problem, bring him along and we'll get someone to keep an eye on him while you're out having fun. Not that there's much fun to be had.'

She agreed to put the idea to Lovat, who agreed readily. It was a month before he could find a free weekend in his diary, but this appointment was kept, unlike many other social dates since he had begun working for Cheri Tuttlingen.

'Now for God's sake, Lovat, don't go poking around looking at pictures unless you're invited,' Joe warned him as the four of them drove together through the dreary suburbs of Essex. 'Shona's Dad hates it.'

'Has he got some good stuff, then?'

'Supposedly he's got Van Dycks, lad, but don't say anything about that.'

'Daddy completely wrecked my first big romance because he's so touchy about our paintings and what not.' Shona spoke urgently from the back of the car. 'He threw us out of the house and bellowed "Never bring that young man here again – the fellow noticed my *things*." I'll never forget it. So *do* be careful, Lovat, I so want everything to go right this weekend.'

They arrived in lashing rain, which continued for the whole of Saturday. Shona's father, of whom Bianca had only the vaguest recollection, was a florid, elderly man who covered up his essential stupidity in a bad-humoured manner which, on this occasion, was exacerbated by a genuine evil temper.

'I've never known him in such a foul mood.' Shona was close to tears by lunchtime. 'He's had a rocket from the tax people and he's absolutely livid about it. We can't go through with this, he'll just explode.'

'We'll just have to soften the old boy up,' Lovat reassured her, taking more than a polite interest for the first time. 'I can see he likes Joe . . .'

'That's more than I can see, I tell you,' Joe said.

'He does like you, he told me so,' Shona reassured him.

'We'll just have to pour on the syrup.' Lovat made the motion of dolloping treacle from a jar. He was already showing signs of a personality which Bianca hardly recognized, a suave, calculating character, adding a slight sneer to his smile and an ironic mobility to his brows. In this milieu, where the other guests spoke only of livestock and taxes, he set out to amuse with his old ploy of provincial ignorance, and halfway through lunch had mellowed the old man marginally by enduring a discussion on the evils of the European Economic Community.

'What do you do with yourself in London?' the old man inquired at last.

'I manage an art gallery in Mount Street, Sir.'

'Do you now. Nothing to do with your father-in-law's firm, are you?'

'Oh no, Sir. We buy from him occasionally, of course. Most of our business is with the States. Berrisford's always gets the best price for its sellers. I have to work a little harder and try to find what people are looking for without paying the top dollar. And when people are selling, of course, they often like to do it privately. I've even paid people in cash, used fivers in a shoe box, can you believe?'

'I'll believe anything you say, dear boy.' Now the old man was twinkling at him as if there was a private joke between them.

When lunch was finished he seized Lovat by the arm and marched him away upstairs. The house was mostly Elizabethan, and had a long gallery running its entire length which was hung with pictures. 'Now take your time, look around and tell me if there's anything here you'd give me fifty thousand for.' He sat down on a chair whose damask upholstery hung in discoloured shreds and, seeing Lovat hesitate, waved him on towards the paintings. 'Fifty thousand, that's what I need. Find me fifty thousand in that lot.'

From his abrupt manner, Lovat recognized the sense of shame which the English aristocrat has about his possessions. The old man was quite oblivious to the artistic qualities of his hoard. An envious uncle had once tried to explain that some of his pictures were better than others, but he could not remember which. What he could not forget, however, was that the objects gathered to express the superior status of his forebears had been extorted from artists whose genius had been patronized in every sense, from craftsmen reduced to serfdom, from foreign countries plundered without conscience or, worst of all, *bought* by some disgraceful forebear who was unable to control his ostentatious impulses.

The younger man walked slowly up and down the gallery. Any one of the large paintings in it would have fetched twice the price that the Lord Lieutenant had named. Hugh was always setting up tests for him, but it was obvious that this man had no idea what he owned. After some careful calculation, he stopped in front of a portrait of a lady in a wide white lace collar, not obviously by Van Dyck but perhaps by one of his pupils. 'This one ought to do it,' he said, his voice muted with nervousness.

'Right. Now take it off the wall, and when you go back to London pack it in your suitcase, sell it and come back and give me the money. Fivers in a shoe box, just like you said.'

Lovat smiled, slightly faint with relief that the old man had not been out to test or humiliate him, and was indeed as stupid as he appeared to be.

With her father now wreathed in smiles and drinking too much of whatever was within his reach, Shona drew a deep breath and announced, 'Daddy, Joe and I rather thought we'd like to get married.'

After a hideous minute of silence while his yellowed eyes roamed from one face to another the old man heaved himself to his feet, patted Joe on the shoulder and said simply, 'Well done, my boy.'

Bianca, preoccupied with the suddenly restless Tom, knew nothing of what had taken place in the long gallery until the picture was unpacked when they returned home and placed on the mantelpiece.

'Just for one night we can imagine we've got a Van Dyck.' Lovat stood nonchalantly beside it as if posing for a photograph. He had looked markedly heavier and older of late.

They had not reconnected since the birth, and were circling round each other, exchanging only small talk, going through all the motions of being a happy young married couple because they were afraid to admit that something between them had changed. The motions included sex at least three times a week, unless Lovat was abroad, because that was what happy young married couples did, and it comforted them.

'Who are you going to sell it to?' Bianca decided that this, a rare moment when Tom was asleep and they were together and wakeful, might be a good moment to move closer. She sat down on their plain white sofa, but Lovat remained standing.

'I don't know.'

'But I thought, from the way you were so sure about everything, you must have had someone in mind.'

'What I've got in mind is taking this off to your father tomorrow to get one of his boys to tell me if it's really worth fifty thousand. What do I know about this sort of painting? The old man was mad to ask my advice.'

'Oh.' She saw a hard, distant cast settle on his face; he was kicking up the corner of the rug, avoiding her eyes.

'If you ask me he wants to sell something privately because he doesn't want the word getting about that he might be in trouble. No one would give him top prices then, would they?'

'I'm sure you're right, Lovat, but I still don't understand. If you haven't got a buyer and you don't know anything about this kind of painting, why did you say you'd sell it for him?'

'Because I reckon I know enough, after having dinner with your father every week, to make a bob or two.' He folded his arms and looked down on her, alarmed by the plaintive, emotional note in her voice. She seemed small and childlike, and her face looked pinched. 'Darling.' He tried to speak softly. 'I don't understand why you're getting upset about this. You know I've got to take all the opportunities that come my way now you've got a baby.'

'I'm not upset.' But tears were smarting in her eyes. She rubbed them with her sleeve. 'I'm just tired. I'm going to bed.'

Two weeks later the lady with the white lace collar was sold for fifty-three thousand pounds to a buyer who wished to remain anonymous, and Shona's father took delivery of his money in used notes. Two months later, flicking through a Christie's catalogue in her doctor's waiting room, Bianca saw the painting listed as a Van Dyck with a reserve price of £250,000. She was not wholly surprised. Lovat had been secretive about the affair from the moment he sensed that it disturbed her, but she guessed from his furtive manner that he had intended from the outset to have the picture reattributed and sold at a higher price. Without doubt her father had masterminded the operation; the fact that the painting had *not* gone to Berrisford's confirmed it, since the art of these deals was never to be caught red-handed. There had been too many telephone calls late at night, too many late meetings and business dinners, too many private conversations between the two men on Sundays, for her not to suspect that her husband and father together had planned the whole affair.

What did surprise her was to discover, ten minutes later, that breast-feeding was not the fail-safe contraceptive procedure which her doctor had described. She mentioned to him she was gaining weight and felt bloated. He looked at her in alarm, examined her and announced without a trace of shame that she was already in the fifth month of pregnancy.

'Good,' she said, feeling a peculiar satisfaction quite different from the awed joy of her first diagnosis. 'And it's too late now to do anything about it even if we wanted to, isn't it?'

She did not encounter Lovat until breakfast, which he normally ate standing up while she floated up and down their pine kitchen with Tom perched on one hip. 'Well darling,' she began, stopping for a moment to confront him, 'it's a good thing you're going to make a killing with your Van Dyck lady, because we're going to need the money.'

'Bianca, please, why are you so obsessed . . .'

'Darling, I don't want to talk about business.' She put her fingers on his lips which annoyed him disproportionately because it should have been an affectionate gesture but it felt distinctly hostile. 'I went to the doctor yesterday because I just thought I was getting fat, and guess what? We're having another baby.'

'That's impossible.' Shock drained all the expression from his face for an instant and his eyes darkened. 'You can't be . . .'

'Well, I'm as surprised as you, but there's no doubt. He says I must be exceptionally fertile. A little brother or sister, Tommo, won't that be fun?' The baby threw its rusk to the floor as if disgusted at the prospect.

Panic possessed Lovat completely. His heart hammered as if he had narrowly avoided a car crash. When he spoke, he had to struggle to move his jaw. 'You do want to have it, then?'

'Of course I do. How could anyone not want another one of these?' Smiling, she jostled Tom and patted the tip of his nose with one finger. 'And anyway, there's nothing they could do, it's much too late. And who'd give us a termination, nice young married couple living in Chelsea? We always said we wanted two, didn't we?'

'Yes, I suppose we did. Look – ah – do you feel OK, can I do anything?' Now all he wanted to do was leave, be by himself and get control of his feelings. This seemed so much like one of Bianca's impetuous decisions that he could not accept it as an accident. Just when he had begun to get his life into shape, to see how his future might look, what kind of a man he might become, he had been betrayed by his wife and her ambitious biology.

'No, darling, I'm absolutely fine. There's nothing to worry about. You go on to work now, we'll talk about it again in the evening if you like.' And she pushed him out of the door, looking forward to another day of picking up the baby, putting down the baby, feeding the baby, talking to the baby, sorting out the baby's clothes and, if there was time, walking up to the interior decorator's shop and choosing a new marble coffee table for the sitting room.

Lovat's turmoil lasted for a month. He felt that his function as a husband was to plan his family's life, and the surprise of a new baby seemed like a threat to his powers. The congratulations now heaped upon him and Bianca infuriated him. Worst of all was that he could say nothing. With Bianca almost installed as the Madonna of Chelsea Old Church, there was no possibility of a protest.

Hugh and Lovat found opportunities to meet more often. They analysed their business in greater and greater detail, discussed the personalities, traded gossip and advice. They discovered that they had much in common; Lovat, with his own enthusiasms, reawakened in his father-in-law the love of painting which had filled his youth with pleasure but over years in business had become tarnished and almost forgotten. He already leaned heavily upon his father-in-law's experience in managing the little Tuttlingen gallery, and Hugh, always easily flattered, basked in his frank admiration while the younger man preened contentedly in his company.

After some time, Hugh began to measure Lovat against

the men who worked for him, and tell himself that he was quite as able as any of them, and the fact that he did not have a genteel background was a great advantage; the business needed to have a more modern, classless feel and the foreigners seemed to need to be met at their own level.

'Why don't you tell that American woman to piss off and come and work for me?' he asked as they sat in the steam room at the RAC Club one morning. They had formed the habit of meeting to swim there at eight, less for enjoyment or the sake of their fitness than to have a reason to leave their homes before their wives were properly awake.

Through the thick vapour he saw Lovat's red face split open as his jaw dropped in amazement. 'Are you serious?'

'Of course I am. I've just lost a modern art assistant. You know more than he does, anyway. I'll pay you what I paid him . . .' He named the figure. 'You'll never be happy running around in a pathetic little gallery for some hideous socialite who wants to bring her friends over to find something to match their wallpaper. Come on, say yes.'

Lovat said yes. Bianca, when he told her the next morning, screamed 'What?' at the top of her voice. The baby, startled for a few seconds, immediately began to howl.

'Aren't you pleased? It's a marvellous opportunity. He's being terribly kind; he must get a dozen guys better qualified than I am writing to him every week.'

'He's not being kind, you fool! Don't you see what he's doing? He's trying to get us back under his thumb. He'll run our lives now, you see. Oh God, Lovat, don't you understand anything?' She walked forwards and backwards with stabbing steps, too angry to be able to quieten the baby. 'When you met me all I wanted to do was get out of Chelsea and get away from my bloody family and be my own person, and now look – back in Chelsea, back with the family . . .'

'But we've got a family of our own now, and everything's different. I want a good life for us, darling, I want my kids to have everything I had, everything you had, and more. It's all for you and the children. What's wrong with that?' His pose was one of calm reason, implying that her passion was absurd.

Bianca felt suffocated. Her face creased and she began to weep. 'Nothing, nothing. That's all I want too, but why does it have to be *this* way? Why can't we manage on our own?'

'Because we can't,' he said gently, taking her in his arms. 'Not with my background and two kids. This is the way it has to be, believe me.'

CHAPTER 6

St Petersburg, 1907

In the portrait on the end wall of the classroom, the noble expression on the face of the Tsar Nicholas II was warmed by the sunlight as if by a smile. Lydia relaxed her hand along the barre and straightened her right leg under her, feeling the kneecap pull sweetly up into place. She closed her left leg in front and allowed her free arm to float up and outwards in preparation for the exercise. The morning sun trickled optimistically through the classroom windows, the walls gleamed and expanded, the mirrors turned to silver.

Nikolai Legat took the first class. He always gave a long *barre*, long enough to chase the sleep out of her. Every morning her body flexed and stretched in the same sequence, recalling the wisdom of its education. Her muscles squeezed the deadening feelings from her tissues; boredom and frustration drifted away like a mist, and she felt hopeful once more.

Class restored her wellbeing like a drug. Until the exercises began she was afflicted with aches both physical and mental. Movement soothed her sore joints; it also dulled the impatience which inflamed her mind more and more as the months wore on and she remained separated from the world where she knew she belonged.

Lydia had made her debut, and received all the bouquets, the little presents and the approving reviews she wanted. She had joined the company as a coryphée, the second grade, missing out the corps completely, but since then she had done nothing of distinction but learn a few small parts. The eventful social life which she had intended to establish remained a dream. At least once she was dancing it ceased to distress her that the pink mousseline dress had been hers for two years and had been worn only once, to a decorous supper given by the War Veterans' Benevolent Society after their annual benefit performance.

Her shoulders stretched back, pulling up her ribs, bracing her chest forward in a bird-like curve. As she turned out her legs her hips eased forward and outwards, slowly opening the pelvis like a flower. The movement had begun to feel immodest. The day when she would spread out her body for a lover was still unmarked in the endless future, but her heart was clinging now to every handsome face which presented itself, and her flesh was fretting and ready to follow.

The puppyish contours of her childhood were disappearing, and the mirrors which were her daily companions told her that her limbs were becoming ripe and firm. When she pointed her toe, pulling her heel up into the calf, pressing the knee straight, the dimples were so shallow they barely showed through her tights. The foot on the floor held firm, instep steady, ankle strong, all the planes true and every joint supple as she rose smoothly on to half point.

In Theatre Street there was no room for deception, of others or of oneself. So many hours were passed each day in scrutiny, analysis and criticism that everyone knew their faults. Lydia appreciated as well as the rest the secret of her failure to fulfil her student potential; it was in the one quality which had brought her early acclaim; she was too good, too fast, too brilliant, too technically accomplished, too delightfully flirtatious, all together too much like a younger incarnation of her idol Kchessinskaya.

'Such extraordinary gifts our little pansy flower has,' the

great Kchessinskaya had pronounced on the very day of her return to the stage after the birth of her son. 'We must take care of this precious child, the best possible care – how terrible it would be to see a young career ended by an injury.' This had been said with raised voice and a knowing glance at the company's director, and ever since that day Lydia had been denied a place among the friends of Coppelia, the Sleeping Beauty's christening guests or Giselle's neighbours, all the small, brilliant solos which would have displayed her gifts to perfection, and instead given the cameo roles for which she was not at all suited.

'Watch your knees, Lydia, don't let them fall in.' She shot the ballet master a resentful look. Her knees never fell in; he should save his criticisms for those who deserved them, like Anna, two places in front of her, who was already shaking like a young birch in the wind. Leo also had strange knees, no elasticity in them. Now she worked with him in class every day she could see the mysterious tension in all his movements. Even his arms were taut. He had a powerful physical presence, which she reluctantly acknowledged; with his dark hair and slanted, almost oriental features, he was generally held to look like a perfect Mephistopheles.

'Don't think, Leo, you can't dance and think,' Legat scolded him. 'If you must do it, think about your dancing. Press that plié down, make it juicy ... and you, Vaslav, thinking's not your problem is it? But what's happened to your line? And your fingers! Don't bring your Italian port de bras to my class if you please – or are you trying to put the evil eye on me?'

A chuckle ran around the bare room. In flowing succession, like a pack of cards flipping over, the dancers turned to repeat the exercise on the other side. Legat was jealous of young Vaslav, because Kchessinskaya had chosen him as her new partner, and because he and Anna Pavlova were taking private lessons from the old Italian master Enrico Cecchetti, but even in the extremes of envy Legat was too good-natured to resist making a joke.

When the *barre* was finished Nico picked up the watering can and sprinkled the bare boards to give a better surface for the centre work. Then the dancers spread out across the floor, muscles warm and expectant, and eighty legs began to swing in precise pendulum movements as if driven by the same motor. Their accompanist, an elderly violinist, hunched over his instrument and his scalp under his thin white hair flushed red with the effort of playing faster tempi.

Above the noise of flapping skirts and jumping feet, Legat had to shout. 'Pull up, Olya, up! Where's your balance? It's above your head, pull up to find it! Lydia! Have you gone deaf this morning? How can you plough across the music like that – listen, listen! This poor man isn't playing for his own pleasure, you know. Right, now you boys – Vaslav, try to come down with the beat, if you please, I know you can do it. Mischa! I'll shed that blue blood of yours if you don't concentrate. Try going to bed to sleep for a change.'

His long-limbed victim scrambled vainly for the final attitude then lounged towards the barre. 'I bet no one kept him up last night, the mood he's in this morning,' he remarked to the room in general, and then, pouting at the mirror, admired the way his heroic shoulders strained the seams of his grey practice tunic while the girls giggled and nudged each other. Of all the homosexual men, Mischa Alexandrov was the most handsome, the most vain and the most dedicated to his social life. He had confided to every one of his hundred and fifty closest friends that the late Tsar Alexander was his real father.

When the first class of the day ended the men remained in

the humid, sweat-smelling room for their advanced work with Legat, while the women went down the corridor for their own lesson. As Lydia pulled on her wrap and made for the door, Leo ran across the floor to intercept her.

'Tonight – will you come out with us?' He often spoke to her as if they had already discussed the matter in question. 'There's something I really need to talk to you about,' he added, noticing her irritated expression.

'I'm dancing tonight.'

'Oh, of course you are, I forgot. Tomorrow, then.'

'I want to stay in and do some sewing. And who's "us", may I ask? Who else is in this party?'

'Ssh, please, I don't want them all to hear. I'm asking Anna, Inna, Julie, Vera and Leon Samilovich. We can meet at his apartment. And another man, important, you don't know him. And Olga and Marie, will you ask them for me? Please, Lydia. Don't tell anyone yet, but I've got a commission. I've been asked to create a ballet, isn't it wonderful? Nothing big, of course, but – Lydushka, I do need you. Sew your skirt another night, please.' His eyes, light hazel and set deep below thick black brows, were glittering with excitement.

'You're such a tyrant, Leo. You just assume I'll do whatever you want, don't you? I'll ask the others, but I can't promise they'll come. And what time? And have you spoken to Paul?' Permission from Marie's brother was desirable before she allowed a man to escort her.

'Oh for heaven's sake, leave all those silly flirt's tricks alone, will you? This isn't that kind of invitation.'

'So sorry! Since you've been sending me poetry for the past five years, I'm a little confused. I didn't realize you had suffered a change of heart. Do forgive me.'

He almost snarled, plunging his fingers into his springy

black hair and holding his head as if in pain. 'I haven't – I don't . . . look, I feel the same about you, it's my curse, I know it now, but this isn't the same thing, this is important, Lydia. A new ballet! I'd love you even if you had two left feet but . . .' The whine of the violin announced the start of the next class and Legat was throwing impatient looks at the gossiping couple. 'I'll call for you at seven – yes?'

'If you like. Talk to Paul. Now I must go.' And she ran complacently down the corridor, her blocked shoes tapping on the floorboards. He watched her until she turned into another classroom, wondering how, being so utterly and tragically empty-headed, she could make him as inarticulate as a road-sweeper within a few seconds.

Lydia was intrigued. A new ballet might be the very thing she needed to get herself noticed but – what kind of commission could Leo have? He was absurdly young for such a responsibility, although Mikhail Mikhailovich was always praising him. Perhaps it would be some ridiculous provincial tour; in which case, she would refuse to be involved. But the opportunity to meet Leon Samilovich was not to be passed up – the artist was quite the hero of the year since he had designed an exhibition of Russian art organized by Sergei Pavlovich Diaghilev, still nicknamed Chinchilla by the ballet community. In Petersburg the show had burnished the city's national pride, and Diaghilev, for once in favour at the Court, had obtained the backing to take it to Paris and astound the West with the achievements of Russian artists. The dancers felt a proprietary pride in his success.

Leon Samilovich Bakst designed occasionally for the ballet, but Lydia's special fascination with him derived from the legend that he had once been so poor he could not afford to buy paint, and was now fashionable, feted and the husband of the daughter of the cultured Prince Tretiakov.

His apartment near the Admiralty was disappointingly small and ordinary, with grey-striped wallpaper in the salon. Bakst and his well-born wife also supported his grandmother, mother and two sisters, and the apartment seemed inhabited by slow-moving, full-bosomed females with lustrous hair and dark eyes who almost concealed in their skirts the painter himself, a slight man whose smile folded up his face so that it seemed all nose and ears.

'How wonderful to make your acquaintance,' she told him as he kissed her hand. 'I have always loved your designs for *The Fairy Doll*, the prettiest thing in the whole repertoire – don't glare at me, Leo, you know I adore it.'

'Well, and no doubt you will soon be equally fond of this young man's new creation.' He patted Leo on the shoulder like an uncle. 'He tells me that if he could have asked for any dancer in the company he would have chosen you first, so I'm as delighted as you that we meet at last. And this must be Mademoiselle Kolkova?' Marie's social curtsey was as quick and charming as a robin's dip. 'Shall we sit down around the table? There's tea or . . . champagne, perhaps?' Through gold-rimmed spectacles he caught Lydia's eye; for a moment she was unsure what he had said. Leon Samilovich had changed his name from Rosenberg and renounced his religion, but he still spoke with a pronounced Jewish accent. 'Champagne! We brought enough back from Paris to relaunch the navy. And you must try these chocolates, no nonsense about dieting!'

A crystal dish of sweets was placed under her nose and she at once picked the violet cream. Leon Samilovich's red hair gleamed with pomade and the aroma of Hungary water wafted across the room at each of his hospitable gestures. The table was half covered with dishes of small cakes and dainty sandwiches. A maid brought champagne on a silver tray, and gold-rimmed glasses. It tasted sour and she made a face, quickly reaching for another chocolate.

A few minutes later Olga arrived with her brother Pierre, a thin, nervous boy of thirteen who sat at the end of the table without speaking, eating everything that came within his reach and occasionally turning away to cough. The other dancers arrived together, and last of all Anna appeared, clinging to the arm of a haughty-looking man in an astrakhan overcoat.

'Anna – sit here, nearest the stove. Try these, little sandwiches with spiced beef, delicious!' She took one and nibbled the corner, appraising the company with timid eyes although she was the senior dancer among them.

'Everyone – may I present Monsieur Victor Dandré? A City Councillor, a philanthropist and perhaps already known to some of you as a great lover of the ballet.' Leon Samilovich pulled out a heavy, red-plush armchair for his distinguished guest, who seated himself as if taking a throne.

'And a great lover of skinny Anna – he's been chasing her for years,' Marie whispered, pretending to pat a hairpin into place.

'Well, we're all here now so I must begin.' Leo stood up to speak, putting his hands in his pockets to stop them trembling with nervous agitation. 'Monsieur Dandré originally asked Mikhail Mikhailovich to create a new ballet for this year's gala in aid of the Society for the Prevention of Cruelty to Children.' He cleared his throat and continued in a firmer voice. 'But he has already undertaken another new commission and so I am greatly honoured that he has proposed me as his substitute, and that Monsieur Dandré has bravely agreed to take the risk of launching an unknown choreographer upon the unsuspecting world.' Dandré, unsmiling, inclined his head in acknowledgement. 'And Leon

Samilovich will design the piece, which is wonderful news.'
There was a patter of applause, led by Marie. 'So what
remains is for us to decide a theme and style.'

'Oh please – something Greek, with bare feet and tunics in
the Duncan style!' Of all the impressionable pupils who had
been invited to a special performance by the American
dancer, Inna had become the most passionate convert.

'Certainly not!' barked Dandré, obviously angered. 'A
charity performance is the last occasion to defy tradition.
When you're asking people to be generous you want to be as
pleasing as possible, not offend them with ugliness and
certainly not send them to sleep with some dreary classical
nonsense.'

Leo and his designer exchanged glances of resignation.

'Pretty legs in pretty skirts.' Tata had such a guileless face
it was impossible to accuse her of sarcasm. 'Well, that won't
be difficult, we can do that, girls, can't we?'

Lydia reached for another chocolate. 'Anyway, Duncan
style would mean us all crashing about like heifers with our
hooves turned in.' She won a harsh laugh from Dandré and
with it one of Anna's most witch-like expressions. 'Why are
we even discussing this? Leo's made up his mind already,
haven't you? Don't pretend you asked seven of us here by
accident. You haven't thanked us for coming, by the way.'

'You're discovered, Levrusha,' Marie teased him.

'I do thank you all for coming here, sincerely.' Curse
Lydia! Why could she never miss the chance to put him in
the wrong? And now of all times, when he almost had the
whole room in his hands. 'All right, I admit it, I know what
I want to do. And it will be absolutely wonderful . . .'

'He's so modest!'

'But it will, Marie. The Pleiades. The Seven Sisters. The
mysterious constellation, brightest in the Milky Way,

fascinating, elusive, eternal . . . the navigator's stars, do you know the Greeks wouldn't put to sea until the Pleiades were above the horizon? Six stars shining bright and clear but one, Electra, extinguished by the Gods for loving a mortal man.'

'Oh Leo, such a beautiful idea.' Marie regarded him with blatant adoration.

'Oh, I remember the story – she disappeared before the siege of Troy, because the city was under her protection and she couldn't bear to see it destroyed.'

'Tata, you know everything.'

There were murmurs of approval all around the table and the dancers leaned forward, eager to hear more. Leo puffed out his chest with gratification as he continued, 'Shura Glazunov has permitted me to have some of his piano pieces orchestrated, and with Leon Samilovich I have arrived at a scenario. An opening ensemble, pas de cinq, pas de trois, and then the pas de deux, but with all the individual variations between each part. And brilliance! That's the key, all the effects of light, sparkling, glowing, radiant – it will be absolutely thrilling, Monsieur Dandré, the audience will be on their feet, I promise you.'

Dandré gave a nod of condescension, as if he had expected no less. The rest of the company were gazing at Leo with every kind of admiration in their eyes. How perverse love could be, Lydia reflected. Leo was magnetic at that moment; each woman around the table was under his spell, but he bewitched them as a man, not as an artist. And she alone despised the man, and found his ideas ridiculous and his ambitions absurd, but as an artist she knew he was a genius. This intuition had been utterly clear from their childhood. And she was the one he loved, and they were both infuriated by it.

'I thought I would do just a few sketches.' With a hesitant smile, Leon Samilovich laid some drawings on the table and quick hands spread them out.'Quite simple, I think, because I'm sure we can't expect much of a budget. A deep sea blue backcloth – you know how the night sky can be more blue than black sometimes? A mast, some spars – we can borrow them from another production, I know they're in the scenery store. And the stars in the shades of light from red to very pale yellow, and here is our Electra in violet.' He put this sketch into Anna's hands, and every woman watching noted the significance of the choice. Jealousy turned the truffle to ashes in Lydia's mouth. 'Crystal beads, silver paillettes, everything to catch the light – I thought the shorter tutu would be appropriate also.' In the general enthusiasm this tiny break with tradition was accepted without discussion.

'And you are to be this mortal lover?' Dandré inquired of Leo as if it were almost an afterthought.

'I wanted Nijinsky, but Mikhail needs him for his new work. Legat isn't right, Guerdt is a little senior . . . I see the role as secondary to the ballerina, so – well, I'll do, at least I know the choreographer's mind.'

'I don't doubt it.' Dandré seemed incapable of smiling, but his manner was benevolent; Leo had obviously hit the right note with his severe patron.

'My friends, my dear friends. Stay and talk, please, drink more champagne, don't mind me because I have to scuttle off to another meeting.' Their host rose to his feet, smiling and bowing. 'Although it grieves me to leave such a bouquet of beauty, really. But I'm due the other side of the Admiralty in ten minutes, so I must dash away.'

'Sergei Pavlovich's infamous Committee, I presume?' At Dandré's question the temperature of the room seemed to drop as if someone had opened a window on to the icy night.

'Alas, yes. He has a way of persuading one . . . he wants to take *Boris Godunov* to Paris, you know – a designer's dream . . .' With an apologetic shrug, Leon Samilovich backed towards the door.

'You're wasting your time. He'll never get the backing, which will be a blessing because the Parisians would die of boredom long before the end of *Boris*.'

'Well, perhaps you're right, Victor, but for a friend, you know, I promised . . . farewell, goodbye, until next time!' Almost squirming with embarrassment, the little artist slipped through the door and closed it silently as if a noise would release a storm of wrath.

'Surely Grand Duke Vladimir will put up the money? Didn't Chinchilla get him to be the Committee's President?' Only those who knew her well could see that Tata was concerned.

'He'll lose it if he does. My guess would be that he will withdraw. Diaghilev's not in fashion at the moment. The man's a swindler, he says so himself. And he can get away with all kinds of degeneracy in private but when his insane arrogance makes him think he can fight over his catamites in public . . .' Dandré's cold stare sifted the loyalties of the whole room.

'He and that awful cousin of his were thrown out of Cubat's restaurant last week – they were fighting over some boy.' Anna's brooding face was the picture of distaste.

'Well' – Tata turned to the censorious couple with frank eyes and a sweet smile – 'we're lucky he's lost interest in the ballet then, aren't we? We never see him nowadays, since he fell out with the Director.'

Despite Bakst's warm invitation, the party broke up shortly afterwards and Leo walked Lydia and Marie homewards. It was early autumn, and the night sky was still silvery with the afterglow of the aurora borealis, but the wind across the water pinched their faces with cold.

'That champagne was awful.' Lydia stared across the grey river, feeling her anger rise now that they were alone.

'It was just French – drier than our Russian fizz. Haven't you ever had French champagne before?'

'I didn't know you were a connoisseur.'

'I'm not.' For a while they walked on slowly in silence until Leo could not bear any more. 'So, what do you think of my idea, Lydia? Don't you think it's good?'

'You asked Anna to dance the pas de deux.' At last she turned around, but her stony face shocked him. 'So much for your admiration for my dancing.'

'Oh Lydia, don't be hurt. You can see how things are with her and Dandré and he's the boss, after all. Believe me, I'd a thousand times rather create something marvellous for you than have to beat my brains out finding something she can do with those pitiful knees of hers. But don't worry, no one will look at her when you're on the stage. It'll be your night, Lydushka, trust me.'

'Trust you! You get me to persuade everyone to come and then this is how you repay me. You know I'm being persecuted by the management. You say you care about me, but when you do things like this how can you expect me to believe you – or trust you?'

'But what else can I do?'

'I just hope she falls into the prompter's box again, that's all. That'll teach you to respect a real dancer.' She folded her arms crossly and accelerated away from him.

'Oh Lydia, you must understand!' Marie ran to her side and put her arms around her shoulders.

'I understand, of course. But you can't expect me to be pleased, surely. Leo can understand that, I hope.'

'Please, Lydushka. I can't do anything else. And maybe it will work out, you know. I know Sergei Pavlovich wants Anna for his Paris season if it comes off.'

Lydia gasped, momentarily winded by multiple jealousies. 'Paris! Oh, it's not fair!' was all she could say.

'Now what's eating you?' Leo halted, waving his arms with anger. 'You wouldn't join Chinchilla's tour if he asked you, you haven't a good word to say for him, and if it happens it will all be Mikhail's Greek stuff and you hate that too. I'll never understand you!'

'It's not fair! Why should Anna be going to Paris when she hates fun and parties and clothes and having a good time, and she's a prig and a bore and a cripple and she only gets decent reviews because she sleeps with the critics . . .' In the glow of the street lamp Lydia's eyes were so bright and full it seemed as if she were about to cry.

Marie hugged her briskly. 'Lulu, darling! Only one critic, you be fair now.'

'Well, one was enough.'

'But now she's stuck with that revolting Dandré and you and I can dance in his gala and have our pick of all the officers in the Horse Guards. So, who's having all the luck really?' A small sniff wrinkled Lydia's nose. 'And you're strong and she's weak, and you're beautiful and she's got a nose like . . . like . . . a haystack . . . and think what she'll look like in that short skirt, and your legs are the best in · the whole company.'

Balancing on the edge of the pavement, feeling his calves stretch as he dropped his heels towards the gutter, Leo distracted himself from their hideous frivolity by analysing the way the two women were posed to express despair and consolation; this useful intellectual exercise was all that prevented him from screaming with exasperation.

In a little while Lydia allowed herself to be restored to reason, and they prepared to walk the remaining few hundred yards to their apartment, the women arm in arm, with Leo sulking beside them. 'Wait,' he ordered at the next corner. 'We can't separate like this, still at odds with each other. Aren't you hungry? There's a little place I know just over there, we can have some fish with salad and a drink perhaps . . .'

'I know your "little places",' Lydia snapped at once. 'It'll have sawdust on the floor and some drunk scribbling on a napkin and calling it poetry. You only want to bore us with your ideas for another couple of hours. No thank you, all the same. I wish I'd stayed in and done my sewing, at least then I'd have achieved something tonight.' They proceeded miserably onwards until they reached their building, which was entered through a small courtyard.

After the women went inside an overwhelming gloom descended on Leo; he sat on the mounting block in the gateway as if pushed down by a giant hand. Lamps were turned on and off behind the blinds of the apartment, but the shadows were so faint he could not make Lydia out or identify the room where she slept. He shut his eyes and filled his head with imaginary dancers, tireless automata with bright smiles who demonstrated whatever combination of movements he chose to consider. When the lamplighter passed in the milky mist of dawn he was still awake, but so cold the old man had to drag him to his feet and walk him down the road until the blood was again pumping freely in his veins.

They were given the Ekaterinsky Theatre in which to rehearse, a small, windowless auditorium more like a concert hall and seldom used. Lydia worked in a poor spirit. Her anger towards Leo grappled for attachment but found none and so raged unexpressed and consumed her energy. As time passed and *Les Pléiades* took shape it became clear that it was a major achievement for such a young aspirant to a profession which demanded maturity.

The pas de deux proved to be precisely as Leo promised, a romantic piece pervaded with neurotic melancholy, ideal for Anna's emotional manner. Technically it was harder than it appeared, for Leo had borrowed his mentor's style of blending turns and jumps into expressive sequences, but it was within the older dancer's range. The dances for the remaining six stars were charming and gave each the opportunity to do what she did best. In Lydia's case she was to begin by flying diagonally down the stage in two thrilling series of leaps; what followed was fast and brilliant, testing her strength to its limit, until she left the stage with another jump into the wings. Hard as they were, she found it easy to infuse the steps with character and make them into something witty and coquettish.

'Magnificent!' Leon Samilovich was almost jigging with delight when he arrived with the final costume designs. 'The Shooting Star, eh Leo? You'll bring the house down, I guarantee it. What do you think – the white dress?'

'I thought the red.' Leo was demonstrating a gesture to the angular Inna and did not look round.

'Leo, how could you? I look awful in red, you know I do.' She sounded shrewish, even to herself, but was unable to sweeten her tone.

'Whatever you like. I didn't plan the ballet around the colours of the dresses!'

Leon Samilovich shrugged and winked at her. 'The white one, yes?'

As the rehearsals continued the rest of the young company

became a gleeful conspiracy, keeping to themselves the certainty of their success. Their excitement was noticed, and shadowy figures began to appear in the dim hall while they worked. One day Lydia was surprised to see the once-familiar dark mass of Sergei Pavlovich Diaghilev assuming a seat in the exact centre of the auditorium.

'What's Chinchilla doing here?' she asked of no one in particular. Six of the girls were sitting at the back of the stage, watching Inna run through her variation.

'Leon must have asked him, they're really thick still, aren't they? And look at him buzzing over like a wasp homing in on the jam pot.'

'Isn't that Mikhail Mikhailovich, too?'

'Looks like it.' The clean-cut face of the ballet master was easily recognizable despite the poor light.

'And there goes Leo – trust him not to get left out when the gods are gathering together.'

'He's mad.' Lydia pronounced her verdict as the older men shook Leo's hand and kissed his cheeks, congratulating him with obvious sincerity. 'They got the police to throw Sergei Pavlovich out of the theatre last week because he came in and started interfering with the new ballet, and now Leo's giving him the red carpet treatment. If he wants to get on he really should take more care who he makes friends with.'

'Oh do grow up, Lydia.' Anna's eyes never left the conversation in the stalls, though her tone was passionate. 'Leo knows what he's doing. Who cares what those fools in the management think? They're just Court hangers-on, they don't know anything about art. The world doesn't end at the banks of the Neva, you know.'

'I'm sure that's easier to appreciate if you've had the opportunity to travel, Anna.'

'So I've been abroad a couple of times, so what? I can't help it if people want to see me dance.'

The companionable group broke up within a minute, dispersed by the senior dancer's insufferable complacency, and Anna, oblivious of the rolling eyes and insulting gestures behind her, tripped away to join the men. Mischa Alexandrov appeared to help her down from the plank bridge over the orchestra pit, and jumped up to the stage himself.

'Lydia Alexandrovna! I hoped I'd find you here. And is your little blonde friend around? Ah yes, there she is. Marie, isn't it? Let's find somewhere to talk.' With a confidential touch under her elbow he guided Lydia to a corner screened by discarded scenery, one of those disregarded spots which make backstage a natural habitat for conspiracy.

'My dears, I must congratulate you. This ballet is absolutely exquisite! Dazzling, just dazzling. Everyone's talking about it. Our little Leo's going to be a star. You're so lucky to be chosen, nothing like this ever happens to me.' A tragic look passed over his noble if rather coarse features and he sat uncomfortably on a trestle. 'Now, my dears, I've a little invitation for you. Some of my friends – and you know I am lucky in my friends, some of them are really quite well connected – some of them are going to be helping at this gala. It's sort of a tradition for the Horse Guards, you know that too, I'm sure. They want to give a little party afterwards in a restaurant to entertain some of the gorgeous dancers who've so kindly worked so hard . . .'

'Oh, cut the crap, Mischa.'

'My dear, they didn't ask for a little scrubber with a mouth like a fishwife.'

'Oh don't be upset, Mischa darling, Marie's just pulled a muscle and she's fed up this morning, that's all. Now, tell us, where is this party to take place and who are these smart friends of yours exactly?'

'The dinner will be at Cubat's – where else? And the host will be General Ragosin, so his nephew Alexis will be there, and all his crowd, Basil, Andrei, Pierre, the usual people . . .' It was his manner to drop Christian names by the basket-load so that listeners were too afraid of appearing gauche to demand better identification. General Ragosin's nephew Alexis, however, was known to them by reputation for he was assiduously courting one of Tata's friends.

'Isn't Alexis Ragosin the one who's mad about Lulu Kyasht?'

'You do keep up with the gossip, don't you?'

'Be serious, Mischa – suppose Marie's brother-in-law won't let us accept this invitation? If Lulu is there, then Tata might be too, which will be very good because everyone knows Tamara Platonova never does anything improper.'

'Cunning little vixen! My dear, I'm *sure* Lulu will be invited, and her prim friend too.' There was a world of difference between a guest being invited to such a party and her definite acceptance, as all three of them acknowledged with crisp nods of their heads. 'So you will ask this brother-in-law's permission and let me know tomorrow, yes?'

By immediate unvoiced agreement, Lydia and Marie adopted expressions devoid of interest and gave their casual assent. Alexandrov had strolled away reflecting on the silliness of all little tarts who affected virginal poses when they were ready to act like cats on heat at the sight of a dress uniform. As if to prove him right, Lydia and Marie fell into each other's arms miaouing with delight as soon as they were alone.

'At last! Now we're on our way!'

'But do you really think we should go, Lydia? You know

what people say about Mischa's friends. They can be pretty wild and we don't want to get bad names right at the start.'

'Are you serious? The first nibble we get in two years of waiting and you're messing about wondering if we'll ruin our reputations?'

'It can happen – we'll never do as well as my sister if we get a bad name.'

'We won't get bad names unless we deserve them, silly. We'll be as proper as nuns and everything will be perfect, trust me.'

'I trust *you* until the end of creation, pet. It's me I'm worried about – all those lovely *men*!'

The day of the gala seemed blessed by Providence. Lydia had decorated her daily round with a dozen tiny superstitions, beginning with the encounters on her way to Theatre Street. That morning she passed a hunchback, which seemed even luckier than a pair of magpies. Her right foot was leading when she reached the staircase; in class Legat had no words of criticism for her at all, which was quite just since she was moving like an angel. To crown everything, at the Ekaterinsky for the last rehearsal a high wind blew in a window pane, which even Leo agreed was the hand of God breaking glass for luck.

Since the time when she had danced her solo as a child at the Hermitage, she had a private name for the sense of being possessed by a high destiny which had animated her then and had since recurred, although randomly and seldom. She called it simply the Magic Spirit. As she was hooked into the white dress for *Les Pléiades* she craved that blissful sense of certainty in her limbs again, but attempted to smother the impulse, feeling sure that if she was too knowing the spirit would not come.

The ballet was well received immediately, with warm applause breaking out so often there was a danger that they
would spend more time bowing than dancing. Pavlova's
claque had infiltrated the event, no doubt subsidized by
Dandré, but there was so much enthusiasm, and so many
boisterous young men in the audience, that their orchestrated
responses were drowned.

When Lydia took the stage for her solo she felt confident,
but sad that she was correct, and that the Magic Spirit had
been scared away just by her invocation. And then, when
she made the final jump in her first series, she knew it was
with her. All sense of weight and effort left her body, and
she had a split second in which to catch the conductor's eye
before flying away upstage to begin the next sequence.
Throughout the audience she heard people murmur and
gasp, and then applause began to break out even before each
new display of her virtuosity was fully completed.

By her final attitude the audience was in uproar, and she
saw through the haze of the footlights that half the crowd
was on its feet to hail her. She made her curtsies to the
prescribed formula – right to the Imperial box, tonight
occupied by Dandré and General Ragosin, left to the Director, whom she was gratified to see had risen to his feet; two
steps forward, a sweeping curtsey to the stalls, then looking
up with a smile for the final curtsey to the gallery. Looking
sidelong into the wings too she saw her companions bruising
their hands in a frenzy of appreciation, and Leo with his
dark face convulsed with emotion. She heard whistles and
cheers, cries of 'Bravo' and '*Bis, bis*', calls for an encore, but
another glance offstage revealed Pavlova in a shadowy
corner, her face immobile with anger.

The spirit seemed to be with her still, and Lydia found her
arms gathering the love of the mass to her heart and then

asking, with a gesture of modest grace which was quite unfamiliar, to be released. In a few seconds people began to sit down and the noise rolled away like passing thunder, allowing her to skip prettily aside and the next section of the pas de deux to commence.

Her state of grace passed, and as soon as the performance had reached its triumphant finale she was impatient to don the pink mousseline dress at last and be away to supper. Leo's praise, reserved for her first, was rudely brushed aside and she paused only an instant longer to receive the congratulations of Leon Samilovich, who appeared backstage with a tall white-haired man, the eminent balletomane General Count Besobrasov, whose endorsement could well make all their fortunes.

Alexandrov, hitherto in the young women's eyes nothing but an ageing dancer who grew more pretentious with each passing year, suddenly appeared magnificent in his evening clothes, with a monocle which comically magnified one of his large blue eyes. Complimenting them on their own finery, he escorted Lydia and Marie to an open carriage driven by a fat coachman with a groom in uniform beside him. At their appearance the two men jumped smartly down from the box to settle them comfortably with a heavy fur rug over their knees.

Lydia was elated from dancing, from her triumph and with the anticipation of long-awaited pleasures ahead. Her sensibilities were all overcharged, showing in a pink flush on her pale face which the night air heightened to a bright rose. Even Marie, pale as she was, had a little colour by the time they arrived at Cubat's. It was the most fashionable restaurant in the city, the expected venue for all the receptions held after the ballet or opera, with an immense dining room at ground-floor level and a gallery above, from which opened a honeycomb of private suites.

Mischa was an expert with nervous girls. A little care, a little kindness at the beginning always paid off – it cost nothing to put them at their ease at first and they would be much more amenable when they had a little confidence. Stooping fondly to whisper quiet directions in their ear, with a gentle touch under the elbow or at the waist, he guided them through the glittering press of people to the cloakroom, where they shed their coats and velvet theatre bonnets, smoothed their hair and admired each other's dresses one more time.

'I wish I hadn't chosen this red.' Marie's gown was a bold scarlet chiffon trimmed with braid. 'It looks terribly brassy, doesn't it?'

'No, not at all, it's wonderful with your colouring. I feel absolutely washed out in this. Is your heart beating? Mine is, I'm sure I won't be able to say a word.'

'I think my stomach's going to do my talking for me – I'm starving.'

Clutching each other's hands, unaware that they were attracting attention only by their fresh beauty and their state of nervous animation, they braved what they supposed was censure in the eyes of the maid, the swooping waiters and the major-domo. Alexandrov held out his arms and made them walk either side of him – he used the same gesture with which he always led the Polonaise in *Boris Godunov*, which made them giggle – and swept them up the wide, carpeted staircase to the gallery. Lydia felt an uncomfortable knot of tension under her ribs. She had a brief impression of scores of white tables and hundreds of people below them, and then attendants pulled open double doors to a lobby and they heard their names announced.

'The little man with Dandré is your host, General Alexander Nikolaevitch Ragosin,' Mischa murmured in Lydia's ear as he drew her forward.

'Saints alive – it's a banquet! I've never seen so much food,' Marie hissed behind her as the General took her hand. For an instant she thought he would kiss it, but he merely paused. Ragosin was indeed slightly built, but intimidating nonetheless with his chest almost paved with decorations and the diamond star of an Imperial order at his throat.

'Mademoiselle Kusminskaya – ladies, gentlemen – the new star in our heavens.' In a few seconds he seemed to have weighed her character and determined the next action. She found herself being presented to the whole room, where forty or so people turned from their informal conversation to applaud her once more. The majority were men wearing the rich blue uniform of the Horse Guards.

'More arrivals from the theatre.' Tactfully Mischa drew his protégées forward to meet their fellow guests. 'Let me introduce you – the general's nephew, Major Alexis Ragosin, Major Basil Nikonov, Major Andrei Lazarev.' Three expect-ant young officers bowed and the tang of conspiracy in the air told Lydia that the last pair were the men who had asked Alexandrov to provide them with company for the evening. They were very much of a piece with the young Ragosin, although whereas he was baby-faced Nikonov was dark and ruddy and Lazarev appeared colourless and hollow-cheeked.

'We must confess the ballet has not been one of our passions until now, but after your marvellous performance this evening Andrei and I have promised to make up for lost time.' Nikonov patted his abundant moustache, below which he was constantly smiling. His lips were narrow and very red, and with his bright round eyes gave him the appeal of an impertinent little boy.

'Yes, indeed. Now we are aware of the terrible gap in our artistic education we intend to repair it as fast as possible. Perhaps you could advise us on what to see first?'

'Ignore him, Mesdemoiselles, the man's a fool. We shall simply attend every performance decorated by your participation. When are you dancing next? Soon, I hope?'

'Gentlemen, for heaven's sake! If you sincerely want to appreciate our art you must choose what to see carefully. What do you think, Lydia – should they proceed historically, beginning with the old romantic ballets?' Marie was starting to enjoy herself, although she was still so nervous that her fingers picked at the braid on her sleeve.

'Not for Andrei! No romance for him, he's too susceptible, poor fellow, and an officer can't come over all sentimental, it's bad for morale.'

Lydia looked teasingly at her shoes and traced some of the carpet design with her toe. If she could have purred with satisfaction she would have done so – this was precisely the style of badinage she had always envisaged herself enjoying at such an event. 'Are we to understand, then, that you are the hard-hearted member of this partnership?' She looked up at Basil under her eyelashes.

'Certainly!' Andrei interrupted his friend at once. 'He may seem quite civilized here in these elegant surroundings but Basil is a poor unfeeling brute at bottom, alas.'

'You liar. Don't listen to him, Mesdemoiselles, he's slandering me. I'm a serious man, that's all. My poor heart is exceptionally tender, and so I take good care of it. I would hate it to fall into the wrong hands, it's so easily bruised.'

'What nonsense you boys are talking – and improper, too. You've hardly been introduced to these ladies and you're flirting already.' Chirruping like an annoyed bird to discover younger competition, Lulu Kyasht joined them and dropped a possessive hand on her beau's arm. 'Alexis, can't you keep them in order?'

There was an awkward pause, broken by a waiter who

presented a tray of tiny glasses. 'Ah vodka – excellent!' Mischa nodded firm encouragement at Lydia. The spirit felt harsh but was soon nothing but vapour in her throat. 'Try some, Mademoiselle, it stimulates the appetite.'

'My appetite is in fine form already,' Marie told him, then blushed almost as red as her dress as the rumble of her empty stomach emphasized her point.

'Heavens – you must forgive us! You are both famished and here we are standing around making useless conversation . . .' Basil immediately strode towards the buffet, summoning more waiters with a glance.

'Delightful conversation,' Andrei corrected him, offering Lydia his arm. 'Can we find something to tempt you here? If you don't see anything you like you've only to ask – they'll make anything you can name.'

An elaborate feast was piled before them. Around an ice sculpture of seven stars and epergnes stuffed with hot-house roses there were at least thirty hors-d'oeuvre dishes, including red and black caviar, mushrooms marinated in oil and meat balls with a rich cream sauce.

'The fish is always excellent here,' Andrei prompted. In hungry confusion Lydia's eyes roamed over marinated fish, smoked fish, dried fish, pickled fish, fish in hot sauce, fish in wine, fish in pastry, fish poached with herbs, stuffed fish and fish cutlets.

'You must try these.' At Andrei's command the waiter removed a silver cover from a hot dish and a spicy aroma billowed towards her. 'Little sausages sizzled in butter, they're my favourite. And some potatoes – in olive mayonnaise, perhaps, do you like that? Or these, in sour cream? They're delicious. Or those little cheese tarts, heaven, so light and moist . . .'

The vodka was snarling in her empty stomach and Lydia

felt mildly nauseous. Beside her Marie was smiling in helpless adoration as Basil ordered the waiters to pile a little of everything on her plate and, when it was heaped so high that an avalanche threatened, he had a second plate started on her behalf. 'If you can't decide the only thing to do is taste everything,' he told her as if imparting the whole secret of gourmandism.

'The cheese things are nice,' Mischa encouraged her, sensing some difficulty.

'*Olivier mayonnaise* is a must, you have to try that,' Lulu advised over her shoulder while intent on her own selection.

'I really . . .' Andrei hung attentively on every hesitant word. 'I really think I need to eat something quite simple,' she began, feeling more and more certain of her exact desire as she spoke. 'What I would really like is some plain rice pudding.'

There was a shocked silence. 'Please – don't disgrace me just because you've never been to a restaurant before,' Mischa hissed under his breath. No one moved.

'Rice pudding, that's novel.' With a sarcastic look, Lulu invited the company to laugh. She had relaxed. Obviously these absurd girls would never be invited anywhere smart again.

'It really is what I would like.' Lydia turned unhappily to Andrei. 'You did say they could make anything.'

'Well, what are you waiting for – fetch Mademoiselle the finest rice pudding in St Petersburg at once.' The speaker was a tall man with a measured, amused voice. Lydia had noticed him in her panicky first glance into the room because his uniform was of a different colour, a pale blue the colour of spring sky. 'Would you care for jam, Mademoiselle?'

She nodded, feeling ridiculously powerful. 'Raspberry jam would be nice.'

'I'm sure it would.' The major-domo clapped his hands softly, a waiter slipped through the service door and the general conversation returned.

Alexandrov, now obliged to present the stranger, gave an irritated cough. 'You've caught Prince Orlov, my dear. He's a miserable bastard so heaven help us all.' He raised his voice and stepped forward as the man approached. 'Your Highness, will you allow me to present Mademoiselle Lydia Alexandrovna Kusminskaya. Mademoiselle, may I introduce His Highness Prince Nikolai Konstantinovich Orlov.'

'My compliments, Mademoiselle.' He barely touched her politely extended fingers. 'I could not bear to see a dancer of such potential excellence starve in the face of plenty.'

'Your Highness is most kind.' His use of the word potential annoyed Lydia, but hunger was now her predominant sensation and she left her anger aside. She looked up at his face, noting the high forehead and fleshy chin. His eyes seemed inaccessible. The impression was as noble as her imagination demanded of a family who had been close companions of the Imperial house for many generations. One hundred and fifty years ago, his ancestor, Count Grigor, had won their title as the most prominent of the Empress Catherine's many lovers.

'Not really,' he contradicted in a detached tone, and then said nothing more, despite Alexandrov's floundering attempts at small talk. They drifted towards the small tables intended for dining at the margin of the room. The pudding, in a crystal bowl on a silver platter, arrived as Marie embarked upon her second plate of hors-d'oeuvres, with Basil and Andrei now both in attendance.

Orlov watched her consume the dish in systematic spoonfuls, methodical in her greed, taking care to spread the jam over each morsel. Eating in silence, it crossed her mind that she ought to feel embarrassed, but did not. At last he spoke again. 'A rare treasure. You know precisely what you want, don't you?'

'Is that truly a rare quality, Your Highness?'

'In a woman, yes, I think so. You still don't recognize my uniform, do you?'

'Your Highness must excuse me, I know so little of military affairs . . .'

'When we met it was such a dramatic encounter I was sure you would remember it for the rest of your life.'

'Don't tease me.' Now she was fast becoming tired and fretful. 'We can't possibly have met.'

'Forgive me. I am certain and I remember your name exactly. Actually I sometimes wondered what happened to you after that day. I wondered if you would cut your hair.'

Warmth, a full stomach and tiredness were softly overwhelming her. The long preparations for this evening, her irritation with Leo, her eager anticipation of this party, were all resolved but her energy was depleted. She swallowed a yawn before she spoke, but goaded herself to launch her irresistible sidelong smile in his direction; what could she be thinking about, becoming dozy when one of the wealthiest and most distinguished unmarried men in the country was claiming her acquaintance? 'My hair? In some quarters, Your Highness, it is very much admired – I couldn't possibly consider cutting it. I'm afraid there would be an outcry.' Conveniently, one lock had worked free of pins at her neck and she could twirl it around her finger before tucking it back in place.

'It is never an inconvenience, then?' His tone was odd. She felt that he was trying to make a joke but had had little practice.

'Well, I must admit that very long hair is heavy when one

is dancing, and needs to be quite firmly dressed for the stage, but a woman must always suffer to be beautiful and I would rather have my curls than a light head.'

'Another wise choice, if I may say so. Tell me – what would you like to do now?'

The room was hot and noisy, ringing with the officers' loud laughter. Marie had propped her drooping head on her hand and was glancing at her suitors with eyes which periodically closed with fatigue. Lydia herself had a distinct vision of her soft, white bed. 'Go home,' she replied and then, feeling that she might be judged ungrateful, added, 'It's been a simply divine evening, I've had a wonderful time and I wish it could go on for ever, but in the ballet we can't have too many late nights.'

'No dancing at the Aquarium tonight, then?'

'Isn't the Aquarium a night club?' With alarm she saw that Marie was swaying on her chair, although her companions were still chaffing each other and did not appear to have noticed.

'With an American negro tap-dancer. He's quite amusing, you should see him some time.'

'I couldn't possibly think of such a thing.' Instinctively, she felt it important to set high standards at once; to her disappointment, however, he did not press any other invitation on her, but looked around for Alexandrov and called him over with a frown.

'Your delightful companions are quite exhausted – please take my carriage,' he said abruptly and then took formal leave of them all with equal courtesy. Looking over her shoulder as she left Lydia saw him join a tall woman in an extremely fashionable velvet dress; she was long-bodied and languid in her movements, and her jewels seemed to drip from her like heavy dew.

Orlov's carriage was enclosed and the size of a small room. Small braziers under the seats made the interior warm and fragrant, but although there was no need of rugs the coachmen assiduously covered them with sable blankets. Marie at once slumped in a corner and leaned her cheek against the red plush upholstery.

'Do make him hurry,' she pleaded in a faint voice. 'I feel ghastly.'

'You look it as well, dear. I suppose you'd better have the window open.' Mischa hauled up the leather strap and lowered the sash, then plumped back into his seat with a pout.

'Don't be angry, Mischa, we'll do better next time.' Lydia suddenly saw her social career reaching an untimely end.

'I suppose you don't realize . . . no, how could you, you're as green as cabbages . . . that was Prince Lvov I was talking to when I got my orders to take you two away. He and Vaslav have been hot and heavy but now he's bored. He's got a friend who's interested but Vaslav – God, that boy's such a fool, he keeps his brains in his legs if you ask me – Vaslav's convinced it's all true love and keeps moping around Lvov making calf's eyes at him . . . so Uncle Mischa's got to sort it all out. Oh believe me, girls, it's not all cherry pie keeping the aristocracy happy. Whoa there! Steady on, you fellows!' The oversprung carriage wallowed around a sharp bend, throwing the three of them into a corner.

'Our Vaslav? Vaslav Fomitch? I didn't know he liked men.' The cold night air and the prospect of gossip revived Lydia a little; she reflected that the young Pole had been wearing some stylish new clothes lately.

'Nor did he until Lvov took him to Fabergé. Now he's in love – that's the way of all flesh, you'll find out. You certainly will, Lydia dear, the way Orlov moved in on you like the Tartar hordes.'

'I thought he was rather cool,' she said carefully, probing for information.

'God no, that's just his way. He's always in a frost, getting a smile out of him is like getting blood out of a stone. Fancies himself as an intellectual and a cut above the rest because he studies archaeology. Actually I believe he is quite cultured. But you managed to warm him up, my dear – congratulations! I can't say I wasn't surprised – he's been with some German woman for years. I expect you noticed her, very modern clothes she always wears. She'll never land him, though.'

'Why not? She is beautiful, even you must allow that, Mischa.' Beyond a certain point she mistrusted his judgement, because he seldom had a good word to say about any woman, and was most contemptuous of those who planned alliances.

'Got no class, dear, common as muck. Beauty's nothing to an Orlov, it's breeding that counts. You won't catch that great pike without twenty pages in the Almanach to bait your hook, let me tell you.'

'What almanack?' Marie's feeble voice inquired from the corner. The coach lurched again as it turned onto a wide bridge over the Neva, and continued to oscillate rhythmically as the horses gathered speed.

'What Almanach! Listen to the dear dumb kitten! There's only one Almanach you need to consult, the Almanach de Gotha, the register of all the noble houses of Europe, essential reading for every amateur fortune hunter in the Western world. Whoops! Here we go again!'

Another violent shudder marked the carriage's turn along the river embankment.

'Mischa, make them stop.' Marie suddenly dragged herself to her feet. 'I'm going to be sick, I know it. Quick, quick!'

With a good-natured show of mock disgust their escort called up to the coachman to stop, but since he fell back into his seat immediately Lydia assumed that it was her responsibility now to help Marie to the river side as fast as she could stagger.

While her friend leaned over the low wall and vomited her sumptuous dinner into the water, Lydia stood back, discreetly shielding her from view. The three-quarter moon was just visible through a scrim of clouds. It was at that moment that she at last remembered her meeting with Prince Orlov.

Reluctantly, she withdrew from the lowest level of her memory the terrible details of that day, the last time the city had slept with confidence in its future, the last time she had seen her family. Unconsciously, she rubbed the back of her knee, remembering the bruises from his horse's saddle. The glacial detachment of his manner had been the same even then, when murder had been all around and blood had stained these same streets.

A lone seabird flew silently across the moon's path on the surface of the water. A sense of predestination embraced her, crushing her to the point of breathlessness, and she sighed heavily, needing air. Whatever Mischa might say, however vast the social chasm, she was certain that to love Orlov was her fate.

CHAPTER 7
Nice, 1965

Inside the Villa les Gazelles every surface was draped. Fringed wool shawls, with bright flowers printed on dark grounds, covered the chairs, the once-white art deco leather sofa and the iron banister rails. A black Chinese shawl half covered the baby grand piano, disguising the many burns and ring marks on its peeling walnut veneer. Over the metal-framed french windows, faded chenille curtains shut out the Riviera sun. The mantelshelf was covered with a linen runner worked in red cross-stitch, a pink chiffon scarf with a hole burned by a cigarette in one corner drooped like Spanish moss from the parchment shade of a standard lamp.

Alex Wolfe looked wonderingly around him. The clutter in all the rooms was indescribable. It seemed as if nothing had been thrown away during all the decades of habitation since the house was built. Once it had been fashionably decorated, no doubt, with the few matching items of Odeon-style furniture which were now dilapidated and covered with rugs. The contents of a junk shop seemed to have been added since, cheap carved tables, a chaise with broken springs, items in pastel wicker and worn leather each placed carefully so that a few inches remained clear between them. A dog, small, black, and old, wheezed in a basket by the cold fireplace. Along one wall of the sitting room old newspapers and magazines were piled almost to the ceiling, with an empty birdcage balanced on top of them. There were a dozen small tables, each covered with a cloth and crowded with blurred sepia photographs, carved wooden animals, lacquer boxes, ashtrays and vases of cheap lustre glass.

The folds of all the draperies were outlined in dust and more dust rolled itself into clouds of fluff around the margins of the dark parquet floors. Some attempt at cleaning was evidently made, since parts of the floor had been polished. On the walls, which were lined with pictures in dark wood frames, the cobwebs did not begin until the height of about six feet.

His grandmother and her companion conveyed with gestures and chatter in French which he could not understand that he should take off his backpack and sit on the lopsided sofa. A diluted tang of the perfume his grandmother wore lingered in the still air. It was an aroma more exotic than anything he had ever scented, neither sweet nor pleasant, but it suggested the world he had been unable to imagine but always knew lay out there somewhere, beyond the furthest boundaries of his childhood, beyond Cleveland, beyond Ohio, beyond America itself.

His grandmother first sat beside him and hung on to his hand, kissing it and pressing it to her cheek, talking softly to herself and to her companion, then released him and began hobbling to and fro on bowed, arthritic legs, unable to rest for excitement. He called her 'Grandmère', and she made him repeat it a hundred times, her hand to her ear as if miming listening to sweet birdsong. '*Musique, musique!*' She nodded vigorously at him.

Her companion she introduced at first as Marie, and then, with a creaky flourish and an unsteady bob of a curtsey, as La Comtesse Maria Stepanova Nikonova, with a few incomprehensible words added to this appellation, after which they clutched each other's arms, laughing at some private joke.

'*Je ne parle pas très bien le français,*' he ventured, clearing his throat, which made the two old women shriek with amusement; then recollecting the possibility of making their precious guest uncomfortable they embraced him, patting his arms with dry, bony hands.

Marie was stout, her belly clearly corseted for its bulk never stirred and the bones were visible at her sides through the tight material of her dress. She bore it before her proudly. Her hair, although completely white, was smooth and thick, and waved attractively, if unskilfully, off her round, tanned face. Her bulk, on her small frame, made her waddle as she went to the kitchen to make tea, but she still had far more ease of movement than his grandmother.

While the tea was made in a silver pot, set down upon the stained cloth on the dining table and poured into red glasses with gold rims the old woman chattered at Alex, who smiled and shrugged and understood nothing. The French word for milk deserted him and seeing that the women drank the tea without it, he did not like to ask. They pursued a rapid conversation propelled by protesting gestures with their arms, until they evidently reached some agreement.

Marie got up and went to the french door. The latch was stiff and Alex helped her open it, then handed her down the few broken steps into the small back garden, where she made off down a red sand path uttering piercing shrieks. By the time she reached the end wall another old woman appeared from the villa opposite, shrieking in response, a small brown dog with bulbous eyes at her feet. They called to each other like parrots over the straggling purple bougainvillaea, then gathered their skirts around their knees and returned indoors.

Some time later a voice called 'Yoo-hoo, yoo-hoo!' in the front garden and the knocker on the front door, a useless nickel-plated ring, was flapped impatiently. Marie set off and returned with their neighbour, who extended to Alex her translucent, freckled hand, its fingers swept sideways by rheumatoid arthritis.

'Good *after*noon, young man. I am Angela Partridge and as you can probably hear I am English.' She was wearing a pleated silk afternoon dress in some beige print that looked like scribbling, with pale support stockings most carefully darned. The dog sat down at her feet and raised one forepaw. 'And this is Sir Horace, he is a griffon and he would like you to shake his paw. That's right.'

'He's got a cute face.' Alex leaned down and did as he was told, noticing how clean the newcomer seemed beside the others and how the fresh air admitted by Marie's exit was still hanging in a cloud in the centre of the room. 'I'm Alexander Elliott Wolfe and I've come from Cleveland in the United States, but maybe you know that already.'

'Since I speak something like your language, your grand-mother – I believe it is – has invited me to translate, so I shall do my best. I do hope your journey was not too tiring.' She seated herself on a hard dining chair, turning round to ascertain its condition first. 'Did you fly? Simply thrilling! Do tell me – how long does it take?'

She began to conduct an exchange of small talk of the kind which his mother's church friends would have considered thoroughly refined, in that it touched on no subject whatever of any emotional significance to either of them. Each exchange she relayed in hideous French to her companions, until his grandmother at last erupted in a torrent of protest and began to direct the conversation herself.

'And now,' the offended translator continued, reposition-ing her white handbag under her elbow, 'your grandmother would like you to come and look at some of her family pictures.'

'That will be great.' He jumped to his feet, clearly full of enthusiasm, and she looked up at him with cynical surprise. 'You don't understand, I've never seen any of that kind of stuff. Back home my mother doesn't have photographs around. She doesn't talk about her family at all, as a matter of fact. I just kind of found out about my grandmother by accident. I didn't even know she existed – I mean, I know she existed but I didn't know where she was or who she was or anything about her.'

'Good heavens!' Angela Partridge was now moved, and translated quickly, producing a flurry of amazement. 'What an extraordinary thing. You do now know who your grand-mother was, I suppose?'

'Who she was?' He was puzzled. 'Well, not exactly. I just know her name and that she was French, although Kusminska isn't a French name, is it? I thought maybe it was more Polish or something.'

'*Russian*, dear boy. Never say Polish to them, they think they're fools. Obviously Russian, look around you, nobody French would live like this, would they?' Getting to her feet, she indicated the chaotic room with a brief wave of her bent fingers. Automatically he offered her his arm, but she indicated that he should help his grandmother to stand.

A thrill shot through him at her words, the sheer excitement of the forbidden. Russian! Nobody in Cleveland was Russian. Some people, Jewish mostly, said they were Estonian or Lithuanian, but never Russian. Russians, as far as his parents were concerned, were enemies, spies, inhuman fiends forever poised to bomb Cuba, torch Vietnam and destroy American civilization. And here he was, apparently descended from a Russian, with the wicked blood running in his own veins.

'And you come from a *very* distinguished family. Your grandmother was in the ballet, you know, a *great* ballerina. Absolutely the tops. So grand she was just called La Kusminskaya, like that, no Christian name. Even I had heard of her when we were all young, although of course I'm younger than they are. That's why she's crippled now, you see. She really was the toast of old St Petersburg. The lovers she had!' This was added as if lovers were smart accessories. Alex had never heard anyone use the word in conversation before, let alone a well-bred old lady. 'Even the Tsar used to come to her performances. Come along, look at the photographs and then it'll all be clear as mud.'

He had only the most elementary notion of ballet, but felt it to be something else rare and exotic, another manifestation of the unknown world he had set out to discover. As they progressed around the room he was shown a bewildering series of monochrome photographs, solemn children, groups of melancholy people in combination-length bathing costumes, posed portraits, formal studies taken on stage with dancers in strange old costumes.

His grandmother picked up a picture of a boy in a sailor suit, riding in a trap pulled by a small white pony. 'This is your uncle Kolya, Madame's son, you see,' the English-woman informed him. 'He's a grown man now of course and lives in Paris. And this' – a portrait of a fair-haired dancer with a pretty smile, wearing a skirt almost down to her knees – 'this is the Countess here as a young girl. She was in the ballet too, you can see that, but she retired from the stage after her marriage. And here she is with her husband.' Marie laid a hand on the upper slope of her bosom, her smile now disappearing in a wreath of wrinkles.

Next his grandmother led him to a corner of the room which he had not noticed before, where two small icons rested on a shelf with a night light in a green glass jar below them and dead matches scattered carelessly around. Above them was a family portrait of a tall man in a uniform loaded with braid and decorations, a small-featured woman with a frozen expression whose elaborate lace dress was ruffled up to her ears, four nearly identical adolescent girls and a small boy. 'The man with the beautiful eyes is the last Tsar of Russia, and this is his family, who were all horribly murdered' – Angela paused while the other two women continued a lengthy explanation – 'and Lydia says it is so, she is quite certain, and all those people who say some of them escaped or it never happened are wrong, because she herself has met the magistrate who ran the special investigation into the murders in Paris after he emigrated and he told her all about it and showed her the photograph of the bodies. They were found in a mine. And the little keepsakes and trinkets found on the bodies were returned to relatives living here in France who recognized them all.'

Under this picture was a much more modern group, a woman with a full face, vivacious expression and dark hair with a widow's peak, a man with a pleasant, level gaze and sharp nose, and an infant girl. 'This is the present head of the Imperial Family in exile, the Grand Duke Vladimir, and his wife and daughter, the Grand Duchess Marie. There's quite a large number of émigrés living here, poor things, and more in Paris. One does feel *so* sorry for them, having lost everything – except hope, perhaps. The young ones are more realistic, of course. And this man on a horse was her lover, Prince Orlov, and here they are together in the villa they used to have over in Monte.'

'Does she have a picture of my grandfather anywhere?' Alex was not much interested in historical figures and found it impossible to relate this aged shred of a woman to the girl with a tiny waist and out-thrust bosom who stared out from the old pictures, bright-eyed and carefree.

'*Il demande son grandpère*,' the old woman translated in an imperious tone. To Alex's surprise his grandmother rattled off a long burst of delight and decided to kiss him again, then held him by the arms and invited Marie to look him in the face. 'She says you're the absolute living image of him, except you're fair and he was dark. She's looking for a picture of them both together.'

It was at last located on the piano, a stage portrait of a young man with a penetrating stare, kneeling with outstretched arms, while a pretty girl crowned with flowers leaned on his shoulder, holding an arabesque on one point. His black doublet was outlined sharply against her long white skirt, and the tails of the large white bow at the neck of his shirt flowed almost to his waist. Behind them could just be made out a painted backdrop with a ruined wall, a broken column and some leafy branches. The whole effect was ridiculous, dated and artificial, and Alex saw no resemblance to himself at all, except that the man's ears were curious, large and rather elfin, very much like his own.

'Tell me about this, where was it taken?' He ran wondering fingers over the glass, leaving trails in the dust.

'It was taken in Monte Carlo in 1914, at the start of the Russian Ballet season, and the ballet was called *Les Sylphides*. Your grandfather was a dancer and choreographer called Leonid Volinsky, and he was a very, very gifted man who adored your grandmother all his life although she says she was vile to him, frightfully cruel . . . oh crikey, somebody turned on the waterworks.'

His grandmother sank heavily on to the piano stool in an attitude of despair, dabbing at her eyes with a handkerchief produced from the pocket of her wrapper. Her voice sank to something between a soft wail and a whisper.

'Is he still alive?' Alex asked the Englishwoman, feeling raw and tired himself.

'Don't ask about it now, for Gawd's sake. Frightful thing, always sets her off.'

In a few minutes the old woman recovered, crossed herself and got shakily to her feet; in the process she knocked a glass dish in the shape of a butterfly off the piano, picked it up with difficulty and put it back, stroking the wings with her fingers. Then she beckoned Alex and their translator, who was acquiring a martyred air, to a place on the wall where a series of ballet pictures commenced, all identically framed.

'This is your grandmother as Salome in your father's ballet, and this is her as the Princess in *The Sleeping Beauty*, and here's the programme from that performance, and this is her with Nijinsky, and this is with your father again in *Don Quixote* but you see it got mildewed so it's not very good of him, and this is with Diaghilev, the great impresario, I don't suppose you've heard of him, and Picasso and some other people, and this is with the Countess again, and Anna Pavlova – you must have heard of her . . .'

Here there was a violent interjection. 'She was the most frightful bitch apparently, and then this one with the goat in is *Esmeralda* . . .'

'Does she have one of my mother?' The names were all meaningless to Alex, who now felt very tired.

'I'll ask, but since she ran away, you know . . . I've never seen one.' The two women conferred, looking all around the room, until Marie sailed to a far corner and returned with a long, informal group photograph, men in white flannels and women with cloche hats, seated upon a rug in a garden. Almost in the background was the figure of a little girl in a caped coat, her straight hair scraped to one side, holding a wicker hamper that was almost larger than she was.

'This is incredible, just incredible,' he said, not liking to remark that from her expression she seemed as bad-tempered as ever. He had brought a photograph of his parents to show his grandmother, but she seemed so pointedly uninterested that he did not mention it. 'I just can't believe I'm seeing all these things, all these people, my family.'

'Well she says you are a miracle from heaven and the answer to her prayers after all these years of loneliness. It's impossible to express her joy at seeing you here. So everybody's happy. Now are you staying anywhere? She'll want to give you her son's room, I expect.'

He was installed in a small, high-ceilinged room at the back of the villa by Marie, while his grandmother lowered herself into a corner of the sofa and began to call people on the ancient black telephone, pausing frequently to untangle the cord from the earpiece. Angela Partridge warned him to expect a party and in a few hours his grandmother appeared from her room in a sleeveless black satin gown which flapped around her thin body. A rope of blistered artificial pearls was wound several times around her neck and her sparse curls were anchored by pins. People began to arrive, most of them also elderly émigrés, and they brought dishes of food, sticky cold vegetables smothered in mayonnaise, fish in vinegar, chewy bread and pale meat fried in breadcrumbs, which soon covered the table. The piano was opened and a very thin old man sat down to play.

'Oh, is this vodka?' Someone put a tiny glass of spirit in Alex's hand. He sipped it cautiously and heard the English-woman's loud voice above the general protest.

'That's *not* the way at all, dear boy. All down at once – what do they say, no heel taps? Just throw it into your mouth. They'll probably break some glasses, it's meant to be lucky.'

The spirit warmed his throat. A man with a white moustache yellowed from tobacco and a cheroot tucked between his lips took the glass from him, carried it ceremonially to the fireplace and stamped on it.

Alex found a fresh glass in his hand being filled from a stone jar. 'It's the most frightful bath-tub hooch,' Angela Partridge warned him in a loud whisper. 'I've got a little gin in my bag if you'd rather.'

He was repeatedly introduced, kissed, pawed and patted. A thin woman in a dress of bias-cut black crepe with a spray of pink carnations pinned to the shoulder stood up by the piano with a violin, and after some argument with the pianist, began to play a waltz. He found himself shuffling awkwardly around the floor with one tiny old woman after another, and then after a while they ignored him and he sat with the griffon on a couch in the corner and went to sleep.

He had the impression that the party continued for days. His grandmother became very drunk and was periodically taken to her room to recover, but Marie never tired and swooped around the gathering with a permanent smile, making ineffectual attempts to clear the debris. People left with much kissing, other people arrived with more kissing. The air in the room was thick with smoke. Plates were scraped, sometimes washed, and piled with food again. Alex, thirsty and with a headache, drank a tumbler of vodka in mistake for water, and once it had taken hold went on to drink more, until he had to run to the bathroom to be sick. In the half light behind the curtains it was hard to tell what time of day it was.

Finally no more people came, except a young black-haired woman with very brown skin, evidently the maid, who carried piles of dishes into the kitchen and began washing them. Angela Partridge and her dog had long since disappeared, his grandmother was in her room and Marie was poised precariously on a stool, one leg crossed awkwardly over the other, trying to pull her shoe off her swollen foot.

Last to arrive had been a tall man with thinning fair hair, who now went to the windows and drew the curtains. The brilliant sunlight seemed to drain all the colour from the room, leaving it a dreary muddle. He wedged his cigarette between the third and fourth fingers of his left hand and extended his right to Alex, who hesitantly shook it.

'I am uncle,' he announced. His accent was very strong. 'You call me Kolya, Kolya Kusminsky. Welcome.'

He was a man of a kind Alex recognized only by instinct. In the dingy surroundings of the villa he seemed to be standing under a spotlight, fine-looking, beautifully dressed, radiantly prosperous. Properly, he should have been called middle-aged, but there was nothing staid about him, his manner was supple and responsive. Light blue eyes examined Alex carefully, without haste, while the left hand carried the cigarette to his mouth and away again. His cuffs were secured by crested gold links that were an important fraction too large, as was his silk tie with its vibrant abstract print. A powerful aura of physical confidence surrounded him. Alex, uncomfortable with the idea of finding another man attractive, felt a thin trickle of apprehension.

'The son of my sister, that is you.' His tone was inquisitorial.

'I believe so, yes, Sir.'

'No Sir, Kolya. Why you believe it?'

'I found a letter which my grandmother wrote to my mother, Sir.'

'You have letter? Show me, please.'

'It's in the bedroom, I'll get it.'

While the maid trotted energetically to and fro restoring the room to its former order, Alex submitted to a cross-examination. He had prepared for it, and brought all the letters, and a selection of other documents which might attest his identity. The photograph of his parents, taken in his infancy, was scrutinized at length. Kolya posed many questions about the account of her early life which his mother had given, and seemed suspicious that Alex could relate very little.

'She always said her life began when she met my father. I got the impression she didn't want to talk about her childhood, Sir. I didn't even know her parents were Russian, or anything, until I got here.'

'How old you are?'

'Sixteen.'

'Too young. You go to school?'

'I went to school in Cleveland, yes.'

Kolya seemed to have made up his mind sufficiently to decide the next course of action. 'I need you passport, please. Bring all these papers. We visit a friend and maybe American consul. Clean shirt, yes?' His hand, which was warm and heavy, fell on Alex's shoulder. The forefinger lifted the corner of his shirt collar. The panic he felt must have shown in his face because Kolya withdrew his hand at once and said, 'Don't worry.' The sense of conspiracy this generated was still more alarming.

His car was a little white Mercedes convertible, shallow like a cigarette box, which purred out of the suburbs, along the coast road lined with palms and into the bustling heart of the city. They visited a lawyer, a gently spoken young man who had prematurely lost much hair and who seemed familiar with the implications of runaway foreign minors. It was decided that Alex should write home at once, reassuring his parents that he was with his grandmother, was well, and had been compelled to satisfy his curiosity about his origins. Kolya then took him to an elegant small restaurant overlooking the sea, where several other men friends stopped at their table and eyed the boy with curiosity.

Several weeks of limbo followed, which Alex occupied pleasantly in lying on the pebble beach and walking around the town. He struck up acquaintance with two girls from Boston who were studying at the university in Aix-en-Provence, but his lack of money limited their interest. Slowly he woke up to his new environment. Kolya left for Paris, returning for a few weekend visits, and his grandmother dozed most of the day beside her telephone. Shopping and cooking were done by the maid, and Marie played patience and corresponded with her children, a son in Biarritz and a daughter in London.

In due course a stiff letter arrived from his father announcing that he had broken his mother's heart, betrayed their trust and shamed them in front of the whole neighbourhood. It concluded: 'As your parents we will honour our obligation to offer you a home under our roof until you are of age but while you choose to turn your back on us and on your country whatever becomes of you is no concern of ours.'

'This is sad. Sad man. No love, no life.' Kolya read the letter slowly, holding it at a distance because the script was cramped and he needed spectacles but was too vain to wear them. 'So now, it's your life, what shall we do?' His tone was unexpectedly harsh.

Alex was suddenly afraid. Kolya's indulgence was evidently not to be relied upon. He had not expected the door to his old life to slam quite so firmly behind him. There was an immediate sense of freedom, but also a stab of loss, and mistrust of his newly discovered family. Being now

accustomed to the unrestrained emotionality of his grandmother, his father's chilly response, with all natural feeling
hypocritically traduced into self-justification, seemed doubly
painful.

Lunch with Kolya was now an expected treat for them
both, and he could relax with the fact that his uncle obviously
enjoyed the curiosity of friends who saw him with an attractive stranger. It made him feel adult and worldly, both very
welcome sensations.

'What was my mother like as a little girl, Kolya?' He had
drunk more than his share of wine.

His uncle paused, dipping a fork into his bouillabaisse
while he collected his thoughts. 'Never happy,' he said at
last, picking out a small piece of red mullet. 'You understand
my mother was very ill when she born, and afterwards she
can't love the child. When I see her first, after end of war,
she like gypsy child, like beggar, dirty, no shoes. Nobody
cares for her. My mother blame her for everything bad in
her life.'

'I can't imagine her getting dirty. She's just obsessive
about things like that now.' He tried to smile but it was not
easy.

'Yes, yes, exactly. As she grow up, she get very quiet, and
work very hard. Everything in house, she do it. Because then
we have no money, and you understand my mother has
never in her life made one cup of tea. Really this little girl
was housewife. But she never happy. She hate for things to
be dirty, people to get drunk, people smoke cigarettes, people
forget, be stupid, be crying maybe or dancing. Russian
people are like that.'

'And she ran away?' It seemed the first link between them,
for now he too had run away.

'We had bigger house, and people living in it who pay for

their rooms, lodgers. Mostly also Russian. One day – now your mother is almost not child any more – this woman comes, Ukrainian, very good family, now she is teacher. And she has fiancé in New York, and she and my sister' – he held up his left hand with the first two fingers crossed – 'friends. They have same heart. So when the teacher leaves, she take your mother with her and we never see her again.' He emphasized the last words with a touch of resentment. 'One letter. One letter in twenty-five years, when she is going to get married. She is *sténographe*, insurance business.'

'Grandmère never talks about her.'

His uncle shrugged, implying that she was entitled to her little enmities. 'If she don't like something then it don't exist for her. Your mother is a woman who can never be happy. Is impossible. She always criticize inside, always thinking what other people think. She has nothing for another person. Women like that are nightmare. When you are man you will meet them. I think it is your destiny, make women happy, but not this kind.' He raised his eyebrows humorously and wagged a finger across the table. 'My advice if you meet this kind – run.'

'Well, I ran, didn't I?' Alex hoped he was not blushing. He felt both flattered and offended by Kolya's worldly advice.

'Yes, you did. Very good. Now we find where you run to. Next question. First, we get suit.'

They had visited a tailor a few weeks earlier, and now Alex found himself provided with an evening suit and a beautiful ruffled white shirt. Feeling already like a new person, he spread out awkwardly in the back of the Mercedes that evening speeding along the coast to Monte Carlo, watching Kolya's strong grip on the gearshift and listening to his grandmother in front pointing out the villas of her long-departed friends as they passed.

The suit and the drive were already more glamour than he had ever experienced, but what awaited him at the little gilded opera house touched the hidden mainspring of his character. It was a gala evening, attended by a crowd of awesome wealth and elegance into which Kolya plunged without hesitation. Women with smooth hair piled high and long false eyelashes, extraordinarily thin, glittering with jewels and sequins, swooped down on him at once. Alex heard murmurs of 'La Kusminskaya', a few seconds before he was blinded by photographers' flashlights.

On his arm his grandmother suddenly seemed less frail. He felt her usual tremor replaced by a firm touch, and she began smiling and nodding to acquaintances around them, standing erect and ordering her satin skirt into folds with an automatic twitch of her free hand. The dress had a close-fitting bodice and long sleeves, thickly embroidered with jet beads, and he saw that she was beautiful and graceful, and that Kolya, now leaning over her shoulder to point out another face in the crowd, still bore towards her the infinite love of a child.

Footmen parted the throng to let them move forward, and Alex was so overcome by the sight of people being held back to let his family pass that he stumbled and almost fell on the red-carpeted stairs.

'You are going to see Russian salad, not real ballet,' his uncle warned him. 'Little taste of this, little bit of that. Here is your American Princess.' The orchestra attacked the Ruritanian strains of the Monegasque national anthem as Princess Grace, in cerise satin, took her seat behind a bank of flowers in the royal box.

The performance began with *Les Sylphides*, which left Alex in a state of delicate rapture which he imagined must be akin to being in love. The entire confection fell into his parched mind like water into a desert. Connections at last began to form between the faded photographs in the Villa les Gazelles, this dazzling world of wealth and sophistication, and himself. Once my grandfather did that, he marvelled as the poet chased the last woodnymph away in the moonlight.

His head was still palpitating with Chopin when the next piece began with harsh chords from the orchestra. A man in loose oriental trousers tore across the stage as if he were about to kill someone. The audience burst into applause. Alex was electrified. A ballerina appeared, but while she proceeded with the intricacies of a pas de deux the male dancer soared and leaped as if powered by inhuman fury. His feet were soundless, like a cat's, and showers of sweat flew off his half-naked body at every turn, making his thick blond hair dark. He was clearly pushing his body to its limit and was not wholly in control; at one point he ran off the stage, leaving it empty while the music played on until the ballerina made her next entrance.

'Who is that?' he asked of his uncle during the tenth curtain call, when the volume of applause was finally low enough for him to be heard.

'New boy from the Kirov. Nureyev. Good jump but no manners. Grandmère thinks he is scandal.'

'I think he's terrific.'

Kolya looked shrewdly at his nephew, who was showing all his beautiful large white American teeth in a smile and clapping heartily as if he were at a football match. The boy was not dull, he thought, only uneducated, without culture, which was to be expected. He was not clever enough to be dishonest, but he had a fey quality which was perhaps mostly shyness. Obviously he had never been exposed to any kind of art, except perhaps a few books, but his instincts were surprisingly refined. But perhaps not surprisingly, considering his grandfather. Kolya had always regretted being born of the less interesting of his mother's lovers. He was also a little pained that his mother was now lamenting the choices of her golden youth. Undeniably, however, this boy had become the light of her life, and so they must do their best for him.

The next day Alex's head was still full of passion, poetry and music when he sat down with his new family to discuss his education. His grandmother held one of his hands in both of hers while Kolya explained that it would be futile to send him to a French school, he would never surmount the barrier of language in time or catch up with the archaic syllabus. There was an international school in the city, where he could study in English for the baccalaureat which was a recognized qualification in most of the world.

'Can I study the ballet?' he asked hesitantly, unaccustomed to having his wishes respected. 'I thought seeing as how it's in my family and everything . . . it might be kinda fun.'

'You can study here. It is only small museum but very interesting collection.' His uncle waved a hand at the chaotic room, his fleshy cheeks ruddy with amusement.

'No, I don't mean study like books and things, I mean learn it, do it, whatever people say?'

'Dance. You mean dance.'

'Oh yeah, how stupid, dance.'

'Well, why not?' The light eyes appraised him a second time, now noting his level shoulders, open chest, light but well formed musculature and starry eyes. 'My aunt Julie has studio in Cannes, if she is still alive. She always like boys, nice boys.' Kolya translated for his mother, who immediately got to her feet and spun around the room, miming joy, then headed for the telephone.

*

Madame Sedova's saucer eyes filled with tears at the sight of her old friend. She called for tea, and while Kolya smoked patiently the women enjoyed a full half hour of reminiscence before Alex was pushed forward and his origins explained, with much simpering by Lydia and teasing by Julie. At last she called in a younger woman, over-painted and wearing a turban, and a pale, lean man in jeans with close-cropped grey hair. Alex was presented and examined, asked to strip down to his underwear and examined again, then taken away by the man to find practice clothes before being walked up and down the mirrored studio and asked to copy some simple exercises at the barre.

'She says OK,' Kolya translated at the end of the morning, rolling off his chair with relief. 'You have to come on Saturday and Wednesday and you must work hard. They say you have your grandfather's ears but pray God you don't got his knees also.' His grandmother was tapping her chest, explaining that the young man's excellent physique was undoubtedly inherited from her. 'And she will make you practise every day. Every day, is important. Training normally start at eight years old. And please not to grow any more tall.'

A competition reveals the world of ballet at its most cruel. The choice of one gold medal winner, who would carry the unofficial title of the best dancer in the world, and sixteen finalists in the annual Prix Lausanne was a clinical procedure.

They began lying on their backs in straight rows of eight, a white plastic cover over the wooden studio floor clearly revealing their lean silhouettes. The twelve judges, seated on a dais at the end of the room, one by one got up and walked between the bodies, noting rotated knees and uneven

shoulders. Then the hundred young dancers from all over the
world were closeted together for three days with their teachers
and judges, aware as they carried their bags of sweaty clothing
between classrooms and rehearsal halls that their bodies were
being scrutinized in the most pitiless detail at every moment.

Wolfe, Alexandre, with the number 24 pinned to his plain
black practice clothes, floated through the affair with an air
of cheerful unconcern, only the occasional flash of his dark-
lashed grey eyes suggesting that he was at all nervous. A
high proportion of his rivals were eliminated after the
introductory classes. The tears began. He had discovered
that people wept every day in this world, sometimes from
sheer emotion but more often from disappointment heaped
on temperaments already frayed by criticism and weakened
by impossible physical demands.

'We will do this to learn,' Madame Sedova had instructed
him and her best girl pupil, Cécile, a colourless waif utterly
absorbed in herself. 'Learn to go before a public, learn how
good you are compared to the international standard. Learn
to rule your nerves.' She glared at Cécile. 'Learn why you
have to work.' She glared at Alex, but he merely smiled,
secure in her underlying approval. For two years he had
been nagged incessantly about the technique he needed to
perfect, but at the same time he realized that they would not
hammer him so mercilessly unless he was good.

Watching Madame during the competition, sitting contentedly with his grandmother, inclining her head to
acknowledge greetings and letting other teachers of her age
or standing approach her, Alex concluded that half the
purpose of their entry in the Prix was to meet old friends. He
no longer marvelled at the inbred, claustrophobic world of
the ballet, knowing that the accident of his birth had for
ever admitted him to its innermost circles.

More than half the profession was still under the control of his grandmother's friends and contemporaries. Here was Madame Egorova from Paris, Madame Sokolova from London, Madame Nieloshevskaya from Stockholm, Madame Inkina from Rome and others, some younger or with younger assistants in tow, all eager to crowd around and renew a relationship which, he had begun to sense, was uniquely binding to them all.

Even in the few days of the competition the entrants developed a desperate camaraderie, so that when he fell badly during his second solo he was at once surrounded by the other boys, massaging his twisted ankle, solicitously asking where it hurt and how much, commiserating with the despair which it was assumed he would be feeling since the accident would automatically rule him out of the contest. Alex felt no despair. He was still fuelled by the delight of making a dream into reality. It was enough for him to be able to dance. He was confident that he danced remarkably well, and that one day he would be exceptional.

His report commended his lovely proportions, his quality of repose and his elevation, while noting that his technique lacked precision. Cécile was among the finalists; he was watching the presentation ceremony when a tank of a woman in a floral frock barged through the crowded hall to approach him and, after a few compliments and some expressions of sympathy for his fall, asked him to point out his teacher. His grandmother, recognizing her accent, broke into the conversation in Russian. As he anticipated, the stranger reacted when she introduced herself, and when he named Madame Sedova. Grandmère immediately embarked on the recitation of their relationship in which his grandfather's name and hers were repeated as often as possible. The dark woman was evidently delighted to have had her judgement confirmed, and set off in Madame's direction at once, nodding significantly to him over her shoulder.

'Alex, you must have been a cat in your last life; when you fall it's always the right way up.' Madame bustled eagerly through the crowd which was streaming past them towards the exit doors. 'Now I can go to my grave a happy woman, Lydia. She's a teacher from home, and she has invited you before the examination committee in the summer.'

'What examination committee?'

'The examination committee of the Agrippina Vaganova Choreographic Academy in Leningrad. Obviously they're looking for some likely lads to play the stupid peasants.'

'Don't be so cruel, Julie, the boy doesn't know, why should he? Everything's changed now. But wonderful, wonderful news! If it is a genuine invitation.' Grandmère reached for Alex's arm to help her down the entrance steps of the building.

'I know they accept half a dozen foreign students in each year, and it's for real study, not indoctrination. You won't get a young Marxist back, Lydia, never fear,' Madame negotiated the steps stiffly by herself.

'I'm not worried, he likes to eat too well to be a Communist.' She gave his biceps a pinch to indicate their inconvertible substance. 'So, it seems you and I know a few tricks still?'

Alex could see high satisfaction on both faces. 'I still don't get it – what is this place?'

'The Vaganova was formerly the Leningrad Kirov Academic School, and before that the Imperial Theatre School, which for two hundred and forty years has produced all the great dancers in classical ballet, including, we cannot deny it, Kusminskaya my friend and myself.'

'And my grandfather?'

235

'Yes, naturally. And that fool Nieloshevskaya, trainer of the cart horse who just won the gold medal which our Cécile deserved a thousand times more, but let's not criticize, back to work. Yes, yes, it's a marvellous opportunity, if they accept you. But I can't have you disgracing me in front of people who actually know what they're doing, instead of just pretending. Stand up, don't slouch. Seven years too late to be a dancer, you can't afford to waste a minute now.'

CHAPTER 8
Buckinghamshire, 1979

'Oh fucking infinity!' Hermione had stepped on a sharp plastic bat's wing lying on the polished eighteenth-century flagstone floor of her sister's country kitchen. 'Why can't these fucking children put their fucking toys away!'

'Because they're boys, dear. Boys destroy, it's a rule of nature.' Her grandmother, following her in from the garden with a basket of herb clippings, paused to retrieve the rest of the intergalactic vampire transport and throw it into a basket. It was a handsome Tuscan willow basket placed in the corner of the kitchen by Bianca to receive the boys' hideous toys and so preserve the aesthetic standard of the room. 'And with each extra boy the destruction increases exponentially, so three boys destroy nine times as much as one. That's a law of mathematics.'

'Mathematics. Hot, acid, yang, left-brain – forget it.' Hermione massaged her bare foot, tangling irritably with the fringes of her red Indian skirt. 'What are we doing with all this, Bianca?'

'Dill on the chopping board, mint by itself in a jar of water and the thyme can be tied and hung up to dry in the larder.' Bianca came in last, her basket piled high with red and white currants, trailing wearily already although it was only halfway through the bright May morning. 'Can't you put your shoes on?'

'I like to go bare-foot on the earth, it's good because there's nothing to stop the energy flowing up into your spine.'

'Which jar, darling?' Charlotte paused in front of an array of Victorian preserve pots, French *confit* containers and bright modern spongeware.

'The old majolica if it's there.'

The garden's bounty was swiftly disposed about the spacious room, the proper living touch to complete the day's set-dressing of the kitchen.

'So how many has Lovat invited for the weekend this time?' Hermione lived in open-mouthed wonder at her sister's life. Since Bianca was buttressed by every possible luxury and permanently unhappy, she offered reassuring proof that materialism was spiritual death.

'Six. And Joe and Shona are coming for Saturday dinner. And your Russian friend from Paris – the one who does icons and Fabergé, I've forgotten his name.'

'Oh I say – you don't mean Kolya Kusminsky?' Charlotte clapped her hands together over her heart, partly a gesture of joyful anticipation and partly because she was wounded that the young could so carelessly trample the memories of her own youth. 'Kolya's not just a friend, he was my baby! I looked after him as a tiny child all those long years ago! You can't imagine how precious he is to me – why, we escaped the Revolution together. Why didn't someone tell me he was coming? It will be such a treat to see him again. We haven't met since – oh, it must be ten, twelve years. Little Kolya, just imagine. You remember him, surely? He used always to come and have tea with me when he was in London. I know you've met him.'

'Well, I know he was tall and smelt exotic. Ten years ago I was pregnant, my memory's a little hazy. Lovat just saw him in the saleroom a couple of days ago.'

'This will be a wonderful occasion! Wonderful!' Her grandmother was childlike in her eagerness.

'Wonderful if you don't have to cook for them all, maybe. Lovat asked him because he's got some Americans coming next week to look for Fabergé. And the Bainbridges because his uncle's just popped off in Grasse and left them some Braques, and the Llewellyns because he buys for some Japanese bank. Hugh to help clinch the deals, Joe because he thinks Lovat's a living god. I get my sister to stop me going mad.' Making more noise than necessary in order to express her annoyance, Bianca dragged a high stool to the scrubbed pine table which filled the centre of the room and began the laborious business of dragging a fork down the currant stems to free the fruit for her famous red-and-white-currant compote.

'Wow, those look delicious!' Hermione picked out a choice stem of berries and ate them in one gulp. 'I should eat more food like this, raw and light, I'm too *kapha*, I need stimulation. What are we making for dinner?' Without any evident urgency, Hermione pulled another fork from the drawer and drifted across the room to help.

'Home-cured gravadlax, saddle of venison, gooseberry sorbet with elderflower cordial . . . Mrs Harris! That reminds me, have we put the flowers I cut yesterday in the porcelain planter in the music room?' The housekeeper, who was sorting the boys' shoes into the rack in the boot room by the kitchen door, reassured her. 'Oh good, and you gave them a drink afterwards? Good.' Bianca put her hands to her head as if to grope for reminders of everything else that needed to be done before the guests arrived. 'And the American percale sheets are on in the bamboo room? And the clock in the garden room is back from the menders and we've wound it up? Have I given you a cheque for the pool engineer? And am I picking Orlando up from school today or is he being dropped off?'

239

'I bet life wasn't as complicated as this in old St Petersburg, eh, Charlotte?' Hermione watched a currant fly off her fork into the far corner of the room and decided not to retrieve it. The mice were part of the ecosystem too.

'Everyone had armies of servants – and God knows how some of those people would have lived otherwise. A man in the equivalent of Lovat's position would have had at least twenty staff.' Charlotte fetched a basket of clean washing and began pairing up the boys' socks.

'And when your Kolya was a little boy did he rip up his toys and drop bits of them on the floor?' Hermione's foot was still smarting.

'Yes, but it wasn't even my job to pick them up. There was a children's nurse and two maids under her. Of course they didn't have all these labour-saving devices. Someone had to wash everything by hand. But Madame would never have considered even coming into the kitchen. There wasn't all this pressure to be a mistress of all the domestic arts. Even when they went to the dacha and played at simple life in the country she never lifted a finger. That wasn't her place in life.'

'Lucky Madame.' Bianca had resumed her seat and was gazing at the pile of prepared fruit with a dull expression, wondering what task it was now demanding of her. After a few moments she got up again, fetched a copper preserving pan and piled the berries into it. Charlotte put the laundry aside and went to rub her granddaughter's shoulders, noticing their boniness.

'Why don't you leave this and go and lie down? If a woman can't rest when she's pregnant, then when can she?'

'I'm only three months pregnant and there's so much to do. I have to finish something in the studio this afternoon, as well.' Bianca knew that Charlotte and Hermione between them would not prepare the food to anything like the standard she needed. Mrs Harris helped, but the cook lived out, and would not appear until the next day for the major dinner of the weekend. Lovat liked the personal touch of offering his guests food prepared by his wife and nobody, in truth, took as much trouble as she did over things. 'Lovat will be in a bad temper if everything isn't perfect, you know what he's like. I don't look tired, do I?'

'No, darling, you never look tired, heaven knows why. Sad, maybe . . .'

Bianca sighed. Charlotte, as usual, was correct and was, in her subtle way, implying much more than she said. A heavy melancholy had crept up on Bianca in the last few weeks, leeching away her energy and blunting her emotions. It seemed impossible that she should be sad with so many blessings in her life, so she had hardly acknowledged the feeling to herself.

Since their existence was a picture of perfection, few people understood that Bianca and Lovat Whitburn had been waging war against each other for years. Both were doing only what was expected of a man and a woman, she raising their family and he providing handsomely for it, so they could not be faulted – indeed, the family was frequently held up among their acquaintance as an excellent example of folk who had everything.

They had a London house, in Holland Park, a few streets away from their newlywed apartment in terms of distance but a world apart in affluence. They had a farmhouse in the Dordogne, with a *pigeonnier* and a swimming pool. There was also a pool at their home in Buckinghamshire, where Bianca and the children lived most of the time. Parts of the house dated from the fourteenth century and the garden was famed among horticulturalists and open to them for two days each year. In all these homes they had antique furniture, pedigree pets and contented domestic staff. Three cars, his, hers and the housekeepers', ferried personnel to and fro.

They had three sons; Tom was gangly, dark-haired and quiet, Benedict was round-faced and mad about football and the youngest, at the age of five, was Orlando, hyperactive and given to climbing any solid-seeming object he encountered. For each boy the parents, after careful discussion of his temperament and abilities, had selected an individual educational path, so Tom and Benedict attended different prep schools in Oxford. Orlando ran riot with their blessing in the village school, saw a child psychologist weekly and was destined for a smart academy for under-achievers.

They had two careers. Lovat was a director of Berrisford's, and the effective leader of the firm. Shortly after he arrived at the dusty, cluttered offices off Jermyn Street, Sir John Crawford-Pitt, gasping with indignation at the size of his latest tax demand and 'bloody socialists hellbent on bleeding this country to death', summoned him and asked him to sell the entire contents of his gallery.

'I'm not a rich man,' the baronet had whined as he watched his paintings disappear into packing crates. 'I've got nothing in the bank, live off an overdraft like everybody else. All I've got is what my father left me, and what his father left him. Now I've got to sell it all off and what for? So that I can afford to die and leave something to my son, while the government pays the bloody dustmen to go on strike.'

It was Berrisford's most important collection to date, and it established the firm immediately in the international arena. Lovat grasped at once that Sir John was only one minor representative of a whole section of British society whose wealth was being pillaged by the government, and who

needed sympathetic, but not overly scrupulous, help in realizing their assets. He also proved to have an almost infallible
instinct for fakes.

'That husband of yours is a wizard,' Hugh Berrisford told
his daughter. 'It's not natural, the way he can smell out a
dud in thirty seconds. We had an African bronze in today
valued at fifty thousand and you know what the boy did?
Took a paperclip off my desk and scratched it, classic trick
to check the depth of the patina. He didn't know that, he'd
be the first to say he knows fuck-all about bronze from
Africa or anywhere, but he just had an instinct and he was
dead right.'

Bianca received this judgement badly. It seemed to her
that Lovat was manoeuvring himself into a position in
which he had her whole family in his power.

Within a year he had persuaded Hugh to add a tax adviser
to their staff. Berrisford's rapidly became known as
champions of the beleaguered estate owners, the Scarlet
Pimpernels who would rescue aristocrats from the penal tax
regime. Five years later they also became what Lovat termed
'poachers turned gamekeepers', and were employed to advise
the Inland Revenue on valuing works of art offered in
settlement of taxes.

Lovat, while spending half his time abroad and almost
every evening at business meetings, refused to have it be said
that he had in any way oppressed Bianca by denying her the
opportunity for artistic self-fulfilment. Hugh and Olivia,
equally, did not consider a full-time housewife an appropriate daughter for them. Among their acquaintance they
selected the curator of the metalwork collection at the
Victoria and Albert Museum as the right mentor. While she
lived in London Bianca drove to his office in Kensington
three mornings a week, to watch him run his nervous,

tapering fingers over Saxon silver and art deco enamel as if to divine their provenance by dowsing. He had a stammer, and her main function was to make his telephone calls for him. The work was interesting and pleasant, but not of her choosing.

When Orlando arrived, and did not sleep for more than ten minutes at a stretch during his first two years, she had an ideal exit excuse. Calling for space, peace and clean air, she moved the family to the country and prepared to retreat into domesticity again. Then there was the studio, and the expectant faces asking, 'Now what are you going to do with yourself?'

Guiltily, she cast about for a new medium to disguise her limitations, and hit upon collage. Lovat brought people to see the work, and as if her own creations were plotting against her, it began to sell. She composed a series of pictures in cut paper, wire and papier mâché on the theme of mothers, rounded, grinning fertile figures with big breasts and bellies enclosing children in their curves. Being amusing, feminist and prettily coloured, they were very popular and a small gallery at the end of their street in London had offered her an exhibition as soon as she had enough work finished.

All the things which they owned were intended to demonstrate their own personal excellence. They themselves were convinced by their possessions that they were whole and contented. When Lovat drove his Ferrari with its interior of tan leather and birch veneer through the gateway and the vista of his house, its ancient brick front smiling amiably down on the village from the knoll, he felt soothed as if by a mother's touch and the internal void in his life was temporarily filled. When he picked out the spot where the helicopter pad would be built it evaporated all the doubts he felt about the corporate development strategy which he had manoeuvred his father-in-law and co-directors into accepting. When Bianca saw her boys run into school in their specifically preferred clothes, uniform for Tom, denim for Benedict and miniature American football jacket for Orlando, she had the full experience of being a good mother, a warm, powerful satisfaction which the actual acts of mothering did not bring her.

Nevertheless, the whole accumulation of their goods was the pile of armaments for their personal war. Even their children were acts of aggression. Bianca's unintentional first offensive had been Benedict, and seeing how disturbed Lovat had been by his unplanned conception, and how much acclaim and attention every birth attracted, and how she could buy time out of the family's obsession with achievement, she had conceived babies at points of crisis in their marriage. For Orlando she had made a ritual of throwing her daily contraceptive pill down the waste disposal unit in the kitchen every morning as soon as Lovat left for work. Three years later she had taken to flicking it into the compost heap on her morning tour of the garden – she had conceived as readily as ever, but miscarried at seventeen weeks. For the baby she was expecting now she had popped the pills down the ancient well in the stable yard. The only person who knew that the babies had not been accidents was her sister.

'Hasn't he ever suspected about you being pregnant again?' Hermione asked as soon as Charlotte left them to make some telephone calls and they were alone in the low-beamed kitchen, with its decorative baskets, oak carpentry, stainless-steel *batterie de cuisine* and hand-painted modern ceramics. 'I mean, four accidents? You aren't thick, or anything.'

'He may have, but what can he do? He can't make me get rid of them.' Bianca smiled at the quince she was peeling for her quince jelly, the most sought-after preserve in the county.

'Although he certainly tried this time. We had a hell of a row.'

Hermione picked up a knife, selected one of the speckled yellow fruit and gazed at it thoughtfully. 'He's full of anger, Lovat. You can see it in his face. Do you notice he's always covering his heart *chakra*, always walling up his emotions? Too much pitta, he ought to eat whole grains and vegetables, cool out, balance all that ambition. There's a lot of negative energies in there.'

'Well he let them out last night, sure enough. We were arguing on the phone for hours. Do you know what really pisses me off?' She quartered the fruit and threw the pieces into a pan of water. 'What really annoys me is he talks like it's all to do with me, as if I'm spontaneously conceiving all these children by myself. He's never once asked me what I'm doing about contraception, not once in eleven years. If he doesn't want any more children there *is* something *he* could do about it, but I know he won't. Men are so weak, aren't they? The minute they get into bed they just want to fuck.'

'Every time?'

'Well, now we live down here only at the weekends, thank God. But no question of laying off just because I happen to be superfertile and he doesn't want any more kids.'

'Well, at least you know he isn't fucking around in London while little wifey keeps the home fires burning in the country. That's the usual set-up, isn't it?'

Bianca paused, wearily pressing her free hand into the small of her back although she was not nearly pregnant enough for it to be aching. 'He might be. I don't know what he does. Maybe he's just screwing me in case I suspect something if he stops. You haven't heard anything, have you?'

'I don't gossip, it's just circulating negativity. Anyway,

246

what would I hear down on the farm?' Hermione was about to steer the conversation towards her own concerns when she caught a cast of genuine anxiety in her sister's face. 'Look, I'm sure he isn't screwing around, he's always with Hugh and Olivia. Whenever I call them he's there.'

'Sometimes I think he's turned into the son our father never had.' Bianca looked reassured. 'Isn't it odd my husband should get on far better with my parents than I do? I suppose you're right, they wouldn't tolerate him playing around, I'm sure. Maybe he ought to have an affair. He couldn't get away with just sticking it into some other woman the way he does with me. Twice a day, the same thing every time. Change would be as good as a rest.'

'Twice a day! Still? Tell you what, let's do a life-swap. You'd love Seumas, he only wants it once a month.'

'Once a month? Is he OK? I mean . . .' To her sister, Hermione was a mass of shimmering sensuality. Her opulent body was always in motion, buttocks rolling, breasts oscillating, thighs like pillows inviting repose. She could not imagine a man not desiring Hermione.

'He says his energy is like really low. I've got him eating Ayurvedic, so that'll help. He's trying to meditate to raise some zap. He calls it stroking the python. Pumping up the life force from the earth into the spinal chord through *chakras*. You have to see your body as a channel, open it and get it like lined up to receive . . .'

'I'd try stroking something else if I were you.'

Hermione sensed that her sister's tolerance for mysticism was minimal at this moment. 'So why doesn't Lovat want any more kids? You love them. You can afford them.'

Bianca paused, wiping her hands on her plain white chef's apron. It wrapped around her in a tight sheaf. After three pregnancies her body had a rangy, emptied look, its bones

247

prominent and the hollows below them deep. Without clothes, she reminded herself of Picasso's goats. Running around after the boys kept her thin, and she had no real interest in clothes. Her jeans were always loose at the waist, worn with plain shirts or T-shirts designed by old friends.

'I do love them, and Lovat loves them in a way. He loves them because they belong to him, that's all. But he doesn't love them as children, and all this . . .' She waved her arm around the kitchen, indicating the plastic cups, the fruit juice and the hamburger buns, the basket of toys, all the detritus of family living. 'He loves his sons but he hates the way of life they impose on us. Actually I think it disgusts him. He always was too bloody immaculate to change a nappy, my husband.'

'And you're really into it, aren't you?' Hermione hitched up her flowing Indian-print skirt and sat on the table top. 'You really dig being identified with the infant level of consciousness. You are Demeter, the nurturer of new life, finding fulfilment in seeing the fruits of your womb grow to adulthood, Demeter whose sacred functions are so demeaned in modern life.' Goddess mythology was the discipline for which Hermione was currently radiating enthusiasm.

Hermione fell for theories the way other women fell for heartbreakers, never believing that they would let her down, each new attraction painlessly erasing the memory of the last. She believed completely that her latest inspiration would unlock every mystery of life and reward her faith by giving her whatever satisfaction she currently craved. After astrology, she had given her allegiance to transcendental meditation, EST, Celtic paganism, rolfing and Native American spiritualism. With every theory there was a diet. To date, all these various creeds had reneged on the deal, bringing insolvency to the wholefood restaurant she had opened off

Portobello Road, blights and epidemics to the organic farm she now owned in Somerset, crippling depression to her significant other, Seumas, and malignant bureaucracy to the Social Security office which supported them both.

'Oh give it a rest, Herm.' Bianca smiled wearily at her sister. 'I can't stand all that goddess stuff before lunch.'

'You're resisting!' She stabbed the air with a forefinger, her unrestrained breasts quivering under her rust-coloured T-shirt. Resisting was the worst sin which Hermione recognized. 'You must let *go*, Bea. Just go with what you are, be who you are. What you resist persists, it'll keep coming up in your life. You are a wellspring of the life force, the fullness of the moon, the ripeness of autumn, what you should do is just *be* that, not chase after ego-rewards . . .' Contemptuously she dropped the one fruit which she had prepared into the pan already filled by her sister.

'The boys are all I chase after.'

'No, no, don't you see, I mean all this, the house, the garden, the other houses. Possessions aren't for you, Bianca. Possessions are a trap, a drain on your psychic energy . . . just think of all the time you spend worrying about them, arranging them, getting them cleaned, mended, serviced . . .'

With strength developed in nine years of hauling children around, Bianca carried the heavy pan of quinces to the scarlet double Aga. She pulled the tray of warmed sugar from its slowest oven and tipped the crystals into the pan, reached for a comically large wooden spoon and stirred the mixture. The thought was in her mind that although her sister talked crap most of the time, it was sometimes very accurate crap.

After lunch she crossed the stable yard and went into the converted barn which housed her studio. Fat female forms cavorted everywhere, their comical round eyes depicted in glass beads. She had some new blue ones for the picture that lay on the worktable, waiting only for its eyes to be completed.

The glue had hardened in the end of its tube and she found a pin to clear the blockage. At the first attempt her hand slipped and she stabbed herself. Ignoring the pain and the tiny drop of blood oozing from her arm, she picked up her tweezers and began to glue the beads to the collage. When the eye was complete she sat back, accidentally smearing blood across the figure's breasts. She wanted to cry. She drew a deep breath and leaned forward again to begin the second eye.

It occurred to her that she should try to remove the bloodstain before it set, but before she could do anything the entire field of her vision blurred and she found that tears were pouring from her eyes. A grimace distorted her mouth painfully. She was weeping, silently at first and then with great gasping sobs which echoed back from the roof beams. She threw down the tweezers in anger, chipping the figure's arm. The picture was ruined. She threw it across the room then sat down on the floor and howled, all the time wondering, with a part of her mind, what in the world she was doing.

'What in the world are you doing?' It was her husband, in one of his dark blue business suits, standing in the studio doorway. Even in her distress she noticed that his latest affectation was a gold Georgian fob chain running from his lapel buttonhole to his top pocket. 'Bianca, are you all right?'

'I don't know.' The question seemed impossible. She could not be all right, because she was crying and screaming. Lovat expected an explanation. He always expected things.

'You must know. What is it, tell me?' He picked his way

across the litter of offcuts on the floor and knelt beside her.
'Has someone upset you? Tell me.'

'No one's upset me. Why must I know, I don't have to
know.'

'Of course you don't, it's OK, everything's OK.' He put
his hand on her shoulder but she shrugged it off at once.

'You're talking to me like a child.'

'I'm sorry, I didn't mean to do that.'

'Yes, you did. You always mean everything. Why don't
you go and talk to your own children for a change?'

Now he waited by her side in silence and after five minutes
or so she felt calmer and was able to stand up and accept his
handkerchief to dry her face.

'You're tired,' he announced as if it was evidence he had
just discovered which conclusively proved a theory he had
been advancing for some time. 'Early to bed tonight.'

'We can't, we've got guests, remember? Why are you so
early anyway?'

Normally, Lovat did not appear on Friday evening until
around 6 p.m., in time to wash and change before receiving
his weekend guests. The habit of entertaining Berrisford's
clients was something which Bianca had resisted with every
argument she could command, but as in everything else
Lovat's logic seemed invincible.

It had been an escalation typical of their style of conflict.
In the early days of their marriage she had tried to avoid
going out to restaurants with business associates, saying that
with Tom and Benedict both of pre-kindergarten age she
was too tired. Lovat had considerately suggested that they
entertain at home instead. This in turn had necessitated a
larger house, and grander furniture, and more elaborate
meals, and a larger salary to be earned by Lovat, meaning
longer hours and yet more entertaining if he was ever to be

at home at all. Bianca had pleaded that with the addition of the ever-wakeful Orlando the dinner parties were too much strain, and that with three active boys she would prefer to live in the country. Lovat's counter-move was the weekend houseparty, without which, he most reasonably said, he would need to remain in London and never see his family from one month's end to the next.

Now invitations to Kintbourne Manor were boasted of in all the art capitals of the world. Lovat Whitburn was becoming celebrated for the skill with which he picked guests who would be impressed by his standard of hospitality, and by each other, and by the seeming intimacy of being invited into the heart of his family. He was also famous for the cunning with which he would choose a moment after a game of tennis, or during a match between visitors and the village cricket team, or while walking through the orchard at midnight before departing to bed, to plant ideas in his guests' minds. Two or three times a year he hosted sumptuous parties; they began with the village brass band – the whole rural community was slowly being sucked into his field of influence – and ended with fireworks. There would be *son et lumière*, recitals by renowned artists or a discotheque in a marquee on the lower lawn, according to the composition of the guests. Bianca found herself acclaimed as the hostess at these glorious fetes, but she resented the annexation of the home, her territory, to the business, which was Lovat's.

He had become precociously mature; a tall man when they married, he was now big in proportion, his face fuller and becoming grooved deeply with lines. His eyes were always serious and the droop of his eyelids, which she had once thought sexy, now gave his face a supercilious cast. His dark hair was short and disciplined and even when he resumed jeans or wore tennis clothes at the weekend his dress had a formal air and was always pristine, laundered by the housekeepers under Bianca's command. He was a fine-looking, rather glamorous man, and Bianca knew other women found him attractive, but for some years now she had been immune to his appeal.

'You're home early,' she accused him again.

'Yes. I wanted to talk to you before everyone got here.'

The barn had a new concrete floor and a gallery over half its area, with an industrial steel staircase leading up to it. Bianca sat on the third step, her arms folded across her stomach.

'What do you want to talk to me about, Lovat?'

'Well, it's like this, love. We had a bit of a row last night about this new baby, didn't we?'

She nodded, giving him no help. 'You said I should get rid of it, if I remember rightly.'

'I didn't mean it; I was angry. But I've been thinking about us and – our life and everything. Are you happy?'

'I ought to be happy, shouldn't I? I've got everything a woman could possibly want.'

'No, but are you?'

The feeling of being backed into a corner, of a trap closing around her sentence by sentence, point by point, began to take hold. She felt that she had given herself away by weeping.

'I can't be happy if I'm sitting on the floor crying, can I? Maybe it's just my hormones or something.'

He was walking slowly around the studio, looking at her collages without seeing them, his arms swinging awkwardly away from his sides. 'I was wondering if maybe we could go and see somebody.'

'We see people all the time. And who would have us to stay with three boys?'

253

'No, I mean a counsellor or something.' Now he was standing still, grinding one fist into the palm of the other hand and speaking brusquely because he was annoyed to have to operate in this messy emotional area where it seemed impossible ever to get a straight answer. He had known before Bianca herself that something in her had changed. For the past five years he had felt terrible loneliness in his own home – whichever one he was occupying it made no difference, because he defined his home as the place where his wife was. Bianca, the person he wanted to rely upon to hear his anxiety, see his weakness, to heal his wounds and restore him simply by her attention, had become inaccessible to him. It was as if she had stepped behind a glass wall, where she looked the same but he could not touch her.

'What do you mean, a counsellor? A marriage guidance counsellor?'

'Not necessarily marriage guidance, I think there are other kinds of counsellor. Or a therapist maybe . . .'

'You mean you think I'm mad and you want me to see a psychiatrist?' She could conceive of only one motive for this suggestion and it burst out immediately. 'What you mean is you want me to see someone who'll talk me into having an abortion, isn't that it?'

'No, no, that isn't it, you're misunderstanding me.' He felt helpless. It was impossible to win an argument with someone who at once pushed your words to the limit of their logical meaning and used them as an accusation against you. Lovat's mother had believed that it was a wife's duty to agree with her husband. Lovat thought he believed that it was a wife's duty to retain the capacity for independent thought, but he had never expected Bianca to disagree with him. 'I just thought you weren't happy and . . .'

'You mean I'm not making you happy? What does it take

to make you happy, Lovat? I bring up our family, I run our homes, I do my pictures and even get people to buy them. I do everything I'm supposed to do and everything you ask . . .' She stood up, hitched her jeans over her hipbones and shook back her hair, which was long and held off her face with combs. For something to occupy her hands, she pulled one comb out and repositioned it. 'I don't know what more I can do. Except have an abortion, which I'm not going to do and neither you nor anyone else is going to bully me into it. How can you even think of it when you look at our kids? Think of killing one of the boys and chopping him into bits and throwing the bits down a drain – maybe you'll understand how I feel.'

'You're getting emotional. I didn't say that.' Now he was desperate to regain control of the encounter. 'I admit, I don't want us to have another child, but I respect how you feel. And I care about you, Bianca, you must know I do. I know you're not happy . . .'

She stood up and brushed the dirt off her jeans with angry slaps. 'I'm pregnant, that's all. It's normal to be emotional when you're pregnant.'

He glared at her. Arguments based on female biology were invincible, since she could claim superior knowledge. 'As you wish,' he muttered, retreating backwards towards the work table. Turning, he took in the smashed picture and the scattered tools. 'What happened here?'

'Nothing.'

'What are these bits of picture everywhere?'

'Don't *bully* me, Lovat. You're always bullying me.'

'I was only asking what happened. Here's a picture been smashed to pieces – anyone would be curious.'

'It's none of your business what happened.' Decisively she made for the door, controlling her shaking voice. 'And I'd be grateful if you stopped looking around for any more evidence that I'm crazy. Your dinner is cooking in the kitchen. Your children are playing in the garden. Your rugs are straight, your furniture is polished, and your wife will be dressed and smiling by the time your guests get here, so there's nothing for you to worry about, is there?'

She marched out of the studio and across the yard to the house, leaving Lovat to sit on the edge of the table and reflect. He did not like things to go wrong, especially when there seemed to be no obvious way of setting them right.

Their bedroom and its adjacent suites occupied almost all the second floor of the house, with separate bathrooms and dressing rooms contrived so that Mr and Mrs Whitburn could prepare to entertain without being obliged to speak to each other. An hour later Bianca was standing on the west terrace in a cream linen dress by some new Japanese design genius, feeling the evening breeze lift her freshly washed hair.

The car bringing Kusminsky was the first to arrive. A young man with dark curly hair got out to help his companion. Bianca took in the black glacé kid trousers and the gold bracelet, cursed under her breath and dived back into the house to call the kitchen on the internal telephone.

'Mrs Harris, lay an extra place and send someone up to make the bamboo room ready for two not one. Someone's brought his boyfriend down.'

She was outside again, smiling and serene in a few seconds, in time to see the stooped figure in a camel coat emerge from the car.

'You must be Kolya Kusminsky, how good of you to come. Of course I remember you from many years back. We've always heard so much about you.'

'But how good it is to be here, Madame Berrisford. How

256

kind you are to invite me. So beautiful!' He straightened his back with difficulty, leaning over his silver-topped stick, and looked up at the rich brick walls glowing in the evening light, early roses tumbling from the trellises, swallows darting out from beneath the eaves. He had the padded face of a man who liked to live well, his small mouth overhung by once-cherubic cheeks. 'And where is she, my Nounou?'

'Here I am, here I am.' Charlotte came running from the house, covering the distance rapidly in short stiff strides, her blue silk trousers flapping. *'Comme tu es bienvenu, mon petit.'* They embraced, laughing, for although she called him her little one he towered over her, and now that he was nearly seventy and ill, and she, although her face was riven with lines, was fit and in her eighties, they appeared to be the same age. 'You have lost weight, are you eating, my dear? You were such a big man . . .'

'Too big, the doctor says.' He patted the slack front of his shirt with a rueful hand. 'But I am well looked after, Nounou. Not as well as when I was with you, of course, but as well as an old man could be. Now, you remember Etienne Sokolov.' The young man stepped forward and shook hands with both women. Bianca caught his bright, bird-like eye, which seemed to acknowledge that his position was equivocal, and that people might think ill of him for befriending a much richer, much older man, but that in himself his conscience was clear.

'Come inside, my dear, come and sit with me and we can gossip in Russian before everyone else arrives.' Charlotte took his free arm and Etienne supported the old man on the other side as he proceeded over the uneven stones towards the french windows.

'Heart is not too bad, they tell me, but arteries are terrible. Especially in legs. Cigarettes!' As if to illustrate the point, he

257

paused and coughed violently. His voice was heavily accented and each sentence closed with a wheeze like an old harmonium. 'They told me to give up smoking, but I would rather die happy man with cigarette in my hand than miserable one with no pleasures left.'

'Nonsense! Don't talk about dying, not to me anyway . . .'

At dinner he was quickly installed as the star of the table. As soon as they sat down he spread his napkin over his knees, smoothed it out without speaking for a few moments, then looked up and fixed Lovat in his watery, old man's stare.

'Now, young Monsieur, grandson-in-law to my Nounou, what would you say if I told you I had heard where is one of lost Fabergé eggs?'

'I'd say I'd like to see it,' Lovat replied with simple directness, forking a slice of fish into his mouth. His habit was to eat very fast, as if begrudging the time wasted. 'I've some folk coming from America next week whờ might be interested if it's genuine. Which one is it supposed to be?'

'The Rosebud. It would be good one to find. Authenticated Imperial design, made 1895, actually Tsar's wedding gift to his wife. There is photograph, in Wartski archives, published 1952. It's quite in modern taste too, very beautiful, not too decorated, gold laurel wreaths, diamond arrows, ribbons . . . but I haven't seen it myself yet. Armenian friend in Paris says he knows someone who has it.' Content to have stimulated interest, he turned to his plate and prodded the gravadlax with his fork.

'What's your instinct about it?' Lovat's plate was now empty and the beam of his attention was fully trained on the old man.

'Good, I think. I've dealt with Vartanian many years, he doesn't waste time. Yes, good, good instinct.'

'He knows how to tease, doesn't he?' At the far end of the table, Bianca whispered to her grandmother and was heard with a sudden bright smile.

'What does it mean, a lost Fabergé egg?' The wife of the heir to the Braques was a round-eyed blonde rumoured to have been a stripper and a Scientologist before her marriage.

'Decorated Easter eggs were a Russian custom. Ordinary people painted ordinary eggs, but the rich had them made in gold and jewels. Fabergé was the court jeweller in St Petersburg before the Revolution; the eggs he made for the Tsar . . . I suppose they're the most precious single objects in the world,' Lovat replied, taking excessive care not to sound patronizing. He misjudged his tone; the woman was accustomed to condescending flirtation from all men and was mildly insulted by what she saw as lack of interest from the youngest heterosexual male at the table.

'But if they're so precious how can they be lost?' She directed this inquiry towards Hugh, whose reserve had been visibly thawed by their conversation earlier.

'An immense number of objects went missing at the time of the Revolution.' Hugh, much taken with his companion, was delighted to have the opportunity to expound. 'Luckily with jewellery and with the eggs the people who made them kept excellent records, with drawings even, so we know what was made. Many treasures were simply destroyed by people too ignorant to know what they were doing.'

'Or they hated the aristocratic class and wanted just to smash everything to do with our way of life. Very sad. Perversion of human instincts.' The fish, tender as it was, seemed too resistant for Kusminsky to cut it. Etienne, at his side, took the plate and used his own knife in a few unobtrusive movements.

Olivia's gold earrings tinkled as she flexed her long neck

like a heron and prepared to pull the conversation back on course. She never classed herself with her daughters as a woman whose allocated role was fretting about domestic operations. Instead, when she chose, she allied herself with the men in steering the conversation into profitable channels. 'But Kolya, the jewellery – small, easily carried ... wasn't a lot of it simply looted?'

'Undoubtedly it was,' her husband continued. They were a well-trained team. 'And not only by the workers during the Revolution. In the Twenties the Russian government was desperate for cash, and they just emptied all the bank vaults and sent boxes of stuff out to be auctioned.'

Kusminsky nodded in agreement, the candlelight shining on his high, bare forehead. His hair had thinned to a border of white around his head. 'I went myself as young man to sales all over Germany. Priceless, marvellous things just heaped into fish boxes, with sailors or soldiers guarding. When you collected what you had bought they would give you receipt and you saw they could hardly write. And they started gold at good prices because they recognized it, but jewellery they had no idea about – "small items set with coloured stones", catalogue paper might say, and they meant diamonds and emeralds!'

Now the room was hanging on his words, so the old man paused to finish eating and let the plates be cleared. The conversation broke up around the table while the venison was brought in and served. Bianca confirmed automatically that it was cooked, glazed and decorated to perfection and watched the diners prepare to consume it. They seemed very small, like actors on a distant stage, and their voices, talking three languages, were muffled.

Her mother, she noticed, was unusually animated. Olivia always looked the same to her, impossibly polished, with a predatory alertness in all her movements. Her beauty was maintained with the benefit of plastic surgery, which everyone suspected but she denied, visiting a clinic in France and calling it a holiday. Bianca felt that she did not age, but a more distant observer would have noted a little blurring of her contours, deeper lines around her eyes and a certain squaring of her lean hips. She seemed to have fewer lovers now, or to be more discreet with them. Her social strategies were still designed to elicit men's admiration, if not the men themselves, but tonight she was playing the part of a good guest, doing a fine job of drawing out Etienne. The young man had been sitting with a half smile fixed on his face throughout the meal, attentive to Kusminsky but saying little apart from a few soft words in Russian exchanged with the old man.

Olivia's girlish squeak, a wholly uncharacteristic exclamation, suddenly pierced the murmuring conversations. Bianca noticed her mother's blue eyes dart fiercely towards Lovat, demanding his attention. 'Kolya's never told Etienne the story of how he and Charlotte left St Petersburg! You know his mother was a great ballerina, I'm sure, yes. It's a wonderful tale, and quite apropos, Kolya, please, tell us again, do!'

It was clear that the old man was reluctant to retrieve this memory, but he had been trapped. Etienne's gentle smile was expectant. 'Well, I was boy seven years old,' he began, drawing in a long, rattling breath. 'And this lady and I were in Petersburg and as you know she was my governess. And it was 1917 – was it?'

'Yes, the spring, 1917.' Charlotte's oval eyes were wide with fond nostalgia. 'And it was Petrograd by then, they renamed it because they hated the Germans once the war began. And fighting was still going on in Europe and your mother had fallen ill in the South of France.'

'Kolya's father was a prince,' Olivia informed the company, a piece of vital information which she knew the old man himself could not contribute without seeming boastful. 'And high up in the government, so he knew what was going to happen.'

'He was a clever man, you know. He had foresight. Most of them had no idea.'

'Revolution had begun,' Kusminsky continued, looking down at the table top because it was too painful to talk directly to another person. 'I was little boy, to me it was all games. Soldiers, shooting, lorries going up and down our street filled with men who waved red flags. But my father said it would be safer for us to go to London, and then to Monte Carlo where my mother was.'

'He knew the Tsar was going to abdicate, you see,' Charlotte added. 'I remember him calling me into the sitting room and standing with one hand up on the stove and saying, "The Kaiser or the Reds, what a choice we have. God knows what will happen, Charlotte, but everything precious must be sent to a place of safety at once." Oh, how we had to run around, his valet and I, taking silver to the bank and his old coins to the Friendly Society.'

'This is really wild,' the Braque heiress whispered to Hugh, who inclined his ear gravely. 'These two are real living bits of history, aren't they?'

'But he didn't send everything away, did he?' Olivia clearly had an end in mind for the tale and would not rest until she had extracted it.

'What I always will remember,' Kusminsky obediently began, and then paused, coughing into his napkin. Etienne refilled his water glass and when the spasm had passed placed it in his hand, tenderly closing his slender fingers over the old man's gnarled knuckles. 'What I always remember was him coming up to the nursery with my mother's jewellery – the things she had you could not imagine, a mountain of diamonds, a king's ransom, our little room was like Aladdin's Cave – and piling it all on the table where I was eating my supper, and the women sewing it into my clothes.'

'What a romantic thing . . .' Now the young woman was totally entranced.

'It wasn't in the least romantic,' snapped Charlotte. 'It took us all night and our fingers were absolutely blistered by the time we'd finished.'

'And I was furious because she had to cut open my teddy bear – well, I had a lion actually – but she cut open his stomach to put big diamond necklace in it. Oh, I was so angry!'

There was general laughter. Bianca raised a weak smile, noticing her mother lean back to exchange a private word with Lovat.

'And do you know, to finish story, after wounding my lion who I loved so much, they still could not get necklace into him without it being easy to discover, so they decided to leave it behind. And you' – he pointed to Charlotte with his fork – 'you said that they would be sure to find safe, and that it was best to hide all the valuable things somewhere else. So down in kitchen my father himself, who never picked up hammer in his life before, made hole in wall, hid everything and put all bricks back like before. And then, when we arrived in Monte Carlo, months later after travelling in terrible danger, my mother was absolutely in rage because we did not have her necklace.'

'You were just a little boy!' Sympathy shone from every ounce of Hermione's body. She leaned forward, accidentally trailing her red silk sleeve across her plate, and touched the old man's arm. 'What a terrible trauma for you.'

'My dear, there had been war, revolution, traumas for everyone, far worse than your mother being in bad temper.' Nevertheless, he patted her hand kindly, feeling overcome by the force of the emotions stirred up by his memories.

'I don't know why my children should think that an angry mother is worse than war and revolution.' With a complacent toss of her head, which set her earrings tinkling again, Olivia reclaimed the company's attention. There was one final point which she wished the story to cover. 'Go on, Kolya, tell them what happened to the things.'

'Well, back in Russia the Bolsheviks shot my father and confiscated everything belonging to all the aristocracy and so we had nothing. First my mother mortgage our villa, then she sell jewellery, first one piece, then the next . . . very hard, very sad for my mother, she can't bear it. All memories of my father and her career and her wonderful life as young woman all disappearing. So I used to go to dealer for her, and in time our friends gave me their things to sell also, because they trusted me, I was one of them, a Russian too. So then I become dealer. I bought shop in Paris, I began proper business and so . . . well, that's my life.'

His voice faded away. Charlotte had fallen silent, all the vitality drained from her face. A pall of melancholy descended on Bianca, weighting her shoulders with guilt for having always seen her grandmother as an old woman with her own kind of hard tranquillity, and not as a tender girl compelled to love and then give up another woman's child. She felt that there had been something unseemly about the whole reminiscence, coldly drawn out by Olivia for the sake of glamorizing the Berrisford name, and probably endured by Kusminsky for the sake of getting Lovat hot for the Fabergé egg.

After dinner the company adjourned to the *toile de Jouy*

music room for coffee. Etienne helped Kusminsky upstairs to bed almost at once, pleading that the old man was exhausted but, to Bianca's eyes, protecting him from the crass curiosity of strangers.

As she turned after bidding them goodnight she saw from the corner of her eye her mother leading Lovat outside. Olivia had taken hold of his arm, her hand under his elbow, and was again speaking confidentially, her mouth close to his ear. The picture was one she had seen many times before, whenever her mother had been cutting out a man she wanted from the herd. Perhaps now she wanted Lovat.

Once the thought had entered Bianca's mind it took hold like a brush fire. Her memories swiftly arranged themselves to prove that her mother and her husband were lovers and perhaps had been for years. She felt pain, and panic, and wanted desperately to find somewhere to run away to where these terrible feelings could not follow her.

A tiny voice told her that she was being absurd, that the suggestion had only been born of her weak and distressed condition. Needing to hear a rational opinion before flames consumed her sanity, she looked wildly around the room for Hermione but her sister was nowhere to be seen. Charlotte also had gone to bed. Her father was standing in front of the low fire, talking to the two remaining men. Stella Bainbridge sat on one of the small sofas asking the banker's wife where she bought her clothes with a creditable show of lively interest. Breaking into either conversation would seem odd, and the longer she stood there in the doorway the greater the risk that this too would appear bizarre.

'If you'll excuse me, everyone, I'll be off to bed now.' She noticed that these important business associates for whom she had so laboriously picked currants that morning were barely moved by the loss of her company. 'My mother seems to have stolen my husband, but you'll say goodnight for me, won't you, Hugh?'

As she walked across to her father, feeling as if she were walking on thin ice, she took care to look at him directly. Perhaps if there was some truth in the awful random suspicion now trapped in her mind his face would show it. And he turned towards her sharply, looking almost frightened.

'Certainly, my dear. You've had a long day, let me take care of everything now.' He had left the fireplace and was walking towards her. 'Is there anything to be done in the kitchen for tomorrow? Has Mrs Harris left?' With a graceful 'Excuse me one moment' to the Llewellyns and the Bainbridges he left the room with his daughter.

'You look very tired,' he told her as they crossed the softly lit hall. She stumbled over the corner of a rug and he caught her arm. Because Lovat believed that fitted carpets would never be found in a gentleman's home, the floors were of oak boards or stone, uneven and highly polished, covered with oriental rugs of even more irregular plane.

'I *am* very tired.'

'You are all right, Bianca? I worry about you being stuck down here in the country by yourself all week.'

'I'm with the boys, that's hardly by myself.'

'They're children . . .'

'I like children. You know I'm having another one, don't you?' In the pell-mell routine of her own family she had grown careless of details and could not remember whether she had broken the news to her parents or not.

He halted and suddenly put an arm around her shoulders. Nobody could make an embrace seem as threatening as her father.

'My dear, no I didn't. Lovat hasn't mentioned it. But it's early yet, surely, you're as thin as a stick . . .'

'Don't *you* start telling me to get rid of it. God, why do all men hate children?'

'Bianca, I would never dream of intruding on your personal affairs in such a way. You know I believe that every woman has the right to control her own biology to the limits of what science . . .'

'Hugh, I know what you believe, and I know what you say you believe and what you do are quite different things. Now please let me go, I'm tired. Goodnight.' She reached up to give him a dry kiss on the cheek and climbed the stairs rapidly without looking back.

She pretended sleep when Lovat came to bed, then lay beside him thinking back through the years of their marriage. In time she recalled the day Lovat announced that he was going into Berrisford's, a decision she had felt ever since to be in some way a betrayal, of her and of his own ambition. She had wanted him to rescue her from her family, and instead he had merged them both into it. Maybe it had been because he wanted to be near her mother. Admiration, compliments, laughter, Olivia's coldness, the way Lovat never seemed to be on her side in anything – Bianca could find evidence in everything to prove her suspicions.

In the morning Lovat rolled over and reached for her. It was a habit of his to climb on top of her for a short, utilitarian fuck before the day began. The sheer calculation of the move disgusted her – he was never late for anything because of it. He seemed to know to the second how long it would take him to come. Would he even notice if she did not respond?

His hand was stroking her thighs, moving her on to her back, pushing her legs apart. When he felt for her clitoris a nick from his fingernail caught the head and a stab of shrivelling pain dispelled the last shred of sleepiness in her

267

mind. She shut her eyes, leaving her hands lying inert on the pillow. Now he was probing inside her. It was not a caress, just an exploration to see if she was lubricated enough to penetrate. Her opinion, if anyone had asked it, was that she was merely damp, but also cold and unexcited. Heat and juiciness would take a few minutes of attention she did not expect to receive.

The weight of his body was lifted, the fingers withdrew, there were some urgent, blind movements and then she felt the head of his penis stab inaccurately once or twice around her lips before pressing inside. The weight returned. His unshaven chin scraped her cheek. The friction became more uncomfortable as he pumped. Bianca made no movement, wondering if, with a variation of the exercises physiotherapists gave new mothers to recondition their pelvic muscles, her vagina could become capable of vomiting him out.

His average – for she had counted – was twenty-two thrusts. After the nineteenth he paused, raised himself off her a little way, and felt again for her clitoris.

'That's OK,' she muttered immediately.

'Sure?'

'Yes.' She tried to sound merely sleepy, hoping not to be asked for another explanation.

In four more thrusts it was over. He kissed her closed lips, lay still for a polite thirty seconds, then got up and went into his bathroom.

A little later Bianca went into her bathroom and looked at herself in the mirror.

'I don't think I can do that again,' she said to her reflection. There was a catch of nausea in her throat.

'Mummy, why are you talking to yourself?'

Their eldest son had presented himself in the doorway,

fully dressed in his school sports kit and apparently washed, a cricket ball in one hand. She realized that she ought to feel worried about the boys; if she left Lovat, or he left her, they might be expected to suffer. Here was Tom, self-possessed as ever but only a child, and yet she felt numb. Love had become impossible. The only sensation her son aroused at that moment was a weary curiosity about the purpose of his visit so early in the morning.

'I felt like talking to myself. What is it, darling?'

'There's net practice this morning. I forgot to tell you.'

'And you have to go?' He nodded. 'Go and ask your father to take you.'

'He says he can't.'

She suppressed a flash of rage. 'He means he won't. Can you ask Mrs Harris for me? Say I'll do breakfast.'

'OK.' He ran away, and she embarked upon the routine of the day, grateful for any trivial chore which could distract her from the bleakness of her heart.

As the day progressed, the longer she was silent the more Olivia seemed to shine. Never the kind of woman who enjoyed the company of homosexuals, she was now making much of Kusminsky and his young companion, drawing forth more memories of his boyhood during the Russian Revolution. The party drove to Newmarket for the races and she remained in their box with the old man the whole afternoon while Hugh and the younger adults scattered over the course.

Bianca drifted in the wake of Shona, who invariably found a score of cheeks to kiss at any upper-class resort within two hours of London. Joe had opened his own design consultancy five years earlier and now, at the cost of half his hair and two stone around his waist, was so successful that the company was about to go public.

'I feel absolutely cheated, darling,' Shona told everyone she met with beaming satisfaction. 'I tried to run off with a penniless artist and now he's being floated for millions. Isn't it a swizz?'

'Have I any reason to feel cheated?' Bianca asked her in a quiet moment when they were alone by the paddock rail.

'What do you mean? This is something serious, isn't it?'

'Lovat, I mean. You're in London, Shona, you hear things. I think he's having an affair.'

'My goodness, I thought you were looking a bit flat. I never hear anything about Lovat except how well he's doing. He and Joe hardly see each other nowadays, although my husband still worships the ground your husband walks on. Do you want me to ask around – I mean discreetly, of course.'

'Yes, if you can.'

'No trouble, consider it done. Girls must stick together.'

It was all too light, too frivolous, too far from the degree of pain she felt. A shadow had crossed Shona's open, foolish face, confirming to Bianca that there was at least a secret about her husband which others knew and she did not.

The evening was almost a replica of the last, except that Saturday's dinner was formal and old Kusminsky told tales of Paris during the Occupation. He retired with Etienne at the same time. Bianca returned to the music room, hoping to find her mother and husband still there and decorously seated far apart, but once more they were together and making their way to the terrace outside.

'Lovat. Stop.' She felt like a schoolgirl reciting melodramatic lines from a bad play. But he stopped and turned, and Olivia at his side did the same.

'What is it, Bianca? Has something happened?' Yes, there could be no doubt, there was a veil over his eyes now and he was struggling to get a note of superiority into his voice.

'Yes, I think something has happened. What exactly is going on between you and my mother?' From the corner of her eye she saw Charlotte's hand fly to her mouth.

'Nothing, love. We're just going outside for some air, that's all.'

'There's more to it than that.' The feeling of nausea which had persisted all day had vanished and Bianca felt strength flowing back into her body. She looked at Olivia and saw her mother step back, tangle her high heels in her long draped skirt of grey silk crepe, and become suddenly ugly and awkward as she struggled not to fall. Her eyes were narrowed to triangles and her whole face had taken on a set, pinched look.

'Let me get this straight – are you making some sort of accusation about me and Olivia?'

'Yes, that's right, that's what I'm doing.'

'Well, you're being ridiculous.' He was glancing uneasily at the remaining guests, and they were edging forward in their seats, preparing for a tactful retreat. Hugh, in his accustomed position in front of the hearth, was holding his glass of brandy tightly in both hands and looking at his feet.

'No I'm not. You can't tell me that this time, Lovat. You always tell me whatever I think is wrong but not this time.'

'Love, you *are* . . .' He swiftly crossed the room, preparing to embrace and reassure her, and above all take her away before she made this embarrassing scene any worse.

'Tell her the truth,' Hugh almost shouted.

Lovat stopped with his arm around Bianca's shoulders, looking from Hugh to Olivia and back again.

'Tell her now. You ought to have done it in the beginning. Now get it over with.'

'Hugh, thank you.' For an instant Bianca was warmed by the first filial affection she could remember feeling, but then she saw that this was not a move made out of loyalty to her, much less from care or love, but of the desire to protect the clan. Another unfamiliar emotion was dawning, a feeling of power so radiant that the dim pinpricks of hurt or care were healed.

Lovat tightened his grip around her, and she angrily broke away. 'I think some of our guests might be more comfortable in the drawing room – the fire's still good, I'm sure,' she said. Shona rose and led the four strangers away, rolling her eyes at Bianca as she went. 'Lovat, I'm waiting.'

'I can't . . .' he stammered, his face breaking up into a random mass of distorted features. His mouth, always so stern and so arrogantly furled, was soft and gaping, out of control.

'I'm sure you can. Why should the words be worse than the deed?'

He let out a furious snarl and Olivia, now visibly frightened, stumbled forward. 'No, Lovat, don't be angry. Let me do this. Bianca, I'm really the guilty one. Why don't you leave us two together . . .'

'Oh no. You'll just say I made the whole thing up, I know you all, you are my family, let's not forget that, let's never forget it. Everyone stay where they are.' Bianca folded her arms, the better not to feel pity for her mother who was now, so unskilfully, so out of practice, trying to be kind.

'It was years ago, Bianca. Before you were married, before you'd even met. We had a party, someone brought him to the house, he'd had too much to drink, so had I, I expect . . . you know what my life has been like. It was only once . . .'

'I don't believe you,' she said immediately, guided by her instinct alone. Lovat sat on the piano stool, his face turned away to the wall. 'Of course I know what your life was like. I always thought you must have rather enjoyed it.'

Olivia refused to be provoked. 'Maybe he did come round again, but there was nothing in it, nothing. He really wasn't right for me . . .'

'You mean you thought he was a bit of rough from the North and beneath you, that's what you mean, isn't it?'

Lovat suddenly turned around. 'This isn't easy for her,' he announced in his old superior voice.

Bianca opened her mouth and felt a breath like the wind of heaven under her ribs. An aria of rage poured from her lips. Olivia collapsed weeping into a chair and she stood over her, raining her anger at the unspeakable crime around her mother's ears, and when that was spent she followed with the fossil-hard furies of her childhood, so long silted down in secret while she had kept a compliant look on her face and behind it placated and manoeuvred and planned her escape.

Her father she lanced with contempt and he took it well, accepting blame for his damaged marriage and his part in conspiring to keep the secret, but Hugh could sidestep real responsibility and lay the burden of guilt on outsiders. Charlotte retreated into silence. She could not find words. Emotion overwhelmed her and muddled her mind. She took on a pinched, aged appearance all at once. Joe, who sat as if deflated in a corner, admitted he had known all along. She passed over him, knowing he would plead loyalty to Lovat.

At last she came to her husband, the father of their three – no, four children, the man who had married her with so much sweetness, care and style, knowing all along that he had already committed a terrible betrayal, and would compound it every day of their marriage. As she let loose her feelings she discovered that they were close to hatred, but she began to choose her words, seeing him now calmer, still looking to her father for support, anxious no doubt that

273

his precious career, the venal, compromising, dark-suited role he had claimed he never wanted, might be in danger. That, of course, was his real concern. It did not really worry him that she was angry, that he had hurt her, that he had lied and cheated, brought children into the world to find their very lives founded on deception. She cast about for a weapon to penetrate the armour of his selfishness.

'It's over.' She was calm and very clear. 'I want a divorce. I want you out of this house now, and I want a divorce.'

'We'll talk about it in the morning,' was his reply and there was something close to a smile on his lips.

'I'm not joking. I want you out of this house now and I want a divorce. God knows I've got enough grounds.'

'Best do what she says now.' Hugh nodded to him across the room. On the upholstery the blue shepherdesses in panniered gowns tripped after their fleecy sheep. On the table the bowl of white peonies, roses and alchemilla shed pollen in the silence of an abandoned battlefield.

Joe heaved himself to his feet. 'Come with us for the night,' he offered, extending his hand to Lovat.

'Thanks but I'll stay.'

Hugh at last left the neutrality of the hearth and came to stand between Bianca and her husband, ignoring his wife as he crossed the room.

'It would be better if you did as Bianca asks.' He put his hand on Lovat's shoulder and the younger man looked at him, knitting his heavy brows in anger. He had an instinctive grasp of power dynamics, and understood that Hugh had deserted him.

'Whose side are you on?'

'My daughter's.'

'You are, aren't you? I suppose you've got a reason.'

'I don't need a reason.' His tone was infuriatingly sententious. 'Bianca is my daughter.'

'Don't give me that. Blood thicker than water, thicker than liquidity, thicker than capital, thicker than everything I've done for you. Right then. Right. I'll do as she asks. But if I leave this house I'll not come back and you'll not see me at Berrisford's again except the day I come in to take your bloody firm over.'

Now Hugh was pale and tense with anger, but he tried to maintain a calm façade. 'We'll talk on Monday. Just go now . . .'

'Right, I will.' Lovat leaped to his feet and was out of the door in seconds. The noise of his feet on the stairs died away.

'This is good of you, Joe.' Hugh felt a need to fill the silence.

'Least I could do. He'll calm down, you'll see. I know him, he's always been like this, the storm blows itself out. He doesn't mean half what he says when his temper's up.'

There was another painful pause, and Bianca sensed that she too might think better of her hasty words in the morning. She reflected with annoyance that a dispute which she had started, and in which she was the wronged and innocent party, had somehow become a fight between the two men, an antler-clashing exercise to which she and her suffering were irrelevant.

'Don't imagine I'm like that, any of you,' she said at once. 'I mean what I said. I want a divorce. We've been living a lie for ten years and I can't stay with that man one more minute.'

There was another rumble of feet on the stairs and Lovat appeared with a grip stuffed with clothes in one hand.

'We'll be off then.' He nodded to Joe. With reluctance, looking from one face to another in the hope of a last appeal, his friend said goodnight to Charlotte and Bianca, to

Olivia who seemed not to hear him, and to Hugh, who prepared to walk them to the door.

'We can see ourselves out,' Lovat told him at once. 'You'll have my resignation on your desk in the morning.' Bianca saw his back disappear and heard the front door open and slam shut. She felt light, as if she could float to the ceiling if she wanted. Satisfaction was a rare sensation and she vowed to have an increase of it.

CHAPTER 9
St Petersburg, 1910

'*Dear Nikolai, my only love,*' wrote Lydia, then paused to admire her pen of translucent white agate banded with tiny diamonds. It always gave her pleasure to use it, most particularly so this morning when she was about to play a final hand for double or quits with the man who had bestowed it upon her. '*I beg you never to doubt that my heart longs with all its passion to grant your request. For the whole of my life I will treasure the memory of our moments together and count myself blessed to have attracted your admiration. I have felt such happiness in your company that I know no other affection can ever diminish my feelings for you. But you must know that I am unable to grant you what you ask of me. The sad circumstances of my origins, the terrible precariousness of an artist's existence, make it impossible for me to order my life according to my own heart.*'

She paused and pushed the folio across the writing table to Alexandrov, who nodded as he read it. 'It's not too much, is it?' she asked him, her face very pale. It was nine in the morning and she had returned only a few hours earlier from a mad trip with Prince Orlov to dine in Viborg, more than eighty miles distant. With a large, noisy party they had travelled two-by-two in open sleighs, pelting through the icy night in a cocoon of furs and sipping vodka to keep warm.

Orlov had courted her for more than a year, and in the last few months had issued an invitation to dine almost every week, always with an air of disinterest and always, as propriety demanded, proposing a party with others. The summer months, when half the ballet company decamped to the neighbourhood of the Tsar's summer palace, had been a period of enchantment for her. The Prince had been a frequent spectator at rehearsals, and in the relaxed atmosphere of the season their relationship had bloomed.

There had been many gifts, at first impersonal tokens like her pen, progressing to oblique tributes to her femininity, jade scent bottles and a boudoir clock of white enamel decorated with bows and rosebuds of rubies. In due time she was able to accept jewellery, diamond earrings in the shape of vine leaves, on her birthday a beautiful brooch set with cloudy Siberian emeralds and diamonds, and lately an emerald pendant to match it.

That night the hectic excitement of the long fast sleigh ride, the drink, the hours alone except for the coachman's impervious back had all at once destroyed Orlov's characteristic detachment. The man had forgotten himself. The impression of his fierce grasp burned around her waist like a brand. Involuntarily, she swallowed again and again; she could still feel his mouth on her lips.

When she had repulsed him he had at first been angry, then withdrawn. At last, as they were reaching the outskirts of the city, he made the proposition. 'You must be mine,' he began abruptly and Lydia, still in distress, had simply begged him to be silent and say nothing more. In consternation she had sent a message to Alexandrov immediately and was reassured when, far from expressing dismay at her stupidity, he had rubbed his hands and suggested that a well-worded letter might secure the ideal outcome of the affair.

'It's absolute perfection,' he assured her, waving the page to dry the ink. 'All this passion and pathos is just the ticket. He knows the score, they all know the score. We just want him to get a good sense of what he'll be missing if he doesn't come across. Stick a good long languishing farewell on the end and we'll have it delivered immediately.'

'I do truly adore him, you know. I really believe we're meant to be together, I know it, I've always known it,' she repeated with vehemence, as if to bring about the desired conclusion to her love affair purely by the power of her speech.

'I think this will get us what we're after, in fact I'd put money on it.' He winked at her as she handed him the signed letter.

'That's no consolation – you'd put money on anything.' Nowadays the commissions which Mischa collected from his friends for effecting introductions in the ballet company stayed in his pocket a short time since he had become devoted to the game of roulette.

'Only if it's red or black, dear, don't be so hard on your old friend. And when you're established in your dear little house with your jewels and your motor car and your entourage just remember who held your hand while the stakes were raised, eh?'

'I have done the right thing, haven't I?'

To her surprise Mischa flung his arms around her shoulders and hugged her to his beautifully tailored chest. 'Your old uncle Mischa's guided many a shy virgin along the perilous paths of love and nobody ever tripped along as nimbly as you, and that's the truth. You're a credit to me, if you want to know. I do believe you love the man, and heaven knows why but that's not my concern. You've kept your head and never given way to any sentimental romantic rubbish or let hot blood get in the way of good business. You really are a star, Lydia. Now go and lie down, have some verbena tea and decide what colour you want your chauffeur's uniform.'

'I can't, I'm dancing tonight and I'm late for class already.'

'But you haven't slept a wink!'

'I know. I can sleep later but I can't get stiff today.'

'The dedication! What's the ballet?'

'*Don Quixote*. I'm the lead, it's my first night!'

'Oh my God! And Orlov is bound to be there, isn't he? Do you want me to see if I can get you something?' Among Mischa's vast acquaintance were a few pharmacists with much experience in formulating tinctures to make good deficiencies in a dancer's willpower, mixtures to numb pain, suppress the appetite or supply extra vitality.

'Oh, darling Mischa, would you? I really think I need it today.' Lydia hardly hesitated.

A clean, intelligent boy, a grandson of Alexandrov's housekeeper, presented the letter to the doorman at the Orlov Palace and when the Prince rose in the early afternoon the missive was brought to him in his study. His taste was for the classical; bas-relief columns of red Kushkuldine jasper lined the plain buff walls. The moulded frieze of entwined military symbols was picked out in white and gold. In his early twenties he had obsessively collected Greek and Roman antiquities and his choicest purchases were kept where they would be always under his eyes. Vases crowded the mantelpiece, small statues adorned the low bookcases and four busts of Greek philosophers stood on marble plinths in the alcoves. The very first acquisitions, a set of medals inherited from his grandfather, were displayed in a special case like a circular table. The most treasured possession, an eager bronze Hermes hardly six inches high, stood poised for flight on his plain mahogany desk.

Alexandrov had slandered him when he judged the Prince uninterested in beauty. It was the only quality capable of moving his heart and he was acutely aware of it in art or nature. However, his temperament was profoundly cerebral. Emotion, sensuality, even comfort appeared to him as corrupting distractions and when his senses were aroused he was quick to rationalize his feelings.

His responses to La Kusminskaya, as Lydia was quickly becoming known, yielded incompletely to this process. He had disdained the ballet as an entertainment for the undemanding intellect, and despised those of his colleagues who were pallidly embowered by ballerinas and actresses. He told himself that curiosity – and social diplomacy – had led him to accept an invitation to the box of the senior Ragosin a few weeks after encountering the dancer at supper.

She appeared in a short ballet before the main offering of the evening, a piece called *Le Jardin Animé*, which by chance mirrored one of his own adolescent fantasies. An unhappy poet moped in a sculpture garden by moonlight and the stone nymphs, moved by his grief, came alive and stepped down one by one to console him. The music was not the usual tinselly trash, but a suite in quasi-baroque style. Out loud he criticized the historical inaccuracy of the costumes, which for reasons of tradition and propriety had all parties absurdly overdressed, but his eye was imprinted with all the lines of Kusminskaya's body and his intellect toyed with the notion of a dancer as a living work of art.

At her curtain call, when bouquets suddenly filled the stage and a palpable wave of adulation roared down from the gallery, he was touched in another sensitive place. Orlov, for all his generations of high breeding, was most susceptible to public acclaim; although he scorned to court the attention of common people, or even acknowledge the gratification it inspired in him, recognition as trivial as the naming of his coat of arms on his carriage door by a passer-by could inflate his vanity.

He was on leave for a few months pending his appointment to a post in the Ministry of Defence. Being learned in theoretical strategy but inept as a commander of men this was a predictable development in his career and one to which he looked forward. Since the approaching winter made travel difficult, he had planned to beguile his leisure reading some of his favourite Latin texts. He took Cicero and Caesar down from the shelves of his library, but with them Ovid's *Ars Amatoria*, and all at once poetry seemed far more challenging to his intellect than prose.

Step by step his own excellent mind led him along the path to erotic fascination. He told himself that good relations with as many generals as possible would be of importance in his new role, and General Ragosin, to whom the pleasure of forty saucy pairs of knees flashing to and fro under short skirts was an essential highlight of every week, was eager to secure the favour of a fledgling statesman for whom much was predicted.

Following the success of *Les Pléiades*, the talents of both Kusminskaya and Leo Volinsky were acknowledged by the ballet's management. Kchessinskaya's attention was distracted, first by the task of building herself a sumptuous new townhouse, then by the virtual rebuilding of her summer residence, and finally by a season in Paris organized by Sergei Diaghilev, which she claimed as her own personal triumph despite the reports that Vaslav Nijinsky and Tata Karsavina had enjoyed greater success. Whatever the truth, all these affairs diverted her influence at home in the ballet and Lydia at last began to receive opportunities to display her gifts.

Among these were new works by Mikhail Fokine and by

Leo, and both were eager to challenge the old order and advance their art. Lydia appeared adorable in white lace as Columbine; with much initial protest, she wore unblocked shoes and gauzy draperies as the Persian sibyl, and was surprised to find that she was considered to have a gift for suggesting pagan eroticism. The tempi of Schumann and Rimsky-Korsakov were as easy to disregard as those of lesser composers. From Ragosin's box, Orlov responded to the aestheticism of both choreographers. He found around him new friends, some of them undoubtedly men and women of deep culture, happy to explain or to argue the merits of the modern styles.

It had always seemed to him indicative of the self-indulgent, emotional response which ballet evoked that the lovers of the art called themselves balletomanes, implying that their appreciation was a mania, a kind of madness which possessed them. Now he found something profoundly romantic in the appellation, and sought the company of balletomanes the better to learn the styles of his new devotion. An artistic revolution was under way, and he seemed to have appeared in its centre. His German countess, for all her exquisite taste in jewellery, found his new enthusiasm tedious; the best that Poiret and Paquin did for her could not hide the fact that her legs were disproportionately short. Orlov saw an increasing resemblance between his lover and her pet dachshund.

Lydia Kusminskaya, to his eyes, appeared a living goddess. Her legs were beyond perfection. The elongated diamond-shaped swell of her calves was extraordinary. The neat articulation of her knees, the filigree delicacy of her ankles, and lissom extension of her thighs all fascinated him. He adored her white arms, her long neck, the dove-like thrust of her ribs. At rest she was beautiful; in movement she was divine. The unique quality of her grace sang to him like a siren, promising ecstasy beyond mortal comprehension. By the time he resolved to court her he was sinking in a quicksand of sexual obsession, into which he had been lured by his own intellectual arrogance.

He turned Lydia's letter over several times with his fingertips, feeling that he hardly needed to open it. Deep in his mind he had already made his decision. The question was not whether he would pay to possess this treasure, but how much she would ask, and from another compartment in his ordered mind, which knew and judged Alexandrov, he had already estimated the price. Money hardly concerned him – the house of Orlov was accustomed to epic expenditure; mortgages on their land from the Imperial exchequer subsidized it now, for the Tsars had felt it only fair to protect their extended family of nobility from the consequences of transforming millions of serfs into landowning peasants.

The cost to his self-respect of installing a ballet dancer as his mistress weighed more heavily, but as a man accustomed to the satisfaction of all his needs it was now a necessity which he accepted. He was ready to join the ranks of noblemen who allied themselves with glamorous women of the artistic *demi-monde*, although he did not see himself going as far as the Grand Duke Gabriel, who shared a roof with the ballerina Nina Nesterova, keeping open house for half the Court with rare wines and finest foods and games of poker which lasted until dawn.

Gabriel was a fool, as weak-minded as his brother Igor who cared only for horses and should have been born a groom. Orlov saw himself as a serious man, despised all hedonists and remained suspicious of pleasure. Eventually, he recognized, he would do his duty and marry, and until then what he needed was oblivion rather than enjoyment. The German countess had an earthy sexual appetite which it pleased him to feed, but he never had the sense of losing himself in her arms. The awareness of his own imperfection oppressed him; at times the hopelessness of the whole human condition made him feel that life was not worth living. He craved relief from these truths, and as a younger man had tried to reach it through sport, drink and opium, but he could not accept the way of life which each dictated.

With a woman he could find peace. Whores and low women provoked disgust, but a woman with something of the exotic always excited him. For some years he had been in the habit of visiting a gypsy cabaret on the outskirts of the city with his brother officers. There he released his stifled desires with one or more of the singers, sinewy creatures with obsidian eyes who stank of sweat and cigarette smoke, spoke in curses and worked with a keen sense of value for money. Lydia, when he gave her a present, snatched it like a child beggar, her eyes flashing wide as if amazed at his gullibility, arousing a similar feeling.

He broke the seal on her letter, noticing with annoyance that the cheap wax crumbled into his coffee. He rapidly scanned the text, then rang for his valet to fetch a clean cup, finished his breakfast and moved to his writing desk to compose a reply which protested his eternal adoration, sympathized with her position, pledged his care for her welfare and proposed that they should meet, perhaps with his steward and her guardian, to agree arrangements which would satisfy them all.

Little of the afternoon then remained; within a few hours he dressed for the evening and took the route which had become so familiar to the Maryinsky Theatre and settled into his usual armchair in the corner of General Ragosin's box, separated from the wide Imperial box only by a gilded barleytwist column.

As a ballet, *Don Quixote* is not much occupied with the old man crazed by dreams of chivalry of Cervantes' stories; its focus is the dream of Spain which crazes every milk-and-water northerner, a black and red tapestry of the hot blood, high passion, fierce women and proud men. At the centre of this flamenco-spiced romance is the fiery young heroine, a role for which even Lydia's harshest critics admitted she might have been expressly created. Orlov found himself leaping to his feet to applaud again and again, amid a packed auditorium moved to the same pitch of ecstasy, and after the final pas de deux a rare event occurred. With her partner she repeated the coda as an encore. Whistling and stamping, the audience demanded another, and after modest protestations which allowed them to catch their breath, the young pair performed again.

Then the benevolent uproar in the theatre, instead of dying down, redoubled, and a third repetition was demanded with loud chants of *'Bis! bis!'* from every level of the great blue and gold auditorium.

'If we're going again for God's sake let's get on with it,' Leo, her partner, whispered in her ear under cover of a tender gesture collecting her for another presentation to her public. 'My legs are getting cold and I've ripped a hamstring, I know it.'

Never solicitous of her colleagues, Lydia barely heard him and continued her sequence of curtsies. 'You need permission for a third encore – go on, ask now!' he hissed as she turned towards the Imperial box, and at last recalled that as she had waited offstage that evening Nicolai Legat had given her a kiss for good luck and muttered, in the manner of a kind man anxious not to prepare her only for disappointment, 'If they do want three encores, little girl, don't forget the permission.'

She rose from her curtsey with knees that momentarily lost their strength. Since his son had fallen ill the Tsar nowadays spent more and more time at his palace in the country, and the box was occupied that night by his mother, the Empress Maria Fyodorovna. Her beauty always carried the grave tint of a woman who had been widowed unfairly young, but tonight she seemed as full of delight as the rest of the house. Hardly knowing what she was doing, Lydia demonstrated their ardour to her with a quick, expressive gesture and dropped another curtsey of supplication, immediately followed by a third of acknowledgement as the Empress gave an animated nod. Orlov, standing not six feet away, tried in vain to catch Lydia's eye as she rose.

When *Don Quixote* was at last finished an avalanche of people flowed into the square outside, but had no intention of dispersing. Orlov accompanied General Ragosin, who intended to pay court to his particular fancy through the window of her dressing room, which conveniently overlooked the private entrance used by the Imperial Family. They were soon surrounded by the most ardent balletomanes, who remained close to the theatre and jostled their way to the stage door. The gallery regulars, nicknamed 'the chickencoop', were calling Kusminskaya's name; they were all young men. Orlov picked out the uniforms of all St Petersburg's most distinguished scholastic establishment, and smiled with tolerant amusement at the high school students in their best grey overcoats twirling newly-sprouted moustaches. Looking down on them, the undergraduates in their elegant new cloaks struck poetic attitudes under the street lamps.

'Aren't those ladies taking an age to get their make-up off

tonight?' observed a freshly hatched intellectual of twenty or so to his much older companion, who grunted agreement through a plume of cigarette smoke from the depths of his beaver collar.

At last the stage door opened and the musicians began to leave, pulling their coats tight against the cold. The dancers of the corps appeared, slender and humble, and the respectful horde parted to let them through. The public was waiting for the stars and if it took half the night they would stand in the snow until their idols appeared.

'She's coming, she's coming!' called a voice close to the door, whose owner had glimpsed the adored one in the hallway.

'La Kusminskaya's coming!' The word passed from mouth to mouth down the wide street. From nowhere a chair appeared, a simple bentwood café chair which was passed above the heads of the crowd by a hundred strong hands and set down by the doorway.

Orlov stood quietly aside, shaking visibly with vicarious pride in the demonstration. He was gratified almost to tears to see that Lydia, the object of this passion, was wearing the blue fox wrap which he had recently given her. Her face was a poem of sweetness in its soft frame, but in silence he promised her all the furs of the Arctic come the next day.

She exclaimed on stepping outside into the crowd, who surged around like an angry sea to make a respectful space for her. Laughing, unaware of the Prince in the shadow of a pillar, she was installed on the chair amid ceaseless cheers and shouts of 'Bravo!' and shrieked with alarm as it was raised to shoulder height. Marie, with her sister and brother-in-law Paul, followed behind her like a bride's train, carrying the bouquets and collecting more posies which were pressed on them from all sides.

'Where is your carriage?' the worshippers demanded.

'You darling boys, I have no carriage!'

'Nonsense!' they shouted, thinking she was teasing. 'Every ballerina has a carriage!'

'But I'm not a ballerina yet, I'm only a *première*.'

'Impossible!'

Orlov was transfixed by the scene, but at his side General Ragosin barked, 'Permit me, Mademoiselle!' and stepped purposefully forward. The young men quietened at once and let him speak. 'Permit me to offer you my carriage, Mademoiselle Kusminskaya. You can see it there, just at the side of the square.'

Lydia was so breathless with elation that she could barely speak; with an effort she controlled herself sufficiently to accept his offer and the chair, swaying crazily, turned at once.

'Are you quite safe, Mademoiselle?' Ragosin inquired, raising his voice even more to quell the excitable crowd.

'Of course she is!' the students shouted at once. 'She's our goddess, nothing can harm her when we are present!'

'Let the lady speak for herself!' he commanded.

'I'm sure it looks precarious up here and indeed it feels it, but I will put my trust in these dear gentlemen,' she gasped, her eyes alight with a pure happiness which, Orlov later reflected, was quite unlike her response to him.

'Hurrah for La Kusminskaya!' cried a tall, blond youth who gripped the front leg of the chair in one huge hand and conducted the cheering with the other as she was carried across the square.

'Your little one has a great instinct for the mob.' The General was regarding Orlov with blatant envy. 'She'll get her promotion before long, even if there are more generals than ballerinas in this country.'

'She's not mine yet.' Orlov liked to be precise.

'Well, man, what in the world are you waiting for?'

'Tomorrow morning, General.'

Alexandrov and Paul called upon him early, swaggering a little with the memory of Lydia's triumph still fresh. Only mildly intimidated by the splendour of the Orlov palace, they squared up to the Prince and his steward, a thick-set man of only middle age whose cropped hair, nevertheless, was already white.

Their bravado was unnecessary, and in an hour they resumed their coats with brilliant smiles and brought back to Lydia the Prince's offer to install her in a suitable house in the best part of town, furnished in every detail to her exact taste, with a household, carriages, horses – and, yes, an automobile if she had the fancy for one – a little white wood dacha in the country with a small park, and a positively lavish capital endowment to maintain the whole. Paul clutched a wheezing black pug puppy with blue leather collar studded with diamonds. Alexandrov concluded the recital of generosity with an invitation to accompany the Prince on his spring tour of France and Italy.

Lydia, sitting upright at the breakfast table, turned so pale that her white wool gown seemed almost yellow. For an instant the two men thought she was going to refuse on an idiotic pretext. Marie thought she was going to faint and rushed to her side. Instead, she wordlessly held out her arms for the little dog, which settled on her lap and snuffled for crumbs.

'Well?' Alexandrov demanded at last. 'What do you say?'

'I can't believe it.' Her eyes were genuinely troubled. 'It isn't some kind of joke?'

'No. It's all written down and sealed.'

'I can't believe it.' She abstractedly pulled the puppy away from her tea glass.

'I don't care whether you believe it, you fool – do you agree to it?' Alexandrov was becoming irritated.

'Oh, *yes!*' And the conspirators embraced and sent out for champagne, telling each other that soon they would all be able to bathe in the stuff if they chose.

With so high a price offered for her, Lydia had been assailed with terrible doubts about her ability to honour the bargain.

'Oh, God, I wish I had a mother I could talk to,' she confided to Marie as they crammed her few possessions into boxes and baskets the day before her departure for her new home. 'What will he expect? Suppose I can't bear it?'

Tatiana, Marie's sister, appeared with arms full of freshly laundered petticoats. 'You'll get used to it, every woman does,' she assured her. 'Of course it can be unpleasant at first – isn't everything? But drink a lot of champagne and have a good warm bath afterwards and you'll be fine. And when you get used to love you'll adore it, I promise you. You're the type, I can see it in your eyes.'

'What about me? Am I made for love, can you see it in my eyes?' Marie pulled playfully at her sister's sleeve.

'Oh, shut up! The way you've been carrying on with Basil you ought to be giving this lecture yourself!'

'Mean to me, my big sister's always so mean to me!' The Guards officer, Basil Nikonov, had courted Marie energetically ever since the dinner at Cubat's after the première of *Les Pléiades*.

Lydia sat on the end of her narrow bed and enviously watched them teasing each other. Living with the affectionate sisters had made her painfully aware that she had never felt so easily intimate with anyone.

'And it will improve your dancing ...' Tata continued with authority as she folded the garments.

'No it won't – she has a one hundred and eighty degree *penchée* already,' riposted Marie, straining one of her own legs vainly towards her ear to demonstrate. 'The Prince is going to have a really good time.'

'How can you be so crude? You'll frighten the poor child. The sooner Basil takes you off my hands the better, you're getting quite impossible. But love will help you to be a better artist, little girl. When you understand what passion truly is – then you can really express it.' Lydia nodded. 'Look at her, the little rosebud, she hasn't the faintest idea what I mean! Don't worry, you'll be fine. Until you get pregnant, then your troubles really begin. But there are things to do. We'll go and see my Finnish woman who knows about plants and she'll fix you up.'

Orlov claimed his purchase as he did everything else, with elegance and restraint. He consulted the Maryinsky programme, to find a run of days in which Kusminskaya was not billed to dance, and called upon her with flowers and a gift, an evening purse of green gold with a diamond clasp. Marie and Basil were invited for familiar, amusing company. Upon the new porcelain dinner service, painted with pink convolvulus flowers and edged in turquoise and gold, the new footman and the new downstairs maid served a delicious light supper prepared by Denis, the new Swiss cook. A fine French champagne, for which Lydia had now acquired a taste, was brought up from the cellar.

'Do you like your house? Are you happy?' he asked her. She was the picture of a creature softened by luxury, curled in the corner of her new Empire sofa feeding the puppy with turkish delight, picking up each titbit with fastidious finger-tips and flicking sugar specks off the white lace of her skirt. At once she understood his intention and her expression of alarm, although rapidly wiped away by one of forced sweet-

ness, was so ridiculous that he half laughed, then kissed her
sticky hand. 'Forgive me, such a hackneyed question and so
tactless. Don't worry . . .'

'I adore my house but – oh! it's so annoying! How can a
person be calm when everyone tells her not to worry?' She
tipped the pug awkwardly off her lap. They were briefly
alone; a game of charades had been proposed and Basil and
Marie were in the next room preparing their tableau.

'You are anxious, my little love, you shouldn't deny it.
And what could be more natural . . .'

All at once her breath seemed trapped in her chest and she
felt she was going to cry. The thought that her timidity was
unkind to him lived for a gnat's span before she crushed it,
but still she was conscious that she was not acting as she
wished. This mistrusting, withholding creature was not the
bold woman who last night enthralled a thousand men by
her mere appearance. She turned to him. 'You know I only
want to please you.'

'You are the loveliest thing I have ever seen.' He spoke
with complete gravity as if reciting a catechism. 'Every
movement you make, every word you speak is precious to
me, every minute spent in your company is a delight.' A
nervous tremor in her throat, as slight as the shadow of a
fish in water, caught his eye and he leaned forward, paused
momentarily, and kissed it. His mouth was soft and warm,
and she told herself it must surely be more pleasant than the
wet nuzzling of the puppy. 'Live for the moment, my darling,
that is the real secret of happiness.'

As the evening continued he made sure her glass was
always filled; their companions were a pair of natural
comedians and by midnight Lydia's ribs were sore from
laughing. Marie asked to leave early, since she had to dance
the next day, and as Lydia followed them across the marble-

floored hallway, admiring her own Chinese vases crammed with flowers from her own hot house, thinking of her pretty English-style bedroom, a mass of chintz and ruffles, she felt whole and complete for the first time in her life, and suddenly resolved to bestow herself on her lover with all the thoughtful generosity which he had shown to her. She dismissed the servants the instant the door closed, ran back to the salon and threw herself joyfully into Orlov's arms.

Inside the gauzy silk gown her body was a light, tensile thing; sinewy arms twined around his neck and she kicked away her satin slippers like a happy infant. She had been so long accustomed to manhandling by her partners that the embrace with which her lover lifted her seemed almost smothering in its carefulness.

His touch was delicate, his fingers as light as breath on her skin. The white-painted bed waited for them, warm and fragrant, its rosy cover folded back over a little ocean of pillows foaming with lace. Lydia was so charmed with the beauty of it and so dizzy from the champagne that at first she hardly felt his caresses.

Without haste, he kissed her lips, her neck, her ears, her throat, again and again in strict order. Passion dissolved her consciousness like a dream. Hairpins fell among the pillows, buttons evaded their loops, her stockings unrolled themselves and slipped from her toes.

'I don't need this now, do I?' she inquired, smiling, emboldened by passion. She pulled off her chemise before he could answer then attempted to push his own coat off his shoulders. 'And why are you wearing all these ridiculous things? I don't believe you always go to bed in your boots.'

As her body emerged from its fine wrappings he became lost in fascination, discovering warm, firm swells of muscle, fine blue veins, bones so prominent he could slide his fingers in the grooves between them. Her breasts were tiny, marble-white tear-drops welling below the brittle span of her collar-bones. Apart from the fleshy peasant girls of his youth, Orlov had never touched a woman in good physical condition. His previous lovers seemed half dead in comparison to this vital, squirming creature who sighed from the depth of her being at each new touch.

A residue of fear remained in her, enough to quicken her happiness as he held her waist, so that she strained eagerly against his hand, longing for its inevitable downward progress. Her thighs, narrow and blood-warmed, parted readily at his touch, inviting, rather than merely allowing, the exploration of her inner secrets. Now his decision to proceed slowly was joined by a mystical sense that this was a ceremony they could perform only once, and so he delayed, ignoring the acute demands of his own flesh, and touched each hidden part of her lingeringly with his finger-tips.

'Angel wings, it feels like angel wings,' she whispered, half to herself, her head turning from side to side among the pillows. 'I'm in heaven, darling, I can't bear it, I can't wait any more, I won't care if it hurts me, only do it now, please, now, please . . .' As he entered her he felt a brief spasm of her muscles, and then no more resistance, only the heat of her flesh around his, and her back arching in response to new instincts for pleasure, and ecstasy consuming him like a white fire.

They soon slept, but within an hour Lydia roused herself and, accustomed throughout her life to obeying injunctions to her physical care and finding them well-founded, stirred the servants to help her bathe. Then she returned to bed, but woke early and began to discover that Tatiana was correct in all her predictions. Orlov was enchanted to be detained the whole day by an apt pupil who announced that she wished to master all the arts of love immediately.

'Don't you think I'm made for it, darling? Just like I know I was made to dance. It was my destiny to love you, you know that?' It was the height of the afternoon and the city outside cowered under a snowstorm, but in the bedroom the roses bloomed unblighted and the lovers restored their strength with cake and chocolate.

'I don't believe in your destiny nonsense,' he answered in a vague tone, bewitched by the pretty greed with which she picked every crumb and poppy seed from her plate.

'You don't believe I was destined to kiss you – like this? And then like this . . .'

'That's your will, not your destiny. You're doing it because you want to.'

'Well, that's true, but you wanted to kiss me for a long time and it wasn't destined so you didn't. You can't argue with that, can you?' She was sitting on his lap, wriggling provocatively, her wrap slipping from her shoulders, and he was in no mood to argue with anything.

'No. And now it's my will to kiss you like this . . .' Her small pale nipple puckered at the touch.

'You can't do that – people don't do that, do they?'

'Yes, don't you like it?'

She sprawled thoughtfully in his arms and pretended to consider. 'I suppose it's quite agreeable . . .'

'Oh, well, in that case I'll stop. "Quite agreeable" really isn't good enough. Only the best caresses are good enough for my precious one.'

'Oh no! Don't stop!'

'Don't stop! Don't stop! You sound just like my old riding master.'

'How complimentary! Thank you so much!' She flounced

away to the centre of the room, still holding half a sugared pastry, and the puppy bounded after her on his stumpy legs.

'Forgive me! I didn't mean it that way!' As he rose to pursue her he saw himself for an instant from far away, a man of learning and respect chattering idiotic nonsense to a dancer, and noted how keen an edge abasement added to ordinary pleasure.

There followed a period in which they considered themselves madly in love. They were reclusive, saw no one, went nowhere and, apart from Lydia's dancing commitments, stayed in her little house delighting in solitude à deux. As Tatiana foresaw, Lydia's body was quick to display its new wisdom in a capacity for fiery languor which soon won her another major role, in *Le Corsaire*. Orlov filled her dressing room with orchids at every performance and gave her a pair of diamond bracelets.

His custom was to leave for his annual tour of Europe in May, and for the sake of accompanying him before the end of the season Lydia pretended to injure her knee, and begged for a month's leave from the ballet. The Director, undeceived but mindful of the influence of a man of Orlov's breeding and stature, agreed.

They boarded the train for Paris with so much luggage that an extra carriage was needed. The pug slept on the finest beds on the continent, while the lovers tried the effect of every sophisticated stimulus on their ardour. In Paris it was foie gras and Cartier, in Monte Carlo lobster and baccarat, in Venice they bought a mirror too big to be transported in a gondola, while Florence was afterwards remembered for the truffles and a new set of trunks to carry their purchases. In all these cities Lydia yawned through cathedrals, slept in the opera and dismissed the paintings of the great masters because they depicted only fat women, and

Orlov was the more enchanted by her crassness and looked back to previous visits, when his pastimes had been reading or sketching the great classical ruins, as an arid waste.

In September they returned to St Petersburg, arranged their treasures and agreed that their native country was a dreadfully backward and rough place and that they would travel every year. Lydia was aghast to discover that she had gained a great deal of weight, and resolved to order no new dresses until she had returned to her former slenderness.

'Kchessinskaya does it every year, and so shall I,' she announced, referring to the prima ballerina's schedule of a summer of indulgence followed by weeks of diet and exercise before her first appearance on stage in the autumn. She began work, and found her body sluggish. She had her maid knit thick wool stockings to help her sweat. From the Finnish herbalist she bought a selection of evil-smelling laxatives, diuretics and potions to melt fat or suppress the appetite, then complained that they did not work and made her feel sick. The old witch, whose face was as brown and lined as polished oak, broke an egg into a bowl of water to look for omens, then examined her eyes and tongue, crossed her palms with twigs and burned them, and finally announced, 'Not fat, Madame, you got child.'

The thought of pregnancy was so far from her mind that Lydia sat for a full minute in silence with her mouth open.

'You want?' The old woman reached for the large bag of cracked black leather in which she carried her wares. 'You want child or you don't want?'

'I don't know,' she said distractedly. 'I hadn't thought . . . didn't you give me something to stop it?'

'Yes, but . . .' A revolting expression crossed the sunken light blue eyes. 'It don't work on honeymoon – you make too much romantic, eh?'

'Oh go away! I'll send for you if I want you again.' Lydia
walked abruptly out of the sitting room into her winter
garden, where a huge pot of jasmine, having been deceived
as to the season by the gardener, was flowering vigorously
and scenting the warm air. Orlov was reading his newspaper
and thinking about leaving for the Ministry. She decided to
consult a doctor at once – one way or another the old witch
had to be wrong.

The doctor confirmed her pregnancy immediately. 'A
Christmas child, if I'm not mistaken,' he told her. 'Don't
worry, my dear, I wish all my patients were as healthy as
you. You are young and strong, just take care to get enough
rest now and you will recover completely by Easter, I promise
you.'

'But my . . .' She paused, realizing that she was unable to
use the word 'husband', and suddenly wanted to weep.

'His Highness will be delighted, I'm sure. Gentlemen usually are – and this will be his first child, I believe. In my
experience the loss of a few months of comfort is more than
compensated by the pride a man feels in his children once
they are born.'

She doubted him, knowing how much her lover valued her
for her beauty, but it seemed that the doctor was correct. Orlov
professed himself delighted, and willingly indulged Lydia in
acquiring every fashionable accessory for their offspring. A
room was chosen for a nursery, redecorated and filled with
toys which, if absurdly inappropriate for a baby, delighted the
deprived child in Lydia herself, who sat on the rocking horse
every day until she grew too awkward to balance. A nursemaid
was hired, and since every good household in St Petersburg
had either a French or English governess, Lydia put in hand
the engagement of a girl from London with the help of the wife
of a young diplomat at the British Embassy.

The birth, the day after Christmas, was short but so terrible that Lydia vowed at once, from the very bottom of her heart, never to undergo such agony again. When Orlov was called and presented with his child he seemed hardly to see it, and instead went directly to the bedside to touch her face. She lay dreadfully still, her complexion lustreless, her eyes sunken and dull. She made a small, defeated motion with one hand, attempted a smile but dissolved into tears.

'What have they done to you, my poor child? What have I done to you?' He embraced her awkwardly, frightened by the limpness of her body.

'She may be too weak to reply just yet.' The doctor touched him on the shoulder. 'Nature is remarkable, Your Highness, she never takes without giving. Madame will be restored to health very soon, I can assure you. And you have a fine healthy son, a big boy although he gave his mother very little trouble for his size.'

'When will she be able to dance again?'

'She may begin light exercise in a month, and then continue by degrees. But she must take care not to over-exert herself.' The midwife, seeing that the baby had attracted little interest, prepared to bear him away to the nursery but Orlov seemed to remember suddenly that he had a child.

'Let me see him,' he demanded. The red-faced, chubby infant, his eyes almost lost in plump creases, blinked at his father. 'What a beautiful child, quite beautiful! What a wonderful colour! And he has black hair like my mother.' The conspirators around the bed exchanged glances. 'Oh yes, we shall certainly take care of them both, Doctor, you can be sure of that.' Behind this show of concern, however, he felt bewildered by this new acquisition. The infant had a disconcertingly specific presence; Nikolai Nikolaivitch Kusminsky, as he was to be christened six weeks later, was one of those babies whose whole manner evokes their inborn character in the cradle. Orlov sensed that he had acquired a person whom he had not chosen, and he had a definite instinct that this person was completely outside his control. The baby's arrival had already banished the gleaming enchantress he had installed as his mistress and substituted a wretched shadow. His first meeting with his son alarmed him profoundly.

CHAPTER 10
Leningrad, 1968

'It's Anya's birthday, it's Anya's birthday.' Alex lounged at the barre, singing under his breath to the tinkling of the practice-room piano. 'Let's have a party, let's have a party. I'll get some vodka, and some sausage, and in my suitcase, I'll find a present. Happy birthday Anya, I love my little Anya, she's so be-yoooo-ti-ful!'

'Ssssh! Everyone will hear you.' She blushed and turned to the wall to hide it, worrying a corner of the peeling cream wallpaper with her toe. The first group of students finished their exercise and cleared the floor. The boards were bare and bleached to an exhausted grey, their surface pulverized almost to splinters by the countless students who had worn out their shoes there.

Anya blew upwards at the fringe of her curly blonde hair, hoping to stop it sticking to her perspiring forehead, and stepped out into the centre of the room. He could see that she was pleased by the swing of her hips. With her round face and curled upper lip, Alex thought she looked adorable.

'You look like a goldfish blowing bubbles when you blow your hair like that.'

'How sweet. I suppose when you drop me you'll say it's my fault for being wet and slippery.'

'I thought maybe we could get around to that later.'

'How dare you make pornographic suggestions to me in pas de deux class?'

'I'm so sorry, when would you prefer me to make pornographic suggestions to you?'

'*Quiet!*' Their teacher, who was normally noted for his reserved dignity, glared at them from beneath his heavy black brows. 'Now remember, children, pas de deux is always the expression of love and harmony. Your movements must twine together, develop together.' He wrapped his hands around themselves to illustrate. 'Balance, timing, all movement of you both should be as one.' He always felt foolish explaining this when he had a pair of real lovers in the class; Kirilova and the American boy, the picture of coltish romance as they whispered together in English, made him feel ashamed to be teaching. Even allowing for the effect of young love, Wolfe had a gift for projecting tenderness. Exasperating that he was so lazy – a good-looking boy like that, with his noble manner and sensitive temperament could have a good future. The teacher clapped his hands loudly. 'So, now, begin – after four. And one!'

The five girls rose on points, steadied by their partners' hands at their waists. From the portrait wall at the end of the classroom the face of Agrippina Vaganova, the school's first director after the Revolution, looked down on the couples dancing in the centre of the floor. Elsewhere her pictures revealed that she had been cursed with a long bulbous nose, receding forehead and thin hair, with only a bright smile to save her from downright ugliness, but for this portrait the artist had prettified her features so unsubtly that the students joked his real vocation had been painting official corpses for their lying-in-state.

Anya trusted herself to Alex's firm grasp, blessing God for having sent him. She was not a popular partner now, being one of those girls whose hormones had outwitted the centuries of expertise with which the examiners of the

303

Vaganova Academy selected their children. For eight years she had been as light, slender and clean-limbed as the others and now, in her final year, a disaster was happening. Every day she grew more voluptuous. Rounded hips and breasts spoiled her line, her thighs were almost ham-shaped. Her bones themselves seemed to have become thicker and heavier. The boys struggled to lift her. By the unsparing aesthetics of the ballet school she had become ugly, so her status had plummeted and her ambitions been denied. She had to forget the legendary Kirov company; at this rate she would be lucky to get a place in a folk dance group.

None of this seemed to concern the American boy. Here he was, crazily in love with her, bringing her clothes, make-up, contraceptives and medicines every time he went to his family in Paris. The fuller her breasts grew, the more he smothered them with affection. He was strong enough to toss her around like a football if he chose, but miraculously gentle, unlike the Russian boys who considered a few slaps an essential part of courtship. Inside and outside the classroom, Anya luxuriated in his chivalry. Fascinated, the other girls claimed that he could not be very masculine but even the most intimate secrets could not be kept long in the school and those whose curiosity kept them awake long enough confirmed her assertion that the American could stay in the saddle for a couple of hours on a regular basis.

Pas de deux was Alex's best class; in the rest of the work, he had his problems. Undeniably the boy was a prodigy, born with immense integrated strength, but he too had grown unpredictably, first bolting upwards like a bean plant then broadening across the shoulders; now he was losing speed and lightness. He was a late starter – well, so were quite a few male dancers, even Konstantin Sergeyev, the director of the Kirov ballet company and omnipotent ruler of their world; this could be overcome by hard work, but Alex was not able to work. His faith in his vision of himself as a dancer fluctuated, and with it his concentration. On days when he was convinced he belonged, his expressiveness was so sublime that his faults became insignificant; when he felt at the bottom of his heart he was just a dull American kid with ridiculous artistic pretensions, he was so uncontrolled that the other boys sniggered openly and the teachers despaired.

There was also the problem of his attitude. A peculiar arrogance, gentle but stubborn, framed all his responses to discipline. Every other student at the Vaganova Academy was ecstatically grateful to be there, but Wolfe seemed unmoved by the honour extended to him. He lacked the proper reverence for the institution. The constant criticism of the teachers, which he ought to have accepted eagerly, went in one ear and out the other, as if he could not believe that he was not already perfect. He was like a small child who was unable to understand the difference between dancing and merely jumping around to music.

The ballet master frowned as his pupils concluded their exercise, then walked across to an exceptionally thin girl with dark hair parted in the centre, and took her by the hand.

'Boys! What is this?' They looked at him blankly. 'Is this a carcase? No! And what are you, porters in the abattoir? No! This is a beautiful woman, the woman you love, and you want the whole world to see how beautiful she is – so, what do you do? Throw her over your shoulder like dead meat? No! Wolf, please . . .' The whole school called him '*Volk*', the Russian word for wolf, routinely now, but at the outset they often used a mocking inflection imputing a predatory character to himself and his country.

The teacher gestured to Alex to assume his position behind

the dark girl, who waited expectantly, unable to keep a complacent smirk from her thin lips. It made her resemblance to the Mona Lisa even more marked.

'Look, all of you, this is where it begins. The placing of the hand, sensitive, natural, simple as a sigh but everything comes from this. Then when you lift' – he indicated that they should demonstrate a small jump – 'like magic, like a conjuring trick. More than easy, it must look as if it happens by itself.' The dark girl sprang silently into the air and floated back to earth as if by reluctant choice.

'But this does not happen by itself, does it? It happens because you use this . . .' He slapped Alex's back where his white cotton shirt met his black tights. 'The back! The centre of control! Not this!' He pinched Alex's biceps. 'And girls! Your pliés! You get your power here – the mainspring of your action! Don't be mean and make the boys do all the work. And above all, boys, you must use this' – he folded his hands over his own chest. 'The heart. Love this woman. Worship this woman. Show her to the audience as if she is a beautiful flower unfolding in the sunshine. Now, again. First group, please.'

In sulky silence, the students exchanged places and the dark girl fluttered back to her partner. Nadia was the golden child of her year for two reasons – she was a superb dancer and a party snitch. That pure Madonna's face masked a compromised soul. She threw Alex a languishing stare under her eyelashes, but to this he was oblivious. As far as he was concerned, Anya was the only woman in the world.

His roommate Vitya raised a laugh, mincing up to his partner and planting increasingly lustful kisses from her fingertips to her ear. Alex caught some resentful looks from the boys, and tried to turn them away with a self-deprecating shrug. He appreciated that in their eyes he did not really deserve to be singled out to demonstrate; in all the other classes he was picked out for his faults. His only real friend was Vitya, cursed with a stocky build and a humorous but undeniably porcine face, who had already given up all pretensions to being a ladies' man.

At the end of the lesson the ballet master had one final word for him. 'You may have your grandmother's strength, Alexei, but I wish you hadn't also inherited her deafness. Listen to the music. This poor woman is not playing for her own pleasure, you know.' The accompanist spoiled the lecture by shaking her head, smiling so much that her eyes disappeared into her plump face. Another reason that he was unpopular with the boys was that Alex Wolfe affected women like catnip affected cats.

He sloped along the corridor to the changing room, bored now that physical activity had ceased, his spirits further lowered by the shabby austerity all around. Eighteen months ago he had entered the school which had been held up to him as the sacred cradle of ballet through an archway from which half the stucco was missing and the rest blistered. The unbroken façades on both sides of Rossi Street, painted pale apricot but streaked with grime, seemed institutional in their symmetry. The thrill of being in this forbidden country began to drain away almost immediately. He noticed that the street itself was unswept and nameless dirt filled the gutters.

The Director was a woman whose looks were of a style which would later become familiar to him. Her portrait photographs, in costume and make-up, witnessed her youthful beauty, but even as a young woman there had been nothing dewy in her gaze, no tenderness in her mouth, none of the faun-like vulnerability shown by her contemporaries. A career of petty betrayals and small rewards, of serving herself before her art, of slavery to a whole hierarchy of crass political satraps, had stolen every shred of loveliness from her face. In middle life she was suety and coarse, expressionless, her grey hair dyed a harsh yellow, her grace replaced by awkward bulk.

In the course of his first term Alex noted that she shared her particular ugliness with many other administrators, and concluded that corruption was a poor guardian of beauty. He compared the women with his grandmother, who at twice the age had vivacity, expression and a fragile but proper pride in her bearing; he noted that the pure features of Nadia the snitch were setting a little harder, a little narrower for every classmate informed upon for such anti-Soviet practices as wasting hot water in the showers.

He considered the link between a woman's beauty and her integrity a fascinating discovery, and began to form the theory that only women were capable of true goodness, while men were condemned to struggle in vain against their self-seeking instincts. He had no way of communicating these thoughts, and no companion receptive to them. He treasured his ideas alone, adding them to a store of female mythology, unconsciously collected to bestow on the woman he loved.

After his formal welcome, he had been taken at once to the museum which adjoined the Director's office, where the Curator, middle-aged but with an air of naive devotion, showed him round. She had the stance he now recognized, the mark which the dance had left on her, erect, still graceful in the upper body but stiff from the consequences of a thousand strains from the hips downwards.

In the museum he received his formal introduction to the ghosts who flitted hourly through the hallowed classrooms of Rossi Street. Around the plain white walls in historical progression were photographs of all the great names he recognized from his grandmother's nostalgic conversations, whom the Director and Curator talked about as if they were not only still alive, but their close friends. 'Karsavina – very talented but she had no technique, her legs would not turn out. She never made the thirty-two *fouettés* but she was always developing herself, her character. She turned her mistakes into her qualities,' they said, gazing approvingly at the soulful face crowned with silk flowers. 'Pavlova – wherever she worked she left a little bit of the Russian ballet, she gathered children and she taught them some exercises. A great romantic ballerina but weak, with many faults. She died at the right time because younger dancers were having more success. Whereas next, Spessitseva – the last Imperial ballerina, the first modern ballerina. Diaghilev said that Pavlova and Spessitseva were two halves of the same apple, but Spessitseva was the one which is turned to the sun. Her family put her in a mental hospital for thirty years to get her away from a bad love affair.'

They were proud to trace the lineage of their own authority. Here was Christian Johanson, who taught Nikolai Legat, who taught Agrippina Vaganova, who taught both of them, who in their turn had taught Kolpakova, Osipenko, Makharova and the dancers in the company now and also – here the Curator dropped her voice – Nureyev, who ran away from the family, after which she had been ordered to remove his photograph from the wall. Of course, from a patriotic viewpoint, it was right to condemn him for his desertion, but she felt personally that officialdom could take a kinder view of the frailty of genius.

The tiny, empty shoes, the lifeless costumes, the busts and statues, the bronze cast of Pavlova's right foot all seemed to Alex unconnected with the luminous enchantment of ballet. He was most attracted to the portraits. Grandmère had been painted full length and almost life size, in an off-the-shoulder pink evening gown with a feather in her hair, and she smiled at him with uncanny vivacity.

'Ah, *yes*, Kusminskaya. Very brilliant dancer, very athletic, but she wants the music to follow her, not to follow the music, so she always make the conductor crazy.'

They found him also a photograph of his grandfather, in a small, thick gold frame below the much larger portraits of Mikhail Fokine and Leon Bakst. He knew enough of Lydia Kusminskaya's life in St Petersburg to understand that his descent from the man who was thought of as her partner and choreographer, not her lover, would need explanation, and since he spoke only a few words of Russian at that time, he had not attempted to claim the relationship, merely asked questions. None of Leo Volinsky's ballets were still performed in the Soviet Union, they informed him sadly. *Salome* was still given in the West, he countered with excessive politeness, and he would like the opportunity to see *Les Pléiades* one day.

Later, he heard the story of Volinsky's death, told pointedly by a senior teacher with the aim of instilling a proper humility in him about his background. He had been caught out cutting a class in the history of the ballet. 'You know, Wolfe, you have sprung from barren soil? America is no place to breed an artist. You must work to make up for your lack of culture. Look at our choreographer, Volinsky, a man with an absolute vocation for the ballet, a very serious artist. Do you know what happened to him in America?'

'No, Sir,' Alex had replied with a show of alert contrition.

'When the war began in Europe Volinsky went with the Ballets Russes to America but Diaghilev lost interest in an artist once he had made him successful, and he wanted to make his lover Massine the chief choreographer. So he tired of Volinsky, who was offered a chance to stay in America and open his own choreographic academy. He had a family by then, there was the Revolution here at home, so he decided to accept, and so did many others who were cast adrift by Diaghilev in the same way.'

'Where did he settle?' Alex hoped to divert the lecture completely into his personal history.

'In a desert! In the middle of the country, where there was nothing but cornfields. And the others also. Now you will learn, Wolfe, that a dancer is always a child. The world is not for you. You cannot be businessmen. And Americans have no interest in art, no respect for culture. Ballet to them was just a passing fashion, they also grew tired of it in a few years. So soon Volinsky was bankrupt. His friends all suffered terrible failures – they were reduced to giving tango lessons in dance halls, dancing in cabarets, giving classes to fat women who wanted to lose weight. Diaghilev died, Nijinsky had gone mad. And Volinsky wrote a last letter to Fokine, who was still his idol but was also out of work, and then he went to a big waterfall and threw himself off the cliff into the torrent.'

'The Niagara Falls?' Alex's eyes were wide with a peculiar joy at hearing such a note of pure romance echoing from his past, chiming with his own wild impulses. In his early days in Leningrad he had been so crushed by loneliness that he too had been teased by thoughts of suicide.

The teacher, never having heard of Niagara Falls, did not understand and went on to lecture Alex about cultural deficiency. Later he had asked the Curator to rehearse the story again, and learned that Cleveland was the desert where his grandfather had despaired. The poetry of this coincidence resounded in his mind for weeks. Finally he was able to integrate all of his past, his dull experience and his exotic heritage, into one convincing life story.

As Alex peeled off his sweaty practice clothes and stood under the rattling shower-head, Anya was on his mind. He adored her so vastly he felt weak when he thought of it. To him she was all legendary women of Russia in one person. In her misty eyes he saw not short sight but the frailty of Anna Karenina. When she pinned up her hair and despaired of its fluffy curls, he saw a hundred heroines of Chekhov and Turgenev at their toilette. With the serious face she wore in class she was the queen beloved of Ivan the Terrible, whose death drove the tyrant to an orgy of destruction. And at night, when they bribed her roommate to disappear and Anya lifted up her bedclothes and welcomed him into her warmth, she was Lermontov's tribal princess of the Caucasus.

He dried himself and dressed, mentally promising his half erection its proper exercise in the evening as he settled it into his jeans. At the door the white-haired concierge scuttled out of her booth squeaking, 'Cold, cold!' She tried to fasten the snaps on his anorak and insisted that he produce his hat from his pocket and put it on.

Outside snow was falling, tiny flakes like a shower of powder, thin at roof level, thick as it approached the ground. There was no breeze. The end of the short street could just be made out, the sky was invisible. He drew in a breath and felt the clammy air spreading like fatigue through his body. The atmosphere in the city was so saturated with damp that on still days like this it was an effort to fill his lungs. The air seemed almost viscous and reluctant to yield oxygen; within a few hundred yards he felt smothered and tore open his anorak again to free his chest.

He turned into Lomonsonov Square and loped across the empty streets to the embankment of the little Fontanka river, hardly bothering to turn his head and look out for traffic; when a vehicle approached he was warned by the noise of its engine ringing across the ice and echoing between the buildings.

'On the corner which Kamenovsky Street makes with the Rimsky-Korsakov Prospekt. So you go past the Yussupov Palace – such a beautiful garden, the lilacs in the summer had such a wonderful scent you could smell them on the far side of the canal. So where the canal joins the river you follow it.' Grandmère had drawn him a map and he held it now in his bare fingers, noticing how the thick pencil lines showed the grain of the wooden table top.

He loitered without urgency, by now familiar with the route. When he first left for Leningrad, she had said nothing about the city to him. He had returned, both enchanted and appalled by the great half-empty avenues and their blistered façades, and shocked by the wilful neglect, the locked cathedrals and palaces used as offices with their marble floors unswept and their mouldings smashed to fit ugly lights. He had begun to pester her with questions about the days before the Revolution. She had refused to answer, raising her hands to push away his words and straining her stiff neck to turn aside her head as if avoiding a blow.

'It's no good, there's no point. You're going to tell me that everything's gone now, everything beautiful. I don't know this place you're talking about.' Now he understood: she was afraid of hearing that her Russia, so vividly remembered, no longer existed; she was like a soldier's mother whose son had long ago been reported missing in a battle but who still dreaded to hear that he was dead. 'The city I knew is gone,' she had declaimed. 'The life I led is over. The people I loved are dead. We lived in beauty, don't you see? I know it isn't like that now, it's all ugliness everywhere. You don't have to describe it to me, I know already. The past is the past, it's gone, finished – except in my heart, in all our hearts, there it is eternal. But don't try to tell me about this place, Leningrad. I never lived there. And you haven't been sent to make me sad.'

To reassure her he began to drop details into his conversation, mentioning the sun on the gold church domes or a statue in a park, and after some weeks she snapped suddenly awake from an afternoon doze and demanded, 'The bombing. What did they destroy? It wasn't much, they said it wasn't much.'

'In the war, the Germans?'

'They said they never got to the centre of the city.'

'That's right, Grandmère. In the siege the front was three miles out, they took us there.'

'But the centre?'

'It's all still there.'

Then she quizzed him, street by street, drawing a chair up to the table to scrawl maps on the paper which had wrapped the morning's bread, until his memory was exhausted and it was evident that the buildings still stood but many names had been changed. Marie sat down and tried to join the conversation, but stalled at the simple task of remembering the street on which she had lived. This unexpected failure almost visibly deflated her, and she sat in silence, patting her white hair.

'When you go back, go and see my house,' Lydia ordered. He was sharpening her pencil with the old penknife which lived with two peacock feathers and an ivory letter opener on an enamel tray. 'Here, I'll draw you the way. It must be there if Turgenev Square is there. When you see my house, then you'll understand what I was, what really La Kusminskaya was. You must take a picture with your camera. But don't show it me if it's ugly.'

Later another thing occurred to her. 'Don't expect a

palace. They requisitioned my house, you know. Nobody told me but I heard in the end. Made my cook serve them, drank all my wine and took my car. So who knows. I had such beautiful things, such beautiful things. No doubt they burned the furniture, maybe even the floors. I hung the drawing-room walls with yellow silk – it's a good thing to do in a northern climate, the colour gives the impression of sunlight.'

Angela Partridge, visiting for the first time after a fall which had kept her in hospital for a month with a broken wrist, rasped agreement. 'Absolutely right, she's absolutely right. I remember my own mother telling me the same thing. Of course, we never see the sun in England either.'

'The furniture was from Meltzer, everyone went to them. Except the bronze bits and pieces, they were from Paris. Who knows what will be left of it all now? One thing I had, which nobody else did – I had a safe in the house for my jewellery. Even Kchessinskaya didn't have that – she kept all her big pieces at Fabergé. A nuisance, sending couriers to and fro every day. She was really envious of my little safe. You go and take a look – the corner of Kamenovsky Street and Rimsky-Korsakov Prospekt. Everyone wanted to move out that way, it was terribly smart.'

'There were no factories there.' Marie was gratified to have one useful memory to contribute. 'But the prices went right up – Basil couldn't possibly have afforded it.'

'I say, it would be too good if the house was still there.' The Englishwoman lifted her bandaged hand on to the table with her free hand, enabling her to turn confidentially to the young man. 'You will have a look, won't you? It does mean a lot to your grandmother. I do believe she's talked about that house every single day ever since we met.'

When he first took to the streets with her map Alex

discovered that Grandmère's geographical recall was poor. For the most part, and once the Curator had found him a simple plan of the inner city as it had been before the Revolution, she had the names of streets correct, but their relationships to each other were all wrong. He found Rimsky-Korsakov Prospekt. It made corners with six other streets, and crossed a small canal, but none of these carried the name Kamenovsky.

A day or two after this setback, Anya proposed a solution. 'Six crossroads, twelve corners . . . why don't you just take your little camera and photograph all the buildings on the corners – then Granny can pick out her old house for herself?'

'They'll arrest me.' Random photography was among the many activities which, he had been warned by the American consulate, were forbidden in Russia.

'No they won't – or only for half an hour, until they find out who you are. Hide the camera in your pocket and just be casual, don't make a fuss about it. Do you want me to come with you so we look just like any other young couple?'

'You're a darling but this is something I want to do alone,' he told her abruptly, unwilling to explain. If they were caught he knew that the consequences for her would be serious.

The camera was buttoned into his anorak pocket, with a pair of gloves stuffed underneath it to bring the lens up to the edge. He could bring his hand up as if pulling his collar around his ears to keep out the cold, and press the shutter. It might be difficult to frame the shots but he was prepared to waste a film on a trial session this term. He set off at a brisk pace down Rimsky-Korsakov Prospekt. The people on the street in Leningrad mostly moved swiftly and purposefully, three shifts a day hurrying to and from their work and the metro stations in silent herds.

To avoid crossing the road too often and attracting attention, he decided to work down one side of the street, then
cross over to the other side and return. Living in Russia
made everyone paranoid; people spied on each other
routinely, normal actions were crimes and fear of the KGB
shaped daily life. To his relief, there were no more intersec-
tions with the city's major thoroughfares after the first canal,
and the crowd dwindled to a few self-absorbed pedestrians
who kept their heads well down against the cold.

His nerves had settled by the time he passed the church of
St Nicholas of the Sea; the gold cupolas on its slender spires
carried a visible sprinkling of snow on their windward side.
Surely Grandmère would have mentioned such a landmark,
even if it was less massive than the central cathedrals. If the
house had overlooked a canal she would have told him that
as well – or would she? Her reminiscences were always so
emotional. Best to be utterly conscientious and record
everything – if the less distinguished buildings were certainly
not what he was seeking they might still stimulate her
memory.

On his way back, with the church just appearing in view
once more, he had almost forgotten his fears, and took his
time to photograph a building whose frontage was partly
obscured by scaffolding. An official sign informed him that
the renovation of the Palace of the Young Pioneers was two
weeks ahead of schedule already. Some of the workers who
were hacking at the green-painted façade were female; the
sight of women doing manual work had first shocked and
now intrigued him. He delayed until one was clearly in view,
swinging her pick-axe in profile like a bas-relief figure on a
Soviet monument.

Before he could press the shutter there were shouts of
alarm and the sound of falling rubble from the interior. A

317

cloud of thick white dust burst from a hole where there had once been a window and obscured the heroic worker. Alex waited for it to clear, absorbed in capturing the picture he wanted.

He heard the command 'Stop!' bellowed as a group of three men ran out of a small doorway directly in front of him, and froze with fear. Although they were covered with plaster dust he saw that they were violently agitated; a fourth man leaped across the cracked doorstep and seized the nearest by his shoulder. 'Stop, you fools!' he repeated in a lower voice. 'Think, boys, think! Do you want . . .' The terror drained from Alex's body as he realized that he had not been discovered. The men were quite unaware of him, although they were separated only by a row of iron railings.

The four now drew together confidentially, their furtive manner amusing Alex. Russians normally hammed their emotions like silent film actors – naturally the drama coach thought his own subtle style was wooden. She just didn't understand, in the West audiences would laugh if he did what she wanted.

The men were examining something which one of them had hidden in his jacket. There was a sudden agreement, a quick back-slapping which raised more dust from their clothes, and they returned inside. The woman on the scaffolding was swinging her pick-axe again. Alex shook himself and stepped back to reframe the photograph before continuing on his way.

In half an hour the assignment was complete. The cold pinched his cheeks and toes unbearably, and he ran back northwards along Garden Street as fast as the icy surface would permit to stir his blood and warm his limbs.

The next destination was a small apartment above a fish shop on the Nevsky Prospekt where he went twice a week for Russian lessons. The shop window amused him when he was in a buoyant mood, but depressed him otherwise. It was decorated with flat wooden images of boats, fishermen and the god Neptune, painted in dull shades of blue. Real fishing nets of knotted twine were draped between the boats, carrying a catch of dummy tins of salmon and herring. Today he was able to smile at them and be charmed by the old salts and their cheery, two-dimensional grimaces. He was relieved to find that the shop was empty; one day there had been a long queue, and the impatient people at the head of it assumed he was pushing past them and set on him, ready to knock him down until the shopgirl screamed at them that he was only her mother-in-law's pupil.

The teacher was a wiry woman whose energy and black frizzy hair belied her stated age of sixty. Alex spoke and understood the language reasonably now; with a working knowledge of three languages he had revised his opinion of himself as a man without words. When he heard himself talking French and Russian comfortably he was so impressed to be communicating at all that the disparity between his deep feelings and the simple words he could command seemed insignificant.

On paper he was less confident. The teacher gave him a story from the Leningrad edition of *Pravda* to read aloud, then rewrite in flowing Cyrillic script. He did both lamentably. Perhaps there had been a sign for Kamenovsky Street after all, and he had simply failed to recognize it. He asked the teacher to write the name for him; she said the name was familiar, but could not find it on her street map. Alex fidgeted and was plainly anxious to be away. When she discovered it was his girlfriend's birthday she sent him off early with two mushroom pies and a gay smile.

At the ballet school's hostel he unloaded his camera and

hid the film in his canvas summer shoes, then set out to complete the preparations for the party. Across the corridor was the room nicknamed the Little Caucasus, inhabited by two Armenian boys and Andrusha, a Georgian, who had returned that weekend from a family funeral in Tbilisi. All Georgians were dealers, adept at playing their vast networks of contacts and favours to procure anything for anyone at a price, and Andrusha, charged by the American to supply the celebration in exchange for a pair of genuine Levis bought to his own measurements and a bottle of whisky, had returned with a suitcase containing a box of cherries, sticky honey and almond cakes, and a small jar of caviar. There was also the sausage, a salami so fragrant, meaty, tightly packed, perfectly rosy in colour and handsome in proportion that he suggested to his client it might be wiser to consume it immediately since on sight of it Anya was likely to transfer her affections. Alex immediately blushed.

'Oh hell, now what have I said? Look at him, he's turned into a beetroot.' The wire bed frame squeaked as Andrusha got up, flicking his thick black hair out of his eyes. 'Please, my friend, forgive me for dirtying your elevated feelings with my coarse imagination. I had forgotten it is love we are dealing with here, not everyday lust. Now, what else have I got for you – ah, yes . . . just one moment, if you please.'

He slipped out of the door and returned almost at once with a bunch of perfect red roses wrapped in newspaper. 'I put them in a little spot I know at the end of the hall where there's a hole in the window frame so it's always cool.'

'Oh wow – these are beautiful.'

'Naturally. My sister knows someone who works on the farm where they grow them. Any time you want to give your girl a nice bouquet just shoot one of my relatives to give me the excuse and I'll be delighted to pop home and get it for you. In my country we have the most beautiful of everything – women, roses, sausages . . .'

'I must give you something for them.'

'Forget it – they're my gift to you.' By this Andrusha meant that he would store the goodwill to be called in at a later date. 'I'm only doing my patriotic duty. When you go home to the West you can tell everyone what a happy existence we have here in Russia. How can these pitiful Americans have any concept of the joys of life, eh, guys?'

The Armenians, lounging on their beds, waited expectantly for the punch line. 'How can they understand the delight of a man who has acquired a sausage at a good price for his friend and had a blow-job from the sausage-maker into the bargain? Pure happiness, eh? How can you compare such a sublime experience with merely handing a few dollar bills over a shop counter?'

Next Alex called on Anya's waif-like roommate, Irina, who was fortunately resting a strain for two days and so able to get the bread, which cost him a Christian Dior lipstick. The champagne he had imported himself, and the vodka was contributed by Anya's closest friend Elena, whose stepfather was KGB and could get the best of everything. She had asked for stockings, but he had only pantyhose, and his assurance that in the West only old women still wore stockings was eventually accepted after much argument.

The guests were the contributors to the feast, with the addition of Alex's roommate, Vitya. He was the son of two famous veterans of the Kirov company, and Alex found him obsessed with his own physical imperfection, but they covered up for each other in so many minor crimes that he counted him a friend despite his character. It was suicide to omit from the circle of favour anyone whose influence could prove harmful.

They assembled as soon as the rest of the students had left for the canteen. Alex had a record player on which he obligingly played whatever the company chose, only occasionally trying to impose his own tentative taste for Steppenwolf and Fleetwood Mac. Anya obediently sang along, although she preferred the Rolling Stones. She wore her present, a pink angora cardigan with pearl buttons, a luxurious complement to her muzzy style of beauty.

For a couple of hours they drank and ate merrily, Alex sticking to the champagne and the others somewhat put out by his generosity. 'Come on, man, toast your girlfriend in the proper fashion at least.' Andrusha put a glass of vodka in his hand.

'It's perfectly proper to drink toasts in champagne at home. You know I'm not trained to drink vodka like you do and besides, tonight I want to save myself.'

'What for?' One of the Armenians looked up, hopeful of further entertainment.

'Not what for, you idiot!' Irina slapped him crossly on the thigh. '*Who* for!' The boys still looked puzzled.

'Old American custom,' Anya explained, snuggling complacently into Alex's shoulder. 'The birthday fuck. Extra special. The birthday person can have whatever she likes.' She rolled her translucent blue eyes.

'Absolutely daft,' announced Vitya, refilling the glasses. 'Give a woman what she likes and you'll be stuck with her. You can't keep a woman in her place if you indulge her. Always leave her wanting more – that's the secret.'

Irina spat delicately at the metal wastebin. For all her ethereal looks, she had the manners of a street-sweeper. 'Well, Vitya, when you have a woman wanting more of you we'll believe you know something.' She tossed her head and examined her new lipstick in her compact mirror.

'That's not the way it is with us Georgians.' Andrusha, who was obsessed with blondes, spoke as if to no one in particular. 'We can't take that puritanical line. My mother always said it was the warm southern climate which made people warmer, pleasure-loving, sensual . . . and our culture has such strong Indo-European elements, the erotic sophistication of the Kamasutra is something that's still in our blood.'

'Rubbish,' muttered Vitya, putting down the bottle with a crash. 'I can't stand listening to this crap. Excuse me, my legs are so stiff they're killing me. If neither of you girls wants to give me a massage I'll have to do something about it myself.'

'You don't fuck enough, Vitya, that's the problem. You need to get the hormones flowing to loosen you up.'

'Listen to the expert here – if fucking was anything to do with it our Wolf would never hear a word about his turn-out again, now would he?' He sat on the floor and began pummelling one of his thighs with his fists, pausing every now and then to refresh himself with more vodka. Nobody took much notice, because Vitya was always bemoaning his tight muscles and always practising some new technique which he was sure would make him looser than ever before.

Elena put on a scratched Johnny Mathis album of which she was particularly fond and invited one of the Armenians to dance with her.

'Have you ever done it when you're high?' Andrusha whispered to Irina. 'Your ears are so tiny, they're just like little petals.'

'What do you mean, high?'

'High like you get from smoking grass.'

'I've never smoked grass.'

'I can't believe that, you're always up with all the latest things. It's the most fantastic feeling.'

'Honestly, it's true – why, have you got some?' Her eyes were positively glittering from flattery and excitement. Andrusha decided that he was probably home and dry.

'Sssh! There isn't enough to share.' He indicated the number of people in the room with a toss of his head, allowing her to admire the well-cut flop of his glossy black hair.

'And the birthday girl will be wanting our place to herself tonight. Where is the stuff – have you got it with you?'

'It's in my room.'

'Oh yes?'

'Why, what's your problem?'

'What about your friends? Are we talking about grass or the daisy game here?'

'What daisy game, I don't understand?'

Irina smiled to herself and smoothed her hair behind her ears. The daisy game was all the rage with the smart Leningrad kids; Andrusha could not be half as sophisticated as he pretended if he had never heard of it. It was simple, really – three girls, six legs spread like petals, three boys, everyone comes when somebody gives the word. Or they say they do.

'Oh nothing. It's just you and me, then?'

'Of course.'

'OK, what are we waiting for? Let's go.'

They left the room quietly, bidding Anya goodnight in low voices. Elena danced with first one then the other of the two Armenians, and when they both were too drunk to co-ordinate she continued swaying about the room by herself. Vitya lay on the floor, wriggled towards the skirting board and extended his legs up the wall.

'Lazy boy,' Alex chided him with affection.

'What do you want me to do? I'm too tired to stand up.

My thighs are like violin strings. Anyway, this way you get the best stretch. Lend me your weights, Alexei?'

'Of course.'

'Well, do I have to lie here all night waiting? If you're going to lend them to me, do it now please.'

Alex rummaged under his bed for his leg weights, bands filled with lead granules, each weighing one kilo, and buckled them snugly around his friend's ankles. Vitya opened his legs into a wide V and bounced them gently, feeling a grudging extension in the muscles of his inner thigh. 'That's good. Half an hour like this and I'll be a new man tomorrow. Andrusha's talking out of his ass, isn't he? About fucking, I mean. I can see a girl might loosen up, but not a guy, never.'

'Get pregnant, Vitya, that's the best.' Elena rebounded dreamily from the wall.

'Sodding biology! Why do I get the short end of the stick every sodding time? Now pass the bottle, please.'

'Are you sure you ought to drink more?'

'Yes, absolutely. It'll help me relax. Give, give.'

He clicked his fingers, winking happily. Alex put the vodka bottle within his reach, then signed to Anya that it was time to leave. They drifted back to her room and settled into bed. For months he had cherished the ambition to make her come while he licked her. She was sceptical, at first because she considered the area between her legs irredeemably unsavoury and did not believe that he could possibly enjoy nuzzling around there. Once coaxed into allowing a demonstration, she had admitted that since his cock got as hard as stone during the process, he must get some enjoyment from it. Alex, with a subtle instinct for sexual personality, could sense a barrier and was determined to lead her through it into full possession of her own sensuality. It was past midnight when her body became insistent and uncontrolled;

at last she gave a small scream and he felt her lips pulse against his and his tongue clasped by all the mysterious inner folds of her sex.

They lay together in the darkness, their skin damp with perspiration. Anya considered the best way to bring up the subject of marriage. Should she act vulnerable and play on his sympathy – he must be soft if he really wanted to eat her out all the time – or give him a bit more air, maybe flirt with one of the others, make him miss her a little, then pitch for the ring? He's the closest I'll ever get to an exit visa, I must tie him down, she promised herself.

Alex remembered their first real meeting, in a small studio where he had gone to practise alone, in the depths of loneliness and despair during his first month at the Academy. When he had stepped into the middle of the floor the emptiness around him had been so overpowering that he had dissolved into tears. After a few minutes she had entered the room with the same purpose and, seeing his distress, had simply run to him and held him in her arms. He had felt enveloped in soft femininity, his pain soothed immediately. Now, with her body truly his and the sweet, salty taste of her in his mouth to prove it, he felt completely at peace.

The sensation was brief. There was an urgent tap at the door and Irina stumbled into the room.

'Quick, quick, get up, get dressed, that bitch Nadia's raising hell.'

'What's the matter?' Anya's head left the pillow immediately and she struggled to be free of Alex's arms.

'She went looking for Elena, someone told her she was with Alex. She must have just walked into the room. The first we heard was her screaming that Vitya was crippled. Thank God she made so much noise.'

'Better get moving, Alex, she's taken off like a bat out of

hell looking for the Director.' Andrusha was a silhouette against the light from the corridor. They could tell from his voice that he was still smiling.

'OK, give me a minute.' He scrambled reluctantly to his feet, pushed Irina out of the room and felt for the light switch as he closed the door.

'Anya had better stay here,' the Georgian advised. 'Then at least only one of you will be in trouble.'

They ran back to his room, in which a grotesque tableau was posed. One of the Armenian boys lay slumped in a corner, the other was more decorously laid out on the bed. Elena had collapsed into a chair and vomited over the arm; the acrid smell tainted the atmosphere. By the far wall lay Vitya, also unconscious, the empty vodka bottle on its side by his outstretched hand. His legs had flopped apart like those of a puppet, one bent at the knee and twisted awkwardly against the wall, the other lying almost flat to the floor at a hideously unnatural angle.

'Oh my God! Vitya – he's passed out. Is she right, has he really crippled himself?' Alex turned to Andrusha in terror, longing for the reassurance of his sophistication.

'Search me. That hip must be dislocated for sure. Maybe the ligaments have gone. I've heard of people doing things like this, but I never really believed it was possible.'

'Suppose he's dead?' A profound cold spread from the centre of his body to the tips of his fingers.

'No, of course he's not dead – can't you hear? He's snoring like a pig. We can't move him, it might make things worse and Nadia will spill the beans anyway. Let's get the boys out of here at least – come on, stop shivering, give me a hand.'

This robust common sense calmed Alex a little, and together they dragged the insensible bodies back to their own beds across the corridor. Irina ripped the quilts from the beds and covered them up, shoes and all. The double windows had been flung wide to dispel the fumes of grass, and now Andrusha closed them before the temperature dropped to freezing. Irina had already made herself scarce.

'And Elena, we must get her back,' Alex insisted, in an agony of guilt that a girl who had abetted his love with such good humour might suffer for it.

'It'll look great if we meet the Director in the corridor.' Andrusha was peeling off his shirt and vest, preparing to change into his nightclothes. 'She's fucked anyway if you ask me, Nadia will sneak to her father, try and do herself some good. We'll be lucky if there isn't a police inquiry.'

'It can't look any worse than it does now – please, Andrusha.'

'Go on, move her yourself if you're so concerned. She's not so heavy – use *this!*' He prodded Alex in the back with audible jealousy.

Without wasting any more time, Alex ran back to his room and dragged the girl out of the chair and into his arms. He heaved her over his shoulder like a rug, praying that she had spewed her last for that night at least. Her dead weight was indeed heavier to lift than her animated body in pas de deux class.

He met no one in the corridor and restored Elena to her own bed without incident. By the time he returned to his own room, the lights were on all over that part of the hostel and the students were standing sleepily in their doorways, asking what the noise was about. The Director, who had taken the time to dress, was standing in the centre of Alex's room listening to Nadia's vociferous description of the scene as she had discovered it, while one of the senior male teachers, in his ugly brown dressing gown, knelt beside Vitya, tenderly stroking his face.

'We could bring him round but what's the point?' he was saying as Alex halted in the doorway. 'The poor lad will be in such agony he'll probably pass out again. Better leave him as he is. How long is it since we called the hospital? Surely they're on their way by now.'

'There he is!' screamed Nadia, suddenly catching sight of Alex. 'It's his fault, he bought the drink!' The others turned, and in a second the man was in front of him raining slaps and punches on his head.

'Stop it, stop it, Fedya. You'll mark him, it's not wise . . .' The Director took a couple of steps towards them but paused, fearing that she would only provoke more violence. In her mind, where humane considerations were not uppermost, this was not a major tragedy. After all, Vitya's parents were the kind of fools who thought that being artists excused them political alignment; they had been thoroughly out of favour for a decade, and were likely to remain so until old age or alcoholism terminated their careers.

'Not wise! Was it wise for this degenerate with his criminal behaviour to destroy the future for one of our boys? What kind of sick mind could do such a thing? Were you drunk, too? Obviously, but that's no excuse. Even a drunken tramp in the gutter has more care for his friends. You're subhuman, an animal . . .' Alex was frozen with shock at the attack and the force of the man's anger. He opened his mouth to protest that he had only broken one small rule, not committed a murder, but his Russian deserted him and he knew that if he expressed himself in his own language it would anger them all even further. He was saved by two ambulance men, who struggled along the corridor with a stretcher, followed by a much older man from the teaching staff who exhorted them to be careful in moving their patient.

In a few minutes two more men arrived, middle-aged strangers wearing suits, and a conversation ensued which he could not fully understand. Vitya, still unconscious, was loaded on to the stretcher and carried away, with both teachers following. Nadia was thanked for her prompt action by the Director, and told to come to the office the next morning to write a report. The rest of the party adjourned across the street to the Director's office. She left Alex to sit outside in the care of the two newcomers and, from the clicks and rings behind the half-closed door, made several telephone calls.

Tiredness numbed him but lurid fears that he would be interrogated, tortured and sent to a prison camp made even a shallow doze impossible. He wished desperately that he could speak to Anya, telling himself that she would be anxious and distressed, but really wanting the comfort of her touch.

After some hours there was a faint lightening of the sky outside, still obscured by falling snow, and shortly afterwards it became clear that a decision had been reached. A man with extremely short fair hair arrived, a junior official at the American consulate. After an interview with the Director, he called Alex in Russian to join them.

'You're being expelled,' he explained in his light, nasal voice. 'If you were Russian you'd be in jail by now. They don't want an incident any more than we do, so they're just throwing you out. We can go and pack up your things now and you can stay with one of our people until we get you on a flight.'

'Can I just say goodbye to my girlfriend?'

The man looked at him as if he were the living embodiment of foolishness. 'If you must, I suppose.'

CHAPTER 11
Britain, 1979

The sun came up eagerly over the village and Bianca was awake to see it. She stood by the bedroom window and watched the new daylight race over the rooftops in the middle distance, warming the red brick walls of the cottages. Skimming the tree-tops, the last bats to return home made for their roost in the studio roof. The church weathervane, a silver trout, glittered as if it were alive and about to shiver its tail and glide away into the sky.

The position of the house was seigneurial, next to the house of God, looking down on the humbler dwellings. No more of that, Bianca promised silently. No more performing beside her lord as the gracious chatelaine, dispensing smiles and compliments at the church fete and the Christmas bazaar to villagers who for the most part were London commuters like themselves, enjoying the feudal pantomime that was the expected perk of converting a picturesque rural slum into a complex of luxury leisure homes.

Bianca had woken before the dawn and lain awake in the bed, smoothing the pillow and the sheet, enjoying the knowledge that Lovat no longer had any place beside her. The defence and protection of her nightdress were not necessary now; she threw the horrible demure white lace thing across the room and pulled on her jeans. Freedom was effervescing in her veins.

The sun lighted her garden. The currant bushes, trained at her direction in docile espaliers, called her to pick their fruit

331

and she ignored them. She hoped the guests invited in her name would have been embarrassed into leaving during the night; entertaining them was no longer her responsibility.

From the children's rooms above she heard small feet on the floorboards, Orlando getting up to play. From a greater distance came the sound of coughing, a prolonged, congested, old man's cough, Kusminsky clearing his ruined lungs. There's no time to lose, I must escape, she whispered to herself in the mirror, chuckling as she ran downstairs. In the hall, the fifteenth-century oak dower chest, which she had recently been gratified to recognize as a mere collection of boards in a barn, called out for more beeswax in vain.

In her studio she looked around at her collages; idiotic faces rolled glass bead eyes, their gambolling limbs suddenly seeming grotesque. Once again, Bianca felt nauseous. She fetched a wheelbarrow, loaded the canvases into it and carried them at a run to the rubbish tip. One barbecue lighter and they caught fire readily, the flames invisible in the bright light. A line of foul-smelling smoke rose vertically in the still air.

'Wow! The burning ghat of Buckinghamshire.' Hermione appeared on the far side of the blaze, bundled into a pink towelling bathrobe. 'What's all that going up in smoke?'

'Rubbish.' A mischievous smile twitched her sister's lips.

'They're your pictures! Bea! What is this – are you all right?'

'I'm great. They aren't pictures, they're crap – trite, coy, nauseating, hypocritical crap. I just looked at them and wanted to throw up. I only did them because everybody expected me to create something. Now they can all just get off my back.'

'I get it – this is death and regeneration, the eternal cycle. Like Persephone you've got to go down into the darkness before you are reborn . . .'

Beneath her diaphragm, Bianca felt the unmistakable first flutter of the child she was carrying. She had forgotten that she was pregnant; the knowledge lay like a pool of dread in her body, something that could render the fine new edifice of her life unstable, because at its foundations she was bonded to Lovat and ruled by her body. She had presented that body as the ungovernable director of her destiny for so long that she believed in it herself; now she wished violently to control it. Was it too late for a termination? Was there no excuse, no explanation she could fabricate to rescue herself? Did she really love children, or was that too something she had put on as a disguise?

The mild ecstasy of the early morning gave way to practical things. Last night she had conquered her family; now she had to consolidate the gains of the victory.

'Are they all still here?'

'Who? The guests? Yes, Charlotte's taken over. She just told the boys that Lovat had been called back to London for business. Isn't she incredible? Breakfast is proceeding as normal – well, actually not, she's brewing up kasha for the Russians. She is *so* cool; you'd think her granddaughter threw her husband out of the house with accusations of incest every day of the week.'

'It's not incest and they admitted it. They all admitted it, don't you remember? They all knew.'

'That really blew my mind.' Natural soft sympathy was all Bianca heard in her sister's voice, which pleased her. A kaleidoscope of possibilities had been spinning in her mind and she had fleetingly considered that Hermione might also have been part of the conspiracy.

Tightening the belt of the robe, Hermione walked around the edge of the fire to see her sister more clearly. Bianca looked younger. There was no bitterness or anger in her face. Despite the trauma of the night, she had taken off her make-up and brushed her hair, and her eyes were clear, without any sign of weeping. In the weak light of the early morning they were dark and her gaze flickered restlessly about, as if agitated by the thoughts behind.

'Oh Bea, you do run full tilt at life, don't you? I just drift along, taking what comes.'

A burning section of a frame fell out of the fire and Bianca kicked it back into the blaze. 'I don't see any reason to hesitate if there's something that has to be done. I was dying, Herm. Yesterday I really felt as if I was fading away, turning into a shadow. I had to be free, that's all. You *are* free already, that's the difference. Your life's your own, what you want it to be.'

'Except I don't know what I want most of the time.' They stared at the fire in silence until the paint and paper had burned away and only the largest pieces of wood remained to be pushed into a smouldering heap. 'Do you think he'll try to make you change your mind?'

'Who, Lovat? No. Lovat left years ago, Herm. Me telling him to go was just a formality. Maybe he was never really here in the beginning. Here, with me, for me, on my side. We were so young, I needed so much to get out of the family – now it's difficult to remember how things were. I know I believed he loved me, but maybe he just needed me.' A light breeze suddenly swept the garden and blew the smoke towards them. Bianca retreated, folding her arms against the sudden chill, then turned to walk back to the house.

'He wasn't one of those aggressive, chippy Northerners at all.' The memory of Lovat standing stiffly at the side of the Chelsea drawing room, his fingers twitching with nerves, softened Hermione's feelings for a moment. 'I used to think that the whole London scene just scared him shitless.'

'Lovat was never frightened of anything. I used to love that about him, the way he would never let anyone put him down or push him around. I thought that was what talent did for you, took away all your doubts. I believed I loved him. So much it made me feel as if the love filled me up like a baby fills you up when you're pregnant, no room to breathe or eat, all you are is a vessel carrying a miracle. But again . . . the same thing. Maybe I just needed him.'

Hermione, now filled with loyal loathing for the man, searched for something to pierce her sister's disturbing calm. 'Are you worried about the boys?'

'No. They won't miss what they never had either.' She paused on the steep path, aware that Hermione was out of breath. 'I think in a way he hated them. Not hated them as children, but as part of my life that he couldn't control. Tell me something, since we're telling the truth . . .' The blue-grey eyes under their level brows searched Hermione's face. 'What about our mother in all this? Do you think she did it deliberately?'

'Seduced Lovat? I had a real intuitive flash on that. She wasn't exactly accepting of us as sexual women, was she?' Hermione combed her long hair off her face with her fingers and set off up the path again. 'She's always been so into herself, into her looks.'

'They both swore it was before Lovat and I met, but what else could they say?' Bianca gave a short, harsh exclamation of amusement, the first sign of tension she had displayed. 'All those years and they all knew and nobody said a word.'

The church bells began ringing for the morning service as they reached the kitchen door; with the belltower so close to the house the noise was aggressive. The kitchen and breakfast room were disarrayed, a child had left a half-eaten piece of toast on the staircase. A sudden longing for a home that was

335

hers, and a body that was hers, possessed Bianca. At least she could free the house of strangers; at once she set off to reassure the English guests with graceful apologies; her invitation to them to stay and enjoy a lazy country Sunday contained the exact proportion of sincerity necessary to enable them to refuse without feeling that they were giving offence, and by eleven they had all thankfully driven away. Charlotte took charge of the boys, ordering them into their clothes and marching them off to church with Kusminsky and his companion, leaving Bianca to deal only with her parents.

They sat, in poses that verged on the histrionic, at opposite ends of the drawing room, the largest room in the house. Olivia had dressed as stylishly as ever, but the ruffles, buckles and fringed suede skirt of her current cowgirl ensemble had a bedraggled air and she herself, sunken-chested and haggard, looked as if she had woken from a nightmare.

'You two look like a Hogarth cartoon.' When Bianca greeted them her mother reacted with so little energy that compassion for the woman drained by shame and defeat almost threw her off her course.

'After *Mariage à la Mode, Divorce à la Carte*, perhaps?' Hugh, smiling briefly at his own wit, did not seem moved to defend his wife. There was a sense of estrangement between them, but not of coldness.

'This will be a difficult time for us, all of us as a family.' Bianca assumed a high, formal voice and instinctively moved to stand in the centre of the room with her back to the fireplace. 'First of all, I want you both to know that I don't blame anyone except Lovat. Naturally, I do feel ...' She paused, searching for the right word, aware that she had them both at her own advantage at last. 'I feel hurt, not by what happened, but by your silence all these years. But the responsibility for telling me was Lovat's from the beginning and I feel that he is the one who has betrayed me.' Again she stopped to gather her thoughts, testing her power. If I can shoot down their protests before they open their mouths, she told herself, then I'll have won, the air will be clear and they won't stand in my way again. Her father, to her surprise, did not interrupt.

'I'm sure things would have been different if we hadn't got married so quickly, while you were away. At the time, I suppose, it was my way of rebelling, claiming my independence.' Now her father was nodding, a degree of relief showing in his pale face. 'Everything I said last night, I meant. I can't live with Lovat any more and I want a divorce, as quickly as possible. I will come up to London on Monday and see a solicitor. But for the rest of today, I think I'd be more comfortable on my own with Charlotte and the boys.'

'I think that's – that's a very understandable request,' Hugh broke in quickly. 'And I'm glad that you've taken the initiative in making this – this very lucid summary of your position . . .' He was talking like a teacher commenting on her homework, but she forced herself not to get angry. 'I think we all need to cool off and consider our next actions.' Could he be ready for a change too, Bianca wondered. He had accepted his wife's tasteless infidelity for so long, and with so much dignity in spite of his vitriolic tongue, that she had lost sight of the fact that her father had ample grounds for divorce.

Olivia cleared her throat and her hand, loaded with silver rings, moved to disguise the lined skin of her neck in a habitual gesture. 'Bianca, darling, I do want to make one thing clear to you . . .'

Rage flared briefly, but she controlled it. 'I can't discuss anything now. I think I understand as much as I need to at the moment.'

'Let's make a move.' It sounded very much like an order, and Hugh crossed the room and took his wife gently by the elbow to enforce it. She rose unsteadily and allowed him to lead her to the door.

The church party, wearied and red-faced from walking up the hill in the full heat of the summer day, returned in time to wave off the Mercedes in which Olivia sat as stiff as a doll. Hugh delayed to take leave of his mother, and to squeeze Bianca's arm firmly, telling her, 'You've behaved admirably over this, my dear. Dignified, generous, self-possessed, everything a woman should be. And for your mother's sake I think it was wise not to indulge in recriminations. I was proud of you, I want to tell you that.' To her own annoyance, she smiled at him in gratitude. It was the first time he had ever praised her. 'You're not to worry about the future, especially the next few months. Try to relax now and enjoy the new baby, I know you will do that. We'll be on your side. Whatever's gone on in the past, this is an opportunity to begin again.'

Bianca watched him walk to the car and drive away, reluctantly feeling a twinge of sympathy.

'Well, dear, you're clearing the house out with a vengeance. Who's next? Do you want to get us out of your hair as well?' In the hall, cool and dim after the sun outside, her grandmother looked brightly up at her from the low window seat where she sat to change her shoes. For church she wore a dress, a slightly bizarre assembly of brown silk ruffles with a peplum which only emphasized her gamine angularity. 'I mean it, I'll take the boys off your hands for the afternoon if you want to be alone. Kolya needs a nap after lunch so you won't be disturbed.' She had left the two Russians sitting outside in the shade of the young wisteria leaves, cautiously sipping tall glasses of Pimm's.

338

'I want the boys around.' There was not a shadow of remorse in her grandmother's manner and Bianca, still hungry for revenge, searched the bland face for signs of emotion.

'Don't look at me like that – I tried to tell you but you flew into a temper.' She stood up and twitched the unaccustomed dress at the back of her neck, hoping that the unruly frills of fabric would arrange themselves properly. 'Don't you remember?'

'No.' How annoying to have her thoughts read and refuted immediately. 'You can't have tried very hard.'

'There was no point, you wouldn't listen. You were madly in love with him, anyone could see that.'

Bianca was suddenly so interested in an eyewitness account of the condition in which she had given herself to Lovat that her annoyance seemed to evaporate. 'Was I really, Charlotte? I can't remember.'

'You used to light up and glow even when you talked about him, and when he was there in the room with you – well, it was difficult to be in a small space with the two of you, I certainly remember that.' Her papery complexion suddenly showed blotches of red. All her life when she had seen people ruin themselves for passion she had been grateful for her own cool temperament; it disturbed her even to talk of violent feelings. 'It was like something magnetic between you, just drawing you together.'

'I can't imagine it.' What she felt now was a powerful force repelling her from Lovat.

'You're in love with him now, if only you knew it. It's just that there's too much going on in your lives.' Before she could contradict her grandmother, Benedict ran into the hall with a football rattle, and in the effort of swinging it tripped over a rug, fell, picked himself up, yelled 'Lunch is ready!'

339

and then, finding that he had banged his elbow painfully, began to bawl. The thread of conversation was lost in the confusion of comforting him.

At lunch three adults, three children and two elderly people sat down with appetites honed by events to a meal planned for twice their number and consumed a remarkable quantity of it. Bianca had intended to dispatch Kusminsky and his companion next, but time had raced away and Charlotte so obviously enjoyed their company that she relented. The Russians retreated tactfully behind their bad English.

Afterwards the company dispersed; it always gratified Bianca to see people lured by the mystery of her garden to wander from one enclave to the next and finally settle wherever matched their mood. Kolya and his young man strolled away to the orchard, the boys and Hermione drifted towards the swimming pool and Bianca joined her grandmother on the sun-loungers by the water garden, where the large dragonflies darting under the giant leaves of the gunnera made the whole world seem momentarily over-sized.

The breeze had died away and the heat, trapped by the close-clipped yews behind them, was so intense that after a few minutes they moved to the shade.

'I do wish I could doze off.' Charlotte, who hated to have idle hands, emptied a tangle of petit point wools from a basket and began to pick it apart. 'At my age I really ought to be able to go off for a little sleep in the afternoon like everyone else, but here I am, wide awake. It's not fair, is it?'

'When Hugh and Olivia were married . . .' Bianca was still anxious to drain her grandmother's memory. 'Were they like Lovat and me?'

'Oh no. Hugh's like his father, not a cold man, exactly, because he feels deeply, he really does, but reserved. That's the word. And terribly proud, terribly. It's the death of him, that pride. And of course, Olivia was very beautiful when she was young. Oh! The delusion that beauty is goodness – men do suffer for it, your father certainly did.'

'You never liked her, did you?'

'It isn't my business to like her or not. Hugh wanted her to be his wife.' Her lips pursed as if to stop disloyal words from escaping, she began extracting a length of wool and reached into her bag for her spectacles. Charlotte always carried a capacious black leather shoulder bag in whose folds everything she needed was elusive. 'Don't sigh like that. You know I'm like Switzerland, permanently neutral.'

'I think I'll be Italy under the Borgias – thirty years of war, terror, murder and bloodshed.' Bianca frowned, feeling the baby move again. 'All that and they produced Michelangelo, Leonardo and the Renaissance. While Switzerland had five hundred years of democracy and peace and what did they produce? The cuckoo clock.'

'Why are you talking in that ridiculous way?'

'That's how Orson Welles said it.'

The response was a disdainful cluck. Charlotte would not be impressed by anything American. 'I refuse to be a music-hall mother-in-law. You can't interfere in another person's life. I tried to once and it was a terrible mistake, so now I've learned my lesson.'

'Don't you even talk to Hugh about her?'

'He talked to me, once.' She pinched the end of a length of pink wool and threaded the needle in one triumphant move, proud that she could accomplish such a delicate manoeuvre at her age. 'It was just after you married. He does love you, Bianca, in his way. You must never doubt that. I don't think he knew about Lovat and your mother in the beginning; by all accounts there wasn't much in it. But

341

she told him and he was angry – I've never seen him so angry. Absolutely white with rage, his face was. He actually called her a whore and he could hardly say the word out loud. And then he said, "I won't find looks of her quality in another woman of our age, and I won't run around making a fool of myself with some young dolly." '

'That was all he said about her?'

'You were the main topic of discussion then, dear.' The needle descended unhesitatingly on a tiny hole in the tapestry.

'So that was when you all conspired to let me go on living a lie?' Would nothing shake a reaction out of Charlotte?

'Nobody conspired. Actually I agreed to take on the task of telling you. I just wasn't very good.' Another stitch the size of a pinhead was added to the design. 'But I think I was glad I made a mess of it. All that modern no-secrets nonsense Hugh believes in – a family needs secrets, they're part of what hold people together. Everyone knows there is a secret, of course, but they don't all know what it is and they agree the family is more important than something that's all in the past anyway.'

In the months that followed Bianca found she was finally grateful for her father's dynastic ambitions. He paid her attention – not in the oppressive style of her early years, but a respectful, even kind interest which made the physical arrangement of her separation as easy as it could have been. Her lawyer was the domestic specialist in the firm which acted for the house of Berrisford; she never saw a bill and Hugh asked her so delicately if he might take care of it that she agreed. Olivia made a few awkward moves towards reconciliation with her daughter, then drifted away to New Mexico on the pretext of a year's teaching at a new design college.

342

Life for Bianca at first continued in the same rhythm as before, but her father began almost to compliment her by talking over his own affairs with her. Since her troubles occupied much of his time it seemed a fair exchange; she sensed that he was lonely, perhaps always had been. Olivia's final response to her daughter's divorce was a brief radiant return from America, with a face which had clearly been lifted once more. Then she disappeared again, and in a few months filed quietly for her own divorce.

Hugh's life seemed to have no real companion, and now that they could meet for the first time as independent adults Bianca was touched to discover he was an anxious man for whom decisions were not easy. A few times she came to London at his request to look at a troublesome painting or escort him to a big reception.

Lovat argued over very little, and a separation agreement was quickly accomplished, to be followed in two years by the divorce. When told that Bianca wanted to sell all their property he proposed that he buy the London house since the boys would not then be deprived unnecessarily of a familiar home, but she prevaricated, saying she wanted to dispose of the Manor first. So inbred was the world of London's dealers that Berrisford's competitors made Lovat no offers, fearing the embarrassment of a family rift being played out in their own salerooms. A Japanese financial group offered him a consultancy, which he accepted for a year.

As if sensing that it was resented, Bianca's pregnancy became more and more irksome. Every part of her body developed its own particular discomfort – stiff shoulders, tingling wrists, heartburn, shooting pains in her abdomen and legs which stung and smarted if she stood for more than a few minutes. She was horrified to catch sight of them in a

343

long mirror one evening and see that they were becoming corded with swollen veins. Her complexion, normally clearer than ever when she was pregnant, erupted in rebellious spots. The baby itself was restless, the wrong way up and obstinately keen to make a mockery of the obstetrician's assertion that it would soon turn over.

The plan for her future was formulated easily and she was impatient to act on it. She would move to Somerset and with her capital she and Hermione would turn the unprofitable sheep farm into a nursery, specializing in the rare old-fashioned garden plants they both loved. Already the greenhouse at the Manor was crammed with viola seedlings and cuttings of obscure herbs. Seumas, who Hermione observed lived an almost vegetable life himself, vanished behind a wall of wartime husbandry manuals and ancient herbals and began to murmur of cordials and vermouths, remedies for club root and the afflictions which might be cured by infusions of feverfew or poultices of lungwort.

The baby arrived as annoyingly as it had grown. Bianca enjoyed driving fast, even in the family Range-Rover which handled ponderously, and in the pleasure of devouring the twisting country back roads between her sister's home and the Manor she was oblivious to everything else. The police car which eventually pulled her over was the first surprise, the second was the pain which seized her abdomen as she opened her door.

The constable, all of twenty-three with a thick Hampshire accent, was lecturing her from a great moral height when another contraction came, then another. It was humiliating to ask to be driven to the nearest hospital, more so to be disbelieved; she flew into a temper, scrambled back into the car and drove away at top speed. The child was delivered on a trolley in the car park of a cottage hospital. A nurse kept demanding 'Somebody fetch 'er 'usband'; the other patients were all over seventy and greatly disturbed by the police sirens.

'He doesn't look premature, does he? Thank God or they'd have kept me in. A month early – I'm never early,' Bianca protested, giving the fretful baby to Hermione to hold while she pulled crib sheets from the linen cupboard.

'Every soul chooses its own time.' Hermione jostled the child hopefully. Babies always made her feel clumsy.

Bianca pulled a cover over the little hypoallergenic mattress with one hand and snapped the French cot bumper appliquéd with sail boats into place with the other. 'There, that'll do. You can put him in now.'

'Her.'

'Oh God, it's a girl. I keep forgetting.'

Hermione gently laid the infant in the cradle on its stomach. Spasms agitated its tiny limbs, it tried with all its pitiful strength to raise its head, and it cried. 'Maybe she doesn't like lying on her front.'

'They have to lie on their fronts in case they spew up and choke themselves.' The baby uttered cry after cry, spluttering and fighting for breath. Bianca shut the linen cupboard with a perplexed expression.

'She's going to choke herself anyway.'

'She can't possibly.' It was a remarkably loud cry for a new-born, let alone one who was supposedly premature. The baby looked apoplectic, its face and neck flushed dark red. 'Oh all right, let's try him on his side. Her side. I hope this one isn't going to be a pain like Orlando.'

'I'm sure girls are different.' Hermione pulled back the quilt and let her sister pick up the frantic bundle.

'I don't see that they can be that different.' Once soothed and returned to the crib the baby fell asleep immediately.

She proved to be from the same mould as Tom, healthy and contented, but, Bianca had to acknowledge, different. Naming her took some weeks, since a girl had not been expected, and Bianca eventually chose Elizabeth because it was the kind of name she had always wanted herself: plain, common and traditional. As an afterthought she added Marjorie, Lovat's mother's name, which everyone assumed was a thoughtful gesture towards the maintenance of family ties beyond the divorce but was in truth a choice made out of sheer malice because she knew he thought it was embarrassingly genteel.

Little Lizzie was pleased to accept other blessings which Bianca had missed. She seemed to have a powerful fascination for all the males in her orbit. Hugh said she was the only really pretty baby he had ever seen. Orlando insisted on pushing her pram, Benedict, the most contemplative of the boys, kept volunteering to watch her 'In case something wakes her up when she's asleep', and Tom, who never normally wanted to superintend his brothers, was sure no one else could protect her from their enthusiasm.

It was Lovat, however, who was most markedly charmed by his daughter. He paid her all the besotted attention which Bianca had craved for the older children and never extracted. It was cruelly unfair, and she could do nothing but bite back the observation and let the boys instruct him in the best methods of rocking, feeding and changing their new sister. Her instinct was to keep the child entirely for herself and it hurt a great deal to be reasonable and make Lovat welcome on his visits. He seemed to be spending more and more time in America, and she began to hope that he would move there permanently.

In a few months Lovat's direction became clear; a new dealership was launched on Fifth Avenue, in the name of

Whitburn-Tuttlingen. In her dentist's waiting room, Bianca saw photographs of the opening party in a glossy magazine and felt a stab of hostility. What a mass of teeth Cheri Tuttlingen had for such a little woman, and what a volume of hair, standing out against Lovat's dark suit. The caption described them as 'long-time associates', whatever that implied. Their opening exhibition was of Ottoman arms and armour, one of Lovat's personal obsessions, exquisite metalwork and all very photogenic on the boys they'd hired to model it, but no way to get New York to take you seriously. She had never been so pleased to hear that the dentist was ready to see her.

Soon there was a more serious reason to be angry with Lovat. 'Were you planning on coming up to London next week?' Her father was trying to sound casual but his face was set in a preoccupied frown. 'There's something you could look at for me if you've got the time.'

'Can't you just tell me about it?' Hugh seemed to believe that no problem surrounding an object could be properly assessed without laying eyes on it. He would also never ask directly for her company.

'It's an unusual thing, very. Actually unique, I'm told. You know I like to have your opinions.'

'Well, I suppose Lizzie doesn't need me any more.' The baby had weaned herself with unflattering lack of hesitation as soon as she had been offered a bottle of milk.

The problem was a small faded box some three hundred years old, covered with satin panels embroidered in silk, the colours faded but the charm still fresh. A lion and unicorn sat face to face on the lid, figures of women representing Faith, Hope and Charity posed among flowers on the front and the rest was a fantasy landscape filled with animals, insects and fish. Bianca recognized it at once. It was the most important item in a collection of needlework done between the ages of eight and twelve by a girl named Mary Hodlin. Berrisford's had negotiated a private sale for one of her descendants a few years earlier; the buyer had been one of Britain's wealthiest men, a member of the ancient City Guild of Embroiderers, to whose museum he donated the collection. Lovat had been particularly proud of negotiating a double tax remission.

'The Embroiderers decided to sell the collection, brought it back to us, we called in the same man as before to do the authentication and he turned round right here in this office and said he'd changed his opinion, if you please. New techniques, new tests . . . probably a Victorian copy, at least two hundred years later. I just don't know what to do. If this gets out . . . I told Lovat it wasn't our thing in the first place.'

Bianca considered the box, and considered how one might set about faking satin worn to shreds and stitches so small they were almost invisible. The entire collection, a dozen samplers and some smaller boxes worked with beads, had been in the same style, with the initials MH worked into the corners; and some of the motifs, the ladybird and the snail, recurred in every one. The child had received silver charms as rewards for her work, and a written commendation from a school inspector. Bianca had brought Tom and Benedict to see them, knowing how one child could understand another's vision, even through three centuries.

'There was a blaze of publicity – that was all Lovat's doing – so now there'll be a scandal. And they'll sue us, and they'll win.' Hugh was walking around his office, gesticulating, and Bianca sensed that he was trying to avoid his own share of blame.

'Who authenticated it? I remember him, wasn't he Scottish, bright and not very tactful?'

'Bloody rude, I'd say. That was another thing, it was a nightmare tracking him down. Gone to work in Washington. We had to fly him over and it had to be Concorde.'

'What new tests did he do, exactly?'

'I don't know what people do with sewing.'

He chewed the word disdainfully as he said it, and Bianca realized that Hugh thought needlework was just a woman's pastime, valueless as art or history and not worth bothering about. Hence his panic and his blindness to a very ordinary manoeuvre which, had it happened with sculpture or painting, he would surely have spotted at once. 'Will the casket get an export licence?'

'It won't need one if it's a Victorian fake, will it?'

'Will the collection without the casket get an export licence?'

'I should think so, without the casket it's not nearly so important. It was being a unified body of work with direct descent in the family of the vendor that made it exceptional. And it's *cute*.'

'Well, my advice is to get a second opinion, and from within this country. Surely there *is* a world expert on English needlework in England?'

'My dear girl, we can't have this getting around . . .'

She heard a note of absolute terror in his voice and reached across to touch his hand in reassurance. 'Hugh, my instinct is that it is perfectly genuine. If a foreign collector wanted to acquire it – and let's face it, the collection is unique, and this little box is a star – there'd be an outcry and the licence would be refused. But if the box is a dud . . . nobody's got a problem. I think that canny lad's got a buyer up his sleeve, folk art's always big in the States, isn't it?'

Hugh looked at her in surprise for a few seconds while he assimilated the idea that a small girl's schoolwork might be termed folk art. Then he shook his head. 'It's too risky, you know how gossip gets about in this business. A whisper over breakfast is being shouted all over Bond Street by lunch.'

'Finesse him a bit. Call him up and tell him in the circumstances you might consider advising another private sale. See what comes up. If he says he could introduce a buyer – then you know.'

'I can't do that!'

She smiled, feeling a distinct adrenalin buzz, and reached for the telephone. 'Then let me do it. What's the number?'

In five minutes, with the conversation amplified around the room on the telephone's conference speaker and Hugh listening from a distance as if he might be seen if he came too close, they knew that her suspicions were correct. Her father was so relieved he was almost affable and wanted to take her out for dinner. Bianca was gratified to be right, happy to have his praise and excited as well. She did not consider that she had done more than support her father through a moment of quite uncharacteristic confusion.

The sale of the Manor proceeded slowly but surely to a conclusion, but she could not find a house in Somerset that was large enough for four children, close to Hermione's farm and what she had in mind for her new home. Schools for the boys were a problem – never close enough, either too academic for Orlando or not enough for Tom. She never seemed to find an outlook she liked, there was so much flat land, so many hills. The estate agents grew exasperated with her as she looked at one lovely stone mansion after another and could never quite say what was wrong with each one.

Hermione and Seumas prepared themselves for the vile world of business by travelling to an island off the coast of Northumberland where, aided by crossed ley lines and ancient Celtic standing stones, they took a course called

Spiritual Money. With their prosperity consciousness thus raised and their understanding of the cosmic law of increase deepened, they fixed notes all over the farm. One on the bathroom mirror read, 'I am a money magnet.' One on the fridge proclaimed, 'Increase is the law of the universe.' The telephone announced, 'I love my work and that love brings me all the money I want.'

Bianca was annoyed that they forgot to switch on the watering system in the greenhouse before they went, and most of her seedlings died. 'That's your poverty mind-set talking,' Seumas argued earnestly. 'When you realize that the world is full of abundance, that your creativity is infinite, then you will understand that there will be more seedlings.'

'Somebody will still have to water them,' Bianca said crisply, catching Lizzie as she reached for a hypodermic full of the sheep antibiotics, despised and forgotten under the greenhouse bench.

'Hey, I've got a great idea,' he announced. 'Division of labour. If you take care of the growing side, Herm and I can do the office and the books and that, yeah?'

'He hates getting wet and cold,' her sister muttered as they toured the area where an Elizabethan herb garden was planned. It had rained for several days without stopping and the area looked like a World War I battlefield, all mud, holes and duckboards. Bianca found her enthusiasm for horticulture ebbing. Perhaps it was another of those womanly accomplishments she had mastered because everyone approved of her doing so and, she had to admit it, because her mother despised them. Certainly a well-grown erythronium no longer seemed like an achievement.

Hugh relied upon her more and more, until she was travelling to London almost every day. His interests, she realized, extended beyond the firm itself. He admired and advised the National Art Collections Fund, a charity which made grants to galleries and museums to help them acquire important works for the nation. Now a European foundation with similar aims, and an added interest in harmonizing the EEC legislation on exporting works of art, was being formed. He spent as much of his time travelling, and meeting politicians and civil servants, as he did in his office. It made him feel that his grip on the firm was unsure.

Berrisford's headquarters, the saleroom, strongrooms and offices, once strange and forbidding, began to seem like a third home and the people who worked there became friends. Friends – people to whom she was attracted through common interests and values – had been absent from her life for some years; instead she had used the parents of her children's friends and Lovat's associates for company.

When the contracts for the sale of the Manor had been exchanged, Hugh invited her to join the firm. She refused, but the next day one of the directors telephoned her. Martin Pownall was said to be the best business-getter in London; he was a handsome, dark-haired volatile man whom she favoured because Lovat had always dismissed him as 'smooth'. 'I do wish you would change your mind, Bianca,' he began. 'Hugh promised to give you to me if you said yes.'

'Are we talking about Mayfair in 1980 or the slave market in Algiers?'

He giggled, being the kind of English public-school casualty who had to laugh at any sexual inference to make embarrassment sound like enjoyment. 'I admit he drove a hard bargain. Joking apart, I asked him. We'd never have got those Post-Impressionists without you.' Bianca granted the truth of that; her father, by his diffident manner, had unconsciously offended the young provincial solicitor who found himself, as the executor of a collector's estate, obliged to deal with the kind of metropolitan sophisticates he had despised all his life. Knowing that he had failed, Hugh left his daughter to take the man to lunch. She chose the Caprice, talked about painting, pointed out Tina Turner at the end table, and, without knowing it, flattered him silly. 'So are you going to let us sell your paintings or not?' she asked him, feeling she would not be worth much if she never put the question, and was almost shocked when he stammered, 'Well, yes, I think so.'

'You couldn't call it nepotism if you worked for me, could you?' Martin had accurately identified the main source of her scruples.

'No, not really.' She made up her mind. 'All right, tell him you've twisted my arm.'

CHAPTER 12

St Petersburg, 1912

'Take The Catastrophe away, Charlotte, and have the maid bring us some tea.' Lydia picked up her son as if he were some household object in need of cleaning and dumped him in the arms of his governess, whose tranquil face under her smooth black hair showed no surprise at hearing her charge routinely designated a disaster. The child immediately screamed a furious protest, flinging a wooden soldier to the floor. 'For God's sake, get rid of him, we've got to dance this evening and we need some peace.'

'Here, little one.' Tata bent to gather up the remaining wooden dolls from the floor and tuck them in the bib of the boy's sailor suit. 'You're adorable but it's time to play upstairs now.'

'You want him?' Lydia did not appear to be altogether joking. 'Have him, darling, he's all yours, tuck him into your bag and take him away. Just hope he doesn't ruin your life like he ruined mine. Hurry up and get rid of him, Charlotte, he'll give us a headache. Then you can join us for tea.'

Without expression, the girl curtsied briefly and carried out her noisy burden. 'How calm she is.' Tata joined Marie by the window and the two women exchanged glances wondering how the servants managed in this lax, chaotic household.

'Charlotte? She's an absolute treasure, my life would be madness without her. Of course I was a fool to engage a governess for a baby, but nobody told me. I decided to keep

354

her anyway, she's cataloguing the Prince's books for him.'
The pug dog, now a wheezing sphere of black fur, squeezed
out of his sanctuary under the sofa and scrambled up on it.
'Charlotte sees him more than I do, alas. But I don't worry
on that score, she's quite immune to romance. They say all
the English are. At least some good may come out of this
disaster.'

The older dancer's Byzantine brown eyes enlarged still
further with sympathy. 'Oh don't talk like that, Lydia, not
about your son. What have you lost that could possibly
compare to such a lovely child?'

'His father for a start.' Lydia threw herself on the *chaise*
in an attitude of despair. 'I'm sure I've lost half a dozen
ballets, I could have been a prima by now. My youth, my
beauty, my strength – what have I got left, Tata? And all
because of The Catastrophe.'

Carillons of laughter echoed around the salon. 'Youth
and beauty! I won't hear a word more, come here at once.'
Marie seized Lydia by both arms and dragged her to the
mirror. 'Now look at yourself and if you don't admit you're
lovelier than you've ever been I'll pinch you.'

The face in the mirror – the same Venetian glass which
had almost sunk a gondola on their honeymoon trip –
portrayed a thunderous sulk. Lydia had been in a bad
temper with life for two years. It suited her; with the added
edge of malevolence her looks departed from prettiness and
became compelling. The depth of her eyes was deadly, the
bow of her lips cruel and her most mundane movements
seemed on the border of savagery. This dramatic beauty was
lost on its owner, who mourned her old flower-like charm.
'You'd better pinch me then,' she shrugged, trying to
straighten the bow of black and white chequered ribbon at
the bosom of her afternoon dress. 'I look like an old crow.

355

No wonder he's straying, who would want me looking like this?'

'He's coming tonight, isn't he?' inquired Tata in her most reasonable tone.

'Later, he told Charlotte. You know what that means, later or never. Tata, what am I to do? He must have found another woman, somebody married or at least not so cursedly revoltingly fertile . . .' Tears began to collect in the corners of her eyes. 'And it was the baby, it was! As soon as I was well enough I knew it had all gone wrong. He was like a stranger, I hardly knew him. I tried to be sweet, but it wasn't the same, how could it be? And we'd been in paradise, Tata, I swear, I didn't know it was possible to be as happy as we were and now . . .' She could hold them back no longer and the tears began to pour down her white cheeks. 'Now I can't even remember what it was like, not really, not the real feeling of happiness. All I know is that I was happy, but it's gone, I can't feel it any more.'

Marie, who had at last chivvied a proposal out of Basil Nikonov, gave Lydia a handkerchief. Her blue eyes seemed full of sympathetic tears; she was feeling sorry for herself, since marriage now threatened to be a terrible ordeal.

The real purpose of the afternoon was to distract Tata with the child and help her relax before she made her debut in *Giselle*. Instead the warm-hearted Tamara Platonova set her own anxieties aside to comfort Lydia. Surely, she argued, it was natural for love to mature, for an affair to grow, deepen and, inevitably, change? Surely a child was a bond which no man, let alone a man of Orlov's character, would ignore?

'And he is a good man, Lydia, I know that, a fine man, serious, intellectual . . .'

'But I'm not and so he's bored and he's run off to some fat old bluestocking who can talk about poetry . . .'

The maid brought in the tea and slunk quickly away when she sensed the atmosphere in the room. Madame could throw things when she was upset. The pug, catching the ominous mood, decided that it would be prudent to retreat beneath the sofa once more. Charlotte appeared silently a few moments later and seated herself a respectful distance from her tearful mistress.

Tata embraced her, now almost moved to tears herself. 'Oh don't cry, darling Lydia, you can't do the peasant pas de deux with eyes like beetroots . . .' Lydia was also to appear in *Giselle*, partnered by Leo, in a minor part in the first act.

'I could do the peasants blind if I had to! I've being doing the bloody peasants for four bloody years! Why aren't I getting anything better, Tata? I've only been given two ballets since I was promoted. Tell me truly, you are a good judge and you wouldn't lie, am I really finished?'

'Of course not! You're dancing better than ever.'

Marie agreed. 'Everyone says so, you're always improving.'

'I just don't trust myself any more. I don't feel the same – in my body, I mean.' Lydia struggled for the right words. She felt for her body the implacable hatred reserved for a friend who had committed an act of treachery. Although she had regained fitness almost immediately after the baby's birth, she could not forgive the instrument on which she had counted for every benefit in life for first betraying her with sensuality and then, through pregnancy and the birth itself, disobediently changing all its properties while she, the rightful inhabitant, was powerless to control it. The memory of the uncanny flexibility of her joints in the first few weeks after she returned to classes still made her shudder inwardly.

'I promise you, you are as strong as ever. You haven't lost

357

anything. And think what you've gained . . .' Tata argued the point with an earnestness which prevailed on Lydia far more effectively than the sympathetic outpourings of other friends. 'You are magnificent, you're a marvel, a wonder and – now, forgive me for this cruel point but it is the sad truth of our lives as artists – wonderful as you are, you will be so much better because you are suffering now. It is only when you have felt terrible emotions yourself – pain and rage and grief to the degree of madness – that you have the depth in your own soul to reach into and pull out that feeling in your dancing. Trust in Providence, Lydia. Everything is for good in the end.'

Lydia kissed her friend and thanked her for her wisdom, biting her tongue on the observation that since Tamara Platonova's destiny seemed to be to be loved by many and moved by none the discussion was hypocritical on her side. Marie silently brooded on the tragedy of an artist's life. The governess quietly refilled the tea glasses, and Tata pursued her argument.

'You're not being overlooked, I assure you, and if there is a conspiracy against you – more than the usual bitchery, I mean – I haven't heard of it. You're only twenty-three. Why, when I was your age I hadn't even been made a ballerina. Have patience, everything will come in good time. The critics praise you, the gallery is in an uproar every time you dance. And you have some very distinguished admirers, you know.'

Lydia rubbed her nose with her handkerchief. 'Like who?'

'Sergei Pavlovich admires you, he told me so. He said you danced like a living flame, isn't that a beautiful compliment? In fact . . .' Here she paused and her warm olive skin turned almost brown with blushing. Duplicity was not Tata's forte. 'He asked me to ask you if you would consider joining his company.'

'Chinchilla? What company?' Irritated, Lydia struggled upright from her attitude of despair on the *chaise-longue*. Was this whole pretence of sympathy and interest in her son just to gain her confidence before passing on Diaghilev's proposition?

'You know we've done two summers as the Ballets Russes in Paris now? And it has been a stupendous success.' Seeing Lydia's sceptical expression, she emphasized her words with a grave face. 'I know people say he's still in debt, but Lydia – I was there, I saw the audiences, I *know* . . . the Paris seasons have been an absolute sensation. Sergei Pavlovich has had offers from all over Europe – Germany, England, Austria, Italy, Sweden, Monte Carlo, everywhere.'

'My parents wrote to me from London that people adored the Russian Ballet,' the governess confirmed in a quiet voice. 'People were desperate to get tickets – there was almost a black market.'

'Sergei Pavlovich has decided he can't possibly tour everywhere we've been asked in our break from the Maryinsky in the summer, and he's tired of having to rely on the Court's favour to get the dancers, the scenery and the costumes for the classics. So he's forming his own company, with Mikhail Mikhailovich as choreographer. I will dance as a guest artist in the summer break – it's all been properly arranged, with contracts. He says Anna Pavlova and Kchessinskaya are signing up too. And you could do the same.'

'Mikhail Mikhailovich is leaving?' Marie pulled the pug dog up on to her lap. 'So he can put on his silly barefoot ballets, I suppose.'

'Yes, he's already resigned. And so have a couple of others.' Tata mentioned their names, two young women and Adolph Bolm, who partnered her often but was close to the end of his career. Lydia made a disparaging grimace.

359

'I can see some advantage to Adolph, he'll get better roles in a smaller company. But the man's mad, he'll lose his pension and then what? Apart from you, Chinchilla won't set the world on fire with that selection.' Lydia dismissed the new company with a sniff of complacency. 'What about Vaslav?'

'He's thinking about it. He'll tell me tonight. I'm sure he'll join. They just worship him in Paris. They adore us all, but Vaslav really is next to God as far as the French are concerned.'

'And Chinchilla worships Vaslav everywhere.' Marie rolled her eyes and sighed. 'That man's such a degenerate, Tata. It doesn't seem like you to be part of his circus.'

The ballerina put down her tea glass with a prim compression of her lips. 'I think it's a cruel misjudgement to give an ugly name to a condition which is just an oddity of nature. People's private lives are their own to live in peace, I believe. When I think of his genius – and Lydia, he truly is a genius, even though he isn't an artist himself, he is a man of such culture, so much energy, so many ideas and such a vision of what Russian art can be – when I think of that then everything else is irrelevant. He has done so much for me, Lydia. He has such intuition, he just says, "Let's talk things over a while", and then you begin to find that in your own mind you know the answer to all your problems.' She saw that her enthusiasm was falling on deaf ears. Lydia had slipped off two of her rings and was trying their effect on different fingers. 'Well, that's all, I've done what I promised, I've asked you to join. Now let's not argue, let's take a nap ready for tonight.'

Lydia admired the new arrangement of her jewellery at arm's length as she rose. 'I like to rest in the winter garden, the flowers are always so pretty. Charlotte, bring me my cashmere shawl and see that The Catastrophe doesn't disturb us. Take him out for a walk or something.'

From the moment they arrived at the theatre Lydia was aware of a peculiar atmosphere in the dressing rooms. The normal hum of anticipation seemed muffled. The scene-shifters and the dressers hurried about their work without cracking jokes. Even Mischa Alexandrov had no gossip to exchange and stood silently in the wings with his huntsman's cloak wrapped closely around him, casting oblique glances to either side.

Leo, who was to partner Lydia, appeared at the last moment with an agitated expression. 'Where's Vaslav?' she whispered as the overture began and there was still no sign of Nijinsky.

'There's been an argument about his costume – now shut up,' was the stern reply.

He appeared very quietly a few moments before his en-trance, wearing a short velvet jacket and tights, and stole to the wings with his eyes fixed on the ground, like a child pretending that if he looked at no one then no one would see him. The Renaissance trunk hose of slashed velvet which normally completed the costume were missing, and the thin tights revealed his lower body in embarrassing detail.

'The fool – he's forgotten the hose. Trust a dumb Pole to do something like that,' Lydia whispered again, with a giggle. 'Go and tell him, Leo.'

'No, he hasn't forgotten. That's the costume they designed for Paris.'

'But it's disgusting, it shows . . . well, everything. You can even see the seams in his jockstrap.'

'I know. He says it gives a better line. Everyone's been arguing with him.'

361

'He's right, though, the line is better without the hose, much more *esthétique*.' This opinion was conveyed in a patronizing hiss by Inna, who stood close by with the other five dancers who portrayed the heroine's friends. Having fallen out with Vaslav over her admiration for Isadora Duncan, Inna had taken up with Leo. They had married while Lydia had been travelling with Orlov, and she had been so uninterested that she had never even got around to congratulating them. In the past year, however, she had noticed that Inna never allowed Leo to have two words alone with her.

'Vaslav can't possibly dance like that!' she murmured, ignoring the interruption. 'It's offensive – and the Empress is here tonight, too!'

'He won't listen.'

The stage manager glared at them and they fell silent, knowing that a pause in the music was imminent and they would certainly be heard.

Nijinsky was never communicative; he was by nature shy, but his gifts and his Paris success had brought him precocious advancement at the Maryinsky. Few men could have attempted the demanding debut in *Giselle* when barely twenty-one. Before a performance he was always so withdrawn as to seem half conscious, and then the miracle took place, and this unprepossessing, thick-set youth with slitty eyes flew into the light and was transformed into a god. That night he seemed to be more than ever in a world of his own, biting his nails as he waited to make his entrance.

The applause was rapturous throughout the first act and if the audience were disgusted by the Prince's unusual exposure they showed no sign of it. Lydia and Leo were happy to give two encores, and Tata, who had been practising her dying fall for weeks with a mattress to save her bruises, collapsed without undue pain.

Backstage was in an uproar during the interval, and the Director himself erupted through the door leading to his box, coat tails flying as he rushed in pursuit of Vaslav.

Lydia, who was not needed for the second act, washed and changed while the elation of the performance drained away. She had hoped at least for a token from Orlov, but all her bouquets were from her fans. He had not sent so much as a rose. Was it foolish to hurry home and prepare herself for his arrival later? Common sense told her it was. He would not come. The dresser, who admired all her clothes, lovingly stroked her sable wrap before settling it around her shoulders, but nothing would warm her heart.

As she made her way to the stage door she passed one of the management offices where Alexandrov, still in his costume, was in deep conversation with another man who was unseen behind the desk.

'Are you sure, Mischa? She really was offended? I couldn't see into the Imperial box from where I was.' It was the Director speaking.

'I'm positive. I could see everything, she was white with shock. It's my belief she didn't make a fuss out of respect for the other artists – she's a wonderful person, so thoughtful about things like that.' Once she had passed the doorway Lydia paused to eavesdrop.

'Did you hear what she said? If only I could be sure. Vaslav's a prodigy but this ... it would be too much if the Empress had been offended. If that stupid boy causes a scandal at the Court I'd have to resign myself ... the little fool, he's running with a fast pack now he's with Diaghilev. He's just a kid, he doesn't even know he's being manipulated.'

'Let me find out, why don't you? I know the Empress's lady-in-waiting well enough to ask her what was said.

Although really I'm in no doubt. I've never seen her look so horrified as she did at his first entrance. If I can make use of your telephone later tonight I'll find out from the horse's mouth.'

She heard the flap of his heavy cloak as he stood up, and hurried on before she was seen. To her surprise Leo, also in his street clothes, was waiting for her by the doorkeeper's office.

'I just thought . . .' he began abruptly, then changed his mind and started again. 'You've got quite a crowd tonight, I thought I'd see you to your carriage. Inna's in the second act so she'll be a while.'

To her surprise she was pleased to see him and taken with his thoughtfulness. The ecstatic scenes of her early days of success had died away, but there was a small, loyal band of her admirers waiting outside, not nearly enough to make an escort necessary. 'I suppose this is one way to pass the time – what do you usually do if you have to wait for her?' she inquired casually as she signed some souvenir postcards for a dapper old man with a crystal-topped cane.

'There's a bar over there, the Stray Dog.'

'Shall we go then?' She tossed him a flirtatious look as she put the last picture back in the febrile kid-gloved hand, smiled gaily and tucked her arm through his. He hesitated, nonplussed, then muttered, 'Well, just for half an hour', and led her across the square.

The Stray Dog was more of a night club than a bar, a wide, smoky room full of raucous conversations which almost drowned the saxophone trio on the small stage. Enjoying the attention she attracted with her smart sable evening wrap, Lydia boldly led the way through the crowded room to a vacant booth and asked for vodka.

'Leo, tell me, could you see the Empress's reaction when Vaslav made his entrance tonight?'

'What reaction? She didn't move. At least, it's hard to tell from the wings . . .'

'Mischa's putting it about that she was scandalized.'

The vodka was set in front of them without ceremony and Leo poured her a glass. At the next table a tall, melancholy woman in lilac silk, whose hair fell in a limp fringe to her Roman nose, complained to her escort that happiness made her feel smothered and was quite unbearable.

'That's rubbish.' Leo gulped his drink without taking his eyes off her. 'It's all a plot, I'm sure of it. This is Sergei Pavlovich at work.'

'How can it be? He's in Paris.'

'Don't act dumb, it doesn't suit you. We both know that man's got long arms.'

The woman with the Roman nose flung a black shawl around her shoulders and Lydia was forced to duck to avoid tangling with it. 'You know he's putting his own company together?'

'Precisely. And he can't move without Vaslav, he's the trump card in Paris, and they'll never let Vaslav go. He's a sensation but he's too young and he hasn't got enough clout to bargain with the Director.'

'So this way, Vaslav creates a scandal, Mischa's paid to fan the flames, the Director is forced to chuck Vaslav out . . .'

'And he's free to join Sergei Pavlovich at once. Clever, huh?'

Lydia finished her glass and, unconsciously companionable, pushed it towards him to be refilled.

'A hard-drinking life, is it, among the aristocracy?'

'Don't be bitter, Leo.'

'I'm not bitter, just surprised. I thought it would be French champagne every night.'

'It is. Tonight I fancied a change. Have they asked you to join this famous Diaghilev company?'

'Yes.'

'And . . .' There was a commotion as the woman with the Roman nose was joined by two friends. They pulled out sheaves of paper from their bags, passed them around and began to read out loud around the table.

'And I refused.'

'But you could do anything you wanted with him – all those dreams you've had, new ideas, new styles . . .'

'I know. I was tempted but it wasn't really a hard decision. He asked Inna too, and she will go, but I need my salary. I wouldn't get much of a look-in with Fokine in the company already. Leon Samilovich has fallen out with him, he expected to be appointed artistic director and Sergei Pavlovich chose someone else. And for all he's so persuasive, he can't get really first-rate dancers. Kchessinskaya's broken her contract with him, which says a lot. And we all need to eat, it seems. He's got Tata, granted, and I think Lulu Kyasht will do a season, but he's scratching round in Moscow looking for people and I heard he's had to go to Warsaw for the corps. Fatal. They just aren't good enough.'

The poetry reading at the next table was gradually dominating their corner of the room, as more and more people fell silent to listen. Lydia sipped her vodka without speaking for a while and let her thoughts wander. Would her sable wrap be stolen in this rough dive? If things went badly with Orlov this lousy place would be what she would be reduced to for amusement – but was she really so desperate she needed to lead on poor Leo?

'I'd go with Diaghilev if you went,' Leo said suddenly, shooting one of his old penetrating stares at her.

'I won't go. I hate the man, I don't trust him, I don't

believe those stories about Paris and I want to stay here in Petersburg . . .'

As she spoke the shadows of sadness deepened around her eyes. He had heard gossip that her protector was neglecting her, but decided not to pry for fear of making her angry.

'You're very beautiful tonight.'

'You're very corny.'

'That's not so bad, is it? Would you like me to get one of these poets to be my Cyrano and give me better words?'

A weak smile illuminated her face. 'Aren't they ugly? Look at that man with a pointed head, like an egg on legs.'

'But what about his soul?'

'I can't see that, can I? All I know is he spoils the view right now.'

They fell silent again, although she glanced furtively at her little diamond watch and saw that nearly an hour had passed. The thought of Inna in a jealous fret was comforting.

Leo drained the last of the vodka into his glass and drank it as if he needed courage. 'I've been given a new ballet after Easter, quite a big number.'

'Well done.'

'*Salome* attracts me very much.'

'She had that effect on men, so I understand.'

'Leon Samilovich will design it.'

'Wonderful for you.' Their eyes met as if by long-arranged appointment. The poets concluded their reading to a ragged outburst of clapping and stamping.

'So whose head would La Kusminskaya like on a plate?'

'Better not ask,' she smiled and, before she knew what she was doing, leaned across the table and kissed him.

Her spirits in general were so low that within two days she was on the point of changing her mind. Orlov visited her, but had little to say other than to warn her that he would be travelling the country for some weeks. He admired the boy, bestowed a brief embrace upon her then unwound her arms from his neck and departed.

Lydia collapsed in despondency. She rehearsed their conversation a hundred times in her mind, searching for double meanings in her lover's words, and then fell prey to violent doubt about her life in general. Was it really wise to agree to do another ballet with Leo? He had been clever, but everyone knew that at bottom he was another revolutionary like Fokine, and the association surely would harm her. He had done his last two ballets with Inna, who obviously fancied herself a far better dancer than she really was. And if Tata and one or two others joined Diaghilev, there would be more good roles for younger dancers. On the other hand, Tata's advancement, and the great improvement in her dancing in the past year, were due to her success with Diaghilev; had she been wise to spurn his approaches?

'Are you quite well, Madame?' the governess inquired, hearing her sigh deeply. It was the late afternoon, when the baby Kolya was brought to play with his mother, but Charlotte had long ago ceased to expect Lydia to take much notice of him. She watched him closely as he staggered cheerfully around the room. The tables were crowded with trinkets – snuffboxes, picture frames and the little animals carved in agate or quartz with diamond eyes which the Prince used to pick up at Fabergé to charm his mistress in happier days – and if the child was not supervised closely he would amuse himself by throwing them into the fire.

'I'm well, Charlotte – it's just that life is so difficult. Everything used to be simple, and now – I can't make up my mind about anything. What do you think – should I agree to do a new ballet with Leo Volinsky?'

'Oh yes, Madame.' The girl had a very definite way of speaking, using few words with an air of absolute certainty. 'You've told me that he is the best young choreographer in the company and it seems to be a general opinion.'

'But it will be a lot of work and I may lose the opportunity to do one of the big classic ballets if I do it.'

'It will attract a lot of attention though, being a première.'

'That's true. But suppose . . .' She was about to say that if the Prince renewed his affection for her she would need to give him all her time, but the possibility seemed sadly unlikely.

Charlotte guessed her train of thought. 'His Highness has always admired Monsieur Volinsky's work. I think he told me that it was his first ballet which brought you together?'

'Yes.' Lydia sighed again. She did not feel it was proper to discuss her love affair with the governess, but since the girl visited the Orlov Palace every day to work in the library she might have heard useful gossip. 'Tell me what is your impression of His Highness, Charlotte? What are people saying?' She felt her cool expression breaking up as she tried to control her emotions. 'You know what I mean, Charlotte, I mean – what's the matter? Is it something I've done, does he talk about me at all? I'm at my wits' end with him, I don't know what to do . . .' She silenced herself, afraid of breaking into tears.

The girl straightened her angular shoulders, having clearly anticipated the question. 'He is preoccupied with his work, Madame.'

'Oh, that . . .'

'He has been charged with implementing the Tsar's plan for the reorganization of all the armed forces, Madame. It must be a terrible responsibility, he talks of nothing else.'

'But that doesn't take up all his time, for heaven's sake.'

'Davidov, his valet, has to wait up until past midnight for him to return from the Ministry, Madame. I do assure you that if he is able to leave at a reasonable hour, then he calls upon you and nobody else. And if I have a query for him I have to wait for weeks sometimes before I can see him.' Incomprehensible as Lydia found this explanation, she knew it must be the truth. Charlotte was a transparently honest creature without the imagination to invent anything, even when it would be politic to do so.

'Still, if he loved me he would contrive to pay me more attention,' Lydia murmured, half to herself.

'His Highness recalls all your ballets with real pride, Madame. He often tells me how much pleasure your dancing gave him, how incomparable is your talent.' Flattery was also beyond this plain girl's capabilities, so Lydia pondered the significance of this observation.

'Do you mean you think he would be pleased if I did something new?'

'I believe he would, Madame.'

The notion pierced her despondency like a sunbeam. All at once she was resolved. 'Then that is what I shall do.'

The young governess could not guess, and her mistress herself chose not to contemplate, a more personal reason for the blight on their love. Both Lydia and Orlov had been scarred by the suffering and ugliness which had attended the birth of their child, but in agreeing never to inflict the experience on Lydia again they had put a curb on their passion. The restraint was fatal to the Prince's desire. He came to bed to lose himself, and the need to be careful prevented it. Calculating her least fertile days and monitoring his sensations to make sure that he did not ejaculate inside her body left him too conscious for true abandoned pleasure. Lydia also had changed. The delight she had first felt in making love had evaporated; most of her feelings seemed dead, and in their place had arisen a queasy terror.

Being a man of considerable pride and some conscience, Orlov could not resolve the decline of his libido by discarding his mistress and his child. If challenged – but she had been careful not to confront him – he would have protested that he loved her as much as ever. He found Lydia's company relaxing for a short time but irritating in long periods. Cerebral distractions could not blunt the desires which she had awakened in him, but the call to serve his Emperor, protect his country and apply his intellect to ordering a small part of the chaos which amounted to its government was more powerful. The Imperial decree to restructure the armed forces of all the Russias had not only relieved his frustration, but allayed some of the despair which had precipitated it. He allowed himself to drift into this new obsession without ever acknowledging that the old one had passed.

Orlov travelled the immense breadth of the empire on a self-imposed mission to see his orders carried out. It was not an inspiring journey. The army and reserves accounted for more than six million men; the navy, desperately depleted since the defeats of the war with Japan, raised the total closer to seven million. Russia's potential defenders were as numerous as the population of the largest cities in the world, and throughout this multitude he heard the same complaints, with cynicism from the Uhlan commanders in Poland, fatalistically from the Kalmuks in Mongolia, with passion from battle-scarred Cossack leaders who hacked their boots with their whips in frustration, with no expression from the Caucasians whose men put their trust in Allah and silkily, diplomatically from the admirals commanding what the Japanese had left of the Baltic and Pacific fleets.

All these men were wary, being sure that a high official from Petersburg could not be visiting their distant province simply to see the plans on his desk in operation. He had needed to gain their confidence, and then they had offered him a single opinion. The plan was unworkable. Its emphasis was all on mobilization, the question of supplying the troops in the field had been neglected. It did not answer their needs, which were urgent. There had been mutinies, fomented by Bolsheviks, anarchists and democrats in the ranks. The commanders had been tough, but brutality alone treated symptoms, not the disease. Morale was low and training was a priority. At this point his informants to a man had paused, gazed thoughtfully at their boots or stroked their moustaches, then approached with the greatest delicacy they could manage the suggestion that training officers, especially senior officers, was the most pressing necessity of all, especially since – and here the speakers had regained their confidence – so many experienced commanders had died heroically in the war with Japan.

Orlov returned dismayed but resolute. The plan needed immediate modification, but since this opinion had been impudently advanced by the new parliament as soon as His Imperial Majesty had announced his intentions, the Prince gave much thought to the best way to get his views accepted, but he was no diplomat, and his superiors dismissed his proposals with alarm. A man of his stature could not be dispatched to the kind of post which usually removed a thorn from the government's side, commanding the labour camps in Siberia or the garrison in Vladivostok. Within a month of his return to the capital he was elevated to the office administering the Imperial Household Regiments and the Tsar himself invested him with the diamond star of the Order of St Gabriel, a decoration in his personal gift.

Thus on the night of the première of *The Legend of Salome* he was driven through the April slush to the Maryinsky Theatre in a troubled mood. Attending the event was, as he saw it, another duty necessitated by his position in the world. His guests, whom Lydia had invited, were General Count Besobrasov, an erudite elderly balletomane whose conversation he had much enjoyed in the days of his first enthusiasm for the dance, and his wife. They sensed their host's abstracted mood and, after a few gracious remarks, fell quiet, content in the expectation of the great spectacle to come.

Orlov's mind was busy placing facts in an acceptable order. As an aristocrat, he had no concept of achievement and thus no appreciation of failure, but his pride was bruised. Beneath what he thought of as superficial responses, his personal despair had been deepened. What could the future hold for this unhappy federation of nations governed by so many timid mediocrities? In such gloom enlightenment was blown out like a match, as he had now been shown. Russian soil was soaked in blood. All his life he had witnessed horrors: war, uprising, mass executions and, most terrible of all, harmless gatherings at which the masses had been seized by a self-destructive frenzy and virtually murdered themselves.

He remembered as a young officer in a small town presiding over the distribution of souvenir mugs for the Tsar's coronation in the square. The milling crowd had broken through a cordon around the site of a new building, stumbled into the ditches dug for the foundations and trampled each other; three hundred people had died, half of them helpless children. 'So it always has been and so it always will be,' his superior, the Minister of the Interior, had remarked when given the news that another workers' demonstration, at a gold mine in Siberia, had turned into another massacre. Orlov's mind, ever ready to cool his feelings by argument, turned to wondering how it should be that familiarity never dulled the Russian people's response to such scenes of carnage, and how their hearts could always be ready to respond with volcanic outpourings of pity and rage.

He took his seat, oblivious to the brilliance of the scene in the theatre. The curtain rose on Fokine's *Carnaval*, a pretty, elegant extrapolation of the Commedia dell'Arte scenario. Columbine was the languid Olga Spessitseva whom he compared to the memory of Lydia's piquant interpretation and found dull.

'Quite miscast, poor thing,' Besobrasov's gruff voice rumbled in his ear. 'She hasn't the technique. Mikhail Mikhailovich demands more of his dancers than one imagines.' The audience were of the same mind; they were eager for the main event. The word on the street was that *Salome* was a sensation. The auditorium tingled with impatience.

Orlov did not leave his box during the interval. Champagne was brought, and he surveyed the crowd, becoming aware that they in turn were watching him. He caught the whisper of his name and the occasional twinkle of a lorgnon catching light from the numerous crystal chandeliers. Besobrasov, whose tall, imposing figure with pure white hair automatically drew all eyes, leaned over the edge of the box to hold a long conversation with Svetlov, the critic who had once received Pavlova's favours, and from their confidential manner the Prince deduced that they were discussing Lydia. His old identity, Prince Orlov the aesthete, the balletomane, the owner of many priceless cultural artefacts and the patron of a great ballerina, settled around his disappointed shoulders like a cloak of glory.

'Ah! At last.' Besobrasov settled eagerly into his seat as the lights dimmed. 'Now, my friend, I believe we shall really see something tonight.'

Orlov did not miss the edge of reproof in his voice. 'Forgive me, General, I am a little distracted this evening.'

'Believe me, I know what it is when one has responsibilities,' the elderly connoisseur reassured him with a touch on the arm. 'But now you can forget for a while, eh? Give yourself to Terpsichore for an hour.'

Salome seized the audience by the throat from the moment the curtain rose. Bakst's decor was a cavern of indigo draped in immense billowing curtains which alluded at once to Salome's veils. In the centre of the dark stage Herod was discovered on his throne musing on the evil omens for his rule. Shafts of intense light splintered the gloom as the dancers appeared, placed them in prominence but cast deeper shadows all around. When Lydia appeared, her skin gleamed like mother-of-pearl through her crimson draperies.

In the company it was clear that the suffering which that heartless chit Kusminskaya had inflicted on young Volinsky had been turned to excellent account. He had found the courage fully to embrace the modern style and reach new heights of expression. The steps seemed to scream with yearning, sing seduction, scorch the stage with sensuality, and he used the very shallowness of Lydia's own character to create Salome as a monster of self-absorption. The music was a magnificent vehicle for dark passions, an assembly of fragments by Rimsky-Korsakov collected from chamber suites and opera intermezzi.

The first act concluded with a long pas de deux in which the temptress taunted her wretched victim, for which Leo had appropriated two movements of a cello sonata, a sobbing adagio and angry rondo allegro. It was violently effective.

375

The encores began immediately and by the time Salome stood alone in a pool of light vowing vengeance on the steadfast young prophet the audience voiced a constant roar of romantic adoration.

'What a marvel she is, your little girl!' Besobrasov beside him was bellowing to be heard. Spring flowers, for which Lydia's fans had raided the market early that morning, hailed down on the stage at her first curtain call, and as she began each round of curtsying she turned by instinct towards Orlov with a triumphant smile. Immediately his heart inflated with pride.

Besobrasov himself was bowing involuntarily in all directions as if to appropriate some of the ballerina's glory merely by association with her lover. All around him Orlov heard cries of 'Incomparable!' and 'Magnificent!' and his heart was thrilled because this wonderful object belonged to him. The highest degrees of her art flowed from the love they shared. Every sensual illusion she had created proceeded from delights which he had shown her. All the perfection of her body, its breathless grace, its fluid precision, its steel strength and suppleness, the ferocity, the tenderness, the élan, the delicacy, were gifts she would place in his hands in a few hours' time.

The dark speculations of two hours past were driven from his mind. He accused himself of neglecting his most precious treasure. Guilt, fear and panic suddenly laid hold of his imagination. She had achieved this miracle without him – what now if he proved unnecessary to her, if another, more forward admirer had claimed her in secret? A maelstrom of concern swept his thoughts to one point – a special gift. There was no better way to consolidate his love. Ungrateful fool that he was, he had been so immersed in his own affairs that he had neglected the simple chivalrous duty of selecting an appropriate memento for his beloved's triumph. In another hour she would be surrounded by flowers and trinkets and his own presentation, which ought to have been the most imposing of all, would be awaited in vain. She would be wounded, she would be angry, he would be shamed.

The Grand Duchess Vladimir acknowledged him from her box with a knowing nod, and he noticed her tiara of rubies, one of the early consolations of her widowhood, with the Beauharnais ruby once owned by Napoleon at its centre. Immediately his mind turned to the casket awaiting his future bride. He sent his coachman to fetch the imperturbable Davidov, who reached the theatre as the light dimmed for the ballet's last act. The necessary instructions were written and sealed in a few seconds.

At the ballet's end the audience erupted into a frenzy of acclaim which endured for almost an hour. The Prince, enervated by the uproar, retreated a few steps to the rear of his box, and then resolved that he must be the first to pay his private tribute.

With his gift gripped firmly in both hands, he half ran through the cool grey corridors of the theatre, found his way through the concealed door to the backstage offices and arrived breathless at her dressing room where the maid was fussing over the surplus of flowers crammed into all manner of containers, half of them on the floor as there was no other place for them.

He caught his breath, smoothed his hair, and chose a place on the dressing table on which to lay his gift. He cast his eyes over the presents from the public which the concierge had already heaped on a side table. There were over fifty. The cards proclaimed the givers from every walk of life, from the laboured script of a group of railwaymen – 'Your devoted admirers in the gods' – to the engraved copperplate of his own friends and associates.

At last there was a commotion at the end of the corridor and in a few more instants the door was flung open by Alexandrov, and Lydia entered, her skin white against her black silk costume embroidered with gold and pearls, one hand still pressing a spray of lilac blossom to her bosom. The Director walked attentively at her side. The choreographer and designer followed, and behind them two stage footmen, sweating under their white wigs, followed with their arms full of bouquets.

In that moment Orlov was filled with the most exquisite sense of possession. He turned from the table of offerings, held out his arms and the goddess seemed to leap into them directly from the doorway. After months in which he had hardly known what to say to her the perfect phrases of praise bubbled effortlessly from his lips, and she, still intoxicated after her exertions, responded with practised grace.

Alexandrov, Bakst, Volinsky and the Director stood aside. 'A few moments, gentlemen,' he ordered them in a confidential voice, and they immediately withdrew, Volinsky directing a lance of pure hatred from his pale eyes. The maid shooed out the footmen and retreated after them, rolling her lumpy hips under her black skirt in sympathy with the general excitement.

Lydia looked expectantly at him, her hands folded at her breast. In these periods of transition between performance and everyday existence she still used the exaggerated gestures of the stage. She was euphoric from dancing, swaying as she stood, flushed and breathing deeply, her eyes luminous. He kissed her forehead, tasting the salt sweat.

'There is nothing that I have which is as beautiful as you,' he began, turning to the flat case of birch wood which he had laid down before the mirror. 'Nor is there anything under the sun more precious to me. This is our family jewel, intended for my bride' – he opened the box and was gratified to see her gasp at the blazing mass of diamonds which it contained – 'and I know now that there will be no one ever more worthy to wear it than you are tonight. Please do me the honour to accept it, and with it all my love, now and for ever.'

For an instant the old greedy Lydia appeared and stepped forward to grab her trophy; then she paused, filled with the new grace engendered by her triumph, for an instant too excited to think clearly or to know what she should do. A heavenly tension gripped the centre of her body.

'Such an exquisite thing ... I can't say a word,' she whispered, finally dragging her eyes from the necklace to gaze into his face with rapture. 'I – darling, forgive me, it's too much, my heart is full, I'm overcome ...'

'Say nothing, my love. But will you wear it now? I should like you to do that.'

'Not as I am, in my poor costume? No, no, the effect will be wrong ...' She was as concerned as he was to present the necklace to the world in the right light. 'Let me call the maid and change, then I can wear it properly.' The first intimation of the significance of the gift began to reach her consciousness through her agitated mood. 'Oh, but first – my love, my wonderful, generous Nikolai – let me kiss you.'

She had to jump to reach her arms around his neck and all the delight he had first taken in her body burst out anew. The costume, contrived with decades of skill to resist violent movement, was clawed away somehow by two pairs of equally passionate hands and upon the red plush couch at the side of the room he sank into the hot, tight heart of her, glimpsing in the mirror the white thighs raised and crushed against his black evening clothes. They returned to each other as if they could fuse into one being, and the fears of the past years were blasted to faint memories.

It was some time before the world was readmitted; she insisted on sending home for a dress with a better décolletage to display the necklace to its best advantage. It was an hour before the door was opened, but the throng of well-wishers waited patiently and came in with due humility to make their own offerings. Among the treasure which Lydia at last carried home from the reception given in her honour was a silver bowl from the railwaymen and a black feather fan from a schoolboy who begged her, if she had any pity for his desperate love at all, to carry it when she next danced in *Paquita*. The Director gave her a diamond arrow brooch, and Leo received a gold lyre also set with diamonds. Besobrasov appeared with a brooch of modern design which echoed the sweeping lines of the decor and was set with blue topaz, amethysts and pearls. From the Dowager Empress Maria Fyodorovna, who once again had occupied the Imperial Box, she received a diamond aigrette and a personally inscribed card. She squealed with delight at every gift, but even as she displayed the hoard to the little audience squeezed between her bouquets she looked into Orlov's eyes with adoration and he was glad he had given her a part of his heritage.

Dawn was struggling reluctantly through low smoky clouds when she turned to Orlov in her bedroom wearing only the necklace and assured him, with a strange ecstatic light in her eyes, that none of these tributes delighted her one hundredth as much as his own.

They began a new period of happiness, deeper and more satisfying than the first months of intoxication with each other, but not destined to endure. For a year Lydia considered herself so perfectly blessed that she would be satisfied for eternity. She understood at last that her public life was the most vital part of her fascination for her Prince. The malaise which had sapped her energy during the clouded months of their affair was defeated, and she applied herself to her dancing with a steely resolve. One triumph followed another, and it seemed that Fate was on her side at last. The Directorate gave her new ballets – *Swan Lake*, *Coppelia*, and finally the role relinquished in her favour by the ageing Kchessinskaya in *Esmeralda*.

Then Victor Dandré was arrested and charged with embezzling millions of roubles from the city funds. When he was released on bail he fled the country, taking Anna Pavlova with him, and so the Directorate was obliged to redistribute her roles. Diaghilev was equally bereft, since Pavlova's first act as a free artist was to break her contract with him. Karsavina was absent for longer and longer periods; other soloists were seduced by the huge fees offered for Ballets Russes seasons, and the younger dancers at the Maryinsky found that they no longer had to wait for retiring ballerinas' shoes. Olga drifted into the more romantic roles, and the bravura fell to Lydia. She learned with prodigious speed, so eager was she to put the proper pzazz back into parts which her enemy had taken purely for their importance rather than her ability to dance them.

She was feted by the public, praised by the artistic elite and treasured by the Court. She was pestered as never before with invitations, most of which she was forced to decline because her stage commitments were overwhelming. Her photograph was sold on street corners, Orlov commissioned a life-size bronze sculpture which he kept in his own study, and her portrait was painted three times for other admirers, including a banker from Moscow who dispatched a fashionable artist from that city, installing her in the best hotel for as long as she needed to finish the painting.

Diaghilev courted her persistently. 'He'll never give up,' was Tata's parting advice as she packed for her summer in Europe. 'When that man wants somebody she gets telegrams served with every meal until she surrenders.' Lydia discovered that she was not yet on sufficiently intimate terms for the notorious impresario to put her on his telegram regime. His strategy was to use intermediaries to plead his case, and with the Ballets Russes company on a triumphal tour nonstop through Europe and then, to Tata's extreme excitement, making a long sea voyage to South America, he had no other option.

Tata herself, when she returned for the winter, never ceased to sing his praises to Lydia, but was too wise to press her directly. Leon Samilovich, once the coveted post of Artistic Director in the company was awarded to him, was more direct.

'She is young, she is beautiful, she is a great, great artist – why is La Kusminskaya hiding away in this half-civilized country when she belongs to the world?' was his constant demand, his eyes behind his pince-nez humorous, taking the edge off his words. Whenever their paths crossed in the salons of St Petersburg or the waterlogged lawns of the Imperial summer palaces she heard him wheedle in his distinctive, aspirated accent. 'Won't you at least come to my home one evening and meet some of the Artistic Committee? I'd love you to hear Sergei Pavlovich's plans for next year, so, so exciting . . .'

The Committee, convoked by Diaghilev to raise money for the Ballets Russes tours, was chaired by General Besobrasov who, despite his failing health, had also been recruited to the campaign to capture her. He took a different tack. 'You would weep to see the honours which are showered on Anna Pavlova now – everywhere she goes – London, Vienna, Milan, even Paris, where they have seen some real ballet at least. I tell you I could cry with shame to hear that feeble creature hailed as the greatest Russian ballerina of all time by people who have no idea what our country can really produce.'

This argument even persuaded Orlov, who was quite fascinated by the idea that Russian art, vital and full of passion, was sweeping away the played-out conventions of Western Europe. When they resumed their summer tours to Europe and went, at his insistence, to see the Ballets Russes company give the new ballet by Nijinksy, *The Rite of Spring*, he changed his opinion.

'How wrong I was to question your judgement,' he told Lydia with genuine contrition. 'This isn't a ballet, it's chaos – like the Moscow station when the train's just arrived. And that isn't music, it's just noise, a cacophony, like the railway yard. No wonder half the audience walked out on the first night! I presume Diaghilev thought they would like anything avant-garde, no matter what its artistic merits, but he doesn't understand the Parisians, they're not fools. How arrogant you must have thought me, my love, to argue with you over your own territory.'

'I forgive you,' she announced with condescension. 'I should know what an oaf Vaslav is, he's been treading on my toes since I was ten years old. The idea of him attempting choreography was always absurd. Promise you'll listen to my little opinions in future?'

But Diaghilev's tentacles inexorably squeezed her. Wherever she went another tormentor would sing his praises and question her judgement in resisting him. The last card was Leo. While Lydia appeared now to be an artist with no inner doubts, Leo's resolution began to falter. He had been eager to step into the creative vacuum left when Fokine joined the new company, but once he had been set upon a pinnacle he seemed to be attacked by vertigo. He clung to Lydia like a talisman, creating only for her and, when he mistrusted his own judgement, allowing her to fly into the cloud which obscured his path and find their way by instinct. In two years he produced four new ballets, each more sensational than the last. Then, to her dismay, he announced that he planned to renegotiate his terms of employment and work with the Ballets Russes the following year.

'I feel I'm suffocating here at the Maryinsky,' he told her, avoiding her accusing eyes. 'I want to try new ideas, new music – and I want to travel. My mind is just freezing up here, I need stimulation. But I can't work without you, Lydia. You know that, you've always known it. Won't you join, just for the summer? Please, I need you.'

Seeing this exacting and brilliant man plead so humbly for her help gave Lydia a fine sense of power, but she refused him all the same. 'We like to spend the summer travelling.' She knew that this intimate manner of alluding to her lover would rub salt in the wound of her refusal. 'The Prince couldn't bear to be parted from me for months while I traipsed all over the place with a touring company. And I'm worn to a shadow as it is with my commitments here – I simply couldn't work any harder. As it is it's a miracle I haven't been injured these last couple of years.'

All the glory and satisfaction which accrued to her proceeded from her body, an instrument of marvellous strength and expressiveness which rose to the challenges imposed upon it by shedding the very last hint of childish roundness, becoming a filigree of muscle and sinew woven around ethereal but seemingly unbreakable bones. She worked like a horse, but joyfully, although she woke in the morning stiff and sore all over. Every day in the mirror Lydia looked less at her face, which she felt was becoming gaunt, and more at the pure beauty of her line. She saw at last the mysterious extension of her limbs' geometry in the air for which she had worked in ignorance for so long.

When it was not to be displayed at the greatest occasions – and many of the less great ones, since she was most attached to wearing it – the necklace lay in the wall safe in her writing room, concealed by the rich apricot damask which draped the walls in severe pleats. It was usual for such large pieces to be kept in the strongroom at Fabergé when they were not to be worn, but Lydia found so many occasions for which it was simply the ideal thing that Orlov resolved to indulge her and ordered a safe to be installed in her house. It had been in place for more than a year when her maid, a pale Latvian girl who blushed very easily, inquired whether Madame had any linen to be laundered.

'No,' she answered without reflection, but then remembered some particularly lavish lawn chemises which she had not seen for some time. She had formed the habit, when something exceptional caught her eye, of buying half a dozen versions of it. 'Why do you ask? Is anything missing?'

'No, Madame, I check everything carefully and the laundress is a good woman, careful and reliable. But she did remark last week . . . and I had noticed myself . . .' Now the girl was as red as a geranium and whispering with embarrassment. 'Not that we would presume to discuss such a thing, Madame, but it was my impression that you have not given us any napkins for some time.'

'My goodness, I haven't, have I?' The girl was referring to the lint and gauze cloths which were used to absorb the blood during her period. Involuntarily Lydia looked down at her abdomen, as if the hideous growth of another pregnancy could swell there in an instant, then recollected herself. 'Well, that's none of your business, is it?' The girl backed towards the door, and Lydia realized that in her ridiculous way she had been moved by concern. 'Still, I suppose I should be grateful that you're keeping track of things. Just check that all the napkins are accounted for, and while you're about it see if you can find my new lace chemise with the eau-de-Nil ribbon. I'll wear that tonight.'

Lydia was anxious, although her instinct was that she was not pregnant. The old Finnish witch had given her a new remedy and had sworn it would prevent her conceiving again. Marie and Tatiana also took it and had avoided pregnancy successfully so far. She consulted the herbalist specifically, and was reassured, but also had the physician call.

'You are very thin,' he commented. Chivalry was not his style.

'A ballerina cannot be fat,' she returned with mild irritation.

'Do you have a good appetite?'

'Excellent, but what can I do? I have to dance so much now I'm just melting away.'

He examined her eyes and tongue, took her pulse and blood pressure, questioned her about all her bodily functions and palpated her flat stomach briefly.

'Certainly there is no sign that you are with child. When a woman is not well nourished she often does not conceive; it is normally a phenomenon of young, sickly girls, and those with neurasthenic complaints, but you appear to be in perfect health. I have remarked lately that several of my patients who have also been called to follow Terpsichore suffer occasional cessation of their female signs. If you wish to add to your family, Madame, I would suggest you take a little more rest and allow your body to recover from the demands you have made of it.'

'When I wish to add to my family, Doctor, I shall certainly take your advice.' She favoured him with a small pleased smile and rang for tea. Her instinct was to withhold truth from any man and since the doctor was attached to the Orlov household she had no intention of disclosing to him any information that could be distorted before it reached the Prince's ears.

'And since you plan to travel this summer I would advise proceeding at your leisure. Let all the little delicacies of Europe tempt you. A spell at a spa would be most beneficial. Dax, perhaps, the waters are excellent for all medicinal purposes and particularly orthopaedic complaints – we must consider the future, Madame – and Dax is most convenient for Biarritz.'

His tone of voice alarmed her. The Prince had not suggested a summer tour; on the contrary, he had wearily announced that his duties would make travelling difficult that year. Strikes were breaking out more and more often. To improve the people's morale the Tsar had decreed that the tax on vodka would be lifted, but parliament had reacted petulantly; the Prime Minister, a man whom Orlov admired, had resigned, and further disturbances were expected. And yet here was his physician discussing the event as if it were already planned.

When she was alone, she recognized that she was angry. Worldliness had calloused her heart. The possibility that she was no longer loved was a minor concern. Weeping for the death of her own high emotions was far from her intentions. No longer a girl to pine in obscurity when her affair waned, she was now forced to contemplate public humiliation. Her first move was to consult Alexandrov, who was himself preparing to leave for Paris with Kchessinskaya and the Grand Duke André in a few days' time.

'Oh my dear, it's true then?' he asked, taking her hand with a concerned gesture.

'What's true? What have you heard? All I know is that the wretched doctor assumes I'm travelling, and yet when I asked Nikolai point blank he said he wasn't. He said he had state duties to take care of. And I was so disappointed, and so sympathetic. But if he's lied and he's making a fool of me ... come on Mischa, spit it out, what's been going on behind my back?'

A pimp in that exalted milieu acquired skills which many a diplomat would have envied. Alexandrov slithered through a tangle of compliments and qualifications to impart the sad news that Prince Orlov had recently been seen paying excessive attention to the wife of one of the aides travelling with the French President on his state visit to St Petersburg.

Lydia had become the essential ornament of every great state occasion, a new national treasure to be displayed whenever a member of the vast family of European royalty visited their Russian cousins. Lately the visits of heads of foreign states had been given equal prominence. The French President was honoured by her appearance as the sea goddess Thetis at a pageant which, since the Tsar and the Imperial Family had now withdrawn from Petersburg almost entirely and lived in their summer palaces outside the city, was staged in the gardens at the palace of Pavlovsk. Lydia's entrance was made across one of the ornamental lakes, posed on a mirror mounted on a raft so that she appeared to be drifting across the water itself.

The night was so close that the dancers felt torpid; she was thankful to be marooned on the cool water where the spray from the famous fountains refreshed the air. She felt tranquil, suspended at a distance from her troubles. The piece had been choreographed for such events, and was more a series of sumptuous tableaux than one requiring athleticism of its chief protagonists and rousing mazurkas from a large corps de ballet.

When the ballet was concluded Tsar Nicholas himself, his hair now receded entirely from his broad temples and his whole face deeply etched in careworn lines, made presentations to the dancers. His children accompanied him. The four grand duchesses resembled each other closely with their thick hair and round cheeks; in their lace gowns they were like a border of beautiful white flowers. The Tsarevitch, for all the tales of his terrible illness, was a well-built boy with an impish face and intelligence in his narrowed eyes.

Lydia was engaged in conversation with them for some time, and bidden to show off her gift, a small mahogany chest bound in gold which contained a selection of yellow diamonds. 'To fashion any jewel La Kusminskaya desires' read a small card enclosed in it. At last she was free to dress and join the reception in the shimmering cavern of the ballroom, wearing a Lanvin gown of dark red taffeta embroidered with gold lilies, with the necklace as her only jewellery, her fears rolled back like thunderclouds.

Orlov was at first hard to distinguish in the haze of gilt and mirrors but when she made him out he was deep in conversation with a woman who was just as Alexandrov had described her: tall, voluptuous, very dark and elegant in the same striking style that his old lover had achieved. Her turquoise gown was decorated with huge stylized roses of black velvet, a design so boldly modern that all the other dresses in the room, including Lydia's own, appeared stuffy and timid.

They were introduced. She was the Comtesse de Chalus-Lupiac, and as pretentious as Lydia had expected. 'Such a charming pageant,' she trilled, looking down her long nose. 'Of course, we have seen the famous Russian Ballet in Paris, but to see it here, as you perform it for your own people, is so interesting. Were you really presented with a chest of diamonds? Is that always the custom?'

'Yes, at special events such as this.'

'Only you, because you are the prima, receive such a gift . . .'

'Tonight my partner, Leonid Volinsky, received a gold watch set with diamonds, the two dancers who took the roles of the sea nymphs were given enamelled powder cases with gold frames and the corps were presented with little silver vases. It is usual in Russia to show one's appreciation of an artist with a small gift.'

'You mean the Emperor chooses them himself . . .'

'For a particular artist, and a particular occasion, perhaps. Usually there is some consultation between the Chamberlain and the Director to discover what one would like to receive, or what would be appropriate.'

'And it is paid for by the Emperor . . .'

Lydia was momentarily dumbstruck at the vulgarity of the question, then muttered a vague protestation of ignorance.

'And what do you intend to do with your diamonds – make them into a necklace? But you have a beautiful *collier* already . . .' The Comtesse realized that she had made a *faux pas* and was paying compliments to soothe the offended company; Lydia saw no reason to be charitable.

'Certainly I do.' She laid her hand across the diamonds at her throat with a reverent gesture. 'This is the Orlov *collier*, the most treasured of all my possessions, Madame. It has been in Nikolai's family for generations.' She paused, allowing the implications of her remark to sink in. Orlov's face was expressionless; he found the encounter awkward; his mistress was determined to be vindictive and the Comtesse, whom he revered but did not much desire, was embarrassingly innocent of protocol at such events.

'Indeed.' The woman was nonplussed. 'How lucky you are to have it now.'

They exchanged a few more frozen remarks and a page arrived to request that Lydia attend the Grand Duchess Xenia, the Tsar's sister, in an adjoining room. As she followed him away, Lydia understood the basis of the woman's insulting manner. The French, indeed most foreigners, had difficulty in understanding that in Russia formal manners were a charade adopted only for the benefit of the outside world, and that in fact emotional liaisons carried as much weight as legal ties. Thus a man's mistress was accorded the same status as his wife – perhaps even greater status if the mistress was a celebrity in her own right. It was not the custom in Petersburg to relegate all artists to the *demi-monde*.

To Lydia's annoyance, Orlov led the Comtesse in to dinner, and danced with her twice, before moving smoothly on to several other partners and finally reclaiming his mistress. 'I have to convey the Comtesse's apologies to you. Since part of the business which has brought her husband here is the negotiation of a loan from France, she was confused by the spectacle of wealth displayed this evening. I explained to her that the Imperial purse is separate from the national exchequer, something I suppose a citizen of a republic, even if she is a well-born one, might easily fail to appreciate. I hope you were not upset.'

'Oh, not at all,' Lydia assured him with a pretty smile. 'I

simply thought she was jealous. Her own jewels were very poor, after all.'

The Comtesse had in fact observed, with a cynicism Orlov found totally captivating since it voiced thoughts he himself hardly dared admit, that it was most bizarre to think that the fruit of the famous industry and parsimony of the peasants of France was to be applied to alleviate the misery of the peasants of Russia, when their own rulers could have achieved the same end by a small reduction in their scale of ostentation.

Two days later he casually announced that he was to be transferred back to the Ministry of the Interior that autumn, and sent to Paris for the summer as part of an exchange of senior military advisers which had been agreed during the French President's visit. The alliance of Russia, France and England was alarmed to find itself locked in a race to stockpile arms with Germany and the Austrian empire. Every year each country voted more money for weapons and warships, and the alliance had pledged itself to make plans for an arms treaty before the whole business got out of control. It was an important posting, and he had been honoured to accept it. She congratulated him with a warm smile and a cold heart, thinking of the struggle to come.

Lydia's next actions were decisive. She demanded that the Director release her for the summer, and then sought out Leo, who had recently been appointed as a ballet master with the company, when his morning class was finished.

'You must forgive me.' She touched his arm and lowered her eyes, the picture of sympathetic remorse. 'I must have been mad to quarrel with my destiny. We have had so many triumphs together I felt quite jealous thinking that now you would conquer a new world without me. Of course I'll join you. Tell Sergei Pavlovich he has at last worn me down.'

'I'm glad,' he said simply. 'I knew that nothing could prevent you that would be worth the loss. And I wanted to tell you that . . . that love might die, but art will endure for ever.'

She was annoyed to think that he, too, had heard the gossip, and tempted to prick his pomposity once more with a pointed retort, but some perverse instinct guided her to hold both his hands in hers and ask, 'Is that how things are for you at home? No! Don't answer, I had no right to ask that. Ignore me, I'm a little stupid today.' His eyes seemed to shrink with fear of being wounded, and she realized that she had guessed his secret, and that he was, as ever, too self-obsessed to divine hers.

A few months later her circular hallway was crammed with trunks and she stood with Charlotte double-checking the lists of her possessions while Kolya persistently mountaineered over the luggage and a nursemaid hovered in attendance. The furniture in the main rooms was already covered with dust sheets, and in the salon the housemaids were on ladders sewing calico covers over the chandelier. More dust sheets draped the statuary. Her carriage, with its three grey ponies of the Orlov breed, waited at the door. The Prince had already departed for London on state business and had agreed, with hesitation, to meet her in Paris.

'Davidov! At last, whatever kept you?' She greeted Orlov's valet with impatience.

'My apologies, Madame, I called at the station first to confirm that the train was running.' His barrel chest heaved and perspiration stuck his auburn curls to his forehead, which he mopped rapidly with a handkerchief. 'The strike may have been settled, but when things have been disrupted the rolling stock can be halfway to Kiev and it takes a few days for things to get back to normal. Is this my package?'

He indicated a small black lizard-skin case bound with brass which Charlotte held possessively in her arms. It contained the most important pieces of Lydia's jewellery, which the house of Fabergé had undertaken to send by courier to their Paris office. Chief among them were the Tsar's yellow diamonds, which she had set most extravagantly in a simple collar that rose high at her throat. Their colour made her white skin gleam like mother-of-pearl, and the design emphasized the beauty of her long neck.

'Whatever shall we do with the receipt?' Charlotte was inclined to panic whenever her careful arrangements had to be changed. 'You'll never have time to go to Fabergé and catch up with us now?'

'I shall send a rider with it to meet the train at Pskov. The station master has already been telegraphed. Never fear, Madame.'

'I never do.' She smiled, flattered by his kind tone. If the Prince's closest servant was still at pains to cherish her she must still be in good standing with his master.

'The *collier* will be the talk of Paris, I'm sure.' He patted the case with his gloved hand.

'I don't want to disappoint you – or the Parisians – but the *collier* is staying here.' She read through the inventory one last time before handing it to him. 'I simply dare not take it. It's an heirloom, a piece of the Orlov family history, a piece of Russian history, even, and I have a feeling about it. It ought not to leave its own country. So it's quite comfortable in the safe and it can have a good rest while I'm away. Instead I shall take the diamonds which His Imperial Majesty presented to me.'

'Yes, Madame.' He resumed his usual servile impassivity, bowed, and was gone.

Charlotte picked up a smaller brass-bound case containing

Lydia's everyday jewels. 'Besides' – Lydia spoke as if to no one in particular; although Charlotte had become a confidante in the past two years, and understood fully the significance of her mistress's trip, she was not quite comfortable with direct confessions – 'when the whole of Paris is on its knees before me, the Prince will certainly wish he had paid me more attention. He'll be furious to see me wearing another man's diamonds, although if they're the Tsar's he can't possibly complain. I can't go out without one proper piece of jewellery, can I? Now, little Catastrophe . . .' Kolya jumped off the last remaining trunk as the porters dragged it outside. 'Come and kiss me goodbye and don't wreck the place while I'm gone. Papa and I will be back soon. Come and wave to me and wish me luck.'

CHAPTER 13

France, 1968

'Is our nestling ready to take to the air? And if so, in which direction should he launch himself?' In her cluttered salon, Lydia presided at the head of the table over a conference called to determine her grandson's future. With his developing instinct for the essence of a woman, he had chosen a present for her in Paris, a mohair stole woven with a mixture of dark wools. She wore it now around her shoulders like a robe of state, her ruined glamour confirmed by its rich setting.

Aunt Julie was installed at her right, with her ballet master at her side. Alex had been sent to call on them immediately after his return. Realizing that the true story of his shame was unlikely ever to reach further than the end of Rossi Street, he had simply announced that he had been overpowered with loneliness in Leningrad and, seeing that his emotional condition was inhibiting his work, the directorate had agreed to send him home.

All the old women had accepted this story with sympathy and capped it with memories of their own apparently desolate youth. The ballet master assessed the taller, broader Alex with a sceptical eye and remarked that homesickness at school was nothing compared to the bitter loneliness of touring with a company; he then suggested that Alex join a class to demonstrate his current level of achievement.

Marie, at the far end of the table, busied herself with the tea. She was alarmingly changed in the few months since

Alex had last seen her. The comforting mass of her body had shrivelled and her dress flapped limply from shoulders which had finally given up their proud line. 'I've no appetite,' she complained with a foolish smile. 'Eating takes my breath away, lately. I don't understand it.'

The conference was completed by three men, since Grandmère considered that a decision was not made unless a man had at least ratified it. A very old Russian sat silent and smoking through the whole affair; an equally aged but more animated Frenchman, who occasionally contributed dance reviews to *Nice-Matin*, squinted speculatively at his feet as if wondering if he had laced his shoes correctly. At the end of the table a tall, elegant man of about sixty, apparently one of the last managers of the final incarnation of the Ballets Russes company, reclined in his chair with an air of weary condescension.

The ballet master was called first to give his opinion. 'Well, our Alex will always have technical limitations. His turn-out is much improved but still needs to be better, and with a fault like that it is impossible to achieve really good placement. But he's a man now, his bones have finished growing – it's too late. I think it's time to go to work. He's a good-looking lad, he'll get something, I expect.'

'Something! Our child is worth more than something, surely!' Grandmère bestowed an aquiline glare on both the speaker and Julie, as if to accuse her friend of having hired an imbecile. 'He's a prodigy, a sensation! How many boys are given scholarships to train in Leningrad? And think of his heritage, my name, the publicity . . .'

'Perhaps he should try his luck in London,' the teacher continued, refusing to revise his assessment. 'The language won't be a problem for him and they're always desperate for good boys.'

'I'm told that now they have Nureyev things are different,' the critic announced with a self-important glance around the table.

'Yes, that's what I've heard too,' the elegant one confirmed. 'Suddenly they're all jumping at last.'

'Surely he should try Paris first?' With her full bosom leading, Madame Sedova sailed forth to meet any challenge to her authority. 'Lifar at the Opéra will see him if we ask him, I'm sure.'

Her ballet master shrugged. 'He'll see him, but whether he'll take him is another matter.'

'Contemporary, perhaps that's his future,' the critic suggested, one finger upraised.

'I hate contemporary,' Alex murmured in alarm from the far side of the room.

'It's much less demanding,' the teacher told him with a sympathetic nod.

'I hate it. All that modern music . . .'

There was a general sigh of agreement. The company fell to dissecting the reputations of lesser Paris dance companies, considered briefly the merits of Amsterdam, Stuttgart and Milan and finally came back to Paris for their decision.

'The Opéra it shall be – I'll telephone Lifar tomorrow.' Madame Sedova seemed thoroughly satisfied although Alex could tell from the ballet master's calculated reticence that his old teacher did not consider he had much chance of acceptance.

'Oh, what a tragedy! No sooner do I get my beautiful boy back than he is torn out of my arms again. Let me kiss you . . .' Grandmère struggled to her feet and embraced him, a puddle of tears stained with mascara already forming below each eye. 'A new life – another new life! Exciting for you, but for us old women who have to wait by the telephone for news . . . this is it, this is what my life has come to now. Well, I'll call Kolya and tell him to expect you.'

Alex was kissed and loaded with tears, fresh advice, more blessings. They drank more tea, smoked more cigarettes, reminisced and gossiped, then Marie, with an effort, took the squat yellow bottles of Zubrovka and glasses out of the carved wooden cupboard.

Fetching dishes of food from the kitchen she announced each one, pausing frequently when she ran out of breath. 'Meatballs with cream sauce, and these are some pancakes the girl made, but she makes them too thin. Little salted Korkun cucumbers which dear Kolya brings from Paris, and fish cutlets – I tried but these French fish don't like to be mashed. Still I did my best.' She sat down, perspiration trickling down her neck although it was a cool autumn day. 'Oh yes, I forget everything nowadays – and potato salad, and cucumbers with salt . . . please, eat, everybody must eat. And the halva, I know there was some . . .'

Alex ate and was comforted. The loss of Anya was still an open wound, but he was aware that Grandmère's world, faded and inward-looking as it was, had the maternal power to restore him. He recognized now that these gatherings were a ritual in which the émigré colony asserted their national identity. In a subtropical climate they opted for dim light and food designed to pad the ribs against cold. In poverty they made their own society an elite more exclusive than any club. Among strangers, they exaggerated all the characteristics of their race, revelling in drink and emotionality as affirmation that they were still Russian, although they would never see their country again.

At the end of the afternoon the company took their leave. In the hallway the ballet master, kind-hearted as well as clear-sighted, took Alex aside and suggested that the world of revues and musical comedies might perhaps suit him, and scribbled down a few telephone numbers on a page torn from his diary. Then he left with Madame Sedova. Marie sighed, then hauled herself to her feet and began to clear the table.

'It's good she's eating less,' Grandmère announced to Alex. 'She was always a bit of a glutton, you know. If she hadn't retired when she married she would have been in trouble. And once the babies started, that was the end, she let herself go. I never did that, not even after your mother.' Her hands settled proudly over the small, melon-shaped swell of her own stomach.

'My dear Lydia, if your friend hadn't been a little bit of a gourmand she would never have become such a marvellous cook.' A current of fresh air and the tapping claws of the griffon on the floorboards announced Angela Partridge, who suffered to be kissed by them all before taking her usual chair. 'And then you would have *simplement* starved to death. I saw the coast was clear so I thought I'd pop in. How do you feel today, Marie? It's better now the weather isn't so hot, isn't it?'

'You say it isn't hot today?' Marie was sweating so heavily that wherever her flowered crepe dress touched her body a dark stain appeared. 'It's enough for me, I tell you. Please, eat – there's salad left, and some fresh bread . . .'

'You sit down, I'll look after myself.' The Englishwoman was neither hungry nor anxious to trouble her friend, but she knew that it was impossible to refuse food in a Russian home. She returned from the kitchen with a plate strategically loaded with titbits. 'And how's the golden boy? Happy to be back before old Brezhnev decided to conscript you and send you off to Czechoslovakia?' She reverted to English and extracted from Alex his sanitized account of his departure from Russia. 'And do tell, I'm dying to know, did you find your grandmother's old house before you left?'

'I got pretty close, I think. I found Rimsky-Korsakov Street, or Prospekt, whatever, but the other street must have been renamed, I just couldn't find it.'

'What about the gates? Iron gates with olive branches? Frightfully elegant, even today I expect.'

'None of the buildings had old gates or railings. An old man told me they were all sawn off and taken away to make nails or something when there was a shortage of metal. So what I did was take some photographs of all the corner buildings, and I thought if Grandmère could look at them herself maybe she'd see something she recognized.'

'And did she?'

'Well to tell the truth, Miss Partridge, with everything that's been going on since I got back I haven't had a chance to sit her down with them.'

'But let's do it now! At once! My dear Lydia, your palace! The boy has found your palace!'

'I hadn't forgotten,' came the haughty response. 'Marie forgets things, but I never do. I was just waiting for the right moment to ask him.'

From the little room at the back Alex fetched the envelope of prints and explained anew, in French, how he had resolved the dilemma of Rimsky-Korsakov Street. Then he laid out the twelve photographs on the tablecloth.

'They aren't all that good, I'm afraid, some of them I couldn't get the roof in, but over there you can't just walk around the street with a camera.'

Marie got to her feet and leaned over Lydia's shoulder, affecting to sneeze as the mohair shawl tickled her nose. The two old women scanned the photographs in silence.

'Snowing,' Grandmère said at last.

'Yes, that didn't help either.' Alex stuck his hands in the pockets of his jeans. It had seemed such a clever idea at the time, but now he felt foolish. 'They are in order, from the little park to where the two canals join. If you could remember the church, or how many turnings . . .'

'No.' Something like Marie's old sweet smile creased her shiny cheeks as she pointed out one particular picture.

'Absolutely, no.' With disdain, Grandmère pushed the Constructivist concrete villa aside.

'Could be.' Now Marie picked up the picture of the Palace of the Young Pioneers; the woman on the scaffolding a blurred shape because she had moved too fast. Grandmère blinked at the picture in silence.

'Here, let me see.' Angela Partridge opened her bag for her spectacles, kept in a petit point purse with a scrap of chamois. 'The vainest creatures you could possibly imagine.' She seized the photograph and focused on it. 'Can't see what's under their noses and not even a magnifying glass in the house. Ah – oh, now, it isn't the best photograph in the world, is it, dear boy? What have we got? Half the house is missing, scaffolding all over the place but I can see it's green, very pretty sort of cucumber green, and quite symmetrical. Porch in the middle with white pillars, and steps up, then one, two, three . . . four windows each side, long windows, plus a little round one over the porch . . .'

'Give it to me, give it to me!' Her mouth working with eagerness, Grandmère snatched back the picture and, as an afterthought, held out her hand for the spectacles. 'Yes! Yes! Look, Marie, you can see! God is good, to keep my house for me all these years. The winter garden is gone, that's what confused me, but I had the only porch with steps like that, and our little *oeil-de-boeuf* window to let light in on the

staircase. Oh, you're useless, you don't remember anything.'
Marie made no response.

'Do you feel quite well?' Miss Partridge, who had been
standing back with her hands on her hips, suddenly moved
forward and took Marie's arm an instant before she
attempted to sit but fell beside her chair, pushing it aside
with a screech of wood on wood as she collapsed on to the
floor. 'Oh God, I was afraid of this.'

'What is it, what's the matter with her?' Lydia did not
immediately understand, and spoke with irritation, as if she
suspected her friend was playing some silly trick.

With a crash as it hit the floorboards, her friend's head
fell helplessly to one side, the eyes open but seeing nothing, a
trickle of saliva running from the side of her mouth. Alex
rushed to the old woman and tried to gather her into his
arms; her flesh through the thin dress felt limp and cold.

'Just let her lie down on the floor, where she is. We can
turn her on her side. It's all right, I did some nursing. Take
care, don't bang her head again. Now draw up her knees,
that's it . . .' The Englishwoman reached for a wrist, then
pressed her fingers into the loose swag of Marie's lowest
chin. 'Something's moving, but it's pretty faint. We need an
ambulance.'

'Is she ill?' Grandmère was standing at Marie's feet, pulling
the wrap more tightly around her shoulders, anxiety dawning
in her eyes.

Miss Partridge was at the telephone, every vestige of
French inflection deserting her as she urgently commanded
an ambulance. '*Mal au coeur, très grave. Une femme de
quatre-vingts ans.*' She was almost shouting. Then it seemed
that she had been understood, for she dropped her voice and
hung up the earpiece.

'She's not eighty yet, she can't be. We're the same age.'

Lydia was still standing over the fallen body. 'She never said she was ill.'

'My dear girl, she's been feeling sick and breathless all week, I heard her say so myself. You only had to look at her to see.'

'But she was always complaining.'

'Who wouldn't, the life you led her?' There was no sting of blame in the question, but the Englishwoman did not use the widened eyes and crooked grin which normally signified a humorous understatement.

'We are Russian, what do you understand of the way we live?' Lydia stepped stiffly over her friend's ankles to strike a pose in the centre of the room, flinging wide her arms as if to embrace the attention of an audience. Her stole flapped, stirring a pile of papers on the table. 'If we have tears to shed, we cry. If our heart is full, we love. Our soul is deep, full of passion . . .'

'For the love of God don't start all that nonsense again. If you want to do something, call up Father Vasily, that's his name, isn't it?'

'What for?'

'Don't you Russians fetch a priest when someone is dying?'

'Naturally we do, we are not animals.'

'Well, then, you need him now, don't you?'

'What do you mean? Tell me what you mean – she isn't dying. She can't be!' The arms, so thin that they were widest at the elbow joint, faltered in the air and returned to clasp each other in the folds of the wrap.

'Yes, Lydia, I think she may be, I really do. Didn't you see the way she looked, haven't you seen it before? The way a person is when they can feel death creeping up on them, but they can't be sure because they've never felt it before and all they know is that they don't understand what's happening to them. You didn't see it so much in the war, death is always on a soldier's mind I suppose, but even then you'd get the ones who never believed it would come to them. I used to think it was one of Nature's tricks, to help people slip away quietly, not in a dreadful panic. Is that the siren? Alex, you've got young ears, go outside and listen.'

In a few moments the low-riding white Citroën swung around the corner and pulled in outside the villa. He heard his grandmother howling 'No! no!' from the interior of the house. Marie was carried out on a stretcher, a rounded shape under the red blankets with only a lock of her white hair visible. It was the last Alex saw of her; she died that night and the priest, citing the climate, advised against the traditional laying out of the body at home.

At the funeral service in the Russian cathedral the incense seemed to choke him. The effort of suppressing his urge to cough brought tears to his eyes. Feeling faint, he willingly allowed Kolya alone to support his grandmother on the long walk to the side of the open coffin. Wreaths and bouquets were stacked around it and the edge was lined with white carnations. Lydia had wept incessantly since her friend's last moments. Her cheeks were wet under her veil, but she was quiet and moved as if in a trance. As the last of the mourners moved away, Kolya gently pulled a small icon in a silver case from his mother's hands and laid it inside the casket before it was closed.

The next day she seemed calm and at first the vinegary tone of her remarks persuaded them that sheer selfishness had saved her from suffering too much grief. 'At least that girl knows how to fillet fish properly – Marie always made a hash of it,' was all she said when Kolya explained that he had negotiated with the maid for her to come in every day and take over the cooking and the rest of Marie's work.

'You shouldn't have taken the icon away from me like

that,' she complained a few hours later. 'I didn't intend to give it to her. That icon was a gift from Sergei Pavlovich. I was keeping it.'

Kolya muttered something under his breath. 'Imagine' – he turned to his nephew as soon as they were outside the salon – 'what it was like for me as a child. Who do you think put food in front of me, and noticed when I had outgrown my shoes, and haggled in the market just before it closed to get everything at the rock-bottom price?'

'Not Grandmère.'

'No, indeed. She is my mother, but Marie mothered me, truly. Actually, she mothered us all. Now one little icon is too much.' It was the only harsh thing Alex had ever heard him say about Lydia.

In the morning the old woman was up and moving about very early, which obliged Alex to wake up himself. He found her sitting upright on a sofa in a new black dress.

'She's so happy to be with Basil and her little ones.' Her mouth, approximately painted with fresh lipstick, curved into an optimistic crescent. 'She was here, she's been here half the night. She was worried, you see, about how I would manage. Had to come and see for herself. But I could tell she was happy. They're all together now, even the girl she left behind who died of inflammation of the lungs. Don't you like my dress? Mourning clothes don't have to be dreary, not if you're clever about them.'

'Is she going mad?' he asked his uncle as soon as he arrived. 'She said she'd seen Marie in the night.'

Kolya drew in a sharp breath, offended by the boy's careless judgement of insanity. 'She always does that when somebody dies. Claims she's had a spiritual visitation. She can't really accept that they've gone and it's her way of pretending they're still alive. Just humour her, don't argue.'

The next day the old woman gave more conventional evidence of grief. 'My friend, my only true friend in the world! You know, it was a formal arrangement for us, friendship, when we were girls? We swore the oath together. The only friend I had.' She retreated to her bedroom and sat at the dressing table of stained maple veneer, sorting through the jumbled drawers for mementoes. 'A good thing I have no jewellery left, now that I've no daughter to leave it to when I die. Soon it will be my turn, I know. There's no point to life when you are unloved.'

Other women friends came to call, but after a while she asked Kolya to turn them away. 'They don't care about me. They just want to look at my things. Jackdaws! I know. Beady eyes on what they're going to steal when I'm gone.'

'That's a good sign,' Kolya confided. 'She's fretting about her possessions as usual. I think we'll be able to get back to Paris in a few days now.'

Alex tried to mute his enthusiasm for this news. He was itching to begin the business of getting a job and had feared that he might be deputized to remain with his grandmother while she adjusted to her loss. But, sure enough, they were able to leave three days later.

In Paris he found a different community of exiled Russians, larger, more diverse, more inclined to go about its business than to idle away the days in a haze of vodka and nostalgia. They recognized two races within their nationality – Russian, by which was meant an exile, and Russian-from-Russia. Uncle Kolya was something of a social focus; newly arrived visitors were brought to his door by acquaintances who said, 'Have you met Kolya Kusminsky? Oh, but you must. Every Russian in Paris knows Kolya. His mother was a great ballerina, some say the greatest. He's in antiques, Fabergé, silver, that kind of thing. Every day he has lunch at the fish restaurant on the corner, and after he shuts up you'll find him in the little bar just opposite. Come and meet him, he'll be so glad to see you.'

His uncle welcomed him to his apartment by marching him down the hushed, deeply carpeted and immaculately swept staircase which they had just ascended and out into the street.

'Now,' he began in the voice of a benevolent schoolmaster, 'you are in the square which was once called the Place Royale and now, God forgive us, is called the Place des Vosges. And why? Remember you are in France when you answer.'

'Er – because of the magazine?' Alex hazarded, tired from the long train journey and longing for a drink of anything, preferably Coke.

'Magazine? No, no, dear boy, *Vosges*, not *Vogue*. Listen, listen! French is a precise language, not like Russian which is meant for screaming and mumbling. No – this enclave of architectural harmony, this jewel of Renaissance decoration, was called after the department of Vosges because after the Revolution the citizens of that region of France had the great stupidity to hand over their taxes before all the rest. That's all that counts with the French, their lousy taxes. Now, let me point out to you some of the important features of the place . . .'

'Can I put down my bags?' Alex hoped for a reprieve but was disappointed.

'Of course, just drop them by the concierge's door, she'll keep an eye on them for you. Now take a look around and notice that there are thirty-six grand houses here, each with four arches, none quite the same but unified by the subtle relationship of the details, the stone-work, the brick-work, the gables and so on. If we start here at number six, the former home of the writer Victor Hugo . . .'

The tour concluded almost an hour later, by which time Alex was ready to sleep on his feet. Having devoted almost four years of his life to his physical development, he found mental work utterly exhausting. He had a brief impression of immensely tall windows, heavy dark furniture and tapestries in the apartment before sinking into a modern leather chair and closing his eyes.

The weekend, which Kolya had generously set aside for his elementary education, passed in the same style. Obediently he walked through museums and monuments trying to assimilate the stream of facts which fell from his uncle's lips while statues, paintings, buttresses, spires and carvings blurred before his eyes.

Kusminsky's shop was in a little courtyard off the Rue Jacob; almost every day the Sorbonne students found something to call them to the barricades, but only the noisiest demonstrations disturbed the quietness of this enclave. Kolya continued his education. With ten days in hand before he had to present himself at the Opéra, Alex, who cherished passionately the rare privilege of being able to lie in bed late, was dismayed to be issued with a cultural objective every morning. Within a few days he pleaded the necessity of attending a dance class every day, but he was still expected to meet his uncle for lunch at the fish brasserie, and then to preside behind the little lapis lazuli table in the outer showroom all afternoon while Kolya received visitors in the office at the rear.

As he became familiar with the routine of his uncle's life, he discovered that the affability which the older man showed him masked something darker. Lydia telephoned her son at his office every morning; she asked about Alex, and Kolya would reply that he was out, lightly but with an indefinable innuendo of laziness or even degeneracy. He never mentioned the calls to his nephew, or passed on the old woman's good wishes.

With a young man's thoughtlessness, Alex did not telephone his grandmother, who soon involved all her coterie in the supposed problem of her grandson's wayward behaviour. The deception came to light when Angela Partridge, who made a monthly pilgrimage to Paris to visit a niece working at the British Embassy, called at the Place des Vosges at 9 a.m. and found the young man rushing with a bag of kit to his first class of the day.

'If I were you I'd make a point of keeping in close touch with your grandmother yourself,' she advised after an uncomfortable lunch *à trois* with Kolya. 'Mad as she may be, your uncle really is absolutely devoted to her. He was her darling boy for half a century before you poled up, don't forget. It's only natural he should be a tiny bit jealous.'

'Are you saying he was deliberately trying to stop her talking to me?' Alex's clear grey eyes were wide with amazement.

'No. But with Kolya an awful lot happens without it being exactly deliberate. His right hand can be terribly dense about what his left gets up to.'

In the afternoons the silence in the shop was smothering. The air was still and always tainted with Kolya's cigarettes. A few hundred yards away the crowds surged up and down the broad pavements of the Boulevard St Germain, and those whose objective was to find some expensive treasure among the Left Bank antique shops circulated purposefully towards the Seine, but few of them were washed up in the courtyard. Indeed, most of Kusminsky's visitors came with the specific purpose of seeing him; browsers and carriage trade were discouraged. The shop, for all its subtle spotlights, pristine white walls and smearless glass cabinets displaying a king's ransom in treasures, was merely symbolic. The turn-over of the business, which Alex was awed to discover usually amounted to billions of francs each year, was almost all generated in deals done intensely over tea in the back office. For Alex, sprawled on an uncomfortable small chair between the case of tiny Fabergé masterpieces and the case of Moscow-school art deco jewellery, it was a major event if the paulownia tree in the courtyard dropped one of its large leaves.

When he telephoned Grandmère she often sounded drunk even if she was not. There were times when she obviously did not know whether it was winter or summer, whether she had eaten or not or what day of the week it was. Sometimes she would demand to speak to Kolya, who would take the call with the merest hint of bad grace.

At seven each evening another unpleasant development took place; his uncle's lover appeared from the direction of the Faculty of Law. By all the natural laws of attraction, Kolya, approaching sixty with thinning hair and a small soft paunch rising under his beautiful hand-made shirts, should have been consumed with anxiety that his beautiful boy would fall for his equally beautiful nephew. Instead, Etienne seemed to express all the jealousy which the older man repressed. He sat all evening with his bony hand draped over Kolya's shoulder, glaring at the interloper. In the course of the studies for which his protector was paying, Etienne's wide shoulders had developed a pronounced stoop, and with his sleek, thick black hair and taste for black high-necked sweaters he had the malevolent air of a vulture.

When his audition at the Opéra took place, Alex thought he did well. The examiners, two men and a woman, decided flatly that he was too tall, which angered him.

He telephoned Madame Sedova in Cannes at once. 'You

really must do something. I didn't see Lifar himself, just his deputy and the *régisseur*. I don't think they even realized who I am.'

'My poor Alex, they realized quite well,' came the throaty reply. 'Lifar telephoned me yesterday. You haven't been exactly frank about your reasons for quitting the Vaganova, have you? Perhaps you thought a few silly old ladies would never suspect the truth. But this is such a small world, and everybody knows everything sooner or later.'

'But I didn't do anything wrong!' In his own mind Vitya's accident was already almost forgotten.

'You broke the rules, that's the worst wrong you can do in their eyes. So many boys would have given anything for your opportunity, and you wasted it. I shall keep it from your grandmother, she has had enough tragedy in her life – well, we all have. And that poor boy will be crippled for life. The girl is pregnant into the bargain.'

'What girl? She can't be, not Anya, I brought her . . .' He remembered that Madame's favourite, Cécile, the daughter of two obstetricians, had supplied him with forged prescriptions for the contraceptive pills on which so much of his happiness had been founded. 'Let's say I took care of her properly. And as for the boy, that was his own fault, I wasn't even in the room.'

He heard her take a deep breath and had a mental image of Madame's bosom heaving with indignation under one of her favourite ruffled chiffon blouses. 'So, it's all true. How dare you try to justify yourself! And lie to us! What kind of fool do you think I felt I had been when Lifar called? Nobody wants a boy with your reputation in their company – one undisciplined dancer, one bad apple – and the rot soon spreads. My advice to you is to go back to school and try to demonstrate that you've changed your ways – or else, give up and get yourself a job in a cabaret. It might be a better life for someone with your kind of morality.'

She rang off with an angry clatter of plastic. Alex threw the telephone into a corner of the room and paced about until he mastered his disappointment and annoyance. He had imagined that his Leningrad life had been a fantasy episode, and that the ballet school, like some enclosed religious order, would never make contact with the outside world, and so his sins within the walls would never be discovered. Now he had again been expelled from a family, another family in which he had felt no sense of belonging, which had detected his bad heart and rejected his attempts to conform.

In a panic he sat down at his uncle's desk and wrote at once to six small touring companies whose addresses his old teacher had sent to him. On his way to lunch he called at the photographic shop and ordered more prints of his photographs. His golden, glamorous future was suddenly dissolving like a mirage, and the present was becoming uncomfortable.

While his uncle was outwardly kind, Alex felt ill at ease in sharing his life. They disagreed profoundly on the subject of women. Kusminsky had female friends, a handful of stupendously elegant women of around his own age who joined them for viewings, gallery parties, and formal social events. They were posed amidst his life like statues, required only to be beautiful and commented upon. If ever they asked for attention beyond ritual chivalry, or sympathy for their personal concerns, Kolya judged them pitiful, neurotic and emotionally voracious, and held them up as proof of the hopeless inferiority of their sex.

Apart from these women, who had no idea how viciously they were criticized behind their backs, Kusminsky's circle was exclusively homosexual and his life was orderly and dull. In addition to the social functions for which he summoned female company he and Etienne moved in a sedate cultural orbit plotted to take in every event necessary to be considered familiar with the arts. At weekends their friends entertained, lavishly, in a style which made Alex's jaw drop, but mostly for the benefit of other homosexuals.

It was always necessary, and always irritating, for Alex to confirm his own sexual orientation. He learned that if he strayed from Kolya's side he would inevitably be propositioned. One evening at a party given by a conductor he had met an American boy of around his own age in Paris on a concert tour with a choral group. They had fallen into a long, pleasant conversation and Kolya, explaining afterwards that he had not wished to disturb him with a new friend, had left with Etienne.

When the gathering broke up in the small hours of the morning Alex found himself alone with his host, who declared that there were no taxis at that hour and then pulled Alex's face to his with both hands and kissed him. 'Oh, you're going to be too good – but wait! First, more champagne!' the man commanded, flinging out one arm as if cueing an inattentive soloist, and taking Alex's shocked immobility for consent. In the time it took the man to find a new bottle, Alex fell on the multiple door locks with both hands and escaped into the street. He said nothing to his uncle, who neverthless advised him the next evening that he should behave with more consideration.

But Alex now mistrusted his uncle, which poisoned the simplest of their exchanges.

'You look so pale – do you feel well?' Kolya asked one evening when they returned to dress for the theatre. This warm sympathy immediately alarmed Alex.

'Oh no, I'm fine.'

'April is an enervating month, I find. The atmosphere is unsettled. I have asked a few friends to drop by and meet us for dinner afterwards, but if you would prefer to rest I can always rearrange things. You haven't said anything for a while, I wondered perhaps if you were a little tired?'

'Well, yes. And I was listening to you talking about those enamelled things you bought today. You were saying something about Fabergé introducing colour into his jewellery.'

'Yes, that's right, with his enamels, and with the hardstones like nephrite, jade, quartz, and semi-precious stones as well as the rubies and sapphires. Before Fabergé jewellers despised stones that were cheap, so they had a very limited palette from which to create. But enough of that, we're talking about you. Sit down, relax, we'll have a little cocktail.' He indicated the sofa, piled with rich cushions, and then leaned over Alex's shoulder to press the bell for his manservant, who appeared from the rear recesses of the apartment for orders. 'I do apologize, I know I get carried away. Beautiful things give me so much pleasure, and I can sense that you, Alex, also respond to beauty – indeed who doesn't, it's natural, after all. I just wanted to share some of my pleasure with you. But perhaps you are a little sad? Disappointed about the Opera – have you heard from any of the other companies?'

'Yes, not good news, two of them wrote back at once saying they don't need anyone right now. The others haven't replied yet – it's been a couple of weeks.'

'Easter is only just over, people are still on holiday. Perhaps I could ask around, I've got a few friends who might be helpful.'

'Oh no, please don't put yourself out for me. You've done

415

so much already.' Having seen how effective the homosexual network was in advancing its members' careers, Alex was terrified of becoming inextricably tangled in its web. 'I've just got a lot on my mind at the moment.'

'Has something else distressed you?'

'Well, yes, there is something.' The perfect defence occurred to him. 'I'm really missing my girlfriend in Leningrad. We didn't have – well, we weren't able to say goodbye properly. And of course she can't write very easily. I just think about her all the time and wonder how she is. I heard a rumour that she was pregnant, so now I'm really worried.'

'You weren't able to say goodbye properly – what do you mean?'

'She – ah – she wasn't around when I left, I couldn't find her.' In fact, although he had defied the embassy official and run to the girls' quarters, Anya had been so deeply asleep that it had been difficult to rouse her. They had a conversation, he had explained, she had murmured a few words, but he doubted that in the morning she would have remembered anything.

'But she knew you were leaving?' Was this genuine concern, or did Kolya know that his story of acute loneliness was a lie and was probing for inconsistencies?

'Oh yes, of course, she just wasn't expecting me to leave when I did, if you see what I mean. At least, I suppose that was the reason.'

'Yes, perhaps it was. But I shouldn't be too concerned. In my experience, Russian girls have always got an eye out for their main chance.'

'Oh no, Anya isn't like that at all.'

'They're all like that, dear boy, you'll find out.' Alex was insulted at the implication and his face said plainly that he doubted the value of his uncle's experience with girls of any nationality. 'Oh believe me, Alex, I know what I'm talking about. I wasn't always a member in good standing of the green carnation society. I was married for twelve years – it wasn't much of a relationship, I grant you, but that wasn't my fault.'

'Was your wife Russian too?' The lingering bitterness with which his uncle had spoken roused Alex's curiosity.

'Yes, well, almost. A Latvian girl, they're famous for their stupidity. I was twenty-six, already quite well off, and my mother nagged me constantly to marry, of course. Every old woman wants to be a grandmother.' He selected one of the modern chairs, a low-slung construction of russet hide and chromium, and reclined, crossing his legs and smoothing out the already creaseless fabric of his fawn trousers. 'She used to cut out the lonely hearts advertisements in the émigré newspaper, *Illustriovannaya Rossia*. There was one that obsessed her, I can see it even now . . .' With one tapering, contemptuous hand he outlined a rectangle in the air. 'A Russian girl from Latvia is lonely and would like to cor-respond with an understanding Russian Parisian and receive his photo. He should be under forty years old with a steady job and a taste for music and the arts.'

'Not much to ask.'

'So it appeared. So Mama actually wrote to this girl and told her where my shop was and invited her to call on me. Matchmaking all the time, even when she was at the other end of the country. So – to please her – we were married. And I discovered that the most intense loneliness in this world is to be found in a home where there is no communication.'

'She was quiet, was she?'

'On the contrary, she talked nonstop, every waking moment, about nothing. It's a facility all women have.

417

Fortunately business took me away quite a lot, but I didn't know about myself then – at least, I knew somewhere in my heart, one always does, but it was only when the war came and I joined the army that I discovered my true identity. And so at the age of thirty-five my life actually began.' All this was delivered with an emphasis so delicate it was as barely perceptible as the vermouth in their martinis, but Alex, while admiring the subtlety, resented the invitation to open the question of his own sexuality.

'So you got divorced?'

'Happily there was no need for that. The Germans came, there was a great flight of people from Paris, Mama wanted my wife and the children to come to her in Nice, but my wife had no gratitude towards Mama. Two women can never share the same kitchen, you know – not that Mama has ever known what a kitchen was, of course. And so my wife refused to leave Paris until the last moment, and then decided to go with our neighbours in their car. There were millions of people on the roads going south, and the German planes came over with bombs and gunfire – they were killed.'

'How sad.' This drop of politeness sank without trace into the arid atmosphere. Alex was chilled to the core of his heart by his uncle's unfeeling recitation. In that instant he knew that he could not exist in Kolya Kusminsky's elegant, bloodless, misogynistic world for much longer. Warmth and care were the oxygen of his spirit, women's warmth and care. He felt that his being could not survive without them.

Some weeks passed. His former teacher urged him to begin classes in jazz and American tap, but Alex was unwilling to let go of his classical dream. He entered one jazz class; it was not to his taste. Afterwards in the showers the regulars traded gossip of new productions and rumours of auditions in an atmosphere of desperate, petty rivalry which disgusted him.

Few answers to his letters arrived. A small ballet company
in Lyons asked to see him and he set off full of confidence.
Faced with the reality of grimy, ill-equipped studios, low
wages and a claustrophobic company riven by rivalry, he
performed below his best. A position was offered none the
less, but he refused it.

Then the telephone rang in the apartment early one morning. '*Mamasha* is in hospital,' Kolya informed him, hastily
knotting his tie as he walked through the apartment to get
his suitcase. 'I'm going now, I'll call Etienne and you must
go to the shop and do the following things – get a paper and
write them down. On my desk in the office is my diary, just
call everyone who has an appointment today and tomorrow
and put them off. You know where the telephone numbers
are. Then in the middle left-hand drawer is a small cash box
with some dollars in it – take them to the bank, the Société
Générale, the book is under the box. And then if you have
reached everyone just shut up the shop and leave a notice
saying the owner is absent for a few days on family business.
Otherwise stay for the day to explain. OK? Got that?' Alex
had scarcely nodded when Kolya ran out of the door, his
coat flapping about him as he struggled into it.

In the empty shop he sat in his uncle's chair making
telephone calls; one appointment, the four o'clock, entered
in Cyrillic simply as 'Gotz', had no counterpart in the
Roladex of numbers and so he was obliged to wait until the
afternoon. After a few hours of idle reflection the notion
formed in his mind that if Grandmère were dying Kolya
would try for the last time to have her to himself. He called
his ally, Miss Partridge, but she was out.

Gotz proved to be a soft-bodied man of about forty with
dark, curling hair that receded at the temples but fell forward
over his nose as soon as he removed his grey hat. He was a

Russian-from-Russia, but with an air of assertive wellbeing which suggested he was of good standing at home and accustomed to the West.

'You must be the nephew?'

Alex greeted him in his own language and Gotz's wet, dark eyes flickered curiously.

'I am, yes. I have to apologize to you – my uncle can't be here, an illness in the family. I did try to reach you . . .'

'Kusminsky has no family – ah, of course! The mother! Not serious, I hope?' Gotz's whole face became mobile with interest.

'I don't know, but then she is almost eighty . . .'

'Eighty at least, I should say. I met her once, years ago. What a life she had, eh? We can't imagine it now. Kolya left yesterday?'

'This morning.'

'So he can't have arrived yet – it is Cannes, isn't it? No, no – Nice, I remember. Well, I've a lot to do in Paris this trip, I'll give you a call before I leave and see if he's back. Give him my best wishes, eh?' He settled his hat on his head once more, pulling the brim down sharply, then left with a spring in his step as if he had received good news.

Alex ran down the steel mesh shutters and, before he left, tried Angela Partridge's number once again. She was there, and immediately confirmed his anxiety. 'Dear boy, they think it's a stroke. She's come round but she's dreadfully weak and of course there's always the risk of another one. I thought you were both coming, fool that I am. I should have spoken directly to you. Get the train, you'll be here when the sun comes up.'

The clinic was on a promontory outside the city, overlooking the sweep of the Baie des Anges and the sparkling sea. Alex took a taxi directly there from the train station and arrived as the white-robed nursing sisters were settling the patients after their breakfast. Grandmère was alone, lying almost flat in a small side ward, with an oxygen cylinder against the wall near the bed and a monitor with several dials and a screen at hand on the other side. The old woman was the livid colour of an antique waxwork, her blue, distended veins snaking down her neck and arms, her flat chest rising and falling with each hoarse breath.

Shyly he asked one of the sisters, 'Is she conscious?'

The woman approached, her long starched skirt swinging, and leaned over the tiny body. 'Maybe. I thought she heard me when I came round to see if she wanted something to eat. She did speak yesterday, after a fashion. Madame, your grandson is here to see you.' There was no response. Her hand, its rounded fingers red and roughened from scrubbing, reached for the old woman's wrist; after a few moments she leaned forward and pressed the bell above the bed.

Alex heard rubber-soled shoes running along the corridor. Two more nuns entered and between them moved the oxygen to the bedside and fixed the mask over the patient's face. Next a doctor burst through the door and ordered Alex to wait outside.

It was there that he encountered Kolya an hour later, striding purposefully down the corridor. Anger flashed through his uncle's pale eyes, but he covered his annoyance at Alex's presence by lighting a cigarette and said nothing until the doctor emerged from the room, pulling his stethoscope from his ears.

'Another stroke,' he confirmed, 'more serious, much more serious. One can never be certain, but I think we may be close to the end. Her condition deteriorates all the time.'

They sat with her, the two men on one side, and a nun on the other, silently watching the needles flicker on the dials.

The air was overheated and had a sickly tang. Sounds and movements of breath had almost ceased. Alex felt compellingly bored, and berated himself for this inappropriate response. He fixed his eyes on the body beneath the blankets, trying to imagine the bones clothed with ripe, strong flesh, free-flowing blood in the veins and skin glowing with health, the skilled limbs confidently accomplishing their tasks.

In an unexpectedly sudden movement the nurse got to her feet and searched once more for a pulse, then again pressed the overhead bell. This time only the doctor came.

'She has slipped away from us,' he told them, and Alex noted that the doctor was also annoyed, as if Grandmère had purposely outwitted him. Kolya seemed to shrink inside his jacket, and the other man touched him lightly on the upper arm. 'There was undoubtedly extensive brain damage; you would not have wished for anything else. It was a merciful end for her.' The words triggered tears. Turning away from then, Kolya groped for his handkerchief and for a moment it seemed as if he was going to vomit.

Instead, Alex saw his uncle's fists clench and open again several times. His spine slowly straightened although he was trembling with the effort of mastering his emotions. When he spoke, his voice was not at first controlled; he stammered a few syllables, whispered, then almost shouted.

'Are you sure?'

The doctor, used to expect bizarre behaviour at the onset of grief, replied in level tones. 'There can be no doubt at all. All the signs of life have ceased – it is finished now.'

'Can't you . . .' Kolya's eyes seemed about to burst with the effort of containing his feelings.

'There is nothing more to do.'

Kolya stepped towards the bed, paused as if he were afraid of falling, then leaned down and began to gather the small, limp form into his arms. The nurse unobtrusively unplugged the leads which still connected the body to the monitoring equipment. As he embraced his mother a horrible liquid sound escaped from her lips, the last breath squeezed from the slack tissue of the lungs by his embrace.

As instinctively as a cat, Alex leaped back at the noise, but his uncle began to murmur soothing nonsense, as if quietening a baby.

'There, beautiful angel, it's all right, everything's all right. You won't get cold, angel, I know you hate to be cold. Tropical flower, little white orchid, the cold isn't for you. You like to be warm. I know, I know. And beautiful, so beautiful. Beautiful white dress, oyster silk-satin, pearls like a bride . . .' He picked disdainfully at the edge of the hospital nightgown as if noticing it for the first time. 'Everything you like, little white orchid, we'll take care of you.' He felt for one of her hands and pressed it to his chest.

The doctor moved towards the door and, seeing Alex transfixed by the tableau, touched his arm to get his attention. They left the room silently, the nurse sweeping after them.

Despite the heat, Kolya insisted that his mother should lie in state at home. It seemed that he had planned the honours in the greatest detail beforehand. Alex was ignored as soon as Etienne arrived from Paris with a young man who was a window-dresser at Galeries Lafayette. The grimy clutter of the villa disappeared behind lavish swags of silk and potted palms. Since the table was too rickety to support the coffin it was raised on trestles and planks disguised by more drapery and banked by orchids.

From the apartment, the young men brought a portrait of Lydia costumed in a romantic white tutu for Les Sylphides, which was erected at the head of the coffin, with photographs, stage accessories and yellowed newspaper reviews in an album displayed at the sides.

An argument broke out – the only disagreement Alex ever witnessed between Kolya and his lover – over the appropriate headdress for the corpse. Kolya favoured the jewelled cap she had worn as Salome, with rows of pearls over the forehead. Etienne recommended a *kokoshnik*, the traditional Russian crown, set with pearls and diamonds, with a veil over the face. After a day of waspish silence during which the casket remained closed, Madame Sedova arrived from Cannes and called on the patriarch of the cathedral to mediate. Pointing out that Salome, although the role in which La Kusminskaya conquered the West, was also a pagan temptress responsible for the martyrdom of a saint, he ruled in favour of the crown. Kolya assumed an air of indifference and the casket was opened.

Bouquets soon crammed the room, wilting in the heat, and a sophisticated stereo system played Tchaikovsky's Symphony No. 6. An extraordinary crowd of people passed through the villa; most of them were strangers to Alex, although many had clearly been dancers once and others were as obviously marked as devotees of the art. Kolya's own circle was strongly represented, the slender, deeply wrinkled men and women in exquisite clothes gossiping together with as much animation as was seemly before setting off for lunch or dinner.

'Must be a marvellous aperitif, paying one's respects to the dead. Seems to give 'em all a healthy appetite – my God, how the French love their stomachs.' Angela Partridge flapped her mock-ivory fan for emphasis. She showed emotion only in two spots of colour on her cheeks and a tightening of her throat when she spoke. Rudely disregarded by Kolya, she had retreated to the kitchen with Alex and the maid to preside over the samovar. 'I hope Lydia's enjoying this circus, wherever she is. If it's as hot as this in the cathedral they'll all keel over like guardsmen.'

Soon they stood again in the perfumed interior of the cathedral, where sonorous hymns echoed in air that was now warm although the full heat of June blazed outside. Alex forced himself to the coffin side, determined this time not to cede one duty to his uncle, but he could not look at her face. The skeletal hands had been arranged around a garnet crucifix and a pair of old worn satin point shoes lay against the paper lace of the interior.

Back in Paris again the sense of drifting grew upon him. There was no post, not even refusals in reply to his letters. The leaden routine of his days continued and Alex embraced it, eager for anything that would prevent him dissolving into anonymity. Angela Partridge called upon him, carefully presented as ever in a silk afternoon dress and mended stockings. She brought an old grey office folder containing signed duplicates of La Kusminskaya's most famous stage portraits, and more of Grandmère's sketch maps of her house. 'I promised I'd explain these,' the Englishwoman hissed, under the impression that they would be overheard.

'Uncle is out,' he reassured her.

'It simply tortured her that she hadn't anything to leave you. They sold everything years ago, of course. She said Kolya would always look after himself, but she was desperate to do something for you. So what this is' – here she pulled out the largest diagram, executed in purple ink – 'is the ground plan of the house, and that' – she pointed to a spidery star at one edge of the paper – 'is supposed to be the location of the safe where all her jewellery was kept. Including the famous necklace Orlov gave her, which she's wearing here in this picture. So, dear boy, all you have to do is go back to Russia and find it, dynamite the wall, pick the lock and you'll have a king's ransom in diamonds.' They laughed unsteadily, moved by this last manifestation of Lydia's faith in the material world.

Alex redoubled his efforts to find work, rising early to take classes and sitting all afternoon at the lapis lazuli table with a sheaf of freshly printed photographs and a list of names and telephone numbers copied from the studio notice board. They were not enticing prospects. Dancers were needed on a Caribbean cruise ship. There was an audition for a provincial tour of the musical *Hair*. At Evian the cabaret director at the Casino was looking particularly for tall boys. He wrote letters, then tore them up. He went to auditions, arrived late, behaved insolently and ensured that he received very few offers of work. The life of glamour he had always wanted seemed to be unattainable. Kolya was increasingly irritable and Alex anticipated daily his insincerely regretful announcement that it was time for them to part company.

The silence of a July afternoon was broken by a small human noise. In the doorway stood a tall woman wearing a panama hat low over her eyes. From her square shoulders to her ankles she was enveloped in a double-breasted riding coat of some heavy matt silk printed like python skin. He had become accustomed to seeing magnificently dressed women wherever he went in Paris, but even so he was temporarily tongue-tied by the effect.

'Can I help you?' he managed to say at last. Of her face, only her full, sad mouth and sharp jaw were visible.

'I hope so. I want to buy something but I don't know what, exactly.'

'Is it for a special occasion?' Since most of Kusminsky's business was with other dealers, personal buyers were unusual; this was the first unaccompanied female customer he had ever seen.

'In a way.'

'A ball, perhaps, or a birthday . . .' Alex moved towards the jewellery cabinet, searching for the keys in the inside pocket of the jacket which Kolya insisted he wear despite the summer heat. Sometimes when his eyes strayed over the necklaces and tiaras in the case he imagined them being worn by exquisitely dressed women of the kind he only read about in *Paris Match*.

'No. A divorce . . .'

Momentarily bewildered, he busied himself with the security routine, locking the door and setting the alarm. 'A divorce . . .'

The mouth smiled without inhibition, revealing strong teeth. 'My divorce. Today it's final so – I have to do something, why not go shopping? I always wanted a piece of jewellery that wasn't just stones, you know, something with a little history to it, a little romance.'

'Well, you've come to the right shop, of course.' He pasted a courteous expression on his face, hoping that his amazement would not show. Kolya seldom bothered to tell him the price of items on display, since he did all the negotiation himself, but he had naturally asked, and knew that there was nothing there worth less than twenty thousand francs. 'Is there anything particular I can show you?'

'Oh, I don't know . . . let me see.' She joined him beside the case and pointed to a bow-knot brooch with a large, milky-blue gem set at the centre. 'What's the stone in that brooch there, at the back?'

'It's what Fabergé called the Mecca stone. Actually that's not the correct name, because a Mecca stone is a sort of pinkish cornelian, and this is a translucent blue chalcedony.'

'It looks like a piece of the moon.'

'Yes, it does, doesn't it?' He wanted to tell her how poetic she must be to see such significance in the jewel. 'And those diamonds around it are little rose-cut stones set so as to enhance its sparkle. That was a particular innovation of the house of Fabergé.'

'What a lot you know. Are you studying jewellery design?'

'No, I – this is my uncle's shop. I'm a dancer, at least, I hope I am.'

She drew out the bare facts of his life expertly, all the time switching attention from his face to the jewellery. He wished passionately that she would take off her hat, and as if the intuitive message had been received she removed it shortly afterwards, releasing straight tawny blonde hair which fell to her shoulders.

'Let me see how tnat necklace looks.' One by one the large coat buttons were unfastened. Underneath she wore a halterneck beige silk dress. He helped her out of the coat and laid it over a chair.

'I know that necklace ought to be about two million francs.' His voice cracked with anxiety.

'I'm not going to buy it. The appropriate compensation for losing my husband to some Mexican whore is around half a million, I decided.'

'Oh, yes, I see.' Reverently, he picked the necklace out of its birch wood box and approached her. Her eyes were speckled green, the colour of some of the Siberian emeralds, but unless she smiled they had a wounded darkness in them. With her right hand she twisted up her hair again, allowing him to put it round her neck. She had a light suntan and her skin was fine-grained and taut. He had to touch her. At the last moment he made it look accidental, brushing his palm against the ball of her bare shoulder, but she started immediately, then caught his eye in the mirror.

'So, what can I get for half a million francs in this shop?' The question was accompanied by a very level look and a half smile. He knew he was blushing violently, and took excessive care in unfastening the necklace and putting it back on its white satin cushion.

'I don't know the price of everything, I'll have to ask my uncle.'

He moved rapidly towards the rear office, knocked and blundered through the door.

The two men were so intent on their task that they did not hear him. Alex hesitated, remembering too late that Kolya had asked not to be disturbed. It was a routine order; most of the business transacted in the back office was less than legal.

Fragments of rainbow danced all over the white walls, refracted from a high-powered lamp by the facets of the jewels which Kolya was examining under his most powerful equipment, a surgeon's lens mounted on a bracket. Gotz, the dealer from Moscow, sat opposite him at the desk, globules of perspiration standing like blisters on his forehead. In spite of the heat he still wore his grey overcoat.

'This dust is terrible.' Kolya spoke in his mannered, old-fashioned Russian. With delicate strokes of a paintbrush, he was trying to clean the stones. 'The way it clings – terrible.'

'What do you expect? You knock down an old wall, there's bound to be dust. The cut is still quite recognizable, isn't it?' Gotz was showing the usual anxiety of a seller encountering Kusminsky's legendary bargaining style.

Kolya gave no answer, but turned his attention from the jewels to the books open on the desk top; he always identified potential purchases from his library of reference works, sale catalogues and copies of the Fabergé ledgers. Alex noticed that he had also opened one of the albums bound in blue watered silk in which the photographs and mementoes of La Kusminskaya's career were mounted.

'It's the old cut, undoubtedly. But that's no help – if it was a twentieth-century piece I might have workshop records, but just from these little photographs . . .' He shook his head.

Through the half-open door, Alex saw the woman walk restlessly across the shop. Should he interrupt the negotiation now, or wait for them to finish?

'They gave me the exact address.' Gotz set his jaw, implying that he had worn down tougher men in his time.

Without haste, Kolya countered, 'Alas, we never even knew it. Her memory . . .'

'But they have it in the records at Rossi Street – it will be very simple to verify.'

Kolya blew thoughtfully across the gleaming stones and a little cloud of white dust settled on the album of photographs. The woman was gazing out of the shop window with a discontented frown. Alex's patience gave way. He coughed.

'What the hell do you want?' Rapidly, Kusminsky covered the jewels with a corner of the white cloth on which he had spread them for examination. Gotz seemed to jump out of his skin with alarm.

'Oh God, I'm so sorry, Kolya. I forgot you didn't want to be interrupted.'

'Well, now I've reminded you. Fuck off out of here, I'll see you later. And shut the damn door.'

His uncle so rarely swore that Alex felt as if he had been assaulted. As soon as he drew the office door shut behind him he heard the heavy iron bolts being turned on the inside.

'I'm really sorry, Madame, my uncle's in a meeting right now and . . .'

'Whatever did he say to you? You look quite upset.'

'Oh, it doesn't matter. I made him angry, I suppose.'

She was holding the Mecca stone brooch with the finger-tips of both hands, admiring the mysterious light in its depths. The compulsion to connect made him bold.

'That was such a beautiful thing you said about the stone just now – do you think the moon really is like that?'

'We'll soon find out, won't we? Your countrymen are supposed to be arriving there tonight.' Now she had an air of confidence about her, and the dark pain in her eyes had gone.

'Oh, my goodness, is that tonight?'

'The first men on the moon, imagine. Where are you from?'

'I must have a terrible accent still.'

'No, it's very good, but I have an excellent ear. I was an actress before I married.' She put down the brooch and reached for her coat. 'It's so hot, I'm dying for a drink. Why don't you join me? At least you won't be disturbing your uncle.'

He promptly put away the jewellery, unlocked the door, reset the alarm and followed her into the courtyard. By the end of an hour he thought that she was the most beautiful, kind, clever and amusing person in the world, and even if she never allowed him to make love to her his existence would have been enriched for ever by their conversation. In two hours she knew the full story of his life and had disclosed the most recent events in her own. His heart overflowed with tenderness for her pain and he wished aloud that he were a professional hit-man and able to give her brute of a husband what he deserved. In another hour, he had confessed the truth of his last night in Leningrad, and felt light-headed with relief. She invited him to watch the moon landing at her house.

'The surface is like a fine powder. It has a soft beauty all its own,' reported Neil Armstrong, his breathy communication proceeding from the moon to the earth, from Cape Kennedy back to a communication satellite and thence to the television in the corner of the woman's bedroom in the middle of the night. The blue-grey light from the screen flickered over tangled bodies and disordered sheets.

'A soft beauty all its own.' Alex traced the centre line of her stomach with his lips and kissed her navel. His fingertip felt her response, a quiver of the wet, hot, satiny folds – it had seemed impossible to give up possession of her body because their most acute pleasure was past for the moment. Juice ran down to his wrist and he felt drunk with her female smell.

The woman considered that such soft beauty as she possessed was the consequence of being forty-two years old and the mother of children, but said nothing. He seemed a very genuine boy. He was the youngest man she had ever slept with; the flattery was thrilling. With his nerves and his timidity, he seemed to be no more than he claimed. Surely a gigolo would never be so passionately affectionate?

He was so beautiful that when she half-closed her eyes it looked as if a marble statue of Apollo was lying between her thighs. The first time he had been too anxious to do himself justice, but she could see that he was aroused again, and in that area he was of more than classical proportions. She sat up and kissed him, caressing his chest and feeling his nipples harden at her touch and a moan escape between their fused lips. She decided that if he did cost her half a million francs, he would be worth it, perhaps even only for that night.

CHAPTER 14
New York, 1984

In his head, Lovat talked to his wife all the time. How could you do this to me, you unbelievable bitch? How could you do this to our children? Haven't you any feelings, don't you understand you've destroyed a family here? You've wrecked five people's lives just as surely as if you'd murdered us – and for what? For the pleasure of getting your own way. You are the most monstrously selfish creature on earth. You're not fit to be a mother, you're nothing but a child yourself. You're mad, you're a psychopath, right and wrong don't mean anything to you. You've broken all your promises, run away from all your responsibilities. A dumb animal would know better.

The sum of these endless conversations was one word – why? The word screamed itself inside his head when he woke up. Why? All he had done was be a good husband. He had loved her, made love to her, given her children, given her a good life, given up everything for her, given her everything she wanted. Why would a woman do such a thing? Women didn't destroy families, they created them, fought for them, struggled for them. Bianca had gone against all human instinct.

The question seeped into all his conversations, especially his conversations with women who he felt must have special understanding of their own kind. So much anger radiated from him that he was often left talking to a politely vacated space or a tactfully turned shoulder. 'I don't *know* why,

Lovat!' Exasperation eventually robbed even Shona of her good manners. 'Do stop going on, you're just being obsessive. Every time you come round here you just mope around asking me why. You should know, for God's sake, you were her husband.'

He slept badly and woke early, opened his eyes, shut them at once before the tastelessness of the bedroom in his rented house assaulted him, and fantasized about killing Bianca. Machine-gunning her on the steps to the water garden, the blood running over the lovely old lichen-spotted stones and dripping into the pool. Or stabbing her in her bathroom, and the blood flying up the marble-tiled walls and dripping down like raindrops, and her hands smearing it over the taps as she fell to the floor. Or bludgeoning her in the music room itself, with the poker? Would that be heavy enough? A hammer would be better, a heavy one, one blow! Ker-splat! Chips of skull and gobs of brain spattered over the blue and white *toile de Jouy*. Then this nightmare would be over, and he could settle down with the boys and a new woman – a vague figure whose details did not interest him at that point – and make life good again.

Another fantasy occasionally offered itself. He would make himself reject it, refusing to contemplate even in imagination the possibility of a reconciliation. In this scenario Bianca appeared in the hideous bamboo, eau-de-Nil and peach sitting room of the rented house while he was watching the news on television. She looked the way she did just after she had a baby, bony and colourless, although she had made a pathetic attempt to be attractive. Weeping hysterically she told him she had been a fool, that she realized he was the most wonderful man in the world, that no one could have been a better husband or father, that she couldn't live without him, that she begged his forgiveness and wanted him back.

Unmoved, he would continue watching television, perhaps favour her with a look of utter contempt. She would begin to scream and sob, fall to her knees, try to kiss his feet, plead to suck his cock, beg to have sex if only for one last time and then, finally understanding that she had wounded him beyond the limit of human decency, she would run out into Bayswater Road and throw herself under a car – usually some kind of flashed-up Ford Escort driven by a spotty boy racer, stickers on the rear window and 'Errol and Sharon' across the windscreen. The body would be tossed in the air like a doll and impaled on the railings of Hyde Park.

In the terrible days after his marriage ended the fantasies of killing Bianca could occupy an hour or two if necessary. Then, feeling energized but slightly ashamed, he would get out of the *faux*-bamboo bed and be equal to the ordeal of pulling up the taupe and peach ruched blinds in the bedroom.

The violence of his hatred scared him. He was genuinely afraid that if he passed much time in his wife's company she would drop one of her oblique insults, his control would snap and he would do in reality what he had so often imagined. Such a volcano of rage was smouldering in him that even the idea of provoking her was frightening, and so he kept a distance and took care to be civil. In Bianca's estimation he was as insensitive as ever, completely unaffected by their separation, continuing his life without interruption, as self-absorbed as he had been throughout their marriage.

Lovat also wanted to keep his innocence spotless, so that he could stand before his children with a clear conscience for the rest of his life and say, 'This was not my choice, I did not want this, I did not deserve it. This is what your mother has done to us.' That and his pride made him agree to all the

435

terms of the separation in spite of his lawyer's advice. He wanted the boys to know that he was right and she was wrong, and with children actions meant more than words. They were always so silent, except Orlando who seemed to act out a perpetual comic strip under his breath. The truth was he never knew what to say to them.

Of the one crime of which he had been justly accused, he had no real memory. Intense guilt had long overlaid his recollection of floundering on the floor with Olivia, half drunk and thoroughly scared of a powerful and much older woman. The pile of the white wool rug in his nose and mouth was the outstanding physical sensation. Before Bianca almost every sexual encounter had been equally meaningless. Olivia was one of the governors of the art school; they had met at a party in the studio of one of the tutors, and in his naivety Lovat had believed that he was obliged to fuck her if she asked him, or be expelled.

Afterwards, however, he had respected her for cutting through his shame and confusion, taking the initiative immediately when he appeared as a significant figure in her daughter's life and suggesting that they should forget the whole episode for Bianca's sake. It had seemed so naturally correct; the way intelligent, civilized, thinking people like the Berrisfords would behave. Why should he now suffer this terrible punishment for a forgotten misdemeanour of which he as much as anyone had been a victim?

Divorce meant failure to him, and it meant shame. His father had once boasted that his mills never employed a divorced woman. No doubt Bianca would call the notion bourgeois, but it seemed to Lovat to have some sense. At the bottom of his heart he had always considered that divorced people were weak, people who made promises they could not keep and did not really care about their children.

Losing his job – that was another horror story from family folklore. In the North everyone had a story about the Depression. It was a bigger event than either of the world wars in the lives of ordinary people. His father often told him how, at a younger age than he was now, he had laid off hundreds of mill girls, grown women who were already the sole financial support of their families. 'The boss sent me to do his dirty work because he said I was young and soft-looking but they turned on me just the same and I had a broken nose before I got off the floor.'

When he opened the thick white Berrisford's envelope which contained his five-figure severance pay, and another enclosing a handwritten note from Hugh expressing civilized regret and good wishes for his future, Lovat felt the fury and despair of losing a job, even if he had to acknowledge that he was some way away from a dole queue. He was grateful to hide himself in a consultancy for a while, fly to Japan twice a month and avoid his former associates. The guilt for accepting the charity of his wife's family, successfully suppressed for years, broke into the forefront of his mind and undermined his confidence. Would anyone else have employed him then? Would anyone employ him now?

Never, ever, would he have wanted to get into the ghastly artificial business of access and weekends, being a Sunday father forlornly trailing his children on outings none of them enjoyed because he could not get the knack which women seemed to have of being with their kids, making the mysterious difference between a house and a home. It was only a knack, a technique he could learn himself, he was sure of it.

He went to visit his sister, married to a professional showjumper in Yorkshire; her little boy just ran around her while she stuffed haynets and washed out buckets. 'Move out of London – with boys you've got to be able to turn

437

them out into the open air,' she advised. He made excuses to drop in on Joe and Shona at weekends; Shona had started an interior decorating business and never left her drawing board except to flip through sample books, but there was a Spanish student who looked after the two little girls and Lovat observed her earnestly. Being in the kitchen a lot seemed to make things natural, and watching junk television, and taking too long to put things away. She seemed to do a great deal of teasing, tickling and giggling.

Lovat felt a fool when he tried these techniques himself. Being in the kitchen itself seemed awkward to him, and talking to Tokyo while the boys threw chips across the breakfast bar was, he realized at once, professional suicide. They ran away if he touched them. 'Ben isn't at all ticklish,' Tom informed him with a serious expression. 'Actually, none of us are much. Are you all right, Dad? You can go and lie down if you don't feel well, we can cope.'

Then the last baby arrived and it seemed to him that his wife deliberately gave birth early and bolted back to her own territory at once to cheat him of any opportunity to share the event. She dumped the baby in his arms as if it was something he had squabbled over that she was bitterly wishing him joy of, and the tiny thing looked at him and then averted her eyes, her cheeks rounded with a hint of a smile. Could a baby be shy? Surely a mite only a few weeks old could not be naturally provocative?

He felt her stirring, and it was a sensual movement, as if she was enjoying being held and being close to him; the boys, he remembered, had struggled and squirmed, always wanting to be put down so they could get away. The idea that this innocent scrap might grow into a woman like Bianca suddenly appalled him. He had a vision of a sullen twenty-year-old with long brown hair embarking on a lifetime mission to defy all sense, decency and civilization. If he lost her, it might happen. But what could he, a man living by himself, do with a baby all day?

Donald Tuttlingen called him on a Sunday morning. 'I'm at the Dorchester,' he announced and the sound of his vestigial Georgia accent took Lovat back ten years to the early days of his marriage, when he would occasionally answer the telephone in the gallery in Mount Street and hear the same ironic voice say, 'I don't suppose my wife is there?'

'I thought I'd call you since I'm in London,' he continued. 'Why don't you come over and have lunch with me? I have some ideas I need to toss around. I heard about you and your wife. Seems like a shame. Inconvenient, it being the family firm. Gonna cost you much?'

Lovat was lost for a response. Two feet away Orlando was about to hit his pile of dry cornflakes with a spoon. Tom frowned at him and passed him the milk.

'I guess you don't know what the damage is yet. Have you got your boys there? I thought I could hear something.'

'It's the TV.' Orlando gazed thoughtfully at a wad of wet flakes stuck to the tip of his spoon. Benedict was not eating at all.

'Why don't you all come over? We'll eat here, there's damn all else open in this city on a Sunday. I'll see you about one in the dining room. I used to prefer the Terrace but it's getting afflicted with kiwi fruit.' Orlando flicked his spoon and the wad of wet cornflakes hit Tom, who launched himself across the table, upsetting everything on it and kicking Benedict in the face.

'Cut it out,' yelled their father, hanging up the telephone. 'Get out of here and get cleaned up and get changed, we're going out to lunch.'

Orlando yelled, 'I won't eat it unless it's McDonald's.'

439

Benedict said, 'What are we going to get changed into? We've only got pyjamas.'

'Dad' – Tom was already searching for a cloth – 'I think Benedict is having one of his nosebleeds.'

Because he assumed that the American merely wanted advice, Lovat was only slightly embarrassed to bring three boys, two dirty and one wearing a pyjama jacket, into the baronial gloom of the dining room at the Dorchester.

'Well, Lovat, it's a pity you didn't keep going – you could have raised a football team.' Donald Tuttlingen smiled at them while the waiters flicked napkins.

'In England, we are inclined to play rugby,' Tom informed him. 'There are fifteen men in a team. It might have been a bit hard on my mother.'

'Indeed it might, I hadn't thought of that.' One of Tuttlingen's large blue eyes winked at Lovat across the menu, implying that grown men knew that nothing could be too hard for an ex-wife. He had the once-boyish face of an American politician, pleasantly grizzled by good living, with a rectangular white smile and sandy hair that sprang up vigorously from his forehead. Lovat remembered that he liked the man; like his father he was proud to be a plain dealer, open about his simple tastes and lack of sophistication. There was a dry edge to his humour which kept people on their toes.

A Kuwaiti family wandered randomly between the tables like straying sheep, their patriarch taking care to pull the skirts of his robes clear of the clawed chair feet.

'Dad.' The high, reasonable voice of his eldest son claimed Lovat's attention. 'Dad, why is that woman in a long black dress wearing a letter box on her nose?'

'The boys were brought up in the country,' Lovat offered by way of explanation.

'She's a nun, dumbo. Who wants my roll?'

'Don't throw it, Ben. Just leave the roll on your plate.'

'How does she eat her lunch?'

'She doesn't eat, she's fasting. That's why she's got that thing on, isn't it, Dad?'

When the boys' mouths were full of roast beef and yorkshire pudding, Tuttlingen leaned across to Lovat and made his pitch. 'I have it in mind to expand that gallery operation of my wife's. What direction would you suggest I considered?'

'What are you looking to get out of it? Cash? Excuse to travel? Mop up your excess liquidity?' He presumed that entertaining Cheri was no longer the business's primary function.

'You can forget the travel.'

'At Berrisford's the hottest area was investment. There's a big international market building there. And in this business, supply is everything. You can more or less manipulate demand.' The older man liked that idea.

'So I'd forget sculpture, it's unpredictable. Concentrate on flushing out pictures with important commercial qualities – easy to like, easy to understand, easy to document, hard to fake. Something that's beginning to happen, fashionable, maybe not completely international yet. And plenty of them around.'

He noted a clouding of the American's brow and decided to specify. 'Not late Titians, for example – they're all in museums already, only a couple would ever come up for sale. Or Rembrandt drawings – I could knock one off right now on the back of the menu. I'd go for Impressionists, the banks love 'em. Quickly. The market's a bit groggy now, but it'll recover. It's inevitable that France will open up in the next few years, with the EEC moving forward. And there's

441

nothing much will come out of this country now the tax laws have changed.'

He paused and looked down at his plate, from which very little had been eaten. The waiter removed it and from the corner of his eye he saw Tom urging his brothers to put their knives and forks together and wipe their mouths. A fork still impaling a potato fell to the floor when Orlando tried to pass the waiter his plate. Tuttlingen looked up and beckoned the maitre d'.

'Gaston, can these young fellas take a tour of the kitchen before dessert?' Alarmed but obedient, the boys left their seats and allowed themselves to be led away.

'Europe?' Tuttlingen prompted.

'Yes. Buy all the Impressionists you can now and feed them out into the market over the next few years. And in the meantime, start developing new markets. A small dealer who specializes can really clean up when his field goes live. You could look at Victorian narratives, Pre-Raphaelites, Arts and Crafts metalwork, photography . . .'

'I get you.'

Lovat felt inspired. Since losing contact with Hugh Berrisford he had lacked a sounding board for the ideas that boiled all day in his brain, and in truth he had been so wretched that his thoughts over the past few months had scarcely been worth sharing. Tuttlingen said a few words here and there but drew him out with what he recognized was great skill. Since the man knew little of his world, he began to sketch it for him, comparing the art market to a coral reef, a vast, complex and beautiful symbiosis in which dealers, salerooms, institutions, private collectors, museums, governments and countries were delicately related. It seemed immense and static, but in fact it was made up of sensitive, growing organisms and when one altered, the next responded.

'Who are the sharks?' The American pushed himself back in his massive pseudo-Jacobean chair, obviously entertained. 'I want to be a shark, a great white shark.'

'The sharks are the guys who get there first and eat the competition alive. You could be a shark. Sotheby's are struggling right now, overstretched in the US – it'll take a billion, I reckon.'

'Dollars? That much, eh?' Tuttlingen clearly had not realized the potential of his wife's little sideline.

'Dad, look what the chef gave me.' Benedict appeared silently at his father's side and held a fish sculptured from carrot under his nose. 'I saw him make it. He was so fast . . . he's doing one for Orlando.' And he ran away as quietly as he had come.

'You've been very patient with my family.' Lovat sensed that the purpose of this meeting was not merely to pass time and pick his brains.

'I know how it is. When my first wife and I split up we had a couple of kids. She took them up to Chicago, not my favourite city, but with the courts women hold all the cards, or they did then. You have to do what you can.'

There was a silence. Outside the hotel the sun came out, and motes of dust danced in the rays that slanted down across the massive oak tables.

'I don't believe Cheri ever did seduce you, did she?' It was a statement not a question, and it was true, but Lovat was offended and snapped upright in his seat. 'I apologize, that was an intrusion. She was always telling me how crazy you were about your wife and I knew what that meant. I held that in your favour; Cheri is one of those women who'll never take no for an answer. But I guess you don't consider this a proper subject for discussion?'

'I . . .'

'Never mind, I can see by your face I never should have mentioned it. The gallery made good money when you were there, I hold that in your favour also. So tell me Lovat, do you think you dare go back in the water yet?'

'Sure, I'd like to get married again. Very much. It's a natural state for me. This thing with Bianca wasn't my initiative; I was very happy being married and I thought that she was too. Obviously there were things I didn't know . . .' Lovat made this speech at least three times a day. He was beginning to wonder if it was not getting over-rehearsed. People who he had imagined would react to it sympathetically tended to listen with glazed eyes and then change the subject. He must try to keep it fresh and heartfelt – clearly he was getting so fluent that it sounded like bullshit. Don obviously wasn't buying it, he was shaking his head.

'Have I expressed myself badly? I should know by now it's a waste of my time being subtle, I just end up confusing everybody. I'm offering you a job – there, how's that for a simple proposition?'

Lovat blinked at him once, which was all the time he needed to reframe his understanding of their meeting, suppress his severe embarrassment about the children, evaluate the offer, consider his options and compose an answer. 'I'd very much like it, Don, in principle that is.'

'Very good.' They shook hands. 'I want you to come to New York and see the set-up and then we'll get down to what kind of money your principle comes down to. Agreed? Can we get to the dessert now? They do a passion-fruit soufflé that's like an angel's kiss. I usually say it's like eating an angel's pussy, but I don't like to lie on a Sunday and the truth is I never yet have had that experience.'

When the cigars were offered Lovat decided to join his host in a Romeo y Julieta. He had five minutes in which to

444

savour its cool, aromatic smoke when a drowsy Orlando climbed on his lap and snapped it in half.

Having walked the boys through the park to the hotel, hoping to take the edge off their energy, he found they were now too tired to walk back, and so he needed a taxi. On the spotless steps of the Dorchester Benedict's nose suddenly gushed blood once more. The first cabbie refused to take them. The commissionaire looked up at the trees. Lovat noticed a chauffeur polishing a stretch Mercedes limousine with a new yellow duster but he judged it an impossible shame to go over and ask to borrow it for his son's nose. An elderly maid eventually appeared with some tissues.

'Lovat, I am relieved you intend to marry again.' His future employer looked down at him from the top step with a smile that was slightly but perceptibly less wide than pure amusement would have prompted. 'A family's a fine thing. Don't you waste any time about it. You'll like New York, there's eight single women to every straight man under the age of sixty. See you next week.' Lovat caught sight of his reflection in the dark windows of the limo; his hair was too long and he seemed to have gained an alarming amount of weight. Was that a burn mark or blood on his Paul Smith tie?

Twelve months later he walked through light rain around the corner of Fifth Avenue and Fourteenth Street, gave his invitation flecked with gold leaf to a security guard and his umbrella to a coat-check boy in pink zouave pants and a gold cummerbund, reached for a glass of blush Zinfandel and wondered why he had imagined that there would be anything pleasant about another opening of another show by another good painter whose work did not sell.

He had two reasons for being there. One was that the

painter was an old Chelsea friend and he had promised her that he would look in; even in a year he had made enough of a name for himself in New York for his attendance at an opening to be considered a valuable endorsement. The other reason, of which he was mildly ashamed, was that the party was his best chance of getting laid that night.

His bruised libido had recovered when he first climbed into the Tuttlingens' car at JFK. Now he had a sexual persona for each side of the Atlantic. In London he was calm and celibate, a devoted father paired thoughtfully with one bright, sweet, lovely woman after another but too responsible to get involved until he was sure he had met the right one, and too caring for casual sex. In New York he was, as Cheri Tuttlingen had sourly reproved him, so cunt-crazy that any decent hostess would have to introduce him with a health warning. His good looks and European manners saved him from more widespread disapproval. There was a carved eighteenth-century four-poster bed in his apartment and his general aim in a relationship was to get a woman out of it before he found out what kind of drugs she was on – they all seemed to be on something.

He found the visitor's book on a table in the corner, signed it, asked for a proper drink and checked the walls. It was hard to see through the crush of guests but it seemed as if the show was devoted to pastel erotica of massive proportions. On the nearest canvas were pale blue thighs four feet long, luxuriously parted, and a violet penis rising from a mound of pale yellow curls.

'Pom at eleven o'clock high.' With a clank of her silver earrings the taller of two diminutive women at the opposite end of the room leaned forward to touch her companion's bare shoulder.

'Where? I can't see him.' In case he could see her, Izza

McKinnon raised a black-gloved arm to brush the back of her cropped red head, checking the effect in the floor-to-ceiling mirror which conveniently reflected the entrance.

'Sizing up the purple number. Dark blue suit, black hair. Could be an eight.'

'No Pom could be an eight.'

'Definitely an eight. I'm serious.'

'Gina, you gave that creep last night an eight and he had a gut on him like a spinnaker.'

'I couldn't see him in profile.' Gina pulled out a strand of her wild black hair and teased it rapidly with her fingers. 'Anyway, you only rate Richard Gere nine and a half. He was loaded, wasn't he?'

'They're all *loaded*. He was in insurance in Florida, for Christ's sake.' Izza believe that she had reached the stage in her career where she needed a man to assist her progress; if he were merely wealthy she would suffer from the Ivana Trump syndrome. She needed a man who was intellectual because she had brains and socially prominent to prove that she had status. No baggies need apply – a baggie was a man who was unfuckable without a bag over his head. Random promiscuity in pursuit of a career was over; for a long-term monogamous relationship it had to be someone she could find attractive if she tried.

'I'll give it ten more minutes. If an invisible Pom's the best this dump can do I'm out of here. Jeez, where are the photographers?' If she paid for her own dinner, met nobody famous or went home without being photographed Izza McKinnon considered she had wasted her day.

It had already taken her twenty years to get out of South Australia, another five to leave Sydney behind and if she didn't get a move on she'd still be nobody at thirty. Harakiri time. The goal was national TV, a couple of novels, maybe a play and the cover of *Rolling Stone*. Or *People*. Plus at least a spread in *Architectural Digest* on her witty int dec. Now she was on cable in New York, but suffering a crisis of her wacky hand-crafted identity because in Sydney she had been rated a celebrity but here she was just another spunky kid scrapping to get noticed; the press she'd had in the States so far amounted to some crud from *New York* magazine snapping her at a rock benefit under the impression she was Cyndi Lauper.

Gina's long magenta fingernails touched her shoulder again. 'He's glad-handing the Ghoul now.'

'Stop pawing me, we'll look like a pair of lezzos.' At last she identified Lovat, reacting politely to the cold, clammy handshake of their Miyake-draped host, who then wafted him in the direction of the painter, a plump woman in khaki linen. 'OK, I got him in focus.' Romantic, broody-looking, tall, dark, Gucci shoes, skin untouched by UV, maybe bit of a square-head. Actually there was something a little bit tragic about him. No wedding ring. Query a friend of the artist – he was holding both her hands while they talked. Query gay, but that wasn't the vibe he gave out. 'Wow, I get it. Heathcliff plus handsome lessons, yeah? OK, let's go for it.'

'Let's you go for it.' Gina's eye was drawn towards the two leather-wrapped young men who had emerged squawking and sniffing from the door to the toilets. As a hunting buddy, she was becoming a drag. They had been working on a cabaret act, Placenta Pizza, post-punk, post-feminist, and now, Izza decided, postponed until further notice. The girl had no focus – if she had a choice between sex and drugs, Gina went for the dope every time. The minute there was even a whiff of weed in the air she was on the trail.

'So long, Bong Brain, I'll catch you later.' Izza tightened

the seven buckles of her little black Gaultier and darted away like a bondage dragonfly.

Lovat was convinced for the rest of his life that he had simply noticed this dazzlingly original girl, a friend of an old friend, in the crowded room, discovered that she was remarkably nice and asked her to dinner. One advantage of being five feet four was that a woman of childlike proportions was seldom thought to be pushy even when her behaviour was utterly brazen.

They ate at One-Fifth, which Izza considered hideously *passé*, and the waiter recommended a wine as being 'loquacious' at which her laughter pealed around the room.

'Why did I leave Australia? There's just no culture. Especially the men, they think art's for queers. Too much sun – their brains get fried. And when it comes to women they're all hung up at the sheep-station stage – get on, get it, get off and count the legs. You know the Australian word for foreplay? Sheep-shearing.' Lovat thought she was the most amusing woman he had ever met.

Izza had evaluated him as dull, perhaps crucially so, and probably a social lightweight, but worth once around the floor in the horizontal bop because she considered it was kind of winding up the Almighty to pass on a straight eight in the Apple. Lightning would probably fry her on the spot.

'I hate to be a stickybeak, but what happened to your wife?' She listened to his answer, heard the hostility and checked the time frame. Some of these retreads seemed to carry the grudge forever and you didn't want to end up dunked in the chop left by some other woman's takeoff. Over the double decaff espresso she swallowed a sigh. The trouble with looking for a long-term monogamous relationship was all the fucking around you had to do to find one.

At three minutes past seven the following morning Lovat

heard the switchback inflection of a television announcer. 'And for your comments on today's happy headlines, over to our girl on the spots, Isabel McKinnon. Where are you today, Isabel?'

'Here I am, up on Columbus, the stretch they're calling Yuppie Gulch because there's more Armani on the sidewalks than there's worms in a sushi bar. I've died and gone to foodie heaven. Pignozzi's, the deli with most alfredo fettucine in town, and this is my friend Zbigniew. Did I say that right? Zib, how about I call you Zib? C'mon be a sport. OK Zib, now the question is, what do you think of the US invasion of Grenada?'

'Asshole.' It was the same voice. Confused, Lovat cautiously raised his eyelids. In the midfield of his vision was a bare back, narrow as a child's, a white arm raised and a hand tousling the geranium-red hair. The other hand was waving the TV console like Darth Vader wielding a light sabre.

'Oh my, did we invade Grenada? Is that what you said?'

'*Asshole!*' In the distance the TV screen was occupied by Izza in a fluffy suit of searing pink and a grossly obese man with black hair in a pony tail. Behind them half a dozen people with wire baskets gawked at the camera and a few committed shoppers browsed the vegetable cabinet.

'You're right Zib, that's not the happiest of happy headlines, is it? Now they're gonna make Martin Luther King's birthday a national holiday – how d'you feel about that?'

'I think it's great, I really do. I just love national holidays, especially in the summer, I like to get out to Fire Island . . .'

The mattress rebounded as Izza sprang off it, swept up her clothes from the floor and disappeared into the bathroom. On the screen the animated pink figure pulled a face at the camera.

'That's terrific, Zib. Now here we have – gimme your name again . . .' Her earrings clattered against the microphone as she took a giggling woman in a red polyester pants suit by the arm.

'June, dear.'

'June Dear! Well, June Dear, how about that lady in Eugene, Oregon giving birth to seven children after treatment with fertility drugs. What are your feelings here, June?'

The woman in the pants suit laughed heartily at the camera. 'I'm sure glad it wasn't me.'

'Right! Let's see, can we take a peek at your shopping, what've we got here, we've got refined flour, cherry tomatoes, avocados, *virgin* avocados, *extra virgin* olive oil – tell me June, do you feel you have a thing about purity at all?'

A bar of harsh light fell across the bed. Izza flung open the bathroom door and noticed that Lovat was awake. Intending to leave before he woke up and skip the morning formalities, she had mentally dismissed him already.

'Oh God, I'd have died rather than you see that. I'm so embarrassed by it.' She put one foot on the edge of the bed, the better to zip up her ankle boots.

'Why? You're really good, it's funny.'

'You're being kind. It's crap.' She changed feet and smoothed her stocking under her knee before pulling up the second zipper. The sound made Lovat's blood tingle. 'I can't believe that's me up there asking those idiot questions. In Sydney I did an arts show, you know – exhibitions, the opera, kind of stuff – and late night so you could get a little challenging, choose some really provocative topics. They don't do that here, it's a total issue-free zone.' She paused, thinking that he looked better out of clothes. A bit pale and fleshy, but for a Pom he was pretty clean. Polite and gentle, too, which made a change.

451

'Why don't you come to London?' He hardly knew he had said it – the words had hopped out of his mouth like frogs. 'I know a few people in TV . . .'

London had been her second-choice destination; she had passed through the city, and been intimidated by the old world, strength-in-depth culture. The Brits were a devious bunch, not exactly welcoming, and her competition looked fierce – what was considered an outrageous style statement in Sydney seemed to be what they wore to the office. With the right entrée, however, things could be different.

'Do you have something I can sit on?'

'Huh?' While Lovat was wondering what could have happened to his chairs, she threw back the quilt.

'I was thinking of something kind-of big and hot and hard . . . maybe this would do.' Her hand was so tiny that the fingers and thumb did not meet around his penis, even allowing for the long red nails. 'You're not using this at the moment, are you? I always do a little bit of cock before breakfast, it really sets me up for the morning.' With her free hand she was scrabbling in her purse for a condom. Her dress rolled up as she stepped up on to the bed and sank slowly down, settling her narrow thighs tightly around him. 'Have you noticed that's something else they don't do in New York? The morning quickie. Dorph-head city – gym before work, work before life. You can move too, it is allowed by the way. Ooh, yeah! Me, if I've got to sit in an office for hours, I like to sit on a smile. C'mon baby, fuck me good now, gonna be a long day.' Her first employer in the States had been a telephone sex line; after a week they fired her for making the other women laugh, but it had been a good learning experience.

In London, Lovat found himself reeling in the slipstream as she launched herself into the city. Izza saw a town as a

452

celebrity chessboard. In the past she had been a mere pawn, but as Lovat's consort she was a back-row piece, able to make the big moves. It was so simple. You wanted a TV break, you chose your channel, found out which party the director was going to attend, made Lovat take you there and hit in half an hour. In a month, she was getting her own invitations and no longer needed to sort through the stack on the marble mantelpiece at his house.

He would never have considered a relationship with an Englishwoman fifteen years his junior, but the fact that Isabel was Australian made a difference. She was so witty, so dynamic and so eager to flaunt her creative credentials that she seemed almost his equal, while in fact, as a stranger in his town, she was almost completely in his power for the first few weeks.

This interlude seemed to restore his masculinity, but it soon came to an end. She found an apartment above a designer dress shop in Chelsea in which she spent a worrying amount of time. A late-night television programme claimed four evenings a week, then a radio show on Sunday morning wrecked the weekend. A book on British style was commissioned, and although she hired a researcher, her own diary became crowded with fashionable names. Friends flocked to her, and many of them he did not like – they were young, rude and weird in appearance and the men all found her as entrancing as he did.

At the start of their affair, Lovat had marvelled at her ability to reach orgasm from cold in two hundred seconds or less; now it seemed like a time-management trick. Her body was so small that it seemed childlike, and his desire began to fluctuate. Touching her was not exciting, there was no flesh to hold, no lush contours to caress. The teasing he had found so thrilling at first gave way to sharp cracks and perfunctory sensuality.

They argued about the condoms. He accused her of only using them because it was trendy, she accused him of out-of-date language and irresponsibility. When his divorce was granted and became final, she seemed to become even less available.

'I'm taking the boys to Northumberland for the weekend, why don't you come?' Benedict and Orlando also considered that she was the most entertaining female they had ever met. Tom, while alarmed that she was cheeky to his father, allowed that she made him happy. 'You can tape the show, you've done that before.'

'Oh great. Six months of no connection without erection and now you want to row me in on your kids. What's the matter, the nanny give notice?' Lovat's protectiveness towards his family appeared to Isabel to be an insult to her; the last thing she wanted was to be lumbered with kids, whatever their parentage, especially three precocious, noisy brats and a drooling baby. 'Count me out, I've got proofs to check.'

Panic knotted his stomach when he considered the possibility of another rejection, and a more public one since Isabel had procured a high profile for both of them in her progress across the celebrity chessboard of the city. He had nothing with which to restrain her, since she ignored his opinions and laughed at criticism.

The business stabilized his life. Isabel was uninterested in anything old, and did not appreciate the glamour which his stock in trade held for him, or how sweet were the triumphs of his new career. From three separate sources he borrowed half a million pounds which, added to Don Tuttlingen's stake, gave him enough to buy a Van Gogh landscape from a small French dealership. He knew, and the joy of that certainty was enormous and swelled his heart every time he looked at it, that it was a far better picture than the dealer had rated it, and he knew that the Metropolitan Museum of Art was assembling works for a major exhibition of the painter's Provençal landscapes. In New York he picked the right ears to hear of his acquisition. The painting was included in the show, and sold on handsomely afterwards. He kept the catalogue in his office for months, open at the page bearing his name as the owner of the work.

'They insured that show for a billion dollars' – Isabel was unimpressed. 'That's sick. How can a little heap of paint and canvas be worth a billion dollars?'

'You don't understand. Insurance valuations are usually done by auction houses, who quote the maximum price on a painting to maintain the image of its market value. Then people are tempted to sell.' Lovat thought he was helping her to be better informed.

'That's bent,' she announced without hesitation. 'Why don't you take up stealing and cut out the middle men? Send the insurance money to Ethiopia.' But she came to the opening on his arm, in a Lacroix toreador suit and hat.

The art market was rapidly turning into a casino, and there were going to be more losers than winners. Lovat was enough of an inverted snob to relish the new atmosphere, although as a dealer, the game could go either way for him. The big auctioneers were trying to by-pass the professionals and sell directly. An auction sale, once a calm, discreet affair attended largely by the cartel of dealers, became a major social event, crowded by people in evening dress who applauded winning bids as if they were operatic arias. Berrisford's began the trend with a sale of Pre-Raphaelites, and knowing that Hugh had no taste for the genre Lovat suspected the influence of his ex-wife. The champagne flowed and the publicity department – Berrisford's had never before considered such a vulgar enterprise – orchestrated coverage by *Vogue* in four countries.

'She's a fool, going into the business. I don't know what she's doing it for – she always said she hated it, she doesn't understand it and she'll ruin them if they give her a chance.' He was not aware that he was smiling when he spoke, but such signs never escaped Isabel, who simply demanded:

'Why are you so down on her all the time? Most men are thrilled when their old lady goes out to work.'

Isabel seemed to see no reason to support his business in any way. Indeed, she openly complained about it. 'I don't *have* to eat dinner with some cruddy bankers,' she announced. 'They give me toxic schlock syndrome. Can't three guys make conversation without a woman to oil the wheels? What's the deal with them anyway?'

'I want to open up a line of credit for the firm, I need backing.'

'You want to lend people money to buy piccies they can't afford. Lease another brain cell – the one you got must be getting lonely.'

The more wayward she was, the more attractive she became and the more his life without her seemed a dismal wasteland. Isabel in fact considered that he was the perfect springboard for the next phase in her career, and was determined to marry him because where she was going she needed all the straight credentials she could get. But the idea of behaving pleasingly towards an intended spouse seemed ridiculous to her.

Since the one acceptable gift he had to offer her was his social position, Lovat chose the most glamorous date in his diary for his proposal. A sale of Fauve and and late Impressionist pictures was to be staged in Monte Carlo as part of a benefit for Princess Grace's children's hospital. The major works on offer were by Cézanne; Lovat had been commissioned to acquire one by his old Japanese associates and on his own account he had his eye on some Matisse cut-paper pictures about which he had an instinct. Isabel was persuaded to knock a five-day window in her diary, and he rented a yacht.

By the time they flew back to London they were both tanned, relaxed and married. The wedding had been conducted in the middle of the Mediterranean Sea by the British consul who had waited all his career to be roused by a romantic couple demanding a special licence. That had been Isabel's idea. 'Why wait? If we're going to do it let's do it. We couldn't go home and plan anything half as romantic as this, you clever old possum.' Maybe it had been the cramped cabin, or perhaps the word 'old', or the way Isabel suddenly lay back and expected him to thrill her because it was their wedding night, but consummating the marriage had been an unexpected struggle.

In his office, Lovat met another unforeseen difficulty. A fax from the shippers informed him that the export licence needed for the Cézanne had been withheld, pending a submission to the French Ministry of Culture and Communication from the European Heritage Foundation. He imagined this body to be some offshoot of the European bureaucracy, and set his assistant the task of research, confident that a telephone call to the right person was all that would be necessary to free the painting for his buyer.

'I don't think you're going to like this.' The young man sidled into his room, holding a sheaf of fax messages against his chest. 'I've checked out the board, they're mostly museum people, a few politicians and academics, but look here . . .'

He put the Foundation's letterhead on the desk, pointed to the list of patrons at the bottom and retreated towards

the door. Lovat's eyes immediately locked on one name –
Hugh Berrisford.

'If he wants a fight, he can have it! Hugh Berrisford can't
think he can screw me for two million – if he does, he's a
bigger fool than I thought.' Lovat reached for the telephone
and dialled the number of Hugh's direct line.

When Bianca answered, his blood seethed. 'You can't
speak to my father, he's in Paris today.' Her voice had the
cool, liquid tone that maddened him. 'I know all about this,
I dealt with it for him, but there's nothing we can do, Lovat.
It was a board decision . . . nothing to do with us.'

'Don't give me that crap. The painting isn't a significant
work . . .' If she had been involved then without doubt this
was an act of hostility. Not content with destroying his
personal life, she was starting a business vendetta. That must
have been her whole purpose in joining the firm. The clear
flame of Lovat's fury was burning higher with every second.

'The board considers that it is. They've submitted a request
for the licence to be refused, but it's up to the French and
the minister. You can make a counter-submission . . .'

'Don't tell me what I can do.'

'Lovat, don't shout at me.'

He took a deep breath and spoke with all the menace he
could command. 'Don't let's kid ourselves, shall we? You
know what this is about. If you take me on in this, Bianca,
you'll be ruined. You've enough arrogance and stupidity to
shoot yourself down and bring the whole of Berrisford's
with you. And if you don't ruin yourself, I'll do the job for
you. You're dead either way, I promise that. I'm the one
who keeps promises, remember?'

CHAPTER 15
Monte Carlo, 1914

Nothing delights a newly qualified sophisticate so much as the opportunity to initiate another into the pleasures for which she has only just acquired a taste. On the long train journey across Poland, Germany, the Low Countries and finally France, Lydia travelled in a private stateroom in the greatest possible luxury; in addition to the comforts she had ordered herself, she was welcomed with an ornamental bucket of caviar, chocolates, a small icon in a silver case and a bouquet too large for the table with a card which assured her that Sergei Pavlovich Diaghilev eagerly anticipated her arrival in Monte Carlo. Leo, who travelled by the same train, had only the second-class ticket purchased for him by the company; with no motive other than her own diversion, she invited him to join her every day and there was hardly a haystack which she did not point out to him to explain its exotic foreign significance.

They left Russia in the muddy exhaustion of early spring, when half-melted snow still lay in dirty strips by the hedges and lumps of ice floated in the turbulent rivers. Here and there a few small leaves unfurled or some thin blades of grass struggled from the waterlogged earth, but the landscape as a whole was a picture of chill desolation.

As the express thundered southwards they had the impression of hurtling through the season itself. Once past Warsaw the countryside was in the full enthusiasm of spring, carpeted with blossoming orchards. The ditches had swollen into rivulets. Mating birds perched on the signal posts, joyously proclaiming their attractions. In the meadows beside the railway track, newborn calves, alarmed by the monstrous train, rolled their soft eyes and started juvenile stampedes.

Lydia was adept at passing time, and found Leo for once willing to lay aside his books and play cards with her to beguile the tedious hours. She sat with the pug dog curled on the seat in a fold of her blue velveteen travelling costume and produced one amusement after another from a deep leather-covered box with brass fittings, a larger relative of her jewel case. Beneath the brim of her little toque hat covered in lapis blue ribbon rosettes her eyes shone and she laughed easily. This new phase of her life, and the renewal of her love, filled her with eagerness and she was impatient to arrive and to begin work. Leo was showered with information, words in German and Italian, descriptions of the delights ahead.

Nothing marked the train's progress more tellingly than the quality of the food which the maid fetched from the restaurant car. Cabbage and haphazardly butchered meat were replaced by good roasts and potatoes as they sped through Germany, and by the time the Belgian border was passed she was able to press him to try foie gras and truffled poussin. In her company Leo was enthusiastic, but when he returned alone to his uncomfortable narrow compartment his mind was overcast and he criticized himself mercilessly.

He acknowledged that he was jealous, unable to forget that every new delight which she showed him now she had first shared with Orlov. Jealousy indicated that he loved her still, even though she had grown from a silly girl whose greed for high living was excusable to a worldly, selfish woman whose light-mindedness was almost a crime. And he was married now, to a fine soul worth a thousand of Lydia, so why should his heart leap every morning when he heard Antra, her Latvian maid, exclaiming softly in her own language as she struggled down the swaying corridor to summon him?

In four days they arrived at Monte Carlo, where the newly inaugurated Ballets Russes tradition required the season to begin. 'Ah! At last! Can you smell it, Leo? That divine spicy smell of the Côte?' She hung playfully from the handrail, feeling her light muslin skirt blow in the balmy air. Although it was still early in the morning, the sun cast hard-edged shadows across the platform. Palm trees waved above the low station buildings. 'It's all so bright, so hot! How I love it! Look at the flowers. Look, you can even see the sea already. I shall dance so much better here, the air is so warm. You know, I do believe in Russia even in the heat of summer we never feel truly warm, our poor limbs can never forget the bitter cold of winter.'

Leo was silent. A sheen of perspiration appeared immediately at the roots of his hair and he ran his finger round the edge of his uncomfortable collar.

Among the figures in soft pastel clothes who met the train were Inna, who at once seized Leo by the arms and reclaimed him with many kisses, and Serioza Grigoriev, the company manager, who greeted Lydia with a small bouquet. Diaghilev himself was in Moscow and would not rejoin the company until the season had begun. 'And whatever you do,' Inna counselled her with flaunting condescension, 'when he gets here, don't mention Vaslav to Sergei Pavlovich.'

'Why not?'

'Haven't you heard? You're so cut off in Petersburg, I forget. They had a terrible bust-up. Vaslav ran off and married some Hungarian girl in Buenos Aires. That was a bolt from the blue all right. Chinchilla's madder than the

461

seventh level of hell. They say he's been out of his mind all winter. He can't be wounded so much personally, they were coming to the end of the road anyway, but for the company he is quite distraught. He's sworn he'll ruin him. And in the meantime he'll do anything to get some excitement into this season.'

This was clearly a jibe at Lydia, which, in the confusion of arrival, she did not register. Inna wound herself around Leo's arm. 'At least we won't have to struggle with Vaslav's choreography any more – out of bad comes good. You'll be the star of this season, my love, no doubt about that.'

On their last trip Prince Orlov and Lydia had bought a house on the Cap d'Ail, which he had named the Villa Cassandra for some reason which Lydia had not understood but which had given him some cynical amusement. She travelled directly there, eager to see the new tennis court which he had ordered to be built in the park, and the redecoration which she had commanded. The servants were permanently in residence and had been telegraphed to expect her arrival, and in addition Tata and Grigoriev had thought-fully inspected the house the day before to make sure the preparations were faultless.

The site was dramatic, the buildings with their balustraded terraces tumbling down the side of a steep hill overhanging the sea, with cascades of pale blue plumbago growing wild amongst the red crags. The four guest rooms were at the highest level, with the suite occupied by Lydia and Orlov below it, the reception rooms yet lower and the servants' quarters and the garage at the level of the winding lane which linked the estate to the coast road.

She found the whole place as charming as she had hoped. Orlov's classical predilections had dictated her new decor; the artist had just retouched the *trompe-l'œil* ceiling in the dining room, a copy of a Roman mosaic in which Neptune presided over gambolling dolphins. The principal bathroom was also in Roman style, copied shamelessly and, she intended, flatteringly from Kchessinskaya's bathroom in her new house in Petersburg, with which the ageing prima was so taken that she regularly used the room for parties.

The bronze, Empire-style lamps and fittings, which had been ordered from Paris, were exactly as she had imagined them. A pleasing aroma of beeswax and lavender rose from the dark wooden floors; the interiors were dim and cool, in contrast to the bright glare outside, and white curtains blew at the french windows.

Her butler presented her with a young dove with cinnamon-brown plumage which had flown into the garden that morning. From its exhausted condition they concluded that it had flown from Africa, and she named it Dido. In a few days it recovered and became tame, arriving at her breakfast tray on the terrace each morning to peck croissant flakes from the white cloth. She found that she was lonely; longing for Orlov was forbidden, the better to play him in Paris. Charlotte's company was more acutely missing; she needed a permanent audience now, someone to respond to every word and applaud her smallest move.

'I feel like someone who looks in the mirror and sees no one there,' she wrote to her son's governess, 'or Narcissus bereft of Echo. There are plenty of English here, but they don't care for the ballet, I'm told most of them have never seen it, that when they go to London Lulu Kyasht and Pavlova are relegated to interludes between the comedians in their music-hall shows. All the same, when I hear their accents I think of you.' She had sealed the letter before remembering an omission; the envelope was torn open and she scrawled a postscript, 'Kiss Kolya for me three times and tell him I will bring our dove home for him when I come.'

Each morning she was driven through the town to their rehearsal rooms, in a square, five-storey building the colour of yellow ochre which was built right on the edge of the Mediterranean. The rooms were cooled by sea breezes. When the shutters were closed against the heat, stripes of bright sunlight fell across the floor. Here the dancers took classes all morning, then rehearsed in the afternoon, or stood patiently while their costumes were fitted.

Her Paris debut had been planned in the imposing pas de deux from *The Sleeping Beauty*, and the Black Swan pas de deux from *Swan Lake*, both partnered by the reliable Adolph Bolm. With Tata she was to appear in Mikhail Mikhailovich's *Sylphides*. With Diaghilev's new discovery, Leo Massine, a timid, large-eyed lad of eighteen from Moscow, she was to dance in *Scheherazade* and in a new ballet, *Joseph*, as the seductive wife of Potiphar; *The Legend of Salome* was to be revived, with an extended solo for her at the finale. But Lydia found to her chagrin that she had been scheduled to alternate in the role with Inna.

'Not my choice, Lydia, I swear to you.' Leo's pale eyes begged to be believed but she did not waste a single thought on his possible motives. She needed the status of a prima ballerina, unrivalled by any other except of course Tata, who after all had six years of seniority on her side.

'Inna can't dance Salome,' she announced in a final tone. 'She's brittle and spiky, and about as sensual as an umbrella frame. And you're telling me this new dance is intended to be wild and full of animal sexuality and cause the kind of sensation that Vaslav used to raise? Inna's not up to that – she'll look absurd.'

She was pleased to note that Leo did not dispute for one

instant her low opinion of his wife's erotic potential. 'I know, I know, but what can I do? Sergei Pavlovich promised it to her.'

'As a reward for recruiting you, I suppose. We'll see about that. What happens here is of no consequence, anyway.' All her energies were focused on the future, on Paris, on the moment when she would be acclaimed by the huge auditorium of the Opéra, by the most discerning audience in the world, in the centre of the fashionable hurricane that the Ballets Russes season had become, and Prince Orlov would once again be forced to claim her before them all.

In the meantime, she was well supplied with distractions. The dancers were the smart guests of the season. The rich and well born fought to entertain them. All along the Riviera the cry of 'The Russian dancers are here!' turned hostesses emerald with envy. Incessant invitations to dances, suppers and parties, to this villa, that yacht, the Sporting Club and the Eden Hotel arrived at Grigoriev's office and, following Diaghilev's policy of inducing word-of-mouth success by expert social manoeuvring, they were encouraged to accept. Many of the most cosmopolitan society figures in St Petersburg were already installed in their own villas, and Lydia found herself sought after in addition by princesses and grand duchesses with whom she was barely on nodding terms back home.

By day, Lydia worked like a machine. Her spirit was abstracted, fuelling an inferno of rage in Leo, who at first showered her with criticism. Their initial rehearsals were marked by the airing of every ancient difference between them. 'You heathen, you philistine – God, why did I ever agree to work with you again? If you despise me, can't you at least have some respect for the music? You're as expressive as a windmill today. The audience will die laughing at this rate.'

Fortunately his attacks rolled off her complacent heart like water off a duck's back. 'Oh have a heart, Levrusha,' she would respond without much concern, 'I'm hung over this morning, you must know how much champagne I drank last night. You were pouring it for me so attentively after all!'

'I don't know how you can behave like this – you've done nothing but eat and drink since we arrived and look at you!'

'That lobster was heavenly – you ate your share, I saw you.'

'But you're putting on weight, ruining your line . . .'

'Oh, so you agree I had a little beauty to spoil?'

'For the love of God, can't you ever be serious?' He refused to soften his harsh tone, but her old flirtatious tricks were unexpectedly reassuring. The sunwarmed pleasure-stuffed life of Monte Carlo filled him with suspicion, and, temporarily unable to occupy the creative high ground, he felt disoriented and aware of working alongside artists who were far more at ease in the daring atmosphere of the Ballets Russes.

The ideas that were dangerously progressive in St Petersburg were here accepted as the norm, and the avant-garde was flirting with cubism, surrealism and jazz, influences he did not understand. The opinion in the company was that Mikhail Mikhailovich was finished as a choreographer; it was expedient to give the public the Fokine ballets which had been so successful in the first years, like *Les Sylphides* and *Scheherazade*, but by now they were creaking old standards which Diaghilev was always threatening to sell, scenery, costumes and all. Leo remained a little in awe of his former mentor but dared not defend him.

Everyday transactions reinforced his sense of inferiority. He discovered that his French accent was poor and he needed to speak carefully to be understood, that if he went into a café for a drink he was never certain whether he should leave a tip, or how much it should be. The company was made up of dancers from all over Europe, who had learned a variety of styles and had all manner of strange expectations. When he faltered, Inna thoughtlessly corrected him. They squabbled continually and he felt his control of his life crumbling.

Lydia, without any particular intention to be kind, introduced Leo to this intimidating foreign world with the same thoughtful grace that Orlov had employed in initiating her. She seemed always to be at his side, telling him what to expect in a light tone which carried no implication of gaucheness on his part, which was generous considering his inability to remember two new names in an evening.

'You can leave your cocktail, the servant will bring it,' she would whisper, effectively leading him to supper. 'How delightful, you're seated between our hostess and the Marquesa Passano – that's her husband with the black beard; they have a villa on the Cap. She's Russian, the daughter of Shchedrin, the writer.' At work it was the same. 'Get the porters to move the piano now,' she would advise as midday approached. 'Or they won't be back until four – they all take a siesta after lunch.' 'We can let this pose just flow into the preparation for the next – they don't wait for encores here like we do in Russia.'

To blow even more fiercely on the never-quenched embers of his love, the new dance for Salome became something which extracted from them both a strain of sexual inspiration which they had never found in the sexual act itself. Salome was required to dance with the head of John the Baptist in a way which indicated that her child's innocence had for ever been corrupted in the decadent milieu of Herod's court. The dance expressed the first passion of her body fatally perverted to the total possession of her trophy, which she would at last kiss lingeringly on its dead and bloody lips.

After a day or two of hesitation, the entire dance was created in an afternoon and neither of them quite knew what had taken place between them. It was as sensational as Sergei Pavlovich had demanded, beginning with a sinuous evocation of the veil dance which had won Salome her trophy and degenerating into wanton writhing on the floor. Lydia instinctively added to Leo's instructions the things which he had imagined but dared not say in words. She ran on legs which trembled in sexual frenzy, froze with her back arched like a cat in season and held the severed head to her bosom with a gesture so subtle, but yet so vile, that it shocked them both.

They fell into the habit of rehearsing into the evening until the point came when they were tired and spoke no more. Then they would change, and dine together at a little restaurant with a balcony overlooking the harbour, and within an hour the bizarre enchantment of their work passed and Lydia became her old eager self. 'Let's try every single cheese they've got,' she suggested, her eyes large as a child's. 'I've always wanted to do that.'

'Lydia, how can you? On top of that chocolate mess . . . you can't possibly let yourself get fat now.' Although, he had to admit, it suited her to carry a little more weight; it never settled around her legs, but softened her neck and shoulders. With round cheeks and a little cushion under her chin she looked herself like a tempting morsel.

'*Bavarois*, my love, not mess. Wasn't it absolutely luscious? I cannot understand it, I've tried asking for recipes and taking them home but Denis never gets them right. He says the chocolate in Petersburg is hopelessly inferior, it won't do anything it should. Now tell us,' she commanded the waiter with a flick of her glove, 'what's that one with the black crust? Is it good? It looks strong . . . is it goat? How can you resist, Leo? Here, try a piece. Don't waste this wonderful opportunity – with all the goats in the Caucasus we can't make anything so delicious at home.'

Hardly knowing how her feelings were changing, she began to see an awkward little boy beneath the old intellectual tyrant of St Petersburg and the maternal care which she was quite unable to feel for her own son flowered in smoothing his path. She had a pleasant sense of being needed for the very qualities which he had always despised. Teasing him was a delicious game.

'Your trouble,' she lectured as he sat morosely on the beach one Sunday, 'is that you can't distinguish between what is trivial and what is frivolous.' Half the company met on this little private cove on their rest day; it belonged to an American millionaire, who had retired after a lifetime of dealing in pig meat, intending to deal in beauty instead. For the sake of having two or three girl dancers to worship, he was happy to entertain their colleagues by the dozen.

'They're the same thing.' Leo threw a pebble at the azure sea, then scraped up a small pile of sand, looking for more missiles.

'They are not. That's just the point. Frivolity is something to which one can devote one's life. Triviality is death. Now, tell me! Baccarat, for instance – is it trivial or frivolous?'

'This is too stupid, refuse to answer, Leo.' Inna jammed her hat over her eyes with contempt and leaned back in her deckchair with her book at the end of her nose. But Leo, half lying on the sand, was looking lazily at Lydia under his eyelashes. Maturity had confirmed the hollow-cheeked, demonic cast of his face, but his eyelashes were still childishly long, thick and silky.

'Baccarat? I think it's frivolous. Especially when I lose.'

'Correct. I award you one shell.' A pink clam shell, as tiny as a baby's fingernail, was deposited by his feet. 'Now, eating strawberries? Trivial or frivolous?'

'Little strawberries or big ones?'

'Big.'

'Big hot-house or big garden strawberries?'

'Imagine us having this conversation in Petersburg!' Tata was listening with her head on one side, an indulgent smile hovering around her little Cupid's-bow mouth. Her King Charles spaniel panted in the shade under her deckchair.

'That I can't do,' Inna replied. Her shoulders were hunched with annoyance and she looked like a crow. 'It's the kind of conversation people only have on the Riviera, thank God. There must be something in the water which makes people decadent.'

Leo's eyes met Lydia's. 'Hot-house or garden?' he murmured.

'Garden.'

'Frivolous. But only if you eat them in the garden itself.'

'Correct again.' A minute mussel shell joined the clam. 'Now, tell me – this is a hard one – romance, trivial or frivolous?'

Now he avoided her eyes, drawing a face in the sand. The low sun of the afternoon was casting deep shadows, making vivid the sculptured musculature of his body. 'Trivial.'

'Correct again. I think you've been taking lessons.' She awarded him the other half of the clam shell.

'It's obvious, surely,' he announced in his characteristic voice of lofty omniscience, the same voice in which, three months earlier, he had spoken for the entire clientele of the Stray Dog in arguing that the departing Prime Minister was the only decent man in Russian politics and therefore his dismissal by the Tsar had been an inevitability. 'Romance is only of value in life inasmuch as it can illuminate a person's qualities, inspire great art, courage or loyalty. Of itself it has no value.'

It was then that the notion of seducing him occurred to her. A piece of mischief to alleviate the tedium of this period of *reculer pour mieux sauter*, a challenge to her femininity, a practice for the task awaiting her in Paris, an appointment with destiny which she had, perhaps, avoided for too long – a dozen reasons popped up to promote the idea. She extended her bare foot idly and massaged his outstretched ankle. 'I am really impressed, Leo. Your aptitude for this field of study is truly phenomenal.'

'The credit belongs entirely to my tutor.' How exotic her little foot now seemed, with its white skin and meticulously buffed nails. He had held it a thousand times while dancing, but now it was new and magically alluring. 'Come on, ask me another one.'

'All right then: decadence. Trivial or frivolous?' She tickled his instep with the tip of her toe.

'Frivolous.'

'You're sure?'

He became aware of a pressing, sweet discomfort. At her touch he had become half erect and, loose as they were, his shorts felt constricting. Violently embarrassed, he curled up with his arms around his knees, hoping to hide the burgeoning contour of his penis. 'Naturally.' There was no breath in his lungs. He coughed, embarrassed. 'Decadence is frivolous because it is only through the pursuit of decadence that art can be purified and renewed. Another question, please.'

Unhurried, she perused her shell collection and awarded him a tiny white whelk. 'Isn't that pretty? It's almost pretty enough to wear in a necklace, isn't it?'

'It's exquisite but if I get five questions right I want a special prize.' Covertly he watched his wife, who was pretending not to listen. She too seemed different in the penetrating light of the Côte. Instead of the interesting, serious woman he had married, a woman he had imagined to have a mysterious centre of gravity, a lodestone of ancient wisdom directing her actions, he saw an insecure, posturing girl who greedily consumed the luxuries of the West with no appreciation of their true value.

'The judges will have to confer.' Lydia raised the silky flap of the pug dog's ear and whispered, making the animal snort with surprise and jump to its feet. 'What is the nature of this special prize?'

'I will decide when I have won.' She had an intuition it had come into his mind to ask for a kiss.

'Fined one point for arrogance!' Half the clam shell was snatched away. He tried to stop her, shouting, 'Unfair! Cheat!' and grabbing her wrist. She was unbalanced and they both fell sideways on to the sand, laughing and wrestling like children. The pug jumped indignantly aside. Inna sighed heavily.

Lydia sat up and brushed sand from her Breton-striped bathing costume. 'The judges are incapable of cheating. Please apologize and fetch us some lemonade or you will be fined all your points so far.'

Obediently Leo rose and motioned the servant who waited attentively in the shade of a parasol to run errands for his master's guests. Inna shut her book, placed it carefully in her chair and suggested to Tata that they should stroll along the shoreline. The lemonade arrived, was poured and drunk, and for a while Leo and Lydia listened without speaking to the shouts of the others and the yelps of the dogs splashing in the water. The tension, the mood of conspiracy which they had shared persisted but without the safety valve of Inna's presence the pressure of their attraction was too much for comfort.

A few days later, after half a dozen false alarms and delays, Diaghilev at last arrived. His train was due in the evening, but all day the company was on edge with excitement. In the morning, when Leo had the whole company for the final scene in *Salome*, he called upon them in the rehearsal room, appearing silently, as if by magic, in the corner by the piano. He was taller and broader than she recalled the old Chinchilla of St Petersburg, his hair receding, his smooth cheeks full and freshly shaved apart from his debonair moustache.

'Mademoiselle La Kusminskaya, at last. Can you find it in your heart to forgive me?' He greeted her first and kissed her hand. 'You must wonder what kind of man could lure such a great and celebrated artist as yourself all the way from St Petersburg and then withhold his company so inexcusably. My problem is my schedule, I never seem to have enough hours for everything that has to be done. But here I am at last.' He flapped his arms, his heavy brows raised with an appealing smile.

Lydia responded with icy grace. After years of listening as Tata recounted the machinations of this man she evaluated his personality as three parts Lorenzo di Medici and one part two-year-old child; when manipulation failed to get him what he wanted, he threw a tantrum. Fortunately, she herself had some skill in these areas. Her strategy with him was to attack at once, reserving the advantage of surprise. 'Of course I am delighted to make your acquaintance properly at last,' she assured him without sincerity, 'and I hope your schedule will permit you now to clear up some of my little problems.' Nothing in her manner suggested that her problems had been adequately represented by this description.

'You shall have my entire devotion – tell me at once what I can do to secure your complete happiness?'

'My complete happiness, Sergei Pavlovich, is sadly not in your gift. You could, however, repair some of the dreadful damage you have done to me.'

'Damage?' His sideways glance at the listening dancers all around told Lydia that he appreciated the gravity of the offence she had taken. 'I am deeply grieved to hear of it and of course we will put things right at once but – is this a propitious moment?' He indicated the rest of the company.

'Yes. It may not be a propitious place however.'

'Very well – Leo, is there somewhere we can talk?'

The building had a shaded terrace on its landward side and it was here, with the cicadas shrilling incessantly in the hot, resinous air, that she flew into a rage, accusing him of all kinds of treachery and double-dealing. Salome was her role, created for – no created *by* herself, with Leo, and never to be danced by anyone else. How dare he propose that she should share it with another dancer, let alone one so thoroughly unsuitable as Inna, and, to add insult to injury, allow her to find this out from Grigoriev? And her billing was absurdly inadequate, and incorrect, and her Black Swan costume was hideous, and as for expecting her to stay in the Hotel whateveritwas, in Paris, instead of the Ritz – well, she had never been so shocked in her life.

'I must apologize, most sincerely,' he answered calmly at once. 'Madame Volinska assured me that the role was one she had danced many times at the Maryinsky and of course I had no reason to disbelieve her. I take your point about her style, but of course she is one of the most loyal members of the Ballets Russes, and I wanted to reward her. I'm sure you appreciate how difficult it was for me to find good dancers in the early days.'

'With Petersburg echoing to stories like this, you cannot be surprised. People told me that you were like Lord Byron – mad, bad and dangerous to know. I told them I didn't believe it, that you were a sincere, cultured and courageous man who believed in your mission to bring the arts of Russia to the West – now, of course, I'm calling myself fifty different kinds of fool for being so gullible. I have told my maid to be ready to pack up this afternoon if necessary . . .'

She saw that she had succeeded in convincing him it would be less trouble to placate her than not. He did not make the mistake of trying to belittle any of her concerns. Instead, he took both her hands in his and said, '*Mea culpa*, Madame. *Mea maxima culpa.* I should have been here to make sure that things were properly arranged. You have beaten me up and wiped the floor with me, and I thoroughly deserved it. Give me a day, two days, and let me put all this right immediately.'

'Very well, Monsieur Diaghilev, two days.'

'Satisfy my concern on another point, if you are not too furious with me – this marvellous new variation we have inserted in *Salome*, are you happy with it?'

'Why yes, we are both very excited about it. Was I not in the middle of it when you came into the rehearsal room just now? Then you've seen it for yourself – it will cause a riot, I suspect. Everything Leo does is extraordinary as I'm sure you know, but this goes beyond everything he has created before.'

'It's not too difficult?'

She realized that he was trying to unsettle her by simultaneously smothering her with flattery and sowing seeds of doubt. 'Monsieur Diaghilev, those words are not in my vocabulary. If the ballet requires it, I do it, however difficult. Yes, it is testing, there are a lot of attitudes on one point which have to be held a long time, but I believe we will alternate with the opera in Paris so I expect there will be time for my feet to get used to it.'

'Excellent. You will come to me, of course, if you are concerned about anything, however small? I want you to take Paris by storm, you know that?'

'That is my own intention also.'

'And Paris has expectations. Our first season was a miracle. People had never seen dance like it, or dancers like ours, or a *mise en scène* which combined magnificent music and decor by the very greatest artists. Everywhere we went we spread a sacred fire. Everything dazzling, intoxicating, enchanting, seductive and brilliant was on the stage. The record of that season is written in letters of gold and so far we have repeated the success every year. But people are hungry, they always want something new . . .' She realized that he was talking half to himself, to reassure himself about the reception ahead.

'*Salome* never failed to get an ovation in Petersburg,' she reminded him in a level, confident voice. 'People believe that Volinsky is a greater choreographer than Fokine. I think you have every reason to anticipate another triumph, Monsieur.'

They parted amicably, each with the satisfaction of knowing that they were worthy adversaries, and true to his word Diaghilev came to her villa on the evening of the second day, with Grigoriev in attendance. She entertained them on the terrace while the setting sun threw a nimbus of orange over the black edge of the hill.

He showed her the new posters for *Salome*, *Scheherazade* and *Joseph* with her name as large – indeed, given the exotic

476

pseudo-Arabic style of lettering perhaps even larger – than that of Karsavina. 'And Madame Volinska understands the position, I think. *Salome* is yours alone. So, we have had a proper Russian falling out, sobs and storms and shouting the place down – can we be reconciled now?'

He opened his arms wide and she kissed him on both cheeks, aware that the peculiar electric charm of the man, about which she had heard so much, was now directed at her. The combination of his coarse body, massive as might befit an industrialist or a banker, his eloquent expressions and the insinuating eyes of an odalisque was quite mesmeric.

'Inna's position is based on jealousy,' she told him, suddenly anxious to be frank. 'Leonid Sergeyevich courted me before he married her, and she feels unable to trust me now.'

'Ah yes, well that would explain a great deal. What a pity you did not marry him, then you would both have belonged to me. Leonid Sergeyevich is a genius, no question about that. I love to see a man like that, on the eve of a stupendous success, when there is still something almost maidenly about him. He has no awareness of his gifts. But tell me, Mademoiselle . . .'

'Lydia, please. We can't be formal after everything we've been through together.'

'Lydia, you're too kind. I am most anxious for your opinion – the other Leo, Leo the younger, little Massine from Moscow. What do you think of him?'

'Such a good-looking boy – and for someone so young he is remarkable,' she told him. 'He is intelligent, he learns quickly, his technique is sound and he's very funny, the comedy parts suit him. Some of his ideas are a little strange . . .'

'How's that?'

'He likes everything at a slower tempo – the pianist is

always complaining. But they are different in Moscow; I think he finds the new repertoire something of a challenge.'

'Unlike you, to whom it seems to be second nature.' She nodded over the rim of her champagne glass, wondering if he was sincere. It was difficult to know. She felt that he was at least asking her opinion from genuine concern to develop his new protégé as fully as possible. 'He is rather provincial, but we'll soon put an end to that. When we play Milan shall I send him to study with Cecchetti?'

'Perhaps – but I think the old Italian style is overrated. It's no help when you have to learn Volinsky's choreography. Massine could take some pas de deux classes though.'

'Very delicately put – eh, Serioza?' The company manager looked uncomfortable. 'You mean he's been hauling you around like a carcase and you're positively black and blue – am I right?'

'No, no, not as bad as that – he's only a boy, he needs to fill out, build himself up a bit . . .'

'More pas de deux work and into the gymnasium tomorrow! Thank you, my dear. You'll have a new partner by the time we get to Paris. Ah, how charming it is here! What an exquisitely arranged house this is. Has His Highness brought any of his famous collection from Petersburg?'

'No, but he bought some Roman glass and a few sculptures for the house last year. Would you care to see them?'

It was a pretext to explore the whole villa. Diaghilev admired everything he saw so fulsomely that she was inspired; the prospect of receiving similar praise from many people suddenly seemed irresistible.

'Nikolai and I had always planned to throw a big party when the villa was finished, but he's stuck in Paris and I would so love to give a reception here just before the season begins – everyone has been so marvellously kind to us, we've been feted everywhere.'

'What a generous thought,' he responded at once, obviously considering the value of her Orlov connections on the Côte, 'and I am sure that, since you are surely as magnificent a hostess as you are an artist, it will be the social event of the season. When His Highness hears of it he will only wish he had not been so devoted to counting guns in Paris.'

'No doubt – and will your secretary help with the invitation list? I know all our Russian friends, of course, but I'm not sure who we should ask among the friends of the Ballets Russes.' How much did Sergei Pavlovich really know? Tata would have said 'everything', and since he undoubtedly extracted every shred of gossip from that sweet, open soul, Lydia considered that he certainly knew all the secrets she had entrusted to her friend.

The reception was the sensation which he had predicted, she made sure of that. She knew full well that telephone lines between the Côte and Paris would hum the following afternoon with reports of the style in which the new Russian prima ballerina entertained, and she saw the event as an important part of her strategy to ensure that she would capture Paris triumphantly. Ostentation moved Lydia as no other endeavour could; she knew that spring on the Côte was nothing but a succession of fetes and fantasies, so to be memorable it would be necessary to employ all her creative powers.

The automobiles filled the small pine wood above the villa, and the overspill lined up in the lane itself, and from them descended two hundred guests, princes, aristocracy, millionaires, patrons of the ballet and, for their decorative value, a few dozen flower-like debutantes and their fresh-faced escorts.

Lydia heard that a great violinist from Moscow, Mischa Elman, was in Nice and begged him to play. Floodlights and seating were hired to transform the new tennis court into an outdoor auditorium, and Massine and three of the young newcomers in the company performed *The Awakening of Flora* in front of a backdrop of cypress trees and marble columns. A hundred myrtle bushes in pots scented the air.

The gardens were illuminated by torch flares procured by the property master of the company, giving a pagan touch to a night which would otherwise have been merely elegant. A hundred lobsters were sacrificed for the buffet, which was prepared by a chef loaned by the elderly Grand Duchess of Mecklenburg-Schwerin who lived along the coast at Eze. There were fireworks at midnight. Lydia wore a gold tunic by Fortuny secured with tiny gold beads at the shoulders, with a draped underskirt of gold-encrusted dark red silk crepe. Cursing the fact that the Orlov necklace was in Petersburg and the yellow diamond collar in Paris, she wore it with a five-stranded collar of small pearls draped between vertical bars set with rubies, and had her French maid, for the Latvian girl was far too clumsy, mount a thin ruby and diamond collar on a red silk headband set off with a single black plume.

Anxious that his company should get a reasonable night's rest before their opening the next day, Diaghilev made sure that the party broke up at 2 a.m. by removing Tata, Massine, Bolm and Grigoriev in a group. Jean, the young artist who designed their posters, swooped out of the throng to take his arm with casual possessiveness. The two Germans on whose play *Joseph* was based followed, and Pablo, a young Spanish painter whom Diaghilev was trying to convince that cubism and ballet could be combined, was called to join them. At the rear trailed the thin, bespectacled figure of Igor

Stravinsky with his equally diminutive wife, protesting mildly that in Russia no party ever started before 2 a.m.

Within an hour the glittering crowd had drifted away, reminding each other of their deep understanding of the ballet by agreeing that dancers needed to follow an abstemious regime while they were working – hence, they all agreed at once, their imperishable beauty. A few couples deep in sentimental conversation remained, and on the tennis court a small group had turned their gilt chairs round in a circle and were enjoying a passionate argument on some musical topic.

Lydia drifted triumphantly from room to room, supervising the servants with unusual benevolence. Six hours of uninterrupted admiration from all quarters had almost sated her. She felt deliciously drunk.

Laughter floated up to the terrace on the warm night air; leaning over, she saw the group on the tennis court break up and walk towards the stone staircase, tossing their cigars into the bushes as they left. The last of the group was obviously a careful man, who lingered to extinguish every smouldering butt. She recognized him at once from the peculiar intensity of his movements. It was Leo.

'You adorable man.' He climbed the last few steps to the terrace and found her holding out her arms to him. 'How beautifully you take care of me. Everyone else enjoys themselves without a thought of anything but pleasure, but Leonid Sergeyevich is wise, and thanks to him a forest fire is put out before it starts.'

'It was nothing,' he muttered, clearly flattered. As he drew close she noticed a film of perspiration on his forehead and his upper lip. His eyes involuntarily roamed over her body as she stepped forward. His normal wary tension was gone; he was quite drunk from vodka. She recognized the signs. The rest of his companions were out of sight.

'Nothing! But for you, my love, my garden would be scorched earth. My rosemary and lavender, my myrtles – didn't you like my myrtles, their smell is so delicate and sweet? Everything would have been burned, the inferno would have swept the whole hillside . . .' She kissed him lingeringly on the mouth, her arms around his neck.

'You're exaggerating.'

He seemed mesmerized, unable to move. She walked away to the balustrade and watched him watch her.

'How long have we known each other? Do you know it's almost twenty years?' The words stole from her lips like a zephyr. 'I'm so pleased. It makes me feel wonderful to know that, do you understand?'

His mind was empty. She was moving again, a feline prowl in a circle around him. Perhaps if he stayed still, did not turn to face her, nothing would happen. Warm breath was on his neck, his ear. She was behind him. Her hands stroked his shoulders. Above them the quarter moon was bright as a newly minted coin.

'And what would I have been without you – or you without me? Oh Leo, we have grown up like two vines, our destinies are wrapped around each other. You will always be in my life, won't you? Whatever happens?'

'What can possibly happen?' She had spoken with childlike anxiety, which irritated him.

'Anything can happen, Leo.' He felt her body rise behind his, press against him. She bit his ear. He felt her lips against his neck, heard her breathing. Still he could not move. She realized that he was completely in her power, that whatever she chose to do he would follow.

He felt her move away and his skin seemed suddenly cold. Hands reappeared around his chest, loosened the buttons of his jacket and pulled it away by the lapels. She was warm against him again for a moment while fingers tugged at his tie and discarded it, then his collar was unsnapped and her lips touched the nape of his neck. Again she withdrew and he stood swaying with longing until she touched him again. There was a whisper of falling silk and something brushed lightly against his calves. Then her hands tugged at his shirt tails, his back was exposed to the air and he felt her naked body, burning hot and soft as feathers, pressing against his skin.

'You will always be with me, I know that, and I will be with you. You are in my soul, we can't be separated. I have resisted you, I know. I was fearful of life, I wanted to be safe more than anything. But there is nothing to resist now, our spirits are together, they always have been. We are already one being. And I don't believe in fighting Destiny, it's impossible. Now I want to vanish into you, I want you to vanish into me, and where we once were there will be a new person.' Her hands slowly roamed his bare chest; her spine undulating, she brushed her breasts against his back. Then she took his arm and turned him to face her. 'Look at me, Leo. Remember me – no one else will ever see me like this. This is who I am with you.'

The dress was a pool of gold around her feet. Above the ruby and pearl collar she held up her head, raised her white arms and began to pull out her hairpins. They fell to the ground one by one, the tiny metallic noises of their impact blending into the shrilling of the night insects. Her silk stockings gleamed in the moonlight, pale but not so pale as her skin. She plucked out the last pin and shook her hair free, deliberately displaying her trembling breasts.

His mind was torn in two; half hated her for profaning his own sacred emotions, the love he had buried deep and secretly in his heart, which he cherished for its very hopelessness. But half of him was filled with joy and wanted only to seize her. He saw himself fall on his knees before her, but feared her contempt. Inertia finally lost its grip on him and he threw himself at her feet, kissing blindly whatever was under his lips, her shoes, her knees, a garter, her thighs. Her legs were shivering. She parted them for an instant, releasing the sweet, wet perfume of her sex, then tangled her fingers in his hair and pulled him to his feet to kiss her.

In her bedroom the belief came to him that he could in truth consume her through making love, and so possess her for ever. She willingly yielded her body to his; after Orlov's soft limbs and familiar movements this hard body, bursting with force and power, excited her. She snarled and scratched like an animal. They fell from the bed and, uncaring, pursued their passion to its climax on the floor.

He slipped immediately into a doze and she left him, sprawled with a sheet tangled around one foot like the victim of a massacre painted by Delacroix. The villa was quiet and restored to cleanliness and order. She walked from room to room, allowing the beauty to soothe her, feeling her legs heavy with the deep fatigue of satisfied lust. Then the need to care for her establishment gave her new energy, and she busied herself checking that the china and silver had been counted and stored away. Her imagination leaped a month ahead, to Paris, to Nikolai. She saw herself bringing to him the animalistic appetites which she had just discovered. Leo was forgotten as she perfected the choreography of her erotic scheme for Orlov.

It was an hour before Leo awoke and found himself alone and chilled on the floor. He had the sensation that his heart was open like a full-blown rose in the warmth of the sun. A blazing happiness filled him, although he became aware that his body ached and his mouth was dry. He found water in the bathroom, then set off in search of Lydia.

484

She was in the kitchen, where the draining boards were wet and the rich aromas of food still lingered, standing in the centre of the floor in a black silk kimono and frowning at the remains of the one glass which had been broken, faithfully retained on a dustpan for her inspection.

'Ah, Leo, that's good. Now you're awake I'll get the driver,' she said, looking at him with well-mannered concern, as if they had only just met.

'No, wait . . .' Foreboding quenched his joy at once. Yes, what they had just done could have meant nothing to her. She was shallow enough; after twenty years he knew that at least. His dark-fringed eyes narrowed in disbelief.

'It's all right,' she assured him, totally misunderstanding his concern. 'I told him there was one last guest and not to fall asleep. Can you find your clothes?' She moved to the service telephone in the corner and turned the handle. 'Gaston, we'll be ready for the car in five minutes.'

Leo's pride was as terrible as a madman's rage, although the destruction it enacted was contained within himself. Lydia, who hardly paid him more than courteous attention until he left, did not remark that his old awkward tension bound his limbs once more, that his eyes seemed to sink under his brows and his lips pressed so tightly together that the skin above them turned white. The open portals of his spirit were walled up in those moments, all the tender surfaces of his soul were cauterized. He buried his love once more, considering it now an undead thing, a vampire which would leech his lifeblood unless he could discover some ritual of exorcism. In that vague hope, although he had vowed atheism all his life, he asked the chauffeur to take him to the cathedral where he joined the first mass of the day.

CHAPTER 16

London, 1986

The fight between Bianca Berrisford and Lovat Whitburn was a duel of two champions struggling hand to hand while behind them two armies roared encouragement. Their personal battle was caught up in a war which broke out between auctioneers and art dealers. They fought over the new clients, whom Hugh Berrisford drily dismissed as the species *Billionairis ignorans*, men who had never thought much about art until they got rich. They used a new weapon, finance, and the strategies of the stock market to procure higher and higher prices. Art was an investment; buy the right Picasso and you could watch it appreciate at an adrenalin-pumping twenty per cent per annum, net of all costs. What's more, art was sexy, it was instant public relations: buy paintings and a glamorous international profile was thrown in with the deal. Pictures, sculptures, furniture, ceramics, carpets – any decorative object might represent serious money.

Dealers used the skills once polished on connoisseurs to court bankers instead. The auction houses offered loans for potential buyers, fifty per cent of the hammer price at four per cent over base. No peacemaker was foolish enough to complain that paintings were becoming nothing but currency, with no meaning other than their price, because the prices leaped higher at every sale. A few disgruntled museum curators, unable even to dream of acquiring important works when they came on the market, bleated bitterly that art was the common property of mankind, but they were drowned in the din of combat.

The whole of Europe became one big art auction, because the *Billionairis* species was not found there, but in the United States, Japan, Hong Kong or Australia. Hugh Berrisford persevered doggedly with the European Heritage Foundation while his colleagues wrote bitter articles for their periodicals accusing him of being a poacher turned gamekeeper. The concept of art as an investment, which had once offended him, became more acceptable when he was faced with the hypocritical onslaughts of his rivals. He had always felt a private uneasiness in selling Van Gogh, knowing that the painter never sold a picture in his life; trying to keep the artist's work near his landscape, or in public galleries where it was accessible to all seemed an acceptable penance for the price Berrisford's could extract for it. He strove to find a connection between the dead painters whose work fetched millions and living artists who could not make a living from their work, countering criticism with rambling editorials published only because of his position.

After Sotheby's opened their financial services department in New York, voices within Berrisford's pleaded for changes, and Martin Pownall was loud among them. He was the most brilliantly persuasive man Bianca had ever encountered and he turned all his powers to the task of winning her to his side, knowing that Hugh was indecisive and relied on one chosen loyal associate to crystallize his thoughts. The role Lovat had once taken was now fulfilled by Bianca. Beneath his superior manner her father was hobbled by inner doubts, whereas she had the gift of conviction. Despite her ignorance and inexperience, he trusted her.

Thin limbs agitating in acquisitive frenzy, Pownall scuttled across half the world in a quest for collections and estates, empathizing, flattering, reassuring. He had a matador's sense of timing, knowing precisely the moment to press a cautious executor for a decision, but in his enthusiasm for the new he dashed from one deal to the next, leaving the details to Bianca. She rushed after him in a snowstorm of paperwork, which he regarded as a waste of his abilities. '*Bor*-ing!' he would sing, scribbling 'BB to deal' on files barely a month old and tossing them into her lap as he reached for the telephone to set up his next target.

Sitting in on his negotiations, she showed a quick grasp, a clear mind and an instinct for negotiation. Their first victory was the Tollemache estate: neo-classical sculptures collected in the nineteenth century by a biscuit millionaire, an eccentric who bought on impulse and displayed great pieces side by side with junk. His grandson, on inheriting a chaotic estate, offered the collection to Berrisford's and then changed his mind.

'A dealer's given him a guarantee,' Martin briefed Bianca as they left the office. 'We're going to have to match it at least, or lose the business. This sort of thing is happening more and more. Sharp little bastard, too. Trust him to shop around.'

'He's not still in biscuits, then?' Bianca climbed into the taxi first, conscious of her legs. Her new red business suit made her feel like a majorette. How curious that it was right for a woman in business to wear short, tight bright clothes, but a mother was expected to be colourless and on the dull side of demure.

'No, father sold the company to a multinational after the war, sank a fortune in a farm in Kenya and lost the lot after independence. The kid's in property now, doing well I believe.'

'They always want to do better, though, don't they?'

He was in his middle-thirties, spruce and confident in shirt sleeves. His office was in a former warehouse in Hackney, converted by a fashionable architect to a cavernous workspace criss-crossed by steel walkways, and views from the vast windows were of derelict sites, scummy water and cranes. Always curious about artwork, Bianca looked at the plans on the draughtsman's desk; under the title Nutmeg Wharf: Phase II were elevations of a thirty-floor building decorated with broken pediments and black marble.

'At Berrisford's we are wary of guarantees.' Martin crossed his etiolated legs and adopted an avuncular tone. 'Our experience in the Seventies was that they created a false market, an inflationary situation.'

'That's your problem. Doesn't concern me, I'm only selling once, aren't I?' Behind his black marble table, the quarry leaned back in his steel-framed chair, his teeth bared in a cocksure smile.

'And naturally the best price is important to you. A dealer almost certainly won't get you the best price at a sale, because he'll take his commission.'

'The figures take account of that. He's giving me three point three mill guaranteed on seven pieces, so what have I got to lose?' A light flashed from one of the three telephones and he excused himself to answer it, not troubling to lower his voice. 'Tell him I'll be out of this meeting in a couple of minutes,' was his first response. Bianca considered that he was overdoing the pretence of having already made up his mind. She stood up and led Martin across the room out of earshot.

'He knows we can do better. Why don't we offer a guaranteed price on the whole collection? He's desperate for cash and he doesn't want any hassle. And if he's stuck with that grotesque one-armed Pegasus he can hardly put it in the

489

atrium here. With the publicity we can get for the sale the lesser pieces will go for more than they're worth, won't they?'

'OK, but you pitch it.' Martin was annoyed with himself; instead of feeling confident in an old-established firm, the man had obviously felt patronized.

Bianca remained on her feet, looking with obvious disdain at the framed Hockney prints on the walls. When the phone call was over she spoke without haste. 'The reasoning is obvious – half this collection is rubbish, quite frankly, not worth a dealer's storage charges. We are in a position to do something about that – there's a lot of hype around a big sale. The very fact of being included is often enough to enhance the value of an item. Of course, that can't happen with a private sale. In this sort of case what we can do is fix a price for the whole collection – it's known as a global reserve.'

'How much?' He was editing his body language, holding his arrogant pose, but his nasal Yarpie accent was suddenly pronounced.

'I'd need to get back to the Fine Art Department, but I'd guess three point seven.' This was not a man to be charmed by coyness.

'Right – when will you call me?'

'This afternoon.'

Within thirty seconds they were waiting for the glass-walled lift. 'What's this global reserve idea?' Martin asked as soon as the doors closed.

'I made it up.' She flashed him a smile full of devilry. 'Flashy little hyena – he annoyed me.'

Martin took on the task of persuading Hugh to agree to the offer, but she noticed that her father's face had the familiar closed expression which meant that reason was never going to penetrate his defences. 'Whether we like it or not, there is competition and it's getting more aggressive,' Martin argued. 'There's nothing new in this; auction houses have been lending money for years. It's a traditional way of keeping the market moving.'

'Not for us. We've never needed to dabble in finance.' Hugh was fiddling with his white agate paper knife, a sure sign of irritation. 'If that Chicago cowboy who bought Sotheby's wants to overheat the art business that's his affair. Roaring inflation won't do anyone any good in the end.'

'Least of all us if we can't keep up with it.' Bianca knew that Hugh would never be swayed by an argument once his pride was challenged. 'We'll have to lose this one, Martin. It was my fault, I should have kept my mouth shut. He'll be stupid to sell to a dealer, but that's the kind of man he is.' She made as if to leave.

'You think he's stupid?' Hugh now felt responsible for the buyer's impending mistake.

'Not stupid stupid, but he doesn't know anything about art – and why should he, growing up in Kenya? Of course we're here to advise people like that, but if they don't have confidence in our advice they won't take it.'

'No confidence?' Now her father was concerned for Berrisford's good name.

'He understands finance, all right. From his angle he can't see our difficulty, so he's bound to wonder what our motives really are. He's a developer, he's used to doing business with sharks.'

'I see.' He made a tent out of his long fingers, an affectation which drove Bianca crazy. She looked away, knowing that any pressure from her would tip the scales the wrong way. 'You are right in a way, Martin. A guaranteed reserve is something we've done before, not for quite a few years but we have done it. There are some important statues in the collection – I wouldn't like to see the best of them quietly disposed of without the right people getting a chance to bid for them. Wouldn't be good.' From being corrugated with anxiety, Martin's forehead began to clear. 'We'll save this chap from himself, then, shall we?'

Before he could change his mind, Bianca made the call in front of him, and a mood of expansion seemed to infuse the room.

'Lending to sellers is only taking a gamble on your own expertise.' Satisfaction laced Martin's mobile face with smiles. 'Lending to buyers will be the next thing. Pre-financing. Where Sotheby's lead, the market is bound to follow.'

'I can't see how that can do anything else but create a conflict of interest and compromise the trust that people have in us,' was the starchy response from Hugh.

'That argument just doesn't butter the peas with the buyers we're seeing now. They don't understand; they think that if they can borrow to finance any other kind of investment, why not art? If our business doesn't keep pace there'll be a loss of confidence. Values might even drop.'

There was a pause while Hugh considered this terrible possibility. 'It has happened before.' His voice was diminished.

Martin quickly restated his opinion. 'We need a credit mechanism, we need to smarten up our act and we need to boot the dealers out of the market.'

Afterwards he told Bianca, 'When you were a little girl your father was a lot bolder and he got his fingers burned. Guaranteed a murky little Canaletto that didn't make the reserve. Sheer bad judgement. But he was humiliated in public, and the firm was knocked back by it as well. He's never forgotten.'

'It's so strange – I've never thought of him as conservative – as parents they were so modern they embarrassed us.'

'I wouldn't say he was conservative. His ideas are progressive, but he doesn't enjoy taking risks. If you want to be a high flyer you must never look down, it breaks your nerve.'

The smartening-up operation was delegated to Bianca, who was appointed Senior Marketing Executive, but she found nothing challenging in purging the firm's literature of technical language, finding a faster printer and hiring a decorator to transform the Mayfair building from something that might have been mistaken for a lumber room into a headquarters fit for an image-conscious international company. The Tollemache collection realized over £4 million, and a new optimism flooded the freshly painted corridors.

Having discovered the thrill of snatching a sale away from a rival, she was eager to repeat it and once her mind was focused on new business, she discovered that many useful memories had been banked in her years with Lovat. Inevitably, he was the rival who most often discovered that Martin Pownall from Berrisford's was giving him hot competition. One loss – of a series of searingly coloured London river scenes by Derain for which he had a red-hot buyer in Canada – was enough to turn Lovat's thoughts to new tactics.

He canvassed support from other dealers, who sank their rivalries willingly to attack their common enemy. Editorials appeared in glossy periodicals, civil servants were consulted, politicians lobbied and questions asked in the House of Commons. A few months later a letter arrived at Berrisford's from the Department of Trade and Industry announcing that a review of the legislation and guidelines relating to auctions was planned.

Shortly afterwards a team of investigators invaded Mayfair, determined to penetrate the wall of gentlemanly reticence which hid traditions that in any other business would have been considered sharp practice if not outright fraud. They expressed schoolgirlish distaste for secret reserve prices and phony bids designed to drive up prices, and a vulgar cynicism about the industry's moral health. Bianca, who until then had considered these things dubious, joined the chorus of outrage and asserted that civil servants did not understand the market's reactions. In the report, Berrisford's escaped specific criticism, but joined the larger houses in a counter-attack. The Minister promised stiffer regulations, a committee was formed, but after eighteen months nothing more happened.

In this period Lovat and Bianca met rarely and communicated as little as possible. Once the decision to join her father had been taken, Bianca moved her life and family to London. The two eldest boys were accepted as day pupils by a public school in West London; Orlando was enrolled in a special school for dyslexics close to their old home north of the park.

When it came to choosing a new house, her resistance to Chelsea had not diminished; she found she was so full of loathing for her childhood home that she wanted a substantial distance between them. Charlotte found a tall Regency house on the river at Hammersmith, where watery reflections shimmered on the drawing-room ceiling when the sun shone. She fetched Orlando from school and visited almost every afternoon, attracted to the house by a magnetism which Bianca at first did not understand.

Had Olivia ever performed an act of motherhood beyond giving birth, her alienation would have been a double blow. As it was, Bianca passed through a period of horror and loathing for her mother, then reached a plateau from which she was to be seen quite clearly as a woman so afraid that she would never measure up to the conventional criteria of goodness that she had renounced them defiantly and condemned herself to empty rebellion for the rest of her days. Bianca found that she was able to pity her; Charlotte, who had often stifled her urge to mother the abandoned, bewildered child, was now free to give her all the maternal care she needed.

It was a healing, a strange, beautiful restoration of the parts of her soul which had been denied since her infancy. Bianca luxuriated in her grandmother's care: the fussing, the worrying, the advising, the undemanding presence in the background of her life in which she could root her energy. Charlotte seemed always to be there when the weekends were impossible to plan, offering to ferry the children between their hard-pressed, hostile parents. She greeted every new development in Bianca's life as if she had specifically predicted it, saying simply 'Oh yes,' when the tailored suits replaced the self-consciously interesting clothes of her married days, and trips to Geneva or New York were scheduled instead of meetings with the Jacob Sheep Society. Charlotte said little, but she buffered the connections between all the members of the family, helping to weave them into a new pattern so that the hole torn by Lovat was covered and the fabric stronger than before.

Bianca thrived. The wretched exhaustion of the last months of her marriage was hardly even a memory. A day, which had seemed interminable, was now a delicious succession of incidents, over too soon. The anger which she felt towards Lovat was diffused between her father and her male colleagues, transformed into initiatives and tough competition. Ideas welled up in her mind and instantly flowed out as

495

actions. She disposed of herculean work-loads and then, with equal ease, delegated the tasks that weighed her down and instinctively reserved for herself the work that had the most leverage in raising Berrisford's profits. Her skin glowed, her eyes gleamed, and her body quickly acquired shape and a vibrant energy of movement.

The endless maternal patience which had previously been her cardinal quality evaporated. Lovat was startled to find that her tolerance for changed schedules and last-minute replanning dropped rapidly. She developed a sharp tongue and a temper to go with it. He often felt forced to cancel or rearrange the boys' visits because none of his associates took any account of his family feelings. She ought to have understood, being now in the same business, but she did not.

'I refuse to take out my feelings on the children,' Bianca told herself and anyone else who would listen. 'I've got to be civilized about this even if their father screws up all the time.'

'My children have suffered enough, it wouldn't be right to turn them against their mother, no matter how strongly I feel,' Lovat explained to Isabel, who was uninterested. Neither of them were able to live up to these noble intentions.

Benedict, who sat for longer and longer in front of his computer, was most markedly affected by the ugly atmosphere between his parents, but all three boys lost a degree of confidence. Tom simply looked anxious and a few Bs appeared on his report cards where nothing but As had been before. Orlando became so violently energetic that he needed to be tired out before he was capable of sitting quietly at school, and was summoned half an hour early each day for an exercise period.

The little girl was a joy to Bianca and an innocent thorn

in her father's side. Lovat had never really understood why having a family should mean that doorways were barred with unsightly half-gates, cupboards were locked and the stereo moved to an unreasonably high shelf. Nor did he believe that he needed to cut short important conversations because there were children in the house.

An inkling of understanding came when he wound up a long call from Don tying up the ends of the Derain affair and Tom guiltily suggested that his sister might have toddled out of the garage door. He found her in the main road which adjoined their street, standing in front of a builder's van, her whole body scarlet with rage, screaming 'Bad cat!' over and over again. On the pavement an alsatian dog was chewing one of her shoes. The builder, two West Indian women at a bus stop and the skinhead leading the dog all abused him for his negligence.

After her rescue Lizzie continued to scream for an hour and nothing would comfort her. When Charlotte arrived she suggested that gripe water might be calming but Lizzie fought against swallowing it and finally vomited the whole contents of her stomach. When she was returned to her mother, wet and retching, Charlotte worked very hard to stop the inflamed Bianca from calling her lawyer immediately.

On another occasion Lovat was putting away some clean shirts in his dressing room when another call made it necessary for him to run downstairs to find a catalogue in his briefcase. After ten minutes of conversation he returned to find that Lizzie had taken all Isabel's boxes of powder and tipped them out over the shirts. The child was happily flinging handfuls of the scented pile in the air. It was fine and clinging, extraordinarily difficult to wash off the walls. The curtains had to be dry cleaned – just taking them down was half an hour's work. The shirts had to be re-laundered, and some of his suits sponged and pressed.

Both Lizzie and Isabel slapped him, and Isabel also hit the child, hard enough to knock her to the ground. Lovat, shocked, lost his temper, but Isabel showed no emotion. 'Don't chuck a mental at me because you can't control your disgusting kids. Dickhead – can't you see what this means? I'm going to have to go on wearing the shit they use in make-up – I wouldn't hang wallpaper with it. I'm late already, I'm out of here,' was all she said, before stepping disdainfully around a screaming Lizzie and walking out of the house. She did not return until the next day, but his anger was still hot and they did not speak for a week.

These episodes were minor in comparison with the day that Lizzie returned from her father's house to Hammersmith with a small plastic envelope among the contents of her treasured miniature handbag. 'S'opping,' she announced, and tipped out the bag on the kitchen table. Hermione, now four months pregnant with her first child, picked up the envelope with the tips of her finger and thumb.

'Tom,' she called out as the boys ran past, 'where did Lizzie get this from?'

'I don't know.' They were heading for the television.

'It's important, kiddo, come back here and think about it.' There were some flecks of white in the corners of the envelope. Hermione blew on it to open it and sniffed the interior. 'Was this at your father's house?'

'I know where she got it, it was in the downstairs bathroom on the floor. There were lots of them.' Benedict was anxious not to miss the football which was due to start at any second.

'Bea, come and look at this. Benny, now, tell me, was it empty like this or was there something in it? Sugar or something?'

'I don't know.' He looked blank.

'Did you see her eating anything or licking anything?'

'She's always eating, she's a pig,' volunteered Orlando.

'But this afternoon, anything out of this little bag.' The boys shrugged and Hermione turned to her sister and lowered her voice. 'There was coke in this, and when it was full, there was enough in it to kill her. I'm going to phone the hospital.'

At the back of Bianca's mind a small, rational voice argued that her sister was speaking with the paranoia of the pregnant, that Lizzie would have reacted already if she had ingested any of the drug, and that unlimited bureaucratic harassment could be provoked by a hospital visit. But the joy of having Lovat in the wrong was very tempting.

'They say to take her to casualty straight away.' Hermione put down the telephone, her eyes wide with almost superstitious anxiety. 'Lovat never *ever* did drugs. Do you think the Aussie has turned him on?'

'Who knows what Lovat does nowadays?' Bianca reached for her daughter's jacket, trying to pretend that she was not delighted to be able to accuse her ex-husband of a major crime. After three hours avoiding drunken derelicts in the casualty ward and an overnight stay in the hospital she was smouldering with righteous anger. Then a junior doctor, a man hardly twenty-five years old, discovered that she was a single parent with four children and a full-time job; being unable to interpret the signals given by her Chanel blouse and Kenzo jeans, he called her into an empty side ward and questioned her, clearly suspecting that she was an addict, a drug dealer and an unfit mother. She returned home in an icy rage, related the affair to her lawyers and instructed them to inform Lovat that he was to be denied access to the children.

499

At the front door next morning appeared what Hermione described as 'a typical bourgeois cow of a social worker with her eyes on stalks thinking that this was some sort of drug-sodden temple of ritual child abuse'. Hermione did what her sister, enraged as she was, had decided was unworthy behaviour. She invited the woman to recline on the Aubusson cushions, contemplate the self-portrait of Walter Berrisford, R.A. with his grandchildren, have some Earl Grey tea in a Bridgewater spongeware mug, and, once fully aware of the privilege, luxury and high aesthetic heritage of the home, discuss the possibility that the peculiar girl on the television, with the pink hair and horrible voice, who was the children's stepmother, was not merely taking cocaine but also dealing in it.

If Lovat was angry when a mini-bus full of police officers woke him at 4 a.m. and searched the house, Isabel was hysterical with fury. 'I don't use drugs, my friends don't use drugs, your fucking ex is trying to get me deported and you're doing fuck all about it!' she screamed. 'Jeez! What's the matter with you? Why don't you just peel your balls and let her whizz 'em up in the blender?'

It was five months before he was permitted to see his children again, with their grandmother or their nanny present to make up for his inadequacy as a parent. It cost him the price of a good English watercolour in lawyers' bills, and severe damage to his self-esteem.

His relationship with Isabel also suffered, but this was almost a benefit. She only spoke to him when she wanted him to escort her in public, and only touched him when she wanted sex. Why she wanted sex was something he did not understand. She performed without enjoyment, but it seemed to be a component of the personality she had constructed for herself, less essential than the red hair, the outrageous clothes and the lurid slang, just an ugly part of the sub-frame which made her femininity look genuine. She said she would rather have a lobotomy than children.

Meanwhile Lovat felt alarmingly little desire for her mini-ature body with its sharp angles and ridiculous little pads of flesh. It did not invite exploration, or offer warm contours to his touch, or lie softly, heavily, receptively against him drawing out the heat of his lust. Isabel had a technique, the calculated application of one orifice after the other, which was efficient but nothing to do with pleasure. He felt as if she was merely raiding him for his useless sperm.

Soon Lovat and Bianca found themselves in direct competi-tion. Martin Pownall became Berrisford's director of financial services, and Bianca was gratified to take over his responsibility for new business. Lovat, with as much prime stock as his plan required, embarked on the next phase, choosing and opening a new market.

They reached the same conclusion by different routes of reasoning. Lovat saw clearly that among all the options he could have pursued, the work of the Russian avant-garde in the early part of the century fulfilled most perfectly all the criteria of highly commercial art. A huge volume of paint-ings, sculptures, designs, textiles, and decorative pieces had been suppressed within Russia from the time of Stalin. Now they lay in obscurity like a lake of undiscovered oil, and the first person to sink a well would tap an inexhaustible fortune.

All her life, Bianca had been abnormally sensitive to the glamour of all things Russian. The most insignificant vodka cup seemed to emanate enchantment. The country resonated with tragedy, struck chords of morbid romance, wild joy, despair. Surrounded by the heritage of every other nation in the old world, she had always strained for the Russian voice and had an instinct that there were others who did the same. She could even sympathize with Malcolm Forbes and the lesser Fabergé egg collectors, hoarding their derivative diamond-studded trinkets as much for their history as their craftsmanship.

Bianca and Lovat responded identically to the artistic qualities of the work they were considering, loving the clear, Northern colours, the vitality which gleamed in the tiniest brush-stroke, the courage of artists who saw themselves as evangelists of a new order. The energy made Western European work of the same period seem weak, even decadent, lacking the love of humanity which glowed in the Russian canvases.

When they looked at the future, they saw the same vision, sketched over the years by Charlotte's network of elderly émigrés and confirmed in months of conversations with more informed sources. The old guard in Moscow would soon die out, liberalization of some kind would be inevitable, and then an avalanche of masterpieces would roll towards Britain.

Charlotte became a pivot in both their lives, but it was as if she chose to decline this unlooked for prominence in the most effective way. She began to fade before Bianca's eyes, growing thinner every day, the lustre draining from her already pale face and grey eyes. Her appetite disappeared, and when she ate she complained of indigestion. For months she refused to see a doctor, but then Bianca came home to find her sitting at the kitchen table looking at her hands, brushing one with the other as if they were covered in dust. 'I can't look in the mirror.' She looked helpless for the first time in her life. 'My hands are a funny colour – tell me, Bea dear, what about my face?'

'You look a little yellow.'

'I think I look quite a lot yellow, don't I? I have seen jaundice before in my life.'

'Oh, all right. You are yellow, your eyes especially. You're going to let me call a doctor now, aren't you?'

'Yes, I shall have to.' Her voice was quiet but irritated rather than resigned. Cancer was suspected, and Bianca last saw her grandmother smiling with the serenity induced by her pre-med injection, a tiny figure under a sheet on a hospital trolley. The exploratory operation found cancer of the pancreas and liver, both well advanced, but while the surgeon was considering whether to remove a tumour Charlotte's blood pressure plunged, her pulse shuddered and her heart began to fail. Within a few minutes she was dead.

The loss numbed Bianca, and shocked the four children who until then had believed that death only claimed four-legged creatures. One after the other they woke in the night, or interrogated her with aimless questions as they tried to make sense of their loss.

Life had teased her, letting her have a few drops of mothering then snatching away the bottle before she could even take the edge off her lifetime's thirst. Whose love would anchor her in the future? She would love her children, and they would love her, but that was not the same as the love of another woman, a nourishing, strengthening foundation. Her sister was an eternal child, her friends had all been distanced in her years of marriage.

As for the love of men – Bianca considered that it did not exist. The word had a different meaning for them. Men might claim to feel love but their actions belied them. They expected you to love them, to prepare banquets of care, sympathy and acceptance every day, with your very soul dressed and decorated to their specification as the centrepiece, and in return they would toss you the cold left-over scraps of their attention, and expect gratitude.

Hermione, with her new baby, plunged into deep depression but Bianca was so muffled in her own grief that she was unable to help. Only one person, the last she would have predicted, seemed to understand precisely how she felt. 'She was so quiet.' Hugh Berrisford spoke at the precise moment when a fresh wave of sadness broke over her. 'I used sometimes to think that you hardly knew she was there, but you did, of course. Now just look at the hole that's left. I know it will fill up, in good time, but just now I can't believe that.'

It was Hugh who broke the news to Lovat, in a conversation which he then instinctively phrased to suggest that he should not attend the funeral, but that he might come to the memorial service in Chelsea Old Church the following month. The younger man was profoundly offended. Although Hugh himself was responsible, it seemed to Lovat that this was Bianca's decision, full of a woman's inhuman malice. To spite him she was even ready to insult her grandmother's memory, for Charlotte had too big a heart for such petty cruelty. A cold thread of fear ran through him, a man's fear of the alien female, unpredictable and merciless. He had been too restrained, for the sake of the children's loyalty and Charlotte's peace of mind, and made himself vulnerable. Now it was time to attack and hold nothing back.

CHAPTER 17

Paris, May 1914

On Thursday 14 May the sixth season of Diaghilev's Ballets Russes in Paris opened at the Opéra with the European première of *The Legend of Salome*. 'Welcome to the Gare de l'Opéra – can you believe that a hundred architects could produce still such a hideous building?' Leon Samilovich seemed slighter than ever, a dapper little doll, standing on the monumental steps at the front of the building to greet Lydia when she arrived for the first day of rehearsals. 'But, ugly as it is, the old place loves us so we must love it in return, eh? Come, I'll show you the way to the stage door. If we start now and step on it we'll get there by lunchtime.'

Even the regular company members, accustomed to the colossal building from previous seasons, felt overawed by the Opéra's massive proportions. At the first rehearsal the vastness of the stage disoriented them; the pit was a chasm, the auditorium a void. Leo called endlessly for wider gestures and bolder mime, and cursed Fokine for having significantly failed to warn him that his trademark subtleties would be lost in the bigger theatre.

Among the fifteen floors and the labyrinthine corridors, the multiplicity of staircases and the acres of rehearsal rooms, dancers got lost every day. They blundered into sewing rooms, wig rooms, offices, the classrooms of the resident ballet school, the engineers' workshop and rooms full of musical instruments, shrouded harps and cellos in their cases like so many Egyptian mummies. They asked the way of one or two of the thousand people who, even in the summer, were fully employed at the Opéra, but were inevitably too confused to regain their proper location, gave way to fears of being lost for ever or claimed by the famous phantom, and then were at last discovered and conducted tearfully home like lost sheep.

The fortunate few in the company who had friends to show them around the institution were the more intimidated to discover that its wonders included stables occupied by stage-trained white horses under the forecourt and a lake of water below the basement which was sucked into the hydraulic machinery which raised the curtain every night. The Maryinsky had nothing to rival the great foyer with its high painted ceiling, and seemed like a toy theatre in comparison.

For all its monumental proportions, the flower of Paris society was crammed in the auditorium on the first night, and the company also brought its own suite of admirers from St Petersburg; balletomanes, fellow artists, critics, lovers and admirers. The principals were permitted to slip through the door leading to the stage box and watch the audience arrive.

'A sell-out as usual, my dears. Congratulations!' Mischa Alexandrov turned his opera glasses on the stalls. He now had the overblown looks of a handsome man who had encountered many temptations and resisted none of them. He danced less and socialized more, always believing that it was his royal blood, not his genius for sexual introductions, which made him popular. He had travelled from Cannes with Kchessinskaya and the Grand Duke André, en route from a state visit to Italy, and had broken his journey in Paris while they continued homewards to St Petersburg. 'And what an audience – I'm sorry for anyone in Paris who

isn't here, obviously it's still social death to miss Diaghilev's
first night.'

'He is so clever, our Sergei Pavlovich, look how he plans
everything.' Tata, already garbed as a yellow butterfly for
the opening piece, stood at Lydia's shoulder pointing out the
faces she would need to recognize. 'They're hand-picked,
every one. He gives tickets to everyone who has backed him
and everyone who he hopes will back him in the future, and
a box to every interesting artist, whatever his field, because
he's sure one day he'll be able to get his tentacles around
them and draw them into the ballet.'

'My, what a show! Who are all those unescorted ladies?'
In the light of the huge chandeliers Lydia saw one elegant
woman after another take her seat in the Grand Circle.

'Don't they look dazzling? Have you ever seen so many
beauties? Fifty free tickets to the loveliest women in Paris,
allocated so that there are never two of the same hair colour
together. He stole the idea from his business partner the first
year. The poor man went bust, of course. But isn't it clever,
to dress the house just like you decorate the stage? Absolutely
no gentlemen in their boring black suits. People call it the
Diamond Horseshoe, or the Flower Basket because of all
the jewels and the pretty faces crowded together.'

Lydia's eyes raked the huge auditorium, looking for
Orlov's tall, still figure. At the Ritz they occupied separate
suites, which was her choice since she did not want to
diminish her position with Diaghilev by saving him money.
They had spent their evenings and nights together since she
had arrived with the rest of the company ten days ago; yet
despite this handsome share of his company, she fancied
she had detected all the signs of an unfaithful lover: the
abstracted manner, the plans for the future only vaguely
discussed and, most telltale of all, a new way of holding and

touching her which she felt sure carried the undeniable imprint of another woman's body.

Prince Orlov's mind was certainly on other matters, but not on the superior Comtesse, as Lydia feared; she had chosen to flirt with him in St Petersburg out of sheer boredom, and here in Paris, where he seemed awkward and at a loss among her own set, she was in any case fully occupied with her long-standing lover. Orlov found the dry reserve of the French deadening; he needed emotional people around him to lift him out of himself, and when Lydia arrived with her bright chatter and general air of energy and bustle he was pleased.

Clouding his thoughts perpetually were the implications of his mission to draft an arms control treaty, which posed irreconcilable paradoxes to tease his brain and subdue his spirits. On one side his associates in Russia argued that all the wars in Europe would in future proceed from the rivalry between England and Germany; Russia, with a German empress and innumerable links with that country, should not be allying herself with England. He had spent time with one statesman in particular whose warning resounded daily in his ears – 'Only the Jews will benefit!' Once in the West, he found himself part of a team cataloguing a massed arsenal large enough to procure an apocalypse, and talking to war office officials who saw positive merit in boasting that for every gun their German counterparts ordered, they would order ten.

He had promised in an abstracted manner to attend the première. Now Lydia scanned thousands of faces and when she found him she hardly recognized him at first because he was, as ever, lost in thought, physically present but mentally elsewhere. Tata, unaware of her anxiety, prattled on.

'You'll see the Comtesse de Greffuhle, Robert de

Montesquiou, the Ephrussys who always give a *fête champêtre* for us at the end of the season, and then you can see all our friends in the boxes. Every artist you've always wanted to meet – Maurice Ravel is there, do you see? He's working on a score for us. And Rodin, up there behind him. And do you see Jean, with that beautiful Misia Sert? She bails us out every year when the bills come in. Isn't she lovely? Everyone's painted her and her first husband's still crazy about her, which is convenient since he owns *Le Matin*. My God, look who's with her, it's Vaslav!'

'*No!*' At once every eye in the party was straining to make out Nijinsky in the depth of the Serts' box. He was standing silently at the back, apparently alone.

'So, he couldn't bear to stay away.' Mischa was delighted to have chanced upon a choice morsel of gossip for his own return to St Petersburg. 'Will he come back, do you think?'

'He wouldn't dare – he's so shy, even now. I hope he doesn't, it will upset Sergei Pavlovich, I know it will. How sadly life can turn out! We were all such friends. I'll wave when he looks this way . . .' Tata was as good as her word and blew a fleeting kiss when the blank, oriental eyes seemed to be looking in her direction. 'Oh, and look Lydia, there's your Monsieur Paquin . . .'

'I buy a frock or two but I don't own him, you know.' Lydia's tone was surprisingly harsh.

'Oh! Are you nervous, darling? Forgive me, chattering on about all those grand people. Don't worry they'll simply eat you up, I promise. Come, let's go backstage, walk up and down a little and then start to warm up our feet.'

The older woman's sympathetic arm pulled Lydia away. As she swallowed she felt her throat rasp. She was indeed in a real paroxysm of fear, by far the worst she had ever felt. Under her wrapper she was clammy with sweat.

When their train had pulled into the Gare de Lyon one of the youngest dancers had fainted clean away with the excitement of being in the fabled city of Paris. For all of them it had been a Shangri-la of style and elegance, a magical city where the streets were polished like ballroom floors and the buildings made of silver. The idea of taking the most exacting artistic community in the world by storm suddenly seemed pathetic, ridiculous.

An hour later she waited in her dressing room for the stage manager's call. Everything irritated her to madness. Her dresser had not let out her costume as she had asked, and it cut uncomfortably around the arm holes. She had chosen to wear the yellow diamond collar on stage, for the second act, but that again, once reclaimed from Fabergé, had proved too tight for her new, indulged contours. There had been no time to alter it, so it was to be fastened with silk cord at the nape of her neck, and felt precarious.

She began to fight for breath, feeling panic squeeze her like an iron hand. Once her years of triumph had begun, the episodes of possession by her old Magic Spirit had ceased, and she had hardly remarked the loss. When she had confided in one of the teachers at Theatre Street that her random sense of inspiration had deserted her, the elderly woman had brushed aside the idea with a wave of her knotted hand and answered, 'You are never without inspiration, little girl, but now I think you have trained it to come when you call it, you don't have to wait upon its caprices any more. That is the mark of a true artist, never fear.'

Her old superstitious habits had also been forgotten and she had skimmed brightly through her life with not a cobweb of doubt to obscure her confidence. Now she felt helpless and frightened. She wanted Charlotte to be cool and quiet and make her feel better. She wanted her dog to be stupidly faithful. She wanted to be able to turn to Leo for comfort, but he was dead to her now and she reproached herself for wronging him. The small icon with which Diaghilev had welcomed her on to the train – it seemed so long ago – was on her dressing table, and another, larger picture of her own showing St Nicholas. Lydia moved them to a clear space and, placing a towel on the floor in order not to mark her costume, knelt down to pray.

Once she was on stage her fear was transmuted into a hectic excitement. She saw that Leo was as white as paper under his make-up, and that Massine, all long limbs and big eyes, startled like a colt at every unusual sound. Inna, who had ungraciously accepted the role of Herodias to secure her position in the season's most talked-about new production, seemed more than ever an unattractive composition of sharp elbows and brittle knees. As the overture began, Lydia kissed them all on both cheeks, letting loose all the magnetism at her command, willing them into animation.

Nevertheless the opening moments of the ballet were stilted. Leo forgot a piece of mime and was ahead of the music for a tense six bars. Lydia looked into his eyes for the first time since their night at her villa, and saw that his meticulous temperament had been shattered by the mistake and he was on the point of collapsing under an avalanche of panic. She placed her hand firmly on his shoulder and added some gestures of her own to absorb the delay.

The audience, who had applauded the butterfly piece only tepidly, were now seeing what they understood as Russian ballet, a fabulous pagan spectacle, all colour, excitement and eroticism, and they responded immediately. At the end of the first act she stepped out with Massine to applause which, reverberating around the tiers and up to the domed ceiling, was like the roar of the ocean.

As the second act came to its finale she had a palpable sense that triumph was in her grasp. A little slave-boy in a turban brought her the head of John the Baptist on a silver charger, she seized it by its curtain of matted hair and began the new solo. The huge theatre was now utterly silent. It had never been the custom in France to halt the action of a ballet for repeated encores, and it had become one of the Ballets Russes traditions, promoted firmly by Fokine, for the audience not even to applaud until the end.

Lydia found it strange to perform without noisy appreciation, but in the dazzling lacuna of the stage, here where illusions were created, where she was insulated in light from her companions crowded in the wings and from the invisible audience, she began to feel that she was being drawn into herself. All the fiery intensity which she normally projected across the footlights seemed concentrated into her limbs, even into the marrow of her bones, so her body was transmuted into a glow of white heat.

Never had she possessed such strength or felt so free. The perverse eroticism of the dance seemed mere irrelevant decoration on a pure exercise in space and time. Her will seemed to slice the air like a sword, carving it into beautiful shapes which lingered fleetingly in the mind's eye before recombining and flowing into new forms. She felt herself to be some exotic hot-house lily, budding, unfurling, scattering her inner riches on the humid air, then dying down only to be immediately reborn. The illusion was so vivid she had the distinct sensation that her own pollen, a warm, fragrant powder containing her spirit's essence, was falling on her bosom and her outstretched arms.

Leo, who had remained frozen with fear throughout the ballet, strode forward to command Salome's execution and the men of the corps who portrayed Herod's guards lifted her up for the final tableau. Then the unthinkable happened, and Lydia's strength suddenly failed. The trance in which she had performed her final solo was wearing off, its departure helped by the manhandling of the guards as they lifted her. All she had to do was brace her body in a defiant arc as they held her above their heads, but her joints seemed suddenly spongy and there was no power in her muscles. A feeble tremor seized her. As the curtain descended she lost control of her body entirely and slumped in the men's grasp; they staggered under her dead weight. Unable to support her, not knowing what to do, they allowed her to slip limply downwards. One man caught her under the armpits. When her feet reached the floor she regained a little co-ordination and stood up unsteadily.

'Are you all right?'

'What happened?'

'Lydia, poor thing, what's wrong?'

'She's ill, she must be ill – but that solo was a sensation, I've never seen her dance like that before.'

'Can you say anything, little one? Little girl? What's the matter?'

It seemed as if every single one of the watching company ran instantly onto the stage and surrounded her. The applause thundered behind the curtain and voices on all sides called to her. Lydia looked around in surprise, still uncertain what had taken place. The black bulk of Diaghilev, nimble on his small feet, rushed towards her.

'Don't be alarmed, poor dear child, no one saw anything. It looked quite as if you intended it, very effective. How do you feel, can you go out to take calls?' His deep voice seemed to spread calm around them both.

'I don't know . . .' She motioned to the man who was still supporting her to step back, and stood by herself, trying one foot, one point after another, holding her arms in front of her. She stepped forward a few paces. 'I think so. I just feel tired, that's all. Everything suddenly seemed very far away.'

'Leo, Levrusha – both of you give her your arms, keep hold of her. Now, everybody else off the stage!'

At once the crowd dispersed as rapidly as it had congregated, Bakst pausing to flick the corner of one curtain, disturbed in the stampede, back into its proper shape. With Leo and Massine on either side, Lydia arranged herself in preparation for her curtsy, drew a deep breath and nodded to Diaghilev in the wings, who ordered the curtain to be raised. The applause crashed in their ears. Her legs were firm, she no longer felt dizzy; things seemed to be returning to normal.

'They love us,' Massine whispered in her ear, squeezing her hand as he held it. 'It's a great, great success, isn't it?'

She was uncertain, not knowing how to read the responses of this foreign crowd, but then their conductor appeared, and after him Diaghilev, flashing his huge smile all around with obviously genuine delight, and Lydia realized that she had indeed secured the triumph which she had so desperately wanted.

First among her bouquets was a huge arrangement of pale gold Gloire de Dijon roses from Nikolai, and when she returned to her dressing room he was there already, his normal stiff reserve warmed by the pink glow of her reflected glory which she recognized so well. In her weak mood she was irritated, but automatically suppressed the feeling and nestled in his arms with every appearance of happiness. His present on this occasion was a pendant in the shape of a fish, an oval Indian sapphire supplied with a head, tail and fins of diamonds set in platinum, flowing in shape and cleverly jointed so that it moved very naturally. It was a lovely object, but Lydia knew that he despised anthropomorphic jewellery, however fine, and was the more suspicious.

'Let me stay while you dress?' This too was uncharacteristic, but she agreed, and he sat stiffly on the small blue damask sofa provided for visitors and talked to her through the mirror while the maid began the lengthy task of unpinning her headdress. He wanted a moment of simple closeness, but immediately there was a knock at the door and Diaghilev appeared.

'My dear, you were quite marvellous. I've never seen such a public, you would have thought their seats were on fire they were so quick to leap up at the end.' He ignored Orlov and pulled up a stool. 'But I'm worried about you, you're so white . . .'

'It is her usual colour, La Kusminskaya has always been noted for her lovely pallor.' Orlov was annoyed. The two men rose and greeted each other, shook hands, exchanged compliments with complete insincerity and resumed their seats.

'Have you felt well since you arrived in France? Since you arrived in Paris? Perhaps we should get my doctor to attend you . . .' The impresario clearly had visions of being obliged to give money back all over Europe if his new star broke her contract.

'I've felt marvellous, Sergei Pavlovich – how could I feel anything else? It's all been like a dream come true.'

'You've eaten well? What did you have for lunch?'

'We ate here, you remember, you had the food sent over from that restaurant we went to last night to console us for having to work nonstop all day. I had oysters and some pâté, and chicken and salad . . .'

'Oysters! That's the problem solved! It's too late in the

season anyway, they're bound to be treacherous. No more oysters, that's an order.' Satisfied that he had discovered the cause of his star's sudden faltering, he rose to his feet, replaced his monocle and made for the door. 'My dear, Your Highness, I shall leave you now, and see you at the Embassy later. There is a car waiting, he knows the address.' The Russian ambassador had claimed the honour of celebrating their opening night with a reception.

'He never stays anywhere long, does he?' Orlov spoke in a peevish tone, annoyed to be cheated of the tender moment he had suddenly craved. 'What did he mean, anyway? You're not ill.'

She registered, without great concern, that he had not noticed her collapse, and therefore the audience as a whole would have seen nothing at all amiss. 'It's nothing. I made a mistake on stage, that's all. I do feel rather weak, though – can we leave early, darling?'

'Was it nervous exhaustion, perhaps? So much travelling, so much hard work . . . I think it's true what they say about that man, he certainly gets his pound of flesh from his dancers.'

'Work and nerves! You're so clever, you know me so well – I'm sure that's what it is.' She rose quickly to kiss his cool cheek, feeling a little restored by his concern for her.

The rest of the month was tinged with magic. Paris was once again captivated by the barbaric splendour of the Russian Ballet, and once more ready to lose head and heart to a new dance deity. Lydia scored another success in *Joseph*, and found herself mobbed in the street, and cheered and toasted every time she entered a room. Her letter box at the stage door was stuffed with envelopes every day, containing praise, adoration, invitations and even poetry. To Orlov's amusement an elderly industrialist took his obsession so far as to wait all day for her arrival to issue a dinner invitation in person.

She rehearsed every day in a room crowded with Diaghilev's influential acquaintances, and usually with an artist in the corner of the room diligently sketching her. She was photographed repeatedly as well, posing in her sumptuous costumes and in gowns from her favourite French couturiers for the benefit of *La Mode Illustrée*. Every day a new drawing appeared, a vivid line portrait by Pablo, a witty caricature by Jean, a chalk sketch by Bakst himself.

Her lover, as she predicted, was dazzled again, and took immense pride in driving with her in an open car to catch the admiring looks of passers-by. He was calmed and satisfied by every evidence that people went about a business other than war, and allowed himself to forget his anxieties. One day a crowd of youths, not filthy street-arabs but a group of smart young cadets from some distinguished academy, ran after them for the whole length of the Avenue de l'Opéra cheering and calling out *'Vive la belle Kusminskaya!'* When the crowd claimed her thus, he seemed to need to repossess her immediately, once even throwing her to the floor of her dressing room with so little care that she screamed and bit him, then burst into tears and accused him of bringing the manners of the battlefield indoors.

After *Joseph* another experimental work was premièred, *Le Coq d'Or*, a marriage of dance and opera staged by Fokine with music by Rimsky-Korsakov. This too was hailed, with perhaps a little less enthusiasm, but it was undoubtedly another triumph for Bakst. An atmosphere of stardust and witchery enveloped the whole company, a subtle gaiety which dissolved old enmities and put a smile on every face, from the simple-minded messenger boy to Sergei Pavlovich himself.

The sudden fatigue of the first night did not return, but she was alert for signs that it had been more than a reaction to oysters, which she had eaten in quantities for years with no ill effects. A light-headed sensation persisted, but as the whole company was walking ten centimetres off the ground on a carpet of pink clouds she did not worry about it.

The season concluded, as ever, with an open-air fete in the garden of the Ephrussys' house. A performance of *Le Jardin Animé* was staged on the lawn, with the pergolas, laden with white roses, serving as scenery and a pair of seventeenth-century stone shepherdesses, life size and carved with wonderful animation, placed among the living dancers in the opening tableau.

The air was still and the atmosphere humid and breathless. In the far distance thunder could just be heard above the hubbub of talk. Orlov stood stiffly at Lydia's side, her hand on his arm, and his own free hand clamped possessively over it, content to bow, smile and say very little while she chattered. His willingness to be overshadowed had begun to disturb her; she had discovered that the balletomane set in Paris, always tickled by the train of aristocratic admirers which the Russian ballerinas drew after them and quite unable to appreciate that she and Orlov were permanently attached, had nicknamed him the Ice Prince. Irritably she pushed him into the conversation.

'Yes, we are going on to London now, but Prince Orlov will remain in Paris, won't you, dearest? You haven't finished with the War Ministry yet, have you?'

'The War Ministry,' he repeated, not knowing how to pick up her lead.

'Tell me' – their hostess suddenly showed more than social interest in the foreign statesman she had inadvertently captured for the evening – 'will there be a war over this

Serbian nonsense? Why can't they agree anything? My husband explains but I don't understand a word of it.'

'What is your husband's opinion?' His face was softening with an indulgent smile.

'He says there won't be a war, nobody wants it and they can negotiate their way clear.'

'That is the general view.' His voice was clipped, which implied to those who knew him that the Prince was maintaining a diplomatic reticence.

'We want to know what you think, Nikolai.' Karsavina took his free arm in hers confidingly. 'We want the prince's view, not the general view, thank you.'

At this there was a ripple of nervous laughter. 'My own view – nobody takes it seriously, so why should you?'

'Because we are your friends,' Alexandrov pledged him with a cheerful smile over his champagne.

'I would like to believe in mediation,' he replied after a pause. 'But they are a passionate race, Slavs, after all, like us, and we are hot-blooded as a rule. And my role in this mission, the reason I would be here even if it were not for Lydia's sake, is to draft a treaty for arms reduction in England, France and my own country, and I cannot say it is an easy task. Everyone is very attached to their guns, not least the people whose factories make them. Last night one gentleman was explaining to me that he would be ruined if he had to cut down production next year. He said he'd even have to give up racing.' There was more uneasy laughter, since Orlov had a way of being so drily ironic that strangers were uncertain of his meaning.

'Oh dear, you've made me feel so sad.' Tata's round face was a mask of tragedy. 'I've been horribly homesick today and now all I want to do is go straight to the station and jump on a train immediately.'

'Sergei Pavlovich will curse you good and proper if you even think of it again,' Alexandrov warned her, and at the mention of his name they all looked around for Diaghilev's black bulk, but in vain. 'He's left,' Mischa confirmed. 'I saw him go half an hour ago, looking lousy. I think the thing with Vaslav gets to him even now.'

Melancholy stole among them like evening mist, to be passed off as sadness to leave such good hosts and to desert the beauties of Paris. The night was airless and hot. Over the distant suburbs a storm was brewing, and the thunder grumbled a bass line under the swell of general conversation.

The next morning Lydia caught the general mood of sadness, and suddenly found tears dampening her morning croissant. Shortly afterwards she was sick, and continued retching all morning until Orlov insisted that he would call a doctor.

'Very well, but not the company physician, for God's sake. I don't want the position of every mole on my backside relayed to Sergei Pavlovich, thank you.'

The man who came was recommended as one of the most eminent personal physicians in Paris. He was certainly one of the most discreet. He looked her over intently, which, since he was an absurdly handsome man in early middle age, was not unpleasant. She struck him as a healthy young woman in radiant good health – in fact her blooming complexion and plump bosom on a body otherwise lithe and muscular immediately suggested his diagnosis. He asked permission to examine her internally, admired the picture of Kolya in its small yellow enamel Fabergé frame just as he performed a painful manipulation of her organs, left the room briefly to reassure the Prince and then returned to a chair beside the chaise on which she was curled up with her little dog hugged protectively to her side.

'Your son seems to be a fine boy,' he began with disarming lightness. Lydia agreed politely. 'Do you have other children?' She shook her head as if this would have been the most ill-advised decision. 'And the pregnancy, the birth, they were quite normal?'

'No, they were appalling, though I'm told that is as it should be.'

'Mothers say to me that the first one is always the worst. And are you and your . . . and the Prince . . . fond of children, Madame?'

'Why?' she demanded, suspicious at once. 'Don't for God's sake tell me . . . not again, I'm not having another child, I can't be, surely? Oh please, don't tell me that . . .'

'I believe it to be so, Madame.'

'Well, I won't. And you're wrong, you must be wrong.' The words came so violently from her mouth that they were almost shouted. The dog, alarmed, jumped off her lap and hid under the bed. She ransacked her memory of the past few weeks for evidence that he was mistaken. A few moments of faintness, a little queasiness – they amounted to nothing. True she had gained weight but everyone did in Europe; the food was so good and she had as usual eaten her share. But she had had no menstruation at all for two years, and that, surely, must prove him wrong. 'Listen, a woman who has no bleeding every month is not a woman, isn't that right? If you don't bleed you can't get a baby. Even if you make love three times a day. You are not fertile. That's what the doctor in Petersburg told me. Was he lying, then? He said we didn't need to be careful if there was no menstruation, and it often happened with dancers because we were so thin.'

'That is normally the case, Madame, and certainly it has been my experience that irregular menstruation is more often experienced by women of slight build. But Nature . . .'

521

'Forget about Nature, I'm only interested in *me*. I've had no bleeding for a year, almost two years. So how can I be pregnant?'

'Irregular menstruation can be deceptive in this respect, Madame. The bleeding occurs at the end of the fertile cycle, and the best period for conception is normally about two weeks before that. I suggest that you did, in fact, begin one fertile cycle, and conceived at once, since when, of course, you will have seen no bleeding and everything would have appeared normal – or normally abnormal in your case.'

'This is no cause for humour, Doctor.' His cat-like smile and his generally light manner now infuriated her. He clearly subscribed to the fashionable opinion that the Russians were marvellous but all a little mad, and would not take her seriously. 'If what you say is true I shall be forced to cancel my contract with the Ballets Russes and the company will lose millions of francs in bookings as a result – I shall probably be sued myself . . . it will be an absolute disaster for everyone.'

'Forgive me, Madame. I appreciate you may be concerned about your commitments. Although I believe that Monsieur Diaghilev is quite accustomed to surviving difficulties with his artists. And you need not give up the stage quite yet . . . in the general way I advise mothers not to exert themselves, but at your age, in your state of health and as you have been in the habit of exercise it would be quite possible just to reduce the number of performances for a month and then retire.'

'Retire! You must be mad. Retire? When I'm the toast of all Paris, my picture's in every newspaper and I'm contracted for another four months for millions of francs! Millions, you understand! You're wrong, you must be wrong.'

He said nothing, but sat opposite her on the hard fake

Louis XV chair, his elegant legs crossed, a sympathetic look in his grey eyes. She picked irritably at the edge of her white satin kimono, her mind in turmoil. There were ways to get rid of babies but she could hardly send to Petersburg for the Finnish witch to brew up something. The best course would be to ask for this man's help. 'Have you told my Nikolai – the Prince?'

'No, Madame. I merely reassured him that you were not seriously ill.'

'Well, that's one thing. Now, what are we going to do about this?'

He looked uncomfortable. 'We can rejoice in the blessing of a new life and celebrate the miracle of creation, Madame.'

'You can rejoice if you like, but I have no plans in that direction. I prefer to rejoice in bringing the great art of the dance back to France, where it truly began. I want to celebrate the miracle which happens on that stage every night, when the whole of the Opéra trembles in a unison of emotion. That, to me, is a real creation. Any village slut can fall down drunk under some halfwit and drop a baby nine months later. So, I ask again, what shall we do?'

'I regret, Madame, that I am unable to help you.' He reached for his hat and prepared to take his leave, but since he was still courteous and she was desperate, Lydia pressed him further.

'I appreciate your sentiments, Doctor. You are obviously not a lover of art, but a man of religion, and I can admire that. I am sure, however, that you know of other members of your profession, or perhaps of an allied discipline, who are not quite of the same mind.'

'I know there are such, but I regret that I cannot assist you . . .' He walked to the door and she rose and ran after him, wanting very much to tell him to go to hell; however, he had one important area of power over her still.

She clung to his arm and looked up with a pleading

expression, well aware that the kimono had slipped off one of her shoulders. 'You will not, at least, tell the Prince of my condition? I assure you he is of the same mind as me. We had resolved to have no more children, and I know he will be angry – I would at least like to choose the right moment to give him the news.'

His eyes, which had appraised her so closely half an hour earlier, now skimmed over her as if she were some Gorgon capable of turning him to stone. 'Everything that has passed between us is confidential, Madame.'

'Of course. How wrong of me to even suspect that your principles were not of the highest in every respect.'

Now thoroughly uncomfortable in the company of a woman he recognized as manipulative, hypocritical and immoral, the doctor bowed briefly and departed as fast as good manners allowed.

Lydia returned to the couch and reclined prettily for Orlov, hoping that no sign of her inner turmoil would appear in her face. She felt a cold pit of despair opening under her feet. If she were pregnant she would lose her lover and her public by the same token. This life of acclaim and luxury would simply crumble to ashes in her hands, leaving her with nothing. Without her beauty she would be unable to attract another protector, and without her strength her career would reach an immediate end. In a year, as she saw it, she would be transformed from a gilded nymph into one of the shapeless bundles of rags who rolled drunkenly about the streets, begging by day, fighting by night, shuffling on wooden clogs and tied together with twine. Instead of basking in the love of princes and the adulation of all Europe, she would see people avert their eyes and hurry away when she approached. Her best hope would be to freeze to death quickly and unawares as soon as the winter came.

When Orlov appeared a few moments later she banished her fearful musing and greeted him with a wistful smile. He was easily reassured that her indisposition was due to nothing more sinister than too much rich food. A squabble ensued, since anxiety had now made her hungry and she had a definite desire for an omelette Arnold Bennett, which he cherishingly vetoed as oozing with cheese sauce and thoroughly indigestible. She waited until he had left to call upon an aunt staying at the George V, ordered the omelette and had eaten half of it when Céline, her French maid, announced a telephone call from Diaghilev.

'I heard you were unwell,' he began without any particular pretence of sympathy. Suppressing a hiccup, she pushed the remains of the omelette aside and gestured to the maid to remove it, annoyed that she could not finish it and that Nikolai had been correct.

'I am not unwell, Sergei Pavlovich. Are you sitting down? I am in excellent health, I have that on high authority, and I am also pregnant.'

She was pleased to hear a horrified intake of breath at the other end of the line. This was the very man who would help to the utmost of his ability.

'So – what shall we do about it?' Now there was an exhalation of relief. 'I can't be more than a few weeks . . .' Suddenly she remembered the night at her villa when she had seduced Leo and knew, with absolute certainty, that the child she was carrying was his. At once it took on a form in her mind's eye, one of those serious, large-eyed little boys, with dark curly hair and rosy lips, the miraculous kind who never seemed to get dirty like their playmates. She saw this child ever present in the corners of her future, consoling and comforting, privy to all her feebleness, a confidant for all her secrets. The vision was hypnotically attractive. Once in her mind it would not leave, though she tried to squash it like a cockroach crushed underfoot. Diaghilev was speaking softly in her ear. Finally she sank her teeth into her own arm, desperate for a violent sensation to drive the picture away.

'Are you all right? Has something happened? Lydia Alexandrovna, is everything . . .'

'It was the dog, the damn thing nipped me. What were you saying?'

'I was rather feebly protesting that this was a problem I had not encountered before . . .' She caught a whiff of disdain for the female in all its manifestations and for a moment feared that he would terminate her contract out of sheer misogyny.

'You cannot really expect me to believe that.'

'It is true, alas. But I believe that among my acquaintance there may be someone to whom they are more familiar. Let me have a day, Lydia Alexandrovna, twenty-four hours, that's all, I promise, trust me . . .'

After a few farewells the line was cut. Lydia endured the day with difficulty, anxiety now increasing her sickness tenfold so that she was almost constantly ill. In her brief moments of clear-headedness she reflected that at least she had little opportunity to be infected by regrets.

The following afternoon Diaghilev's secretary called to say that a Madame Arbeau would call upon her, and a few hours later the name was announced and a tall, slender woman with hollow cheeks, dressed in a plain but well-cut afternoon gown of aubergine silk and carrying a small carpet bag, presented herself.

'I have had the honour to attend many of the most illustrious artists at the Opéra,' she announced with a reassuring, confidential smile. 'And many members of the aristocracy also. I am told that you believe that your condition is not long established?'

'I do not think it can be more than two months or so.'

'That's very good. It may be that some tablets will be all that is necessary. May I be permitted to examine you?'

From the bag she took out a white apron. She had cold hands and strong arms, and performed the same manoeuvre as the doctor without causing quite so much pain. 'I agree, two months seems quite correct. This will be simple.' The apron was briskly removed, for all the world as if she were a cook finished with making pastry, and tucked back in the bag, from which she then removed a plain white pillbox.

'Take two of these tonight. They should produce some painful cramps, for which I regret that you should not take any remedy at all, especially not laudanum or any spirits. Just be brave, bite a piece of leather if you like, if it helps, and soon it will all be over. Shortly afterwards you should see some blood, actually quite a significant amount. If you do not, take a larger dose one week later – three or four. You have enough here. That should be all that is necessary. Then you should feel quite well, because it is a natural process that we activate this way.'

'Thank you, Madame. You have saved so much of my life with this little box, you can't imagine . . .'

'It is nothing, just my calling to help sisters in distress, Madame. Life is hard enough for a woman, I see no justice in the curse of Eve. I will leave you my card in case you should perhaps wish to recommend me to anyone.'

With a self-effacing gesture she slipped the small piece of pasteboard into a silver dish on a side table. It described Madame Arbeau as a *corsetière*. 'You are very elegant,' Lydia remarked with curiosity.

'Well, I could hardly walk through the streets in my apron, now could I?'

As soon as she was alone Lydia opened the pillbox.

Within were ten white tablets the size of peas. She decided to leave nothing to chance, and take four of them immediately.

They had no engagement that evening, and she was due to leave early in the morning. Orlov returned at six, looking forward to a few peaceful hours in her company and hoping to find her recovered. She was able to sustain a bright conversation for half an hour before a terrible pain wrenched her bowels and she doubled up on the sofa. 'Oh God! I feel like the water the blacksmith puts the red-hot horseshoes in! I'm going to boil, I know it! Aaaargh!'

He leaped to his feet, upsetting the ice bucket which had cooled their last champagne in Paris. 'Céline! Fetch the doctor immediately!'

'No! Céline, stay where you are. I promise you, my love, this is just what he warned me to expect. I won't have the poor man dragged away from his family on my account. He said just a few hours of pain and everything would be fine.'

'But my precious one – I can't bear to see you suffer so.' Protestations of this kind were not his best speeches. He stood awkwardly at her side, wondering if he should touch her or not.

'Then please, if you love me, leave me alone now. We have to part tomorrow and I won't have you remember me like this.'

With a few more entreaties she drove him away to his own room, then lay on the bed and screamed into the pillow until the convulsions passed.

In the morning she was as white as a corpse, with deep mauve circles under her eyes, and he kissed her tenderly and held her tightly to his chest on the platform at the Gare du Nord where the boat train for London stood releasing little columns of steam into the cool air.

'Four weeks of separation – how shall I bear it?' She said

528

this with all sincerity, feeling desperately unprotected now that they had to part and she was destined for a country whose people she did not know and whose language she had never learned. He was obliged to stay in Paris for another month, and then planned to travel to the Villa Cassandra where she would join him in a few days. The next phase of her engagement with the Ballets Russes was to be a tour of Germany in the autumn.

'Always remember that I love you,' he said suddenly, his flat voice at odds with the words. Her frailty, when she was always brimming with crass vitality, struck at his heart. He felt as if he had deceived a child. 'Always, my darling. Nothing gives me more pain than to know that I have given you cause to doubt me. I shall never do so again. God forgive me if any action of mine should ever injure you.'

She looked deeply into his eyes, defended by lids narrowed in emotion, and saw that he was sincere. 'You knew what was in my heart, then?'

'I confess that I did. I knew I had wounded you, which I regret more than I can say. It – she – it was all of no consequence, except that you were hurt by my actions, which was unforgivable.'

'Not so.' She reached up to stroke his head lightly with her fingertips. It was the moment to be sweet and in any case she had not the strength for harshness. 'I have forgiven you, Niki. You are so dear to me, I can't be angry with you for ever. However shall I live without you?'

'The time will pass quickly. You will have a big success in London, and you'll forget me while you're counting all your bouquets. And I shall write to you often, and telephone you if I can. A new country, new people to meet, that will make the days pass, surely?'

'Nothing can compare with the happiness of being with

you.' This was said in a feeble whisper as an involuntary shudder passed through her body. He tenderly accompanied her to her compartment and saw her comfortably installed. Her last glimpse of him was an aloof figure among the gay well-wishers on the platform, waving stiffly, the morning sun polishing his noble forehead with its pale rays.

The Channel crossing made the entire company as sick as dogs. Lydia found the London public as enthusiastic, although nowhere near as refined, as her Parisian admirers, but away from the stage she found the city oppressive. The Savoy in London was grimy and noisy compared to the Ritz in Paris, and her dressing room at Covent Garden too cold and clinical to feel comfortable. Her pains past, the nausea seemingly also overcome, she quickly regained the greater part of her strength and even managed to lose a little weight, since the London food was disagreeable in every way.

The show of blood did not appear. She went on stage in perpetual fear of a scarlet flood breaking out and disgracing them all, but nothing happened. In accordance with Madame Arbeau's instructions she took four more of the pills on a night when she was not scheduled to dance, and suffered if anything more severe agonies than before.

Another week passed and still no bleeding took place. Now fierce anxiety took hold of her and she awoke before dawn every morning in a frenzy of panic. Her dancing suffered, for she was now always tired, but the London crowd was an unrefined mob who seemed to detect no difference. Her sense of isolation deepened. Few members of the company spoke English, and they were all the more bound to each other by their common languages, so that by the third week of the season the majority hardly ventured outside the Savoy hotel except to travel to their rehearsal room, a dreary drill hall in Bloomsbury, and to Covent Garden in the evenings when they were performing.

In this enclosed atmosphere the news that the heir to the Austrian throne, Archduke Franz Ferdinand, had been shot in Sarajevo, had little impact. They did not remark the few stern faces about the opera house, nor the subdued mood of their audience that evening, and Leo, ever ready to consider himself the intellectual of the group, pronounced *The Times'* opinion that the assassination had shaken the conscience of the world to be a typically militaristic British delusion.

Lydia was surprised when a yellow telegram envelope arrived with her breakfast tray. The message was from Orlov, announcing that he had been ordered back to Petersburg but hoped to be in Monte Carlo as soon as possible, and did not want her to change her plans. She had scarcely read it when Céline announced a telephone call from him.

'Pray to God this is merely an alarm and will soon be forgotten.' The line hissed so badly she could hardly make out his words. 'The Balkans are a perpetual wasps' nest and now it has been broken open in a big way. I hope it will all die down. Are you well, my darling?'

'I feel well now but this climate does not agree with me. And we are a big success, just as you predicted.'

'God keep you safe,' was his answer and despite the poor connection she did not miss the note of apprehension in his voice.

Their final performance in England was also a matter of tradition, a private engagement in the presence of the Dowager Queen Alexandra of England. Their English patron, the Marchioness of Ripon, had erected a beautiful little theatre in her ballroom at Coombe House for the event, designed by Bakst in his favourite green and deep blue – *bleu Bakst* was currently a very fashionable colour all over Europe.

Gwladys Ripon was a woman who spread serenity around her. The soul of loyalty and generosity herself, she seemed to extract the best from everyone who entered her charmed circle. Even Diaghilev, who knew full well that she had welcomed Nijinsky and his new wife with equal hospitality only a few weeks earlier, was unable to reproach her once inside her aura of harmony.

The dancing, this time *Les Sylphides* with both Lydia and Tata partnering Massine, was over in the early evening, but the women were begged not to change their long romantic tutus for an hour or so, so that the guests might enjoy the effect of the ghostly white figures drifting among the French parterres in the garden. The evening was one of those soft July nights in England which are made to seem unreal by the random gusts of wind and sudden draughts of cool air which are a prelude to a storm. A few days earlier they had witnessed the worst thunderstorm in living memory in London; four inches of rain had fallen in three hours, and several people had been killed.

Now the calm of the hour held a sense of premonition, as if the next phase of the apocalypse was soon to begin. A soft, veiled light, dimmed early by gathering clouds, shone on the white balustrade of the verandah. In the distance the leaves of a line of willow trees gleamed silver as if already in moonlight.

'Aren't you longing to go home?' Tata asked her, gazing at the lovely scene with sadness in her eyes. 'I cannot wait. When I see beauty like this and I'm far from where I want to be it just seems like a cruel joke, as if some malicious devil has conjured the whole thing up to make me feel unhappy.'

Lydia frowned, unwilling to endure half an hour of mournful nonsense from her friend. Tata was a bore in her over-sensitive moods. 'Come on, show me your portrait,' she demanded, catching her hand and pulling her firmly to her feet. 'I've seen those wonderful chalk drawings, now I want to see the real thing.' Five years earlier Lady Ripon had commissioned John Singer Sargent to paint Karsavina; the picture now hung with his companion portrait of Nijinsky in the Marchioness's study, while the artist continued to be fascinated by Tata's beauty and returned every year to sketch her in rehearsal.

The portrait was only a temporary distraction; soon Tata continued her previous train of thought as if uninterrupted. 'Normally I'd be happy to stay in London for a few more days, but this year I feel different . . .'

'You'll be on your way to Petersburg tomorrow,' Lydia reassured her. 'And I'll be on my way to Monte Carlo to wait for my darling Niki. Home is where the heart is as far as I'm concerned.' False conviction gave her words too much emphasis. She was resolved to stay in Paris for as long as it would take to see Madame Arbeau and dispose of her pregnancy for good.

Her predictions proved to be untrue. The following morning Tata burst in on her behind Céline with her breakfast tray, her hair flying loose like a maenad's and her eyes positively sparking with annoyance.

'The nerve of this man! I'll never work for him again, never! I know I always say that but this time I mean it! Can you believe this?' She brandished a note under Lydia's sleepy nose. 'Take a good look, it's a note, and Sergei Pavlovich never writes notes, so this is a collector's item! Do you know that man owed me two years' money? *Two years!* I knew it was too good to be true, just this week one of his backers came to my dressing room and gave me two thousand pounds. So I banked it. Now Diaghilev wants to borrow back £400, and begs me to delay one more day in London to go to the bank with him! And he knows I'm dying to go home. Fool that I am, why did I ever believe I'd be paid in full?'

'You're not a fool, you're an honest person and you can't understand how the mind of a cheat would work.' Lydia pulled herself up to rest against the pillows which Céline arranged behind her back and waved the breakfast tray away. The mere smell of coffee made her feel ill.

'He's not a cheat, he's a genius, I do believe that. I just wish he would pay more attention to his contracts – heaven knows he's tough enough when he negotiates them. Wait! Céline, don't take that tray away . . .' Another envelope, identical to her own, was tucked into the toast rack. She passed it to Lydia and watched intently while it was opened.

'Oh dear. Tata, I'm the cause of it all – he owes me £400 and here he is promising that I'll be paid tomorrow! Robbing Peter to pay Paul – isn't that typical? Well, I'll tell him to pay me in Petersburg then we can get out of here.'

'You will do no such thing.' Tata was suddenly composed. 'After all this time I'm used to Sergei Pavlovich's little ways but there's no reason you should make allowances for him. I feel responsible, I got you into this after all. I won't hear of you doing anything but accepting your full fee. At least if I have to wait in this wretched place for one more day I shall have good company. We'll make him buy us the best champagne in town. Oh look, they've brought you that wonderful cream for your coffee – if you're not having some, may I? My own must be quite cold by now. You're sure you aren't hungry – look, there's that bacon stuff, it's delicious the way they do it in England . . . isn't it nice to be able to eat whatever we please now we've got nothing to do for the next two months?'

Long afterwards both women were never able to see a silver jug of cream without remembering that morning, the last carefree hours they were to enjoy for many years. One day's delay for the sake of their improvident impresario was to cost them more than they could possibly have imagined.

The evening brought another telegram from Orlov. 'Come home at once, fastest possible. My worst fears confirmed. No peace until I see you, Niki.' She hesitated. They had already waited a dreary hour with the concierge, who had difficulty in changing their carriage reservations, and was able only to offer Tata an ordinary second-class seat for part of the journey to St Petersburg.

Diaghilev called on her before dinner with a grave face. 'Tata tells me you still intend to stop in Paris – don't do it, Lydia Alexandrovna. I've heard from Petersburg that the order for general mobilization will be given tomorrow. The embassy will advise all Russian nationals to return home immediately. Then there'll be a mad stampede, so go now, I beg you.'

'But why? I don't understand.' She was still reluctant, looking forward to the sybaritic life of the Riviera. Madame Arbeau's ministrations were not so vital, since at home the Finnish woman would be just as capable of freeing her from her stubborn burden.

'There's going to be a war.' He nodded with raised eyebrows, as if teaching a simple word to a small child. 'Russia is going to declare war on Germany, and with any luck our allies England and France will pitch in. Don't worry, if they do it'll all be over by Christmas. But you mustn't be caught in the wrong country or you'll be interned – or worse. There have been riots all over London today, mobs turning on anyone they consider a suspicious foreigner. We've all got to leave.'

'But there are no reservations to be had – Tata's had to go second class half the way.'

'My dear, would you rather travel second class or spend six months in a rat-infested prison and be grateful because you've escaped lynching on the streets?'

She saw that he was serious and sighed with annoyance. 'Very well. I'll change my plans.'

'Here are your tickets.' He pulled them from his jacket pocket, neatly wrapped in the Thomas Cook folder. 'I took the liberty of having the concierge change them as soon as I got the news. You leave together at six a.m. God go with you. Now let's go down to our last supper.'

'Won't you travel with us?'

'Alas no. I shall be sailing for New York tomorrow. The Americans have pleaded with me every year to take the Ballets Russes over there, and now I think the time is right to give them what they ask.' He extended his arm and she took it with every outward show of grace, feeling nothing but dislike and distrust. 'I'm so excited about America. They have no ballet, indeed, scarcely any culture at all. Can you imagine what an impact our dancers, our composers, our artists will have on them? It will be extraordinary, a once-in-a-lifetime experience. How thrilling to appear before people who have no idea what to expect, to step out on the stage and capture their entire hearts – but not by the tired old expectations of tradition, no! Raw emotional impact – that will be all! Do you know, I've heard that even savages in the jungles of Brazil will respond to the music of Mozart played on a phonograph . . .'

He was still painting the picture for them when they sat down for dinner. Lydia waited until he drew a new breath and then remarked, 'How gratified my Niki will be to see his mobilization strategy in action at last. Do you remember how proud he was, Tata, when His Imperial Majesty honoured him with the order of St Gabriel for his work on the plan?'

Diaghilev paused, open-mouthed. She imagined him to be properly reminded that she was one of the most powerful women in Russia, even if she had agreed to return there in a second-class seat.

As their train crawled through Berlin it stopped at every station and yet more Russians embarked, thrown into a panic by the mysterious rumours which they trusted totally while ignoring official statements, and consequently desperate, terrified and determined to return home no matter what dangers or discomforts lay ahead. They were a few miles from the border, late in the day, when the news passed from mouth to mouth that the German Kaiser had declared war on his cousin the Tsar.

As if to confirm the words, the train ground to a halt a few minutes later, and a detachment of German soldiers stationed themselves along its length. The passengers were allowed to leave the sweaty, airless carriages and walk along the track while the sergeant argued with the train driver and signals were sent back and forth.

Russia lay only a few yards away. Every time she had crossed at this point in the past Lydia had looked with contempt at the tumbledown houses of unpainted wood, surrounded by scrawny chickens and haphazard haycocks, on the side of her own country, and preferred the solid stone cottages of the Germans, with their neat, abundant vegetable patches and flocks of fat geese.

In normal times she despised the Russian porters, who scrambled forward to welcome each traveller with the words, 'Safe homecoming!' They intended no goodwill, it was done to get a good tip. The chief Customs officer, a balletomane, had once recognized her and come running from his office to order that her luggage be treated carefully. Orlov had smiled with satisfaction at that. 'Your face says more than my coat of arms ever could,' he whispered in her ear as they followed the caravan to their new stateroom.

Russia was now dark and quiet. The German sergeant ordered them all back to the train and as they wearily boarded their carriage Lydia heard one man tell another that the first shots had already been fired.

It was still light when they reached Berlin. As they walked from the station down Unter den Linden, kicking up crumpled proclamations like autumn leaves under their feet, they clutched their silk wraps around them and tried to conceal their jewel cases in their folds, uncomfortably aware that they were sufficiently elegant to attract attention. Behind them their maids dragged their feet fearfully. Lydia felt her petticoat cling to her thighs with more than the mere clamminess of perspiration. She was aware of a faint raw ache in her lower abdomen and, convinced that she was bleeding at last, shook off her weariness and strode forward with new energy.

The Russian Embassy was like a house where a death had occurred, shuttered and still. She remembered it blazing with light and noise the year before, when she had attended a ball for the Kaiser. Now there were only two obdurate officials in the hallway, facing a desperate crowd who waved papers and shouted their demands to the empty rooms.

'I can't help you, Mademoiselle. The embassy train is completely full. Look, look – here is the list of passengers. We can't even get all of our own staff on it, let alone people who walk in off the street . . .'

'How dare you refer to me in that manner? Do you know who I am?' Lydia flew into a tantrum of rage. She shouted her name, the name of Prince Orlov and the names of every prince and duke she had entertained in Monte Carlo. The tirade immediately produced a result. A door at the far end of the hallway was unbolted and opened, and a clerk appeared to invite her and Karsavina to the Ambassador's office. Their maids scuttled after them.

The Ambassador was hastily struggling into his jacket. The room was in chaos, with packing cases full of papers stacked on every surface and more clerks frantically writing labels and lists.

'I most deeply regret that I cannot offer two such honoured artists immediate conduct out of Germany, but the authorities have told me that anyone travelling on the embassy train who cannot produce a diplomatic passport will be executed summarily as a spy.' He spread his manicured hands, asking mutely what one could do with such people. 'What I can do is commend you to the embassy of a neutral power. His Excellency the Spanish Ambassador has been a dear friend to us here in Berlin and you may have complete confidence in him.'

He gestured to a clerk to bring pen and paper, and a note was rapidly written and sealed. To their relief a car and a driver were summoned.

The Spanish Embassy was also shuttered, but it was clear that the kindness of the Ambassador had been well known to all his colleagues, for the building, large as it was, was bursting with English, French, American and Russian people, shepherded from one room to another by dark young men who glanced uneasily at each other as if for reassurance. The atmosphere was tense but ordered. Their introduction took them directly to the Ambassador's office; Lydia was immensely embarrassed to notice that she was indeed bleeding heavily. Dark red streaks marked her

stockings and so much blood had collected in her shoes that
her feet made squelching noises at every step.

The Spanish Ambassador gave them shelter for the night
in his own home, but by morning pains like knives were
tearing at Lydia's stomach. A Spanish doctor came, treated
her with contempt when he realized her condition and gave
her tablets which she did not take. Tata, from whom she
could no longer conceal the truth, hovered over her like an
anxious angel.

'What are we to do? What are we to do?' she asked no one
in particular over and over again. She was the kind of
woman whom everyone was always alert to help. Lydia began
to run a fever. She had lost a great deal of blood, and was
dramatically pale and immobile.

The events which took place thereafter were recounted
to her by Céline. She herself was only rarely conscious.
She felt as if she floated through each day, dimly aware of
people in the distance expressing worry and distress. The
pain in her abdomen raged and throbbed. Her head was
like a baby's, too heavy to hold up. She was eternally thirsty
but vomited even water. After a while she saw no more
faces, but heard only voices telling her she was leaving, but
she did not know where she was or what her destination
would be.

As she surrendered to her illness, the Ambassador
consulted his wife, and the three of them had a long,
awkward discussion. The embassy could not shield them
without risking its own status. Paris had just declared war
on Germany, the border with France was closed, and might
shortly become a battleground. Karsavina could have a pass
to Holland and might, from there, be able to get a boat to
England, from whence she could travel on to St Petersburg,
but Lydia was in no state to endure such a long, uncertain

and dangerous journey, and with such a handicap Karsavina herself might be unable to find a passage.

Immediately a perfect solution presented itself. The Monegasque consul, no longer able to share a roof with the French Embassy, arrived to open a temporary office in this welcoming pocket of Spanish territory. On seeing his car and trunks, all emblazoned with the Monaco arms, Tata proposed that Lydia travel in the care of her maid to her own villa in the principality, there to recuperate and travel north again when her health was restored.

In a day she was provided with temporary Monegasque documents. Tata travelled with her in the embassy car to Hamburg and saw her settled aboard a Swedish liner bound for Marseilles. She revived slightly once at sea, and took a little liquid, but at the end of the week-long voyage she was still feverish and too weak to speak. The driver came from the Villa Cassandra to fetch her. It was some weeks later when she woke up to find a pink face peering into hers.

'There you are,' she heard a voice heavy with the accent of the South of France purr above her. 'You've come back to us at last. You've been very ill. You've had pneumonia. But our prayers have been answered. And don't worry about your baby, Madame. Everything is fine.'

CHAPTER 18
Leningrad, 1988

When he heard that Mikhail Gorbachev was the new Soviet leader, Lovat decided to telephone Kolya Kusminsky and suggest that he drop in for a chat. 'Is better you come evening.' The old man gave a hoarse laugh. 'Evening I am good.' The shop in the courtyard off the Rue Jacob now sold stationery, Florentine paper, Mont Blanc pens, sealing wax in a dozen bright colours, under the management of Etienne Sokolov. Kusminsky worked from the apartment.

An entryphone admitted Lovat from the street, and another opened the door of the apartment itself. Kusminsky's voice called, 'Come, please,' from the half-open door of the sitting room and Lovat found him at his desk in a swivel chair. Age and illness had shrivelled him; he was now a small figure and his glow of good living had dimmed to a grey greasiness. His eyes were invisible below the slack overhang of their lids. He wore an opulent jacket of midnight-blue brocade, and a cashmere rug covered his legs.

'You drink champagne.' It was somewhere between a question and an order. He retrieved a bottle from the deep, brass-rimmed ice bucket on a side table, patted it tenderly with a napkin and removed the cork with a chromium contraption. Pouring was a test of his strength, and when he passed a glass to Lovat he swayed off balance and a few drops splashed to the floor. 'Excuse please. I give last year one leg to cigarettes. *L'artériosclérose.* Is difficult.' He patted his left thigh, producing a dead, metallic sound. In-

542

voluntarily, Lovat's eyes went to the feet. Two black velvet slippers embroidered with stars rested on the floor, one foot less symmetrical than the other, although the black silk socks made it hard to tell.

'I am sorry.' How chilling the difference in the man in only five years.

'I also. *Nostrovya!* Cheers!' They touched glasses and sipped, then paused in appreciation to watch the bubbles rise. 'I expect you. Your wife come . . .'

'We are divorced.'

'Of course. I remember. She come, she ask if you also come, I say no, she say very good. But he will. He will come. And then – you telephone.' He seemed to be thoroughly amused. Suspicions teemed in Lovat's mind. Did Kusminsky consider himself loyal to Bianca, because she was Charlotte's granddaughter? Would he offer bad advice or send him on a false trail? 'You also looking for early twenty-century Russian work, Constructivists, Blue Rose Group – Popova, Larionov, Goncharova?'

'Yes.'

'Stage design, ballet design, backcloth . . .'

'No, my buyers are less interested in that area.'

'Textile? Popova design in factory after Revolution. Poster, commercial art, architect drawing?'

'Not textiles.' Bianca was bound to go for the rest of the list. She was sentimental about textiles and he had to acknowledge she had a good instinct for collectables, the area where art met shopping. She could keep that market, it was too small for him.

'Silver, metalwork, jewellery, little *objets*?'

'Maybe.'

'*Maybe?*' Histrionically, Kolya dropped his head and raised his eyebrows. 'Very big market, very good.'

'Is there much new stuff coming out?'

'All time.' He leaned unsteadily forwards and from behind a stack of papers dragged a silver candelabra, upending it to show the hallmark. 'This one, I buy yesterday, come from Kiev. Mark is Kiev, see here. In Soviet Union, every week, workman knock down a wall and inside – silver, gold, diamonds, porcelain, coins, certificates, banknote – everything family hide from Bolsheviki. Even my father, I see him do this. I tell you . . . before. In your house.' His hand made an irritated sideways movement, pushing away a troublesome memory. 'So – workman give everything to Soviet government? What for – he get nothing. Black market he get dollars, pounds – hard currency.'

Every detail of his last weekend under the same roof as Bianca was branded in Lovat's recall. He examined the candelabra with interest. This was the area in which he was most acutely interested. He knew better than to ask outright who sold the piece. 'I thought exporting from Russia was illegal.'

'*Y-e-e-s!* In USSR, everything is forbidden. Simple. So you get three sources.' He held up three fingers of his right hand. 'Official negotiation. No good now, today, but for next year – it will come. My advice, begin now, it will take a long time but you will be one of first. Two – works already here, in West. You know already some, I give you names. Three – black market. Everything forbidden, everybody cheat. My advice, come here to France, because nobody ask many question. In England, law is different, always problems.' He refilled the glasses.

Lovat made it clear that he had American buyers, specific interests and no great difficulty with black-market goods although he was planning a London show for which he needed authenticated works. Kusminsky, satisfied that there was business here for himself, pulled the tattered Roladex towards him and gave the younger man contacts. 'I make deal with Miss Berrisford,' he explained. 'She get Moscow, you get Leningrad. Good?'

Lovat bit back his annoyance but the old man tapped his hand like a co-conspirator. 'Leningrad is more open city, I think things leave more easy. Moscow is better for art nouveau, costume, textile – better for woman. Paintings better in Leningrad. Moscow is more difficult, believe me.'

Sitting in a café on Boulevard St Germain an hour later, an anxious melancholy clouded his thoughts. The instinct not to trust Kusminsky was strong. He chafed at the inevitability of encountering his ex-wife around every new corner and was angry with himself for letting her get to the old man first.

In the stream of passers-by his eye landed on a woman plainly dressed in a grey skirt, white shirt and cardigan, with light brown hair pulled loosely off her narrow face. Her undulating walk, which moved her full breasts at every step, attracted him. His gaze lingered an instant while he tried to analyse her elegance, and a few minutes later he was aware that she was sitting at a table behind him.

He had forgotten about Paris – more truthfully, he had never dared to share the city's obsession with erotic adventure. The woman leaned forward and asked him for a cigarette. Feeling stupid, he replied that he did not smoke. She did not smoke either, but she liked a little glass of wine on a fine evening, she found it *sympa*. Unhappily, she was alone, her boyfriend was out of town. She crossed her arms, her breasts pressed together, one hand raised and a fingertip toying inside her blouse with the satin strap of an undergarment. When she left him, early the next morning, she stroked his cheek, purred in his ear and called him a real animal. It was the most genuinely affectionate gesture he had won from a woman in ten years.

The world looked brighter afterwards, and as a consequence he allowed himself to trust Kusminsky. There was no point in fighting Bianca too fiercely for the Russian pictures already in the West, since a major sale at Berrisford's could only generate interest and drive up prices. If he mounted his own exhibition first it would be in danger of going unnoticed. Let her go to Moscow with the Minister and endure a formal banquet with the Politburo, she would get nothing out of it. He contented himself by sending on to their saleroom a dealer with two dubious pictures ascribed to Lubov Popova, and a third which was an outright fake, over-restored and signed on the front, which was not the artist's custom.

It was eighteen months before he travelled to Leningrad; he had dim memories of a student visit, of his philistine companions leaving him to wander alone in the Hermitage, through room after room of Meissen and Sèvres, until he sat down exhausted on the staircase below a colossal canvas by Picasso.

With four other cultural businessmen, a film director, a concert entrepreneur and two actors, he was escorted on a brief tour of the neo-classical sights of the city, then left to follow his approved itinerary with an interpreter. She was a short, stocky woman who conversed eagerly from the moment he met her in the bustling lobby of his hotel. The excessive make-up favoured by the Russians did not disguise her white Scandinavian complexion, fresh although she was certainly not young. Her bushy blonde hair hung in a firm pigtail that reached to her waist.

At meetings mediated by Anya at least as much time was devoted to the two Russians assessing each other's position in the web of influence as was taken up by Lovat's ambition to buy paintings. He made little progress in three days. In her bright conversation, questions soon appeared to test his own integrity. Appreciating that he was in a country where the question to be asked of a citizen was not if they took bribes but what they wanted to be offered, Lovat was relieved when she began the preliminary negotiation.

'You like caviar?' They were waiting for lunch in the hotel's cavernous restaurant. A smell of non-specific soup hung in the air.

'No, I don't.'

'Russian caviar is the best in the world. You try it?' She picked a packet of Benson & Hedges out of her red shoulder bag and extracted a cigarette.

'Yes, but I don't like it.'

'Caviar is very healthy food. When I was little girl, my mother make me eat caviar sandwich every day. Good for slim, no calories. Your wife like caviar?' She tucked the cigarette between smiling lips and waited for him to light it. The idea of a man who did not smoke carrying a lighter just in case a woman should want a cigarette was hilarious, but it also made her feel sentimental.

'No.'

'Vitamins in caviar very rare, vitamin E, vitamin K. Make more sexy. Your girlfriend like caviar?'

'I haven't got a girlfriend.'

'You learn like caviar, you get girlfriend.' When she laughed her breasts shook inside her camel polo-neck.

'There's no point buying caviar, it's illegal. You can't export it without the receipt from the state shop at the airport.'

'I show you how to pack it so no one ever find it. How much you like?'

'All right, I'll buy a tin.'

She chuckled as if he had said something idiotically stupid. 'The more you buy the better the price. Look, when you make your exhibition in your gallery, you have party with real Russian caviar, everybody is very pleased, very impressed – it will be good, I think. Fifteen tins.'

'Two.'

In the end he agreed to ten, she exchanged a few words with the waiter and he brought them from the kitchen under a napkin. As they left Anya strode off in the same direction, swinging her hips, and returned with a plastic bag in which he glimpsed packets of butter.

Her next move was to test his interest in black-market goods. It was obvious that she had very little appreciation of art and when he began to mention particular painters' names she looked blank. Her opening offer was an introduction to a man who traded in icons, well known for the number of forgeries he supplied. 'And the market for icons in the West is dead, I'm really not interested. I'm after early twentieth-century pictures, nothing else.' Eventually, she made him write the names down.

As a token of advancing trust, she conducted him to his appointments and left him alone with the dealers, whose English was in some cases better than hers. He was thus able to negotiate freely for five excellent pictures, to be exported by processes into which he would not inquire and paid for in dollars in cash.

He was noticeably more cheerful by the end of the day. Anya suggested that they should drop in on a friend, and had their taxi leave them near the Bank Bridge. She seemed unfamiliar with the address, and with the arrangement of the apartments in the old building, even though their destination proved to be the principal dwelling in it, on the second floor over the street door, with a balcony along four long windows.

The door was opened by a man of around thirty-five with a loose-fleshed, Ashkenazi face and receding brown curls. 'I am Mitrokin, Simeyon, good afternoon.' His keen eyes looked Lovat over as he shook hands, leaving a trace of moisture from his palm.

Despite the failing light of the autumn afternoon and the heavy velvet curtains the colour of claret, the main room blazed with gold, reflected from ormolu statuary, cloisonné vases, silver-gilt table ware, chalices and icons encrusted with gems, brass votive lamps and the massive gilded picture frames which crowded the walls. Several glass cases displayed jewellery and precious trinkets. One was devoted to Fabergé, mostly minor items, photograph frames in pastel guilloche enamel and hardstone carvings. Marble statues, some of life size, were arranged in an alcove beside the fireplace, behind a table of magnificent bronzes.

For thirty seconds Anya looked around the Aladdin's cave of treasures with wide eyes and a mouth gaping in astonishment, then recollected that she ought to be giving the appearance of familiarity with the place and asked briskly about early twentieth-century paintings. The dealer drew Lovat to the long rear wall, which was crowded with pictures, and began to talk him through them. Two portraits were outstanding, an elderly woman in black smiling merrily as she held on to her hat in a strong wind, and a young woman with a ripe smile standing by a balustrade at night. This picture was so subtly coloured it was almost monochrome. The figure was pale against the satiny darkness; large cream roses were pinned in her dark red hair, and a few more blooms lay by her feet. She wore a trailing dress of white silk and lace, and rows of diamonds sparkled around her long neck. The only focus of colour was the split-fruit mouth.

When he expressed interest, Mitrokin told him it was a portrait of a ballerina, executed for the famous artists' bar, the Stray Dog. He had other pictures from their collection – Akhmatova, poet, another dancer, Karsavina, sketches by Larionov, caricatures by Legat ... An instinct prompted Lovat to ask the name of the woman in the portrait. It was Lydia Kusminskaya.

'Her son is a dealer in Paris.' Lovat looked the man briefly in the eye.

'Kolya. I used to see him sometimes. Now he is very ill.' The dealer was searching for words in English. 'Doctor cut' – he struck his knee with the side of his hand to illustrate – 'cut his leg.'

'Very sad.' Now a real introduction had been made. Lovat was suspicious that Mitrokin was not among the names that Kolya had provided. Obviously he was well connected, a business on this scale could not survive without substantial protection, obviously he was not a friend of Anya, but perhaps found through a contact, or perhaps part of a conspiracy to mire him in illegal activities; Kolya would know.

An elderly man in a cardigan brought tea and the three of them sat down at an inlaid fruitwood table crowded with massive silver ink-wells. Lovat slowly assimilated the significance of the room and its contents. Most of the treasure belonged in a museum, nothing he could see was less than a masterpiece, and some things, especially the nineteenth-century realist studies of peasant life, were surely of significant worth as historical documents. These things were the country's birthright, and Mitrokin's avidity to sell them, and the whole clumsy conspiracy which had brought him to the room, saddened Lovat. If the man was genuine he could make a killing here. The metaphor suddenly seemed ironic. There was no dignity in the affair.

He decided to give the man the respect he was not claiming himself, and establish his own connection with Kusminsky. Perhaps, in a minor way, it would put the dealer in touch with his heritage if he heard the story of the old man's flight from St Petersburg as a small boy. Mitrokin's eyes widened at the description of the jewels sewn into the child's clothes and the necklace – presumably the very one in the portrait – left behind. Anya was moved to jump up and examine the picture again at close quarters.

'Perhaps it is still there.' The dealer did not speak frivolously. 'House is well preserved. It's Pioneer Palace. Headquarters for Soviet boy scouts. Pity you don't know where they hide it.'

'As a matter of fact, he described exactly where it was.'

'To look for something like that – it can be done, of course.' Nothing further needed to be said. Anya was drifting around the room, marvelling at the untouched pre-Revolution decor, stroking the pink damask wallpaper and fingering the silk tassel at the end of the brocade bell-rope. Tactfully, she slipped through the door, but Lovat was not tempted to advance further along the line of conversation until he had spoken to Kolya.

There was a scream in the passage outside. She had found a lavatory, panelled in glowing mahogany, pink and red art nouveau carnations writhing decoratively around the bowl, the wash basin and all the matching porcelain fitments. There was a red silk cord to pull the flush. Having alarmed the men, Anya herself was pink with embarrassment.

Lovat invited her to have dinner at the hotel and she flirted with him heartily. 'You are handsome man, you don't like your wife – yes, this I can see, I know it – so why no girlfriend?'

He muttered something about morality, unsure what to say, unsure, since the question had been bluntly asked, what the true answer was. Isabel had a deadening effect on his libido, but at bottom he was afraid to endanger even the hollow shell of his marriage.

'What about you?'

She was transparent. That tense, retreating smile, the narrowing of the eyes, hiding them in supposed merriment. 'You want to know if I have a boyfriend?'

'Isn't it a fair question?'

'No!'

'You asked me.'

'If I had a boyfriend, would I have dinner with you now?'

The hotel had a basement bar that called itself a discotheque. She pulled him through the weekend crush of drunken Finns to the dance floor and as soon as he put his arms around her he resolved that he would make love to her that night. Then he thought of his dismal room, the coarse sheets on a lumpy palliasse and the pillow which was redolent of a thousand greasy heads, and changed his mind. He was acutely sensitive to beauty, and in its absence had less heart for living.

Her hands barely reached around his neck, but somehow she pulled his head down until she could reach to kiss him. It was a competent, energetic kiss; momentarily it became languorous but when it was completed she pulled away and patted his lapel with an air of finality. Perhaps she felt his depression, or read disappointment in his eyes, because she said, 'Tomorrow evening you come to my apartment, yes? You bring caviar, I cook for you.' It was after she had gone, as he was walking down the interminable corridor to his room, that he felt a surge of desire, and an immediate counter-flow of disgust. She was pathetic, an ageing woman prostituting herself for a few paltry comforts – but would he be any better if he raided her for synthetic intimacy and phoney passion?

She lived on the western outskirts of the city, on the top floor of a modern five-storey building, with a view out across the grey water of the Gulf of Finland. The wind hummed in the power cables and thrashed the young trees whose tops were level with her green-painted iron balcony. The smell of frying butter filled the room. He looked at the cheap attempts at decoration: theatre posters, a large red Chinese fan, photographs of Anya with unrecognizable celebrities, strings of beads draped over mirrors.

She hummed around the stove in the cooking alcove, a frayed apron tied over a red wool dress. It was soothing to sit and watch a woman cooking, and in a primitive way, he supposed, flattering. It no longer happened in his life that anyone cooked for him, personally, specifically, voluntarily, with the sole purpose of making him feel good. Lovat found that he felt good.

She passed close by him, crossing the room to find matches, and he put out an arm to catch her around her thighs and pull her to the arm of his chair. They began to kiss, and he wanted the touch of her flesh more than anything he could imagine. The dress, and the ill-matched underclothes, were pulled off and thrown to the floor. In nakedness she was magnificent, spine braced with regal pride, her skin matte like velour and evenly pale, all her rich contours firm in motion. He thought of ripe tomatoes bursting, swelling pumpkins, of opening a pomegranate, splitting a watermelon.

Giggling and scolding, she lay across his lap and offered

him whichever portion of her flesh he wanted to kiss, or suck, or crush in his fingers to try its density. She stroked his hair and then, feeling him hard, slipped to the floor, opened his jeans and pressed his cock between the cushions of her breasts. Her eyes glistened with desire, her curled cat's tongue bathed him. Desperate to collect himself before it was too late, he pulled her up into his arms, and then fell to the floor; her hospitable thighs parted and he lay in their heat, feeling that he was truly taking possession.

Afterwards he expected her to make a pitch for whatever the larger agenda was, and was saddened when it came. They ate first, companionably half naked; she made blinis to eat with the caviar, and fried chicken with potatoes. He had brought a bottle of imported champagne; imported from where it was hard to tell, but it was a relief after the sickly Russian substitute. It was still half drunk when she raised the question of Kusminskaya's house and the location of the valuables in it.

Was there any point in honesty? Was there anything to lose – he had no faith at all that the necklace would be lying untouched in the wall after seventy turbulent years. He had made love to her, he felt connected, and so he explained that he was uncertain whether Mitrokin could be trusted, and in any case did not deal in jewellery.

Soon afterwards he left for London, committed to return in three months with cash deposits. Anya was discreet with him in public, particularly in the hotel, where it was clear that every member of the vast staff was some category of informer. It was the one thing which punctured his mistrust of her.

Anya visited Mitrokin as soon as their mutual acquaintance, the Georgian Andrusha, next appeared. A recurring cartilage problem had ended his dancing career in his twenties, and he was now a full-time social parasite, a big man among the gangsters who supplied the city with the necessities of life, and a big man in literal terms since with inactivity and high living he had run grossly to fat.

He sat like a pasha on the Empire chaise that was the dealer's finest piece of furniture and delivered his judgement. 'I find no justification for knocking holes in the walls of the Pioneer Palace. If those disgusting little brown-noses have left any walls standing. Too much trouble. He says he's not really interested, so why don't we just believe him?' Anya had always been soft about foreigners, but surely even she could understand that there was nothing in this?

'Not really interested – that's like saying a little bit pregnant. He'll go for it if we set him up right.' She pouted in disappointment.

'She's right, Andrusha. When he sat here and looked at this picture, I was watching his face. He'll do the job, all we've got to do is give him a hard-on for it. But you're right, leave the Pioneers to gallop their maggots in peace. There's a deal here, but we don't need to disturb their innocent pleasures to get it.' Mitrokin pulled an envelope from the only working desk in the room and took some photographs from it. 'Someone I know in Moscow, jewellery is his big number, he knows the market and he has much more stock than I, suggested that we could tempt him – and use this. Look at the picture, it's a near-enough match.' The photograph showed a diamond necklace displayed on a dark background so that all its details were clear. He took it over to the portrait. The rendering of the necklace was not precise but both pieces were of similar overall shape. 'The only difference that you can really see is the drop stones here at the front, but these can be added, for a price. If the man comes back and says he's changed his mind, or suddenly finds he knows someone who's into diamonds, we can just give him this. Simple, yeah?'

Anya was enthusiastic and so he agreed to sanction the scheme – after all it would cost him nothing and with the country opening up to the West, who knew where a contact might lead? 'I hope he gave you some nice presents, this art pimp. How are you keeping, by the way?'

'I'm great, really good, thanks to you, Andrusha. I can't thank you enough for fixing this job for me.'

'Any time. What's an old friend for, after all? You get any more problems, just get in touch and I'll do what I can. And your toy boy?' Anya had taken up with the deputy manager of the hotel, ten years younger than her and thoroughly bad news. From the Georgian's point of view he was thick with all the wrong people, mostly the gang with which his own organization was most often at war. Plus the man was a tightwad, he neglected her, screwed around – and now it was common knowledge that he'd set up his new secretary in an apartment.

'He works too hard, but he's good to me so I can't complain, can I?'

Poor girl, such a dummy. Life was terrible for a woman without a man to take care of her, especially at Anya's age. 'Glad to hear it. I thought the younger generation were a bunch of skiving halfwits, but maybe I'm wrong. That freezer I promised you is on its way, the boys will bring it round next week.' He heaved himself to his feet to kiss her goodbye. 'Good luck with your necklace scam – maybe you'll get a collar on an exit visa at last, eh? And if you need anything, don't forget, you know where I live.'

Lovat consulted Kusminsky, who gave a good opinion of Mitrokin, and offered the explanation that he had withheld his name only because he knew him as a dealer in Fabergé and small objects and never considered that he might also trade fine art. He offered more detailed advice but Lovat had a powerful instinct that the real information, whatever it was that was crucial for him to know, was being withheld.

The deal for the two portraits and three small bronzes was done with Mitrokin, the goods shipped through Zimbabwe as tractor parts and arriving via Kusminsky with false French provenance covering their ownership since 1911. The dealer was as good as his word throughout the transaction, and, wanting to keep such a valuable source sweet, Lovat allowed that he might be able to place the Kusminskaya necklace if it could be recovered. He asked for a photograph, which he showed to Kusminsky; the old man dismissed it after the briefest examination as nothing like anything that had ever belonged to his mother.

'She had two diamond necklaces, and she was painted in both; one made from rather poor stones given to her by the Tsar, which was shipped by Fabergé to Paris, recorded in archives with drawing. She sold it in 1920 for very bad price but what to do, it was not the time to sell diamonds. Other one, Orlov necklace, is priceless. Now only I know where it is.'

For the opening of the exhibition, Lovat hired a public relations firm, who christened the event A Night in St Petersburg', had half the gallery tented in gaudy, glittering fabrics and hired a balalaika trio. The Tuttlingens flew over with a party and the Russian Ambassador made a twenty-minute speech about *glasnost* which was laboriously constructed to leave him politically untainted while remaining quite incomprehensible to his audience.

The guests whispered among themselves, and the least discreet was Isabel, conspicuous in a small black dress

encrusted with lurid graffiti in sequins and beads. Lovat
thought that his wife looked like a parrot when she was
trying to fascinate a man, the way she shrieked, preened and
bobbed her head. The performance was for the benefit of
one of the Americans, a man with expensively messed blond
hair. A bright blue silk scarf was draped around his neck
over an ensemble of loose clothes. On his hollow cheeks
grew half a millimetre of designer stubble which, being
blond, imparted a sheen like good velvet. Since Isabel
considered the deconstructed Armani look to be utterly
passé, Lovat was surprised that she was paying him so much
attention.

'That gentleman is accompanying one of my wife's
friends,' Don growled in his ear as relieved applause broke
out at the end of the speech. 'Always running around the
world with some ballet company, which makes as much
sense as digging a hole in the back yard and throwing money
into it. He's supposed to have trained in Russia, although he
is American. She is a widow, and her trustees would be
extremely relieved if she dumped Terpsichore and took up
with a muse that didn't need so much investment. Cheri tells
me she's about to come around to their point of view so I
thought we'd ask 'em along. They will be dining with us.'

At the meal, Isabel gave a virtuoso performance. She now
defined herself by what she did not do – she did not drive,
smoke, drink alcohol, or eat meat. She seemed also to have
given up sex since his return, but Lovat had an instinct that
her celibacy was specific only to him. The simple meal was
turned into a three-hour spectacle starring her own ego.
First, she disdained the common Perrier water on the table
and produced her own bottle of Welsh spring water, supplied
by a rock star friend from his own farm. Between the first
and second courses a box of Nicorex gum appeared in her

fingertips and was manipulated unceasingly until someone invited her to explain that a magazine editor friend in New York sent it over for her.

With operatic verve, she returned the salad to the kitchen for the crime of containing croutons fried in butter. Finally, when the conversation turned to the environment, she struck a series of absurdly tragic poses – face contorted in caring agony, hands wrung in the depth of her hollow belly, fingers pinching her temples, perhaps in a vain bid to extract a thought.

'You remind me of Martha Graham's Sophoclean heroines,' observed the target of these histrionics, obviously unmoved.

'It must have been just physical with her and Scott Fitz, don't you think? She was kind of androgynous, he was basically gay – I mean, that's what the impotence was about, really, wasn't it – so she was the next best thing to a boy . . .'

The American's eloquent grey eyes looked at her as if she were speaking in schizophrenic voices. Lovat laughed out loud. 'Martha Graham the choreographer, dear. You're thinking of Sheilah Grahame . . .' The end of his sentence was muffled by a slab of monkfish which hit his mouth. Tomato *concassé* dripped on to his shirt. Isabel had thrown her plate at him. The legs of the Philippe Starck chair squealed as she rose and by the time she reached the door it had clattered to the floor.

'She is your wife, I mean, you're married, aren't you?' There was a hint of wonder in the American's voice, implying that a man must be powerfully stupid to marry at all, let alone to marry a creature designed to make life a misery. His own companion, who was seated within earshot, bridled visibly.

'Can't you tell? She's from Australia.' Lovat offered the

only explanation he had. He was surprised to hear an expression of sympathy from this man – why, he could not analyse. Instinctively, he recognized his sexual aura and in the primitive depth of his psyche he saw him as an enemy.

'Mmn – beautiful country but no culture. It's a great deficiency, one has to work hard to remedy it. Still, I am grateful personally since now I can talk to you. What a great thing you have done in bringing these wonderful paintings to the West.'

Lovat was unused to flattery and it went to his head at once, allaying his gut distrust.

'We haven't been introduced. I know your name, of course; I am Alexander Wolfe.' A slight pause, as if he only half expected a reaction. 'It was a particularly moving exhibition for me, because one of your pictures is a portrait of my grandmother. The lady by the balustrade, the ballet dancer . . . so strange, to see her as a young woman, when I remember her as elderly. But still magnificent, in her way. When I was at ballet school in Leningrad I saw their portrait of her, but it's nowhere near as fine as yours.'

'I'm glad to hear that, of course.' Lovat had a shred of recollection; Kolya had once mentioned a boy, but not kindly.

'What an extraordinary coincidence. Were you very close?'

'Absolutely. She brought me up, I ran away from home when I was quite young to live with her.'

'And her son Nicolai . . .'

'My uncle Kolya, yes. He was living in Paris by then, but he was very protective towards me, especially when I was starting out in my career. Now –' He made a beautiful gesture of regret. 'My company tours all over the world, but I'm based in New York . . .'

'He hasn't been very well.' Lovat would have put money, a lot of money, on this being news to Alexander Wolfe. Such a shame there was no one to take on the bet.

'Really – I hadn't heard. How sad. My uncle always radiated good health, good living – he used to absolutely glow with it. He's an antique dealer, but the foundation of his business was selling my grandmother's jewels when she first went into exile.' How eager he was to clothe himself in any shred of importance within his reach. This was a man with an ineradicable sense that in the judgement of serious men he was worthless. He was like an orphan, all sham swagger betrayed by his hunger for care and protection.

'It was quite strange seeing that portrait, and seeing her in her diamonds at last. She always talked about them.' He shook his head. The melancholy seemed genuine, but Wolfe had the curse of a highly persuasive manner; he was so compelling that he believed himself, and therefore could not discriminate between his own real emotion and play-acting.

'Kolya must have sold those very diamonds.'

'No, there you must be wrong. The story in the family was that in the Revolution the best diamonds – the Orlov diamonds which her protector gave her – had to be left behind in her safe.'

A notion appeared in Lovat's mind which he at once rejected. Undaunted, it restated itself in more elaborate form. It was irresistible, he had to comply. The more he considered it, the more flawless it seemed. It begged to be executed.

'Whoever has them now is sitting on a goldmine.' Be cool, be noncommittal. This man may be stupid but he may not be naive.

'Well, I suppose so many diamonds are worth quite a bit.'

'Oh, but that necklace would be worth more than just the

value of the stones – far more. Ten times, a hundred times
more. It's a historic piece. They belonged to Prince Orlov, I
take it, the descendant of the lover of Catherine the Great. If
it ever went on sale it would be worth a huge sum –
probably the most historic piece of jewellery outside the
royal collections of Europe.'

Childlike, the grey eyes widened. 'I don't believe anyone
has it now. Grandmère' – one word of French, but remarkably well spoken – 'believed the necklace was exactly where
she left it. She said she wanted me to have it, when she died.
I'd even gone off and looked for her old house, and it was
still there. She drew me a map of all the rooms, with the safe
marked on them.'

'When was that, when you found it was still there?'

'Sixty-eight, sixty-nine . . .'

'And where was it, do you remember that?'

Wolfe assumed a sly look, absurd on a face which was not
able to register any mental process in detail. 'What a lot of
questions – are you interrogating me?'

'Not at all. Forgive me, I'm fascinated by the story. The
idea of that magnificent treasure just lying undiscovered for
seventy years . . . I don't deal in jewellery myself, but if I did
I'd be dying to get my hands on it.'

'Would that be possible?'

'Oh yes. Look, this isn't the best place for a proper
conversation – come and see me at the gallery tomorrow,
have lunch if you're free – and we can talk it through.'

Wolfe appeared promptly at midday and toured the
pictures in the manner of a five-star general inspecting troops:
leisurely, condescending, uttering a few encouraging mono-
syllables through barely parted lips. He was nervous and at
pains to hide it.

Lovat hardly recalled Kusminsky's judgement on him.

'What makes man become gigolo? He's lazy, he's a *tapette* – at the bottom, he wants to deny what really he is. That is my nephew – he thinks he desires woman like young dog thinks he wants tin can tied to car bumper. Making much noise, make whole street look at him, never see that he does not desire her at all, that is not his sexuality. I try, I Kolya, his uncle, I talk to him, but always he deny this. And then woman come with money – he goes. Then another one, and another one. Now he is women's dream, that's all.'

Cheri Tuttlingen had been less analytical. 'He's been telling my friend he needs ten million for the next season – I mean, no cock is worth that much, right?'

In another man's company, insecurity was written all over Wolfe. The only fear Lovat had for his scheme was that the man would not have the guts to act. Lovat assumed command of the lunch, took him to Harry's Bar and noted the looks he gathered from a table of property-developers' wives who tossed their hair and flicked about their salads, restless like antelope scenting a lion.

'Leningrad people are quite passionate about their heritage, I expect you know. While the rest of the country was pulling down statues, they went to extraordinary lengths to preserve the Imperial palaces, for instance.' Lovat ordered a magnificent bottle of wine and watched him drink it as if it were Coca-Cola. 'What I'm thinking is that if Kusminskaya's house was intact in the late Sixties, and it was presumably in that lovely old part of the city which has been preserved intact, then it will be there today. You could go and simply claim your birthright. If your grandmother left a will you might even be able to do it legally – the Foreign Office negotiated with Shevardnadze a couple of years ago for claims for foreign assets seized in the Revolution to be settled.' He watched Wolfe's mobile face closely. No, there was no will. 'Even without a paper claim, it shouldn't be too much trouble. I'm sure you've found how easy it is to bribe the Russians.'

'Oh sure, but then what would I do with it? I'd have trouble smuggling it into the States . . .'

'There are ways . . . if it was my problem, I'd sell in France, where they're not so hot on paperwork. But through a British auction house – there's one which is developing a special interest in Russia, Berrisford's. And I'd take it straight to their new business director, Bianca Berrisford, but don't be fobbed off with anyone junior.'

A haze of Giorgio announced the entry of Evgenia Panopoulis, sixteen-year-old daughter of a Greek banker and an American socialite, whose coal-black eyes smouldered on the cover of the current issue of *Vogue*. She paused by their table, Lovat rose to greet her and she lingered at his side, fingering her snaking black curls, complimenting Wolfe on his past season in New York and angling for an invitation for the next. Once he named a theatre and suggested she look him up her smile raked the corner of the room like a lighthouse beam and she almost skipped away.

'Nice kid – but that was so embarrassing,' Wolfe confided. 'I don't even know when we'll be able to open. Our last show was a smash, the first time we've ever been a hit in New York and we've got a great programme in preparation now, but I'm kind of uncertain about the backer.' He sighed again. It seemed to him to be the greatest of human tragedies that all passion was finite. He manipulated a natural end to his affairs, and no woman had ever left him, but there was a first time for everything and the more generous women were in the beginning, the more embittered they seemed to become at the end. The widow was grateful to him for lightening the first years of her bereavement, but what they had was dead now. His need to fall in love again was pressing, but not with a child like Evgenia; he liked confident, independent women, who controlled their own lives and of course their own money. It would be too humiliating to run after an heiress. 'Where were we? You think I should look up this Mrs Berrisford?'

'I happen to know she's very interested in this market at the moment, and jewellery is something she knows a lot about. Let me write down the number for you . . . but don't tell her I sent you. She's my ex-wife, and we're going through a bad patch right now.' It galled him to admit to the hostilities, but if he glossed over the situation there were a dozen people who could relate it to Wolfe and he would then become suspicious.

'Seems like you aren't having much luck in that area right now.'

'And by the way, she also does business with Kolya Kusminsky.' Lovat considered that he had disclosed enough for one day.

'I get you.'

Bianca's secretary could not find a window in her diary for three weeks; she mentioned a board meeting, but Wolfe mentioned Kusminsky's name and explained that he was due back in New York as soon as possible; apologetically, she suggested 8 a.m. on any weekday. 'Tomorrow will be fine,' he told her, eager to appear unimpressed.

Bianca enjoyed breakfast meetings. The office was quiet, concentration was better, much more could be accomplished. And much needed to be done now. Her father, once so tentative on the subject of loans, had finally taken the bit between his teeth. The loans outstanding to buyers at the end of the financial year totalled almost ten million pounds, more than half of which represented a single borrowing by a

Chicago entrepreneur whose affairs at the time were the subject of a government inquiry. The word was that the man would be bankrupt, and that interest rates would be rising in the coming twelve months. With its slender reserves, Berrisford's faced a cash-flow crisis.

Hugh had struck the pose of a high-minded gentleman whose financial ineptitude ought to have been foreseen by his colleagues. He intended to resign as managing director. Several of her colleagues had pressed Bianca to accept nomination in his place. They cited the continuity of the family name, her modern profile, her successes in the past years but she, whose eyes saw more clearly the more she accomplished, knew that the men had smelt a change in the commercial climate. They were looking for a fall guy, holding her responsible for her father's foolishness, reasoning that a woman would not feel failure so badly.

The stranger who had wanted so urgently to see her was late. When he arrived, she was preoccupied with the figures on which she had been working, and since he said nothing arresting in the first ten minutes she was barely aware of him. He talked in a general way of doing business in Russia, mentioned that he spoke the language and, with his dance company, occasionally toured there or visited on cultural exchanges. When he rolled out his background like a precious carpet and pointed out the highlights she gradually became intrigued.

He was remarkably easy to talk to. He admired the decor of the building, the charm of her secretary. As if he felt he had talked too much about himself, he drew her out, asking questions that were uncannily well aimed at pains she hardly knew were nagging her. He saw her force immobility into her soft lower lip as it began to quiver when she mentioned her divorce, and her eyes softened as she talked about her children. She was like some noble, wounded bird. He longed to give her back her wholeness. His eyes spontaneously paid tribute to her beauty – the way her hair sprang from her temples, the slant of her nostrils, the pale skin with its fine, almost dusty texture, the delicate shadows of her neck above her loose silk blouse of steel blue.

In good time he worked the conversation back to Russia; she explained the difficulties of doing business in a country where profit was an unknown principle and bank statements were still handwritten. They discussed the excitement of *glasnost*, the chaos and uncertainty. Perhaps, he suggested, she needed a consultant?

Again, he was accurate. She needed at least a courier to take in the cash payments to Russian dealers. Nothing about this man inspired confidence. To Bianca's hypersensitive faculties he was obviously nervous, intimidated by the whole enterprise, and not particularly honest, but somehow the pressing business of the morning seemed less urgent. It was around 11 a.m. when she identified the long-forgotten feeling simmering in her belly.

He asked her to lunch, suggesting Harry's Bar. It was instantly obvious that he was not a member, did not know it was a club, and probably could not afford it, but instead of correcting him she found herself smiling softly and saying that she preferred the nearby Italian trattoria. They looked helplessly at each other over two halves of roast grouse, wondering how the meal would end.

He was moved when he talked about his grandmother's death – the imminence of love always made him a little morbid – and she touched his arm in sympathy, feeling the hard, rounded shape of muscle. His loose clothes only accentuated the density of his body.

Normally, Wolfe would never expect to make love to a

woman the same day he met her. He cherished the slow burning of emotions, the tension that would finally erupt in seething, devouring sensuality. But he had no money for courtship, only a return air ticket which he could trade if he was able to stay in London. The widow had taken separate rooms at the hotel. She was lunching in the country, but would be back in the evening. All these considerations churned in the dark confusion of his mind, not quite acknowledged. In the full light of consciousness, all he knew was that he was in love.

Outside the restaurant he drew her tentatively into his arms, felt the immediate yielding of her body and so kissed her. When they drew apart she was shivering.

'I don't know what this is, what I'm feeling. You're not offended, are you?'

'No. Did I feel as if I was offended?' Her eyes were wide and dark, deep as forest pools.

'No Oh, no.' He had no words for the dynamic force he could feel in her body, the vibrating energy in the soft flesh, the arms winding around his neck. 'You feel . . .' He kissed her again and sucked her tongue into his mouth. How strong his lips were, how delicately they moved. Impossible not to imagine them roaming over her body, nuzzling every sensitive part. 'You feel wonderful,' he concluded in a weak voice. 'I must see you – when can I see you?'

'I don't know, I'm needed in the office . . .' The board meeting was tomorrow, and the fall-out from it would tie her up for days. He pulled her hand to his chest. His nipples were violently reactive, but he was too shy to tell her so for fear of seeming strange or effeminate. She felt the intake of his breath against half the length of her body. 'Now. It has to be now.'

Being in his hotel room, a gust of fear overcame her. The

force of the attraction he aroused was terrifying; she imagined that her whole life would be overturned by it, but she could not turn back. She was tired of self-sacrifice. This was what she wanted, needed, deserved. It would be hers alone. He found some champagne, kissed her hands and licked her fingers while she recovered her courage and grew impatient to go wherever this golden impulse might lead.

His flesh was straining for hers, to touch, enter, merge with her, to strike the essence of her and pound it until it combined with his, atom linking with atom. At the moment of penetration they were still and quiet, pausing with a single will to feel the act of union as if with each individual nerve.

Bianca felt her flesh parted for the first time since Lizzie's birth, now obeying a different instinct, hot and receptive. Then she had given, now she would be given to. She was being reborn, regenerated from inside to out. His body glowed under her hands, the muscles like the hard ripples carved in sand by waves, his movements fluid and free.

Before he came, Alex made a bargain with God. Give me this woman, but *give* her, all of her, body, mind and spirit, give me this woman and take the rest of my life. Then his mind melted down, stars burst against his eyelids, he heard himself scream, felt Bianca's back arch and the divine crushing tension of orgasm. The bargain had been struck before, but it seemed that both parties conspired to forget it.

The next day when she assumed the leadership of Berrisford's, Bianca put forward a plan for the coming year which rested on two planks: sweeping retrenchment, and concentration on new markets where stock was cheap to acquire. 'We need to do real business, and to prune our ambitions. And we need to get away from the most inflated categories fast – I wouldn't be happy to have another large Impressionist sale in the next year or even two. My aim is for a period of quiet, honest turnover to re-establish our stability.' They agreed easily, too easily, and afterwards Martin Pownall saw her privately and offered to take early retirement.

'Martin, are you volunteering to be the first rat?' It sounded almost flirtatious, but her eyes were fierce. He waffled, surprised to have been so thoroughly understood. 'I can't keep you if you want out. And if you do, it would be better if you went as soon as possible.'

'Yes, I agree . . . we'll work out the details as fast as possible . . .'

'I mean now, Martin. If there's anything personal you need we can ask your secretary to bring it over in the morning.'

He was stunned into stillness, only his fingers twitched in anxiety. 'But Bianca, we haven't fallen out, have we? I don't want to leave on bad terms. We go back a few years now, you and I . . .' For the first time, Pownall understood why Lovat Whitburn acted with such suicidal vindictiveness towards his former wife. She was a villain, that was the only fair description.

'Of course we do, and I don't want this either. But for the sake of the firm, of morale, it is the best way. There's no bad feeling here, believe me.' How many times she had heard her father use the same formula to blow up the emotional foundation of an argument.

When he flung open the door to leave it almost hit Alexander Wolfe in the face. Nevertheless, as soon as they were alone, Alex took Bianca into his arms and said nothing until he had re-established their physical connection. In time, he commented, 'That man was angry.'

'He's a traitor and he didn't like me telling him so, that's all.'

The clarity, the strength – admiration dazzled him. 'What happened today? Did it go as you planned?'

'Yes. And I've put the big Russian sale into the diary for next summer. So you're hired for a buying trip next month. Run all that about your grandmother's necklace by me over dinner, yes?'

It was the best decision for Berrisford's. It was the best decision for him. It seemed to Bianca to be the best decision for her as well, but the symmetry of the affair disturbed her.

CHAPTER 19

Petrograd, 1917

'What shall we call it, that degree of virtuosity when the dancer's body no longer needs to obey its own laws, where it overcomes itself, becomes transfigured? There's no expression in Russian, shall we create one in French? ... Perhaps we could say that it makes itself a glorious entity – *se faire un corps glorieux*?' The French Ambassador, Monsieur Paléologue, appealed to his guests, his starched shirt crackling as his chest swelled with delight at his cleverness.

'Oh, so eloquent! What a sublime imagination you possess, Your Excellency.' Karsavina, to whom his bouquet of semantic pleasantry was offered, clapped her gloved hands softly while Bruce, the pale young English diplomat whom she had recently married, murmured, 'Quite so, yes, imagination!' and added his own applause.

'Well, what can I do? To celebrate midwinter we have delayed our luncheon to embrace the hour of sunset. We have moved our table to the window which, of all those in the most splendid embassy of my career, offers us the best view of your majestic river, but alas! The sun is too modest to lay aside its draperies of cloud and perform for us.' Three years of war had been a worthy challenge to Monsieur Paléologue's highly cultivated aptitude for pleasure. While the city, rechristened Petrograd to disclaim its numerous ties to the enemy Germans, was engulfed in a turmoil of rumours, shortages, panic and lawlessness, he strove to keep his large acquaintance in good spirits.

Each week he entertained on a different theme, turning to

account the possibilities of his embassy; for today he had decreed The Sixty-degree Luncheon, with the intention of wringing the utmost enjoyment from the meteorological phenomenon peculiar to that latitude in winter, namely twilight at noon followed by sunset at 3 p.m., accompanied by a subtle, unearthly display of light and colour as the rays surrendered their strength to the frozen and saturated air.

'Oh – but last week, when you opened your ballroom for us so that we might enjoy the tapestries while we dined! That was unforgettable! After that, your friends could ask nothing more of you.' Tata was smiling, but was perfectly serious nonetheless. She adored the French Ambassador. A few weeks ago he had recounted to her the details of the assassination of Rasputin, adding all the dramatic points which to her mind spelt veracity, the writhing form whom poison could not master nor bullets kill, the body thrown into the river with bound hands but recovered, some days later, with the right hand on the left shoulder, the last position of the sign of the cross. Now the times grew more disjointed each day, she was inclined to believe nothing unless His Excellency said it was so and had a masterly story to prove it.

'You are too kind, but myself I was so looking forward to the spectacle. The enormous shadows growing longer and longer behind the tiniest lump of snow, the seabirds wheeling restlessly across the burnished sky, the last red rays stealing across the ice . . .'

'Like raspberries and cream?' The Englishman was clearly delighted with his own imaginative feat.

'Something more melancholy – and yet, the sunset is never *triste* here in the North, don't you find? The land is so well acquainted with the night, it welcomes the darkness like an old friend. I find the sunsets here in Petrograd are full of hope, more like the dawn in my own country . . .'

573

'So here you would disagree with Pompey, that more worship the rising than the setting sun?' Orlov was a frequent guest at the French Ambassador's parties, and like the rest of the company cherished the man for his gifts as a host. He was an exquisite product of his own superior civilization, but recently his ability to amuse had grated with the Prince. 'But what of our dawn here on the Neva – is our dawn full of hope?'

'Your Highness, I am a lover of the future. Whatever convulsions may take place, I have absolute trust in humanity to save itself, to elevate itself, to overcome all sufferings, defeat all enemies in pursuit of its highest good.' He concluded this flowery evasion with a small, involuntary bow.

'Even Russians? On the basis of my own observations, self-preservation is an instinct which occurs only rarely among *Homo sapiens* at Latitude Sixty.'

Paléologue wagged his finger as if at an excessively flirtatious woman. 'You will not make me call your people beasts, Your Highness. When it comes to humanity, I consider that the Russian can teach the rest of the world the true meaning of the word.'

'I heard they sang the Marseillaise at the opera last night.' The Englishman was anxious to steer the conversation into more cheerful waters.

'Ah yes! I have never heard it sung so magnificently. Your great bass, Chaliapin, led the whole house. Tears choked everybody. Such deep emotion. Even in France I have never felt it. This morning I sent a cable to Paris: "Chaos everywhere. No information. Chaliapin magnificent. Situation normal."' The company laughed and exchanged rueful shrugs.

'We are artists – it's our privilege to inspire the war-weary people. But I think we ourselves are truly fortunate in these

574

dark days to feel the steady, optimistic pulse of our allies beating in the hearts of our companions. Emotional instability is our curse in Russia, we need to be with rational Western spirits or we will lose our minds.' Tata turned to Orlov; her eyes were brimming with tears even now. 'I am doubly blessed, of course, with my dear husband, and you have that sweet English girl under your roof too. And His Excellency, always so well informed, is a beacon to light our darkness.'

Orlov sighed. He too was well informed. 'We are sustained, certainly, but patriotism has become rather a luxury. So indeed, have many of the necessities of life for our people. Chocolate is ten roubles a bar now, shoes more than a hundred roubles, factory wages less than thirty-five a month. At those prices I don't know that an ordinary man would be sustained even by company such as we have here tonight.'

'Ah, indeed. Dear Niki, you're so involved. We are living in an enchanted world, it's true. The only things in good supply right now are talk and newspapers. So tell me, dearest Niki, I have been invited to dance our new production in Kiev – do you think I should go?' She balanced her pointed chin on her graceful hand and gave him an interrogatory smile.

The Englishman leaned protectively over his new wife and added, 'Tell her not to go, Your Highness. It would be madness, surely?'

'The depths of the country have been stirred and the bottom is rising to the top now. Men are deserting at the front . . .'

'Just a few, surely.' Paléologue knew the truth as well, but would not alarm his guests nor offer an unpalatable fact to his host country.

'Thousands. Perhaps – well, quite certainly, hundreds of

thousands. Simple men, trusting, illiterate, foolish – our noble peasant in his millions. I can't blame them, their officers sent them to their deaths rather than deal with their committees. And who can blame the officers? Every one of the men's grievances is absolutely genuine, anywhere else in the civilized world their conditions would be a scandal. What can the officers do? Nothing. But wash down our doorstep and invite Fritz to come in – ah no. After all there is a war to be fought. So – forward! Victory or death!'

'If you don't blame the officers' – the exculpation was heresy to Bruce, schooled as he had been from infancy in the obligations of the officer class – 'whom do you blame?'

'Myself. My peers. We are at the end of the chain of command, we must be responsible. Peasants are truly like beasts, but noble beasts. Like horses, they can sense the limit of their understanding, and they know that it is you who rule their world. Your responsibility is to care for them. And we failed.'

'But what has become of the deserters? Surely they just bolt back home?' The Englishman's eyes were a little bloodshot; he had drunk well of the champagne and the fine wines, and was now finishing with brandy. Orlov imagined his own words, filtered through alcohol, in tomorrow's dispatch to London.

'You can see scores of them here in Petrograd, they're the ones who're even thinner than our own folk. They've come to be in on the real action. The rest of them – they're thousands of miles from their homes, and some of them have nothing to return to in any case. They're swilling around the country like flotsam, stirred up by Bolsheviks, maddened with hunger . . .' His voice died away. He was boring the party, an unforgivable crime. Better to keep his gloomy opinions to himself.

576

'Tata, my dear, I would not alarm you for the world, but there may be worse hazards in Kiev than deserters turned bandits. When will you travel?'

'Early in February.'

'Before the thaw – well, that's on your side. But I believe that Russia herself may be breaking up. The reports we have at the Ministry tell us that every province in this nation is restive – the Finns, the Poles, the Cossacks, the Ukrainians, Siberia, the Caucasus – in every region nationalists are stirring up the people. The Ukraine has even sent their own peace delegation to the enemy. In a few weeks you may need your passport to go to Kiev – I'm serious, it can happen.'

'So I'm right,' Bruce persisted, 'she should refuse to go?'

'But who is asking our Tata to go, and could they be a good friend in the future?' Their host left his dark, disappointing windows and came to join them, picking a grape from the arrangement of fruit in the table centre as he went. 'You may be glad of the permit to travel in the future. And – you may soon be in more danger here. I hear there is now a government committee on the evacuation of Petrograd. There are enough people here who think that if the Germans took the city it would be a blessing, because the Soviets would be destroyed and so would the Baltic fleet, the worst red cell in all the forces.'

'Oh, dear! Why is life so impossible! Please, Niki, give me some proper advice.'

'My proper advice would be that if you believe that there will be no revolution before the end of the war, then go to Kiev, because I know that peace cannot be concluded before the end of the year.'

'I can't bear it! "If I die you will lose your son and your throne in six months!" That was what he said, wasn't it, Rasputin? We can't let that ghastly man's words come true.'

577

'Speaking personally, I'm quite certain there will be no revolution before peace.' Paléologue thought that when women started repeating Rasputin's curses it was only chivalrous to reassure them. All the diplomats in Petrograd kept their doubts to themselves in Russian company. Nevertheless, the Frenchman gave Orlov a keen look, suddenly anxious to sound his opinion more deeply.

Orlov felt that there was nothing to be lost by candour. 'There speaks a Western mind. This is Russia, we don't obey the same rules – anything can happen here. Everything I know of our past, everything I have studied in the past of ancient civilizations, has taught me that a state can reach a critical point of instability beyond which it won't be able to recover. I believe that Russia is close to that point.'

'There you are.' Bruce took his wife's hand. 'Now will you be sensible?'

'But darling, I know how much it would mean to the people for me to go. And after all, I am an artist, it's what I have to do. I've been coddled all my life' – with an exquisitely expressive sweep of her arm she included the magnificent room – 'so that I can perform. And it may be just bread and circuses, but it's my duty and I can't think of my safety any more than a soldier can.' Karsavina was at the height of her powers and the pinnacle of acclaim. In the old days, Orlov would simply have called up a company of men to escort this national treasure through any local trouble, but throughout the winter there had been riots in the city; the best regiments were already at the front, and he could not pledge his help for the future with any certainty.

The optimists, a dwindling class, had predicted that the winter would freeze the rebellion to death, but it was many-headed like a hydra, and every head crushed grew back as two. There was no Hercules to kill it.

Orlov was tired. It was the unnatural fatigue of living in falsehood. His daily business consisted of dealing in monstrous half truths. The table before him was covered with real lace, swagged with silk ribbons and decorated with posies of forget-me-nots forced in the hot-house. It was laid with silver-gilt cutlery copied from Catherine the Great's service preserved in the Hermitage museum, and set with Limoges porcelain. They had eaten foie gras, *quenelles de brochet* and wild duck. Later, he was bidden by Countess Witte, the wife of a former prime minister, to a charity gala in aid of the Disabled Soldiers' Workshop, where Fokine and Kchessinskaya were to dance in the first act of *Don Quixote*.

From the beginning of the war his army – for he thought of it as his although the army, under General Kornilov, now thought of the whole of Russia as its own property – his army had stood against the Germans without arms and without rations. The railways, instead of providing swift, reliable transport for men and supplies, had all but broken down. The men had been heroic, they had been defeated, many had been killed and the survivors reviled by their allies, especially the French, for their lack of victories. When he saw his careful plans sabotaged by rivals and botched by fools, Orlov had despaired.

He left the gay party as early as he dared, dismissed his driver and walked, slipping and even falling on the snow and thin ice. It was around five o'clock, the time at which thousands of men left the vast, barrack-like offices of the government to make their way home. They were for the most part middle-aged or more, stooped from a lifetime at their desks, subdued by the interminable waiting for dead men's shoes, but each according to his rank wearing the splendid uniform prescribed by Tsar Peter the Great, with the imperial eagle on every button.

The small roads were quiet; people were afraid of deserted corners and preferred the safety of crowded avenues. Voices from the distant streets, muffled and distorted, echoed through the cold air and across the watery spaces of the city. A young woman was screaming 'Pavlusha! Where are you? Come out, it's not a game!' He heard the thin young calls of 'Down with the government!' answered with 'Power to the Soviets!' Lowing like cattle, the resonant voices of working men chanted, 'Cabbage, porridge – our life is hopeless.'

As he approached the bridge over the little Moika river he saw a gang of gaunt and ragged men burst suddenly from a side street on the far bank. As he passed below a street light the first was clearly hiding something under his coat as he fled. After them came two young boys, then older men, and finally women, a small and infuriated crowd, with four men of the city police in an automobile behind them, but too late to prevent the marauders scattering with their prize.

'Looters! Why don't the police shoot them?'

'Is that all? I thought they were German spies.' Gasping for breath, the pursuers gathered on a street corner.

'What did they get?' Orlov demanded of the boy who had led the chase, a child with a shrivelled, monkey face who, when he spoke, seemed much older than his size suggested.

'Our boots, Sir.' Two tears fell from his eyes. He smeared them aside with a grimy hand. 'All we had in the shop. They just came in and took them. My mother will kill me. She only left us for a minute.'

'Only a Jewish shop.' People drifted away, feeling the cold after their exertion.

'God save the Tsar! Beat the Jews!'

'Right! God save the Tsar!'

He gave the snivelling child a coin and continued on his way. A few hundred yards further on, near to Rimsky-

Korsakov Street, the deep silence of wealth prevailed. He had formed the habit of visiting his son here every evening, not only because he craved as Tata did the reassurance of a foreign presence in the governess, but also, in those dangerous days, because his only offspring had become acutely dear to him. When he was alone and thought he could feel death breathing on the back of his neck, Orlov craved company and the sight of his child.

'Papa,' his son greeted him, 'you must tell Charlotte not to cheat when she plays Lotto with me. I have thought about it a lot today. I know Mamasha cheated but I don't think it's right that a governess should cheat, do you?'

The nurserymaid took Orlov's coat with its high sable collar and brought slippers which bore his family arms in petit point. 'But this is a grave allegation, Kolya. May I ask how you know Charlotte is cheating?'

'She always wins, Papa, she must be cheating.'

A suppressed smile hovered at the corners of the governess's small mouth as she resumed her seat at the opposite side of the hearth. The little family had taken to living in the morning room, a pleasant chamber at the rear of the ground floor, the chairs protected by slipcovers of fresh blue and green cotton.

'I am not cheating, Kolya, I told you before. I've just stopped letting you win, that's all. You're seven years old now, you could beat me if you tried.'

The child glowered at her. Kolya was a fine boy, fleshy, sturdy, round-faced, with curly hair and a mouth like a Cupid's bow. His eyelids curved decisively, so the upper edge of the iris of each eye was always obscured, giving him a baleful look. 'You made my armour wrong,' he accused her in a sulky voice.

'I know you don't like your armour, but the poem says

"damascened gold armour wrought by a cunning Saracen",
and that's what I made you.'

Discarded in the corner lay a breastplate and greaves of
card, painted yellow and elaborately decorated with black
ink cross-hatching to look like Moorish filigree. 'Why, it's
magnificent armour, Kolya. Don't you like it?' Orlov found
the helmet under a chair and held it up to admire the work.
'Saladin himself would have been grateful to have such a
skilled armourer.' He noticed Charlotte blush.

'It isn't like the picture in the book.' Kolya was fascinated
by one of Pushkin's fables, 'The Son of Wise Oleg'. It was a
morbid story, concerning a warrior prince who banished his
beloved horse after a wizard prophesied that the animal
would be his death. 'Look, Papa, in the picture Oleg has
chain mail.'

'That's quite likely, chain mail was a Saracen invention.
But damascened decoration is inlaid, and that can't be done
on mail. So here I think the illustrator is at fault, not your
governess. And why do you suppose we call it damascened?'

The child's keen eyes searched his face for clues. 'Oh, I
know! From Damascus. Read, Papa, read it again, *please!*'

'Won't you read it to me tonight?'

Reluctantly, the boy reached for the book, but Charlotte
said, 'Our little prince is worn out this evening. In the park
today he was unhorsed in his pursuit of the ruthless hordes
and wounded in both knees.'

'I hope his wounds were borne bravely.'

'I did not shed one tear, Papa. Don't listen to Charlotte,
she always lies.'

'You must speak of your governess with respect, Kolya. If
you want me to read to you, you must apologize to her
first.'

The house had acquired a new atmosphere under the hand

of the English governess. Without Lydia's careless extravagance to disorder things, with the most ostentatious rooms closed, and the war forcing a new way of life on the city, the whole household had an air of bourgeois industry which amused Orlov immensely because his mistress would have scorned it.

The dacha which he had settled on Lydia had become a convalescent home for servicemen, and almost all the staff had been sent to tend the patients. All but two of the horses had also been placed at the service of the wounded heroes, but in exchange Charlotte had surprised him by asking for a cow, a milkmaid and some chickens. He had laughed, thinking of her as a bluestocking, not knowing that her anxious mother in London had written to advise such measures, and not foreseeing that her practical request would prove so wise.

The animals now lived in luxury in the stables and gave the household enough milk and eggs to spare. In the hot house the orchids had been packed into a dim corner, and melons, tomatoes, cucumbers and marrows grew in large pots. The remaining servants, to whom such prudence was almost witchcraft, looked upon the governess with superstitious respect.

While he was reading, Charlotte heard a tap at the door and stepped into the corridor, where the kitchenmaid stood in frightened defiance, twisting her apron in her reddened fists.

'Ma'am, I can't go again, please don't ask me to. I'm not shirking, honest I'm not, just don't ask me to go again.'

'Go where, you silly girl?'

'For sugar, Ma'am. Cook says I must go and my boots won't stand up to it, I swear they won't. Those hours of waiting in the snow and rain. They're splitting as it is, Ma'am . . .'

'But Lena, we must have sugar. How will we make tea without it?'

'Oh . . .' The girl's dull eyes were vexed with the effort of thought. 'I don't know, Ma'am, it didn't come to my mind to ask.'

'Go again tomorrow, Lena, and when you come back we will send your boots to be mended. How's that?'

'But Ma'am . . .'

'I can't send Mischa with you again. He's too old, it will surely kill him.'

'Oh but I'm so feared to go by myself, Ma'am.' Stolid as her nature was, the girl was working herself into hysterics. 'Must I go? Can't it be Ilze's turn again . . .'

'That wouldn't be fair, now would it? Perhaps, though, you and Ilze could both go. It will mean more suffering in one way, but you will be able to keep your courage up better if you are together. Send Ilze to me and I'll explain. And suggest to Cook that she sends to inquire of our neighbours – maybe a man will be going from their houses – you'd feel safer then, wouldn't you?'

'Oh, Ma'am, bless you . . .' The girl darted forward and kissed Charlotte's hand. 'You're so wise and good, Ma'am. I don't know where we would all be without you.'

'What was that about?' Orlov appeared in the doorway. Wan and careworn as his face had become in the past months, she still considered him a fine-looking man, especially in his dress uniform. He looked amused, which he seldom did now. She knew that he thought her ridiculous for talking reasonably to the servants when to be shouted at was what they needed.

'Run along, Lena.' The girl, who had been gawping fearfully at their master, curtsied and waddled away, her square hips shimmying in agitation. 'The younger maids take it in turns to queue. Lena is going for sugar for us in the morning and she didn't want to go, that's all.'

'Did I hear something about boots?'

'You did, but that's not the real reason. The queue for sugar forms earlier and earlier, there are people there before dawn, and she's afraid to go out in the dark. And when the post boy called this morning, he stirred them all up downstairs with stories of another bread riot last night.' Charlotte did not consider it proper to elaborate. On her way to the last sugar queue, the nurserymaid had been set upon and raped by a group of rioters and Lena feared the same fate.

'Tell her not to be afraid, I'll send someone over.' Orlov indicated the slumped figure of his son in the corner of a chair. 'You were right, he's exhausted. Shall I carry him up?'

'Why certainly. How good you are to us.' Apart from Mischa the groom, who was elderly and half crippled from a knee kicked to fragments in his youth, the household was entirely female, and Kolya was not a light child.

The nurserymaid dressed the sleepy boy in his nightshirt and put him to bed. Orlov kissed his forehead, and returned to the morning room to sit with Charlotte by the stove. She would not light the fire, since fuel was scarce, supplies sent from the Orlov estates were often stolen by bandits, and the fire's heat was negligible beside the warmth of the stove.

'The boy brought us a letter from Madame this morning, although the postmark is September in France.' She passed him the single page, covered in an angular scrawl, barely decipherable. 'You'll see she says she is still in bed. I fear for her so much. From her letters, she has hardly had a week of good health in the past year.'

'She is well cared for, Charlotte, and in a healthy climate. We can't do anything to help her here in Petersburg. You worry too much.'

'I'm sure she is suffering because you and Kolya are apart from her . . .'

Orlov smiled, thinking that the Englishwoman, all gentleness and fidelity herself, was imputing her own high motives to Lydia. To him, the letter was nothing but hysterical self-pity. He imagined Lydia reclining on her terrace above the Mediterranean, eating candy and sipping lemonade in the sunshine, quite oblivious to the fate of her friends in Russia who were in real danger of freezing or starving to death.

Orlov thought of how Lydia would scoff to see him gossiping in common comfort with a governess, contemplating with satisfaction the slippers she had embroidered for him. She was now working a cover for a footstool, and he would often stay with her for several hours, half reading a book. The two of them might for all the world be some minor provincial bureaucrat and his wife.

Curiosity about an underling, especially a female, was alien to the Prince's way of life. His own household was administered by a steward and he did not expect to hear anything of his servants' personal affairs. The governess was different. Her status was that of an independent employee rather than a serf, but what had stimulated his interest in her was the difference in his son and in their home once Charlotte had control of them.

Lydia had squabbled with her staff; dismissals and departures were frequent, screaming tirades a daily occurrence. Items were often lost, so there had been many accusations of theft. Things were damaged, repairs never done properly. Fires went out, palms withered, the horses went lame.

On his return from London, Orlov had found a different house, one where order reigned, the servants were cheerful and sometimes industrious and there was a general thriving air. Most extraordinary of all was the difference in his son.

Kolya had grown markedly; his temperament seemed more even, his intelligence more mature.

Orlov was so estranged from domestic administration that he almost imagined that a household regulated itself. He was astounded that one woman in a few months could make such a difference, particularly because Charlotte was such a retiring figure. Wanting to understand the enigma, he began to engage her in conversation, and discovered at once that all this was done from adoration of her mistress. She was dazzled by Lydia and barely recognized the selfishness which she had remedied so well. 'Oh dear – if only Madame was here,' she would say when he recounted his bad news or his latest anxieties. 'She has such wit, such a bright spirit, one could never despair with her at home. I'm afraid I must be very boring company in comparison.'

After the first year of the war, when Petrograd's wave of patriotism had subsided and the food shortages began, he noticed her kindness. Half Lydia's acquaintance seemed to know that the household was well provided and its mistress had a warm heart. Karsavina's elderly and simple-minded maid came every morning to collect milk for the dancer's baby son. Marie Nikonova, with two young children, called frequently. One afternoon Orlov noticed a pasty-faced, hollow-chested youth slipping furtively out of the kitchen door; he carried a basket and a bundle, and around his shoulders flapped a coat with a worn collar of ginger fox fur which had once belonged to Davidov, the Prince's valet. 'It is Madame's young brother,' the governess explained when he inquired. 'He came to the door a few weeks ago.'

'I never knew she had family still living.' He had a clear recollection of Lydia installing a tattered photograph in an enamelled frame and sighing over the death of her devoted parents within weeks of each other in a typhoid epidemic.

'I wasn't sure, she hardly ever spoke of them and then always as if they were dead. It seems only that they were too poor to keep her, and became estranged.' Charlotte spoke with a careful lack of emotion. To her, Lydia had maintained with some passion that her mother had thrown her out of their home.

'He might be an impostor, did you think of that?'

'He brought papers to prove the claim, and he seems quite intelligent. A clerk, but with their mother to support, and he coughs all the time, I think he's consumptive. I gave him left-overs and old clothes – I hope you don't mind.'

He began to find beauty in her. She was a neat woman, with even, unremarkable features. The hard climate, instead of draining colour from her face, gave her complexion an even, burnished tone, so that with her dark hair she seemed more Mediterranean than northern in looks. Intelligence gleamed in her eyes, but her face was always placid and her voice seldom raised.

In time he attributed her reserve to a childhood spent caring for her own mother, a semi-invalid, and her four younger siblings. Her parents were both teachers, and seemed to be liberal thinkers who shared the fascination with Russia that was common among the English intelligentsia.

In her late twenties, she ought to have been married, and he suspected that it was her enchantment with Lydia that had prevented it. Before the outbreak of war she had travelled home to London every second year; when he learned that there was a fiancé, some kind of artist, he had offered to send her home, but she had declined in alarm, explaining nothing.

'Then his loss must be our gain,' he agreed at last. 'But think again in the summer, and come to me at once if you change your mind. The Germans may have overrun the Baltic, but they will never dominate the Arctic Sea.'

He rose and went to the writing desk, where every item lay in its place. The letter from Lydia joined the others in the drawer reserved for her correspondence. 'And what did the post bring you, Charlotte? Have you news from home?'

'How kind of you to ask – yes, there were letters for me. My mother is no better. They have no word of my brother, which means he was certainly lost at Verdun. And an arms factory in London blew up with such a terrible noise it was heard far away in the country – as if' – she pinched the bridge of her short, straight nose in thought – 'as if an explosion here were heard in Viborg. Seventy people were killed.'

He nodded. 'Sabotage, no doubt. They'll give out that it was an accident, for the sake of morale. And your Walter?'

The name of her fiancé also seemed to amuse him. 'He is still recovering, but can't think of returning to his regiment yet. He is patient, but I think it's getting him down.' She looked intently down at her needle, knowing she was a bad liar. Orlov would be appalled to know the truth, that the man she was to marry was a pacifist, and in prison. She had invented a chest wound for him early in the war, and pretended ever since that he was in a sanatorium.

'Would he not recover more quickly with a good woman's care?'

'I am sure he has the care of enough good women already.'

'Aren't you worried that he will fall in love with one of them?'

'You're teasing me.'

'Forgive me, I forget how serious you are.' She was seldom ready to laugh – it was her only fault. He changed the subject and they passed the time happily until his driver called at eight. The Countess Witte would not be happy with a donation instead of his presence, but not surprised since he had become a rare figure at the ballet now that his mistress was absent. He did not forget to order the driver to pick out the toughest lad in their stable yard and send him back to see that the maid came to no harm while she waited for their sugar.

A few days later a party of English, French and Italian statesmen arrived. Although in their eyes the war was almost won, the Russians had lost all belief in victory, but talks about peace terms proceeded. Petrograd society, on the edge of abandoning itself to a mood of impending tragedy, elected to believe that Russia's fortunes could be restored by the intervention of their allies, and embarked upon a new round of festivity in their honour. The delegates, already tired and overworked, found the pace intolerable and were grateful for a two-day trip to Moscow, scheduled as relaxation.

Orlov accompanied them. From the train, he noted the signs of famine and looting throughout the countryside. In the city there was outright panic. The British delegation, who outnumbered the other two nationalities even discounting their separate military mission, were invited to a private meeting by the mayor of Moscow and Prince Lvov, the leader of the local government committee. The aristocracy had always played an active part in the district councils; Orlov not only respected Lvov as a social equal, but considered him one of the few men in the country whom he could admire as a politician. He was flattered when his request to be included was agreed.

Lvov spoke with restraint; his manner was characteristically mild and in addition he was plainly exhausted. Lest his condition should rob his words of their strength, he had also prepared a long report. 'In essence, gentlemen, what we are saying is this: if the attitude of the Tsar and his government does not change, we believe there will be a revolution in this country within three weeks. Any new government will be under extreme pressure to take this country out of the war.' He sat back, and the absolute weariness of movement was more eloquent than writing or speech.

Much of the rest of the visit was wasted on an official banquet which lasted five hours, and while the delegates slept on the journey back to Petrograd, Orlov thought of the future and of his son. If Lvov was correct the country would soon be plunged into a period of terror and confusion beside which the darkest days of the French Revolution would appear a tolerable interlude. By no miracle of national rebirth would Russians become capable of the orderly extermination of their aristocrats; he and his peers would become the people's enemies and be destroyed the Russian way: savagely, senselessly and probably in secret.

He was dispassionate on his own behalf. Politically he had committed the fatal error of independent thought, sat on too many fences, made too few friends. He was no Talleyrand, able to sail through storms by trimming his sails to changing winds of opinion. He was simply a misfit, and he knew the fate of such men in history. Already he had suffered accusations of profiteering, and there had been attempts to load the blame for the collapse of the army on to his shoulders. Socially, he was fatally enmeshed in the net of the Imperial Court.

Nothing would save him. Not for one instant, even in the furthest recess of his mind, did he consider for himself the option of flight.

For his son, he thought of nothing else. Kolya must be sent to safety immediately, and Charlotte with him, the house emptied and closed down. Terrible visions emerged in his mind, of the child's corpse, unburied, face down in bloodstained snow, torn by crows and wolves, perhaps even violated by his executioners. He knew that starving men turned to cannibalism, though official reports never admitted it. The fact that the child was not, and never could be, the legitimate heir to the Orlov name made his innocence seem the more tragic. To his patrician mind, he had betrayed his son by conceiving him with a commoner, but could redeem the crime by saving the child from the curse of his noble blood.

In Petrograd, he still did not sleep, but went straight to the Ministry and ordered passes. He called personally on the British Ambassador, saying only that his English governess, a widow, needed urgently to return home with her child. The man understood at once that he was lying, but saw that in his extreme distress the Prince, whom he had always considered an unemotional man, had not even registered his disbelief. Orlov left with an endorsement adding Nicholas, born 1910, to Charlotte's passport and a letter to the captain of a coal ship due to leave the Arctic port of Murmansk in two weeks' time.

He savoured the tranquillity of the house in Rimsky-Korsakov Street for as long as it took him to draw breath before calling for Charlotte and ordering its evacuation.

'Everything precious must be sent to a place of safety. I am going to send you and Kolya to London. It may be dangerous if people know who he is, so he is to travel as your son on your passport. You will go north by railway to Murmansk – there is a navy train scheduled for tomorrow night. You will have an escort, I hope I can find an officer who can be trusted. You must begin packing immediately – the house will be closed after you leave. Don't argue' – he saw that she was about to protest – 'what I have heard in Moscow makes me certain that this is necessary now. You have a passage on a ship to London, only a freighter, but it may be the last one for some time, I had no choice. From there, you must arrange to travel on to Monaco as soon as you can. I am transferring money to an account in London for your journey, but take as many valuables as you can hide in your clothing . . .'

'Surely we won't need . . .'

'Believe me, my dear, we cannot be sure of anything at this moment. Now where is my boy?'

'In the kitchen. Cook is giving him lunch – one of the nurserymaids has run off, and Lena too.'

'So, it's beginning. There will be a general panic soon.'

She nodded, smoothing down her light blue cashmere dress, thinking of what had to be done. 'Heavens, why am I just standing here? We'll never be ready in time.'

'Don't concern yourself with anything except the boy – and your own safety. Don't worry about the house.' He was halfway down the service stairs as he spoke.

A few hours later he came up to the nursery where she was sitting amid piles of clothing making a list. The room was furnished with a narrow bed, where a maid slept at night, a sofa, table and chairs. One corner was the schoolroom, with bookshelves and the desk where Kolya did his lessons. The electricity in that part of the city had long since been cut off, and two oil lamps lit the room.

In the Prince's hands were the contents of the safe, wooden boxes and leather pouches of jewellery, trinkets and gold coins. Kolya, eating bread and jam at the table, gave a cry of excitement as the load was spread before him.

One by one Orlov tipped out the containers and a heap of jewels sparkled in the warm glow of the lamps. Last of all he opened the box containing the diamond necklace.

'I want you to take as much of this as you can.'

'But – we'll have to hide it all.' Her eyes were wide with wonder at the treasure. 'If I'm to travel as myself, and Kolya as my son . . . how would a governess come to own even the smallest thing here?' She picked up a small ruby and diamond ring and held it close to her. Beside a modest woman in simple clothes, it appeared dangerously gaudy.

'It's Kolya's birthright. Who knows, if the worst happens it may be all I can give him.' He stood like a man distracted, his hands at his temples.

One by one she picked out the twelve twigs which Lydia used to decorate place settings at her most lavish dinners. No more than three inches high, they rested in rock-crystal vases carved to seem half full of water, with gold stems and leaves of jade, agate or emerald invisibly hinged so that they trembled realistically at every movement. The first he had given Lydia as an Easter gift, a birch twig with white enamel bark and catkins of spun green gold, and the rest she had commissioned later. 'She was so proud of these. No one had anything like them. Suppose they break?'

'If they break, they will still be gold.'

'But their beauty will be spoiled. If I am found with things like this I wouldn't blame anyone who said I'd stolen them. Maybe if I can sew the small things into our coats . . . unpick the linings and sew things inside. They will be well hidden in the padding.'

She rang for the one remaining nurserymaid, pulled her scissors from her work-basket and set to work. Kolya, already tired, bellowed with rage when she proposed fitting the necklace into his toy lion but soon afterwards, exhausted with emotion, fell so deeply asleep that she was able to pull it out of his arms without disturbing him.

The lion was made of leather which had once been soft and covered with yellow fur. Now it was stiff and mostly bald. Delicately, she cut open the stitches at the animal's belly, pulled out some of the cotton stuffing and tried to manoeuvre the stiff band of diamonds inside. After half an hour of slow and careful manipulation, she gave up. 'All that for nothing. I'll have to think of something else. Let's hope I can make the poor thing look as if it had never been touched.'

'Can you get this in?' He picked up the jewelled birch twig; she measured against the toy, wrapped it in a piece of lint and pushed it into the stuffing.

He had intended to leave and return in the morning, but the habit of her company was strong. The maid fell asleep over her portion of sewing and was sent to bed. Once she had left them, Charlotte asked, 'What is to become of the staff?'

He had not given this subject any thought at all. 'When you've gone, they can leave. They'll be paid off, of course.'

'But old Mischa . . . he has no family, you know.' She cut her thread, laid aside a coat with small brooches in its hem and began to snip at one of the boy's caps.

'I'll take care of him. He's as good as a veterinarian, with his cures and lotions. He can live out his days in our mews.' As he spoke, he wondered for how long the Orlov mews with its famous greys would continue to exist.

'And the milkmaid? She's halfwitted, but she was promised to a lad in the village before the war.'

'I'll send her back – she can travel with the next ambulance.'

'You won't forget?' She looked at him as if to will him to remember, then licked the end of a fresh thread. Her lips closed on it gently, the upper folded slightly over the lower.

'For the love of God, they aren't your concern, why are you bothering about them now?' He saw that she was scared, and regretted his harshness. 'Forgive me. Please don't be worried. No one will be overlooked.'

'And you? What will you do?'

'What I have to. Nothing. I don't know.'

She racked her brains for conversation. 'Marie Nikonova visited us this morning. A tram driver had stopped to let her cross the road and called out "Come along, Comrade". She was terribly upset – quite hysterical.' At this he laughed, and she was encouraged.

After a while he fetched a map and showed her the railway line and the port, then explained to her all the documents he had prepared, the travel permits, letters and references. Fear made them both short-tempered. She argued, he snapped at her, they apologized, over and over again, intimacy like a sticky web binding them together the more they struggled. All the time she kept up the rhythm of cutting and stitching, and the heap of jewels grew smaller until only the necklace, the little copse of eleven twigs, and a thin, misshapen gold bangle were left. It was midnight when she stood up and stretched her arms towards the ceiling.

'My eyes are too tired, I can't see well enough. There is time to finish in the morning, isn't there?' It would be her last night under that roof.

He rose also, thinking that their amiable quarrelling was even more like the behaviour of a dreary married couple.

Neither of them intended what followed. The dreams of death which had possessed Orlov awakened a primitive need which suddenly overpowered him. He reached for her, held her around the waist, pulled her towards him, looked into her luminous eyes and sensed that fear had stirred her blood also. A gasp of shock was forced from her. His hands felt the breath leave her chest, saw the tremor under her dress that was her heartbeat, felt the warmth of her parted lips against his cheek.

They paused, shivering, knowing what was to come.

'You have been so dear to me,' he whispered.

'And you to me.' Her voice was so low he barely heard it. She lifted her head and the last shreds of control parted. They kissed as if to suck the life from each other, and a frenzied desire took light and consumed them. Charlotte remembered the moment for the rest of her life. The force of her own passion terrified her. She had always denied and evaded, damped down her inner fires and starved them of fuel. Now she tore away clothing, both his and her own, opened out her body to him without shame and gave herself to the violence of her instincts.

At that moment when she felt on the verge of dying, she heard screaming, her own voice, and remembering the child pulled Orlov's hand to her mouth. In their ecstasy he felt nothing when she bit through the fleshy edge of his palm. They looked in amazement at the smeared blood in the morning.

Through the small window, a ray of pale sunlight slowly strengthened, reached the table and brought the brilliant stones of the necklace to life.

'You are right,' he said at last, standing over the jewel and pushing it into a crescent with the tip of one finger. 'This could betray you. It's too big, and even an ignorant eye could see that it must be the property of a great family. My mother was often painted in it.'

'The boy doesn't wake early, but he may hear us.' She was buttoning her dress, shaking out its creases. He did not respond, so she crossed the room and offered boldly to tuck in his shirt. 'It is the Orlov necklace, it should stay with you. Maybe . . .'

'I haven't got any faith in "maybe".' He spoke with difficulty. The instinct that he had given her a child was choking him.

'But you *must* hope.'

Kolya's sleepy voice murmured from the next room.

In the next instant Orlov kissed her for the last time. 'Go and see to him. I'll put these back in the safe.'

The child's bed creaked and he appeared in the doorway, rubbing his eyes.

'But the house will be unguarded. A safe only tells thieves where the valuables are – shouldn't we send them to Fabergé? Or to a bank?'

'If things break down, there will be looting, mobs on the streets – a bank won't be safe.'

They looked at each other uncertainly while the child came to the table and made the jade leaves on the willow twigs swing at his touch.

'Peasants hide things under the floors, in the chimney . . .' They thought of the rooms downstairs, the parquet waxed to the sheen of satin, the walls hung with silk.

'The walls in the scullery are only whitewashed. There is a chimney, it used to be for the copper until we built the laundry room.'

'Very well.' He poured the necklace back into its case and snapped it shut. 'We shall wall up the treasure like Electra. Tell Mischa to bring me some tools, then send him away. No one must know except us.'

Later when darkness gathered the servants became tearful. As the time of their departure approached Kolya too began to weep, and Charlotte's eyes were brimming as she comforted him. All the small household gathered unbidden in the hallway, and together they observed the peasant custom of sitting down and crossing themselves before a journey. Orlov, in a plain coat borrowed from his driver, came with them to the Finland station and saw them installed on the train under the care of a young marine officer.

The journey northwards was wearying but uneventful. The train crawled across flat tracts of snow, whether land or lake it was impossible to tell. They saw a few elk, and men hunting them from sledges. Kolya ran up and down the corridors and the sailors spoiled him, taught him their ribald songs and gave him hard biscuits from their rations which dispatched two of his baby teeth.

Charlotte leaned in a corner by the window, fear and sensuality churning painfully in her mind. Her eyes smarted from gazing at the snow. She was afraid for Orlov, afraid for the boy and afraid for herself, now that she knew what terrible excesses she could commit. Her roused senses would not be subdued, and she forced her mind to find distractions. Never had she imagined so many hues of white. What a strange beauty this desolate landscape had, with the snow to hide its black marshes. Only a few trees, stunted and tortured by the howling winds, stuck through the blanket of whiteness as reminders of the ugliness beneath. She had a pencil and a sketch pad, packed for the child, but seeing him already amused she took them herself and began to draw.

On their first day at sea the news of the abdication of the Tsar was telegraphed to the ship and announced to the handful of passengers by the Captain. The voyage continued through the savage, grey waters until they reached Aberdeen at the end of March. In London, Charlotte found her family in mourning for her two brothers and the fiancé of her elder sister. Their mother was fading towards her own end at last. German U-boats had sunk hundreds of merchant ships in the Atlantic and no line was willing to accept passengers.

She felt a stranger in England, and even more of a stranger in her family home. People bemoaned the bread rationing, and were offended when she told them they had no idea of real hardship. Her sisters were cold, and before long she understood that they were jealous, because she had a man, and he was safe and alive, and did not deserve to be. The older girl called him a coward outright, and Charlotte sensed the hostility of others in their circle. The smug, petty pretensions of the English disgusted her.

She applied for permission to visit Walter at the internment camp, and found him brawny from working in potato fields and as excited as a puppy to see her. 'I didn't think you'd come back,' he confessed, looking at his coarsened hands. 'You seemed so set on being in Russia, even before the war. I wish we could be married now – the day the war's over and they let me out of this place. No more waiting! Say you agree . . . why not Gretna Green, if that's what we have to do.'

Kolya developed bronchitis, and she herself felt weak and blamed the dirty air of London. Two letters came from Orlov, hastily written, telling her of his new appointment under the provisional government of Prince Lvov. They seemed plain and unaffectionate to her, although he signed himself 'Devotedly – Niki'.

The first convoy of merchant ships arrived in London under navy escort from Gibraltar in June. Using money from the account, she paid an absurd price for a passage to Marseilles for herself and Kolya.

In the blazing heat of high summer, they arrived at the Villa Cassandra to find twenty people lunching under an awning on the terrace. Flowers cascaded from every pillar and a miasma of perfumes, cologne, cigarette smoke and garlic hung in the hot air.

Charlotte, having for months imagined Lydia as a frail invalid, was stunned to silence by the sight of her – raucous at the head of the table, her hair cut short and curled, her face heavily made up. She was smoking a cigarette in a white agate holder, and her low-cut afternoon gown of flame-red chiffon caught with black silk roses revealed rounded arms and a swelling bosom. In fact, she was plump.

Kolya ran to his mother immediately and snuggled awkwardly into her side, leaving Charlotte to stand alone, struggling with her emotions. Eventually Lydia greeted her, giving her perfunctory kisses on both cheeks. 'My poor dear, you must have endured a terrible journey. Tell us about it when you have recovered your strength,' was her final word of greeting, and a maid showed Charlotte to a small, stuffy room at the back of the house.

She found Lydia utterly changed, but wondered later if, in her innocence and inexperience as a young girl in Petersburg, she had not merely been blind to the woman's true nature all along. When the trunk of winter clothes was opened, the seams slit and the jewels revealed, Lydia flew into a temper and demanded to know how she was expected to maintain her position on the Côte without the Orlov necklace.

'You lying bitch – don't tell me he sent you here without it!' Even her voice had become shrill. 'You've stolen it, haven't you? Your worthless family in London will be living off my necklace for the rest of their lives!'

For an instant, Kolya's loyalty wavered. 'Papa wouldn't like you to talk to Charlotte like that. It's my fault we didn't bring it, Mama. They wanted to hide it in my lion but I wouldn't let them. Papa hid it in the wall, with your little trees because they were too heavy.'

'Darling boy, such a good heart.' His mother kissed his forehead without much feeling, leaving a smudge of red lipstick. 'Well, who knows what else I've lost? Especially now. Petersburg is in chaos, I hear. Who would have dreamed that His Imperial Majesty would have to leave the throne? Extraordinary. It can't be true. And when is the Prince coming?'

'He did not say. Now that he is in the new government . . .'

'Oh, he's so stupid. I must write and tell him how much fun it is here.' Lydia's interest waned at once; she simply walked away, with Kolya trotting adoringly at her side.

In a few days Charlotte discovered a filthy child who lived around the kitchen and would not speak. Lydia's new French maid whispered maliciously that it was Madame's child, born in the first months of the war, which she hated and instructed the staff to ignore. 'She hates the sight of it,' the girl whispered. 'She's crazy. She pretends it belongs to one of us. There must be something bad, some secret about this child. After all, terrible things can happen to a woman in wartime. The old couple who were here in the beginning, they took it to the priest and he baptized it, so its name is Marie, but it doesn't answer to anything.'

Charlotte felt that her heart was being cut to pieces. The silent waif preyed on her mind. Was she Orlov's child too? Kolya, enchanted with his mother, and the sunshine, luxury and food which seemed to come with her, ignored his governess. She had no position in the unhappy household, and no respect for its members or its guests. There was enough Petersburg aristocracy on the Côte d'Azur for parties every night. For patriotism they disbelieved all bad news, and toasted God, the Tsar and victory. A tragedy was considered to be the rationing of dress fabric to four metres per outfit.

Kolya was safe, his little fortune had been delivered. She could leave, and felt unwanted, but leaving would sever her last tie with Petersburg, and end her seven enchanted years. At home there was the war, her sour family, and poor Walter. And here was the silent child. She resolved to speak to Lydia.

'What child?' She was shuffling a pack of tarot cards,

waiting for the arrival of a new acquaintance, a former opera singer who now made her living telling fortunes.

'The child who hangs around the kitchen.'

'I haven't seen it. What is this nonsense?' She cut the pack, slapping the cards together as she gathered them up again. A cigarette smouldered in the holder.

'It's a girl, she can't speak. I have been told that you . . . that the child . . .'

Lydia cut the pack again, and turned up a card. 'The Empress, but reversed. Hmm. Charlotte, let us be direct. We are grown women. Instead of talking rubbish about the cook's brat in the kitchen – what about *your* child?'

'My child?'

'Yes, yours. Oh, the devil! My cigarette has gone out. Ring for a match.' Charlotte did as she was bidden, carrying out an orderly search of her memory. Was it possible she could have conceived? In the terror of their flight from Petrograd, she had been aware of nothing but their safety, but she had no recollection of having a period in that time, or in England. Her light summer dresses were tight, but she wore them seldom and never felt as comfortable in them as she did in more familiar garments. Was it possible that in that last night in Petrograd, in that fearful, ecstatic surrender to her feelings, she had conceived Niki's child?

The butler brought matches. Lydia told him to return in five minutes, but did not wait until he had left the room before continuing, 'You look to me like a woman who is expecting a child in about four months. And how do you explain these?' From a drawer in the table, she took the two letters from the Prince.

'But . . . they were in my room.' Her eyes were drawn to the mirror and she saw how rounded her face had become. Putting her hands in the pockets of her pink linen dress, she pulled it against her and looked at her silhouette. When she gained weight, it usually settled at her thighs and hips. There was now a definite fullness at her waist.

'*My* room, Charlotte. *My* villa. And my Nikolai, however he thinks he can sign himself to you.' She flicked over another card, making a great show of what a light matter this was to her. 'The ten of swords. These cards warned me, you know. You slut! You viper! All these years under my roof and this is how you betray me. I pray to God my child has not been depraved by your evil influence. Now get out of my sight. I've had your things packed. The driver will take you to the station or wherever you want to go.' She reached for the gold-mounted bell push and pressed its lapis lazuli centre to summon the butler. 'This woman is leaving immediately, the car is waiting for her at the door.'

'Goodbye, Madame.' Charlotte spoke pleasantly, made a small, courteous bow, and walked to the door with a spring in her step. Instinctively, she knew that she was truly carrying a child, Orlov's child, the child of a man so fine and extraordinary she had not dared even to think of loving him. She was to give life to a part of him, a part of the country she loved, a talisman of her magical years there. And she herself would be transformed, her life sent in a new direction as if knocked from its old orbit by a comet.

She knew that Kolya had been sent to the beach. Blessing the disloyalty of Lydia's staff, she made the driver stop so she could walk down to say goodbye to him. But he was collecting shells, and did not show much interest.

CHAPTER 20

London, 1990

'Mum, I know this is really none of my business . . .' Tom had been drifting around the house all day, pretending to pack his things for the new term at university. He had chosen to read history with history of art in Glasgow, and the thought had lain at the bottom of Bianca's mind ever since his first term that he had deliberately chosen a university a long distance from London because he was uncomfortable at home. Tom would never confess such a thing, he had grown into a frighteningly contained individual, so she had to be content with guesswork.

'What isn't, darling?'

'I'm thinking about the summer, really . . .' He was drooping with embarrassment, his thick black hair falling to his nose. 'Are we going to Italy again?'

'Well, that's what the house is for, isn't it?' Five years ago Bianca had decided that she had eaten enough *confit d'oie* to last a lifetime and traded the Dordogne house for one in Tuscany. 'You all seem to enjoy it – don't you want to go this year?'

'No, it's just . . . I wondered who else would be coming.'

'This is about Alex, isn't it? You mean will he be coming?' She could see that he was relieved that she was not angry. 'Probably not, darling. I don't know how much further Alex and I have to go together, to tell you the truth.'

His serious grey eyes flashed optimism. 'Well, you've been together quite a long time. You're not upset, are you?'

She patted his cheek, a mannerism which he hated, meaning you've annoyed me so I can annoy you back. 'We met nearly a year ago, that's not long in an adult life. It's nothing definite, you understand. Don't discuss this with the others. I just know – well . . .' She paused, trying to define the instinct which had prompted her. 'I know what Alex is like, he's a gypsy sort of person, not really wanting to stay anywhere long, and although I have been very happy with him, I know it isn't for ever. That's all.'

'Oh, OK. That's sort of what I guessed, anyway.'

'Considering that your father and I are two of the most pig-headed, dogmatic people we know, I'm amazed we had such a reasonable son. I know you hate him, don't worry, and I wouldn't dream of taking him on holiday with us – that's a promise. Anyway, he has to go to Russia again for me on business. So don't fret.'

'Can I invite someone?'

'Yes, darling, of course, you know your friends are always welcome.'

'I mean, a girl.'

'Do you mean a girlfriend?'

'I suppose so.'

'Yes, of course you can. How nice for you.' Tom had previously regarded girls as a duty, to be entertained in order to placate his peers rather than for their own sake. Bianca was pleased to see him ready to love, but mildly pained that her son should judge her own choice of companion unacceptable to the woman who had finally captured his attention.

'I wondered if you were considering getting married or anything.'

'Haven't I always said I'd never get married again?'

'Yes, but . . .'

'Do I usually mean what I say?'

'Yes.'

'Well, just for the record, I won't ever get married again and if I was even thinking it, you would be the first to know, OK?'

'OK. I was just worried, that's all.'

'On whose account? Mine or yours?'

'Well, yours. I mean, I know he makes you – er – happy and everything but . . .'

'I think I've a right to enjoy being made happy for a few months, don't you? It's a new experience for me, I spent most of my life making other people happy.' She regretted speaking harshly, especially to her son when his own emotions were leading him towards an attachment for the first time, but she also resented having to fight for the right to have just one, single, uncritical person beside her. Alex was dumb, a beautiful loser, but as far as he understood the word he loved her and at the end of every one of her tough days he had been there and had given her what she needed. It was the first time since Charlotte died that she had felt the energy of another human pouring into her, instead of her own energy ceaselessly draining into others.

None of the children had taken to him. Lizzie was dazzled by him, but only because Bianca had asked him to make an effort with them and he, knowing no other way to gain acceptance by a female, had flirted with the demure ten-year-old and charmed her into confusion. He had no idea how to relate to the boys. Orlando greeted his appearance by scowling, relapsing deeper into apathy and playing The Cure at full volume. The two eldest behaved with a politeness which eroded every time they encountered each other. Since both older boys were away at university much of the time, Orlando's point of view was over-represented, but the fact remained that Alex was not a popular visitor at her home. Since he had clearly expected to live there, and Bianca had felt obliged to offer him the company's flat, this had been a treble blow to their future.

In a few more days there was a storm in the kitchen. It was Saturday. Bianca had flown back from New York in the night, and she and Alex were preparing for a long formal evening, the presentation of the European Heritage Awards at the National Portrait Gallery. At lunchtime, the boys had drifted into the kitchen in the hope of food.

Alex compared their childhood to the only other of which he had good experience – his own – and often criticized them for their laziness around the house. Benedict, who was in his foundation year at Chelsea, had spent the entire morning writing a technical drawing programme on his computer, and when he complained that there was no meal imminent, Alex attacked.

'You've spent four hours sitting on your butt in front of a screen – I was younger than you when I was painting the back fence for my parents. You can cook your own dinner, can't you? Your mother has had a tough week, she's had nothing but tough weeks for months. Why don't any of you ever lift a finger to help out? You're just exploiting her, lying around like you do when there's chores to be done.'

'I suppose you do know what you're talking about,' rejoined Benedict, who spoke seldom but usually to good effect, 'but I don't see you showing us the way, exactly.'

There had followed a shocked silence; Wolfe had not understood the jibe and stood looking awkwardly at the youth across the kitchen table. Bianca was infuriated but forced herself not to show it; Benedict's lazy manner belied a very sharp mind and it was never wise to engage him in a verbal battle, particularly when he had his brothers at his back.

'That's not fair, Ben. Alex is employed by Berrisford's as a consultant, he pays rent for the flat and looks after himself. That's more than you do, any of you; I'm not criticizing you for that, you're my children, it's natural, but you've no right to insult someone I care about because he also works for me.'

'He's your boyfriend,' Orlando sneered from the far end of the room.

'That isn't the point,' Tom put in. Sometimes he had the perfect manner for a smart young barrister.

'I am entitled to a boyfriend. I've chosen Alex. Your obligation is to behave decently towards him, as you would to any other person, and to consider my feelings as well.' Orlando kicked the cat's dish, which was fortunately empty, and loafed out of the room. 'But I must say, Alex, that how the boys behave towards me is really between them and me.'

Alex had started an angry protest, but she silenced him with a look. Ben apologized with a good grace, and the boys slunk out of the kitchen in silence.

'You're too soft on them, you shouldn't have let them get away . . .'

'Alex, I meant what I said. I don't think you can tell them how they should act with any special authority. You're not their father.'

He folded his arms, his grey eyes almost black with anger. 'I don't think you should allow some feather-bedded kid of eighteen to . . .'

'Darling, don't you see where this is going to end?' She softened her voice, not wanting to hurt him. 'I don't want to be put in the position of having to choose between my children or you. And that's what it will come down to if you can't all get on.'

'Meaning you'll choose them.'

'They *are* my children.'

'And so you let them run your life?'

'It's not my life, it's our life. The children and I, we're part of the same life.'

'So where does that leave me?'

'Alex, I care about you very deeply, but . . .' Then she saw that he was unable to understand what she was trying to explain. He was comparing her love of her children directly with her feeling for him, blind to the fact that there was nothing causal about a parental bond. 'I don't think you understand this.' She took his hand, and he allowed it, but did not respond. 'You can't compare the two things. I can't stop loving my children because they behave badly, and they can't make me love them by being good. That isn't the point. They're my children therefore I love them, and that's what my life is about. I would put them first, whoever, or whatever, came in conflict with the tie between us.'

Alex had drifted away to a mental distance from which he could camouflage the unwelcome truth. He tipped up her chin and kissed her, a gesture which she usually found endearing, and then said, 'Poor Bianca, the wounded tigress sacrificing herself for her cubs. Why don't you leave all this and come away for next weekend?'

Hermione drifted into the kitchen with Anjelica, her four-year-old daughter, perched on her hip. 'Yes, Bea, why don't you? I'll be here to hold the fort, after all. You need a break, you're totally stressed out.'

'Where shall we go? The world's your oyster . . .'

She looked from one face to the other, her sister rounded and reproachful, her lover intense. He was pulling a strand of her hair free from the band which held it at the nape of her neck and winding it around his fingertips. The force which drew them together was still potent. She gave in. 'No long flights. Actually, no flights at all. Can't we just go to somewhere in the country? Rain and mud and log fires and stuff? I know England's miserable in spring, but I just want to cocoon.'

At Berrisford's, the past six months had been stormy. The board had agreed to prune their American operation severely, and she had been obliged to go to New York almost every week. Making people redundant was a sickening business, not least because, as the true condition of the company became more apparent, she had begun to reproach herself for not seizing earlier the power which had been given to her too late.

'Leave it to me, darling. I'll take care of everything. Just be ready to leave when I tell you on Friday.' Alex held her close for an instant, gave her one of his soul-boring looks and brushed her lips with his before striding out of the door. His physical presence was so strong that whenever he left a room he left a sense of vacuum, and a faint tang of Vetiver in the air.

'Why aren't I more annoyed with him?' Bianca held out her arms to take her niece while Hermione prepared toast and Marmite for her tea. 'He's just picked a fight with Ben, and then ran out on talking about it because he just doesn't understand that the kids are first with me. And he talks to me and touches me as if he was . . .'

'John Wayne? Patronizing sexist crap?'

'No, be fair, Herm, he is sexy with it – let's say Burt Lancaster.'

'Muscle-bound patronizing sexist crap with teeth?'

'Poor love, he wouldn't know sexist crap if he trod in it.'

'Thekthsit cwap!' Anjelica seemed to be in agreement, but it was hard to tell when she spoke through a mouthful of toast. She was a crazy child who fizzed through her little life like a firecracker, leaping unpredictably in one direction after another, beyond any kind of order or discipline. Even finding one ruly curl in her white-blonde head to which to attach a bow was difficult. 'Thekthsit cwap!' She shook her head violently.

'If you spit that toast out you'll be sorry, kiddo. Why don't you ask your aunt if she's going bust this week?'

'Butht! Butht!'

'Not this week. What about you?' Hermione had arrived a month ago, with Anjelica and her new baby who was asleep upstairs. The nursery had lost money since its opening, and she had mortgaged the farmhouse to keep going. With the interest now at fifteen per cent, the business was no longer viable. Since Hermione could at least make plants grow, Seumas had insisted that the administration should be his responsibility, but he had diverted a few thousand pounds of VAT and left the last six months' bills unpaid in order to take a trip to Utah to learn Native American husbandry skills. The bailiffs had arrived the day he left.

Bianca was selfishly pleased, since she missed small children around the house, and missed her sister. The trouble with being one of the most powerful women in any business was that you had very few peers, and you could not afford to be friends with any of them. She yearned for a woman friend and her sister, although her response to bad fortune was to spout more moonshine than ever, was a warm, intimate companion. Yesterday, Hermione had gone to meet the receiver to decide what denomination of bankruptcy was appropriate to her affairs.

'The receiver was really cool. He wants to liquidate the business and pay everybody, including me, because I'm an employee. It turns out Seumas was a closet control freak. He decided he could be a director but I could be an employee. It was my house and my mortgage paying the business debts, but he didn't see that as relevant. He didn't feel it was even relevant to tell me. I called him and he said he felt the stress would be too much for me, interfere with my ability to bond with the kids and why was I hung up on these meaningless words anyway? But it means he's liable, and I'm not – so how's that for what goes around coming around?'

'Sounds good to me.'

'So Berrisford's can fight another day, too, huh?'

Sometimes Bianca believed her sister's claim to have intuition. 'Mmn. Barely, if you want the truth. Let me tell you . . .'

In Martin Pownall's place, the board had announced as one man that they wanted to recruit a new finance director from outside the company. They had chosen Hugh to speak for them; it had been a mistake. He spoke as if giving her an order, and Bianca, knowing that her father was never so authoritative as when he was guilty, had been suspicious. She had looked around at them, eight men dressed identically in dark suits, striped shirts, discreet ties with tiny patterns, silk handkerchiefs or gold watch-chains worn like regimental badges, and seen that they were looking for another fall guy to take the blame – but for what? Undoubtedly for something she did not know about, something worse than the current mess.

'I went over and locked the door, Herm. And then I put the key in front of me on the table and told them they'd better come clean because none of them were leaving until they did.'

'Headmistress trip, huh?'

'Absolutely. Oh, they blustered and blathered, but they didn't dare complain, they knew I was right. And then that ass Bainbridge tried to tell me a cock-and-bull story about loans, but I wouldn't buy it. And I pointed out that the new finance director would be breaking the bad news soon enough, and when he did there'd undoubtedly be a few resignations needed, whereas this way they could all keep their seats – for now, at any rate. And in the end a couple of younger guys cracked. It's a mess, Herm. Actually it's a fucking disaster. Hugh and Pownall decided that we needed a bigger building, and signed some kind of agreement with a developer for a double site in Belgravia. We're due to take possession next month. We don't need it, we can't afford it, commercial property's got pneumonia, we'll never sell the old place, they've sunk millions in the development itself – out of our reserves, for God's sake.'

'You mean you really think . . .' They sat opposite each other at the old pine table, holding mugs of cold tea and thinking of what Berrisford's meant to them.

'Terminal. God! The shareholders could sue the lot of them. The only way I can see out of this would be to find some hole in the contract – it's apparently a pretty idio-syncratic document. That's the only prayer we've got. No wonder Pownall was so eager to retire. I hope his kickback's worth it. I'm just glad I threw him out when I did.'

'What did you do when they told you?'

'Recalled the meeting for the next morning and asked for proposals to deal with the situation. It's bloody easy being the boss, you know, everyone else does the work. Nobody came up with anything worth sneezing on. So I sent the execs away to come up with plans for twenty per cent staff cutbacks in their departments, plus fifty per cent budget cuts. Next week we work out the details. It'll be absolute hell. I say that and I'll have a job at the end of it – a lot of people won't.'

Hermione paused to hand her small daughter a cloth with which to wipe her face, then helped the child down from her chair. She ran away to the toy basket at the far end of the room. 'Will Berrisford's be all right then?'

'I doubt it. It will buy us time, that's all. The market's turned, the big boys are trying to talk it up but it's no use. We've been smart to some extent, diversified, opened new markets, but I need a big sale, Herm. If we can't get a big sale in the coming year we won't have enough cash to carry on. The Russian sale is our best bet, but we need to clear five million on it and I just don't see how we can possibly do it.' They sat silently, looking at the half-empty cups of cold tea. The collapse of the firm that shared their name was unthinkable.

When Alex took Bianca away for a weekend, the bill arrived on her desk a month later in the form of his company credit card account. She had once suggested that she would be happy with a more modest and more genuine invitation, or equally pleased to pay herself, but he had sulked and snapped and accused her of trampling on his feelings and making him out to be a kept man. Since she enjoyed the new sensation of being cared for, she let his leaking logic alone and paid the credit card bills herself.

He had chosen a hotel in the Lake District. They arrived in torrential rain and ate an exquisite meal over which he made her off-load the week's traumas in detail.

'I need a big sale,' she repeated. It was a mantra she recited to herself constantly at that time.

'Won't the Russian sale be big?'

She shook her head, enjoying the motion of her freshly washed hair. 'Not big enough. We need to clear five million.'

'Suppose you had a really magnificent, historic thing . . .'
He had floated the notion of the Orlov necklace, his grand-

mother's mythical treasure, before, and she had dismissed it.

'Are you offering to go and find your grandmother's necklace again?'

'Don't say it that way. I've always felt it was part of me, part of my roots, if you like. And I *know* it's still there, and you can't believe how easy it is in Russia . . .'

'Alex, darling . . . no. It's just too much of a risk and too much of a romance.' From the mutinous way he pushed aside his plate, she knew that he would raise the subject again.

They went to bed, a seven-foot expanse of chintz, and in the morning it was still raining, so they did not get up. By noon, Bianca was saturated with physical wellbeing. The true luxury of being with this man was that she could claim the full occupancy of her body, reacquaint herself with every nerve ending, use her muscles, touch with her fingers, lick with her tongue, enjoy the softness of her skin, the silky length of her hair.

They communicated physically things which, she sometimes saw quite clearly, they did not really intend. In ecstasy, in abandon, in giving their bodies to each other, they felt transcending emotions and called them love. Bianca had no memory of her early love for her husband, only of behaving as if she had loved him. Now intense emotions detonated in her guts for a man for whom she cared but could not fully admire, and she wondered what feelings she had really had for Lovat.

Alex's standard distance for making love was an hour to an hour and a half, and he seemed to feel rejected if she did not want him every night and morning when they were together, and at least once again in addition in every twenty-four hours.

It was bliss to surrender herself to feeling, to wind her limbs around his firm, warm flesh, to explore his body and discover its secrets. She had never made love to a man whose responses were so passionate. There was a place in the small of his back which she could stroke or kiss and make his whole body shiver with excitement. His nipples were as sensitive as a woman's, if she touched them at the right moment the noise would start deep in his stomach and reach his lips as a roar as he began to come.

In the first few weeks she enjoyed the sensation of being awakened, but felt inhibited because his body was not only perfect but radiant with the care he took of it. He was toned and groomed like a race-horse. She confessed that she felt half alive beside him, and when he simply answered, 'Well, you could work out a little, you know,' she pressed for his advice. Alex still took dance classes several times a week, wherever he was in the world, and whoever he was with. She could not lose that much time from her schedule, and so she hired a trainer who took her running along the river embankment in the morning or to a gym near the office after work. She changed shape, her skin lost its dry, papery texture and acquired the voluptuous glow of one of Lely's Beauties. For the first time in her life, it was a pleasure to look at her own naked body in a mirror.

That confidence had led them to higher planes of sensuality; the simple caresses of their early days became themes on which they could compose variations. The freedom to trust his strength and his experience was thrilling, but finally she became aware that he did not feel equally free with her, that he was always alert to the impression he was making, and that his care for her was ultimately care for himself.

'How do you end it with the women in your life?' she asked him on the morning of the second day, when it was still raining.

'Why?' He was guarded, the eyes which should have been

617

open and frank closed off, as if he had run down shutters behind the irises.

'I wondered, that's all. Nothing to do with us.'

'I don't end it, things just seem to come to a natural end, that's all.'

She dropped the subject, and rang down for clean sheets. Perhaps his confrontation with Benedict had been part of the natural ending process, a way of offering her grounds for anger. Her sense was that if he could not live in her house, he would break away as soon as he could. He was uncomfortable living by himself, even though she slept with him at the apartment several times a week.

She left him there on Sunday night, took her own car and drove home. Hermione opened the door as she approached.

'Lovat's here,' she whispered, an anxious look in her eyes. 'There's been an accident. It's Lizzie, she's broken an arm.'

They were waiting in the sitting room, Lizzie with an immense white sling across her chest and her fingers, protruding from a new white plaster cast, visible at the end of it. Her daughter had inherited her own fair colouring; now her face was as white as the bandage and there were dark circles under her eyes. Bianca went over and carefully embraced her.

'I tried to reach you.' Lovat was not trying very hard to sound neutral although she read both guilt and anger in his manner. 'She was calling for you. She fell downstairs at my house today – it's a really nasty break, several places. Fixing it was a big operation, and she's got to go back tomorrow.'

'Poor little Lizzie – does it hurt?'

The child gave her a weak smile and nestled her head against her. 'They gave me tons of aspirin. It tasted disgusting but it doesn't hurt now. I fell over Isabel's shoes.'

'I telephoned the hotel, but they said you couldn't be disturbed.'

'Oh dear, I did tell them that.'

'But why – with four children surely . . .'

'Yes, I know anything can happen any time. I've been on call for over twenty years, Lovat – this weekend I wanted a few days of peace with Alex.'

He had a hungry, restless look, something she had never seen on him before. After their split he had gained weight, and his face had become heavy. Now he had suddenly dropped the excess pounds, and become almost thin. His shoulders seemed bony under his corduroy windcheater. Something of his youthful, classical look had returned. His hair was cut very short, and his eyes were very bright, like the eyes of a cat.

'Did Hermione give you anything to drink?' The journey from the country had tired her and a jolt of alcohol seemed attractive.

'I think she was embarrassed at letting me in, but I had to see you and tell you what happened. I didn't want you imagining things . . .'

'Will you put me to bed now, Mummy?' Bianca took Lizzie upstairs and tucked her in, then came down and poured them both large neat vodkas over ice.

'*Nostrovya.*'

'You're not asking me to drink to your Russian sale, I hope.'

'Why not, won't you be putting some of your mistakes in it?'

'We don't make mistakes at Whitburn-Tuttlingen. And if we do, we don't tell anyone about them.'

'We could drink to getting through ten years of separation without killing each other.'

'All right, I'll drink to that. Pinch any more pictures from me and things'll be different.'

'How did she fall over Isabel's shoes?'

'Isabel walked out on me this afternoon. She dropped the shoes on the way.'

'I'm sorry to hear that.' Bianca tried hard to sound sincere.

'About the shoes or her leaving? I was delighted to see the back of her. She gave me the crap about needing space but actually she's been screwing some playwright and they're both taking off for Los Angeles. She was the biggest – well, the second biggest – mistake of my life, that woman.'

'Oh – what was the first?' He looked away, annoyed to have revealed himself. 'Oh – I forgot. The apologizing gene isn't on the Y chromosome, is it?'

'If this is going to be . . .'

'It isn't. Forget it, sorry I spoke. At least Isabel kept out of the children's way.'

'She couldn't stand them.'

They talked amiably for an hour, mostly about the children. To Lovat's eyes, she was showing no sign of strain, and he wondered if she even realized how she had been manoeuvred into the position of presiding over the fall of the house of Berrisford.

'How are things?' He looked into her eyes, something else that he had not done for many years.

'Things?'

'Berrisford's. You let me pick up those Somov pictures without much of a fight.' Mitrokin had recently offered him a set of four rococo fantasies by that artist, painted as designs for chocolate boxes.

She smiled. Her lips were still sore. The trouble with a love affair fragmented by business was that you never got into training for serious kissing. 'You bought them from that dealer in Leningrad, didn't you?'

'Mitrokin. Amazing guy.' So that was his source – what a fool to let slip the name.

'Leningrad's not my turf, is it? Kusminsky gave me Moscow. Wasn't that a judgement of Solomon?' He did not remember her smiling so much when they had been married. It suited her.

'Kolya just wants to play both ends against the middle. He's always very discreet about you. But I was surprised – I know two of my Somov paintings came from Moscow.'

'He's always discreet about you, too. I can't get excited about Somov, you know. His stuff is either sentimental or just plain bad. The way I think about all those early avant-gardes is Somov them aren't worth the hassle. Pure yuk. I'd have been embarrassed to have them in the saleroom.'

'Pure business – I've a collector in San Diego goes ape for that stuff. Somov us have got it and Somov us haven't, I guess. But seriously, now that Hugh's off the scene, I've heard things . . .' The glasses were empty again, but he did not want to refill them at that critical instant for fear of looking as if he were trying to get her drunk.

'They're all true. We're buggered, that's all there is to it.' She was still smiling, but at the absurdity of life, not from any desire to please. 'Hugh agreed some loans which have gone bad, Martin bought an office which we can't afford. Most of the market has collapsed, I'm running like mad to stay in the same place, but I can't see any way we won't sink in the end.'

'You don't seem upset.'

'What would be the point of that? We can still do our best for our clients, still employ most of our people, I've got a few things cooking and we may squeeze through. Running around like a headless chicken won't help.'

'But aren't you mad at Hugh . . .'

'I've no more energy to be mad at my parents. If that's maturity, I've got there. In his position I'd probably have done exactly the same. Have you heard what I've heard about the Bank of Japan?'

'Planning to restrict loans secured on Tokyo property? Yes, they're announcing it next week, aren't they? That'll freeze the bollocks off a few of my players.'

She nodded, draining her glass and getting up to refill them both. 'You never really liked selling to banks, did you?'

'No. Not the big pictures they were never going to be able to display. I mean, what's a painting for, if not to be looked at? Of course, some of them stick them up in their board rooms . . .' They killed another hour in trading information and discovering that their ideas had hardly changed since the day they met. Eventually Bianca unsteadily got up and told him to leave because she had an early start ahead. He called a taxi, and it crossed her mind as she shut the front door behind him that for the first time since their separation he had been jealous. The idea of herself and Alex, together in a hotel room and not taking telephone calls, had touched a place that was still raw. The thought pleased her. She scrawled 'Mitrokin' on the kitchen memo board and went to bed.

Lovat sat in his house for another two hours, enjoying its emptiness. How well he had considered that he knew Bianca's courage; he had dismissed it as a woman's bravado, born of ignorance and that peculiar, female lack of respect for risk. To get a gambler's rush you needed to be good friends with danger. Bianca, matriarchally self-righteous as wife and mother, had declined even to make its acquaintance. Bianca as art-market raider seemed now to be deeply in love with it. She was so clearly aware of her company's ruin; she blamed no one, she intended to see things through even to the bitterest of ends. He had never given her credit for that kind of guts.

At 3 a.m. he noticed that the bottle of vodka was empty. He put it down on Isabel's favourite table, made of a reclaimed railway sleeper of Australian jarrah wood. It had cost two thousand pounds. The bottle fell over on the uneven surface. Lovat contemplated the still life with annoyance. After a while, he picked the table up and walked out into the street with it. It was heavy, but there was bound to be a skip within a few yards; people were still improving their houses in Holland Park.

In the morning Bianca's desk was piled high with bad news, and worse was to come. Berrisford's shares had been falling slowly but surely for weeks. In the early afternoon she learned that one particular buyer had been mopping up the bargain stock – Whitburn-Tuttlingen.

She was immediately outraged that Lovat had sat in her own home pretending to be a good father, a decent person and pleasant companion all the time knowing that he had been plotting her downfall for months. Her anger was surprisingly brief; she found her better self mocking her hostile instincts. Lovat had pretended nothing – by anyone's standards, he *was* a good father, a decent person and a pleasant companion. Had not she been plotting his downfall for years?

How extraordinarily well-matched they were as adversaries. Many times she had been able to read his mind, and just as frequently he had read hers, and they had feinted, bluffed and double-bluffed until that deal was done and they squared up for the next. The memories made her smile. Until Alex had appeared and coaxed her withered sensuality into bloom, duelling with her ex-husband had been her greatest selfish pleasure.

The fight involved Alex somehow; all her instincts told her that his entry into her life had been too well-timed. He had restored her womanliness, but that was one of destiny's own little jokes. Plans sizzled in her mind – it was time to make a move and trick Lovat into giving away his position.

'Alex, about what you said at the weekend, about your grandmother's necklace . . .' She slipped into his office and sat on his desk, a familiarity that she knew would charm him. 'I've changed my mind. You're right. It is worth a shot. Actually, it's worth our best shot. And there's a dealer you can see for me, if you can find him. Mitrokin. When do you want to go?'

CHAPTER 21

Leningrad, 1990

Anya looked at the buff form in her hand. Three votes to be cast. Should the city be renamed St Petersburg – cross out the word no if you wanted the new name. Or rather, the old name. Would changing the name be an insult to Lenin? Who cared, what had Lenin ever done for her? Would keeping the name be an insult to St Peter? St Peter denied Christ; naturally, he was a man, don't men deny everything when it suits them? That shit at the hotel denied he'd got another woman, and denied he'd got her a flat. Anya thanked God and her own common sense that her flat had been fixed by Andrusha; old lovers were worth more than new ones.

She looked down at her red dress, creased in front and seated behind although she pressed it every day. The hem was becoming uneven; she had resewn most of the seams and the zipper a dozen times. It was made from poor-quality wool, reclaimed probably, there was no heart in it. In the real St Petersburg they had worn elegant clothes. This place was filthy, collapsing into its own mud, there was no food. A miracle it had survived so long. Her father used to say the city had risen from its ashes like a phoenix so many times, it would surely do so again. Maybe the new name would help. She crossed out 'No'.

Now, the party leader. Some self-righteous *babushka* on the metro had told the whole carriage of people that only gays, tarts and spivs would vote for Yeltsin. 'Sounds like everybody I know,' a young man had answered and the

625

entire sardine-tin of people had laughed. They said that strangers met and fucked in the metro without anyone knowing, people were all jammed together so tightly. They said that every Russian woman was a prostitute. Anya preferred to call herself a free-trade zone. She voted for Yeltsin.

Lastly the mayor. Sobchak was a doll, he was a civilized man, rational but not a fence-sitter. She loved watching him on television, that cute chipmunk smile, and the only one with brains. Last night he had said that the only thing worth working for was for your children and grandchildren to live in a different society. She agreed with that. Anya had no living children and had had seven – no, eight – abortions. Not so bad, that was the average so there must be women with more. But it wasn't too late. And hadn't she been working on living in a different society herself all her life?

She voted for Sobchak, folded her paper and posted it into the plain varnished wooden ballot box, giving the huge iron padlock a cynical pat. Of course the election was rigged but you had to go through the motions all the same.

It was the height of summer. Out by the open sea the sweetish smell of the water was pleasant, but as they approached the city on the trolley-bus there was only the stink of dust and sweaty people. The air was like a steam bath and two cars with boiling radiators caused a traffic jam half a mile from the terminus. She struggled through the crush of passengers and jumped down to walk, pleased to have got away without putting her five kopecks in the ticket machine.

On the way to the hotel she saw a queue, not too long either, outside a meat shop. 'Not for those horrible Chernobyl chickens, is it?' she asked the last person. Any chicken was good to find these days, even the mutant ones with twisted beaks or a stump instead of a wing. He shrugged and grunted. People used to be kinder, now they never wanted to talk. She saw a woman leave with a round parcel. Even the radioactive birds were never that shape.

In forty minutes she saw with satisfaction that it was pork and bought all she could afford, snapping abuse at the women behind her. It wasn't rationed so why shouldn't she buy what she could? Walking on to the free-enterprise market she looked for cucumbers and potatoes; you could never count on anything these days. There were some cucumbers, but the price! Two years ago cucumbers were five roubles a kilo, but you paid anything for them now. The only ones left were malformed but she still had to fight over them with some pot-bellied young hooligan who thought he had the right to shoulder her aside just because he pissed standing up. No time to queue for potatoes, even if there were any.

Sometimes she felt like hanging herself after queuing. It was so humiliating, people were so vicious. At the hotel there was a message to go to room 157, which made her even more gloomy. Why had she ever allowed herself to get into hotel work? Because she was too old to be an air hostess and too dumb to have stayed married.

Her husband was just a dealer, not a big noise like Andrusha, but he didn't have a hard life. Could it have been so bad, taking care of him? He was never home anyway. But then before him, with her pilot, she'd been used to the whole imported lifestyle, the magazines with pages like silk, the underwear good enough to go to the theatre in – such a difference between everything she wanted and whatever rubbish had come her husband's way. She had a period every month, God willing, but how often did his gorillas get their hands on tampons? Once in five years, and then they sneered at you for wanting them. How could a woman feel like a woman without perfume – sometimes even without soap?

Maybe her mother was right, if she'd been sweeter-tempered to him, he'd have paid her more attention. Too late now, anyway.

The translating was OK, but the best jobs were going to the younger, thinner girls. The entertaining wasn't exactly arduous, all you had to do was keep your john downstairs while the surveillance team changed a tape or turned the room over. Neither of them were KGB jobs, but you had to sign the KGB pledge all the same, and then, of course, they had you. When their own girls were tied up, you got sent to room 157 and given the dirty stuff. No question of refusing, unless you wanted to end up working the Moskovsky Station tomorrow.

'Here he is, an American, here for a week but he knows the city, he's studied here, and we have to get to him straight from the airport. He's just checked in, he'll be down for dinner soon.' The important guy in the centre handed over the photograph.

'Do we have to use her again? Why can't one of our girls take this one?' Pathetic little whelps, the secret police recruits nowadays. She'd seen pigs with more intelligence.

'We've no option, with the African trade delegation at the Astoria.' He turned to Anya, who was studying the photography. 'What's the matter, not handsome enough for you? Too much like work, is it?' He leaned forward across the desk on his knuckles.

Anya turned the photograph to the light which struggled through the dirty curtains. 'He's an actor, isn't he?'

'No, antique dealer, so he says. Usual job, just keep him downstairs as long as you can, OK? And get moving.' She lowered her eyes shyly. The demure number was what these little shits liked. At least she didn't work for them full time, but what a life they led you anyway. Always pushing it, always after a deal, looking down on you like you weren't fit to lick their boots and you had to smile and do what you were told, and the only reward was they didn't kick you out of the hotel.

The head waiter seated her in a quiet corner at the side of the empty dance floor. 'I'll put him there.' He pointed to a small table close by. 'How about a nice little snack to keep you going?'

'Great, I'm starving.' It was early and the cabaret group were warming up, the drummer testing the tension in his skins and the girl showing off, doing splits and back-flips, while a party of Japanese students dutifully applauded.

The asshole brought her nothing but a wafer of cheese and a few olives, with a beer and a bit of bread. She could have had a better meal off her own lipstick. And the john took his time, so hungry as she was she had to leave food on the plate to make everything look natural and light up a cigarette to kill her appetite.

Anya had her own strategy with these pick-up jobs. Every foreigner in the hotel expected to be approached either by a spy or a prostitute. Therefore it was pointless to try acting the smart Soviet lady accidentally on her own in a foreigners-only hotel. If you pretended to be a hooker they would never suspect you, and if you felt like a quick one with a nice-looking guy with good European manners, you could have it and get a few dollars on the side into the bargain.

Only once had this plan gone wrong, when the crazy bastard had stuffed ten dollars into her bag and dragged her upstairs before the goons were finished with his room. How could a woman put her heart into getting laid when there was a dumb cop under the bed? What a Charlie Chaplin scene, getting the fool out while the john took a leak. She had a good laugh about it with the other girls, and it had put the KGB off using her for a while.

He was being shown to his table. She quickly licked her lips, pulled up her skirt and winked at him over the rim of her glass. Lovely smile he had. Perhaps she was actually feeling a little randy tonight after all. Andrusha said her problem had always been giving it away, but how could she help it with a tempting dish like this under her nose?

'Are you feeling lonely, by any chance?'

To her surprise, he answered her in Russian. 'The truth is, I'm not looking for company, but if you don't mind I'd like some conversation. For the same money – I am serious, my Russian is pretty rusty.'

'It's not so bad. Your accent is good, a Leningrad accent, too.' He stood up, walked around the table and pulled out the other chair for her to sit down. The waiter, arriving with a cheese puff for hors-d'oeuvre, snickered audibly. She could have hit him. 'Shall we have some wine? Bring me the list.' His tone was dismissive and the man slunk away.

'What is this, is it cheese?' Doubtfully, he prodded the food with his fork.

'Cream cheese in pastry. It's very good, eat it.'

'I'll look like a pig by the end of the week if I eat this stuff.' He saw her eye the food, and noticed the meagre plate on her own table. She was a voluptuous woman, everything about her spoke of healthy appetites. 'Why don't you help me? Bring us another fork, and a knife, please.' This was to the exasperated waiter. 'Take my fork, go on, don't be shy. I ate on the plane, I'm not really hungry.'

A more contented stomach improved her eyesight. This one would never have to pay for it, even in a strange town. He must have been a real looker when he was young. His body was still good, you could see that, and he held himself well. The face – nothing wrong with it, but those boyish looks could dry out in the thirties. The hair had lost its bounce, but he had cheekbones, nice eyes. And something else, she could not put a name to it.

'What's your business here in Leningrad?'

'I'm an agent for a London auction house, they're mounting a big sale of Russian works of art, crafts, everything.'

'I see. And where did you learn to speak Russian so well?'

'Here. When I was a kid I studied ballet, and I was a student at the Vaganova Academy.'

Her heart hit the floor. She felt sick. That lousy cheese was halfway down her throat planning a comeback. Was that it, the reason she felt she knew his face?

'Wolfie?' The name came hurtling back through the years and reached her lips before she knew it.

'That was what they called me – Jesus Christ! It's you! It's really you. Anya. Ever since I knew I was coming here, all I've been able to think of is running into you again. My little love. Here ... come ...' And he was on his feet again, walking round the table, holding out his arms, pulling her up, holding her. They were both weeping. The waiter almost hit the table with the plate of chicken, determined to bring the girl to her senses.

'Why didn't you forget me?' she managed to say at last.

'How could I forget you, the first woman I ever loved?' He was about to add 'the only woman I ever loved', but held it back. Not for Anya the big, easy words he used with other women. 'I've always thought of you. Did you remember me saying goodbye to you when they took me away?'

'I thought it was a bad dream.' She wiped her eyes with the backs of her hands. He had a handkerchief, new, clean, smelling very faintly of Vetiver.

'And I heard ...' Few men who were not themselves

obstetricians could talk about women's physical mysteries with less inhibition than Alexander Wolfe, but now he was unable to say the simplest words.

'You didn't hear anything. Our little mistake was taken care of – it was nothing, I was back in class next day. They let me graduate, I went to a little folk-dance group for a year or two, then got a job as an air hostess. I've had a very good life . . .'

'How beautiful you are.'

'Don't give me that crap . . . I'm a fat, middle-aged tart and you're used to those Western girls with their soft lives and proper cosmetics . . .' Shut up, you fool, the best chance you ever had and you're going to blow it twice?

'You don't look any different from the Anya I've always remembered. What about me?'

'Well, you haven't changed, you were always as vain as a peacock.' Self-consciously he ran his palms over his temples, brushing back his hair. 'When they showed me your picture I thought you were an American film star.'

'Stop flattering me. And *they* – I suppose they are in my room?' She nodded, a grimace of remorse stretching her lips. 'Don't be unhappy, we all do what we have to do in this life. Come, sit down, let's finish our dinner then we can go for a walk, yes?'

By midnight they were walking along the Neva embankment by the Hermitage, alone except for a single dogged fisherman. The sky was several shades of grey, with neither sun nor moon visible. The wide river, rippling like a white witch's hair in the pale sub-arctic night, carried sounds of music and laughter from a beach party on the distant bank.

They had exchanged versions of their life stories which they both recognized as carefully edited, but felt no need to question. All that mattered was that they had found each other. Beside that epic synchronicity, everything else was insignificant. For two superstitious people nothing had ever felt more like fate.

'And you mean to tell me that you're actually here to look for the Kusminskaya necklace?' Anya drew him into a semicircular embrasure and leaned against the stone wall with her back to the river. 'That's another one, another incredible coincidence. I translated for an Englishman who was after the same thing last year.'

'And . . .'

'I found it. Or rather, we went to a dealer – we have them, it's legal, it's all free trade now – and he got hold of it. Don't ask me how. They have their ways.'

'So it's already in England?'

'No, it's here in Russia. The bastard keeps stalling on it, saying jewellery isn't his thing.' Alex rapidly confirmed the details of the affair, the location of the house, of the necklace within it, and finally, the name of the Englishman. She could not remember.

'I've got it written down in my apartment, but we'll have to wait until the bridges come down again at two.'

They leaned on the balustrade and watched the river in silence for a while. A small launch weaved crazily across the empty channel, its wake widening over the calm surface until wavelets slapped the wall below them.

'I'd like to see it, you know. The necklace. Grandmère always used to say I would understand what she was when I saw her necklace.'

'It could probably be arranged.' She wanted to tell him the whole story, but forced herself to be prudent. On the street behind them passed two cars crammed with young people, the windows open to release tinny music to the street.

'Everybody's having a party tonight.'

'The white nights get people that way.' She put her hand on his and linked fingers.

'I always thought of you being settled down with a good man and six little ones by now.'

'In this country a good man is a relative concept.' She laughed awkwardly, aware that she sounded harsh. 'Besides, you spoiled me. You were the best fuck I've ever had, you know that?'

He put his arm round her shoulders and looked into her eyes, half smiling, inhaling the hayfield scent of the camomile flowers she infused to rinse her hair. 'I've learned a lot since then.'

'And me.' It was a simple statement of fact. How luxurious to flirt just for the fun of it, not for make-up or a new iron or a job or the privilege of being able to stay in the hotel another week. How strange that being wicked could make you feel so pure. They whiled away a few more hours, then flagged down cars until they found one to take them out beyond the Smolensky cemetery to her neighbourhood.

On the bookcase in her apartment was the picture of Anya at her graduation performance, partnered by one of the Armenians, both posed stiffly with huge, phoney smiles and eyes cast upwards to the supposed gallery. 'It should have been me.' He traced the image of her face with his fingers. 'I let you down, I'll never forgive myself.'

'Darling, you mustn't talk like that. It was my fault, my birthday. Believe me, I never blamed you. I was only glad that you were safe, that nothing happened to you.'

'I love the way you are now.'

'Oh, you're silly . . .' She gave a little half-annoyed puff and although her lips were no longer plump he saw the pouting goldfish expression once more. He could not bear to let go of her, and the bed, uneven under its red divan cover, was beckoning them.

Afterwards she had a cigarette, then remembered the minor purpose of their trip. She pulled on a pink kimono and began searching through an untidy mess of papers in a drawer while he lay in bed, watching. What he loved was the way she sat solidly with her elbows turned out and her head up, making round gestures as if to collect all the knowledge that they had between them and knead it into shape. Everything about her was muscular and sound, even the firm knot which tied her sash under her breasts. She was a goddess of womanly wisdom. He could lie on her altar, confess his sins and be absolved without judgement.

'Here he is, the pig.' She fished a business card from the corner of the drawer and handed it to him.

'Whitburn-Tuttlingen, Inc. Lovat Whitburn, vice-president.' Alex became angry. It was rare for him to feel this emotion, still rarer for him to express it, but his sense of humiliation was strong and it was safe to let out his true feelings with Anya. 'This is him, the guy who sent me out here!'

'But I don't get it, why? We got the necklace for him, he knows where it is . . .'

'He's not straight, whatever the explanation. This is a set-up. He got the whole story out of me, then sent me to see this woman who runs a big firm of auctioneers. And she used to be his wife. I'm being used, Anya.'

'I certainly agree, but by whom?' There was a flash of pain in his eyes. He had not disclosed his relationship with Bianca. But the idea of a man living off a woman was so alien to Anya's experience that he was mistaken in assuming she had guessed it. 'What's in this for him? I don't understand it. Are they still working together, this man and his wife?'

'Nothing like – there's no love lost there, I can tell you. It was a pretty messy divorce, and now her business is in trouble and he's trying to buy it.'

'Ah, so maybe that's what he's after, it's really this woman he's setting up, you're just in the middle.' Anya tested the explanation against all the facts she knew and was satisfied with it. The Englishman was a shrewd operator and she could easily believe that he had sussed the scam with the necklace. 'So – what to do? Have you got money?'

'Some.' He rolled his eyes rapidly round the room, implying that they might be under surveillance. He was right, you never knew. She passed him a piece of paper and he wrote down the sum, and under it wrote 'in cash, in US dollars'. It was more than they had asked the Englishman.

'So – we can do the deal. There's no problem.' It seemed a satisfying short cut to his search. Almost at once Alex began to feel that he had been remarkably clever in finding the necklace so quickly. She reached out her hand and pulled his face close so that she could kiss him. 'How long can you stay?'

'I don't know. Ten days, two weeks . . .' The hopeful curve of her cheek fell back into disappointed lines. 'But, if we can get the business done – I can spend all the time with you.'

It seemed that this was a poor substitute for something, and in four days or so, when he had been presented to Mitrokin as the Englishman's agent, acquired the necklace, hidden it simply in his film preserver, and then been shopping with Anya, and learned to some degree how she was earning her living, he understood.

Alex had never seen himself getting married. He knew that he had nothing to offer a woman in life besides himself, and that was not really good enough. For a year, maybe two, once, when he was young, for four years, his skilful body and his sympathetic mind might be enough, but beyond that there were all the considerations of material substance, and in those he was deficient.

He had come to realize that women came to him always from some dark chrysalis state, when they were soft-bodied, vulnerable, their wings mere gummy membranes stuck uselessly together, and he would blow on them like a warm zephyr, until they reached their proper state of strength and glorious colour, and were ready to take flight into their real lives. He was an interlude to them, a convalescence but nothing more.

Anya was not like that. She faced her miserable life like a hero, fighting it into a corner again and again, but she would never overcome it. He, on the other hand, could for once in his life take the role of knight in shining armour and deliver her from all her suffering, simply by offering her what his other loves had not needed – himself.

On a day which was wholeheartedly sunny, she procured a car and they drove out into the country, along a road lined with decorated wooden houses, each with their potato patch, fruit trees, wood pile, haycocks and family of chickens, nestling behind a windbreak of birches or poplars. Their destination was a track which led off a side road through birch woods. The land was uniformly flat, and half waterlogged, with the pale summer flowers, meadowsweet, ladysmantle and cow parsley, standing among the lush leaves with their roots in water. Here and there were clearings in which a few battered beehives stood, leaning towards each other like groups of drunks on street corners.

In a large, sunny clearing they drew up. Here were about twenty hives, and thousands of their occupants whizzing in the air all around. There was a hut of plain, unpainted wood, and an old canvas awning tied to one side of the low roof shaded a table.

'This is where we buy honey,' she told him, greeting the woman who sat on a crate beside the table with a small girl leaning against her lap. The child ran into the hut and came out with a loaf of bread. It was fresh, still hot, with a strong, smoky tang on the crust. He imagined it being made in some primitive wood-fired oven – yes, there it was at the back of the hut, a stone smoke-stack built into a rear wall. The woman tore the bread into chunks and motioned them towards the table, where half a dozen plates were set out with a pool of golden honey in each. The bees swarmed over the product of their labour, some of them drowning bliss-fully, clutching each other in pairs or trios.

They dipped the bread into the harvest and tasted, discuss-ing the merits of one hive, one blend or one flower over another and finally choosing the linden blossom for Anya and the mixed flowers for her neighbours. The price was ten roubles a pound.

'That's steep!' Alex had never bothered much about the price of anything before. Now that he knew that a hotel prostitute such as Anya had impersonated could expect ten roubles for half an hour, he had some standard of comparison.

'Yes, but what can we do? There's no honey in the shops now, ever. And no sugar quite often. This city – I tell you, it's impossible to live here and impossible to leave.' She argued bitterly, feeling the injustice more keenly than he did. A man appeared from the hut bearing three small glasses of home-distilled vodka, a brew of volcanic strength.

On the way back they stopped where water flowed clear and free under a plant bridge to wash their sticky hands. It was there that he asked her to marry him, but a full two days of assurance that he was serious were necessary before she accepted. By the time Andrusha had pulled strings to get around the waiting list, and the ceremony was performed in the Palace of Weddings, she had been more in tears than not for a week. He left the next day, promising to return as soon as the necklace was delivered to sit out the long wait for an exit visa with her. After all, he would not be needed in London once the diamonds were in Berrisford's safe.

Once back in London, his perspective altered, and he began to panic at the idea that Bianca would need him after all. She never reacted quite as other women did – the business of the apartment for example. How he hated the place, with its little reproach of a kitchen and cold corners smelling of loneliness.

He found her as he always did, in her office in the evening, taking advantage of the calm after business closed to plan the forthcoming day. She looked utterly beautiful, the curved planes of her face enhanced by the hard light from her desk lamp, the folds of the cinnamon silk suit which he had picked out for her glowing in harmony.

'This is it – the Orlov *collier*.' He had kept it for a few hours rolled in a handkerchief in the inside pocket of his suit and when he laid it across the palms of her hands it was warm as if it were alive. The stones threw tiny rainbows over her wrists. 'I'd say it was worth five million of anyone's money, wouldn't you?'

'Yes.' She turned it over, automatically looking for hallmarks, signs of repairs or alterations and the other details which would affect the authenticity or the value of the piece, while at the same time realizing that her future, and that of a hundred other people, rested on the value of this handful of minerals.

'It's beautiful, isn't it?'

'Yes.'

'Just imagine, the last time anyone wore it was my grandmother, going to some wonderful ball in a palace . . .'

'Unless her maid tried it on. Or even *my* grandmother.' She draped it over the back of her hand and admired the way it was articulated, a hundred tiny gold joints, invisible and so supple that it moulded itself over her fingers.

'You're such a realist.'

They smiled at each other. 'Yes, I am. I'm glad I am, it makes life simple. Not pleasant or easy, but simple.' Another luxurious quality he had was never seeming to be in a hurry, never living with one eye on his next appointment, like all the other men she knew. Alex lay elegantly across his chair as if he had all the time in the world to place at her disposal.

She suggested dinner, but added that she wanted to be home early. He agreed, setting a seal on the distance which had opened between them. She kept clothes in the apartment, and while she was showering he chose a plain black dress with thin straps, and he suggested that she wear the necklace.

'Don't be silly, suppose . . .'

'I insured it. This afternoon I insured it to be in our safe until one month after the sale, and all risks for tonight, and for the day of the sale itself. Here's the cover note, I had them fax it. Just for tonight, Bianca. For us.'

She was terribly tempted to kiss him, but they both knew that this was their last supper and she did not want to blow on the quiet embers of their passion and have it flare up again at the wrong moment. 'You think of everything. If you ever want a day job, I'll give you a good reference.' Her throat was tight and the words came out with difficulty.

'You'll miss me, then?'

'Of course I will. What do you want to do?' She was

about to zip up her dress when he crossly pulled away her arms and fastened it for her.

'Go back to Leningrad for a while, after that – I don't know. I can always teach, I've had good offers.'

'There are a few more things you could do for me in Russia, you know. If you'd like to. I could extend your contract six weeks or so.' She had heard that in Leningrad Lovat had found some more paintings by Konstantin Somov and, despise them as she did, she was in no mood to let him have them.

'I wouldn't want you to do anything . . .'

'It would be quite proper. And it would be a help, I can't operate in Leningrad, your uncle decided to award the city to Lovat.'

'The war continues, then.' He allowed her to slip the links into his cuffs, even though she was also far clumsier at this task than he.

'Totally. And I hope you're on my side.'

'Naturally. At your service until death.' He made the most elegant of courtly bows and offered her his arm. 'He was after the necklace too, you know. I met some dealers who told me he'd been asking about it.'

'I can't believe I was married to such a two-faced swine.' She turned to the mirror to admire the necklace and Alex noticed that her face wore an expression he had never seen before, elated, bright-eyed and confused. There was something girlish in it, suggesting the excitement of the first kiss or the thrill of the first ball. He attributed it to the necklace – jewellery had the power to change a woman's face, he had remarked it before. It never ocurred to Alex Wolfe that a woman he had loved could be excited about another man.

CHAPTER 22

London, 1991

Bianca saw Mr Wyngarde to the door and returned to her office. No hesitation, no second thoughts – if she thought about what she was about to do she would never do it. With her pen, in ink, she approved the proofs of the catalogue for the Russian sale: Kusminskaya's portrait on the cover, a full-colour page inside and two more pages of description and history of the necklace which she now knew to be false. The reserve was two million pounds. This too she initialled without pausing.

She gave the proofs to her secretary to send to the printer, then called in the marketing director and the public relations executive and talked through plans for massive press coverage and a parallel word-of-mouth campaign.

'This is going to be the most important sale in the history of the firm. We've got to break ground here, and in a big way. I want to know that we gave it our best shot. Don't hold back on this one, it's the biggest thrill we'll ever get.' After two hours, she sent them away with pages of notes, adding, 'Nobody can talk up a market the way we can – let's show them how it's done.'

It was true, and it was largely her own achievement. When she talked about a sale Bianca had such conviction, such profound confidence in her own judgement, that she could persuade the least interested listener. If Bianca Berrisford – BB, as the whole world of art now knew her – said that Matisse's *Hand of Fatma* was a far better painting than

Picasso's *Lapin Agile*, she was believed, even if she was about to sell the Matisse at the time. BB knew art. That was the whole story.

She had finally come into her birthright as a Berrisford. Upstairs in the marketing office there would soon be a planner with the key people – curators, connoisseurs, dealers – targeted to receive her personal assurance that the Russian avant-garde had been the greatest flowering of talent since the French Impressionists.

It was 7 p.m. Her secretary brought her a spritzer. She telephoned her home and heard her daughter's account of her basketball match. Then she went up to the top of the building, where the apartment was now empty but for a lingering tang of Vetiver. It was the most erotic smell. Did she miss Alex? Not his poor muddled mind, nor his eggshell confidence, but his body, yes. In fact, at times she craved it. Late at night, when she woke in the morning, her flesh screamed for his.

He had taken her on a journey of exploration. Ten years of marriage, five pregnancies, and yet her own body had been a country unknown to her until Alex, with all his beauty and tenderness, had shown her its mysteries. Now she was alone; the pain of it was hard to bear, but not for anything would she want to return to the half life she had lived before him. She envied men, who could pick up a telephone, walk out into the street, sit down in a bar, and have all the sex they could pay for.

She turned on the shower and stepped into it, wondering how much fucking it would take to make you forget a two-million-pound fraud. Twenty minutes of Alex at his best; there had only ever been his best, he was a perfectionist. There had been a few others after her divorce, but none of them could have distracted her from a parking fine. And

643

Lovat? Maybe he could have been a contender, if he had ever put his mind to it, given it the priority. Maybe a man couldn't be a good businessman and a good lover.

Would Lovat have gone ahead and sold the necklace, knowing it was not authentic? Lovat Whitburn, king of the raider-dealers, he deserved the title, even if she had succeeded in snatching the Somov willow-tree series from under his nose. He would have bitched and raged but – yes, he would have done the same thing. But with a worse conscience. Duelling with him in business, she had discovered that Lovat had a severe handicap: there were depths to which he would not sink, a core of morality which would not bend to the shabbier tricks of his trade.

She dried her hair, climbed into the boring little suit she kept for dinners with Japanese clients, and went to Claridge's to meet Mr Kameyama of the Mountain Tortoise Gallery in Tokyo.

Two weeks later, Lovat and Donald Tuttlingen drove to the Mount Street gallery directly from the airport. The American, suffering electronic withdrawal since his portable telephone had declined to receive signals in Park Lane, quickly began a long series of calls. Lovat picked out the Berrisford's catalogue from his pile of post.

'Don't tell me . . .' He looked carefully at the cover, and turned to the centre pages on the necklace. 'I don't believe it, God isn't that good . . .' He read the notes as fast as he could without skimming, re-read them to be certain, then threw the catalogue in the air with a rebel yell. 'Yeee-hah! She fell for it! The dumb bitch fell for it!'

The American turned towards him, eyebrows signalling interest while he listened to the voice from Tokyo in his ear.

'Is it an eagle? Is it a firebird? No! its a fucking *turkey!*

644

We've got her, Don. The shareholders will give us her head on a plate after this.' He rummaged in his desk, an asymmetric neo-surrealist construction chosen by Isabel in which it was impossible to find anything quickly, and pulled out a file containing the picture of the necklace which Mitrokin had offered him and a detailed report from Kusminsky on its provenance.

The American finished his call. 'Run this by me again . . .'

'That' – he flattened the catalogue with a slap and pointed to the description of the necklace – 'is a dud. It's a fake. She hasn't got the Orlov necklace, it's a lousy replica one of those Russian dealers botched together for a few dollars more. Mitrokin offered it to me last year, but I passed on it.'

'So how did Berrisford's get it? I thought you two had the USSR carved up between you.'

'You remember that flake who was walking your wife's widow friend? He came to me, claimed the Orlov necklace was left to him by his grandmother, and said he could get it. I knew he was lying. I sent him to Berrisford's just for devilment. Even *I* didn't dream that my dear ex-wife would be so stupid . . . I bet when he got out to Leningrad, Mitrokin saw him coming.'

'He was a good-looking boy, the flake you mention.'

'Maybe he was twenty years ago . . .'

'You got green eyes, son.' Sometimes Tuttlingen's jocular paternalism annoyed Lovat, but today he enjoyed it. Today, he was ready to enjoy anything.

'Listen, I hope the fucking she's getting is gonna be worth the fucking she's getting. Sincerely. I know what I'm talking about here, my wife is one of those women who never cared to get down and get nasty. Butter wouldn't melt in her cunt, one of those. If the guy's hot tamale, if he's turned her on – I'm glad for her. She needed it.'

'So out of the pure kindness of your heart you had him stripped, washed and sent to her tent . . .'

'You wanted an auction house, I got you an auction house. On a plate. And stuffed.'

'With salsa, the way I heard it.'

'Don't wind me up unless you want me to fly, Don.'

'You went supersonic the minute you saw that catalogue, that's what worries me. Listen, Lovat, I want an auction house, right? The way the art thing is going, in ten years you'll either be an auctioneer or you'll be rabbit shit. But you're emotionally invested here, and you are in way too deep for me to sleep nights. Your evidence is a description in a catalogue, a bad photograph and a painting which isn't exact. That's not enough. I don't want us to move on this until we're certain and we can prove it.'

It was a reasonable stipulation. Lovat booked a telephone call to Anya; the delay was eight hours. He sent a fax to the hotel, then another to Mitrokin, who sent one back regretting that the Kusminskaya necklace had now been sold and, in addition, he had also taken a better offer for the series of willow-tree studies by Konstantin Somov.

'The hell he has.' A cloud of annoyance darkened Lovat's day. 'Who from, for fuck's sake? He won't tell me, lying's the oldest sport in the all-Soviet Olympics.'

'Could be a coincidence.'

'The moon could be green cheese.' Lovat reached for the catalogue again and ran his finger down one page after another. 'But it isn't. Numbers thirty-five to forty-two. "After the birch tree the willow was a favourite subject with the landscape realists . . ."'

'On a plate with butter sauce, boy.' Lovat screwed up the fax and threw it at the grinning American. 'We still need proof positive on the necklace.'

'Wyngarde. They always used him for jewellery.' Lovat
reached for the telephone again.

'He won't tell you.'

'I'll say I'm worried about her, that I think she's been
conned.'

'He won't believe you.'

'Who's side are you on, Don?'

'I'm on our side. I say, no selling the bearskin until we
shoot the bear.'

Before Lovat could dial, his secretary announced Shona
Crawford-Pitt. 'Shit! Help me out, Don, have lunch with
us.' Imagining that he was doing Joe a favour when the
design business was dying, he had asked Shona to
redecorate his house, replacing Isabel's pseudo-aboriginal
murals and Balinese batiks with something – anything –
more soothing.

He at once discovered what his best friend had not told
him, that their marriage was also in a terminal condition.
Both husband and wife had misinterpreted his gesture; Joe
bitterly accused Lovat of kicking him when he was down.
Shona wanted lunch every week and was making amorous
advances. Lovat had never found her attractive and
considered that his loyalty was with Joe, but he had not had
sex for over a year. Not since Anya, and he was not proud
of himself for taking advantage of her. He felt vulnerable.
His life could get out of control.

'Thank you for coming so quickly.' Etienne Sokolov opened
the door of the apartment on the Place des Vosges. There
was a strong smell of pine needles, and Bianca noticed a
scented candle burning in a silver tub on the console in the
hall. Sokolov no longer looked young. He was pale, and his
face in his late thirties was settling into very deep lines. As

647

always, he was dressed in black. 'I was embarrassed to ask you but Kolya absolutely insisted.'

'Does he know?'

He took her raincoat, holding it awkwardly over his arm. 'Oh yes. He had quite an argument with the doctor. Last week they wanted to amputate the other leg, and he refused. Then the doctor said he could have gangrene, a stroke, anything, that he would not be responsible . . .' He waved his hand, dismissing the doctor as if he were nothing but a hairdresser throwing fits over a tint. 'And Kolya fired him. He said when he died it would be as a whole man, not a half. I've got another doctor, more sympathetic, with more respect, and he found this morning one tiny place where there is gangrene. So Kolya told me to light the candles, because you know it can smell pretty bad. The lawyer came this morning, because he wanted to be sure that his will is all OK. And now he's waiting for you. I have to give you these.' He held out three thin steel keys, safe keys, and she took them. 'He may be a little' – he searched for tactful words – 'a little brusque. He has had morphine but there is still a lot of pain.'

The bedroom looked fit for Napoleon, with dark blue wool drapes held back in gold ropes over the massive mahogany *lit-bateau*. Kusminsky was propped against fresh linen pillows, his thin hair washed, his silk dressing gown perfectly arranged over his thin chest. With a stab of foreboding, Bianca saw the Berrisford's catalogue beside him, under the crooked fingers of his right hand.

'You are a stupid girl.' His voice was faint, but how like her father he sounded. She prepared herself to be patient with a dying man. Undoubtedly he knew about the necklace, but if he had not told anyone else then she was safe.

'You don't have the Orlov necklace, so why do you advertise it?'

'The necklace I have was attributed wrongly.'

'Of course it was. But you know. So why?' He was too weak to speak with much expression, but his voice was clear.

'It was too late when we found out.' If she pretended that the catalogue was to be withdrawn perhaps he would drop the subject.

'Your husband says you are in trouble.'

'Yes, we are. Everyone knows that.'

'And you need a big sale.'

'Yes, we do.'

'So you don't need a big scandal?' Surely he was not going to betray her? Not in the very last days of his life?

'Of course not.'

He raised his right hand to point, and she saw that it took all the strength he had. 'The safe is there, open it please.'

Another blue wool drape, edged with gold key-pattern brocade, covered half the opposite wall, and it had been pulled back so that the wall safe was exposed. It was quite a simple design, three locks for the three keys, and she opened it without difficulty. Inside were a number of birch wood boxes, some bearing the Fabergé stamp, and a red morocco case.

'Bring everything to me.' He had an invalid's writing table beside the bed, which she folded out. There were twelve identical tall boxes, one flat case and the other in leather. 'Now open everything.'

She noticed that her fingers were shaking. Excitement was simmering in her stomach, the excitement of a child at Christmas. An instinct for drama made her begin with the red morocco case. It contained a thin gold bangle, bent slightly out of shape.

'From the Tsar's own casket. That was her first gift. Don't do anything with that.' He nodded at her, impatient for her to continue.

649

One after another, she opened the twelve vertical boxes, which contained Fabergé botanical studies, gold twigs in crystal vases with leaves and fruit in precious stones, each one a tiny masterpiece of artistry and imagination. They all represented trees – a birch, a willow, an alder, a horse chestnut with red jasper kernels, mistletoe with moonstone berries, beech, oak, pine, cherry, blue spruce, apple and rowan.

'The most beautiful, the most delicate, and the most rare. They never made another set like this. Not even for the Tsarina. Go on.' He was not looking at her as she opened the flat case. His hand fell on the edge of the table, inched forward on to it, and he touched the birch twig and made the catkins shake on their tiny gold hinges.

The flat case contained the Orlov necklace. When she saw it, exquisite and brilliant even in the subdued light of the sick room, she reproached her own judgement. How could she ever have considered that the feeble thing Alex had brought her could be passed off in place of this?

'That is . . .' He spat the word, and his left hand, which held a folded handkerchief, stirred on the quilt beside him. She saw tissues on the night stand, pulled one out and dried his sunken mouth. 'That is the Orlov necklace.'

'It's beautiful.'

'Yes. Take it, take these' – his forefinger indicated the twigs – 'and sell them, in this sale. Not the bracelet, it's not worth much. I will probably not be here when you sell them. There is a case, there, by the wall, and in it all the papers you need. Get the best price, and give the money to Etienne. He is my heir in any case.'

She stood like a statue, frozen with amazement. He seemed to register her astonished expression. 'Etienne could never sell them, just as I could never sell them before now. Twenty years ago a dealer brought me these from Moscow – except the birch, I always had that. These things are part of me, of my life. But Etienne has given his life to me. I am his profession, really. It is right that I should reward him. Keep your mouth shut until it is done.'

'I am profoundly grateful, Kolya. You must know that you have saved my business, my family. My grand-mother . . .'

'It's not for her. I'm not doing this because you have been stupid, either. I know you will get the best price, that's all. I'm tired. Go away.' He shut his eyes and his hand slipped from the table.

She did as he had directed, closed the boxes and packed them into the brown leather dressing case. The documents inside were in perfect order, his own instructions to Ber-risford's, as good a provenance for the necklace as she could have hoped for and copied pages from a Fabergé order book with sketches of the botanical studies. Then she asked Etienne to call her a taxi, because she felt suddenly very weak.

Afterwards, London remembered the sale, and the guests who had been there told each other that they were glad there were still people in the world who could do things in such wonderful style as Bianca Berrisford.

She had the great saleroom, already one of the noblest spaces in the city, tented in scarlet felt with the Berrisford cipher embossed on it in gold, elaborately caught up with gold ropes and tassels. Benedict, who had decided to video the event, assembled a very funny montage of people walking through the door for the first time and saying, 'Bakst!'

The viewing gallery was painted a pale Scandinavian blue-grey; there were bundles of silver birch branches in the corners, and the gallery was perfectly lit – she despised the trick at lesser houses of showing goods in the poorest possible light. It was perfectly simple to hang the inferior pictures a little too high or towards the corners so that their quality was less obvious. In the saleroom itself the lights were lowered and candles a metre high rose from baskets of red and gold flowers.

The staff, well aware that their futures were also at stake, performed with enthusiasm. The porters, at their own suggestion, were dressed as Russian peasants in high boots, loose trousers and embroidered linen tunics. When they saw the men in costume, the waitresses who poured the champagne looked sadly at their black dresses, and the marketing director went herself to the Ukrainian cultural centre to borrow sarafans and scarves from a dance group. Bianca vetoed all suggestions for music, but finally permitted a pianist to play some quiet Scriabin.

The viewing opened at the beginning of the week, with the sale scheduled for Thursday. Lovat arrived on Monday afternoon, fresh from an interview with Wyngarde who, contrary to Tuttlingen's prediction, had believed his story of concern for the poor duped Bianca and confided all he knew about the necklace he had seen.

The jewellery was in a case raised on a dais at the end of the gallery, with four security guards standing obtrusively at the edges of the room. Lovat went straight there, Mitrokin's photograph in the palm of his hand. The sight of the necklace was like a punch in the face; he stepped back and almost fell off the edge of the dais. When he took a catalogue from the pile by the entrance, he saw that the centre page had been reprinted, and that two diamond necklaces were now on sale. There was also a photograph of the magnificent object which now sparkled on a black velvet stand in the centre of the display.

He left immediately, afraid that Bianca would be told of his presence, and ran back to Mount Street to make a short and difficult telephone call to the officer at the Fine Art and Antiques Squad at Scotland Yard who had been expecting a different kind of conversation. Tuttlingen, whom he didn't call until the next day, was very kind to him, which only deepened his humiliation.

By Thursday evening he had recovered enough to make jokes to himself, and be utterly curious as to how the sale would go. He had an invitation. As a dealer he was asked to most of Berrisford's events. Evening dress was requested and, wanting to look as good as he could, he went home to change and arrived just as the auctioneer started the bidding for the first picture. It was the young Scot, who ought to have been nervous but looked serious and perfectly relaxed.

When Lovat heard other men talk of walking into a room, seeing a woman and wanting nothing else in the world at that moment but to make love to her, he thought they were crazy. Nothing like that had ever happened to him, until he entered Berrisford's saleroom. Something was sizzling even before he saw Bianca, merely because he knew she was there.

When his eye locked on to her, standing at the side of the room by the telephones, the shock was electric. He could not look anywhere else, or think of anything else but pulling the silly silk bow out of her hair, tearing open her jacket by its black satin lapels, eating the half smile off her lips. Even as half his mind told him he was mad, the other half was running through strategies to get her back.

Bianca noticed him immediately, but pretended not to. It took an extreme effort, especially when Patrick reached the Somovs and they went one after another to a telephone bidder in California. She had been going to sales all her life, and always found them thrilling. A hundred nervous people, huge sums of money, duels to the death, victories and disappointments – a sale was as emotional as an opera to her, and this sale, her own triumph, was an epic.

While Patrick disposed of a bronze head of a long-forgotten woman, a little bud of warmth for Lovat swelled unexpectedly in her heart. To come here tonight, her hour of victory after he had planned her defeat, was a brave and generous action. Her eyes were pulled towards him and made contact with his for a second. She smiled, she could not help it.

At last, Patrick was coming to the end of the sculpture. The jewellery would be next, with the portrait of Kusminskaya to go first, and the porters carried it up to the black flat on which it was to be displayed. The room was sweltering and now Bianca felt faint. She put a hand to the wall to steady herself, and realized that after so many months of high emotion she was utterly weak. Shaking her head to clear it, she walked to the side door and left the room.

'Are you all right?' Lovat found her in the corridor.

'I felt shaky for a moment. It's better out here, it's cooler.'

Would she let him put his arm around her? 'Come and sit down. Do you want a glass of water?' Yes! She seemed pleased.

'I think I would. Yes, I'd love a glass of water.'

'You are looking pale.' She was looking heavenly. Her arm was hot to touch. He regretted with passion ever having said anything about that body and butter.

'It's been a tough few weeks, you don't know.'

Lovat did not trust himself to say anything. If she found out now that he had attempted to sabotage this evening, he would be lost.

'What's happening?' She leaned forward to see the monitor screen in the corner. 'Still on the portrait.'

'Do you want to go back in?'

She wanted to say yes, but could not. She wanted to get up, but nothing happened. His arm was round her shoulders, which was – what was it? It was pleasurable. She felt she wanted him to hold her more tightly. It would be nice to kiss him, she could smell the particular spicy scent of his skin. And he was feeling the same, she knew that look in his eye, even if she had not seen it for years.

'I can't go back in, I just can't. I don't know what's the matter with me, it's just too much. Can we walk outside for a while? They're going to take a break before the jewellery anyway.'

Now her legs obeyed her. Her shoulders felt cold without his touch. Walking slowly down Jermyn Street, she racked her brains for a way to make things happen.

'You know we're on CNN?'

'Congratulations. Well done the press office.'

'They came to us.' Suddenly she had the answer. 'I'd love to see it. We took a suite at the Ritz for later, it'll be on there, we're taping it. Shall we go?'

'Will we get there in time?' What did she really mean? He could not read her signals. This was a person he did not know, but she was walking faster, away from Berrisford's, towards the hotel, and whatever she intended, she had given him the opportunity he had prayed for.

The suite was so quiet that they could hear the VCR humming. The television screen was full of President Bush making a speech. Champagne was already cooling in buckets, so he opened a bottle and poured for them both.

'Yes, I'd love some,' she said as she took her glass, and he realized he had not asked. His mind was running on a single track.

She pulled a fake rococo chair up in front of the television and turned up the volume as the Washington report came to an end. A woman reporter took the screen, standing in the viewing gallery in front of the Kusminskaya portrait. She seemed to be wearing no makeup and a loose shirt of unbleached cotton with leggings. The name Isabel McKinnon appeared at the bottom of the screen.

'Did you know it was her?' Lovat took a chair for himself, turned it around so he could lean on the back and sat as close to her as he dared. 'She must have recorded this earlier.'

'Yes, I'm afraid I did.'

'Trying to embarrass me?'

'You don't need my help.'

'She's gone all Nineties, integrity and environment.'

'I bet she was a rotten fuck.'

'Well . . . she was efficient. And she paid her own credit cards.'

She giggled, but wouldn't look at him. 'Well, Alex was worth every cent, if you want to know. You set me up, didn't you?'

He bit his lips, actually drew blood in the effort of not speaking. The urge to confess was strong. He wanted a bond of honesty between them now, and in wanting it he at last understood why she had wrecked their marriage. It was the deception itself that had repelled her, not the reason for it. Even at their closest, that lie had divided them. But if he told the truth now, she would be angry again, he would lose her.

Bianca wondered if she had overplayed her hand. He was looking at her with a helpless expression, lost for words.

'Don't answer, it doesn't matter. Alex was what I needed, he did me good. His necklace wasn't the Orlov necklace, but

656

we'll make a good profit on it and that's also something we need now.' She reminded herself that however thrilling this sale might be, and however good the prices, their profit would only keep Berrisford's afloat for six months or so, but these facts failed to make her feel the proper sobriety. 'Do you want to know where I found the real thing?'

'Of course.' Lovat felt weak from the release of his tension.

'I thought you would.' She crossed her legs and smiled at him, watching his eyes follow as she moved.

'So tell me.'

She shook her head. In amusement, her top lip folded over her lower lip, softly, leaving a sheen of moisture.

'That's not fair.'

'Isn't everything fair in love and war?'

So what was this, love or war? Or both? Lovat was lost for a response.

On the TV, there was a shot of the necklace, then a cut to the saleroom where a model was showing it.

'What are you hoping to get?' He knew how to do it. He knew how to get her, whether she was playing or not.

'Five million pounds.'

'You're mad, you'll never make it.' Keep it light, keep it natural, just insulting enough to sting . . .

'Want to bet?' Patrick started the bidding at two million two.

'Yes, I do.'

Clever man, he'd sussed her. She crossed her legs, feeling that she was juicy and ready for him now, but the anticipation was delicious, the game was wonderful. Was he as excited as she was? 'OK, you're on. Stakes – you choose first.'

'If you lose, you have dinner with me tonight. Alone.' Damn! He'd blown it. Pathetic. She would be tired, irritated, they'd be bound to quarrel. The bidding was rising rapidly, they were at three million six.

She turned her head slowly and gave him a long contemptuous look under her lashes. 'You know how difficult that's going to be. But I'm not chicken. OK. If I lose, dinner.'

She flexed one of her feet, seeming to admire the thin suede strap of her shoe buckled over her high instep. 'I suppose I ought to choose you selling half your Berrisford's stock.' There seemed to be something stuck to her lipstick, she was pouting and running the tip of her tongue over her upper lip. 'Or giving me those Cézanne drawings you're keeping quiet about, but they don't really turn me on.'

Her hair needed rearranging, she put down her glass to do it with both hands and when she was satisfied saw that the glass was empty and handed it to him to refill. As he poured, she continued, 'I think what I want is you, in there, in the bedroom, on the bed.' Champagne slopped over her fingers. 'The bed and any other appropriate surface. Up to one hour of sex, as hot as it gets. You are clumsy, Lovat, look what you've done, you've spilt this all over my hand.'

He took her hand then and licked between her fingers. Very well.

'One hour, with the option to extend. Agreed.'

'Uh-huh.' He turned the hand over and licked the palm.

'We can shake on it when you've finished that. I am serious, Lovat. Only if I win.' Once they had shaken hands, she took hers away and folded her arms.

Patrick was asking for advances on four million four. Three bids came quickly, raising it to four million seven.

'Who's bidding, do you know?'

'Some of them. Four six was off the wall.' She meant it was a dummy bid, either a figment of the auctioneer's imagination or made by one of their own people to force the price up. 'Don't look at me like that, everyone does it. There are two genuine punters in there anyway.'

'Four million eight, in the front here.' Patrick's fresh young face was expressionless as he looked around the room.

'Isn't he . . .'

'Four nine point five, thank you. Four million, nine hundred and fifty thousand pounds.'

'That's the Sultan of Brunei. Isn't he what?'

'Young for a big sale like this?' He wanted a drink, but his glass was empty and he never went well on champagne. Lovat swallowed, his mouth was dry. Somebody go to five. Please go to five. Go to five and let me have her. Please.

'The senior guy's in hospital.'

'He hasn't got the experience, he's letting them go off the boil . . .'

'Patrick's all right.' She drained her glass and let it hang from her fingertips. Somebody go to five. Go to five and let me put that sweet cock where it can do some good. I'll die if somebody doesn't go to five.

'And his accent . . .'

'Don't be a snob. It's a cute . . .'

'*Five million and fifty.*'

She turned to look him full in the face, and let her eyes caress him for a minute. Did he feel different, smell different, touch differently? He looked quite frightened. She was nervous herself.

'Five million and fifty. At the back.'

'You've won anyway.' There was a hopeful note in his voice. He was trying not to smile.

'That's a new bidder.' She reached out and with fingers and thumbs, delicately, took hold of the tips of his black tie and pulled it apart. 'They'll slug it out for a while, I expect.' The top shirt button was a swine, especially in a man who insisted on buying collars half a size too small and then complaining that he was uncomfortable. 'If he's waited to come in at five, he must be serious.' How could she have been married to this man for ten years and never found out if his nipples were sensitive? Oh yes. Yes. What a beautiful look that was, melting.

'I won't . . .' He had to clear his throat. 'Our deal was the bedroom.'

'You've cut your lip.' She touched the raw place. His eyes closed. 'I want to know what the necklace goes for.' She stood up, now unsteady with desire, and took the loose ends of his tie in one hand, pretending to pull him to his feet. 'But there's a television in the bedroom.'

The new bidder was an American hotel magnate anxious to give his new trophy blonde something more than he had given his old trophy blonde. He took the Orlov necklace away from the Sultan at five million seven hundred thousand pounds. Bianca had never felt so happy in all her life.

AUTHOR'S NOTE

The initial inspiration and much of the historical background of this novel came from *Theatre Street*, Tamara Karsavina's record of her life as a dancer in St Petersburg, one of the most delightful autobiographies ever written. Where other accounts conflict, I have generally accepted the authority of the great ballet writer, Richard Buckle.

Karsavina struggled briefly with commissars appointed by the revolutionary government, reluctantly becoming the president of the Maryinsky company's ruling committee. Her husband was obliged to leave Petrograd with the British diplomatic mission and she followed him to London in 1918 with their baby son Nikita.

A loved and revered figure in the blossoming London ballet, she continued to dance with Diaghilev's company until 1926, when she partnered the young Serge Lifar in *Romeo and Juliet*. Before she retired from the stage in 1931 she also appeared with a new British company, the Ballet Rambert. To Margot Fonteyn she passed on nuances of her performances in *Giselle*, *The Firebird* and *Le Spectre de la Rose*, and to Sir Frederick Ashton she taught the mime scene in *La Fille Mal Gardée*. She died in 1978, mourned for her unique artistry, cultivated mind and great heart.

Few of Karsavina's contemporaries enjoyed equally long and happy lives. For some years Sergei Diaghilev, the most gifted impresario the world has ever seen, continued to assemble artists of genius to create miracles for his audiences.

Ballets Russes dancers and choreographers dominated their art for generations; among the legion of musical and visual talents from whom Diaghilev commissioned were Bakst, Braque, Debussy, Matisse, Picasso, Ravel and Stravinsky. In the perpetual frenzy of enthusiasm for his promotions and his artists, Diaghilev, who was diabetic, neglected his health. He died at the Grand Hotel des Bains in Venice in 1929, a fortnight after taking his latest protégé, the sixteen-year-old composer Igor Markevitch, to the opera for the first time.

Anna Pavlova also made her home in London. Dancing with her own company under the management of her husband, Victor Dandré, she toured the whole world with a repertoire ideal for her unique expressive gifts. Pavlova inspired dancers wherever she performed, among them the young Frederick Ashton, who saw her in Lima, Peru. She caught a cold after a rehearsal and died of pneumonia in Holland in 1931.

After he left the Ballets Russes, the behaviour of Vaslav Nijinsky became more and more bizarre. His career ended in 1919 at the age of twenty-nine. Schizophrenia – then a newly named condition – was diagnosed. His wife and friends made ceaseless but unsuccessful attempts to cure his madness; he died in London in 1950.

Olga Spessitseva, perhaps the most brilliant ballerina of her generation, in fact did not graduate until 1912 – for the sake of including this fascinating figure in the novel's background I have taken the liberty of adding a few years to her age. With her powerful poetic style, her perfect legs and feet, her steps which 'unfolded like a flower', she became the star of the company after the Revolution, as well as a favourite guest artist with the Ballets Russes.

Lifar reports that Spessitseva became the mistress of a

senior official in the Communist government; the traditions of the dancers' world at first continued under the new regime, but instead of jewels her lover offered her the honour of choosing the first corpse to inaugurate the city's new crematorium. Spessitseva left Russia in 1923. With her intriguing but neurotic personality, she found it hard to settle in exile and during World War Two was confined to a mental institution in the United States, from which friends released her in 1963.

Fortunately for posterity, Mathilde Kchessinskaya seems to have kept exhaustive diaries. Her memoirs are an assembly of titles and honours, performance dates, rave reviews and lists of jewellery. During the Revolution her palatial home was commandeered by the Bolsheviks; Lenin made speeches from her balcony while she went into hiding in Petrograd, at first unable to understand that her days as 'the most powerful woman in Russia' were over.

With her lover, the Grand Duke André, and their young son, Kchessinskaya fled southwards and left Russia for ever in 1920, sailing from the port of Novorosisysk to Venice with a party of dispossessed nobility. All were virtually penniless; Kchessinskaya had only two dresses, and André's mother, the Grand Duchess Marie Pavlovna, paid their fares with a diamond brooch.

The couple first lived at their villa in the South of France, and married the next year, when the head of the Imperial family in exile gave his permission for morganatic alliances among the Tsar's kindred. By 1928 all the funds raised by selling jewellery and mortgaging the villa were gone, and Kchessinskaya opened a dance studio in Paris. Her pupils went on to dance and teach throughout the world; those from England included Margot Fonteyn, Pamela May and Pearl Argyle. Her last stage appearance, at the age of sixty-three, was at a gala in London, for which she danced a Russian folk piece which she had last performed for the Tsar.